D1053638

The Finest in Fantasy by
Michelle West

The House War
THE HIDDEN CITY
CITY OF NIGHT
HOUSE NAME
SKIRMISH
BATTLE
ORACLE*
WAR*

The Sacred Hunt
HUNTER'S OATH
HUNTER'S DEATH

The Sun Sword
THE BROKEN CROWN
THE UNCROWNED KING
THE SHINING COURT
SEA OF SORROWS
THE RIVEN SHIELD
THE SUN SWORD

* Coming soon from DAW Books.

BATTLE

A *House War* Novel

MICHELLE WEST

DAW BOOKS, INC.

DONALD A. WOLLHEIM, FOUNDER

375 Hudson Street, New York, NY 10014

ELIZABETH R. WOLLHEIM
SHEILA E. GILBERT
PUBLISHERS

www.dawbooks.com

First Paperback Printing, January 2014
1 2 3 4 5 6 7 8 9

DAW TRADEMARK REGISTERED
U.S. PAT. AND TM. OFF. AND FOREIGN COUNTRIES
—MARCA REGISTRADA
HECHO EN U.S.A.

PRINTED IN THE U.S.A.

For my aunts:
Fujiko Harada
and
Nobuko May Sagara

Absent but never forgotten.

Acknowledgments

My life has been deadline heavy in the past year, in part because turning a creative art into a professional one can be fraught. If things work relatively smoothly, the butt-in-chair school of writing works, and absent the usual writing stresses, everyone is more or less happy. When things don't work, they have to be fixed, and if they don't work several times, they have to be fixed several times, which leads to a sudden, rushing vacuum where all the time used to be.

So: for keeping me as sane as I generally get when things are exploding or burning down, thanks go to Ken and Tami Sagara, Thomas, and Terry; to Kristen and John Chew for feeding us all on Mondays, for Daniel and Ross who have a much more realistic and unromantic view of a writer's life (my favorite comment was Daniel's, "Mom, could you *try* to be a little more objective about your own work?" when the hair-pulling had reached epic proportions).

For sanity beyond the realm of the "Oh. My. God this is *never* going to fit in one book" terror, Sheila Gilbert, my long-time editor and friend at DAW, and Joshua Starr. And Jody Lee, of course, for her beautiful art.

Prologue

24th of Henden, 427 A.A.
Terrean of Averda

THE TREE STOOD ALONE in the moonlight. The forest with which it had once been surrounded had withered; dead trees, trunks hollowed, shed dry branches in a circle for yards. Little grass or undergrowth survived in the lee of the tree; no insects crawled along its bark; no birds nested in its slender branches. It lived, yes, but its life was almost an elegy. Where wind dared to touch it, no leaves rustled; it gave nothing back.

Nothing but illumination. Light extruded from bark that seemed, at a distance, to be composed of ice; from branches that seemed sharp and slender, like long, narrow blades. There were leaves on those branches, and in the moon's light, they looked silvered, their edges inexplicably dark. The tree cast a long shadow over silent ground.

Into that shadow two men walked. One wore robes that seemed to draw moonlight into its weave; one wore dusty, sweat-stained cloth. The latter was armed, although this unnatural clearing was utterly silent. Both men paused ten yards from the tree, scanning the ground that surrounded it.

"Can you hear it?" Meralonne asked softly, his gaze held by the Winter tree.

His companion closed his eyes. After a brief pause, he nodded.

"And?"

"Like the others, it cannot be saved. It sings of cold, of isolation, of fear. It will devour all in its attempt to appease its hunger." His breath sharpened as the mage approached the tree, one hand raised. "APhaniel—"

"If it cannot be saved, it must be destroyed."

Kallandras said nothing. Meralonne APhaniel habitually guarded the tone of his words, but it had been a long six days, and even he had grown weary. The bard, not the mage, whispered a benediction to the wind, and the wind intervened. It lifted the mage off the ground a moment before the earth beneath his feet broke and roots crested its surface, moving like misshapen snakes.

"APhaniel," he said again, cajoling the mage as he might cajole the wild wind at its most reluctant, "This tree cannot be saved."

The mage proved more truculent than elemental air; he would not be moved. Roots coiled beneath his feet, snapping at the underside of boots they couldn't quite reach. Like the tree they sustained, they were silver, their luminescence veiled by dirt.

"APhaniel—"

The mage turned, eyes flashing as if they were diamond in clear, sunlit sky—hard, bright, cold. And beautiful. Always that. Kallandras fell silent.

Taking a step into air, the bard cleared ground, hovering above it, weapons ready. If Meralonne was unwilling to countenance the certainty of failure, the bard was not. He remained silent; the single glance had been warning enough. Even when roots erupted in a frenzy beneath his feet, piercing the air upon which he now stood, he did not speak a word—not to the mage.

He spoke to the roots, but he spoke in the silence granted any of the bard-born; only the tree itself could hear what he said, and the answer offered was the sharp thrust of those roots toward his chest; they were hard and sharpened, like long, curved knives, and their tips glittered in the radiant light of the tree's bark. His blades cut three, and slid off three more; he leaped up to a height that the roots couldn't easily follow. Given time, they would; that much, he'd gleaned in the last week, working in secrecy on the borders of the Terrean.

But Meralonne had reached the tree's trunk. The roots that Kallandras severed barely troubled the mage; they did not attempt to pierce, but rather to ensnare. He had gathered them loosely as he moved, and they pooled around his ankles, obscuring his boots, as if the tree were trying to absorb him, to make him some part of its essential self.

Meralonne did not speak. Kallandras knew why: in this place, at this time, he could no longer guard his voice; every word contained the pain of loss and the slow, steady death of hope. The mage reached out with both hands; his palms touched the ice of bark and light shone where they connected; it was bright and piercing to the eye, as the roots meant to be to the heart. The momentary dimming of vision did not impede the bard's weapons; they were meant for this fight, and they moved almost with a will of their own.

The light that was pale and even platinum began to shift and change; what remained beneath the palms of the mage was a red-copper that pulsed. Kallandras had seen that steady transformation every time Meralonne's hands had finally touched bark; he expected no different, and was not therefore disappointed. The mage's hands stiffened, his fingers trembling in place. He whispered a word, and if the word did not carry to the bard's ears over the clash of blade against armored root, what lay beneath the utterance did.

In the clearing made by a hunger that could never be satisfied, even if the whole forest should be devoured, light broke the cover of night, falling in sharp, defined spokes. Meralonne APhaniel invoked the ancient magics of Summer as if Summer would never again be seen in this world. He turned his face away from the bard's view; he could do this much, but not more, for the tree's sudden scream of fury meant the safety of distant kinship was at an end.

Winter rose as roots thinned and sharpened at the ankles of the mage; he did not even gesture before they fell away, melting beneath the sudden heat of Summer, the scorching light of a different desert. He flinched as the tree's screams transcended rage and fury for the territory of pain. Had Kallandras not now been fighting for his life, he might have sung—but his song did not reach the heart of the tree the way the Serra Diora's once had; he had tried.

Summer flames burned; bark melted, roots withered. Only bark and root; the flames did not catch cloth or hair, and where it touched the edge of growth not yet devoured in the spread of this single tree's roots, it burned nothing—but the leaves of undergrowth leaned inward toward that light, and the flats of those leaves brightened in color, the small branches lengthening. These lesser plants lacked the sentience of the Winter tree; they could not and did not speak. Nothing in their welcome dimmed the horror and the loss of the single tree's death, and even as the tree withered, small shoots of pale, pale green could be seen in the troughs and furrows made by the passage of Winter roots.

Meralonne's hands fell to his sides; what remained of the tree was now silent. It would crumble if Kallandras touched it; it would crumble if anything did. Anything, or anyone, but Meralonne APhaniel.

"Come." He bowed head a moment; his forehead grazed what remained of standing ash. "We are almost done."

His voice was the voice of the desert.

Meralonne was wrong. The quiet, grim march across the slender and invisible border of the Terrean came to an abrupt end in an unexpected way. They heard the sounds of fighting. Kallandras spoke softly, as was his wont, and the mage had become so taciturn in his work that words were harder to pry from him than blood. Even in their combat against these unnatural trees—and there had been many, each dissolved, in the end, by the harshest of Summer light—their conversation had dwindled to the wordless syllabus of blades, air, and fire.

Not so the combatant in the distance: he *roared*. It was a harsh, almost guttural cry, in a language unknown—but not unfamiliar—to Kallandras. The bard's blades rose in an instant, and he forced them down as he glanced at his companion; Meralonne's robes shifted as he nodded, becoming a fine, heavy mesh of something that might have been chain, had chain been light and magical. Significantly to Kallandras, he did not draw his sword; he gestured briefly, and wind played in the sweeping fall of platinum hair as he turned toward that roar and began to walk.

His stride was supple and wide; Kallandras kept pace with some difficulty. But he was grateful in some fashion for the interruption. The mage's gaze was now brighter, the line of his shoulders, straighter. He took the lead; Kallandras was content to follow. If he did not relish the possibility of combat, he prepared for it; it had become a fact of life, as necessary as breath if one wished to continue to breathe.

Through the night forest, in the light surrendered by moon in a clear, dark sky, they at last approached a clearing similar in shape and size to one they had just left. Kallandras could see the edge of living foliage as it circled fallen branches and the husks of great trunks. But there was no stillness, no silence, in its center. Each time Kallandras and Meralonne had approached such a clearing, there had been a tree of ice awaiting their arrival; what stood in this dead clearing barely resembled a tree, it was so misshapen. The earth was overturned where roots had broken free of its confinement; they rose like armored tentacles, slashing and stabbing at the only thing present that was not likewise bound in a similar fashion.

He was as tall as Meralonne APhaniel, if not as fine-boned, and his hair was ebon to the mage's platinum; his skin looked all of red in the light cast by the shield and sword he bore. Where Meralonne had touched the tree with his exposed palms, the *Kialli* did not; he slashed at its trunk. Fire gouted from the edge of blade as roots writhed and coiled. In one wide sweep of sword, they fell, but they were almost instantly replaced.

Kallandras was silent; Meralonne, silent as well, although the mage exhaled sharply. The bard glanced at him, seeking direction; in response, the mage drew sword for the first time in this long march of days. It was blue, its glow harsher than the red illumination of *Kialli* sword.

Invoke the Summer, Kallandras thought; he gave no breath to the words—he had no time. Meralonne APhaniel leaped above the circumference traced by dead foliage; he leaped above the easy reach of roots coiled like armored snakes. The sword crossed his chest as he gestured with both arms. Blue light cut a trail across the bard's vision. When it cleared, Meralonne was a yard above the ground; roots flew where they sought to attack him as he cut his way toward the heart of the moving trunk.

Kallandras whispered a benediction to air and it came; he leaped, as Meralonne had done, landing at the same height. He did not attempt to make his way to the heart of the trunk; instead he fought a rearguard action. He had no desire to strike the killing blow; if APhaniel or the *Kialli* now engaged in combat brought a ferocity of exultation to their battles, Kallandras did not. Nor had he ever. Necessity was his only guide.

Not so, these two: the *Kialli*, seeing the direction Meralonne took, roared again. Kallandras almost froze at what he heard in the demon's voice. Had he, he would have died, and if he had no desire to claim a kill as his own, he had no desire to die in this forsaken place. He leaped beyond the reach of both *Kialli* blade and piercing root, changing his trajectory in the air as he did. If the tree in this form seemed a nightmare of bestiality, it was not without its cunning.

He did not choose to alight; because he rode the currents of the wind, that choice was his to make. Air was caprice personified, but without rage, it had little malice. He landed, cut roots and parried them before vaulting into air again, losing some part of his boots in the process. Although at each stage of this isolated search he'd been forced to defend himself against the oppressive hunger of trees such as this, he had yet to see the earth erupt so violently.

Because it had, he could only peripherally observe what occurred beyond his immediate fight for survival—but the sky flashed red and blue and white and the song of swords clashing implied a sword-dance. He wanted to turn, to watch; he wanted to survive. The *Kialli* did not roar again, and Meralonne did not speak; the clashing glow of colored light grew faster, the brightness more intense, and then, in the space of a breath and a heartbeat, both were gone, and the roots that had gathered in such number stiffened, stilled.

Sheathing the weapons that had been Meralonne APhaniel's gift, Kallandras whispered his thanks to the wind and released it; he stepped upon upturned earth, between the dying roots. As if it had been struck by bladed lightning, smoke rose from the tree's trunk; bark hung in tatters, like flayed skin. Where blades had cut wood, gashes remained, but no sap flowed from the wounds.

Meralonne APhaniel's sword was no longer in his hand. He turned to the armed *Kialli*. "This is not your task," he said, his voice clear and resonant.

"No more is it yours, Illaraphaniel, and yet you are here." The smile he offered was slight and sharp; it was framed by small scratches, which surprised Kallandras. So, too, his cape, although his armor was clean and untouched. He sheathed sword in the way the mage did; it faded from view, the red, red light dimming. He surrendered shield in the same way.

"Were it not for your presence," the mage replied, "there would have been no fight."

At this, the demon laughed. It was the first laughter that Kallandras had heard in almost a week. "And are you now so old and so enfeebled that you decry the necessity of combat? You?"

Meralonne gestured; his sword returned to his hand.

The demon, however, remained unarmed. "You will need your sword in the time to come." Mirth ebbed from his voice as he spoke, light from APhaniel's hand as the blade once again vanished.

"Why did you come, Anduvin?"

The *Kialli* was silent for a long moment, studying Meralonne; at last, he shrugged. "I wished to see for myself the damage done. A road existed here, where no roads travel that were not made by mortals; it was fashioned by the roots of the Winter trees. I do not know what treachery allowed those seedlings to leave their master—but they are gone now."

"You were not aware of the plans of the Shining Court." It was not a question.

"I? No, Illaraphaniel. I am not a member of the Lord's Fist, and I spend little time in their councils, except as called." He watched as Meralonne once again sheathed sword. "She will not leave her Court, now."

"She cannot, as you know, or you would not be here." The silence that followed these words was thick and heavy, and it was the mage who broke it. "In your travels did you find one tree that might be saved?"

"Not one, and I assume from your question that you were likewise unsuccessful."

Meralonne nodded; his hands clenched into brief fists, open and shut, the externalization of heartbeat or word.

"You can go where I cannot," Anduvin said.

Silence.

Kallandras, aware of the mood of the two, hesitated. "APhaniel, you speak of the Winter Queen?"

"We speak," the mage replied, his voice shuttered, "of the Summer Queen. The Wild Hunt rode."

"I know. I witnessed some part of its passing."

"The Winter King died."

"This, I did not see."

"No. No one of us did, who are not part of her host. But the horns were sounded, the Hunt called; the Winter Queen rode."

"And the Summer Queen?"

"She is also Ariane. It has been Winter in the Hidden Court for many, many mortal lifetimes. There were those who felt that the old seasons would never turn again—but the Hunt was called. She rode. The horns were heard across the length and breadth of the hidden ways; they were heard above the howl of the Winter winds."

Anduvin lowered his head and turned away from them both.

"There is no end to Winter while the Winter King lives," the mage continued, his eyes shining silver as he lifted his face. "And the Winter King could not be found for centuries. But he was, Kallandras, and bards whose voices you will never hear if you are very, very fortunate will sing of that long wait, that long hunt, when you are dust and none remember your name.

"But when the King is dead, the seedlings must be planted."

Kallandras' eyes widened.

"Yes," Meralonne said. "These trees were rooted in the flesh of mortals, sacrificed for that purpose. But the Summer trees? They are planted in some part of the Winter King's body. And it has not happened, not yet."

Kallandras did not ask him how he knew with such certainty. He heard it in the mage's voice, and that was enough.

"Ariane now requires two things: a Summer King and a seedling. One, even one, will suffice. But the Summer King is not chosen from her kindred. Without one tree to guard and open the way, she will have no King, Kallandras, and if she reigns, she does not reign alone. Not in Summer. Without one tree—and we have salvaged none—she will know neither Winter nor Summer, and until the paths are no longer sundered from the mortal realm, she will know little freedom."

Anduvin turned to the bard, although he addressed his comment to Meralonne. "You have chosen an odd companion for this task; he seems unaware of either the history of these trees or their significance."

"It is not for his knowledge of history that I chose him; he has traveled the hidden paths, and when he speaks, the wilderness listens."

Anduvin's gaze narrowed as he continued to examine the bard. The bard waited. "He did not travel them of his own accord."

"It matters little. You are aware, as I am, that mortals may chance across the Lattan paths and the Scarran paths without knowing the ways; you cannot likewise travel. There is no longer a path that leads from the heartlands of the South to the North, and no path to be found outside of the Green Deepings that might wend its way to the Hidden Court, if then. What the Shining Court wrought here, they wrought well."

"Not so well as they hoped," Anduvin replied.

Meralonne's hair began to move in a breeze that touched nothing else. His gaze narrowed as it traveled from Anduvin's face to some point beyond his shoulder. Kallandras moved as well.

"I did not expect to see you here in the end," Meralonne spoke to the shadows, "when you did not arrive at the beginning."

Into the ruins of their hope, a figure in midnight robes now stepped; like the mage's hair, the hem of her cloak billowed at the touch of a wind that disturbed nothing else. "Well met, Meralonne," she said. She did not lift hands to hood; it was only by the timbre of her voice that Kallandras knew her. She was not young, but not yet at the peak of her power. "Well met, Kallandras." Her eyes narrowed as she looked to Anduvin, but she offered him no similar word of greeting, and it was not clear from that lack whether she recognized him or not.

Kallandras nodded to the woman he knew as Evayne a'Nolan.

"This is the last of the corrupted trees," she said; there was no question in the words.

"And you failed to help us uproot them or lay them to rest." The mage's words were brittle.

"Were it my choice, APhaniel, I would have happily done little else—"

"But you would not have survived it. Not yet. In your prime, perhaps." He grudged her the words and did not trouble to hide the anger he felt. She was not yet old enough not to flinch; although her expression remained hidden by folds of cloth, her mouth tightened briefly.

"My arrival, at this or any age, is not of my choosing."

"So you say. And you have arrived now, at this moment, to accomplish what task?"

"To learn," she replied. So saying, she walked between Meralonne and Anduvin, to reach the ruined trunk of the tree they had between them destroyed. She lifted a hand, touched it; the robes at her feet shifted again, their movements stronger. The dead bark cracked beneath her palm. "To learn and to gather."

Meralonne spun, although Anduvin remained still.

"You were not my only master," she continued, as she lifted a section of wood. She took care, but it cut her palms anyway; even dead, that was the nature of this tree. "You were not even the first—but after I made the long choice to walk the hidden paths, Master APhaniel, you were the most constant of my . . . companions." She rose, her hand bleeding. Her lips curved in what might have been a smile, if smiles could contain so much unshed pain. She lifted her palm. In the scant light, blood was the color of shadow.

Meralonne was not a man to be moved by pain. He watched Evayne, his eyes unblinking, his hands taut by his sides. He was the taller of the two, his hair long and unfettered, his gray eyes shedding light. Her eyes were still concealed by the fall of her hood; she folded her arms around the wood she now carried.

"What will you do with that?" Meralonne asked.

She did not answer.

"Evayne—"

"In truth, I do not yet know. I haven't seen what it becomes."

"And you will not look."

"No. Not here." She glanced around what remained of

dead foliage, her head stopping briefly in the direction of the *Kialli* lord. "What is the year?"

"It is the year four hundred and twenty-seven," Kallandras replied, for it was clear Meralonne would not. "I believe it is the evening of the twenty-fourth day of Henden."

She stilled. Even her robes lost their habitual, constant, rustle. "So late," she finally said, in a whisper. "So close, now." She turned in place, careful to take no step forward or back. It was to Kallandras she now spoke.

He thought her all of thirty, although perhaps she was younger; her voice gave him much, but pain, loss, or fear was not a property of any specific year in a single person's life, and Evayne was no exception. But he saw that she wore no rings, and had she, he would have seen them; he himself wore one.

"If it is Henden of four hundred and twenty-seven, the first battle has come to pass; it is over. You have won."

"It is not," he replied gravely, and without deliberation, "my war."

"It is, in the end, the only war; it will devour our lives, Kallandras, and we will give them—willing or no—to see it to its conclusion." Her grip tightened, as if she now held a doll and not the detritus of a tree that would have blindly devoured the whole of her life had it been able to touch her. "But I will tell you what I know of the year and the time." She swallowed; the line of her shoulders shifted.

"What the Lord of the Shining Court intended failed; the South is not yet under his dominion."

Anduvin stirred, turned; he lifted one hand. Kallandras bent knees, and they stood thus for a long breath—but neither man drew weapon.

"What of it?" Meralonne asked. Of the three, he was the only one to draw something from his robes—but it was a pipe, not a sword. He then cursed—in Weston—and to Kallandras' surprise, Evayne laughed. It was not unkind; it carried, rather, astonishment and rue.

"You have no leaf?"

A platinum brow rose. "I have, as you have surmised, no leaf."

"I—I have some."

He pursed lips, losing, for a moment, the perfect line of unassailable distance. "It is no doubt stale."

"It is."

"And you have taken to the pipe after subjecting me to all of your impertinent lectures about its dubious virtues?"

"Ah, no, Master APhaniel. I have kept it because you never listened to any one of those pleas."

His eyes rounded; Kallandras thought it subterfuge until he heard the mage's voice. "You have carried this leaf across unknown centuries for *my* use?" He was genuinely surprised. "You have wasted the considerable gift of your birth and your talent to comfort an old man in his dotage?"

She snorted. "I had it because you were always so foul if you wanted your pipe and it was denied you. I have never been in one place long enough to set it aside." She was lying. "And you will never, ever be in your dotage."

"Then it has not been many years since I last saw you in the Tower."

"No."

"Very well. I will take the stale leaf with as much gratitude as I can muster." He held out a hand; she reached into the folds of her robe and removed a small pouch. "One cannot always see the ties that bind us," he said, as he began to fill his pipe, "but even I would not have guessed at this one."

Smoke rose in the air like a slender thread.

"There is no path between the Northern Wastes and the Terrean of Averda," Evayne began. "But the trees planted here for just that purpose pulled the hidden paths and knit them together in such a way as to create one. It was meant," she continued, "to last."

He glanced at the dead trunk. "And now?"

"You have destroyed those unnatural moorings. If the demons travel from the Wastes to the Dominion of Annagar, they cannot travel in numbers; not even the *Kialli* are guaranteed to find their way through the paths that are hidden. They were not," she added, "meant for the use of the dead. In the Winter, the *Kialli* can travel with impunity; the Winter was always the season of their Lord. But in the Summer? It will be much, much simpler to hold those roads against such a passage."

"And there will be no Summer?" was the soft, soft question that followed. It came from Anduvin, not Meralonne.

She hesitated. "Understand that the roads were meant to contain and cage those who would not—or could not—

leave these lands when the Covenant came into being; it is upon those roads, and no other, that the gods and their offspring might walk without losing their way."

"I understand the Covenant and its cost far better than one who is merely mortal," Anduvin replied; his voice was Winter ice. The *Kialli* were famed for their pride—for those who knew of them at all—with reason.

"And the hidden ways?" was her soft rejoinder. "Then I will not bore you."

"Bore me in his stead," Meralonne told her; the words, however, were soft and shorn of impatience.

"They have been broken in subtle ways. I am not immortal, but I have walked the roads—in both Winter and in the Summer that is long, long past."

"How subtle?" the mage said, when she fell silent. He gestured the embers of his pipe into a brighter orange and once again lifted stem to lips.

As if his action was at once both comfort and irritation, she continued. "The containment is cracked. The mortal world seeps into the hidden and the wild; the hidden and the wild will seep, in return, into mortal lands." One sharp breath left her lips, and when she spoke again, she spoke with urgency. "I have not seen it all, APhaniel. I have looked, and I have not seen it all—but the war you fought here was not the end; it was only barely the beginning."

"What have you seen?" His voice was the mage's voice; the brief anger that had informed it was gone.

She swallowed. "The firstborn," she replied; the word barely carried. "In the North, in the Empire, in *Averalaan Aramarelas*, the oldest who have lived on those paths are … waking. If you cannot hear them now, you will hear them soon."

The mage's eyes were like silver in sunlight. "Many, many things sleep beneath that city; the city itself is not unaware of the things that are buried." His eyes narrowed; smoke drifted in rings from his lips.

"One of the eldest has already begun to move, APhaniel."

"In Averalaan?" The question was sharper, harder.

Cloth brushed cloth as she nodded.

"It is hard to believe that the gods would allow it, if they were aware of it at all; there are ancient things the city protects, and we cannot afford to have them waken. I will speak with Sigurne."

"Meralonne—"

"The worst of the battle here is at an end, tonight. We have had one victory and one defeat—and the defeat is subtle, Evayne; the Annagarians will barely countenance it as a loss." He glanced at what remained of the last of the trees. "Indeed, for them it might be simple boon; they have never seen the Summer Queen, and their brief experience of the Winter was not to their liking."

"Return to the North," she told him. To the bard's surprise, he nodded gravely.

She turned to Kallandras. He waited; he did not speak.

After an awkward pause, she did. "How old will I become, while I walk this path?" She could not quite guard her voice; he heard the fear and the weariness that informed her words.

"I do not know," was his grave reply. He spoke softly and without anger because he now could; in his youth, he had not been capable of that much kindness. No one had injured him as gravely as Evayne a'Nolan in her youth. But he was farther from that youth than she herself, this eve; he could afford this small act of generosity.

She lifted her hands and finally pulled her hood from its peak, exposing her face and the entirety of her expression. He studied her face, as she intended.

"Twenty years."

". . . Twenty more years." The words were an echo of his, but they had a different texture, a different meaning. She closed her violet eyes, lifted one hand to briefly touch the pendant that hung around her neck.

"It will not hurt you as much in two decades."

Her eyes opened, rounding. "Will I forget?" she asked. She made no attempt to hide what she felt; even the two silent witnesses could easily grasp her apprehension. "Will I forget what drove me to walk this path at the beginning?"

"I do not know; you have not—yet—spoken to me of your motivations." He lifted one hand. "I can only guess, Evayne, and it is a guess based in part on the woman you will become; she has seen much, perhaps more than even I."

"And that guess?"

"No. You will not forget. But you will come to understand the broader imperative, and perhaps that imperative will weigh as much as your personal reasons in the end."

She lifted hood to face again. "I must leave," she told them.

Kallandras nodded, accustomed by now to the unpredictable nature of both her arrivals and her departures. She took one step forward and vanished.

Only when she was gone—and he was certain of her absence—did Anduvin turn to Meralonne. "Illaraphaniel, will you seek her?" He did not speak of Evayne.

"Not yet," was the mage's quiet reply. Smoke, like small ghosts, wreathed his face. "If I find her Court, what have I to offer? She will not be moved by anything now. Your Lord planned well, when he planned this."

"If he is to have purchase upon this plain, she numbers among the most dangerous of his foes." The *Kialli* lifted his head, turning away. "You will be in want of a shield."

"I will."

"Take me with you."

"Your Lord will not be pleased if—"

"You refer to my Queen?"

"Your Queen, then. I do not think she will countenance such a journey."

"Oh? She is mortal yet, Illaraphaniel; I do not think she will care. She lives with the mortals, on the edges of their Court and not in its center; power is not her concern." His tone made clear that he thought it should be. "The mortals are not so enamored of our kind that they seek us out; she does not—she has not—summoned me since the eve of battle."

"And you think she will not?"

Anduvin nodded. "Take me with you," he said again, and then added, "and if you can lead me to the Queen in the dawn of her Summer, I will make you a shield that even the gods themselves could not break."

"You might not survive the finding of that Court."

"I am aware of the risk."

"Even in Summer, the wrath of Ariane is unpredictable; it is wild, Anduvin. It knows no bounds. She will feel the death of each of the trees we could not save—"

"And she will be grateful, Illaraphaniel."

"You are so certain?"

"I play no games this eve; I am certain."

Meralonne smiled; it was a slender lift of lips, and it was cold. "Very well. I will consider your offer, Swordsmith."

Anduvin bowed. "Then I will take my leave."

"Where will you go?"

"To the North, APhaniel. It is why the stranger appeared; she meant to give warning. I will go North."

"Then I will tell you one thing, and perhaps it will ease you. Evayne a'Nolan is mortal, as you surmised—but she is god-born."

"Her eyes—" Anduvin's brows rose.

"Yes. They are not golden. She was not born to a distant god; she is of this plain, as is her father."

"She is—"

"She is kin, in that fashion, to the Queen of the Hidden Court. They are half sisters. It is possible that that robed stranger can more easily traverse the paths that will lead to the Summer Court. Remember it; I am certain you will see her again. It is not her way to give advice—to appear at all—without exacting a price."

"The advice was not given to me; I am therefore little concerned at its price."

"Remember that," was the grave reply. "For it may be, in the end, that her words were meant for you. If you go to the heart of your enemy's stronghold, you will undoubtedly see her again; she may—or may not—recognize you. Have a care, Swordsmith."

"Save your concern for those who require it."

"If you do not live, you will craft no shield for me."

"Do not insult me."

Meralonne laughed, and after a moment, Anduvin joined him. They looked young, then. Bright and gleaming, like new blades.

24th of Henden 427 A.A.
Avantari, Averalaan Aramarelas

It was not unusual for Devon ATerafin, a senior member of the Royal Trade Commission, to work late. It was, however, unusual at this time of year. The offices were all but empty;

the lack of discussion, argument, pleading, and the occasional loud spate of cursing made the silence almost disturbing.

It was not disturbing to Devon. Gregori, his aide, had remained in the office, occupied with the filing, which was both necessary and tedious enough none but the junior members of the Commission were required to do it.

Neither man was particularly surprised when the door opened; they were alert, but unalarmed.

Devon, however, was surprised to see the woman who entered the room: Birgide Viranyi. Her expression was shuttered, but that wasn't surprising; so was Devon's. He rose. "Apologies," he said, "but the Royal Trade Commission is closed for the day."

She entered the office, closing the door at her back. "Yes."

Silence. Gregori left the stacks of letters and moved to the books; in any given day, ledgers and references were taken from the multiple shelves that held them—and their return to those shelves was, like the rest of the filing, the employ of junior commissioners. He began to shelve books.

Only when a majority of those volumes were in place did he turn; he nodded once to Devon.

"Why are you here?"

"I wish to speak with Duvari," she replied. She was stiff, but the mention of the Lord of the Compact often had that effect on the men and women who served under him.

Gregori and Devon exchanged a glance.

Birgide was a compact woman of medium height. Her hair was shorter than either Gregori's or Devon's, and her scars therefore more visible. Her eyes were sharp, a clear gray that was often disconcerting when she failed to blink, as she did now. "I have only just arrived from the Western Kingdoms, but I could see, as I made my way to *Avantari*, the trees that grow on the Terafin grounds. I heard the rumors as I traveled, but it is seldom that rumor contains so much truth."

"Did Duvari summon you from your post?"

"No. I do not imagine he will be overjoyed; he is not a man who appreciates initiative."

"Is that so?"

Birgide grimaced. Duvari's disembodied voice sounded clipped and unamused. No door—no obvious door—had opened; Devon was almost certain that Duvari arrived at the exact moment Birgide had.

"It is, as you well know," she replied.

"Initiative and abandonment of duties are not, surely, synonymous?" He stepped into the room from the farthest reach of the office.

Devon tensed. Birgide did not. Gregori continued to work. Gregori very seldom spoke when Duvari was present—and of late, his silences were the norm.

"Report," the Lord of the Compact said.

Devon considered returning to his chair, and decided against it. He was angry. "Four men wearing the armor of the Terafin House Guard attempted to assassinate the Terafin this morning. This is the second assassination attempt she has survived."

"They failed."

"Yes."

"The manner of their failure?"

"The Terafin moved."

"Moved."

"She threw herself forward and somersaulted across the hardwood, narrowly avoiding two swords."

"There were four men present."

Devon nodded. The nod was controlled. "None of the four survived. One of her cats was on escort duty. I believe he killed two before they could draw weapons." He glanced at his cuffs, as if searching for ink stains. His hands were remarkably steady. "I was to be informed before any move was made against the Terafin."

Duvari said nothing.

"We have lost two tasters in the kitchen," Devon continued.

"The Terafin is aware of this?"

"They were not poisoned."

The Lord of the Compact stepped toward Devon; Devon stood his ground. Birgide idly crossed the room and took Devon's chair. "I would be a better choice if you chose poison," she said reasonably.

If Devon could have ejected her from the office, he would have. Birgide, however, was not his immediate concern—although that might change in an instant. She, as Devon and Gregori, was *Astari*.

"You are crossing a dangerous line, Duvari," he said, without preamble.

"As are you," Duvari replied.

"No. I owe my loyalty to the *Kings*, and the Kings have remained utterly silent on the matter of the Terafin's disposition."

"There is no proof that the assassination attempt was connected to the Kings."

"No. But two of the four were yours."

Duvari did not deny it. "And the tasters?"

"They are not dead."

The lift of a dark brow changed the contours of the Lord of the Compact's face. "You are compromised," he said softly. "You understand what must be done, and you hesitate."

"Until the Kings command otherwise, I owe my service to the Terafin. They have *not* commanded, Duvari."

"That is not what I mean, and you know it. You allowed them to survive."

"The Terafin would have taken their deaths very personally, and I could not have offered any reason for those deaths that would have eased her."

"And so you protect her from me."

"Yes."

"Do you understand what she has done?"

"Yes."

"And can you honestly tell me that she does not constitute the biggest threat to the Crowns that the Empire has yet seen?"

"Yes. We survived the Henden of 410. She is not the danger that we faced then."

"No. No, in my considered opinion, she is far worse. I want her neutralized."

"And I will kill her myself when the Kings give that command."

"She has not yet chosen to subject herself to the judgment of the Kings."

"The Kings have not yet made their decision."

"Have you informed her of the extent of the architectural changes within *Avantari*?"

"No. She is aware of the obvious changes: the floors and the structural pillars. She is not a threat to the Kings."

"You are not impartial."

Nor was Duvari. Which was irrelevant. "Should the Kings decide that she is to be removed, I will kill her."

Duvari did not acknowledge the words. Instead he said, "The Exalted are highly concerned. It is clear that the gods believe the Terafin is a danger."

"To the Kings?"

"Their concern is not the Kings. They feel she is a danger to the Empire. I will grant that they feel the danger she poses is unintentional, but the Lord of Wisdom believes she should be removed—if that is indeed possible."

"And the Lord of Wisdom is *not* the Kings. The gods do not rule here. The previous assassin was demonic in nature."

"I am aware of that."

"If the demons want her dead—"

Duvari lifted a hand. "The Kings have taken that into consideration. They are willing—barely—to wait. I infer, from the words of the Exalted of Cormaris that time, should we wish to remove the Terafin, is of the essence. She does not yet understand the power she wields."

"No more do the gods!"

"They understand it better than the magi or the Kings," Duvari said, voice the cold of ice. "And she *will* grow to understand it. She altered the architecture of the Kings' Palace without once leaving her own backyard. She did so without obvious intent."

"She saved the lives of the—"

"I *understand* what she did. Were it not for that, the Kings would have made the only wise decision immediately upon arriving in the Palace."

Birgide cleared her throat, and the two men turned. Duvari was unamused. "I wish an introduction to the Terafin Master Gardener."

"I did not summon you from the Western Kingdoms. Nor did I request your expertise at this time. If you hope to infiltrate the Terafin manse, you have now made that clear to Devon ATerafin."

She smiled. "I am aware of Devon. There is no way of gaining entrance to the House that would avoid his detection. I have not been briefed about the architectural changes, but such a briefing was obviously not considered germane.

"But I may be of assistance. I may be necessary."

Devon did not argue. He did not point out that both he and Gregori were ATerafin; nor did he claim that they could easily assassinate the Terafin although, were she any other head of a House, he might have.

"What, exactly, do you desire of House Terafin?"

"I am a botanist, Duvari. I wish to study her grounds, her trees, and her rumored forest. Not more, not less."

"I will consider it." He turned his attention to Devon. "Do not cross me."

"If you wish me to revoke the Terafin name, only ask. I serve the Kings, Duvari. I do not believe that the Terafin's death is in their best interests."

"You are not impartial. What you feel is immaterial."

18th of Henden, 427 A.A.
Araven Estates, Averalaan Aramarelas

Hectore of Araven hated no color on earth so much as black.

This had not always been the case; in his feckless, brash youth he barely noticed it, and in his errant first attempt at adulthood, he had considered it a bold fashion statement. Now? It was a public emblem of loss: Black, white, and gold—but black, in this case, the predominant color. His daughter wore mourning white, as the mother, although she wore a black veil; her husband, the white and black; the whole of the Household Staff of the Borden Estate in the seventeenth holding employed were likewise attired.

Even Hugh, the oldest of Rachele's children, was somber and colorless as he stood beside his parents in the long hall that led to the single, modest public gallery, and from there to the grounds in which Sharann, Hectore's beloved grandchild, would be laid to rest. Rachele, the youngest of his daughters, had been coddled, according to Hectore's wife and his many friends; she had not learned that life was a constant test. It was not success that defined a man or a woman—it was their grace and their continued ability to maneuver in the face of inevitable failure. His daughter held her head high, but even through the veil her swollen lips and eyes could be seen.

She had shed nothing but tears for weeks now. She had traveled, when she could bear it, to the Houses of Healing at Hectore's side; she had sat by her youngest child's bed, and dribbled water and broth into her daughter's mouth. She had watched—as Hectore had watched—as Sharann dwindled in weight; at seven years of age, she had weighed well under thirty pounds in the last few days of her life.

She had woken four times on her own, and a handful of times with intervention, but she had eaten so little; toward the end, when she woke, her eyes were dull and she could barely remember how to speak. Hectore had visited daily, absent the usual merchant emergencies; he resented each and every one of them bitterly, now.

Sharann was not the only person to die of the sleeping sickness, as it was colloquially called in hushed whispers throughout the hundred holdings; she was not even the only child. But she was the only one whose death Hectore of Araven took personally.

He hugged his daughter tightly and wordlessly; after a few seconds, she wrapped her arms around his neck and the whole of her body trembled. He didn't much care that other visitants were waiting to speak a few words to the bereaved; they could damn well wait. He didn't care about their time, their convenience, or their much smaller sense of loss. There were only two things he cared about today: his daughter and his grandson. He went to his grandson after he forced himself to relinquish his hold on his daughter.

"Hugh," he said, offering the boy an open hand. Hugh, mindful of his father, took the hand; mindful of his mother, he stepped closer to his grandfather. He was, in Hectore's opinion, just a shade too young to fully understand what death meant. He was not, however, too young to understand his mother's pain. He was, in Hectore's admittedly biased opinion, a good child. "You'll have to take care of my daughter," he said, bending in, speaking softly as if attempting to conspire.

"Da takes care of her," was the quiet reply. "She doesn't want my help."

He glanced at Rachele and then back to his grandson. "She doesn't know how to ask, yet. She doesn't know that she wants help. It's not that her world is over—but she'll never see Sharann again, and that's hard."

And you'll never see her again either, but that's not quite real to you yet. He took his leave of his family, and accompanied by Andrei, made his way out to the gardens. "Well?"

Andrei glanced at the grounds. They were almost impeccable, and they were certainly larger than the grounds Hectore's gardeners maintained; Borden was situated in the hundred, and Araven's main house, upon the Isle. Land on the Isle was at a premium.

"There are no easy answers. There are no answers within the Order of Knowledge that my sources were willing to divulge; the Exalted are involved." He paused and added, "The *Astari* are involved."

Hectore rolled his eyes. "I have no designs upon the Kings; they were not materially involved in my grandchild's death."

"No."

"But I feel that something was, Andrei, and I will know what it is."

"Patris Araven—"

"Do not sling titles at me; there are no eavesdroppers." Hectore's hand was cupped firmly around a stone of silence, in his pocket for just such a conversation. "Had you met me before I was required to depart, things would be simpler. My daughter will be in tears for the whole of this wretched day, and I would be there to offer her comfort."

"Your daughter accepts the death, Hectore."

"She's no other choice."

"She has." Andrei raised a brow.

"Give me the information you've managed to obtain."

Andrei nodded. "It is, as I suggested, scant. It is therefore not reliable."

"But?"

"Hectore—"

"Out with it."

"It involves House Terafin."

House Terafin. First among The Ten, although not by such a wide margin now as it had once enjoyed. Hectore had some dealings with Terafin, although to be fair, he had dealings with all of The Ten in one form or the other. His merchant holdings were not small, and they were not passive. He frowned. "House Terafin. It's where the healer boy lives."

"It is."

"Andrei, your expression could sour wine."

"The boy is not, as you well know, the most significant aspect of Terafin at the moment. You attended the previous Terafin's funeral."

Hectore nodded, lifting a hand to his chin as he began to stroll past the violets. He found them a little on the pale side, but Rachele had always preferred what she called "soft" colors. "I did. It was interesting, and not the norm for such affairs."

"Did you note the young woman?"

Hectore nodded. He didn't need to ask which young woman Andrei referred to; from the moment he was granted entry into the grounds and the outdoor reception, there had only *been* one woman of note. She wore a dress that Hectore could still remember if he paused to close his eyes: a thing that suggested all possible variants of the shade white, mixed with gold and the delicate black of mourning. It had not been particularly daring—and yet, it had. "Jewel ATerafin. She is Terafin now."

The dress, oddly enough, had seemed more significant than the very large, very white winged cat that had sat, like a statue—a talkative one—by her side. Hectore knew he had seen the creature—but his memory would not conjure a concrete image; the woman in the dress, however, haunted his vision, like an afterimage burned there by unwary sight of the sun.

"Yes. In the weeks since she was acclaimed, she has survived no less than four attempts on her life."

Hectore shrugged. House succession was always a tricky affair, especially if the House was one of The Ten.

"Not all of her assassins were reputed to be human."

This, Hectore had not heard. "Why did you not inform me of this fact earlier?"

"It was barely possible to ascertain that it was, indeed, fact. The stories that have sprung up around that girl almost beggar the imagination—and a rational man would assume most lacked substance."

"You, of course, being the definition of rational."

"Indeed."

"Andrei, I cannot run my life without you. You are aware of this, even if your modesty forbids open acknowledgment of that fact. If you do not, however, speak plainly, I will strangle you and consign myself to a life absent your competence."

"The stories are true."

"Pardon?"

"The stories are true, Hectore. She owns giant, winged cats—"

"If I recall correctly, the cats are not suitable as either guards or servants; far too cheeky."

Andrei did not roll his eyes, but this clearly took effort. "—she rides a large, white stag that appears—and disappears—at whim."

"Her whim?"

"Apparently so. She is served by someone the magi deem an immortal—a Hunter."

"Hunter?"

"The Wild Hunt."

"Andrei—please. I know you do not drink when you are on duty."

Andrei inspected the roses; he liked them. Hectore did not care for roses, or any flowers that came with thorns. "It is said she stopped the rains on the first day of the Terafin's funeral—and that, Hectore, you must believe."

Hectore shrugged.

"But she did more—and this is *not* rumored, for reasons which will become obvious. She altered the structure of *Avantari*."

"Impossible." Hectore's eyes narrowed as he turned to confront his most loyal and most necessary servant. What he saw in Andrei's face stemmed the tide of his careless words, and left him only with the careful ones. Andrei was not—and had never been—a fool; his was a skepticism and cynicism that even Hectore found difficult at times. Hectore was not certain what it would take to convince Andrei of the truth of a rumor of that magnitude—but clearly, Andrei believed it.

"Were any of the assassins sent against her *Astari*?"

"Hectore, that is beneath you."

"I am serious, Andrei. If what you have just said is true in any measure, the Kings cannot afford to let the girl live."

"And yet, she does."

"Why, in your opinion?"

Andrei's silence took on a different quality as he considered the man he had served for much of his life. "She is," he finally said, "The Terafin. The death of a reigning member of The Ten is always destabilizing. The fact that her predecessor's death occurred at the hands of a demon adds to the danger. Recent attacks on the current Terafin are also demonic, which makes clear that the demons consider her a primary—possibly *the* primary—threat.

"It can safely be assumed that what demons want and what the Kings want are not the same."

Hectore had made the Araven fortunes by relying on a mixture of instinct and natural shrewdness. And by, admittedly, a certain brash arrogance and a willingness to take risks to get what he wanted. The problem with many of his opponents was that their definition of what Hectore wanted was so parochial and so narrow. Many of the visitants to this particular funeral were such men—and women. They were here to show their devotion to Araven and its merchant trading wealth. They would not believe that Hectore was distraught over the death of a granddaughter, as he had so many of them.

They would certainly never believe that Hectore might choose to take this one death personally.

"You are not telling me what you know, Andrei."

"I am telling you what I know."

"You are not telling me all of it. I will have the rest. I will have it now."

Andrei, to Hectore's surprise, hesitated. "It has been very, very difficult," he finally said.

"It is unlike you to offer excuses in place of information."

"It is very like you to be so impatient."

"This is *important* to me, Andrei."

"Understood. When we attended The Terafin's funeral, I saw Jewel ATerafin when you were briefly presented to the House Council. She was—as you have rightfully pointed out—daring in both her choice of dress and her choice of colors; she made a statement without opening her mouth. So much so," he continued, after a long pause, "that I did not recognize her."

"You would have little reason to do so."

Andrei smiled. "You would think that, yes. You would be wrong in this particular case. She is not someone I have seen often; I have, in fact, seen her on only one occasion in the past."

"The recent past?"

"No, Patris. It was almost two decades ago."

Hectore frowned. "You did not meet the girl in my company."

"No. You were not directly involved."

Hectore's eyes narrowed. "I am involved in almost any action of note you might take; if I am not *present*, I am nonetheless affected. Where did you meet her?"

"In the Common."

Hectore waited. His lack of patience, his fury at his granddaughter's senseless, lingering death, were balanced—barely—by a growing curiosity. Curiosity and a faint suspicion that was hardening as he watched Andrei's expression. *Do you think to save me pain?* Yes. Yes, he did. Hectore was not certain what might cause more sorrow on a day when he was forced, against all prior effort, to finally acknowledge Sharann's death.

But he could guess, if he thought for a moment like a rational man. At times like this, rationality was highly overrated, but it had its uses. "Ararath."

Andrei did not seem surprised to hear the name, although it had been well over a decade since it had been spoken between them. "Yes, Hectore. I met her in an evening, in the Common, while attempting to watch over your godson."

"How was she significant?" That she was, Hectore no longer doubted.

"He did not mention her name in my presence, but it did not matter; it was clear to me that Ararath had become as invested in her welfare as you were in his. Perhaps more. She arrived in the Common in order to protect him."

"Two decades ago? She couldn't have been more than a child."

Andrei nodded. "A child," he said, "who saved your godson's life; I do not think I would have arrived in time, otherwise."

Hectore's brows rose. "You?"

"Even so."

"How could a child save Ararath's life? Was he unarmed?"

"He was not. But what he faced, Hectore, should have killed him, in my opinion."

"You killed his assailant."

"There was more than one, and yes. It is why I am aware of how unusual the young lady in question must be."

Hectore's eyes narrowed. He examined Rachele's roses, eyeing their thorns with suspicion. The flowers, however, were a lovely color. "You have not answered my question."

"It is a difficult question to answer. But it is my suspicion that the child was—and is—seer-born."

Hectore bent his face over the roses which were still in bud. They were sweetly scented, but at this stage in their growth, the scent was not cloying, not overwhelming. He had heard that one or two enterprising Master Gardeners had managed to create roses which grew no thorns, and he was interested in seeing such flowers, because he was somewhat skeptical of the claim. "You never mentioned this."

"Ararath would have died."

"You said that much."

"Ah, pardon; you misinterpret. He would have attempted to silence me, Hectore. You were as fond of Ararath as you were of any of your own children, and there are some things you would not forgive, even of me. I made it clear that I would speak no word of her ability or her existence. I thought her mage-born, at first."

"I cannot believe that Ararath would have been suicidal enough to attempt to harm *you*."

"Men are not always wise where their children are concerned."

"Indeed, they are not. Nor their grandchildren." Especially not their grandchildren. Children were always so fraught with difficulties; they were rebellious, angry, sullen, in their turn—and a parent must tolerate all of these things with a modicum of grace, weathering the worst of the storm until it passed. Grandchildren, however? Those storms were their parents' problem. Not his. The affection was unadulterated by the daily realities of life.

"Ararath's young charge eventually wound up in House Terafin. That cannot have been an accident."

Andrei addressed the first sentence, not the second, not

immediately. "She did. She went to House Terafin on the day that an assassin also visited the manse. The rumors—and these are more easily accessed—are that she proved her value to the House by saving The Terafin's life the day she first arrived at the front gates. She is admired by the House servants, with a few notable exceptions. Do you know that she was given a permanent residence in the Terafin manse from that first day?"

"I obviously knew no such thing."

"I believe she is seer-born," Andrei said again. "I think Ararath knew it. And if it will bring you any peace, I think Ararath sent her to his estranged sister at House Terafin, and his estranged sister accepted her."

Hectore straightened. Ararath. *Did you make peace with your sister, in the end?* But no, that was not Ararath's style. His pride had been both his strength and his downfall. "You think Jewel ATerafin is that girl of Ararath's."

"Yes, Hectore."

"And she is at the center of the strangeness in House Terafin; of that there's no doubt. Why," he asked, his voice softening, "do you feel that the sleeping sickness is connected in some fashion with that girl?"

"I do not; nor would I have ever assumed it. But there is an undercurrent of unease within the Order of Knowledge—and not a little resentment—about The Terafin."

"Resentment?"

"Apparently she is not interested in having her grounds overrun by desperately curious mage-born scholars."

"Really? How selfish of her," Hectore said, raising a brow. "I can see why the magi would therefore assume that she is the source of all evil."

"The resentment has been heavily discouraged by the guildmaster—to no great effect. Discussion about The Terafin within the Order has also been heavily discouraged, to much greater effect. Because there are demons involved, and because the guildmaster's policy in regards to discussion of anything related to the forbidden arts is harshly enforced, there is little discussion. It is why I have had such difficulty, and why, in the end, I have no solid information to offer; the magi are willing to discuss what is known—the cats, the trees, the stag—but they fall silent very quickly when it comes to intelligent speculation and theorizing. I understand why," he added. "Guildmaster Mellifas is as terrifying a woman as I have ever met."

"That is unkind, Andrei."

Andrei nodded smoothly. "For this reason, Hectore, I have been uncertain about the value of any information I might bring you with regards to The Terafin or the nature of the plague. Because it *is* of import, and because you will act in haste when your family has been harmed, it is rather more important that the information have a strong foundation in fact or truth; less would be socially irresponsible. What I have said today is, in the main, hearsay. I am not comfortable with it."

"You are, as always, too strict in your determination of what constitutes solid information."

"As you say."

"I wish to speak with The Terafin."

Andrei evinced no surprise at all.

"But, tell me one thing, Andrei. In your investigation, did you happen to discover if Adam, my healer boy, was living under the auspices of The Terafin herself?"

His servant smiled. "Indeed, Hectore. He is living in the personal apartments used by the new Terafin and her small, unusual court. She has failed to take up residence in the large apartments traditionally reserved for The Terafin's personal use."

"What? Why?"

"I am not certain. Adam lives in the West Wing, where The Terafin currently resides."

"In your investigations, what is the general consensus about her ability to hold the Terafin seat?"

"I believe it would be best, in this case, to meet with her in person, if that can be arranged."

"I am Hectore of Araven," he replied, drawing himself up to his full height with an annoyance that was more real than feigned. "Of course it can be arranged. I will go through the Merchant Authority; I believe it's been some time since I took tea with Jarven."

Andrei's smile stiffened as he bowed.

"Oh, stop. If I have forgiven him our early encounters and rivalries—or perhaps, if he has forgiven *me*—I fail to understand why you continue to harbor such a dislike of the man. Speak to Jarven."

"Yes, Hectore."

The Patris Araven spoke a soft word as he touched the stone in his pocket. "And now," he said, in an entirely different tone of voice, "I will go to my Rachele. I will offer her what comfort I can, and I will tell her that I will personally see that whoever—whatever—is responsible for our loss will *pay*."

Chapter One

THE SERVANTS WERE, as always, efficient. They moved in silence through the back halls, and with grace through the public halls, tending to their daily duties with the starched exactitude the Master of the Household Staff expected. But if one knew them well—and living in the Terafin manse for half one's life allowed opportunity for plenty of observation—it was clear they were excited. There was an expectant air to their work.

Some of that work involved the rooms occupied by The Terafin, although at the moment they were empty on what Gabriel ATerafin referred to as a technicality. Everyone else referred to it as "Jewel being difficult."

Jewel found the transition from member of the House Council to Head of the House to be daunting. She'd expected daunting. She'd worked herself out of hours of sleep while staring at the ceiling in the room she'd occupied since she'd first set foot in the manse, thinking about how to deal with the Kings, their *Astari*, and the mages who served them. She had, thanks to the unsuccessful assassins, managed to avoid *Avantari* and its many Courts since she had been acclaimed, but the time for such avoidance was rapidly drawing to a close.

Speculation about the intentions of the Kings—and the Lord of the Compact—was dire; given the constant press of emergencies that now constituted her life, Jewel avoided those discussions whenever possible.

She'd had less luck avoiding the bards of the bardic colleges, because at this point in her early tenure she had two in residence. They were young enough not to be master bards, and nervous enough—when they thought no one was looking—to be careful, but they were *also* charming bastards. They reported to Solran Marten, the Bardmaster of Senniel College. She, as anyone with the ability to form half a thought knew, reported to either the Kings, or the Queens if the Kings were otherwise occupied.

The Exalted were also uneasy with the newest in the line of Terafin rulers. The Guildmaster of the Order of Knowledge had likewise expressed reservations. Hannerle was, at the moment, asleep in the West Wing, but when she wasn't, her room was a silent battleground of anger, guilt, and fear. Haval could hide it all, of course; Hannerle couldn't.

But again, all of these were things she'd expected.

What was unexpected was the sudden diffidence shown her by every servant in the manse. Every single one. Even Merry. Oh, she knew they'd always stretched all the rules of etiquette when they worked in the West Wing, making allowances—as Merry called them—any time the Master of the Household Staff was absent.

Since the day Jewel had left the Council Hall as The Terafin—with only two abstentions in the vote, those being Haerrad's and Rymark's—the servants had been uniformly perfect in all of their interactions. They replied with actions, and only spoke if words were utterly necessary; they no longer smiled, nodded or—gods forbid—laughed. They looked at Jewel only if she gave them a direct order, but absent that order, they looked through her or past her. It didn't matter whether or not the intimidating Master of the Household Staff was even present.

Jewel felt like a ghost in her own home.

You are not Jewel Markess ATerafin, the Winter King said. He could; he was at a distance somewhere in the wild garden. *You are now an office; you are the reason House Terafin exists; its leader and its rule. It is not an office you made, Jewel. It existed before you, and it will exist when you die. The fact that you fill it lends color, personality, and direction to that office—but it is not you, and it is not entirely yours. They understand, even if you do not, the respect that office* must *be given if the House is to endure.*

She didn't bother to answer. Instead, flanked by six of the Chosen—and Avandar, who stood closer to her than her own shadow at high bloody noon—she examined the library's shelves. She had always loved this library, with its long, empty tables and its high, high ceilings which nonetheless let in light, be it sun or moon. But she had come to realize in the past few weeks that part of what she had loved about it was the quiet, steady presence of Amarais. Paying her predecessor the final respects that were her due and her right hadn't laid the sense of loss to rest.

She should be used to it. She'd done this before.

"Terafin," Avandar said.

She turned to face him, one thick and scuffed leather volume in her hand. "I've got it."

He nodded, as if the book had no significance; to Avandar, it had little. "You have three hours in which to prepare for your first public outing as The Terafin."

She hesitated for a long moment, and then slid the volume back onto the shelf.

Haval was waiting for her in the West Wing in what had become her fitting room. He had already set up the tools of his trade; the stool upon which she might stand for adjustments in length of hem, the spools of thread and needles of varying thickness, and the pins which were such a necessary annoyance. Although Snow lounged in the corner, he had failed to insist on the creation of any new dresses. He nonetheless felt compelled to offer criticism of the clothing she did end up wearing. He was, in cat parlance, *bored.*

"You did not," Haval said, "take Night with you."

"I only went upstairs, Haval. I had six of the Chosen *and* Avandar with me at all times."

"In the last eight weeks there have been four attempts on your life, at least three of which obviously involved magic."

"Believe that I'm aware of that fact. Sigurne—"

He cleared his throat loudly.

"—The guildmaster expects to speak with me tomorrow.

Again. The Order of Knowledge has been given permission to lay down whatever magics she feels will be useful to us in the months to follow. I have food tasters in and out of the kitchens and the dining hall before any meal; I am not allowed to snack without their presence. Daine is in full command of the healerie as we speak, and the previous four attempts on my life, while unsuccessful, caused enough injury that he's unlikely to relax. I feel the absence of one cat is unlikely to make much difference within the manse itself."

Snow hissed.

"I fully intend to have *both* Night and Snow on guard for my first walkabout in the victory parade."

"You will take Lord Celleriant?"

"Yes."

"And the Winter King?"

"No." Although she was grinding her teeth in an attempt to keep half of her annoyance on the right side of her mouth, Jewel found Haval's obvious irritation a boon. If the servants, the guards, and the Chosen accorded the office far more respect than Jewel found comfortable, Haval did not. "Have you heard anything new?"

"Of relevance? Possibly. It is not, however, of relevance *right now*. Standing still, on the other hand, is. Honestly, Jewel, you might spend more time in the company of young Finch; she adapts. You might absorb something."

"I would, if Jarven were around less often."

"I believe he is her central adviser on Council matters."

"He's also her boss—I consider it a conflict of interest."

"Meaning you don't care for Jarven ATerafin."

"Something like that."

"Finch seems fond of him. The inimitable Lucille ATerafin also holds him in some obvious esteem." Haval stilled; he lost his pinched and parental look as his face became expressionless. "What do you see, Terafin?"

"I've had no visions involving Jarven."

"Ah. Why do you dislike him? I will assume it is not for reasons of petty jealousy."

Jewel glared down at him; the stool's height gave her that advantage. "I don't trust him."

"Very well; you are obviously not a fool. He is, however, a valuable source of information. It is my considered opinion that he means no harm to either Terafin or Finch personally."

"It's not that I think he means harm," she said, turning as he nudged her. "I just don't think he cares if harm happens."

"Astute. Irrelevant, but astute." He stepped back, examining his work. "I believe Ellerson is waiting as well. The order of guards?"

"Torvan and Arrendas are in charge of that at the moment." She stepped down, fussed with the skirts; they were a color of blue that most closely resembled the House Colors, but there was a wide swathe of white that ran from throat to ground, and the sleeves and hem were edged in black and gold. Every other member of the House Council was allowed, by mourning custom, to wear white and gold; The Terafin alone was exempt.

"Let me remind you, Terafin, that the victory parade—the return of the Kings' armies after a significant and important battle—is meant to be a celebration."

Jewel nodded. "I know what they were facing," she told him. "Part of me is surprised that there's much army left to return." She hesitated and then said, "Did I forget to tell you that the Council of The Ten will convene in three days in the Hall of The Ten?"

"You did. Devon, however, did not." He fussed with the fall of her skirts, and then folded the cuffs of her sleeves, which she accepted. "The Southern victory was—and is—important, Jewel. You were in the South; you understand why."

She nodded. Morretz had died in order to deliver the message that had summoned her home from the Terrean of Averda. Summoned her, she thought bitterly, in time to witness—but not prevent—The Terafin's death.

Haval's hand tightened. "Remember that you desired the position you now occupy. Attempt to occupy it well. Devon will be situated in the crowd."

"Devon will? Why?"

Haval pinched the bridge of his nose. "Two of the four attempts would have been successful if not for the speed of your response—and yours alone. I believe he takes this fact personally."

"And you don't?"

"No. I am grateful, at the moment, for your survival. Do not tax my joy. If I may have a moment of your time after the late dinner hour?"

"You can have an hour."

"Good." He set aside his needles and turned to the white sprawl of lounging cat. "Snow, I believe it would be best if you accompany Jewel now."

Snow hissed. "She's not *leaving* yet."

"Very well. You may remain here. If she forgets to summon you—"

The cat rose. "I *like* assassins," he said as he padded toward the door. "They aren't *boring.*"

The Terafin garden was almost empty, for the first time in eight weeks. Even the by now familiar robes of the Order of Knowledge were nowhere in sight. Jewel stepped down from the terrace and instantly populated the grounds with her battery of Chosen, House Guards, domicis, and two cats, the latter of whom were arguing and stepping on each other's feet. As Jewel found it difficult to move without stepping on someone she had some small sympathy for their annoyance, although the resultant behavior was fast destroying it.

"Night," she said, choosing one of the two arbitrarily, "go find Celleriant and bring him here."

"Why do *I* have to do it?"

She answered his question with a silent glare, and his belly slowly sank toward the ground. After a minute of this, he moved, complaining as he left. Snow was hissing, because he was spiteful.

A breeze touched her cheeks and hair; not even a full summer storm would dislodge so much as a strand given Ellerson's work. Leaves rustled as that breeze moved through the tall, tall trees that could be seen from the street—any street—on the Isle; they sounded like the sea. She closed her eyes, lifting her chin as she did; she reached out with one hand from the terrace and felt, for a moment, the rough touch of bark beneath her fingertips. She lost sound, let go of frustration; the scent of undergrowth rose, and with it the quiet of a forest seen in isolation. Birds sang in the distance, wordless and insistent.

"Terafin."

The single word brought her back to the terrace, the manse, and the reality of the city. Celleriant strode up the path toward where she now stood; she could see Night in the air, weaving his way around the trunks of the great trees.

"Lady." He bowed.

"Rise," she told him, and he did. He carried no sword, no shield; he wore armor that seemed, in comparison to the armor of the Chosen, light and trifling. His hair fell down the length of his back in a straight, unfettered drape, and his eyes were the color of silver leaves, sharp and cutting. "We travel into the city, to celebrate the return of the victorious Kings' armies."

Celleriant nodded.

If Torvan and Arrendas resented his constant intrusion, they kept it to themselves, wordlessly rearranging their own marching order to accommodate his presence. They accepted Avandar's presence in the same way, although Avandar was domicis, and they had become accustomed to Morretz. They were less copacetic about the cats, in large part because the cats failed to maintain a peaceful marching order. The cats were, however, more or less respectful in the presence of Lord Celleriant, which is as much as Jewel felt she could realistically ask.

Marrick was waiting for Jewel in the foyer. To her surprise, Angel was by his side. He was smartly and neatly dressed, although the current high-collared style of his jacket—a dark blue very similar to Terafin's colors—did not suit his hair. Then again, very little did. Marrick was dressed in full mourning; he offered Jewel a deep bow as she approached. "Terafin."

"ATerafin," she replied, dipping chin. "Marrick."

His smile was the broad and avuncular smile that characterized his presence in the Council Hall. "House Terafin will be given position less prominent than that afforded Berrilya and Kallakar."

"Given their position as Commanders, that was to be expected, surely?"

He chuckled. "It was. Haerrad, however, is displeased. He wishes to know if you argued for position by prominence at all."

She shrugged and began to walk toward the waiting carriages. "He can ask."

"Ah. And if I ask?"

"No, I did not."

Marrick's smile froze in place.

"I was in the South, Marrick, in case you forget. I was in the South, and aware of the enemies the Commanders faced. Their losses there are both a loss to the whole of the Empire and a personal loss; it is in respect of the personal that I declined to play political games. If Haerrad—if *you*— have a problem with that decision, let me make clear now that I expect it to remain your problem."

A gray brow rose as animation once again returned to Marrick's face. "What did you see in the South, Terafin?"

"Demons," she replied. "And death."

"We have not been absent demons ourselves."

"No. But here at least our mages can be said to be functionally on our side. I'm not sure I understand the role of the Sword's Edge or his subordinates in the Dominion; if I ruled there, I'd disband them."

"That is possibly easier said than done. Haerrad has gone ahead. I have not seen Rymark."

"Elonne?"

"She traveled ahead with Gabriel." He bowed again. "I will take a separate carriage as well, unless you wish to make room in yours."

"It's probably safer if you don't, given the last two months."

He chuckled. "I believe that was Haerrad's thought, as well."

She would have laughed—or cursed—but was forced to break away to mediate between the two cats who had decided that they would ride on the roof of the carriage.

The carriage door closed upon four: Avandar, Celleriant, Angel, and Jewel. The cabin, with its padded, velvet cushions and backing, all in House blue, was neither large nor spacious, but Jewel felt herself relaxing. This was as much privacy as she'd been granted in weeks. Even the room in which she slept contained four of the Chosen, Avandar, and two cats at its least occupied; two more of the Chosen stood sentinel on the other side of closed doors. Torvan and Arrendas had, for the better part of six weeks—since the first failed assassination attempt—urged her to expand the ranks of the Chosen.

She couldn't. She was willing to let Arrendas or Torvan make recommendations—but she made the offer with care. The Chosen served The Terafin, and they were called Chosen for a reason; the choice had to be hers. The trust implicit in the choice, hers as well. She needed to make the time to observe—or to spy on—the House Guard, and she had not yet done so.

She could not leave her room without her retinue; not to slip into Teller's room, or Finch's; certainly not to travel to the large offices in which most of The Terafin's records and paperwork loomed. Jewel wondered if a day would come when the constant presence of people who were *not* her den would feel natural. Amarais had never seemed troubled by it.

But Amarais sometimes shed some of her Chosen and her domicis to retire to the garden of contemplation, or the House shrine, a feat that Jewel had yet to duplicate. It was not, however, the only reason she had failed to visit that shrine. It stood too close to the heart of the hidden, the wild. Even with four loud wheels beneath her seat, she could hear the sounds of leaves—gold, silver, diamond—and the crackle of a lone tree of fire, as if each movement was a syllable in a strange, compelling chorus.

She understood her home: it was her den. Her House. With time, it would encompass the Chosen. But the forest eluded all but her dreams—and her nightmares. Those had been bad.

Celleriant said, as if her thoughts were visible and loud, "Lady, will you not reside in the forest?"

"The manse comes with the office." She turned her gaze to the window and watched as the mansion began to recede. Although the carriages were horsed, they could not travel quickly; not today. Fully a third of the Isle, from servants to the Kings themselves, would be traveling across the bridge to the heart of the Common.

"Will you play games with words?" the Arianni Lord said sharply. "The heart of the old woods is yours, here. You are not Queen, and you are not firstborn—but if you will it, the forest will grace your manse of stone and wood, and lend it both splendor and life."

She said nothing.

Angel, however, did. "The Kings, the magi, and the Exalted

are watching every move, every action, and every decision of the current House Council. Turning part of the manse into a forest wouldn't be to anyone's advantage."

"Oh?" was the chill reply. "It would not be to yours, certainly. But since the day of The Terafin's funeral, my Lady has not walked the wild roads, except in her dreams. Had she, at least two of the assassins might never have reached her side."

"Angel's right," Jewel said sharply, turning from the window. "I can't just wander into the ancient forests; the paperwork—and all of the meetings it engenders—still has to be attended. And if two attempts might—*might*—have been prevented, two would not; if I had spent more time being political, and gathering information on the House Council, *they* might have been prevented."

"Do you still consider it unwise to dispense with the current House Council? Excepting, of course, those members who are already in your service."

"This is the Empire. Murder is frowned on."

"This is House Terafin. If the deaths occur within the manse—or any property owned by Terafin—they are not a matter for Imperial Law." Cellieriant spent most of his time in the gardens, lost to all sight; she should have been surprised at what he'd managed to learn in his almost complete absence. She wasn't.

"Whatever else you think I *can* do for—or with—the forest, I can't make wholesale changes just on a whim." He started to speak; she lifted a hand. "If it were possible, it would still be wrong. I understand that the old forests—the deep forests—were the home of your youth, Cellieriant. Understand that the old city, the hundred holdings, were *mine*. I don't know how far my reach extends, and I don't want to take that risk without a damn good reason."

"You are afraid to learn."

"Does it matter? It's *my* decision. If I use the power on a whim, if I change the landscape to no useful purpose, I'll probably turn thousands of people out of their homes. I don't care if you think their homes are hovels, or worse. They probably are. But *so was mine*. Regardless, if I tried, the Kings would be forced to remove me. And I can't depose the Kings. I can't bring down the cathedrals."

"You have already made changes in the palace of your Kings."

She flinched. She had not yet seen the changes Celleriant spoke of, but she knew he was right. It was why Duvari had become so quietly threatening. She was almost certain that none of the four attempts on her life to date had been engineered by the *Astari*, but the distance between that almost and certainty couldn't be breached.

She was more comfortable assuming that they were organized and engineered by members of her own House. How wrong was that? But Haerrad had been difficult in Council—more so than she remembered, although she had never liked him, and they had often clashed. Rymark had been remarkably helpful—publicly. His considerable arrogance had disappeared, like a bad dream. She found its absence perversely unsettling.

He did not, however, treat Teller or Finch with any great consideration, and while she didn't wish Rymark on either of them, it made it hard to forget that he was clearly capable of decent acting. She felt no additional resentment for his almost open dislike of the cats. People were contrary.

Haerrad was the obvious choice of antagonist; Rymark was a not-very-distant second. But Elonne was also a candidate, although Elonne had voted in Jewel's favor. Marrick, Jewel had given up on suspecting, much to Haval's annoyance. Yes, he was capable, and she suspected he was capable of attempting to arrange her death, but so was Haval, and she didn't suspect him.

"Jay?"

She looked up, her gaze sliding off Avandar's instant and glacial frown.

"He's right," she told Angel. "I did. I don't know what the changes are, and I don't want to see them. I didn't do it on purpose, but it doesn't matter. In some ways, it makes it worse." She glanced at Celleriant; ice would have been warmer. Her voice dropped; the words, however, didn't stop. "I did whatever I did at the Palace—and I'm sure someone will helpfully walk me past it on the way to the Hall of The Ten—because of the earth and the air. I could hear them. I couldn't understand them, not the way I understand us—but I knew.

"I was angry," she said, her voice dropping further. "I was angry at the *damage*. I was angry at their presence and their stupid fighting in the middle of The Terafin's funeral. I was angry at the demons, at the death I couldn't prevent. I didn't *think*. I just reacted." She laughed. It was not a happy sound. Angel's silence wasn't, either—but it was a comfort.

"Standing near the terrace—our terrace—I did something to the *structure* of *Avantari*. I might have killed people. I might have injured them—you don't move chunks of stone like that and disturb nothing. I touched things I couldn't even *reach*. Because I was angry."

Angel shook his head. "Not because you were angry. You wanted to protect your home."

"Most people can't—"

"It doesn't matter. They're not you. You're not them."

"I was angry," she said, denying the comfort he'd folded into the words. "I was angry because of what I'd already failed to protect. Morretz is dead," she said. And then, because the bleakness was there and she'd already touched its sharp edge, she added, "The Terafin is dead. I'm not. It's never me."

"Don't expect me to regret that." The words were as low and intensely spoken as her own.

"I wanted the power. I wanted it because I could use it to protect my home. But I don't want—" her breath was sharp, singular. "I don't want a power that I don't control. If I want to kill a man now—I mean seriously want a man dead—I can arrange that. But I'd have to be careful. I'd have to *work*. I'd have to plan my way around even the discovery of it. This way?" She laughed again. "I'd barely have to *think*. I don't want that. I don't want it to be so easy, because I can't bring them back.

"I've had to apologize and grovel for the words that fall out of my mouth so many times I've lost track. But I can't apologize and grovel to a corpse and expect to be forgiven. I can't bring the dead back to life."

"You have not killed," Avandar said, in a voice that matched his expression.

"No. I was lucky." She turned back to the window. "I know I'll have to kill. I *know* it. I don't know who, I don't know when. But I *know*, Angel."

"Let us do it."

"No. If I can't face it myself, if I can't stain my own hands, how can I expect you to face it? I don't want that, either."

"We're not your children," he replied. "We're your peers. Where you go, we go. If you kill, Jay, it's because there's no other choice."

"Yes. Now. I want to keep believing that's true."

"Terafin," Celleriant said, his voice twin to Avandar's.

She grimaced. Half of his word was lost to the raised voices of irritated cats, and she was almost certain that one set of claws had pierced the roof from the other side. She didn't, however, climb out the window to threaten them. The luxury of behavior that practical would never be hers again.

"If you will allow me?" Avandar said, lifting one hand and placing his palm very near where the damage had been done.

"Please. Just don't piss them off so much they destroy the *rest* of the roof."

The roads were, as expected, congested, even at this distance. Although it was early, and the army was not due to appear near the Common for some hours, The Ten, the Kings, and the Priests from the Isle were expected to arrive and arrange themselves before the rest of the citizens grew too numerous.

The Ten and the Kings did not divest themselves of guards, Swords, Chosen. They did not divest themselves of courtiers or attendants, counselors and advisers. If individually these companions were accustomed to the trappings and privilege of power, they were nonetheless constrained by the number of bridges and the guards that manned them. They were also, sadly, captivated by the sight of what Jewel assumed were Night and Snow, perched noisily above. Had she not been The Terafin, she was almost certain she would have been asked for some sort of writ granting permission for the display of uncaged exotic animals, which wouldn't have made them any quieter.

As she was, or rather, as the carriage was clearly marked to indicate that its occupant held the seat, the carriage was immediately waved across the bridge—once it reached that point. If the weather had not been cool, it would have been unbearable. As it was, enclosed in a carriage with Avandar's disapproval and Celleriant's disdain, it was close. Angel, never the most talkative of the den, chose to watch the road.

No one spoke until the carriage reached the holdings. As it did, the noise on the roof receded. Snow and Night were perfectly capable of dignified behavior when it suited them; it seldom did.

If you so chose, Avandar said, *they would behave perfectly at all times.*

Jewel didn't particularly feel like listening to an angry domicis on the inside of her head. "I choose not to."

"It diminishes you."

She shrugged; his frown, which had started before the carriage had pulled away from the manse, deepened. "It diminishes *them*. They're cats in name only; they look like winged, maneless lions. They're a threat; everyone who sees them can feel it. But anyone who has to listen to them for more than five minutes doesn't. I can't get rid of them; not even Haval considers it wise. This is my compromise."

"If they are, as you suggest, terrifying, it suits their role as guards."

"It doesn't. When I lived in the twenty-fifth, I would have avoided any streets—and the market—that contained those two unless I'd heard them squabble."

"You would have avoided the House Guard as well."

"Yes and no. The magisterial guard, yes. They generally threw us out of the Common on the flimsiest of pretexts. House Guards didn't; as long as we kept out of purse-cutting range, they left us alone. When the cats are dignified—as you put it—they look like they're on the prowl. We would've assumed that they'd eat us—or worse—and the magisterians would turn a blind eye. After all, The Terafin is powerful." Her laughter was brief and bitter.

She was. She knew it. She knew what House Terafin meant, both in Averalaan and in the Empire itself; as a House Councillor, it had been part of her job—and not a little of her pride—to bolster that reputation. But nothing she had done since The Terafin's funeral had made her feel more powerful. She was theoretically in charge, but every order of any import at all had to be inspected, measured, and weighed before it left either her mouth or her office. The former was much more difficult.

The assassination attempts had done very little to ease her doubts. Yes, she had been affirmed as The Terafin; Elonne pointed out that given the events of the first day rites and the presence of every man or woman of any standing at all in the Empire the title had already been given to Jewel in all but name. But clearly, affirmation was not the same as acceptance. If she was to be replaced, time *mattered*. She had not yet fully consolidated her power, especially not in the outer reaches of the Empire. Haerrad's duties to the House were his; if she wanted a full review from him, she needed a small legion of incredibly competent spies. He was only willing to tell her what she already knew; he would cede nothing.

It was not Haerrad that troubled her, although she hated him. She had hated him since the day Teller had been taken to the infirmary with two broken limbs — a gift and a warning from Haerrad. She had fervently hoped that Rymark — or Elonne — would succeed in ending Haerrad's life; attempts had been made, but he was, besides being a cruel, power-mongering son of a bitch, clever, cautious, and lucky.

Rymark was different. He wanted power, of course — they had all wanted that — and he was clever, cautious, and lucky. But he was talent-born as well, a member of the Order of Knowledge, and the former right-kin's son. His presence on the House Council caused nothing but disquiet; she knew that if Rymark suddenly retired or disappeared, Gabriel might be convinced to remain.

But Gabriel did not want to face his son.

His son had produced a forged document proclaiming Rymark ATerafin heir to the House. It had been signed by Amarais, witnessed by Gabriel. Neither, of course, had seen the document before he had produced it in the Council Hall. Were it not for Gabriel's bitter silence, he would have been relegated to Rymark's faction by the other contenders; because of it, he had been allowed to rule as regent. His silence, however, included no open disavowal of the forgery.

Blood mattered. Even in a House where its members were required to take an oath that severed those ties completely, it mattered. If she had been Gabriel and Carver had been Rymark — if Carver had been in a position to produce such a document and make such a claim — it would have counted among the worst days of her life. She could not, even in the silence of thought, be certain what she would say or do, but she was certain that she would hold denial in abeyance until she had the time to grab him by the collar, drag him off into a corner, and demand an explanation. She would owe him that much.

What was difficult for Jewel was Rymark himself. If Rymark had been like Marrick—or the dead Alea—Gabriel's reaction would at least make *sense*. Rymark wasn't. He had always been arrogant; he had never stooped to kindness where malice—or veiled threat—would do in its stead. Magic, for Rymark, was a tool, just as assassins were tools. He lived part-time in the manse; all of the House Council had rooms there, and the rooms were grand ones. But the Master of the Household Staff was very particular about the cleaning and care of those rooms. Only specific servants were allowed to tend them, and the schedule of their working hours was strictly enforced and inflexible.

Rumor had it that he was not particularly careful about the servants, ATerafin or no. Especially not the women. Jewel had had some experience with Rymark's certainty of his own irresistibility; she believed those rumors were true. They came, indirectly, from Carver. Rymark had an imperfect history within the Order of Knowledge; he wore their symbol and gained prestige through it, but Sigurne did not trust him. He clearly had funding—but attempting to trace that funding to its source had proved, to date, fruitless. Finch could find nothing in the records at the Merchant Authority; Angel's friend could find no records of manifests or cargo that could be linked with Rymark's external supporters. He owned some land and some leaseholds, but in and of themselves they were not enough to justify a bid for the House, unless that bid was accepted *quickly*.

There was no reason—at all—to give Rymark ATerafin the benefit of the doubt. But Gabriel, by his silence, had done exactly that. Someone like Carver had done nothing but good. No, that was an exaggeration, but Carver was part of her *den*. Rymark, she would never have taken.

You took Duster.

She stared out the window.

7th of Fabril, 428 A.A.
The Common, Averalaan

Jewel was forced to disembark long before her carriage reached the platforms upon which chairs had been placed. Wagons lined the road, and they could not easily be moved to grant passage to carriages; only the Kings were given any exemption—an exemption they did not choose to enforce. What the Kings, and therefore the Queens and the Princes, endured, every member of the patriciate was expected to endure. Even the Exalted. Bards, however, roved the streets that led to the center of the Common, lutes in arms; even when they couldn't be clearly seen, they could be heard, their voices full and sweet.

In her youth, when the bard-born walked the Common during Festival or the Kings' Crown, the sound of those raised voices were a source of unalloyed joy. This was in part because her Oma rarely had a sour word for bards; she didn't like their lutes, lutes being Northern, but she allowed herself to be captivated by their voices.

Oma. What would you think of me, now? The old woman, teeth yellowed by pipe smoke, lips creased in perpetual frown, had never cared for the patriciate, but she'd held them in no more contempt than she did two of the bakers and one of the cloth sellers. She didn't trust them. She considered The Ten to be marginally less trustworthy—not because of their power, because power at least was predictable, but because they weren't *family*. Blood mattered, to her Oma. The Ten eschewed the only bonds for which her Oma would have been willing to die. Or kill.

Her granddaughter, her only surviving grandchild, had claimed the rule of House Terafin. Now, flanked by Night and Snow, Angel and Celleriant, led by Chosen, she walked easily through streets that had once been so tightly packed she could barely see a foot ahead of where she stood in her Oma's shadow. Although the day was cool, the sweat of the men and women who labored here in increasingly cramped spaces filled the air, broken by perfumes, colognes, flowers, and the welcome scent of food.

Enterprising bakers had already extended the lines of their stalls as far as the Common's guards would allow them to go; bakers, their assistants, their families and the slowly increasing press of their customers, stood under colorful spring awnings. None of the merchants hawked their wares at their usual uninterruptible volume at the Royal Party; they were notably subdued when Jewel and her guards passed them by, carrying the banner of Terafin. Its vertical edges moved in the stiff sea breeze, and the heavy chains worked into the end of the cloth clattered against the pole on which it was hoisted. Jewel disliked it; it reminded her not of pageantry but battlefield.

It hung over her shoulder, like a great sign or placard, making her visible and drawing the kind of attention that would have meant certain starvation in her early life in the hundred holdings. She weathered it, lifting her chin and straightening her shoulders.

"Avandar?" Her domicis was frowning.

"Look very carefully at every stall. If you see even a hint of magic, mention it briefly."

"It's the Common. There's going to be trace amounts of magic everywhere."

His silence was both loud and dismissive.

"The magi have been here. The Kings and the Queens will attend. If there's anything the *Astari* missed in their sweep, I'm not going to find it while casually strolling by."

They do not see as you see.

No. Most days, they see better. It was going to be that kind of a day.

The banner went as far as the second tier of the dais erected in the center of the circular road. It was, to Jewel's eyes, a marvel of almost instant architecture, and she could see the faint glow of magical protections and enforcements—at least that's what she assumed the soft blend of orange and green meant. This was not the Hall of The Ten. While Terafin presence was considered a political necessity, the internal politics of the House were considered beneath external notice; there were four large chairs, two to either side of the banner's pole. Jewel was clearly meant to take one, and it was not uncommon for a domicis to stand behind the occupied throne. There was—if they were careful, and honestly, how likely was that—room for Night and Snow at the foot of those chairs; if they weren't careful, however, they were likely to hit the backs of the

Kalakar chairs, which had been placed in front of House Terafin's.

The House Council had arrived, and they were congregated in a loose group; they appeared, as she approached, to be conversing—but it was the type of conversation in which little was actually said. They were waiting for Jewel, and conversation banked as she approached. Teller and Finch were there; so was Jarven. When she met his eyes, he raised a white brow and offered a smile that was slight and entirely without hesitation.

She nodded in turn and moved on. "Gabriel."

"Terafin."

"Elonne, Marrick, join us." She lifted her hands, signed an apology to Teller and Finch, wishing as she did that she could speak to them the way she could speak to the Winter King. She glanced once again at Jarven; he wasn't watching her. He was watching Rymark and Haerrad. His expression was genial, friendly—but Jewel had quickly come to understand that that was Jarven's version of Haval's sudden, neutral mask. The realization also made completely clear that Haval dispensed with the pretense of facial expression as a courtesy to her, a signal that she focus her concentration and attention on his words, or the history that formed their context.

That Jarven watched the two Council members she had chosen to leave on the ground wasn't a surprise. Harraed and Rymark might consider the choice a slight; she'd bet on it. But she was also aware that they had abstained in the Council vote that had placed her in charge, and she couldn't, at this point, slight Elonne or Marrick; as declared allies—if cautious ones—they deserved some acknowledgment. The House Council was not, by any means, settled. It might have been more stable if not for the assassination attempts; those attempts made clear that the assignation of the title alone was not enough to lay the war to rest. Best to show public appreciation for public support; those who were quiet might be moved to reconsider their silence.

No call had yet been made for her resignation—but House history, which existed in the admittedly biased form of the journals of previous House rulers, made clear that resignation, in all but one isolated case, was a synonym for death. Death, on the other hand, had been tried. While it was possible Elonne was still in the hunt, Jewel doubted it. Jarven seemed to doubt it as well; although he'd briefly glanced at Elonne, his attention seemed reserved for Haerrad and Rymark.

Jarven noticed that she was watching him, and winked. It was annoying.

She could, of course, afford to slight Teller and Finch, the two people she would have chosen had she been able to make that choice without consideration for the political costs and benefits accrued. But she trusted Teller and Finch; they trusted her. They would understand why she had chosen Elonne and Marrick over two members of the House Council who had occupied their junior seats for a scant handful of months.

She also knew that would have to change. She trusted Teller and Finch. In order to build a House Council she could trust to actually support her, both of them would have to gain power. Power, in the Council chamber, was not decided by any actions or arguments taken therein; you brought your power to the table and you wielded it with care. Or, in Haerrad's case, like a cudgel.

Jarven was close to retirement—or so he'd said. But Finch pointed out that he *said* this on a more or less continual basis. If he did amaze them all by actually retiring, Finch could, in theory, succeed him—but it was tenuous theory. To make it solid, she had to be responsible for some truly clever, and extremely profitable, trade deals. At the moment, according to Finch, there were three men associated with the Merchant Authority offices who were capable of doing what Jarven had done in his prime. Unfortunately, they were capable in thirds, and three men would not fit in that office.

Jewel shook herself and ascended the stairs; no one else would move if she did not. Gabriel offered his arm; she took it. "You will have to choose a right-kin in the near future," he said, his voice low.

She nodded, that stiff almost regal movement of chin—and nothing else—that Ellerson had so laboriously taught her. "Let us discuss this in two days."

"Terafin."

She did not go to Gabriel for advice anymore. Not directly. Teller did, and Gabriel was comfortable with that. He had been comfortable giving advice to Amarais—but Amarais didn't follow advice; she accepted it, as if it were an offering, examining it for its inherent value before she decided its disposition. She did not *need* Gabriel's advice; she valued it, no more. Jewel, in Gabriel's eyes, was in need of advice and it unnerved him.

Teller was her right-kin. He was the right-kin of her heart; he had served as right-kin in her den, although her den had never required pretentious titles for what he did. But Teller was so junior a member of the House Council he lacked the gravitas of Gabriel. If she made him right-kin now, she would be throwing him into the line of fire.

Gabriel took the chair to her right out of long habit; only when he was halfway seated did he realize what he had done. He glanced at her, chagrined. She couldn't help but smile; she could keep it as brief as possible. Elonne took the seat directly to her left. If there had been some subtle negotiation between Marrick and Elonne, it went unnoticed; Marrick did not appear to be unduly ruffled.

When Snow and Night joined her, Snow to the left and Night to the right, she realized why; he'd taken the seat farthest from the cats. He caught her gaze and winked. It was something he wouldn't have dared to do with Amaris, but it was conversely something he'd frequently done with the den. She knew it was inappropriate to respond to it here; she knew Marrick knew it, as well. It was a game, but as far as games went, it felt harmless. Attempting to avoid making any further eye contact, she looked up, and up again; the trees of the Common cast their shadows. Here, the leaves were in bud, not bloom, and the trees were surrounded by buildings and awned carts, not the carefully cultivated flower beds and smaller trees of the Terafin Master Gardener.

Wind rustled the tips of high, slender branches. It was a cool, biting wind, heavy with salt. Home.

Terafin.

She blinked and found herself staring into the wide, golden eyes of Snow; he had shifted position to face her, and his wings were high.

Avandar. Beneath the tier on which the Terafin chairs stood, The Kalakar and her attendants had arrived. Not to be outdone, The Berrilya, with his attendants, was also present, although the Berrilya House Council had yet to take their seats. The Kings, in a position of prominence, had not yet taken their thrones—chair was too petty a word to describe them—when the wind grew stronger.

It was a wind she shouldn't have felt; the branches it moved were far too high. Her skin tightened; the hair at the back of her neck—what very little of it had escaped Ellerson's merciless attempts to confine it—rose. So did Jewel.

Gabriel looked to her instantly; Night rose and whispered something to Snow. Jewel heard it, but didn't recognize the word. She understood its significance.

"Avandar!"

He was behind the tall back of her chair.

"Terafin."

To the left of House Terafin sat The Morriset; to her right, the deliberately bald Korisamis. Above, on the widest of the platforms, the rest of The Ten. She scanned the growing crowd, searching for Devon, for some sign of Devon; when she failed to find him, she searched, instead, for the magi. The guildmaster was distinctive enough that she, at least, was easily spotted.

"Terafin." Gabriel's voice was low, urgent.

Jewel said, "We need to get everyone off this platform. We don't have much time." To Night she said, "Find Sigurne Mellifas. Tell her."

"Tell her *what*?"

"Watch for fire." She stepped away from her chair and turned to House Morriset. "Morriset," she said, her voice even and steady, "we must vacate these stands." Without waiting for his assent, she turned to The Korisamis. He was a man to whom protocol was as natural as breathing; for that reason, she had always felt ill at ease in his presence. Today, it didn't matter.

"Korisamis, my pardon—but it is imperative that we leave the stand at once."

"May I ask why, Terafin?"

It was the question she dreaded. "I will explain later—any explanation now will be costly." Again, she moved, this time forward, to where the edge of this platform almost touched the back of the seats on the platform below. "Kalakar. Berrilya."

They turned instantly at the sound of her voice, as if they were still on the battlefield; they recognized the tone. The Kalakar's brows rose. "Terafin."

"The platforms must be cleared, now. The Kings and the Exalted must stand back."

The wind grew stronger as she spoke. Snow came to his feet, his fur rising. The Kalakar frowned as she turned to The Berrilya; he nodded smoothly and without hesitation. Their counselors had heard Jewel speak, but waited, stiffly, on the commands of their own leaders, which followed seconds later.

"I will carry word to the Kings' Swords," The Berrilya said. He hesitated briefly before he leaped. Jewel was almost — almost — shocked; The Berrilya was so proper and so exact in all forms of patrician behavior the thought that he would take the most direct route to ground had never even crossed her mind.

As if she could hear the thought, The Kalakar smiled. It was both broad and grim, a slash of an expression. "We recognize the feel of this wind." Her tone matched her smile. "It appears to have followed us home." She turned. "Korama, alert the Kalakar guards. I will make certain that word travels in haste to the army."

The army. Jewel closed her eyes and exhaled. The army that was, in theory, to perform a full dress parade through the center of the Common. She turned to see that The Morriset had already passed word to the platform above; people, some clearly displeased, were abandoning their chairs and heading toward the stairs that bound either side of the almost concentric flats.

The wind grew stronger and wilder — but the wind itself wasn't the threat; she was certain of it.

Certain enough that when the floor cracked a yard beneath her feet, she shouldn't have been surprised. Slats of wood splintered, as something burst through, knocking the now empty chairs in a wide, wide circle.

Snow leaped up, wings scraping air as if to gather it. His claws were extended, his lips pulled back over long teeth that glittered unnaturally in the morning light. Wood cracked again; someone in the distance screamed. Jewel turned to look over her shoulder; Avandar filled her view.

He grabbed her, lifted her—and to her great surprise, threw her. He followed.

Only Avandar hit the ground, and as the platform crumbled, it was a significant drop. She should have joined him. Instead, the wind caught her, buoying her up, as if she had invisible wings. She caught threads of pale, platinum hair as they drifted across her open mouth.

"ATerafin," a familiar voice said. "Ah, my pardon. Terafin."

She looked up into the familiar face of Meralonne APhaniel. Snow circled them both.

"I see Sigurne did not exaggerate," he said, although he spared Snow only a glance. Instead, he faced what was left of the platform as obsidian emerged, shedding planks as if they were splinters.

"Terafin," he said, his face impassive, his eyes narrow, "guard yourself. I believe the *Kialli* has come for you."

Chapter Two

IT WAS NOT THE FIRST TIME Jewel had seen demons, nor would it be the last. But this one was unlike any other she had seen. It was dark, and its skin caught morning light, reflecting it as it unfurled great, glowing wings—of fire. Where they touched the gaping hole left in the platforms erected for The Ten and the Kings, wood began to burn.

Meralonne spoke in a voice that hinted at Winter wind, and the creature turned to face him; as he did, he laughed. The laughter was like an earthquake, a sensation more than a sound. Even caught in Meralonne's spell as she must be to stand suspended above the cobbled streets, she felt it reverberate.

"Illaraphaniel, I did not think to find you here, among the cowering mortals."

Meralonne inclined his head.

"Stand aside, little Prince, and I may—may—be moved to stay my hand. I see no battle here."

"Darranatos." Meralonne, for as long as Jewel had known him, had always become strange and wild when presented with a fight that anyone sane would flee in terror. His eyes would widen slightly, his lips would turn in a feral, perfect smile.

Today, there was no jubilation to be found in his expression; it was a pale mask of grim determination, as terrifying in its way as the slow emergence of the demon had been.

"Snow—"

"He's *ugly*," the cat replied. He flew in a tight circle that went nowhere near the demon, and he looked enormously puffy in spite of the chill wind.

Below them, people screamed. Not all of the voices raised were raised in terror; some were raised in command. The Kings, she thought dimly. The Kings were upon the field. If it was a field of cobbled stone, stone building, wooden wagons, and cloth roofs, it mattered little; the presence of a demon twice the height of a man turned the familiar into a battlefield.

She had walked through these streets while demons destroyed everything in their wake; they had even felled trees before she and Avandar had made their escape. Avandar had been their target on that day.

Jewel! The private voice she found so uncomfortable brought her a measure of relief.

I'm here—I'm with Meralonne. I think he recognizes the demon.

His silence was marked.

Avandar, do you?

He is not an enemy you can fight in your current state, was Avandar's reply. *You have managed to survive significant foes in your time, but there is a limit to what you can avoid by simple instinct.*

He's here for me, was her flat response.

Yes, Jewel. But you do not yet know how to fight him.

She closed her eyes. She knew what he was asking.

Yes, he said. *Lord Celleriant is not wrong in this. You have the tools to defend this city, but you have no will to use them. Not yet.*

These are not my—

They are, Jewel. The Common speaks to you as strongly as the Terafin manse.

But it didn't. The wind she felt did not enrage her; the demon invoked fear, not furious defiance. The trees had no voice.

The fire, however, did.

It spread like liquid, consuming the fallen chairs and the broken slats on which they had once been standing. As they burned to embers, the creature's wings grew taller, wider, brighter; had they not been demonic, they would have been beautiful.

No, they *were* beautiful. Darranatos was, in height and form, beautiful. She had no doubt at all that he would kill anyone fool enough to stand in reach; no doubt that the deaths would be painful and unpleasant, because fire *was*. But her mouth was dry, her voice absent, as she looked at the creature's face; the line of his perfect nose, the angularity of his obsidian jaw, the height of his cheekbones. He was a nightmare, yes. But the Winter Queen had been so beautiful one might be moved to tears at the sight of her—before the Winter Host rode. Even if you were the person they were hunting.

Jewel bit her lip as bright, burning wings rose on the heat of the fires below. The demon flew to face Meralonne APhaniel. In his hands were sword and shield, and fire trailed up from the ground, enrobing him. Wind grew wild around Jewel; wind grasped at fire, tearing it away in chunks.

But fire grew again, regardless, crackling and almost sibilant.

"Meralonne—put me down!"

She might not have spoken; he did not react to her words at all. Before she could speak again, the *Kialli* rose higher. Meralonne cursed. "ATerafin—mount the cat. He will offer some protection against the fire, and he is far faster, when necessity dictates speed, than I. I have no shield," he added, as he raised sword, "and I cannot allow him the advantage of height." So saying, Meralonne rose to follow.

She was grateful that they had taken their fight to air. Grateful until she heard the tenor of the screams beneath her dangling feet: the fire had spread, and where it touched cobbled stone, the stones began to melt.

Sigurne Mellifas was silent. She had passed orders to the magi present, and she had sent word—in haste—to those who now sheltered in the Order on the Isle. She turned her considerable power toward the fire, knowing that—to the people who remained in the building-enclosed circle of the Common—the fire was the greater threat. But in the heat of the fire, she felt cold; as cold as she had ever felt when a Tower had been her prison on the edge of the Northern Wastes. There, she had learned the arts of summoning and control, and she had tested the boundaries of naming and names.

All forbidden. All.

At no point, in service to two masters, had she encountered *Kialli* such as this. She could not even see the shape of his name. In the binding of name and named, there were complicated, complex magics. Only adepts could sense some of that binding—but through it, they might begin to touch the hidden essence of the demonic avatar.

She tried, instinctively, while the magi began the casting of their shields and their defenses. But she stopped before she had truly begun. *No* mortal in the history of the magi— the long and troubled history—could contain the whole of this creature's name. She was certain, as she lifted her hands and began to weave bright, orange light—a light unseen to all but the talent-born—that only the gods could.

The golden light of the Exalted joined her shields, lending warmth and substance to the desperate work of the magi. Against lesser demons, against even the *Kialli* lords she had encountered in her long, unspoken war upon their kind, the three Exalted might triumph. Here, now, she felt it a matter of time.

But the whole of a mortal life was simply a matter of time. Hers had been long, and she did not intend to surrender the time left.

Red lightning changed the color and complexion of the sky as the demon's blade fell. Jewel heard the clash of blades, and knew a blue sword had parried, but that light was meager in comparison. She sat astride Snow; the wind no longer held her. But the cat was warm, the wind chill. Night rose to join Snow, as silent—and ruffled—as his brother.

"This is not for *us*," he said. As he did, she saw one other take to the sky, and she recognized him instantly: it was Celleriant. She opened her mouth to call him back, and shut it, hard. He held both sword and shield, and even at this distance, they were bright, solid; his hair trailed behind him like white fire. She thought she could hear horns, faint and attenuated, above the roar of flame.

One of the demon's wings shifted, spread; it struck the Arianni Prince and sent him flying. The hair that seemed the pride of the Arianni caught flame a moment before it banked, but Celleriant righted himself as it did. The trees were the only thing in the Common that approached the height of the combatants.

Silent, immobile, she let Snow move as he would. As she did, she felt something in the back of her thoughts. It was familiar, but it took her a moment to understand why—and when she did, immobility was forgotten.

Avandar! No!

There is no other way, he told her, his voice distant even on the inside of her head.

Celleriant and Meralonne—

His laughter was bitter and quiet; nothing hampered it. It joined the wail of wind and the crackle of flame. *They are not a match for what they face now. There* is *no other way*.

She was afraid; the fear was visceral. If he did this—if he did—she *knew* she would lose him. She could not be where he was; she could not draw him back, not in time. If the demon died here, so would Avandar—the Avandar *she* knew. She did not want to lose him.

But he rose, now. He rose and in his hands—sword, golden, gleaming. Sword, she thought, and shield. He hadn't the hair or the grace of the Arianni, but watching him, she could see the slow death of anything she defined as mortal. As human.

"What will you *do*?" Snow asked, as if he had heard each silent word. Her arm throbbed. Her sleeves were long and heavy; she couldn't easily pull them up to look at the skin that lay beneath them. But she knew the brand burned there in haste and without permission was bleeding; blood had seeped into Terafin blue.

The Terafin banner was ash. So, too, the banners of every one of The Ten; the banners of the Kings had not yet been placed, and they flew in wind; the fire did not reach them.

"Up," she told Snow. He obeyed instantly. The Common became smaller as she rose; the streets narrower. She could see the movement of crowd as people flowed away from fire, magi, and patriciate. Moving against that tide—splitting it, as large rocks split streams—came the bright and shiny dress parade, composed of the men and women who had survived the war in the South. Today was to have been their day—a celebration of their sacrifice and victory over the shadows that lay across the Dominion.

They'd come home, as Jewel had come home, to find home had changed. Maybe because of their absence—but worse, maybe because of their presence. They hadn't left the war behind, although they'd tried.

Enough, she told herself, hands clutching Snow's fur. Her voice sounded—felt—like her Oma's voice, the word laced with the same biting, sharp anger, the same momentary contempt. The sky reddened, brightened, and reddened, as demon warred with Arianni, sunset with sunrise. There was nothing she could do here but wait, witness; her hands shook.

No, she thought. No.

Avandar—he's here for me. For me.

He is.

Will he remember why he came? Fire lanced sky as Snow hissed and dropped. It was enough of an answer. It was the answer she suddenly wanted. She heard the demon laugh, a sound as wild and unfettered as angry wind, hungry fire. Even at this distance, her spine stiffened, her shoulders tensed; she *knew* that she was not yet far enough away for safety—if safety could ever be reached again. She had nothing to throw back; even had she bow, she couldn't string it, couldn't aim it, couldn't choose a path that defied or used the currents of air.

"Night—find Meralonne."

Night hissed.

"If he is injured, carry him. If he is not, follow."

"To *where*?" His voice cut above all other sounds. He knew she wasn't asking—wasn't commanding—him to fight.

"Home," she whispered. Tightening knees around Snow's back, she bent head to bring her lips closer to his ear. "Home," she whispered again, in an entirely different tone. Snow growled. His voice was a low, low rumble, felt as it moved between them; it was hard to imagine something so bestial could also whine and sneer so effectively.

He wheeled in a tight half circle; his haunches gathered, muscles tensing and releasing as if the air were solid beneath his great paws. Without a single, backward glance he flew directly toward *Averalaan Aramarelas*, where the Terafin manse lay in wait.

*   *   *

The voice of the wild wind grew distant; it did not dog her steps. The fire's crackle receded as well; the streets emptied as she reached the channel that separated Isle from holdings. Not even half a city away, people went about their business, unaware of what now waited in the Common. But as Snow angled closer to ground, she heard the demon's roar—and she saw heads lifted in confusion as people stopped and turned.

Winter King, she called.

Jewel. The manse could be seen before they had left the channel behind—the great trees rose in clusters, obscuring the building's fine roof. Here, leaves caught sunlight in a sky that was neither red nor blue, and it seemed to Jewel that they reflected it in bright, sharp bursts, glittering like unidentified metal. She shook her head; these were not trees of diamond, gold, or silver; they were too tall, too *alive*, for that. But where the wind at the heights of their crowns moved through their laden branches, the rustle formed whispers from which words emerged.

Too many words, spoken at once; she could not separate the syllables into something she could recognize.

Snow did not even try to reach the manse, and for that, she was grateful. Night cut across their path; Meralonne was not on his back. "Night—clear the grounds. Tell the gardeners to go inside."

"The grouchy man won't *listen*."

"Make him listen. Make him listen *without* making him bleed."

Night hissed.

"Don't hurt him *at all*. But tell him—damn it, tell him demons are coming and they'll be safe only if they're indoors."

Night wheeled toward the thickening trees as Snow brought them in. She shouldn't have been surprised to see where he'd chosen to land, but she was: his claws clicked and slid across the hard marble steps of the Terafin shrine. There was no spirit standing beneath the small, polished dome—and no ghostly image of his dying body bleeding into the altar. The shrine was silent. Jewel's legs had been locked so tightly around Snow's back that they cramped as she dismounted; she stumbled, cursed, and rose.

The Winter King stood on the path that led to—and from—the shrine; his eyes were dark, wide, his coat the color of ice on snow. He was a stag, yes, but at that moment she saw in him something as ancient—as wild—as the elements. She couldn't run easily until her legs adjusted to the freedom of movement, but she tried anyway.

"Snow—help him, help Night!"

"No. I will not *leave* you. Not now, not now." He growled, his voice dropping. "Shadow is coming."

"Tell Shadow to stay with—"

"You must command him yourself, *silly* girl."

"*Go now.*" Hands curled into fists as she turned; Snow was already gone. The Winter King approached and knelt; she leaped onto his back as if it were home. Riding Snow was not the same; the Winter King was haven.

She heard dragon's roar.

Not dragon, the Winter King said.

Will he come?

He is coming; the winds carry him. The fire hinders his movement—but he knows where you are.

Take me—

The great white stag leaped as if words were superfluous. She wasn't certain if his hooves touched stone or earth at all; he moved over and around the small ornaments and flower beds as if they were simple illusion, colorful shadow. But as he did, he approached the trees; their shadows were darker, longer, and far more solid. He slowed; before he had come to a stop, she was already halfway off his back. Her feet touched earth, and as they did, the whisper of leaves grew louder—louder and more distinct.

Beneath the bowers of the trees that lined the Common were the trees that existed in story, song, or dream: diamond glittered as she approached, finding the path, finding the way. She did not mount the Winter King again, although it might have been faster. Her hand touched gold leaf, gold bark, glanced off silver. She did not stop moving until she reached the lone tree of fire, around which nothing grew. She did not touch bark or leaves, but watched as heat distorted the air above its many branches.

It was so quiet here. There were no gardeners in sight; no cats. Only the Winter King, the trees, and the darkness of an almost unknown forest beyond her feet. She looked into the distant shadows and saw movement; light surrendered no shape, no form.

Do not leave the path.

I know. I know but—

It is not yet safe, Jewel. In time, you might make paths that touch the whole of this forest—but you have not walked beneath these bowers since the first day.

A roar broke stillness and silence, and in this forest, it became wind, became gale; the leaves flew at right angles to their many branches, and the branches themselves twisted and intertwined.

"He's here," Jewel said. The Winter King said nothing.

She was afraid. She hated it.

Hated it, fought it. This was *her* home. This was *her* stronghold.

But Avandar had drawn his sword; Avandar had taken to air, just as Meralonne APhaniel often did. Both were significant, terrifying acts—but far worse was that in spite of the unveiling of his power, in spite of the presence of Lord Celleriant and a First Circle mage, he was not certain they would triumph.

The hidden forest—Jewel's forest—took the roar of the demon into itself, shaking as it did; the earth trembled beneath her feet, and around the path, it broke, disgorging deep roots—roots of gold, of silver. She cried out; her voice carried, wordless, to where those trees foundered.

She heard the crack of wood and remembered the way the whole of the raised pavilion in the Common had broken like paper when the demon had chosen to reveal itself. Branches snapped and fell, trunks followed. This was her forest, and it was of her. And who was she? Jewel Markess ATerafin, a stiff, strained echo of Amarais Handernesse ATerafin.

The demon did not speak, not in words. He didn't demand that she show herself; didn't accuse her of hiding. It wasn't necessary. The sounds of his carnage approached with him.

But even had he moved silently, she would have known where he was; she could feel his feet break the earth; could feel the burning folds of his wing scorch undergrowth and wild plants. She could almost feel his breath in the wind that reached her upturned face. He didn't belong here; he would *never* belong here. Even so, he knew—and had known, even in the Common—exactly where she was.

And he knew he had lost time to words and the need to assert his power in the presence of the powerful; he had given her the time to flee. He brought his darkness with him, but it was not the darkness of unknown forest; it was wilder, darker, colder. He brought his fire with him, and uncontained, it began to spread through the standing trees.

It traveled far more slowly than it had in the Common, and for the first time today, the smile that touched Jewel's lips felt natural. "I did not flee here in terror," she told him, although he was not yet in her view. She stepped back, drew breath, lifted arm; her palm faced the coruscating bark of the tree of fire. Closing her eyes made the heat more intense, not less.

The Winter King left her side, leaping to the right as fire blossomed beneath her hand, spreading up her arm and across the whole of her body between breaths. When she opened her eyes again, she saw the forest through a flickering mask of red, orange, yellow. She herself was almost white.

The roar of the flames she now heard most clearly was *her* fire. In it, she heard the tinkling of metallic leaves, and, loud as the ocean waves she had heard for all of her life in the city, the rustling of living ones: gold, green, and white, high above where she stood. She saw shadows cast by firelight that were the wrong size, the wrong length, and the wrong shape; it took a moment before they resolved themselves into the outlines cast by buildings when the sun was heading toward its height.

She whispered a word, two, and the trees she faced parted, moving to the right or the left; she knew where the demon had destroyed parts of the forest; she could feel the broken, burnt trunks as if they were fingers or toes. She desired to lose no more of them. But the trees, from a height, seemed to bend toward her; the trees she had moved leaned over the path that their parting had revealed.

Movement drew her eye; it was silver and white. The Winter King stood at a distance, like moonlight in the heart of night sky. *He comes.*

I know. Breathe. Breathe. Breathe. Pause. *Winter King.*

Jewel.

Why is it always night in this forest?

She felt his approbation. *You begin to understand*, he told her. *It is not always night.*

It was night where the demon lord walked.

He carried a red great sword and long kite shield. She carried nothing. Nor did she attempt to force the shape of weapons from the fire that surrounded her; she *knew* that had she, she would die. She might have the knowledge to build them—she did not have the experience to wield them.

He paused ten yards from where she stood; his eyes were red, and his skin was obsidian, glittering in reflected light. "So," he said.

"I am Jewel Markess ATerafin," she replied, her voice steady but thin compared to the richness of his. "And you are *not* welcome here. Go back."

He smiled and began to walk toward her. "Or? A command is rendered a plea if the person who makes it lacks the will—or the power—to enforce obedience."

She gestured. Fire encased her.

She felt the sudden rumble of earth beneath her feet. "No," she told it. "You are not welcome here yet; he does not have the right to invite you." The earth stilled. It did not speak again.

The demon's eyes rounded slightly, and then of all things, he laughed. And oh, the sound of his laughter. It was cold, yes, and cruel—but it was also warm and bright and enticing. Wind came in a sudden gale, and again, she said, "No. Not yet, not now." It stilled.

"They are yours to deny," he told her. "But not yours to command."

"Not yet," she countered.

He brought his sword down.

She raised her arms, crossing her wrists over her head; it was almost a cringe. But it was a defiant cringe, and fire pooled like armor—like a sudden dome—above her head. The impact drove her to her knees, and she raised her face, arms still crossed, to see the very edge of the blade inches from her sleeves. To either side, fire flared, but did not break. Instead, for a moment, it seemed to absorb the color from the blade.

Roots burst from the earth around Jewel's ankles, wrapping themselves around her legs. She had no time for any other defense; he brought his shield in from the side to sweep her off her feet. She shuddered with the impact, and even with the grounding of those roots, she staggered; fire fled from her side as if it were blood.

You cannot triumph here if you do nothing but defend.

Voice dry as ash, she said, *Thank you, Avandar.*

He did not laugh. All of the wilderness in this place was hers. But he appeared by her side, and when he gestured, when he spoke, when he brought his arms up in a circle that ended with his palms, the earth trembled again.

Yes, she told it. *Yes, now.*

If the earth heard the relief in her voice, it gave no sign. Avandar was unarmed. Avandar carried no shield. He carried the weight of experience and the talent of the magi—but he'd always had those and they had never driven him to the very edge of sanity.

I was not *insane,* her domicis said.

We can define sanity later.

Lightning flashed in the clearing she had made; Avandar was its cloud, its gray-green sky. White light struck the demon lord's chest; it drove him back two steps. At his height, at the length of his stride, that was a good ten feet. Claws broke earth as the *Kialli* halted his progress; runnels formed beneath his ancient, unseen feet.

Pillars of stones rose around The Terafin and her domicis. They spoke with the voice of the old earth, and it was angry. Had she thought them pillars? No. They were stone trees; she realized this the minute they stretched out their many, leafless branches. The demon was fast; he raised shield and stone splintered against it without causing any visible damage.

But he had one shield; the pillars, many arms. Nor were they kind enough to strike from only one direction. The great sword rose and fell in a whistling arc; branches clattered to the ground where the earth instantly absorbed them. Avandar, arms raised, head bowed, was pale. The stone pillars moved as the earth trembled, giving it voice; the earth did not break beneath the demon's feet. Nor did it attempt to swallow him.

His knees bent as he pushed himself up in one lean, graceful motion, wings unfurling and taking, as they did, whole branches from the trees themselves. Those branches, like the great stone spears, moved to impede him, and diamond sliced obsidian as it passed. The demon roared in rage. Diamond shattered as his sword rose and fell.

It was not the only sword in the clearing now; it was the only red one.

Celleriant—angry—had arrived. The wind carried him; Jewel whispered a benediction to its rushing, agitated currents. It was not slow in the way the earth was, but it carried the only sworn knight in her very small Court toward his opponent. Like the earth, it was not hers to command; she granted permission, no more. But permission now was all that was needed.

Why is it always night?

Blue blade struck red. When two such blades were drawn, what other outcome could there be? Sky of red fire, sky of blue ice, and the clear, clean sound of metal and metal. The demon had no wind to buoy him; Celleriant, smaller, was in constant motion. He should have been faster; he was only barely fast enough.

It isn't.

Was it only at night that she entered the forest? Was it only at night that she walked the hidden paths that were at once wild and strangely familiar? She was not safe yet, and knew it—but beneath the din of blades, and words that were at least as cutting, she closed her eyes. The fire still enveloped her, offering warmth, not pain. The sun—in seasons that were not Summer—was warm in the same way.

The Summer.

Meralonne APhaniel, on the first day she'd seen him, had called Summer in The Terafin's reception room. There, daylight streamed through windows that were framed by heavy curtains; the Summer was close, the night absent. Here, it was night—but dawn followed night. Always.

She could see and feel sunlight, broken as it was by leaves that also grew toward its touch. It was time, she thought, for night to retreat; to surrender its indigo to the pale purple and pink of morning light. It was time, now, for azure to reign in the skies above the forest. She couldn't call day; no more could she call earth, wind, or water. But she could welcome it. As if she were leaf, she lifted her face, seeking the sunlight that would deny the night the demon lord kept wrapped around him.

When she opened her eyes, she had to squint; the whole of the clearing was bathed in a brilliant, pale light. It wasn't white, would never be white—that was a Winter color, harsh and lifeless. This light looked like burnished silver. She stood in the center of its gentle brilliance and watched it as it spread in all directions, rippling across the familiar forms of standing trees, undergrowth; changing the color of pillars of moving stone and new-turned earth.

The light was not kind to Avandar. In the pale brightness, he was ashen, the skin beneath his eyes, dark. But his lips were curved in a cold smile as he lifted his face.

There, above them both, the demon lord was caught for a moment in spokes of light that passed through his wings as if they were blades. Celleriant was likewise illuminated, but the Summer did not cut or burn him; the wind carried him, and he drove his blade into the demon's leg. Or he would have, had the red shield not blocked his sudden thrust. Even injured, the demon lord was fast.

And if Celleriant's blade had not struck home, the *Kialli* was wounded; the light burned; smoke streamed from his still-perfect skin. The pillars of stone stretched and thinned as they reached for the demon, and even in his obvious pain, he broke them. Not with sword or shield; those were reserved for Celleriant; he kicked them and they shattered.

What is he? Jewel asked the distant Winter King.

He is firstborn, Jewel. Among the Kialli, *he is Prince.*

He's like Ariane?

No; she is Queen, and she is other. But even Ariane would find such a foe difficult. Viandaran is correct; he is beyond us.

The wind buffeted his injured wings; the earth attempted to break him; Celleriant harried him with ferocious concentration. The only thing that had done notable damage was the Summer light. It had not, however, destroyed Darranatos; nor did he seem intent on destroying himself. He was angry, yes; he roared and the whole of the forest shook.

But only when Meralonne APhaniel arrived did the demon lord take the risk of exposing his back. He wheeled, turned, and dropped in a short dive that ended with Jewel.

It should have ended her life, but the trees surrendered whole limbs in a sudden converging of branches; he broke them all, but they slowed his fall enough that she could dive toward the burning tree. It was an instinctive reaction. The fire with which she'd cloaked herself had saved her once; she wasn't certain it would save her again—but she had time to think this only after his sword pierced earth—and stayed there. He could not easily withdraw it.

Nor could he easily avoid the twin blades of Celleriant and Meralonne, who took advantage of the opening to thrust swords through his back. Blood, dark and only barely red even in this light, darkened their swords as they were withdrawn; he had the strength of earth, and the strength to bind those blades. Jewel knew it, and didn't question the knowledge.

He tried, once more, to dislodge his own weapon; earth flew in a wide circle—but it did not surrender blade. His hands, straining around the sword's hilt, were bleeding. Twice more, two men struck, but not a third time; he snarled, roared; his sword disappeared as he released it.

And then, wings flagging, he revealed a whip of fire; with its many tongues he attacked not Celleriant or Meralonne, but the air which carried them. She heard the wind's sudden anger and realized that the fire was not natural—if demonic magic could *ever* be natural—but wild. She did not hear its voice. The wind did, and the earth, and their voices were as clear as thunder. They had been kept from warring with each other by the skill of their summoners—but the fire was one foe too many.

Avandar's jaw tightened; Jewel saw his fists clench. She heard Meralonne's cry of warning and she cried out, wordless, as her own hands curled into fists. The trees had been broken and burned by the demon and his great wings, and they had suffered in silence; this fire enraged them. It was almost as if—as if—

She shook her head and lifting her hands, pulled the trees' branches up toward their trunks, skirting fire as the wind tore it into many smaller pieces—none of which guttered. They were driven to earth and bark; they were blown toward the trailing length of her hem. In each case, they began to burn. But this close to earth, these small fires could not survive; the earth swallowed them whole. Jewel almost fell into the pit that opened beneath her burning skirt; roots caught her legs as she stumbled, leaving bruises.

The earth closed like a giant maw. She could live with the bruises; she was certain she wouldn't have survived the earth.

Day gave way to dusk. Had she summoned Summer? No, she thought, as the season slipped away. She had drawn it from the memories of these standing giants with their roots in the deep earth and their crowns in the wind. But it was not Summer in this forest, and the trees wailed as it slipped away, as if it might never be Summer again.

"Meralonne!" she shouted.

But he knew. As Celleriant continued to harry the injured demon, Meralonne put up his sword and stepped back; the wind drove his hair as if it were snow. He spoke, his voice resonant and clear, and as he did, she saw again the golden, glowing light that had once saved The Terafin's life. It encircled the demon; the demon roared.

"Illaraphaniel, you will die for this."

The mage did not laugh, as he might once have; nor did he frown. "I will not die here, Darranatos. Not so far from my home, and not in this season. If you wish my death to be at your hands, you must find a different battlefield; you will not have victory here."

The Summer light intensified, hardening around the demon lord as if it were shell.

Jewel knew it wouldn't last. It caused pain, yes, but it could not destroy the creature Meralonne had called Darranatos. As if he'd heard the thought, he summoned not dusk, but night. It came like a flood, filling all of the space that existed between his body and the summer shield of the mage's construction.

"Illaraphaniel!" Celleriant's sword passed through the barrier. It slowed in its sweeping arc, and then passed through the night as well; black clung to the edge of his blade as he cursed. The demon had fled. With him went fire, or rather, fire's sentience; what remained, the earth smothered.

Meralonne descended. His eyes were silver. "So," he said softly. "Sigurne was correct."

Jewel didn't ask him what the guildmaster had said. She was staring at the *Kialli*-shaped darkness that lay beneath a thin, thin sheen of Summer light. "You're not—you're not just going to leave that standing there, are you?"

Meralonne reached into his robes and produced a familiar pipe. "No. I will destroy it, with your permission."

The Winter King came to stand by her side. *Be cautious, Jewel.*

The mage lined the bowl of his pipe, but his eyes never left her face. He was waiting for her answer—and waiting with an uncharacteristic patience. "Why is my permission required?" she finally asked.

His smile was slight, sharp; it acknowledged a hit. "Ask your companion," he replied, nodding not to Celleriant, but to the Winter King. The Winter King lowered his tines in what Jewel assumed was a gesture of respect.

It was both that, and a subtle threat.

I'm not sure Meralonne understands subtle threats.

Lord Celleriant had set aside both sword and shield in the aftermath of the interrupted battle; he joined Jewel just before the cats—all three—flew down in a loud, messy rush. They did not knock Jewel over, but it was close. She turned to Shadow immediately.

"Why are you here?" she demanded.

Shadow hissed.

"I mean it, Shadow. There was a demon here—"

"I *know* that. It was a *big* demon." He glanced at Snow and Night, who were now standing to the left and right of him. And two steps behind. "*He* told me you were *alone*. He didn't mention the *ugly* one."

She cleared her throat loudly. Shadow's belly reached for ground, and his ears flattened. His lips, on the other hand, pulled up over teeth that were already too prominent. "We have a guest," she told him evenly.

"Guest? *What* guest?"

"Behind you."

Shadow moved his incredibly flexible neck to look over his shoulder at Meralonne APhaniel, whose pipe remained unlit. The mage was staring intently at the cat.

"They came with the forest," she told him, folding arms across her chest.

Snow, however, sauntered over to the mage, pausing a few yards away. It was, for a cat who assumed ownership—or at least superior power—over everything, significant. "I *know* you," he said.

The mage said nothing. After another moment, he lit his pipe.

Night, not to be outdone, approached Meralonne as carefully as his brother. Only Shadow remained where he was, although he rose and turned toward the mage. "Don't let *him* destroy the shadow," he said.

"Why not?"

"It is not *his* forest."

"I'm not asking him to claim the forest. I just want to get rid of the—"

"Yes, yes." Shadow stretched his forepaws, his back sloping, his wings rising. "*We* will *eat* it."

She raised a brow. Before she could speak, Meralonne removed the pipe's stem from his lips. "It is not impossible for them. How did they come to be with you?"

"They came, as I said, with the forest."

"They are dangerous." He blew smoke rings in the direction of the cats. "Have you bound them to your service?"

Shadow hissed. Snow and Night, however, growled.

"No."

"Unwise."

"Do not attempt to eat him," she told the cats severely. "I need him."

"You *don't*. No one needs *him*."

Meralonne surprised her; he smiled. "No, indeed." He pointed with his pipe hand. "That tree, Terafin, I do not recognize." He meant the tree of fire.

"The demon today wasn't the only demon to walk in this forest," she replied with care. The dense, standing darkness bothered her far more than the tree. "He brought fire with him."

"And you retained it?"

She nodded.

To her surprise, Meralonne turned to Celleriant. "Did you recognize the demon to whom she refers?" He didn't ask Celleriant if he had been in the forest at the time of the demonic attack; he assumed it.

Nor did this seem to surprise—or concern—the Arianni Lord. He nodded. "Lord Ishavriel," he told the mage. "Of the Shining Court."

A silver brow rose; for the first time that day, Meralonne

smiled. It was a Winter smile, at home in his angular face.
"You witnessed the birth of this tree?"

"I did." Celleriant's smile now matched Meralonne's.

"*Can* we?" Shadow asked, as if neither man had spoken.

"Can you what?"

He hissed and shook his head at the sheer stupidity of
the question. "Can we *eat* it? Or will you wait until it dies of
boredom?"

Still hesitating, she nodded. The cats turned as one from
Meralonne APhaniel, and leaped toward the darkness. The
Summer light didn't stop them.

"No, wait—be careful—don't jump—" She might as well
have told them not to breathe, speak, or fight. They hit the
darkness, claws extended, and passed right through it. Unfortunately, they didn't come out the other side.

"They were never terribly bright," the mage said, pipe
once again trailing smoke. "And they were always the antithesis of caution."

Jewel could barely find voice to answer. "Where did they
go?"

"Who can say, with cats? There is a reasonable chance
they will return. Look."

She couldn't look away. The patch of darkness, through
which nothing could be seen, began to change shape; it grew
shorter, squatter; it pressed against the containment of
Summer magic as if seeking escape. It shrank.

That was the good news. But when it was smaller than
the size of a single cat and the cats had failed to emerge,
she approached it; she couldn't quite stop herself. The
Winter King, however, could. He was there, his tines between Jewel and what remained of the demon lord's passage. *Do not touch it.*

She turned to Avandar, wordless.

"In my opinion, you would be well quit of them should
they fail to emerge. They are quarrelsome, difficult beasts; it
is in their very nature to cause damage and trouble if not
carefully supervised. They have not," he added, in case it
was in doubt, "been carefully supervised for the entire duration of their stay."

"They've killed no one."

He stared at her.

"They've killed no one who wasn't trying to kill me."

"True. But had at least one of those people remained alive, we might have been able to retrieve information from them."

"It doesn't matter. We can't bring them back. Avandar—the cats—"

Meralonne exhaled. It was like a loud sigh, but adorned with smoke, which he then blew into rings. "They are only foolish, Terafin. They are not suicidal. But they will not return this way."

"We should have just left the darkness—"

The Winter King and Celleriant turned to stare at her, and she failed to finish the sentence.

"I am still," Meralonne said, "by contract, the Terafin House Mage. If you will allow it, I will remain in service to the House." He glanced once again at the tree of fire.

"I will, if the terms of employment don't radically change."

"How so?"

"I don't want to pay through the nose for the services of the magi at the present time. And I know how much the Order of Knowledge raises its price when they believe the situation might be 'difficult' as they call it."

His brows rose and then he laughed. It was not a quiet laugh.

Celleriant, at his side, was smiling. It was clear to Jewel that they knew each other. They had both been in the South. But there was something about their proximity now that implied, strongly, that the knowledge was older than the war in the Dominion. How old?

"I believe," Avandar told her, voice dry as autumn leaves, "that you are in the unusual position of being able to bargain the Order of Knowledge down in price, not up. The magi are free to accept legal employ—with the guildmaster's permission, of course—at their own convenience. If you attempt to secure his services for *less* than the Order is accustomed to receiving from the House, and you succeed, it will be a point in your favor in the newly constituted House Council.

"The Order may react poorly to the attempt, but they cannot reject it out of hand; Member APhaniel is a First Circle mage, a member of the magi; should he desire to do so, he could remain as the Terafin House Mage for free. It is entirely in the hands of Member APhaniel."

"I rather think," Meralonne said, although he was clearly still amused, "that such a tactic would not stand *me* in good stead."

"And this is a concern of yours?"

He shook his head. "No. Sigurne is likely to be unimpressed, but she will accept it—if I do." His eyes narrowed. "Your tenure is not, in your opinion, secure?"

"That's a bold question," Jewel replied, striving to attain a patrician tone of voice.

"It is, indeed. Your status may have changed; mine has not. If you recall, I was not perhaps the most politic of The Terafin's many servants."

"How could I forget?" She shook her head. "But you would never have dared to ask The Terafin *that* question."

"No; she was who she was. You are who you are. My history with your Terafin was not—is not—my history with you. If you prefer, I will defer to the general rules that govern interaction with the head of a House." He blew another large, lazy smoke ring.

Jewel remembered, as it rose, just how much The Terafin had hated his pipe, and she laughed. She couldn't help it. How many hours had she been trapped in a room with this arrogant, mercurial member of the Order of Knowledge? She had crawled through the dirt by his side for so long she couldn't clean it from beneath her fingernails without an hour's worth of soap, water, and Ellerson. How many meetings between The Terafin and Meralonne APhaniel had she been forced to attend, where she huddled as inconspicuously as possible out of the range of their wrath?

"No, I think I'll pass. I would appreciate it if you failed to mention that decision to any member of my House Council." She glanced at Avandar. "And my domicis, but I suppose it's too late for that."

The corners of the mage's eyes crinkled as he smiled. "Does that mean you will answer the impertinent question, Terafin?"

She swept one arm in a wide circle that encompassed one tree of fire, one tree of diamond, two of gold, and one of silver. "What, by the way, are the tall trees called?"

"The tall trees?"

"The natural ones. The ones that grow in the Common."

Meralonne glanced at Celleriant, whose expression was so neutral it had to be forced. "I am not entirely certain that you deserve *entry* to this forest. But I find myself hungry, and would be obliged if you offered refreshments while we are here."

She hesitated, her demeanor changing. "I'm not sure I can."

"Oh?"

"We should go back to the Common. If the demon—"

"Ah. No. Your ploy was, if unexpected, both wise and successful. Had Darranatos been more certain of your vulnerability, he would have taken the time to cut a large swathe through the patriciate of this fair city before he abandoned the Common in pursuit. He was not. And, to be fair, ATerafin—"

Avandar glared.

"—Terafin. It is not an intentional slight, Viandaran. I have had years in which the *polite* form of address was the one I just misused. You have my word that if we were in more grave circumstances, I would—"

"*More* grave?" Jewel's voice rose in pitch. It was a trait that she had all but abandoned in her dealings with men— and women—of power.

One silver brow rose with the smoke, although it didn't fly free. "You are not dead. If I recall those creatures correctly, you will now have a few moments of peace and privacy. And," he added, as he began to walk away, "you are excused an afternoon of tremendous tedium in the company of preening nobility."

"I have to—"

"You could not defend yourself, Jewel. Go back to the Common, and what guarantee have you that Darranatos, or his kind, will not return?"

"I'm seer-born. I'll have warning."

"Ah, yes. You'll note that I did not say he would kill *you*."

Chapter Three

7th of Fabril, 428 A.A.
The Terafin Manse, Averalaan Aramarelas

THE SERVANTS WERE NOT HAPPY to see Jewel. They were, however, ATerafin, and their shock and concern did not show. It would, however, travel faster than fire through the back halls and the servants' quarters; she was certain most of the manse would know that she was not in the Common by the time she reached the West Wing.

Lord Celleriant did not choose to accompany her, and she knew why. He was injured. He tended his injuries in isolation; he could not abide even the mention of the healerie. The Winter King likewise remained in the forest. But Avandar and Meralonne did not.

She found the walk to the West Wing almost disturbing in its silence; only the sounds of their feet accompanied them. On a normal day, Snow would have walked by her side, and since Night and Shadow had also been present, there would have been the usual snarling, hissing, and misplaced paws; the walk would have taken longer. She shook herself. When had the disruptive and annoying behavior of unruly children become normal?

But she glanced over her shoulder, looking for a glimpse of the cats, aware, as she did, that Amarais would never have done the same. At sixteen, Jewel had been certain that

The Terafin hadn't *had* emotions. Now, she knew that she must have. She had given everything to the House, in the end, even her life; no one who was devoid of emotion or humanity could have done what she did.

It was only a matter of hiding it. Of protecting it. Of keeping it so private, people could assume that its absence meant strength. And why, she thought bitterly, was that how strength was defined? Why was it wrong to show some part of what you felt if you felt it *anyway*?

It is a display of will, Jewel, the Winter King replied. She hadn't meant to radiate the silent question so loudly. *The desire for expression is strong; it is, in part, the desire to communicate. It is fundamental; it is true.*

So is lying.

She felt the momentary warmth of his silent chuckle. *Yes. The desire for approval is also fundamental. The canny and the wise understand this; they can bend it to their use, as if it were any other more corporeal tool. But think: if you display yourself and your truths so easily, you hand those tools to your enemies—or your allies; there is frequently very little that separates them.*

She thought of her den. It annoyed the Winter King.

Strength means many things. Your Terafin was strong enough that she could—and did—choose what to reveal. And when. You will learn to do likewise.

She failed to answer. They were approaching the West Wing. Chosen stood outside the entrance, but only two; there would be four on the interior, no doubt roused by the servants and warned of her unexpected arrival. It was not, however, the Chosen who were her chief concern.

Ellerson was waiting as the doors opened. "Terafin." His tone was smooth, cool, and entirely uninflected; she had brought a guest. His brows, however, rose as he pointedly looked at her right sleeve. Her own gaze followed his as if dragged, and she winced. Blood had, indeed, seeped through the cloth.

"There was some difficulty at the Common," she told him, resisting the impulse to shove the arm behind her back.

"I see. Shall I send word to the healerie, Terafin?"

"No. The wound was slight, and it has long since ceased to bleed. We will take tea in the great room."

Meralonne lifted his chin.

"Or very early lunch, if that is acceptable."

When the doors to the great room closed, Meralonne APhaniel sat—heavily and gracelessly—in one of the large chairs closest to the fireplace. Avandar stood to Jewel's left. She resisted the urge to tell him to sit down, although he looked exhausted.

"Jewel," the mage said, tapping ash from his pipe, "do you understand what you have done here?"

"Maybe. What do you call the trees?"

He looked momentarily astonished at the question. Shaking his head, he said, "they are called many things in many different languages."

"The Weston word?"

He all but snorted in derision. "The Kings' trees, the god trees, The trees. They have more formal Weston names; you will have heard none of them."

"If I had, I wouldn't be asking."

"You have not asked your Master Gardener?"

"No."

"And yet you presume to ask a First Circle mage of the Order of Knowledge?"

"Clearly."

His smile sharpened. The Winter King was right. People wanted approval. *Jewel* wanted approval, even the small scraps this arrogant man occasionally threw. "Very well. One of the oldest words for those trees is *Ellariannatte*. It is not a word in common use; the word is often abbreviated. Ellarian."

"It sounds . . . like a name. I mean, a person's name."

"As you say." The pipe, filled, was lifted to lip, where it paused. It was his punctuation. "But you were wrong in one regard."

"Only one? I've improved."

"Indeed. You called them natural trees. By that I assume you meant they were not magical in nature."

"They're not."

"As I said, you were—and are—wrong in that regard."

"Meralonne, I can *see* magic."

"Clearly you can, as you crudely put it, see *some* magic. There is a reason the *Ellariannatte* grow only in the Common.

And here," he added, as she opened her mouth. "I leave it to you to divine the reason, and perhaps that is unwise." He closed his eyes. "You do not understand what you have done here."

"No. Not in a way I can put into words."

Eyes still closed, he leaned back against the chair, his hair spilling down his arms. No wind moved it, but in the light, it gleamed in a way that implied color. "The stability of your leadership?" he asked, without opening his eyes.

"As you've no doubt heard, I've had some difficulties. This counts as the fifth attempt on my life in the last two months; it's certainly the most public, and easily the most dangerous."

"All of the assassins were demonic?"

"As an adjective, yes, but in the physical sense, no. Three of the five—if you count the Common—were demons."

"They worked alone?"

"Yes." She paused and then added, "To the best of our knowledge. It's probably more accurate to say they made the attempt alone."

"And the other two?"

"Men. Four men in the uniform of the House Guard— they were not House Guards. One woman."

"Your investigations?"

"Are internal. I am willing to discuss what I've learned; I am not willing to compromise my own."

"Very well." Pipe smoke, like fire, could be strangely comforting. She wondered what her Oma would have made of the mage were she here; she was certain that there would be two pipes burning in this room, not one. "You require a House Mage."

Which he knew. "I do."

"I will, for a concession, add in some small way to the political stability of your House."

She considered Celleriant's continual offer to do the same, and wondered darkly if this were similar. But Meralonne was a member of the Order of Knowledge, and he served Sigurne Mellifas; a woman less likely to slaughter the difficult parts of the House Council could not be found. Certainly not in this room, on this day. "Your concession?"

"You are free, of course, to refuse. The Order will second

one of the First Circle to these duties—but if you refuse, Jewel, it will not be me."

She tapped the arm rest of her own chair impatiently. "APhaniel, your concession?"

One pale brow rose. "I am to be granted access—at times of my own choosing—to the Terafin grounds."

She waited. When it became clear that he had no intention of adding further words, she rose. She was, not unexpectedly, exhausted. She wanted word sent to the Common, but knew it was unlikely to be heard; although the demon had followed her, he had caused damage, and the resulting chaos, where it involved the Kings, would be the primary concern of everyone present.

Everyone except Teller, Finch, and Angel. The Chosen as well. She desperately wanted to know that everyone had survived—but Meralonne APhaniel was not the man to ask. She considered asking Avandar to go to the Common and discarded that option; if Meralonne was an acquaintance of long standing, he was also an unknown. She could not afford to give Avandar a public order that he would refuse to obey.

"Why do you require that access?" She knew, before she asked, she would acquiesce. If Meralonne was an unknown, had always been an unknown, she was nonetheless certain that he could do her no harm in the grounds of the Terafin manse. Even the attempt would see him cast out of the Order as a rogue mage—a very, very dangerous one.

"My reasons are my own, Terafin. I mean you no harm."

"And I mean the Empire no harm."

He frowned. "Is there a reason that you are stating the almost criminally obvious?" He might have been Haval. Or Avandar.

She swallowed exasperation and gave reign to the amusement the words had also evoked. "You haven't spent much time with Sigurne since your return from the South, have you?"

"I have."

"And she's voiced no concern?"

"Ah, I see the difficulty. You misunderstand me, Terafin. You misunderstand," he added thoughtfully, "almost artfully. She is aware—most of the Isle is aware—of the unusual circumstances that now surround House Terafin, and in particular its young leader. The magi dislike mysteries as a matter of principle, and they will speak the life out of them if given the smallest opportunity. They attempt, again, given opportunity, to turn magic into rudimentary *mathematics.*"

"And you do not count yourself among the magi?"

"Not in that regard, no. The work is too dry for my taste. You have now wasted minutes of my time at your leisure, and Sigurne has requested my attendance."

Jewel turned. "When you leave to attend Sigurne, please inform my House Council that the situation is in hand."

"Very well. Your decision?"

"I think you understand what I don't," she replied. "And inasmuch as it affects my House, I require you to share the information you gain from the unlimited access you request."

"I am willing to tender reports of that nature at your convenience."

"Good. I also require one of two things in return."

"And those?"

"You will either indenture yourself—and the entirety of your time—to House Terafin for a period of not less than five years," which Jewel knew would be flat out impossible, although the words left no impression on Meralonne's face, "or you come—and go—as your current House contract dictates, without monetary concession."

Meralonne stared at her for a full minute, and then he burst out laughing. It was a deep, rich sound that filled the whole of the room; it probably traveled up the empty fireplace and out the chimney, where it would startle birds. "The guildmaster will not be pleased."

"That is not my concern; it is yours."

"She could order me to refuse the House contract."

"She could—but she's never struck me as foolish. You'll do what you want, Member APhaniel. She's known you for longer than I've been alive; she knows. She may tell you your acceptance of the terms harms the future earning potential of the magi, she may ask that you *consider* refusing it; she may even go so far as to paint it an insult. She won't forbid it."

"Terafin, I believe I am genuinely surprised."

"The demon did not surprise you, the cats did not surprise you, the forest did not surprise you. Even the demands I have made did not surprise you. A single observation about Sigurne?"

"Even so." He rose, tapping ash out of the bowl of his pipe into the empty fireplace. It was not, strictly speaking, for such ash. "I will deliver the message. Both of them. Word will travel," he added.

"If you know I'm not dangerous—"

"I did not say that. I merely said that it is obvious you *intend* no harm. You have touched things that even the magi cannot touch; you have demonstrated that you are powerful. You are content—in a way that almost no mage would be—to wander in ignorance. You *are* a threat."

She was silent as he left.

He did not return to Sigurne, not immediately. Instead, he followed the galleries until he reached the wide glass doors of the terrace. They were guarded, but loosely; most of the House Council was still absent. Meralonne made certain that the pendant that marked the Order of Knowledge was clearly visible as he approached the closed doors.

One of the guards stopped him.

"The grounds are forbidden."

"The Terafin has returned from the grounds, and she has given me leave to examine them for magical interference. *I* am not in danger."

The guard was young. He was not foolish; Meralonne considered many courses of action, but chose waiting. The wait was under ten minutes, and involved a second guard moving with unseemly haste down the hall. In five minutes, a man whose tabard had the subtle marking that distinguished the Terafin Chosen from the Terafin House Guard appeared; he did not run. He was no youth; nor did he appear to be perturbed by Meralonne's gently spoken demand.

"Member APhaniel."

"ATerafin."

"The grounds are off-limits to anyone currently resident within the manse, by order of The Terafin."

"I have just retired from an audience with The Terafin, and I enter the grounds at her request." It was more or less the same claim he had made in the face of the younger guard's nervousness.

"Very well." The Chosen turned to the guard who'd been sent for greater authority. "Member APhaniel is granted a temporary leave to enter the grounds. He is the only exception." Thus, the power of the Chosen in the Terafin manse. The man accepted responsibility for allowing Meralonne to leave when no countermand had been given to prior orders.

Meralonne turned to the young guard who blocked his way, and the man almost gratefully moved.

He heard the voice of the wind. It was playful, light, sweet with the scent of hidden flowers, clear water. He heard the movement of leaves; a different man might be mistaken in thinking their rustle entirely due to the passage of air. His pipe, he put aside as he approached the path crafted by the Terafin gardeners. It did not conform to the forest, but it did not confine it, either. The trees that lined this walkway, tended like the path and the flower beds, nonetheless surrendered the white stag and Celleriant as Meralonne walked.

"I have come," he said gravely, "with your Lord's permission. I am no longer entirely certain that I could do so, otherwise."

The Winter King lowered his tines briefly; the gesture was tense.

"It is not Summer, here," the mage said.

"But it is not Winter, not quite."

Meralonne smiled. It would have shocked Jewel, had she seen it. "No, it is not quite Winter. You truly serve her, now."

Lord Celleriant nodded. He was unarmed, in the way that the Arianni are. "Will you walk the forest, Illaraphaniel?"

"I will." He took a step forward, hesitating in a way that was almost foreign. Lord Celleriant did not hesitate, as the Winter King had; he stepped aside and Meralonne stepped off the tended path, and onto the wild one.

He could feel the difference in the earth beneath his feet almost instantly; could sense the playful breath of the wind. There was, as yet, no water here, although he was certain, if Jewel explored, she would find brooks, streams, perhaps even a significant river. He wondered if she would know what to do with them, or rather, if she would attempt anything at all.

He walked until he reached a tree of living diamond. "It has been so long," he said, lifting a hand to the tree's cool bark. "And I have been so entwined in the affairs of this mortal city I am almost ashamed of my thoughts."

"Oh?"

"Her House might cull a leaf or two and sell it."

Celleriant's silence was sharp and sudden. It did not last. "You have, indeed, been too long in the company of mortals."

"Your Lord is mortal."

"Yet she has never considered such an enterprise."

"Not yet. Would you stop her?"

". . . No. But I would make my feelings quite clear."

"And you would survive it, no doubt; Jewel ATerafin was ever a woman comfortable with an excess of feeling." He lowered his hand. "Diamond, gold, silver."

"You did not expect them."

"No. And yet, they feel natural to me." He lifted face and gazed at the height of the *Ellariannatte*. "But these? One could almost feel young again beneath their bowers. I have served as the Terafin mage for decades; I have worked in this City for longer. These trees are at the heart of the hundred holdings—where any child might play atop exposed roots. Did you not see them?"

Celleriant nodded.

"Did you not wonder?"

"The trees in the mortal city are silent, Illaraphaniel. They do not speak, they do not wake."

"Yet they grow. I do not think they will remain sleeping; before this is over, even in a forest of wood and stone and human foibles, you will hear their song."

"It will not please my Lord."

"No, perhaps not. Perhaps she will be content to let them sleep; they have slept long. But where other trees might wither in mute silence, these do not, not there. In the Terafin grounds they are not mute, but their voices are subtle," he added, "and curious."

"Curious?"

"They do not speak with a single voice. They speak with two, and one of them is Jewel Markess ATerafin's."

"She does not realize how much of a danger you are."

Meralonne chuckled. "No. No more does she realize how much of a danger you are." He turned; the Winter King had followed at a safer distance than the Arianni Prince. "Will you not bespeak your Lord?"

"No. I will leave that in your hands."

"I do not serve Jewel."

"No, you do not. But I perceive that you better understand the subtleties of her thought than I."

"Did you not first encounter her upon the hidden path, Lord Celleriant? Were you not then part of the Winter Host?"

Celleriant nodded. "And I have waited, APhaniel. I have listened. I have remained in this forest. But I have not heard the song of the Summer Queen. I have not felt the call of the Summer Court." He smiled, and to Meralonne's surprise, it was rueful, not bitter.

"What is this?" the mage asked softly.

"The Summer is not for me, now."

"It is not," Meralonne replied as he stepped away from the trunk of the rising *Ellariannatte*, "for any of us."

Celleriant stiffened and turned. "Explain yourself."

"Have a care, Lord Celleriant. I do not wish to engage in combat here, but your Lord will allow it if it does not endanger either your life, or mine. She might not notice it at all if we do not damage her trees."

For a moment the very air around the Arianni Lord's hands seemed to waver. Merlonne's hands, however? They now contained his pipe. "I have become accustomed to mortal arrogance," he said, when Celleriant failed to draw sword. "It never fails to amuse. But you are not as they are, Lord Celleriant."

". . . No. Why has there been no Summer? She called the long hunt against the Winter King; I heard the horns; I saw the host pass."

"She did. The Winter King perished, as he must, at her hands."

"Then—"

"There are no Summer trees."

Celleriant stared at Meralonne APhaniel as if the mage had lost his mind.

"I make no cruel, tasteless jest. There have been no Summer trees, and it is my fear that there will be none. She will not reign in Summer, nor again ride in Winter; both faces of her power will be denied her."

"Illaraphaniel—what could now prevent it?"

"The Lord of the Shining Court removed the Winter seedlings. His *Kialli* planted them in mortal lands—in the newly killed flesh of mortal children."

No words escaped the Arianni Prince, but Meralonne did not expect them, not yet. "I traveled the length of the borders of the Terrean of Averda, at the side of Kallandras of Senniel College."

"Kallandras."

"Yes."

"He has returned?"

"No, but he will. The South holds him until the coronation of the new Tyr—but it is to Averalaan that he is drawn. The trees were planted in such a corrupting fashion along the border of the Terrean. We hoped to find one we could purify without destruction."

"You did not."

"No."

Celleriant closed his eyes briefly. "They will die, for this. Does she know?"

"That the seedlings are gone? Almost certainly. But if the *Kialli* sought to remove Ariane from the game, they have also hampered themselves; there is no Winter upon which to draw power."

"They have never derived power from Summer."

Meralonne was silent for a long moment. "Not never, Celleriant. But if not for the suspension of all natural law, I do not think your Lord would have survived this first meeting. Darranatos was always powerful."

"If he is upon the plane—"

"Yes. He was not summoned. Could not be summoned by any save the Lord of Night. They have opened their gate, and the demons now cross the barrier without the need of name as a binding to hold them here."

"And the Summer Queen cannot take arms against him."

"Not yet. I am not—entirely—without hope, but it is scant." Shadows touched the forest floor and spread. Meralonne frowned, his eyes narrowing. These were not shadows cast by light. They were sharp, cold. Celleriant was angry. "Your Lord does not understand what she holds, here. It is a small miracle that she holds it at all."

The Arianni Lord stiffened and glanced at the shadows that had caught the mage's attention. "She does."

"I have seen that; the *Ellariannatte* speak her name." He continued to walk through the trees until he found the lone tree of fire. "But this, Celleriant, this is a sign."

Lord Celleriant was silent, shuttered; the news had disturbed him greatly. Here, too, the shadows that lay across the forest floor had darkened. The red light of fire did not dispel them; it deepened them.

"Does she understand at least this much?" Meralonne asked. He reached, carefully, for the trunk of this rooted flame; it could not be said to have bark. It was, in height, the shortest of the trees.

"I do not know. She has entered this forest only twice; she skirts its edges timidly, otherwise. She lets the *Master Gardener* play at arranging life as he sees fit; she will not touch his flower pots or his flower beds. She will not alter his tame, tepid saplings, his lifeless stone pillars; there is only one work worthy of note here at all, and it is all but hidden."

"The fountain on the terrace?"

"Yes. She could change all of the lesser things. She might build a garden here, and a palace, that would be reckoned truly beautiful, even by our kin. But she will not welcome the forest into her home."

"You did not expect otherwise, surely?"

"Mortal men once wielded power of this magnitude. They were not terrified of what it signified. They did not doubt themselves because they had touched it. They built, Illaraphaniel." Celleriant lifted his face toward the bowers of fire, his lips curved in reminiscence. "Even I, who seldom had cause to visit the Cities of Man, remember what they wrought. They came, at times, to the Summer Court with gifts for the Summer Queen—and those gifts rivaled ours, not in execution, but in conception, in urgency. We know death," he added softly, "but a life as long as ours so seldom instills that urgency, that bright desire, that obvious desperation." He shook his head and lowered it. "She is not—entirely—at home here."

"Yet she is at its heart."

"Is she?"

"You serve her, Lord Celleriant. Can you not feel her presence? It is at the heart of this tree—and a tree such as this, I have seldom seen planted. Not even the Winter King could hold it in the heart of his lands. It does not burn the trees; it does not burn the undergrowth."

"It will burn the birds that currently fly here."

"They are not foolish enough to land. Tell me, if you will: why did she plant it?"

"It was Lord Ishavriel's fire. I believe she sought to contain it or use it; I am not certain. But its fire has not guttered."

"No. And she did indeed use it. It is one of the few defenses she might have brought to bear against Darranatos. And," he added, slowly lowering his hand. "She did."

"It was sloppy."

"It was." He turned to Lord Celleriant. "They fear her."

The Arianni Lord pretended no ignorance. "No more than she fears herself. It is only when she is pressed—and today, she was—that she overcomes her fear."

Meralonne shook his head. "She does not overcome it; she merely gives way to a stronger, more visceral fear. That fear moves her to protect what she claims to love. Without it? She is afraid to be a threat to the Kings, the Exalted, The Ten. No—it is not even that. She fears the cost of this magic upon the people who dwell in the old city, the hundred holdings."

"They cannot harm her."

"No, not in any way that would be of significance to us—but we are not Jewel, and we are not Sen."

"What will you then do?"

"I? I will bespeak Sigurne Mellifas. I will counsel the Kings. I will serve as House Mage, and in that capacity, I will counsel your Lord."

"To what end?"

"You were in the South, Lord Celleriant. What we saw there is only the beginning. I have never been one to believe in destiny or fate; destiny or fate is something applied after event, when bards create their narratives. But having said that, I will say this: without Jewel, this city faces annihilation."

"And with her, Illaraphaniel?"

"War. But that was coming, regardless. There is power, in this city, to withstand much." He walked away from the tree of fire. As he did, he frowned. "Lord Celleriant, there is a presence in this place that is not hers."

Celleriant fell silent.

"It is elusive," the magi continued, as if the pause were insignificant. He glanced at the Winter King, not the Arianni Lord. "Do you sleep here?" The words were sharper, colder. The mage knelt, touching the ground with the flat of one palm. He spoke a word, two, and the wind grew stronger, pulling at the strands of his pale hair.

The Winter King shook his head: No.

"When did this occur? Is she aware of it?"

The Winter King nodded, but it was a hesitant nod.

The mage rose and uttered one weary sigh. "I will speak with Jewel," he told them both. "But I fear there is now a danger that I did not anticipate. One of the firstborn found this path before it called her here—and what one discovers, the others are certain to discover."

Haval joined Jewel a scant hour after her return to the West Wing; she had, with the departure of Meralonne, successfully dismissed her domicis. The clothier looked pinched and exhausted, and he surprised her by allowing it to show. Suspicion followed surprise; she weighed his expression carefully against known facts. "Did Hannerle wake?"

"Not as such. But she spoke in her sleep, and she spoke clearly and lucidly. I thought she spoke to me," he added, with a trace of bitterness. "And so she did—but no words that I said reached her ears. Her dreams—of me—are clearly not kind."

"But—this is the first time she's talked in her sleep."

"It is. Or at least it's the first time she's done it while I've been present. Can I consider this progress, of a type?"

"Did you call Adam?"

"I did not. I was fascinated, being the object of the rather heated conversation; I did not wish to pull myself away. There is always a certain amount of curiosity about what one's nearest and dearest actually think. There is also a strong incentive not to share the experience, especially not with one as young as Adam." The words were, again, bitter, but he adorned them with an ironic smile.

"You might not have heard—"

"That there was difficulty in the Common?"

"You heard."

"Very little. I did ascertain that you were materially unharmed." He glanced pointedly at her sleeve. "What happened?"

"A much more public assassination attempt."

His brows rose in concert.

"Not one that can be pinned directly upon any member of the House," she added.

"Another demon." His voice was flat, his expression neutral.

She nodded.

"And your injury?"

"Not from the demon."

He raised a brow; she failed to see it—which took a little effort.

"Casualties?"

This was the question she dreaded. "I don't know yet. Word hasn't returned to the House. The army was called into action; the Kings, the Exalted, and the magi were likewise forced to make a stand."

"And you?"

"I flew here."

"Alone?"

"On Snow. I thought the demon would follow me. He did."

"The demon?"

"He left."

"He was not destroyed, then."

She exhaled. "No. I don't believe it was possible."

"Very well." Haval took a seat, dismissing the attempted assassination as if it were no longer of concern. He was a practical man, at heart; it wasn't. He could do very little about demonic assassins. "You will meet with The Ten in the Hall of The Ten on the morrow."

She nodded. "I expect the meeting itself to be interesting. Finch has prepared documents about the three contested trade routes; Devon has added his own information. I'll have that information at hand for the meeting—but I don't think we'll be discussing or negotiating financial concerns if it's at all obvious that the demon was hunting me." She folded her hands in her lap as Ellerson entered the great room with tea. He did not immediately leave, but lingered by the doors.

"The Berrilya and The Kalakar are unlikely to come to the meeting prepared for financial concerns, although they will also have relevant documents to hand. They have returned from the war in the South; your own part in that war was, in the end, small. My suggestion, if it is at all possible, is that you focus discussion on matters of that successful war."

"Likelihood of success?"

"Vanishingly small. I realize it's difficult for you to, as you put it, waste time in the attempt if you're certain to have no success. The reasons for this so-called waste of time?"

"It buys time."

"It does. The meeting may well take more time than anyone has anticipated; I believe every House leader was in attendance in the Common today. Your attendants?"

"Gabriel ATerafin."

Haval sighed heavily. "Gabriel will not remain by your side for much longer. Take Teller."

"Teller's not my right-kin."

"Not officially, no; nor is Gabriel. It is time, Jewel. Take Teller. Given the gravity of the circumstances, he will be noted; it is important that he *be* noted."

"The continuity of the House—"

"Is not a concern to outsiders. If you rely too heavily on Gabriel, a man who has made his intent to retire quite clear, it implies a lack of resolution on your part. In this, you cannot afford to be meek or reliant on an old regime."

"I haven't ditched the rest of my House Council, either."

"No. Nor would you be expected to do so, and believe that The Ten will be aware of this fact. But they will no doubt be aware of the fact that there have been attempts — all failures — on your life, as well; it will indicate that your rule is contested in a way that your predecessor's had not been for decades. They will see weakness and opportunity. Make your stand, Terafin."

She remembered the Winter King's words. Avandar's words. Her own fear.

Haval saw it. "Jewel," he said softly, "if you will not and cannot trust them, you will leave them behind. They are not yet your comrades; they are your responsibility. You are not, yourself, content to sit, to wait, to gather; do not expect—do not impose—that fate on your den."

"Is it wrong to care about them?"

"No. But this is not care. It is fear. Understand that there is a difference between what you do and what you are afraid to do. You are afraid to ask them to face risks you don't face. That is respectable, even admirable. But you are, at the moment, afraid to allow them to face the *same* risks you undertake. That is not." He mimicked the folding of hands and watched her. After a long, long moment of silence, he picked up his teacup and began to drink. During this careful, civilized action, he never once took his eyes off her face.

"You were not always this way," he finally said, conceding ground to her in some small fashion.

"I was."

"No, Jewel. I remember the first day I met you. Do you?"

"Rath brought us."

"He did. I remember why. I considered refusing his request at the time. Hannerle was extremely unhappy. She liked you. For some reason, she doesn't approve of any interactions I have with people she likes." His smile was chilly.

Jewel waited.

"You came with Duster. She was not, then, like you."

"She was never like me."

"No. But you could give Duster orders—subtle orders, to be sure—and she would follow them inasmuch as she was capable of following any order. She did not like you."

"No."

"But she loathed herself."

"She didn't—"

He held up one hand. The other, the hand which held the cup, was perfectly steady. Far steadier than Jewel's would have been.

Jewel bit her lip and then continued. "Duster didn't like anyone except Lander. She didn't like anything. It's just the way she was."

"She is dead. There is no need to protect her from my assessment." He sipped tea quietly. "But that is the point, isn't it? She is dead."

Jewel shrugged uneasily. "She's been dead for half my life, Haval. You're not telling me anything I don't know."

"No. Sadly, I am not. You will find that people frequently wish to ignore the things they know; they can be quite perceptive about the things they don't; it is exceedingly frustrating. Ignoring what you know is unlikely to change the simple facts. So let me now expand upon what you do know."

Jewel rose. She made it halfway to the fireplace, clenched her jaws, and stopped.

"Haval—"

He was watching her with the same hooded, neutral expression. His eyes were so dark in the interior light, they seemed black.

"You gave her an order. You told her to protect the den. You were not with her at the time; you knew what she was like, as you so colloquially put it. She followed your orders, Jewel. She followed them in her own context. She died because she did so—not more, not less."

She hated him, then. At this very moment, she couldn't see a point when the hatred would stop. Her hands were fists, her knuckles white with the strain.

"I have taken the liberty of speaking with Finch and Teller," he continued, as if her hatred, the sudden pit of rage that had opened beneath her feet threatening to swallow her whole, was insignificant. "Therefore, I will continue. Lefty died following your orders. Fisher died following your orders. All of your den present on either of those two days survived; Lefty and Fisher did not.

"Only Lander died because he failed to obey you. His death is not on your hands." Haval continued to drink his tea. In the background Ellerson watched, his expression for the moment as hooded as Haval's. If she wanted rescue, it would not come from that quarter.

It wouldn't come at all.

"But were it not for your order to Duster, your den would be dead. You might have survived, but it was not your survival that was your concern at the time; it is not your survival that concerns you now, you are so certain of it. What would you change, Jewel? If you could go back to the day of her death—the day of your arrival at the Terafin manse—what would you change? What could you change?"

She struggled for a long moment with helpless rage. But when she faced Haval at last, her face was as hard, as neutral, as his. "I can't change anything," she said coldly. "It is a pointless question."

"Is it? Examine facts. She died; the rest of your friends did not. It was not a conscious decision on your part, but that is the truth of it." He sipped tea.

"I am aware of that, Haval."

"Good. You were, on that day, a better leader—for your den—than you are on this one. You have given them safety—inasmuch as safety is possible in these times. They are not starving in the streets; they are not required to steal or expose themselves to different forms of danger, merely to put food in their stomachs. They are, by all external measure, successful.

"They have grown, Jewel. Finch is not the child you rescued in the streets of the holdings. Nor is Teller. But you guard and hide them as ferociously as if they still were. You let them be competent only in your absence. But in your absence, they presided over the slow crumbling of The Terafin's power. They were placed upon the House Council with very little political preparation, but their roles within the bureaucracy of the House prepared them in other ways, and they have yet to disgrace themselves. I do not believe they will.

"Teller is young, yes—but so are you. He is, in my humble opinion, worthy of the title right-kin. Barston will remain as his secretary if you affirm Teller in the role, all of Gabriel's protestations to the contrary aside.

"Finch will not, in my opinion, as easily replace Jarven—and any hope that Jarven will peacefully retire or gracefully expire is a vain one. But she understands the Merchant Authority, the treaties that have been made—and broken—in the last sixteen years. She understands the ways in which the Port Authority and the Merchant Authority are tied, and she has overseen some small handful of agreements with the Royal Trade Commission. She seems delicate and retiring; she will not, however, be moved in the face of threat or danger. Lucille is quick to jump into the breach of Finch's silence—I feel Lucille vastly underestimates her—but absent Lucille, Finch is capable of holding her own."

Jewel lifted a hand. It was shaking. "Haval, enough."

"You even hide Daine, and he is healer-born; he is Alowan's successor."

"Daine is barely twenty! He is only barely—"

"You were a member of the House Council at sixteen years of age."

"*I* was a member of the House Council because I'm seer-born!"

"Daine is also talent-born, as I have pointed out. He is granted the lesser respect because he is forced to hide the symbol of the twin hands."

"Are you unaware of how Alowan died?"

"Jewel, please." He sipped tea, eyed the bottom of the cup, and set it down. Ellerson then moved from his stiff and perfect position by the doors to refill the empty cup. He did not meet Haval's eyes; nor did he meet Jewel's. Jewel was the only one who tried to catch his attention. "Tell me how I am wrong, and I will stop. Convince me that you do not cripple yourself. Convince me, further, that you do not impede their growth. The only people you are willing to trust are the people you cannot bring yourself to openly love: Avandar. Celleriant. Meralonne. The cats."

"Avandar *can't die*."

The words echoed in the large room. She bit her lip and turned away from Haval, and away, as well, from what she was certain she would see in Ellerson's face.

"I will take that under advisement," Haval finally replied, teacup full and once again in his hands. "The others?"

"They're far more powerful than I am. They've always been more powerful than any single member of my den. If Celleriant wished it, he could kill us all. He could arm and armor us first, and then kill us all, without breaking a sweat. I'm not convinced that he couldn't kill most of the Chosen in the same way." She swallowed. "Meralonne is the same. And Haval? They both *love* to fight. They love it."

"To fight, or to kill?"

"To fight and not die, if I had to guess. It's the only time I see either of them look joyful."

"So you are willing to trust them—"

"I don't. I don't trust them the same way. My den, me—we want the same things. We have the same goals. There are things none of us would *ever* do to further those goals. Avandar, Celleriant, Meralonne—with them I have to watch what I say, watch what I do, watch how my words might be twisted if it serves their purpose. They have goals and those goals *aren't* mine; my goals are convenient for their purposes now, that's all. The cats are the same and not the same. They also love to fight.

"But the others, my den—they're like me, but *without* the sight. If someone attempts to slide a dagger through my back, my body moves. I don't even have time to think. They don't have that. When Haerrad had Teller injured—" she lost words. Found them again, but it was hard. She wanted Haval to understand.

She was afraid he already did. "I wanted to kill him. I want to kill him now. I was certain he'd be dead before The Terafin was buried. It was the one silver lining to a House War. I want them to be safe—"

He watched, impassive now. "Do you feel that you are safe, Jewel?"

"I can't easily be killed."

"That was not the question I asked. Do *you* feel that *you* are safe?"

Did she? "I feel that I'm safer than they are."

He raised a brow. Raised a cup.

". . . No."

"Better. You've said that you can't—easily—be killed. I will accept that at face value; I believe it is true. Why, then, do you feel unsafe?"

She let the tension drain out of her shoulders, arms, and fists. What did she know about Haval? Nothing. Nothing except that there was so much *to* know. "What is Hannerle, to you?"

Both of his brows rose in what Jewel hoped was genuine surprise. He then smiled, his eyes crinkling. "That, Jewel, is a palpable hit. Very good. I will not trifle to answer the question you have asked in a trivial way. She is the entirety of the reason I live—and work—in the Common. The choices I've made in my life to date revolve around the fact that she is part of it. She is almost the whole of it. What I am willing to do to preserve her life is almost without bound. But not entirely; there are some things she would never forgive."

"You could hide them. You're good at that."

"I am. But I am older than you, as is Hannerle, and I

understand the ways in which lies of any significance trouble a marriage. They grow roots, the way trees do, and they break foundations in ways that are unforeseen by even the wisest. I lay no claim to wisdom," he added. "Will you tell me that your den is like my wife?"

"Maybe."

"Then I will tell you that you have made all the wrong choices in your life if you mean that statement to be true."

"No."

"No? You are The Terafin. You might have chosen to remain a member of the House Council with all the lesser significance and weight that implies. It is still considerable."

"You know why I couldn't do that."

"Indeed. And so do they. They did not argue against it, Jewel, and in your absence they protected what they could. They want what you want—and not less. They will give what you give—possibly more. I could not live with Hannerle had I not surrendered claim to the greater responsibility."

"But you're here now."

"Indeed. I am. She is not pleased. I think she would be entirely unforgiving had my work here not involved you, and for that I am grateful. She is not suspicious of your activities in the same way she was suspicious of mine—and with reason. She sees to the heart of the matter. I am willing to do what my current life requires, no more, no less. But what I am willing to do to preserve it, you would not do."

"Haval—"

"I do not practice the full range of my options because some of those would destroy the life Hannerle and I have built just as certainly; in all ways, the choices I make are hampered by my desire to live Hannerle's life. But absent that? There is much I would be willing to do that you could never countenance. Not to save Teller or Finch. Not to save yourself.

"But I tell you this to point out that our situations are not the same. The den knows what you know; they are willing to see you do what you feel you must. They will not leave you because they disagree with your choices. They do not hold Duster's death against you; nor do they fear to follow because of it. So: do not speak to me of love, even if you will not name it."

"You're here because you're certain Hannerle would have died had you stayed at home."

He nodded.

"I shouldn't have taken advantage of that."

"Jewel, please. I have already pointed out all the ways in which your attempt to do so was a failure. Do not force me to repeat them; it is almost entirely beside the point, and I wish you to remain on point."

"I don't feel safe," she told him, forcing her hands to remain at her sides, "because Duster died. Lefty died. Lander died." She turned toward the fireplace, and then turned back. "And before them? My mother, my Oma. My father. Rath. It's exactly the same. You're afraid of losing Hannerle. You're here. I'm afraid of losing anyone else I can love. I don't want to be left alone in a silent house ever again."

After a long pause, during which Ellerson refilled Haval's cup, Haval said, "If all of your arguments in Council involved matters of the earnest heart, my dear, your rule would be unassailable."

"Is that a compliment?"

"It is, of a sort. You have forced me to acknowledge a sympathy, an empathy, I would have sworn could not exist. Shall I now tell you why you are wrong?"

"If I say no?"

"We shall sit here in increasingly uncomfortable silence."

She did laugh, then. She laughed, and she returned, at last, to the seat she had vacated.

"You need them."

"You need—"

"I need Hannerle in my store. I need her in my life. But *my* life, with the single exception of this endeavor, is hers. I have accepted the confines and the cage because if I could not, she would not now be mine. You need your den in the same way I need Hannerle. If I were afraid that every prick of a needle would send her to sleep—or death, as devised—if I was afraid that any bolt of cloth she might touch would be poisoned, any customer might be an assassin, I could not have my store. Or my life. I would deny her—and myself—her competence."

"In your case, none of those things are likely."

"Yes. Because in my case, the making of clothing for the

idle rich—or the busy rich, do not make that face—is not political. It is not a matter of power; it is, at base, an appeal to those who have the power I lack. I curry favor.

"In your case, you *are* a power. And, Terafin, it is my belief that you must be more of one before this is out. Not within the confines of your House—although that is utterly necessary—but beyond its boundaries. You must be as near to absolute as it is possible for you to become. And without your den, you have deprived yourself of the *only* people you trust at a time when you cannot afford to falter on any front. You cannot defend yourself against the Kings, the magi, the Exalted, the demonic—and still oversee every other element of the House. Nor can you afford to appoint people you trust less at such a delicate moment in your rule."

"I don't want—"

"No, of course you don't. But, Jewel, I have considered—carefully—what I will do if Hannerle does not survive. I have seen what my life will become. Have you done likewise?"

"...No."

"You must. Unless you intend to end your rule if your den dies, you must consider the alternatives with care. You must even cultivate them. You are no longer Jewel Markess, the youthful and earnest orphan who followed Ararath Handernesse to my store. Your life is not your own. You are The Terafin, now. You have taken the responsibility for House Terafin within the Empire. You cannot cease to function because one, or another, of the members of your House falls; that luxury is lost.

"But you did not cease to function when Duster died. Regret? Yes, of course you regret it. On some days, you regret it bitterly. But that, as they often say, must be *your* problem. It cannot be the House's. Trust your den. I believe they are worthy of that singularly unwise decision. You need them," he said again. He set his cup aside. "And I must attend my affairs and my life, now. I have been absent from her side."

He walked toward the door, but before Ellerson opened it, turned again. Jewel had not moved to see him out. "There are, at the moment, some discrepancies in the House accounts. Those discrepancies can be traced indirectly to the office of the right-kin."

Jewel froze in place. "How large a discrepancy, and is it in his favor?"

"A very large one, alas. No, it is not in his favor. I do not believe he is aware of the full state of his accounts, but it is almost exactly the sum of money one would expect to spend on very short notice if one hired a fully-trained assassin."

She exhaled. "Come back, Haval. Tell me what you know."

Chapter Four

ELLERSON QUIETLY BROUGHT Jewel tea, allowed her to drink half of it, and suggested—firmly—that she might consider changing her attire. Since she knew the events in the Common would bring a stream of visitors that she could not put off for lack of an appointment—and since her day's schedule had been cleared for the purposes of a day-long inspection of troops in the heart of the hundred—she took his advice.

She regretted it slightly when it came to the matter of her hair, because apparently ash, small stones, splinters, and dirt did not magically take care of themselves. But the mark on her arm had, as she'd told Haval, ceased to bleed. It did remind her, as she rose to dress, that Avandar was absent. She hoped he was sleeping, although Avandar's sleep—like her own—was not guaranteed to be restful.

"Ellerson."

"Terafin."

"I will be in The Terafin's—in my—office. I'd like to speak with Teller and Finch the moment they arrive home."

When Ellerson had finished making her look presentable, she walked through the Chosen stationed outside of the room. They followed at a very discreet distance; only in the West Wing—her personal quarters—did they do so. But these quarters also housed the den, Adam, Ariel, and two domicis. In this case, it was the domicis' rooms she approached, or rather, Avandar's.

Not for Avandar Gallais the practical rooms that Ellerson occupied; Avandar's room had no cupboards and no counters, for one. But, like Ellerson's, they were unadorned. For a man who had not spent his life in poverty and, more germane, had lived a very long time, he had very few obvious possessions, and none of these were sentimental in nature.

Jewel still had the old, iron box in which the den's money had been kept in the twenty-fifth holding. She kept Rath's sword, although that had only come into her hands after The Terafin's death. She wore the Handernesse ring on a long, golden chain that hung around her neck. She had the House Council ring, of course—the old one, although she no longer wore it. The new one was styled in a much more ostentatious way; she liked it far less.

It was vastly heavier, its weight an accusation, not an affirmation.

She knocked on Avandar's door. There was no answer; she knocked again. After a long pause, she opened the door. It was not his habit to keep this door locked. Hers, yes.

He was abed. The curtains were drawn, and the magelight that adorned the room had been whispered to near invisibility. She heard his deep and even breathing, hesitated a moment, and then turned in the doorway.

"Jewel."

"I'm sorry. I know it hasn't been very long—"

Across the darkened room she swore she could hear the brief clenching of domicis jaws. Avandar rose. "Your meeting with Haval is finished?"

"Yes."

"Did he have any information of import to impart?"

"Yes. Gabriel's personal accounts."

He shed the robe he habitually wore when sleeping, and began to dress. "They are significant at the moment?"

"Only in one regard. Haval thinks the money that paid for the assassin—the woman—came from Gabriel's account."

"I see."

She took four of the Chosen with her when she left the wing. Avandar, clothed, walked to her left. He did not look significantly better for the rest he'd taken; his face was pale, his eyes lined and dark. She made no comment; they only irritated him, and today, there would be irritants in plenty.

But she worried, and he knew it.

Jewel, I cannot simply expire from exhaustion.

The halls stretched out before her. They were no longer adorned with the symbols of mourning that had marked The Terafin's death; she missed them. *I don't know what's going to happen in the future.*

Ironic, coming from a seer.

She nodded slightly, keeping the habitual grimace from her lips. *But you can't fight—not like that. Not that sword, not that shield. Not that.*

There is *no other way to fight what we faced today.*

Yes, there is. We did fight it.

We did not destroy *it.*

She almost asked him if he thought he could destroy the demon in other circumstances, but stopped herself from forming the words. He would be aware of the thought itself; he was. He chose not to answer. It didn't matter. A sudden, certain implacable knowledge, a flash of conviction, came in the place of the words he refused to offer: he could.

But it would destroy him. It wouldn't kill him, no. But it would break whatever hope he had of escape. Of death.

It was so ironic. The one thing she feared—death, even if not her own—was the one thing he wanted. A reminder, if one were necessary, that eternity was not the blessing the powerful and the mortal believed it would be. She had seen parts of a past that stretched as far as the gods—perhaps farther. Avandar was the one person—the only person— that she thought she could cede to death, if there was some path that would lead him there.

Terafin.

And she *knew*, as she walked, that there was. She couldn't see its shape, its form; she couldn't see its end—but in that moment, between one step and the next, she knew it existed.

Barston was, in no one's estimation, a happy man. He was precise, orderly, immovable within his own domain; no detail was too small to escape his notice. He was not young— Jewel privately wondered if he had ever been young, even as a child. But he was also aware of the relative ranks in the House, and he insisted, no matter what the circumstance, that the respect due those ranks be strictly and exactly observed.

He rose the moment the doors opened and Jewel entered the right-kin's office.

Barston was technically the right-kin's secretary. He was not The Terafin's, but The Terafin did not require one; all appointments, all matters of concern, that were meant for The Terafin, passed beneath the eyes of the right-kin first. Only those matters the right-kin felt were urgent—or political—enough to demand The Terafin's attention were then put before The Terafin's eyes.

Barston, therefore, was responsible for a majority of Jewel's schedule. He knew it, in all likelihood, better than she herself did. She was not of a mind to change this arrangement, although she knew it was not an arrangement followed in the other Houses among The Ten. She liked having the shield of Barston to huddle behind.

Avandar did not approve.

"Rise," she told the secretary. He did. "I apologize for my unexpected presence. The victory parade in the Common was severely disrupted."

Barston didn't blink. Nor did he ask. He assumed that the reasons for her unexpected and unforeseen presence were impeccable. "You have no appointments scheduled for this afternoon."

"No. But Gabriel has not yet returned from the Common; I do not imagine he will be able to extricate himself from the procedural difficulties for at least another hour. I wish to speak with him when he returns—and I wish to speak with him before I speak with any other visitors."

"You expect there will be other visitors of import." It was not a question; Barston was not an idiot.

She nodded. Hesitated. Barston noted that, too. But questions of a very delicate nature could not be asked of Barston in so open an environment—the office was not empty—if ever. "I expect the appointments that arise out of the afternoon events to be long and complicated. At least one of those will be held over one of the dinner hours; I am unconcerned as to which hour it is."

"Which appointment, Terafin?"

"The Guildmaster of the Order of Knowledge."

Barston nodded.

"Offer her that meeting time, and extend an invitation to join me. I am certain, by that time, we will both require refreshment."

"Yes, Terafin. I will inform you if her schedule conflicts with yours in such a way that the meeting cannot occur."

"Thank you, Barston." She turned toward the door, stopped, and turned back, squaring her shoulders. The movement caught the secretary's attention. "I'm sorry. I know you have work that you hoped to catch up on while most of the House Council was occupied in the victory celebrations. My presence here cannot be helpful in that regard, but I must ask for a few moments of your time."

Barston rose.

"May we use Gabriel's office? Or Teller's?"

"Gabriel's office is the more secure."

Jewel deliberately chose to take Gabriel's chair. It was behind his very clean, very fine desk; that the desk was also functional was not in question. Avandar, however, stood to one side of the ornate doors, as if he were part of the furnishing—the tasteful, sparse furnishing—of the right-kin's office. Barston closed the door and joined her, but he chose to stand instead of availing himself of one of the chairs which visitors generally occupied. He had been a fixture in this house before Jewel—and Teller—had arrived at the front gates. He ran the office; if he deferred to Gabriel, it was because the office served the right-kin. The right-kin was the conduit to The Terafin for everyone.

"You know that Gabriel intends—fully intends—to retire."

"Yes."

"You are aware that, were he willing to stay, I would retain his services?"

"Yes." Barston offered a weary smile. "Teller has made that quite clear to Gabriel. He has also," he added, his smile transforming into a tight frown, "made it clear to anyone else who is privileged to work in this office."

"There's no harm in that."

Barston said nothing.

"As I have not yet expired—and not from lack of trying

on the part of my enemies—I need this office." She watched him closely. "Gabriel *can* retire, Barston. It's not what I want, but I understand the difficulties he now faces." She drew a deep breath, exhaled, and made a decision. "Are you aware of the state of his finances as they pertain to the House?"

"Of course." The secretary's expression shuttered. Not a good sign, but not a definitively bad one.

"Are you aware," she continued, "of the state of his personal finances?"

"His personal finances are not the concern of the House."

"They would not be, if my rule of the House were less uncertain." She phrased the statement in a tone of voice that implied agreement, not argument.

He watched her.

"You are aware that I am to meet with The Ten in *Avantari* on the morrow."

"Of course."

"I had intended to take Gabriel with me."

His silence was longer and deeper.

"Let me make things clear, Barston. Gabriel's personal account saw a withdrawal of a significant sum of money. There has been no change in his holdings, and no acquisitions—through any of the regular, known channels, of the items of art that he personally collects. That sum was not paid to his son; nor was it paid to any of the various people Gabriel regularly employs. We cannot trace a recipient."

"Terafin."

"But the sum corresponds to the rather hefty fee one would be expected to pay for an assassin who had any hope of success. I'm sorry."

"There must be an explanation for it," Barston finally said, in the most chilly of tones he might offer the woman who ruled the House. Had she been anyone else, Jewel was certain that she would no longer be standing—or sitting—in Gabriel's office.

"Yes. And I am certain the answer does not rest with Gabriel—not directly. Gabriel is, to my mind, above suspicion."

Some of the ice melted.

"But it is an investigation which must be entered. It is not, of course, public. Nor will it be made so—not directly, and not by me. I am certain, however, that Haerrad, should he gain access to that information, is likely to spread it at least among the House Council."

"What will you do?"

"I will do nothing," was her quiet reply. "Gabriel has said—from the beginning—that he would not remain as right-kin; no plea I've made has moved him, and I do not imagine any plea I make now would. He has remained in this office as ATerafin, because the House is in turmoil. If it were not, he would have resigned the moment I was acclaimed.

"You have remained with him. You have offered no word of your intent to resign."

"If Gabriel is forced from this office, Terafin, after his years of service, I will not remain to guide it."

She nodded; she had expected no less. "If he is allowed to retire, as has been his declared intent?"

"If his retirement is clouded—"

"Inasmuch as it is within my power, it will not be. I have never intended to force him to remain. But if he leaves now, he is unlikely to be drawn into what will no doubt become an ugly investigation." She exhaled again, and said, "If there is irregularity in his accounting, I expect it is entirely due to his very ambitious son."

"He does not support Rymark."

"I know. But Rymark troubles him, nonetheless. We do not, it is true, choose our kin."

Barston raised a brow and cleared his throat.

Her smile deepened. "Most of us do not. In the case of my den, we had little choice."

"It is seldom that lack of choice proves so fortuitous."

"Rymark has always pressured his father, and in a way that Gabriel cannot easily counter—if at all. Gabriel's sense of responsibility will not—yet—allow him to disavow his blood kin. But if we move against Rymark in this, Rymark will throw his father into the wolf's path, and it is Gabriel who will fall. The investigation *must* continue, and its conclusions must come to light—at least within the Council Halls. I cannot prevent it; indeed, my rule will depend on it. I would spare him at least that much. If he is not among the Council—"

"He will surely retain a seat upon the House Council?"

Jewel looked away. "If he has not discussed this with you, then I should not. But I will, regardless. He does not intend to retain a seat upon the House Council. He has suggested, instead, that I take the very unusual step of appointing Jarven ATerafin."

Barston's brows rose. "Jarven is . . . not a young man."

"No. And he is a busy one. I am considering appointing Lucille in his stead."

The brows rose further, which should have been physically impossible. But they fell as Barston schooled his expression. "Let us not discuss the possibility of his replacement before he and I have had a chance to discuss this."

Jewel nodded.

"You wish to spare Gabriel the continued . . . misfortune . . . of dealing with his son." Barston did not deny the truth of any of Jewel's barely veiled accusations.

"I do. I wish it enough to deprive myself of Gabriel's guidance at a time when it is desperately needed. If I allow Gabriel to retire, with honor, what will you do?"

Barston hesitated, which was very rare. He then walked over to the desk and took the chair nearest to it. "Oh, very well. Who will you appoint as right-kin in his place?"

"Does your continued tenure in this office depend on my reply?"

Barston's eyes narrowed. "It is a great pity that Gabriel could not see his way clear to fully supporting you in his former position as right-kin," he said, after a significant and disapproving pause. "While on the surface you have very little in common, it is clear to me that some tendencies have strong overlap. One of these would be asking superfluous questions."

"Superfluous."

"Those to which you already know the answer. Those to which," he added, enunciating each syllable, "anyone who breathes might already know the answer. Of course it does. You could appoint Rymark or Haerrad, and I would not even go so far as to properly pack the office for the sake of my successor."

She laughed. She knew Amarais wouldn't have had she been in the same position, but the genuine amusement his perfectly correct outrage had caused welled up and burst forth before she could even think of containing it. "There is no way I could appoint either man," she said, when she could once again school her face. "I am still breathing, after all." She let the smile drop from her face. "Gabriel feels that you have earned a respectful—and peaceful— retirement."

Barston's smile was withering. "Gabriel also believes that most adults behave with a modicum of consideration and respect for my labor. He has clearly spent far too many of his notable years on the wrong side of these doors." He lifted a hand. "I am, occasionally, wearied by the work; I will not deny it. But I find it stressful to contemplate the state of this office without my guidance."

This could not come as a surprise to anyone who had even a passing acquaintance with the man.

"Were Gabriel's retirement to involve lesser, but similar, work, I might join him. I have considered it. But if he means to absent himself entirely from the responsibilities of the House, no."

"No?"

"Gabriel has always pursued interests of his own; he has his art, and some small handful of artists, for whom he serves as patron, and he has endowed a not inconsiderable sum on Senniel College. He has one standing grant offered to the Order of Knowledge on alternate years; he has some small interest in the study of ancient languages. I confess that my own interests in any of his endeavors is entirely because they are his; they are not my own.

"If Gabriel truly takes the retirement he yearns for, those hobbies will occupy his time and his attention. They will not, however, likewise occupy mine."

"You've no hobbies?"

Barston raised a brow. "I am unaware that you yourself have developed a broader range of interests that do not reflect the business of the House."

"I'm not certain my sojourn in the South reflected the specific interests of the House," she replied.

"It was not, by all accounts—and those accounts were muted, indeed—a voluntary leave of absence. But the needs of the office today will, as you say, require some finesse and the patience of an energetic saint. I will therefore attempt to come to the point, without duly taxing either of our abilities to dance around it."

"And that point?"

"The office of the right-kin, Terafin."

"It is not an office that you yourself have ever considered assuming?"

He looked completely scandalized. Jewel almost laughed again, but this one she managed to contain. "Barston, it is not an entirely idle question. You of all people must be aware of our origins. Your current Terafin was born and raised in the twenty-fifth holding. If, with my background, I can take the House Seat, surely the office of right-kin is not beyond yours? You have both the experience and the education for it."

He stared at her for a long moment, his face almost as shuttered as Haval's could instantly and easily become. "I understand that you mean no insult, Terafin, and I will therefore endeavor to take none. You must understand the difference in our relative positions. You came to the House Council at the unprecedented age of sixteen years. You were accepted on that Council, the usual reservations entirely muted, because of your singular talent.

"It is not a talent with which I was born. I was never invited—or commanded, as Teller was—to assume such a seat. Nor was my employ and the gradual shift of the weight of responsibility designed in such a way as to allow it. It was clear to us—to Gabriel and myself—that The Terafin had hopes for, and designs on, your futures."

"She sent Teller to you."

"She sent Teller to Gabriel, yes. Do you think it was merely to make work for the boy?"

Jewel was silent.

"No. You don't. No more do I. Nor did I, at the time. I have trained him—and I will say that he was an adept student. He is not hasty, and he is more than considerate; he has performed his duties to this office with a characteristic humility and completeness. But as his understanding of the duties of the office evolved, he served as junior aide to Gabriel, and not under-secretary to myself. What he saw of the office and its responsibilities broadened considerably in the scope of those duties. Had Teller been my successor, his duties would have, of necessity, been somewhat different.

"That was never his role."

"And you are content?"

"Were I to reside in this office—were the chair you now so boldly occupy to be, in truth, mine—who would run the office itself? They cannot be a person who exudes little authority—and for that reason, if no other, I would hesitate to put Teller behind my own desk—and they cannot be a person to whom the small, daily duties and information are not essential. Most of the assistants who have been sent my way feel half of their work is trivial. They make small errors because they do not retain the focus required, and those small errors become, as they gather, much larger and more difficult."

Jewel lifted a brow. "You are telling me that you consider yourself irreplaceable."

He reddened, very slightly, but did not demur.

". . . And Gabriel, of course, is not. But irreplaceable or no, if I did not approve the correct man—or woman—as right-kin, you would abandon your duties."

"I am secretary, Terafin," he said, as if secretary was a position only less exalted than the Kings themselves. "I am not the whole of the office; I am half of it. But the halves of the office—both the internal and the external—must work together to weave a consistent, single fabric, and if I am attempting to weave silk while the other is attempting to hammer nails into the threads, the office will not function."

"And Teller?"

"He is not Gabriel," Barston replied. "But he understands no office but *this* one." He folded his hands in his lap and waited.

Jewel rose. "Very well, Barston. I will tell you that I consider to you to be nigh irreplaceable. If you will serve Teller as secretary, Teller will be my right-kin. When Gabriel returns, send him to my office; I wish to inform him myself. But it is Teller who will accompany me to *Avantari* on the morrow."

Barston rose as well. He bowed.

"There is one other matter of concern," she said, as she reached the door. "The matter of your own successor. Please, please find a suitable assistant that you might begin to train."

"Of course, Terafin."

"Well?" she asked her domicis as she headed down the hall.

"You did well. He is, in his fashion, a formidable man. He will not slay demons for you—but the majority of the previous Terafin's life did not require it. Without obvious rank, he is clearly not a man to be crossed more than once."

"I mean, will he find an assistant?"

Avandar chuckled. "I believe he has been laboring under the exact same orders for the better part of two decades."

"Teller says he has high standards."

"Indeed."

Torvan—alone—was waiting in The Terafin's office when Jewel arrived. Two Chosen were stationed outside of the doors, but this was common. Even, apparently, when The Terafin was not within the manse. The sharp, loud clang of a full salute, offered in dress uniform, filled the room. Jewel said, "At ease, Captain."

Ease came to him slowly, and in the only fashion that it ever came to the Chosen whose Lord was still living.

"I'm sorry," she added, when he failed to speak first. "I had no warning of what might occur in the Common before we left the manse, and only warning enough to clear the platforms before the demon emerged."

Torvan remained silent.

"He intended to fight his way to me, through whatever was foolish—or brave—enough to stand in his way."

His exhalation was heavy. "He was there for you, then." It wasn't a question.

She answered anyway. "He was. I had some hope that he might follow if I returned in haste to the manse; he was winged, and the wings were not decorative."

"He did, Terafin."

"Casualties?"

"It is unclear. Many were injured; some half dozen are dead."

She flinched. "Teller? Finch?"

"None of the dead served you. Two of the magi fell, and one Priest of the Mother. We would have returned in haste to the manse, but the three armies would not be easily moved; they were summoned in haste, deployed in haste. The three Commanders took charge."

"The streets are clear now?"

"The streets are not clear at the moment, no. Because the route was lined with both enterprising merchants and the citizens who wished some glimpse of the returning soldiers, they are still not cleared; it will be perhaps another hour before full order is restored. The Chosen, however, are upon the grounds. The House Council will follow; they are no doubt being detained by the *Astari* as we speak."

"I can imagine." Duvari was not going to be a happy man. "I'm almost surprised the Chosen were allowed to depart."

His face perfectly composed, Torvan said, "It is better to beg forgiveness than ask permission."

That did evoke a smile. "How clear was it that the demon was there for me?"

"It was not immediately clear at all. The assumption, given the presence of the Kings and the Exalted, was otherwise."

"When did it become clear?"

"To the Chosen? When you left, and the demon chose to pursue. It was not clear, at the time, that you had vacated the Common; it became clear shortly thereafter when Lord Celleriant made it clear to Member APhaniel. I do not know if it was, at that point, clear to the Crowns or the Exalted."

She nodded. "Thank you, Torvan. Tomorrow—provided the meeting is not, in light of this uproar, rescheduled, I will meet with The Ten in *Avantari*."

He nodded.

"Teller will accompany me."

"Angel?"

"Yes, of course." She hadn't considered leaving Angel behind. But Torvan knew her, and he understood that her silence came from hesitance; he therefore waited. She was silent for a long moment, and was saved the effort of making a decision by the arrival of Gabriel ATerafin.

Jewel wanted to dismiss every other person standing in the room. It was instinctive and protective, and it was a desire she worked to squelch. Torvan, the Chosen and her domicis were, as far as Gabriel was concerned, a functional extension of her body. He would have far less difficulty with their presence than she herself did, at the moment.

"ATerafin," she said quietly, and then, "Gabriel." She took a seat behind her desk, and indicated that he might, should he so choose, take one of the chairs that fronted it. He accepted the offer. His eyes had the gaunt, sunken look of a man who's chased sleep for nights without managing to catch it. He had come from the Common, and splinters still adorned the left arm of his jacket, as did the gray overlay of spread ash.

"Terafin." He lifted his head, straightening his shoulders.

She hesitated. She was aware that Amarais would not now hesitate—and that the hesitation was not, in the end, a kindness to any save herself. "I wish your advice, Gabriel, as a man who has served most of his tenure in this House as right-kin."

He nodded.

"Teller has served in your office, and under your auspices, for almost the whole of his tenure as part of the House. In your opinion, is he capable of assuming the duties that you undertook with such grace for so long?"

Gabriel met—and held—her gaze. "In my opinion, and inasmuch as all men feel they are irreplaceable, he is."

"Good."

"The timing for your question is unusual, Terafin. May I ask why it is of pressing concern at this moment?"

He knew. She was suddenly completely certain that he knew—everything. Embarrassment at having been caught investigating his personal accounts warred with the fact that the accounts merited the scrutiny. She wasn't certain how Amarais would have handled this because Amarais would never have *had* to handle it: Gabriel had been above suspicion.

"You know," she said, deciding. "You know why."

He met her gaze unblinking for a very long time, and then he looked away.

"I will not ask you for an explanation, Gabriel, if you do not choose to offer one. I will make no demands. If you are aware of the ongoing investigation, you are also aware of the ways in which it might be either aided or hindered, and I will not command you, in this."

The stiffness left his shoulders and his neck, draining slowly away into the silence that followed her words. "And if I ask—"

"Can you? Can you now look at me, in this office, and ask me to drop the investigation?"

He glanced at a point just beyond her left shoulder for a long, long moment, and then he surprised her: he smiled. It was a weary, tired smile, but it was genuine. "No, Terafin. No, I could not. Not in good conscience, and at my age, that has become significantly important. I cannot, however, offer you the aid you will not demand. You have my gratitude."

"I would keep you, Gabriel. I would keep you as right-kin."

He said, "No. You cannot. Not now."

"And failing that," she continued, as if he hadn't spoken, "I would keep you on the House Council. But that would not, I fear, be a kindness to you—only to me."

"It would be no kindness, in the end, to you either. It would not have been a kindness to your predecessor; it is always painful to watch a friend fall—and fall, if I remain, I must." She thought he would rise or leave; he did not. Instead, he seemed to relax into the chair, as if he intended to occupy it for some time.

"Amarais chose you," he finally said.

She did not mention the claim—and the document—his son had presented to the House Council, proclaiming Rymark as the chosen heir. Nor did he.

"I understand why she did, and in the end—in the very end, Terafin—I did not counsel against it. I did not, perhaps, see the proliferation of the demonic, but the demons had already begun to cast their long and subtle shadows over the House. It is my suspicion that it is not just in *this* House that such a danger dwells."

Jewel nodded.

"Let me ask a different question. What will you do with Barston? He has worked tireless and thankless hours for decades now, and I would see him—"

"I will retain Barston. He is—as you well know—capable of speaking for himself, and in this, he has indicated a desire to remain in an office that I desperately need functional."

"Then you will appoint Teller as right-kin."

"Yes. Is it mention of Barston's disposition that makes you so certain?"

Gabriel chuckled. "It is, indeed. Teller is more malleable than I, even in my younger years—but when he disagrees with Barston, Barston finds little purchase for actual argument, which both confounds and impresses him. I have done what I could to prepare Teller for this eventuality."

"Have you spoken with him directly about the possibility?"

"No. I have tried, in subtle ways. I have tried in less subtle ways. When I made clear my intent to retire and leave the whole of House politics well behind me, I attempted to enumerate the tasks my successor would be required to undertake immediately. He listened only until the point I attempted to make clear that I desired that he himself be that successor."

"Surely that decision is mine?"

"It is, Terafin. But if we are not to dissemble and proclaim ourselves witless or unobservant fools, it is clear to all involved what the most likely decision would be. I have watched your den, and while they are all loyal to you—inasmuch as they can be—there are few who have the necessary experience, or even inclination, to undertake the role. Teller could. I believe, in time, Finch could—but only in an emergency; you would have to deal with both Lucille and Jarven otherwise, and Jarven is not a man you wish to cross."

"Jarven? Surely you mean Lucille."

"Do I?" He lifted a brow. The conversation, and its finer points, had engaged him, and he looked—for the moment—like Gabriel of old. It was both a joy and a sorrow; she clung to the joy, because the sorrow was likely to remain on its own. "Teller would not countenance that discussion; I believe if it were possible he would nail my feet to the floor of the office and keep me confined behind its desk."

"He thinks highly of you, and always has."

"He will understand, in time, why his respect is both valued and incidental. Yes, Teller is ready. Will you take him to *Avantari* on the morrow as right-kin?"

"That was my intent."

Gabriel nodded, lost in thought. "And will you assent to my suggestion?"

"Which of the many?"

"Jewel."

"Apologies. If you mean will I give Jarven the spot on the House Council that you will vacate in your retirement, I have not yet decided. He is not a man I distrust, but he is not a man I trust, either—he is clearly not Haerrad. He has no ambitions that I can see."

"He is one of the most observant men you will ever meet. It is not entirely comfortable."

"Second."

"Second?"

"Second most observant, I think. The House Council seat that will be vacant could be used as incentive to strengthen my own position within the House. I might offer it to Guillarne ATerafin in his stead; Guillarne is possibly the most successful of our Authority negotiators."

"He is certainly the most flamboyant—and at his age, that is not necessarily a good thing."

"He is not *old*, Gabriel."

"Nor is he young, any longer. I feel, at his age, some conservatism should be practiced."

"I understand that. But if Guillarne's lack of conservatism continues to serve him well, it will also enhance the standing of the House at a time when it would best suit me."

"And if it does not," he countered, "it will tell against you at the time when it will *least* suit."

"Also true. I will take that under serious consideration. But the Council seat is one of the very few incentives I have to offer someone like Guillarne; I would not be at all surprised to hear that he had already been offered it by at least two others, contingent on his support for their successful bid. Given the fact that there were four new employees at the Terafin Merchant Authority Offices within a week of The Terafin's death, I can well imagine that he was offered that seat by all of them."

"You have not asked?"

"No. Will you at least remain in residence in the manse?"

His smile was pained but gentle. "You understand why I cannot."

"I don't. Jarven lives here and he has been neither right-kin nor Council member."

"Jarven is the head of the Terafin's Merchant Authority

operations, and a very real part of the House position among The Ten. As of tomorrow, Terafin, I will not be a very real part of anything but the House history."

"Our foundations are our history."

"They are." He glanced at his hands as they lay in his lap. "I cannot remain here, not in the near future. It will not aid you in any way, and my sudden departure may work in your favor. With your permission, I will return to the office to inform Barston. There are a few personal possessions within the office which I would like to take with me."

"Gabriel you don't need to pack up and leave overnight."

"No, of course not. With your permission?"

She nodded and he rose. Before he left the office, he turned to Torvan. Torvan turned to Jewel, silently asking her permission. She nodded, although she didn't understand everything that lay behind the silent exchange.

Gabriel, Avandar said, *has requested an escort of the Chosen.*

Why?

They are frequently the guards situated at his door—and in his office, should the need arise. That is not, however, the reason why he wishes this particular escort. You said yourself that he knew the difficulties you now face. He does, Jewel. He understands them very, very well. The Chosen will supervise his retreat from the office he has occupied for decades.

She rose in outrage, and Avandar stepped into her path before she could follow Torvan and Gabriel out the doors.

"He is correct," the domicis said, retreating into the speech Jewel found more comfortable.

"I don't suspect him of anything! I won't have him treated as if he's a criminal in his own—"

"It is no longer his office. You offered him as graceful a retreat as it is possible to offer someone; he is offering, in reply, a similar gift. He asked the Captain of the Chosen, obliquely, to serve as his escort. Torvan understood what he asked, and he assumed that you understood it as well. You may, if you feel it necessary, burden Torvan with your anger; it was, however, a decision he left up to you."

And I didn't understand it. She heard her Oma's very clipped *ignorance is no excuse*, and accepted it as her due.

"It will no doubt be a long day, Terafin. Shall I arrange for lunch?"

"No. I've arranged for dinner; dinner will do."

Avandar stood in her path until it was clear that she would not rush out the doors guarded by two impassive men in armor.

Teller—accompanied by a pale Finch—arrived twenty minutes later. Neither had taken the time to change; nor had they taken the time to eat. They were immediately granted entrance into the office by the Chosen who had been informed of their possible arrival, and Jewel once again wished that she could simply empty the room, because she could see that Teller was angry. Finch, like her namesake, fluttered, looking from one anchor point in the room to the other. Her hands flew in den-sign; neither Teller nor Jewel's hands rose in response.

Teller did not shout; he didn't rage. He never had. But his expression and the tight line of his mouth made his feelings plain if one knew him. Jewel did. She didn't take her seat behind the broad desk. She sat on its outer edge instead, palms gripping the desk's edge for balance.

"I'm sorry," she said, in a voice as tight as Teller's lips. "I found out this afternoon."

"The investigation didn't start this afternoon." Of the two, he had the more even voice.

"No."

"How long have you suspected this?"

"I didn't suspect it at all, as you must know." She waited; it wasn't easy. After a long pause, in which Teller refused to carry the burden of conversation, she continued. "The information was brought to me upon my return from the Common."

"And you've checked this report for accuracy?"

"No. I trust its source."

Teller opened his mouth and snapped it shut again. He didn't pace. Jewel would have, which is why she had chosen to literally cling to the desk.

"Gabriel was removing his *paintings* from the office walls."

"They *are* his personal paintings."

"Yes. He was doing so under the surveillance of Torvan and three of the Chosen."

Jewel clenched both jaws and hands. "He requested that escort."

"Jay—" Finch began. Jewel did lift a hand, then, and Finch fell silent.

"If you trust the source of the information that has caused this—" Teller stopped himself from speaking again, and she was glad she'd told Avandar she'd skip lunch. She felt as if there was no ground beneath her feet—and what did remain felt an awful lot like falling. "Gabriel deserves *better* than this."

"Gabriel has never made clear that Rymark produced a forged document in the Council Hall minutes—*minutes*—after The Terafin's death. He knew. He said nothing. Not then, and not later."

Teller's brows creased; his face lost color.

If words were a path, the turn she'd just taken was the wrong one. And had she been speaking to anyone other than Teller, she would have paid dearly for it, because she couldn't then do what she now did. She held up a hand, densign, and she flexed fingers in quick succession. "I know why he couldn't. I've never asked him about it. I've never mentioned it to him." She swallowed. "The House Council—with the single exception of Haerrad—has done the same. But this? The missing funds are almost certainly the funds used to pay the assassin that Snow killed. I know Gabriel didn't hire her. It doesn't matter.

"Someone did. I can't afford to say—and do—nothing. It will make us look incompetent."

"So you surrender Gabriel."

"I accepted Gabriel's retirement, yes." She climbed down from the desk and began to pace. "Teller, if there was *any* chance he would have stayed, I would have done anything at all to keep him. There *wasn't*. Rymark knows how I feel about the right-kin. He knows that my hands are all but tied. If Gabriel doesn't leave, Rymark will continue to use him because if Gabriel is his shield, I won't strike. Come up with a better solution, and I'll listen. I'll listen *joyfully*."

Finch was watching Teller; Teller was watching Jewel. After a long, long moment, Finch touched his sleeve and said, "There isn't a better solution."

Teller closed his eyes, drew one very long breath and exhaled. "Was this his suggestion?"

"The Chosen were his suggestion. He intends to vacate his rooms—and the manse—immediately."

"Jay—"

Her own shoulders sagged, then. "I hate it," she whispered. "But it doesn't matter. I wouldn't have done this on my own—and he knew it. But Amarais *would have*. It's his gift to me."

"It's not a gift to *me*," Teller said.

"No. But you've been my right-kin for most of my life. Barston will stay if you ask him. He might negotiate a higher rate of pay."

"If Gabriel intends to leave the manse, does it mean—"

"He intends to resign from the House Council as well, yes. I need you in that office."

"I know."

"And I need you there now. It's not going to be a *pretty* day, and if I had to bet, I'd bet Haerrad and Rymark are already *in* the right-kin's office. It may put Rymark off-balance; it will certainly please Haerrad. Using either of those facts to buy me a bit of space would be highly appreciated."

Teller left the office. Jewel did not accompany him. She watched him go, but prevented Finch from following. Finch took a seat and folded her hands in her lap, mostly to stop them from moving.

"Where are Snow and Night?" she asked, when the silence had gone on for too long.

"After the demon fled the grounds, they attempted to destroy the shadow that remained in his wake. They . . . jumped *into* it. I haven't seen them since."

Finch absorbed this information in silence; she glanced at the door through which Teller had escaped, as if the impulse to follow was strong. "Will Gabriel be all right?"

"I don't know. I don't know that I would be, in his position. But he's not me. And you're not Gabriel. I want to talk to you about Jarven."

"Jarven? Why?"

"I've met him a number of times, but always as your boss. I know the position he holds in the Merchant Authority, and I know many people assume he holds it because of his prior competence."

Finch nodded.

"But I know you don't believe that's the case. Tell me what you think I should do—as The Terafin—with Jarven."

"Why do you have to do anything with Jarven?" Finch asked, her voice tightening, her arms drawing closer to her body. Jewel knew Finch as well as she knew Teller. "Jarven has no intention of retiring."

"I have no intention of forcing him to retire," Jewel quickly said. "But Gabriel's final advice—his final request, if you will—was that I cede his House Council seat to Jarven. That wasn't my intent," she added softly. "Jarven has, as far as I'm aware, never attempted to gain position on the House Council. The power he holds in the Merchant Authority is of greater weight, in my opinion, than a House Council seat would be. I can't imagine that Jarven approached Gabriel, of all people, with this request, but—" She froze.

Finch tensed again.

"No, let me take that back," Jewel said, rising. "Gordon, Marave, accompany us. We must retire to my personal chambers for a brief period of time." She didn't mention Avandar by name, but it wasn't necessary; he was her shadow.

Haval was sitting with Hannerle when Jewel arrived. He rose when he heard the knock at the door; he knew who it was. The weight of her steps in the hall, the particular tenor of her knuckles against the door, were by this time familiar. Before he could reach the door, she'd opened it, but given the way her steps had fallen, he expected no less.

"I need to speak with you," she said, in a very chilly voice.

He raised a brow. "If it will not discomfit you, speak with me here. Hannerle will not wake."

"Finch is here as well."

He glanced at his sleeping wife. "Very well. Shall we retire to the great room?"

The fireplace in the great room was no longer cold and black; wood burned there. It was a decent hardwood. Clearly, Ellerson had anticipated that the space would once again be needed. Haval did not understand the domicis, but he admired them in his fashion. Had a guild of such men desired power, they would have it; they would be a very, very dangerous entity. Ellerson did not want that power. Avandar Gallais? Haval found him almost mystifying. He did not trust the man—only a fool would. But he did not understand Avandar's ambitions, either. They were not akin to Ellerson's, and they were in no way comparable to Morretz's.

Haval entered the room carefully and slowly, affecting a weariness that was not entirely assumed for his own purposes.

Finch sat gingerly in one of the armchairs nearest the fire, thereby unconsciously choosing where the discussion would take place. Jewel sat heavily, the fingers of her right hand drumming the gleaming wood of armrests. Haval, of course, sat last as etiquette demanded.

"Terafin," he said gravely.

"When you were conducting your investigation into the personal affairs of Gabriel ATerafin, was Jarven ATerafin one of your sources?"

His brows rose; his surprise at the question was not entirely feigned. "I would sooner ask Duvari for aid."

Finch uttered a delicate, deliberate cough.

"I realize that he is in every possible way an admirable employer in his own rather impressive fief. His concerns are not, however, my concerns."

"His concerns may be *my* concerns," Jewel said, before Haval could draw another breath. He studied her, considering his reply. He was indeed surprised that she had asked the question, and wondered idly whether or not he had underestimated her. It did happen, although not nearly as often as he would like.

"Beyond the obvious—he *is* the titular head of the Merchant Authority offices—I fail to see how. I also fail to see how the inquiry is an emergency, given the events of the day."

"Gabriel will, as you know, retire."

"So you've said."

"He has chosen to take his retirement today."

Haval folded his hands in his lap. He nodded, all expression dropping away from his face. Her frown was reward for the effort.

"He had one piece of advice—one last request."

"Please do not tell me it involved Jarven ATerafin."

"You're surprised? I don't believe it."

He smiled then. "No," he said quietly. "You don't. Very well. I will not answer your question; it was clumsy and irrelevant. What does Jarven want?"

"That's what I want you to tell me. You, or Finch," she added. "I don't care which. I'm expecting at least a letter from the Exalted, and some missive from Duvari—if I'm lucky. Haerrad and Rymark will no doubt descend on my vacated office; I expect to see both Elonne and Marrick as well. I don't have a lot of time."

"What makes you believe that Jarven wants anything?"

"Gabriel asked me to install Jarven on the House Council, in the seat Gabriel will vacate. I thought at the time it was an unusual request; I'm unaware of any similar request that Jarven has made in the past. As he is *not* a member of Council now, I assume he has never made one."

"The Terafin would not have agreed to it."

"I'm not sure I will, either." She frowned. "Why do you think the former Terafin would have rejected such a request?"

Haval pinched the bridge of his nose. "While I understand it has been a very trying day for you, Jewel, I feel that the answer to that question is beyond obvious."

Finch very carefully studied her hands.

"Finch," Haval said. She looked up. She seemed very shy and retiring, but her expression was steady. Given time, Haval thought he could make something of the girl; given Jewel, it was a pipe dream. "Please answer the question."

She held his gaze for a long moment, and then glanced at Jewel. Jewel nodded. "Jarven does as he pleases. In the past, that has always worked well for the House—with one or two exceptions. He is observant, and he is adept. He gets what he needs, and he gets what he wants—usually by obfuscating what he wants. But he doesn't, as Lucille is wont to say, play well with others.

"He has power. If Jarven decides that he wishes to hamper any member of the House Council, the Merchant Authority is his weapon. He has done it in the past, at least once. Putting him within reach of the governing body of the House would not gain The Terafin anything."

"You see?" Haval said to Jewel. The implication was clear in his tone.

Jewel, however, refused to play. "Gabriel asked that the

Council seat be given to Jarven. I had hopes for it, otherwise, but to be fair, Jarven is unlikely to occupy it for long.
What did you ask of Jarven?"

Haval raised a brow. "I believe the delicate machinations
of investigation were to be left in my hands."

"And I believe that reports were to be tendered to me
upon request. Gabriel's acquisitions do not flow freely
through the Merchant Authority—that I'm aware of. Those
that do are a matter of House Business and House records."

Haval cast a baleful glance toward the door, and Ellerson approached with tea. Haval considered adding brandy
to the liquid and decided against it. "They are."

"His personal affairs are not."

"No. But the banking is done through similar channels.
Jarven has access to most of the merchant banks, and it is a
friendly—and in some cases obsequious—access. Before
you lose the temper that is rapidly fraying, Terafin, I will
trouble myself to point out that it was not *I* who approached
Jarven."

"Jarven approached you."

Haval nodded.

Jewel's gaze swiveled to Finch. Finch was silent. "Why,"
Jewel asked her, "did Jarven approach Haval, and not you?
You're the most certain conduit to me, and Jarven is well
aware of this."

Finch said, clearly and distinctly, "I don't know." The
question did not please her, in Haval's opinion. When she
lifted her chin, she looked straight at Haval. "But I believe
Haval does. As it is not the information one would normally
hand a clothier, we must assume that Jarven knows something we don't."

"Perhaps he is aware of the role I now play as Jewel's
adviser." It pained Haval to say this.

Finch met his gaze and held it for a long moment. "That
makes sense, given Jarven."

Haval nodded.

"But, given Jarven, it makes too much sense."

"My dear," Haval told her, "it is a small marvel to me
that you are trapped in the Merchant Authority. You are, of
course, correct. There is some history between Jarven and
me, and it is complex, and better left entirely unspoken. I
understand why he approached me with information about

Gabriel's personal accounts—and no, Jewel, Jarven does not consider Gabriel the hand behind the assassin. He is, however, a cautious man; he allows for the possibility."

"I don't," Jewel rather predictably said, tightening her grip on the armrests.

"Understood. I would have more to say about this, but if you have accepted Gabriel's hasty retirement, you understand the political cost, regardless."

She said nothing. He judged the whole of the day in her pinched expression. She was not—yet—at her limit, but she now trod the edge of it. Exhausted, she lacked rudimentary caution, and the subtlety that the political arena required quickly passed beyond her. "If you wish it," he said quietly, "I will speak with Jarven."

But Finch rose. "No, Haval."

He raised a brow.

"I will speak with Jarven." She paused, her expression shifting into almost open anxiety. "Jay? That's all right?"

Jewel hesitated again, and then nodded. "I'd rather he speak to Haval, but I don't think he'll give Haval much."

"I am not incapable of—"

"You'll notice things. He'll notice things. I think there's a better chance that he'll actually talk to Finch."

Haval raised a brow, considered it, and nodded. "I concur. If we are done, I must return to Hannerle, and I believe you must return to your office." He rose, lost for a moment in thought as he considered Jarven clearly. The situation troubled him. Jarven delighted in being an annoyance—especially to Haval; he always had. But the House Council? That was more than just a stage for annoyance.

What game, he thought, as he left both tea and the great room. What game are you playing, Jarven? He sensed a web, a net, something that Jarven was spinning in his deplorably gleeful way, and he could not tell if it was the acceptance or the refusal that would trigger its fall. Jewel saw the House, of course, and she did not trust Jarven—showing an unusually canny perception, for Jewel. But Haval was not certain that Jarven now aimed for the House.

He did not desire to play a game of chess with Jarven when he himself had the lesser familiarity with the board and its pieces.

And that, he thought, his hand on the door that led to Hannerle's room, was a half-truth. Or half a lie, and only a fool lied to himself. Some part of his mind was waking after decades of forced sleep, and the prospect of facing Jarven, and emerging triumphant, was compelling.

Chapter Five

WHEN JEWEL EMERGED from the great room, she ran into Angel, and staggered backward. Angel, arms folded, didn't move. He looked down at her for a long moment, his spire of hair tilted in the direction of her face.

Finch sidestepped them both, which took dexterity given they were almost standing in the door's frame. She signed both hello and good-bye to Angel; he dipped chin in acknowledgment as she brushed past and headed out of the Wing.

"I'm alive," Jewel told Angel.

He nodded. "The demon?"

"Come with me. I have to go back to the office, or Teller will be lynched."

He looked at her, his brows creasing. "Teller?"

"Long story. Well, short story, long explanation."

He fell in to her right, stopped as he realized that nothing large, winged, and spiteful was attempting to trip him, shoulder him into a lesser position, or crush his toes, and asked, "Where's Snow?"

"Gods alone know. I'll fill you in on that part, too."

The first thing they saw as they drew close to the office was Rymark ATerafin.

He was waiting outside of the office doors, which was unusual. Members of the House who lived in the manse—

and all of the House Council had that right—generally retreated to their own quarters when required to wait to speak with The Terafin. There were no chairs in the hall; there were chairs in the waiting room, and Rymark clearly hadn't chosen to avail himself of any of them. This simple fact made clear to Jewel that the waiting room itself would be heavily occupied.

She did not want to speak with Rymark in the open acoustics of the hall. If she were honest, she didn't want to speak to him at all. Avandar, to her left, tensed slightly; the Chosen moved to stand between Rymark and their Lord. They were not required to be subtle, and today, they were not.

"Rymark," she said, offering him a stiff nod. She was certain—they were all certain—that Rymark ATerafin was responsible for at least one of the assassins; Jewel privately thought he was responsible for the fake House Guards as well. She was also certain that he had cost her the guidance and the company of Gabriel—and as that loss was immediate and fresh, her anger—at Rymark, at the games she was forced to play to preserve the House, was visceral. It was *not* a good time to be ambushed in the halls; not by Rymark.

"Terafin," he replied. His usual arrogance was, for the moment, hidden; he was pale, his expression tight.

She lifted her chin, schooling her expression, and remembering—of all things—some of Haval's earliest advice. She was angry at losing—at having to lose—Gabriel. And it hurt her. She drew on that, allowing it to fill her expression. She wasn't certain what Rymark saw, but she didn't care. "You've spoken with Gabriel," she said quietly.

"I spoke only briefly with the former right-kin." Not his father, of course. The former right-kin. "I had hoped, of course, to speak with you in some privacy; the events of today seem to have destroyed that possibility."

"Given the events that occurred in the Common, I see little hope of that in the next few days. Please accept my apologies in advance. The Ten meet in *Avantari* on the morrow, and the office of the right-kin is in transition. If I were not certain to receive both messages and visitors that the House cannot safely dismiss, I would retreat from the office and call upon the House Council. That luxury at the moment is not given to any member of this House."

Rymark bowed. Before Jewel could pass him—and it would have been hard, as the Chosen hadn't budged an inch—he rose. "I wish to speak with you at your earliest convenience, Terafin. I have much to say."

If he offered to turn evidence against his father in the House Council, Jewel would kill him herself. Or, worse—far worse in some ways—she would allow him to be killed. She would allow it to be arranged. She'd even ask that it be done. The grief at losing Gabriel faltered at the sudden incandescence of her rage; her hands, hanging loosely by her sides, stiffened. For a full three breaths, she found no reply to tender, because speaking—at all—would have alerted any occupants of the waiting room behind the closed doors of her utter loss of control.

"Make an appointment," she finally managed to say.

He stepped back. "The information," he said, his voice still soft, his posture still shorn of the edge of arrogance, "involves the Shining Court."

Before she could reply, he turned and left, and she let him go because the enormity of his statement left no room for thought. When thought returned, she was once again in a hall that was empty of anyone save herself, her domicis, and the Chosen. And Angel, who had watched Rymark's back until a corner carried it completely out of sight.

Avandar, he said the Shining Court, didn't he?

He did.

Her hands curled in fists, she approached the office doors. Avandar opened them for her, and she entered.

The waiting room was not as crowded as she had expected, given Rymark's appearance in the hall. It was not, however, empty. Three Priests, in the robes worn by the most senior members of the Cathedral of the Triumvirate on the Isle, were seated. They had no attendants, and given the colors of their robes, this was unusual. Two men and one woman rose as she entered. She offered them a deep bow. They had eyes of brown—brown and blue. They were not god-born. But they served the Exalted directly.

Torvan had said that among the casualties inflicted by the *Kialli* before his sudden flight, there had been Priests. She therefore approached the Priests seated in waiting with quiet, but obvious respect. She didn't really love the Priests, and she didn't understand the varied layers of the hierarchies of the Cathedrals on the Isle—or off the Isle, if it came to that—but in this case, that understanding wasn't necessary. If Priests had been injured—if Priests had, as Torvan reported, died at the hands of the demon lord—they suffered the loss of a colleague, and quite likely a friend.

It was a loss she understood, but could not directly address, not yet. She bowed, instead. A bow was not a strict necessity, but she made it serve in the place of the words she could not, without a formal report, utter. The Priests rose as she did. They did not wear robes of uniform color; nor did they wear the usual dress robes seen on the customary official visits. One wore robes of earthen brown, one wore robes of neutral gray, and one wore robes the color of rust.

It was the man in earthen brown who spoke. "Terafin." He bowed, just as she had done. He was not a young man; she thought him perhaps Gabriel's age. The symbol of the Mother hung from a thick chain around his neck, falling across the robes just beneath his collarbones. There, in gold, wheat lay across two open palms. They were the same open palms that, empty, designated the bearer a member of the Houses of Healing, a reminder of the Mother's mercy. "I have been sent at the behest of the Exalted of the Mother."

Jewel nodded. "Will you join me in my office?"

"It is not necessary, Terafin. I am to convey a message, and I am to wait for your reply."

She glanced at the silent Priests who stood behind him now, like points of a triangle. "Do you also carry messages from the Exalted?" They nodded. "The same message?"

"Yes, Terafin. Your presence is requested in the Hall of Wise Counsel on the morrow."

"After the meeting with The Ten in the Hall of The Ten?"

"Yes."

She felt the tension ease from her shoulders. "I am not certain how long the Council meeting will last. There is much indeed to be discussed there, and I imagine many questions to at least be asked. Perhaps the day after?"

Silence, which she'd expected. She had no objections at all to the request, and none to the day; if the meeting of the Council proved too fractious—and at this point, she couldn't see how it wouldn't—the Exalted provided a respectable excuse to vacate the premises if she felt a need to retreat.

But she chose to be careful about conveying any gratitude to what was, in essence, a demand.

"Very well. I cannot vouchsafe the hour of my arrival, but if that is acceptable to the Exalted, I will meet with them at their request on their chosen day. Will the Kings also be in attendance?"

"They will."

She bowed again, and the three weary Priests immediately retreated.

Which left only a handful of people in the waiting room. One of them was Haerrad. She wondered, idly, what he had said to Teller to be granted the audience Teller had so clearly denied Rymark. The thought set her teeth on edge, but Haerrad was not a proponent of friendly or accessible rulers, and hostility—if it was veiled—was unlikely to cause him any difficulty at all.

"Haerrad," she said, inclining her head. She turned toward her office, and he rose to follow her. Avandar interposed himself between Haerrad and Jewel's back, an action which was unlikely to be lost on the House Councillor Jewel most wanted to see as a corpse. It was, however, unlikely to be resented. Haerrad appeared to *like* the fact that most people thought he was a murderous bastard. Their fear—expressed as caution—made him feel secure in his position.

She walked immediately to her desk, Avandar by her side; she allowed him to pull out the chair so that she could sit in it, the large desk between her and her visitor as much of a barrier as such a meeting allowed.

Haerrad glanced casually around the room, making it seem smaller by the action. He noticed the lack of Snow, but made no comment; Haerrad always noticed anything that resembled a vulnerability in an opponent's defense. Age had tinged Haerrad's dark hair gray; it was the color of steel now. The scars that were his medals from the early, rough years on contested roads had faded with time, blending into the etched lines around his mouth. But the prominence of an obviously broken nose still ruled the terrain of his face, and his eyes were dark enough in the magelights that they were almost black.

"Terafin."

She inclined her chin and waited, folding her hands in a

steeple beneath it. She had, with Haval's help, learned to school her expression, and she channeled the natural suspicion Haerrad evoked simply by breathing into something that looked like attention.

"You've dismissed Gabriel," Haerrad said.

"Gabriel chose to retire."

Haerrad's eyes narrowed. "And you, of course, begged him to remain."

"Of course. His experience and his expertise in his role have been of great value to Terafin, and such experience is not lightly surrendered." She kept her voice smooth and even, and was rewarded by his smile. It was not a pretty reward; it was a wolf's smile. Or, she thought, trying to be fair to wolves, a rabid dog's. He assumed she lied.

It was a neat trick. It was, of course, Haval's trick.

"And his replacement?"

"You are here, Haerrad. You have obviously seen his replacement."

"Very well." His smile continued to adorn his face, and he seemed to relax into his chair. "I have a report to tender. It will be of some interest to you, Terafin."

She waited; he did not speak. Instead, he handed her a slender set of papers. "I am now aware that your information sources are surprisingly good," he said, as she accepted them, "but I think you will find mine are also formidable."

She didn't even glance at them, although that took effort.

"They will, of course, be of lesser import to the day's events." He paused again, his eyes still narrow, but more watchful. He was Haerrad. He went straight for the figurative throat. "The demon was there for you."

"That has yet to be determined."

"By who? The magi? The Exalted? The *Astari*?" He almost spit at the last word.

She forced a sharp, slender smile to her lips. "Indeed. To all of them. I am sure their sources of information are at least as good as our own; let them discuss and dissect. I will, of course, point out that the Kings were present in the Common, and the Kings are a far more likely target."

"The Kings have not faced demons."

"Ah. Your information sources are not, perhaps, as complete as you suppose, Councillor."

A brow, bisected by the fading line of a scar, rose. He did

not, however, look annoyed—or rather, not more than he naturally did. "Oh?"

She smiled again. "I thank you for your report. If I am not mistaken, the magi have arrived in the outer office."

"Do not be so quick to placate them, Terafin."

"Placate them?" Her brows rose in feigned shock.

Feign less, Avandar said dryly. *You are not one hundredth the actor that Haval is.*

"At the moment, Councillor, I have no need to do so. You will no doubt hear, when the House Council again convenes—"

"I suggest that sooner rather than late."

"Indeed, given the unexpected departure of Gabriel ATerafin, it is necessary."

"In two days?"

She shook her head. "Tomorrow I will spend a full day in *Avantari*. If the outcomes of the meetings there require it, I will call Council in two days—but I suspect if I do, Duvari will be present within the manse, and possibly within the Council Hall in some fashion."

"Impossible." The humor drained from his face in an instant.

"He will, of course, make clear that his presence is entirely in service of the Kings and their investigation into a demon that managed to destroy Priests through the barrier of their god-born magic. I will, of course, block him in that regard—but if he chooses, he can be difficult. During normal circumstances, I would ignore the difficulty; at this time, I am unwilling to spend his wrath needlessly. I have no doubt that there will be cause to do so in the near future."

His nod was reluctant, his eyes narrower than they had been. "What news of the magi, then?"

"It is a trifle," she replied, "and as such not grounds to call Council—but the Terafin House Mage will serve the remainder of his contract with the House at no cost to the House coffers."

His eyes rounded briefly before they returned to their normal shape. "What do you hold over the Order of Knowledge that you could gain that concession?"

She merely smiled and rose. "I thank you for your information," she told him gravely. "And I hope that in future, the vote of confidence you have withheld will be offered me, and the previous abstention struck from the records."

Only after she closed the door on his back did she return to the desk to look at what he had offered her. It was not—entirely—what she had assumed it would be.

"Well?" Avandar asked, raising a brow at her frown. "It concerns Gabriel, does it not?"

"Yes," Jewel replied. "But it is not—as I expected—an accusation of malfeasance on Gabriel's part; it is an accusation of sentimentality and willful blindness."

"This would not qualify as information on the part of any Council member."

"No."

"What information, then?"

"The woman did not work alone."

Avandar came to stand by her side. "How does Haerrad claim to know that?"

"It seems his shock at the lack of fee on the part of the Order of Knowledge is not mere dramatics; he hired one unnamed mage in his pursuit of the 'suspicious' activities of Rymark ATerafin. In the course of that investigation, his investigator uncovered the assassin in question, although he claims not to have understood her significance until well after the fact of her death."

"Convenient."

"Far too convenient," she replied with a grimace. "What's interesting is this: Rymark met with an investor in the High Market—at the Placid Sea. He used an audible conversation stone for the duration of their meal."

"Did the mage attempt to listen in?"

She shook her head. "Rymark has always been careful. He would have noticed. There's no record of the contents of the conversation, and the investigative details were split at that point. One man followed Rymark's guest, and one continued to tail Rymark. It was the guest that proved fruitful, in the end, and it was the guest who met with his 'sister' after the meeting. The sister in question matches the description of our assassin, except for the color of her hair."

"Hair is simple camouflage."

"It is. But an eyewitness report based on description, and compared with a description of a corpse? Haerrad is certain—or his source is—that the woman in question was the same one. Why?"

"It is possible that either Haerrad or the investigator recognized the man who clearly handed off the assignment."

"Yes, that would be my guess as well. He does mention the possibility of a large withdrawal from Gabriel's account, but not conclusively." Although it was not information that led her to draw any conclusion she had not already drawn, it was useful in one way. Haerrad, who publicly disdained the magi, clearly had reliable connections within the Order itself.

When Jarven ATerafin returned to his rooms within the manse, he had a guest. She was not waiting in the hall; she was seated in the parlor; nor did she rise when he entered. Instead, she watched him with care. His clothing was in slight disarray; Jarven had not been one of the members of House Terafin who had made their hasty retreat from the Common to the manse. If he liked to play at age—and he did, when it suited him—he was not a young man by any stretch of the imagination.

"Have you just returned?" she asked him quietly.

"Finch," he replied, smiling. He offered her a bow. "I must be addled; I was certain I had locked those doors on my way out."

"You're still certain," she replied, her smile both present and reluctant.

"So I am. I admit I am slightly surprised to see you here." She lifted a brow.

"That is the absolute truth, my dear. You are honestly far too embroiled with Lucille if you can doubt that—and doubt it so frankly."

"I suppose it's the first time I've broken into your rooms."

"I hope it's the first time you've broken into *anyone's* rooms; it would be considered completely inappropriate behavior for a member of the House Council—and risky behavior for a member of your age and relative seniority. I trust there is a reason for it, other than to test the deplorable security of these locks?"

"There is. I want to know why you approached Haval

with information about Gabriel ATerafin. I considered asking Lucille, but thought that should be my last line of offense, not my first."

"Ah. So you are not yet angry."

"I'm not angry, no. Worried. Concerned. Curious in an uneasy way. I'll reserve anger for later use."

"If you are asking why I did not approach you, I had my reasons."

"I have no doubt of that—but I would like to know what they were." She folded her arms across her chest, tilting her chin up as if she were Lucille behind the bastion of her desk.

"Because I had the information. I am fond of you, Finch, but the information, given to you, would be of little value."

"It would reach Jewel."

"Ah." He crossed the parlor and opened a small cabinet. "I have had a rather tiring afternoon—and an unexpectedly exciting one—and I am about to indulge in a drink that is not tea. Will you join me?" He pulled out one glass. "I will take that wrinkled nose as a no."

"I will keep you company while you drink," she offered.

"Good. You can perhaps explain what occurred in the Common since you will not be otherwise occupied."

"Explain? You were there, Jarven. You saw what we all saw."

"I am certain I saw more than you saw," was his friendly reply. He took a small table, dragged it across the very fine rug, and deposited his squat, round glass in its center. He then went back for a chair. "But it is possible that your understanding of what you did notice was deeper than my own. I would therefore be quite interested in hearing your version of events."

"Haval first," she told him.

"Finch, you wound me. I am all but exhausted."

She rose then, and fetched a footstool from the corner of the room farthest from the door. This, she carried—although it was much heavier than it looked. She placed it firmly in front of Jarven's feet, and then resumed her own seat.

"You are not in a terribly charitable mood, I see. Then again, you almost never are, where that girl is concerned."

"Where The Terafin is concerned," she said, correcting him.

"My dear, if I answer your questions, Haval will be ill-pleased."

"Haval is already ill-pleased."

"Oh?"

"You asked for the House Council seat. Whatever else exists between you, that was no part of his plan."

"And you are so certain it is part of mine?"

"Tell me it's not."

"It is not."

"Liar."

He chuckled, lifted his glass, and held it to the light. It was magelight. "Do you understand why I maintain my position in the Merchant Authority?"

"Lucille would kill you if you quit."

He laughed. "I assure you that is not the case. She will not see me forced out—and she would indeed threaten acts of dire violence against any she perceived had that intent. But if I retired, do you not think she would be relieved?"

Finch considered the question with care; it was a serious question, even laced as it was with his laughter. Lucille held Jarven in the highest respect; she valued the service he had offered the House, and she spoke—when she was tired or unguarded—of his feats of brilliance in the Merchant Authority. But she very seldom turned to Jarven for either advice or guidance; Finch did.

Finch did far more often. "It's possible," she finally said. "Why do you think you retain your position?"

"Because it suits me, Finch. I am disarming. I am an old man whose days of glory are far, far behind me. I forget things easily. I lose track of complicated numbers."

Her eyes had narrowed with each short sentence; they were almost closed by the time he lifted his glass again. "You know Lucille hates it when you do that. And you do it almost all the time, these days."

"I do, indeed. I am somewhat more fragile than I was when you were first introduced to my office—and you, my dear, are much less so."

"You didn't get the information about Gabriel's accounts by being a doddering, witless man."

"Ah, Finch—but I *did*." He drank, studying her through the glass.

In truth, she wasn't afraid of this man. She had never

truly been afraid of him. Was he powerful? Yes. Demonstrably. But it was a subtle power, and he leavened it with a sense of humor and a very real sense of sentiment.

"I kept the Merchant Authority because, for years, Finch, the heart of the House activities passed through my office and beneath my eyes. Accounts tell a tale of power, abuse, and grand plots if you know how to read the numbers; they always have. The world—perhaps especially the parts of it that meet with your disapproval—requires money. But in truth, Amarais' reign was so stable until the end that there was very little treachery. Not none, of course."

"You didn't report it."

"I did not wish The Terafin to be as bored as I was."

"The Council seat?"

"Can you not guess?"

She thought Lucille might be tempted to strangle Jarven at this point.

"You have grown so careful, Finch." He set his glass down, glanced up at her, and watched as she sighed and moved to refill it. "So very careful. You give me so little information; I have to watch you like a hawk. I miss the days when you relied on my advice."

She was, however, thinking. About Jarven, about what she knew of him, about the Merchant Authority offices behind the Terafin crest. About the House Council. And, yes, about Jay. About the funeral, and everything that had happened since.

"The Merchant Authority is no longer the central hub of treachery and deception," she finally said.

His brows rose; his smile was almost beatific, it was so content. "Indeed. You see my problem."

"I see *a* problem."

"The demon in the Common was there for Jewel. The army assumed it meant to assassinate the Kings and the Exalted—the god-born."

She didn't deny it.

"I know that demons interact with us; I know that *we* desire power, and power is often money. But in the case of the magi, it is not. In the case of the demons, stripped of dependence on mortals, money becomes strangely irrelevant. It is not *satisfying*, Finch. Yes, there are movements, within the Authority and at the Port. Haerrad is not yet finished, although he now bides his time. Jewel has proven her ability to survive in the face of enemies that would almost certainly have killed any other member of this House.

"But Elonne and Marrick have pulled in their teeth. It is my feeling that they were both deeply impressed by the events in the Terafin grounds—and by the trees that still tower there, after the fact of it. But they do not yet understand the scope of the difficulty."

"And you do?"

"No, not yet. But to fully do so, I must have access to the House Council, because it is in the House Council that I will have access to your Jay. I will have access," he continued, lifting and studying the bottom of a glass that was noticeably emptier, "to the reports of the magi, the demands of the Exalted, and even the annoyance caused by Duvari and his pack of trained dogs. I will see for myself what now moves the House—and what now moves," he added, his voice dropping, "the Empire." He lifted the glass in her direction. "So you understand, Finch, why I want the seat."

She did. She understood it in exactly the way one understands the pit that has opened up beneath one's feet during an earthquake. Jarven wanted this. Watching him, watching him watch *her*, she understood that she had never truly seen him want anything before. She had worked with him for half her life, albeit more as a page than an equal for the early years—if she was even an equal now—and she had never seen the expression that transformed his aged face.

She wondered what Lucille would think, in her position. She knew Haval didn't trust Jarven, which didn't bother her. She knew Jay didn't either, which did. But she felt that she could trust this man. Maybe it was naive. Maybe she had learned to trust him because there was no conflict in what they desired. Finch wanted the safety of her den, and her den's leader; she wanted the health of House Terafin; she wanted a home, and as starving children often squirrel away whatever food they can get their hands on, she had made more than one: in the West Wing, in the Merchant Authority, among the Chosen that Torvan trusted.

But if what Jarven wanted worked against those in any

way, he would still want it. He might be stopped, but not by
Finch alone. She wondered, as she studied him, mirroring
his regard, if anything or anyone could. She had her doubts.

His smile acknowledged them. It was hard and sharp.
"Well, Finch?"

She folded her hands in her lap. "What would you do
with the information?"

"What does a rich man do with his rings and his gold and
his many, many houses?"

"Wear them and live in them, I imagine."

"You do not. You have worked with me for far, far too
long—and I have not fired you or had you sent from my
office, more's the pity."

"Jarven."

"Yes, that was harsh. But you really have become quite
cautious, and at the moment, I feel it is to my detriment.
You have affection for me; that much is obvious. But you
are not exactly on *my* side." He set the glass down. "It really
is a pity that you are so devoted to your Jewel. I feel that in
you, there exists the steel to manipulate and maintain the
House Seat."

"I know you mean that as a compliment," she said softly,
"but it's really not—"

"Nonsense. If you mean to tell me that you are too shy,
too retiring, too tongue-tied, I shall accept it for what it is
worth, and remind you that Sigurne Mellifas is old, frail,
and sentimental. But she has held the Order of Knowledge
for decades, and those who attempted to oust her by violence are no longer among its many rolls. I will not argue
with you about this; I know what I see. Even if you were
certain you could do so, you would not rise to make the
attempt."

"No more did you."

He smiled quite fondly, folding his hands across his chest
and leaning back. "No."

"Jarven, what will you *do* with the information?"

"How can I say? I am unclear as to what the information
is. But you have not disapproved of what I did in the web of
my office to date."

"I disapproved of some of it, when I had the knowledge
to understand it," was her severe reply.

"Very well. It did not cause a war; nor did it cause a permanent loss of status, although I will grant the temporary loss was severe." Neither loss, nor status, of course, had been his.

She exhaled, hands still in her lap, her shoulders turned toward the floor; she looked much smaller in the confines of the large chair. "Would you give up the Merchant Authority in exchange for the House Council seat?"

He did not even attempt to look outraged or apologetic. The harsh, hard gleam of his eyes didn't falter. "Is that your opening position?"

"My opening position is No."

He did not point out that it was not a position she had the authority to take; that would have been an insult. To her surprise, he didn't even make the attempt. Jarven *knew* how to wheedle. He knew how to get around her. He knew, sitting there, eyes hard and bright, that she never truly wanted to deny him anything.

But he knew that she could, or would, if she felt it necessary.

"I am willing to consider a senior aide in the Authority office."

"Would that aide report to you, or to Jay?"

"To me."

She folded her arms.

"*And* to The Terafin, of course."

"To Lucille and The Terafin. You know how Lucille feels about your reputation in the office, and you already use it shamelessly."

"In return for this concession—"

"It is only barely a concession, Jarven."

"In return," he repeated, "I am to be given a seat upon the House Council, and my authority is to be commensurate with my experience in the Authority."

Her brows rose. "There is *no* seat on Council that is commensurate with that, and you know it. If you cannot separate yourself—genuinely—from some of the power you now hold in the Merchant Authority, you will *already* wield more power than any other Council member; it's likely you'll wield more actual power than The Terafin herself.

"I trust you. I know I shouldn't; it's a weakness. But even I would hesitate to give you that much control."

"If I am not given the Council seat," he replied, in an

easy, friendly voice, "you will come to understand just how much damage the Merchant Authority offices can do to the House."

She stared at him for a long, silent moment.

"Ah, yes. That is a threat, Finch, and I am sorry to have to make it so baldly—but you are not the dance partner I expected to have in this discussion, and only the bald will reach you." He frowned. "You may tell Haval that I owe him."

"Please do not threaten Haval," Finch replied.

"You are not concerned about my threat to the House? To your young Terafin?"

"I am. I know you mean it." But even knowing it, she couldn't find her righteous wrath. It wouldn't have done any good. "You can do the damage, Jarven; she can, in turn, replace you. It will be costly—I can imagine how costly you would make it, and I really don't want to continue in that vein. But that war will not give you what you want, and if you begin it—even a small overture, as a warning—she will die before she gives you the seat you desire.

"And if she dies, you will never have what you want."

"Finch, I dislike your expression. I may be forced to remind you that we will still be working together in the Authority offices, and that I am your superior."

"Yes."

His eyes narrowed. "You intend to discuss this with Lucille."

"I'm not certain."

He frowned. As he did, he straightened both spine and shoulders, sitting more formally in the chair he'd dragged across the room. "Is this not the point at which such threats are now affectionately offered?"

She liked, and had always liked, Jarven; that was the truth. Even his threat hadn't changed it; it was immutable, as much a part of her life in House Terafin as—as Jay was. But she had loved Duster, in her time, and Duster had indisputably been the most cruel member of the den. She smiled at Jarven, thinking how like—and how unlike—these two were. "It is, Jarven—but these are real. You know I adore you, you've always known it."

He did not smile; he watched her then, as if she were the

emerging first draft of a difficult and much contested territorial rights contract.

"But I also love Lucille. I always have. She's been like a mother, to me."

"She is like a mother," he said, with a sniff, "to almost anyone who is not immediately odious, and who will stand still. At least if they're female; she tends toward suspicion of the men."

Finch nodded with the smile that Jarven withheld; it was all true.

"I fail to see what this signifies."

"No. You don't."

He sighed. "Finch, please. At least do me the courtesy of pretense?"

"You haven't tendered me the same courtesy."

"You are young. You have decades. I may have a handful of healthy years; time, for me, is of the essence."

"Which has nothing at all to do with pretense."

"Does it not?"

"No." She let her smile fade as she considered Lucille. "I'm uncertain because it will bother her."

"Everything—"

Finch held up one hand. "No, it doesn't. Everything *irritates* her, it's true. But this? It's serious, and she'll know it. Lucille is not you, Jarven. She complains about the House, and the idiocy of some House Council policies—she always has. But she's *of* the House. She respects you because of what you've done *for* the House; she demands the same respect from anyone who's part of the House, and still breathing. You know it, I know it.

"This? It's not something that will irritate her. I think there's a very real chance it will upset her—and in the end, to no purpose. She won't be able to change your mind, and she won't be able to influence Jay—Jewel—The Terafin—"

Jarven chuckled.

"—either. I care about her at least as much as I care about you—and for far better reasons. I don't want to hurt her. I know you won't tell her a thing; if she finds out, it will be because of me—or because of an announcement made in the House itself, should Jewel consider your offer with care." Clearing her throat, she added, "and what *are* you offering in return for the concession you demand?"

He steepled his fingers beneath his chin, a gesture with which Finch was familiar. His gaze was still sharp, still hard. "You are aware, no doubt," he finally said, "that I am exceedingly fond of Lucille."

"You are. You would never deliberately hurt Lucille. If I may be either bold or foolish, I would swear you would never deliberately hurt me, either."

He nodded; there was acknowledgment, but no warmth or encouragement, in the gesture.

"But you would never deliberately avoid it, if you were focused on a goal, a deal, a significant acquisition."

"That is harsh, but perceptive."

"Jarven—if I didn't know this to be true, you'd be impossible. I also understand that you grant me the same courtesy: you know I'll never go out of my way to deliberately hurt you—if that were even possible—but that I won't surrender things that would harm *me* solely to prevent it, either. Lucille is not you—which is why you both trust and like her—and she's not me. She couldn't have this conversation—she'd be too busy trying to change your mind."

"She knows me," he said quietly.

"Yes—but she'd try, anyway. She would feel like a failure, or worse, in the wake of an outcome that you and I acknowledge at the outset is inevitable."

After a long pause, he inclined his head. "Let me grant you that point."

"What do you offer for the seat? A vacant Council chair this early in a ruler's reign is an important strategic piece. If you are given the seat, what will you bring to the table that will be to The Terafin's advantage?"

He did smile, then; it was a very, very odd smile. "I am inordinately fond of you, Finch, but I will say today that you have done something I would not have considered possible, for a variety of reasons. You have made me proud."

The praise moved Finch because it was so unexpected. But it did not change her demands; if anything, it strengthened the certainty that she must be firm and clear-sighted. These negotiations would decide Jay's future in the House, or a great part of it. So much, resting on the shoulders of this elderly, implacable man.

"What does The Terafin want?"

Finch smiled and shook her head. "That is not how this game is played, Jarven. She has something you want. Absent obvious threat—which I am certain, until the end, you will not make—you must now convince her that you have something she needs."

"The threat would be effective, given her precarious position."

"No, it wouldn't—and you won't make it except as a very last resort."

"Will I not?"

"No. Even if you mean it—and I don't doubt that you do—it will break something between you and Lucille that the few years you have left won't be long enough to heal. Only if you have no other option will you play that card."

"Indeed. I rather resent Haval, at the moment."

"Haval has nothing to do with this."

"Does he not?"

"No, Jarven." Finch rose. "This is you; this is all you. I've spent very little time with Haval and Hannerle; I've spent sixteen years in the Merchant Authority offices, bringing you both tea and news. If you have not considered what you will offer The Terafin in return for the Council chair, I will leave you to consider it now."

"Has it not occurred to you," Jarven said, also rising, "that it is precisely because I am uncertain of what she needs that I want that chair?"

"Never," Finch replied sweetly. "And it never will." She turned toward the door, and then turned back. "I'll be in the office tomorrow, unless another demon appears in the Common; given today, I don't expect it will be all that busy." She hesitated, and then crossed the room, bridging the gap between them. She hugged him tightly and briefly.

Elonne, Marrick, Iain, and Gerridon came and went. They offered Jewel renewed support in various ways—Gerridon was the most circumspect, Marrick the least. No other members of the House Council crossed her threshold, and the only one that had who had dared to mention Gabriel was Haerrad, which was not a surprise. She wasn't certain if this was an act of courtesy on their part, because she wasn't certain, in the end, that they understood how much it grieved her to lose Gabriel.

Gabriel, who had served Amarais as her right-kin, her most trusted adviser, for all of Jewel's life in the House, grieved for Amarais' loss in almost the same way that Jewel did. Losing him, losing that lifetime of their mutual respect and admiration, losing the solidarity of their bereavement, was like losing Amarais again. An echo. An aftershock.

But even raging—in silence—at Rymark's very existence, his parting words remained with her. They were not words she had expected to hear in the halls of her own manse.

When Sigurne Mellifas arrived at the end of the day, Jewel was beyond exhausted. Exhausted had occurred hours ago, and because she had failed to surrender to it, she was in a curious half-state. It was possibly the wrong state in which to encounter the Guildmaster of the Order of Knowledge, but when Sigurne was escorted into her office, she saw that Sigurne was likewise graced by the same near-emptiness.

"I have been told," the guildmaster said, bowing briefly, "that you have reserved the honor of dinner for my appointment."

She'd said that, and remembered saying it, to Barston. It seemed curiously displaced in time, although she knew she'd said it only this afternoon. Jewel turned to Avandar, who said, "It is the late dinner hour, Terafin." To Sigurne, he said, "Please follow."

Jewel wanted to return to the West Wing and its large dining hall—or perhaps its breakfast nook. She did neither. Instead, she allowed Avandar to lead the way to The Terafin's personal chambers—rooms that Jewel had yet to occupy, because to do so, she had to leave behind the familiarity of the home she'd built. Yes, both rooms were in the same manse—but her den would never be a part of these rooms.

Gabriel had accepted her reluctance—but not in silence. She wondered if Teller would do the same, and the thought surprised her. Before today, she would have assumed the answer was no, because Teller knew what the West Wing meant to her—and to all of them.

"Gabriel," Sigurne said, as she walked, "is no longer in the office of the right-kin."

"No. He intended to retire the moment Amarais Handernesse ATerafin died, but he remained in the office—as regent, not right-kin—because the situation in the House became so quickly precarious."

"Precarious is a charming word, Terafin, and is oft used as understatement." Sigurne stopped speaking as she mounted the stairs, hand on the gentle curve of the rails. When they reached the upper halls, she apologized. "It has been a very long day. Had it merely been the usual politically motivated form of busy, I would not be here."

"Nor would I," Jewel replied, wanting to offer Sigurne an arm. And why shouldn't she? She paused as Avandar's lips pursed, and turned to the guildmaster, offering her the arm.

Sigurne took it with a wry smile. "I have displaced my cane," she said, "And Matteos Corvel is not in condition to join me this eve. I had to order him back to bed—as the guildmaster. He is likely to be quite put out for the next few days."

"Will you be in the Hall of Wise Counsel on the morrow?"

"Yes. I think it likely by that time that Matteos will either join me, or be forced to wear manacles and chains—and that much of a loss of dignity, I do not think wise."

The arm that Jewel had offered was not decorative; Sigurne leaned heavily on it as they made their way to the guarded, wide doors of the rooms that had been used for so little. Jewel knew that the servants and the kitchen would nonetheless have the private dining room prepared. Nor was she wrong. But she hesitated in the dining room's door, and the hesitation was obvious.

She had seen this room, had dined with Amarais, hundreds of times since she had arrived at House Terafin. She had come here as guest, as confidante, and as counsel. But she had never come here as The Terafin; she had never brought guests of her own.

"It is hard," Sigurne said softly.

Jewel grimaced. "Is it that obvious?"

"Amarais Handernesse ATerafin was a woman worthy of respect and devotion, Terafin. Yes, to me, it is obvious. But I am old, and I have seen much; I do not find your grief—contained and controlled so admirably as it usually is—an offense or a weakness. If I have concerns—and I do, as you must suspect—that reaction calms them; it does not exacerbate them."

Jewel led her to the chair that Jewel herself usually occupied; Avandar pulled it out, and Avandar tucked it in. He wouldn't join them at the meal itself; Morretz never had. But he would be a constant presence, and he would warn her if she crossed a dangerous line in her current state of exhaustion.

He offered wine. Sigurne hesitated, and then nodded, which surprised Jewel. It surprised Jewel enough that she allowed herself to do the same. They sat in silence while Avandar served, and in this, Avandar echoed Morretz. It was surprising, and it was painful. But the pain was dimmer than it had been.

Sigurne drank, although she drank slowly. Avandar lit candles for their ambience, but he also whispered the magestones to brightness. Above them the ceiling opened to let moonlight in; the night was quiet and blessedly cool. "Terafin," Sigurne said. "The demon was there for you."

This was, of course, the conclusion that Jewel had expected Sigurne to draw; Sigurne was no fool. She considered a rote response about the importance and significance of the Kings, and decided against it; the day had been too long. Instead, she nodded.

"You fled. Did you flee to the manse?"

"Yes. I thought the only chance I had of making a difference was upon the Terafin grounds."

"And you thought that he would follow."

Jewel nodded. "I was certain he would he follow." This was not entirely the truth, but Sigurne didn't expect unadulterated truth—not even at an intimate dinner. She spoke to The Terafin, after all.

"He did. In the few moments before he made that decision, he killed twelve people, among them four of the Kings' Swords, two of the Astari and six of the Priests. He also destroyed two of the great trees—an echo of the attack that occurred before your disappearance from Averalaan."

"But—"

Sigurne raised a brow.

"Meralonne and Celleriant engaged the demon."

"Yes. Had they not both been present, the death count would have been much, much higher in my opinion." She cast a speculative glance at Avandar. Avandar, of course, said nothing; Jewel chose, for the moment, to do the same. Sigurne then turned back to her drink. "Some damage was done to the creature by the Kings and the Exalted—but not enough to slow it."

Jewel frowned. She reached toward the table's center, placed her fingertips delicately upon a decorative candleholder, and invoked the room's strongest silence. Sigurne watched, but said nothing. After a moment, Jewel took the conversation in hand, and Sigurne allowed it.

"There was something different about this demon."

Sigurne lifted a brow. "You speak of its power?"

"... No." Jewel's frown was marked; she struggled for words with which to express her growing certainty, and failed to find them immediately. "No, that is not what I meant—although Meralonne and Celleriant agreed that this creature is the most powerful we have faced."

"Yet you are alive, Terafin. And the demon is not here."

"The demon's alive, as well."

"But he is not here; you are. You understand how significant that is."

She did.

"It is not, however, the first demon sent to assassinate you."

"No. It's just the most significant."

"And do you feel it will be the last?"

Jewel was silent for a long moment. She wanted to rise, to pace; she remained in her seat, and kept her hands in her lap to prevent herself from fidgeting with the silverware. "No," she said at last.

"Good. Then we are on the same page, in this. Yes, Terafin. There was something different about this demon. Is it the first time, in your encounters with these demons, that you have noticed something strange?"

"Beyond the simple fact of the demon's presence, yes. Member Mellifas, do you know what it is?"

"I have some suspicion."

"Is it a suspicion that will require my death if I happen to be informed of its nature?"

Sigurne's smile was brittle. "It is not significant in regard to you and the difficulties the demons pose to House Terafin."

Jewel nodded.

"What is, however, is the very fact of your survival."

"Please forgive me if I fail to regret it."

Sigurne did not smile. "Terafin. Jewel. I believe that we would have forced the demon to flee—at the least—but not without a cost measured in hundreds or thousands of lives. You retreated, strategically, to this manse, with the same outcome. You are not magi; you are seer-born. As you are no doubt aware, those born as seers are rare. But there were no deaths upon these grounds. No lives lost, where we would have been forced to spend many."

Jewel nodded. "It's why I fled."

"Yes. I understood that. I believe The Ten will also come to understand it; there was enough confusion that your disposition was not immediately clear, and the fires and destruction of the platforms and the chairs occupied a great deal of their attention. But not all."

"Do the Kings know?"

"That the creature came for you? I believe they will have guessed, yes. Duvari is not entirely certain; it is possibly the only advantage to his infamous paranoia. But it is not an advantage that stands us in good stead." She frowned. "I have spoken with Meralonne."

Not Member APhaniel, Jewel noted. Meralonne.

"Your negotiated position is unhelpful in my own Council at the moment, but I am willing to cede his services to your House regardless—an acknowledgment that his choice has already been made. But that is not my concern; it is the pretext for my visit, of course."

Jewel wondered if Meralonne had accepted her demand entirely for this purpose. It surprised her.

"You are a threat to the Empire, Terafin."

Jewel stiffened.

"Will you deny it?"

"I will. I do."

Sigurne nodded. "And you will believe your denials. But your denials are based on intangibles: your feelings. Your intentions. Even the oaths you have sworn—to House, to Kings. They are based on protestations of love, of loyalty. They are not, sadly, based on anything else. If I accept the protestations you will certainly utter if given leave, it changes nothing of the facts." She fell silent.

Jewel did not speak; instead, she nodded. Sigurne knew what she would say, if she chose to speak; Sigurne did not even deny the truth of the unspoken words. She denied, instead, that they were relevant. They would obviously not come to an agreement on that basis.

"Tell me," Jewel said, when it became clear that Sigurne was waiting for her response. "What are the facts as you perceive them?"

Sigurne inclined her head. Appetizers were carried into the room by Avandar, and set upon the empty plates in front of either woman. They were small, garnished artichoke hearts, and looked more like sculpture than food. They were also of no interest to either of the diners, although Sigurne did move fork first.

"Upon these grounds, you demanded the obedience of the wild elements. I know of only one mage who is capable of a like task—and not even he, at the height of his power, could deny their use simultaneously."

"I can't summon them, Sigurne."

Avandar's brows dipped, but he didn't choose to correct her use of the personal name over the titular one. He assumed there was a reason for the choice.

"So you have said. I choose to believe this, although it cannot be proven conclusively, even by experiment; there is no guarantee that you would genuinely make the attempt." She lifted a hand before Jewel could answer. "I believe you would, but my belief in this case *must* be grounded in fact."

"Continue."

"Upon these grounds, Terafin, you have evoked magics it is my belief you do not understand. There are ancient trees here, in the height of their growth and power, that appeared between one moment and the next."

Jewel nodded.

"Neither of these facts are of interest to the Kings. No, let me rephrase that. They are of interest; they are not an immediate threat. But at the height of your struggle for dominance of your land in the face of the anger of the wild, you touched *Avantari*. You demanded that the earth still; you rearranged some part of the architecture of the palace. I was present in Terafin that day; I heard your words.

"But I was not the only one who heard them, alas. Nor were the rest of the witnesses confined to the Terafin manse or its grounds. Your words were heard across the Isle, Jewel. And in some places—although this was less universal—your voice was heard in the hundred holdings."

"I didn't—"

"No. There are, that we could discern, no changes within the holdings themselves. But within the Palace, yes. It can be argued that air and earth were summoned, and not at your behest. The Crowns are uneasy with the summoning. They understand the necessity for it, and no censure accrues to your followers for using the power they had at hand to preserve the lives of the Princes. But it is clear to the magi, and to the Exalted, that the cessation of those hostilities was at your command, when you were not present.

"You are not bard-born, and you are not magi; there is no way for your words to carry. No known, accepted way. But they did. What we know of seers is scant, but no story that originated in Old Weston contains any hint that the seers could communicate their visions over great distances. You are not god-born. It is true that the god-born can conceal the color of their eyes from casual discovery, but it requires the cooperation of the magi, and you have not had that.

"What are you, Terafin? You must understand that a power that can casually stretch to encompass the whole of the Isle is a power that cannot be countenanced in the hands of any save the Kings."

Chapter Six

IT WAS SILENT in the small room; it was an almost intimate silence. Breath was its harmony; even movement was stilled. The magelights' glow was soft enough that the moons' light almost equaled it; beneath a ceiling of sky, the two woman regarded each other. Beyond them, by the wall, Avandar was as still, assessing danger. He was not, Jewel noted, surprised.

She was.

"Is this the topic of discussion for tomorrow's meeting with the Exalted?"

"It is."

Jewel glanced at her plate as Avandar once again resumed his duties as domicis. She had lost all appetite, but knew from experience that lack of food had its costs. She ate in silence; the topic had not notably deterred the guildmaster from doing likewise.

"This is not, of course, the reason I chose to visit. I am to ask you—and I will—about the demon in the Common, and I am to make my displeasure at your high-handed demand for inexpensive service of the Order known." She smiled; it was a brittle expression, but it held no danger for Jewel. Very little she could now say would.

"I will grant Meralonne his permission, of course, and I will return, disgruntled, to my Tower."

"The Order will be angry at *Terafin*," Jewel pointed out.

"Terafin, oddly enough, will bear the lesser brunt of their outrage; if you do not seek a similar agreement with any other Member of the Order, it is Meralonne they will harangue in their pique. As he will no doubt be absent from the Towers in the foreseeable future, I consider it a small price to pay."

"They'll be angry at you."

"Yes, but again—Meralonne is known. Their anger with me will be the anger of co-confederates, for they do not truly believe that Meralonne APhaniel follows *my* commands, except as it suits his whim."

"But . . ."

"Yes?"

"But he does."

Sigurne raised a white brow. "You are, as expected, perceptive, Terafin. Yes. He does. But it is an intricate dance. I do not attempt to give him orders which I know in advance are too trivial for him to follow. I do not tell him how to dress, I do not command him to attend social events, no matter how it might bolster the Order's reputation; nor do I deny him the use of his *infernal* pipe. I know his measure, and he knows mine." She rose. "I will not tell you to trust him; you have known him for some years now, and I believe you have taken his full measure in that time.

"But I will ask—if necessary, plead—that you listen to what he might condescend to teach. And if in the course of that teaching, you can break him of the pipe's habit, I shall be eternally grateful."

When Sigurne was gone, Jewel lingered in the small dining room. Avandar watched her as she stared at the empty space across the table, remembering other nights, other emergencies, other hopes.

"You did not mention Rymark."

"No."

"You did not ask about the Shining Court."

"No—given the doubts the Kings now have, I thought it wisest to refrain. If I am to meet with the Kings to make the case for my own survival," she added, unable to keep the bitterness of surprise—and, yes, anger—from her words. "It's best to have something in my hand to offer them." She rose. "Shall I go meet Meralonne?"

"Is he waiting?"

Jewel glanced out of the window. "Yes."

Silence. Even in her thoughts, Avandar's reaction to the words was inaudible. "How long," he finally asked, "has he been waiting?"

"Since Sigurne arrived. He is in the forest," she added softly.

"And you have been aware of his presence for the duration?"

She exhaled. "Yes."

In truth, it wasn't Meralonne APhaniel Jewel wanted to see, although she hadn't lied; he was waiting for her in the Terafin grounds, near the garden of contemplation. She wanted the cats. Or at least one of them. She was exhausted and almost overwhelmed, and she wanted nothing so much as sleep.

But she was afraid to sleep tonight. She wasn't certain why, but accepted it; that was the nature of her gift. Avandar would, of course, stand guard as he almost always did, but Immortal or no, Avandar also needed sleep.

"Lack of sleep will not kill *me*," was his response.

"Hush, there he is."

Pipe smoke rose around the mage's face in thin streams, undisturbed by even the slightest of breezes. It was dark, now; the magelights that lit the path through the garden of contemplation were an even glow two feet from the ground. Meralonne seemed, for the moment, to be alone; he was certainly not with the cats.

He glanced in her direction as she approached. "You are later than I expected," he said, as if they had indeed agreed upon not only a meeting, but a time.

"I was with the guildmaster. Apparently my refusal to pay you what you're worth has earned the ire of some of the magi."

"That would perhaps take five minutes of conversational time to discount."

"We spoke of other things as well, all of them relevant to her position as Guildmaster of the Order of Knowledge."

"Very well," was his grudging response; it was framed by rings of smoke. "You are aware that I have been here the entire time?"

"Like a planted tree," she agreed. She glanced toward the path that led to the shrines of the Triumvirate.

"Do not even think it. While you are no longer paying for my time, my time has some value to me. Come, Jewel." Jewel. Not Terafin.

"Have you seen my cats?"

"Yours? They are cats; they seldom acknowledge an owner. But no," he added, lifting his pipe to forestall her reply. "I have not." He glanced at Avandar. "You may follow if you insist, Viandaran; she is, however, under my protection now."

"She stands upon her own ground," Avandar replied. "Even from you, Illaraphaniel, protection is no longer what she requires." To Jewel's lasting surprise, her domicis bowed. "I will wait for her at the Terafin shrine, as a domicis traditionally waits for The Terafin."

Celleriant was not immediately visible when Jewel stepped off the gardener's path and onto the hidden one. She was aware of the transition, but it felt natural now, not abrupt; the great trees of the Common existed no matter where in the gardens one walked. Here, beneath bowers of silver, of gold, and of diamond, they towered taller, and although there was no magelight, the colors of their gold-and-white leaves were visible to the naked eye.

Or to hers.

Jewel. The Winter King stepped out of the shadows between two trees. She had passed those shadows, and she knew without question that he had not been standing there moments ago. She didn't ask where he'd come from; he offered no explanation. Meralonne took his appearance in stride, although he did grimace around the stem of his pipe.

"You were aware," he said, as they approached the lone tree of fire that stood burning in the heart of Jewel's forest. "Of my presence. That implies a strong sensitivity. You were not searching."

"No."

"You were not aware of the *Kialli* in the Common."

She shook her head. "Not until he was almost beneath us." She hesitated. "He wasn't there. He wasn't in the Common while we were gathering for the parade."

"You are certain of this?"

She was. A lifetime of being taken at her word when she spoke with conviction caused a brief curl in both hands before she forced them to relax.

"How?"

Jewel frowned as she watched his expression; it was calm. "I'm seer-born, Meralonne. I know what I know."

"Yes. And you see, Terafin, what you see. Have you perhaps heard the word Sen?"

She stiffened. "Yes."

"From your domicis?"

"Yes."

"It is not a modern word in any way; it is not a Weston word, even at its roots. What do you know of the Sen?"

"Nothing."

"You show a deplorable lack of curiosity."

"What do *you* know about the Sen?"

He raised both brows. "Clever child. Very little. I would, of course, like to know more. And I think I shall, in the end."

"You're lying," she told him, without any heat.

"The bard-born would not be able to pick that up from my voice."

She noted he did not deny it. "I'm not bard-born. I'm seer-born. It's not a reliable gift," she added, as she approached the heat of the burning tree, "but in this case, it's accurate. Where have my cats gone?" She turned to face him, the tree at her back like an angry sentinel.

"They are here," he replied. "And not here. It is a state you should understand."

"I don't."

"Do you not? I sense the dreaming here, Terafin. It is strong." He paused to light his pipe again. "You should sense it, as well. You should sense it almost as clearly as you can sense demons; you should certainly be able to sense it more clearly than you can a simple mage. Where is Lord Celleriant?"

"He's over there." She lifted an arm to point, and dropped it again, turning to stare at the mage. He was smiling; the smile was cool.

"You do not question what you know. You do not question what you feel. You accept, without thought, the instincts that drive you to safety. It is understandable, Terafin. Jewel. But it is no longer enough. You saw Darranatos. Had you the full range of your power, you could have prevented him from arriving in the Common."

She was silent, staring at him as if he'd lost his mind. "How?" she finally demanded. The Winter King drew closer to her, gliding above the undergrowth as if afraid to break it beneath his slender, sharp hooves.

"The land—in your Common and behind your manse—is not separate. There is a reason the *Ellariannate* grow in either place. There is a reason that they now grow here—and they are connected. In the age of living gods, a city once stood across the bay. It was a city such as you have never seen."

But, she thought, she *had*. Not in life, although she had seen the deserted remnants of such a city rise from the desert sands in the heart of the Sea of Sorrows, but in dream. In Avandar's dream. "Many cities have been built here."

"Yes. At least one, of notable power, was built on the ruins of the ancient; it, too, is gone. It will not rise again. People fail to understand the nature of gods, the nature of demons— the nature, Jewel, of the Immortal. Why do you think, in a Henden seventeen years past, *Allasakar* was summoned beneath the streets of *this* city? Do not say because it is large; I will bite off the stem of my pipe in frustration."

"They required sacrifices, Meralonne."

"So they did. But there were many cities more amenable to their intrusion, and many places in which such trifling sacrifices might be found. Yet they chose this city, Averalaan, a city ruled by the god-born—the only city likely to survive a concentrated attack by all but the god himself. Did you think it only due to their arrogance?"

"Truthfully? Yes." She shook her head. "No. I didn't really think about it at all. This is where I lived. This was my whole world. When they attacked the hundred, they attacked the whole world. I was sixteen," she added, as his brows drew together. "I knew nothing about demons except stories. They love to kill, and kill slowly. They devour souls."

"That part is fabrication."

"It doesn't matter. They define evil."

"Yet you sheltered the daughter of darkness for a time. What was she called?"

He knew. It irritated her. "Kiriel. Kiriel di'Ashaf. She didn't choose her father, and she caused no harm to us."

"Perhaps. God-born or no, she is mortal; she has a choice. Let us return to the nature of the forest here. It has lain unclaimed for centuries, and it has been an open path to those who understand how to walk the Winter road. It is not difficult—although it is costly; only the powerful may walk its ways. It is my suspicion that the source of the demons within the Terafin manse was this hidden way.

"It is almost certainly the explanation for the appearance of the kinlord in the Common." He glanced at her. "But he did not choose to come here, and the Common was not the most fortuitous of places in which to make an easy kill; not today. Do you understand?"

"Why did the kinlords not claim this land when they hid beneath the streets of the city?"

"They could not. Do you think such a claim is trivially made? This forest, this path—it is not gold. It cannot simply be grasped and held by those who take a fancy to it. Simple death will not assign its territory; if you were dead, your assassin could not easily step into the breach to claim the power of this land that you now hold. Not yet."

"When, then?"

"When the land was truly his own. It would be centuries, if that."

"I haven't lived that long."

"No."

She studied his face in the light of the tree; although the fire was almost red, it shed sun's light. "Could you have taken these lands?" she finally asked.

"I? No."

"Why?"

"They are not my home."

"But you've lived here forever."

"When dealing with the Members of the Order, it does feel that way, but no, Jewel. If I died on this soil, these lands would still not be my home. Yes, they are home to many— but the many are not you; they are not born with your gift."

"Could Evayne have taken them?"

"A perceptive question. I do not know. It is my suspicion she could not; else, she would have done so long ago. Perhaps she did not choose to do so because she had seen an older Terafin in her travels, and she knew who now holds these lands." This last was said with a trace of bitterness, a hint of anger—but it was only in his voice; his face looked oddly peaceful. "And if she is certain, she can be certain for only two reasons: the first, that she has attempted to cross them without your permission, and you are strong enough to block her way; the second—and in my opinion more likely—is that she has seen what you have built, and she understands what it means."

"But I—"

"You have built nothing yet, no. But she is not bound by time in the fashion you are."

The Winter King touched her shoulder with his muzzle, and she turned to meet his eyes; they were almost black, although the fur that framed them looked golden.

"There is, however, one other who stands some chance of wresting control from you if you do not assert territoriality here."

"Who?"

"I can tell you his name, but it will mean nothing to you; I am not even certain you could pronounce it. He is not *Kialli*, not *Arianni*."

Sometimes Jewel found the magi frustrating. "Tell me who he is."

"I told you—"

"Then tell me *what* he is, at the very least."

"You have seen his hand, Terafin. It has stretched across the hundred holdings; it has moved across the Isle."

She frowned, wondering how it was that Sigurne had not strangled him yet. "Meralonne."

"He calls the dreamers," the mage continued, untroubled by her growing irritation. "And they do not wake."

"Have you told this to Sigurne?" she demanded, when she could speak calmly.

"I have mentioned it, yes. There is very, very little that Sigurne can do in this case; very little, in the end, that *I* can do."

"How long have you known?"

"Since my return. Remember, Terafin, you returned before I could."

"Have you told the Kings?"

"The Kings now understand that it is not a plague, yes. It is not contagious. But there is no certain way for those who are not god-born to avoid it. Even the talent-born have fallen to the illness; two bards are sequestered within the walls of Senniel, at its highest remove. What the healers cannot do, the bard-born cannot do; their commands cannot wake the sleepers. There is, according to Sigurne, only one in the city who can." He raised a white brow, waiting.

She offered him nothing, not yet. But in the end, she had to ask. "Why? Why only one?"

"I consider it a small miracle that there is even one. But there have been no sleepers outside of the city limits. Victims have fallen to sleep only here," he said, raising his face to stare, unblinking, at the *Ellariannatte*, "and within the hundred. Only in these two places. Do you understand? If you cannot yet touch the hundred holdings, the path exists there; you have made no attempt to walk it, if I am not mistaken. You have remained here, near the heart of your lands. But they extend. What you will not take, you cannot hold; Darranatos will come again, and I do not think he will come alone. But he will not come immediately; he is injured. He will gather his power, and he will gather his lieges; if the Shining Court has finished licking their wounds, they might come again in force."

"Why do you mention the Shining Court now?" she asked. "It's the second time today that I've heard those words."

"How could I not? We have seen its hand at play throughout the South. We have seen its Fist, and its armies; we are only lacking its Lord. But he will not remain in the Northern Wastes forever. I speak too much," he added. "It's the pipe. It makes me careless."

"How do you know where the Shining Court is?"

His smile was thin. "The armies of the Lord of the Hells walked the hidden path. No; they did more than merely walk it; they broke it and remade it so that it might carry the whole of its army from the cold, icy wastes to the Southern basket unhindered. The Lord of the Hells," he added, as he began to open his tobacco pouch, "owns his great, cold city, just as certainly as the Winter Queen owns hers. And you, Terafin, could stand among them."

"Mortal, remember?"

"It was not always a word synonymous with weakness and insignificance."

And she remembered the Cities of Man and fell silent.

"To answer your one unanswered question, because I am indeed feeling mellow this evening, you deal not with the gods, not demons and not *Arianni*, but in some fashion, the god-born."

"But—"

"Not all who were born to gods were conceived in the Between."

"But the gods can't—" she fell silent, then.

"You understand. When the gods walked the world, they had children, and the children were born to and of it. Many died. Many of the gods died, Jewel; they were not then what they are now. But the children of the living gods were not mortal, and some had power to rival the gods themselves. Yet when the gods chose to withdraw from this world, their children could not likewise leave—they were *of* it, and sustained by it."

Jewel said, "The Oracle."

Meralonne's eyes rounded, his lips turning up in a pipeless smile. "Yes. She was first, or so it is said, but there were many. One is here, playing at the edges of lands you inconveniently claimed as your own."

"Can you—"

"No. Lord Celleriant cannot either; he is an extremely subtle enemy."

"He is working in concert with the Shining Court."

Meralonne shrugged. "For now, as it suits him. But the Northern Wastes grant him no measure of power; he derives his power from the dreams of mortals. It is not a wonder to me that he is here, and if I had understood what the plague presaged, I might have understood some part of what the Lord of the Hells intended."

"How?"

"He should not be here, Jewel. But he is, and had we known—"

"Meralonne, *known what*?"

"Apologies, Terafin; given your authority over these lands, I assume you understand more than you actually do. That must be remedied. In their attempt to warp and twist the fabric of the hidden ways, the Shining Court damaged the containing walls that divide the two lands, something believed to be impossible. Yet it has happened. Those who were trapped on the hidden path—those with a measure of power—must have made their way through. There are only two nights during which they might otherwise do so: Scarran and Lattan, the longest night and the longest day. But he is here, now. Find him, Terafin."

"But the demons—"

He shrugged, as if the demons—even though they included the formidable Lord Darranatos—were inconsequential. "You needn't search for them at the moment. They will find you."

Jewel returned to the path at the edge of the garden of contemplation. Avandar was waiting for her. He raised a brow as he saw her companion; Meralonne had not chosen to leave the forest, but the Winter King had. The domicis nodded gravely to the Winter King; the Winter King inclined his antlered head in response.

"Do you intend to enter the manse?" Avandar asked.

The Winter King inclined his head again. Jewel raised a brow, but did not demur; unlike most of the animals resident in the manse—the living ones—he broke nothing, made no noise, and didn't leave scratches or other unpleasant messes. He did attract attention, but attention tonight was going to be minimal, and mostly composed of servants on the night shift and House Guards.

"You don't consider his presence significant?" the domicis said, as he fell in to Jewel's right, the left being occupied by a rather large stag.

"Yes."

"What do you intend?"

"Me? I intend to go straight to sleep. I'm exhausted."

He raised a brow. "Terafin."

Jewel did not return to the West Wing that night.

Instead, squaring shoulders, she mounted the wide, wide stairs that led to the empty and familiar grandeur of The Terafin's personal chambers. She felt guilty that she had not done this during Gabriel's tenure, because she was almost certain he would have been close to tears of joy—or at least relief. These were the small and precious moments lost when one failed to accept the fear of change, and she was determined to remember that fact.

Avandar's brows rose higher when he saw the turn she had taken and followed her to the stairs; they descended as she ascended beneath the lights of the chandelier above. The halls were now clean and pristine; the drooping flowers, tear-stained letters and small portraits, some of no great skill and some, minor miracles, had been removed. There were very few signs of Amarais' death—and the subsequent outpouring of grief and loss—within the manse itself. Jewel had, against custom and to the minor disapproval of her domicis—both of them—kept three of the small portraits; one was drawn so simply it would never be considered art, and two—well, two had been composed by Terafin-sponsored artists.

The rest had been buried with her, but gods knew the dirt didn't need to see them, and Amarais couldn't carry them with her when she crossed the bridge. She had no need of mementos now—but Jewel did. It would be nice to have something that she could place on a desk, a wall, or in a cabinet; most of her memories of the dead and gone she carried within her, where only words could express them.

As The Terafin, she was expected to reveal no such emotions.

She had the Handernesse ring about her neck on a slender chain; when she had time—if she ever did—she would have the band remade so she could wear it. Avandar, reliable as sunrise, disapproved, but no one else did. Rath's sword was beneath her bed. She would move it later. She would commission a chest, much like the battered, heavy one that Rath himself had kept his past locked in, and she would eventually place it there, along with the battered iron box that she could not be moved to part with, much to Ellerson's dismay.

But she had nothing of Duster, of Lefty, of Lander, or Fisher, because they'd had so little, and they had disappeared so abruptly. She *wanted* the few things she had that reminded her of the people that she had loved, and no amount of disapproval would sway her.

But this, this mounting of empty stairs, she could do. And there was a reason for it, beyond the obvious—that she was The Terafin now. The Winter King walked by her side, and if the House Guard thought it unusual, they didn't blink and they didn't say a word. Of all of the people who walked these halls at any hour of the day—or night—The Terafin was never stopped, never asked to state her business, and never questioned in any way.

Unless, she thought, grimacing, Duvari was on the premises.

The Chosen stood guard at the door—only two, because she was not, in theory, in residence. They moved to face her as she approached the doors, but they didn't speak a word; she knew, the moment she was safely ensconced behind them, more Chosen, summoned gods only knew how, would appear, and the complement outside the door would number four; they would number at least four on the interior of the apartment. Given the day, probably more, unless she forbade it.

These were, however, the safest rooms in the manse, without exception. There were magical protections on the doors and walls that were strong enough they were visible to Jewel's eyes. She tried to find them comforting, although they were a constant reminder of the fact that people she didn't know were desperately trying to kill her. She found it less upsetting that people she *did* know were also trying to kill her because she didn't like any of them, and she understood exactly why. It wasn't personal.

"It is entirely personal," Avandar said, in a clipped voice.

She laughed. She laughed, and she found the tension easing out of her shoulders, her face, the whole line of her body. "I guess I'll have to find someone else to deal with my hair," she told him.

"Pardon?"

"Ellerson is contracted to the den, not The Terafin." She wandered through the library's many shelves, gazing at spines, a full half of which she had trouble reading. Although these books comprised The Terafin's personal collection—inasmuch as the head of the House could be said to possess anything truly personal—there were three archivists who kept them clean, bound, and organized. None of them would be present at the moment. She would need them if she were to have any hope of unearthing some of the older documents—and, more importantly, understanding them.

At length, trailed by both Avandar and the Winter King, she left the shelves and opened the doubled doors that led to the personal rooms; the small sitting room, the large bathing room, and the bedroom, with its entirely cavernous closets. There was also a small office, with a much more modest desk and a few shelves, none of which were full.

To the other side of the library, the more public element of the private rooms lay: the large parlor—and why it was so large, when few guests of import were ever entertained within it, Jewel didn't know—the small and intimate dining room, the rooms in which servants could warm and present food and drink if the guest she entertained was demanding. In Sigurne's case, Avandar was enough, although no one would argue that the Guildmaster of the Order of Knowledge, and the head of the Council of the Magi, a First Circle mage and confidant of Kings, was not demanding. She, however, chose her fights.

Jewel had learned—bitterly and with difficulty—to choose hers. She wasn't nearly competent enough at choosing the right ones, but at least the wrong ones taught her something about the nature of choice. She glanced at the Winter King.

"Why are you here?" she asked softly.

You will go, tonight.

She did not pretend to misunderstand him. "And you can carry me in my dreams?"

It is the nature of my enchantment, Jewel. There is no terrain over which I cannot run, and none over which I cannot carry my rider.

Avandar said nothing, but the line of his jaw tightened. "There is a danger, Jewel."

"Can I die in my dreams?"

"Can those stricken by the plague die?"

She glanced at the Winter King. "Yes."

"Yes. They die simply by failing to wake. I do not understand the whole of the dreaming, but if you do not wish to empower your enemy, you cannot afford to be trapped in his web."

You knew.

No, Jewel. This is far, far more subtle than any action the firstborn would have taken when they freely walked the waking world. Aloud, he said, "I will keep watch. Let me return to the West Wing and arrange for the transfer of our clothing and your possessions; I will bring the magestone and its holder.

"Can you bring Rath's sword?"

". . . Yes."

"Can you tell them?"

"I will inform Ellerson; he may choose the best fashion in which to inform the den." When Jewel fell silent, he added, "You will continue to live in the same building as the rest of your den. Teller is your right-kin. Finch is your only safe conduit into the Merchant Authority, and she has been a member of that office for long enough that there is little that will escape either her attention or her comprehension. Arann is one of your Chosen.

"I consider it highly unlikely that you will somehow be cast into the outer darkness of isolation." He turned and left the hall as Jewel headed toward the bedroom.

At the end of the half hour, there were, as she'd expected, four Chosen stationed on the inside of the inner doors of The Terafin's rooms. There were four stationed on the outside, as well. None of these eight were Arann; one of them was Torvan. Avandar returned and was immediately granted access to The Terafin, that being Jewel; he was the only person in the manse who would be given such a pass. Not even the right-kin could expect to walk through the guards without stating, in some part, his business.

There were, of course, servants assigned to The Terafin's personal chambers; none of those servants were the ones with which she was most familiar. The servants who guided, cleaned, and—after all these years—still coddled the denizens of the West Wing would of course remain on duty there, as would Ellerson.

She could think that now without a pang of loss. She could be grateful that he was there for her den when she herself couldn't be—not that she had ever been able to do what Ellerson did with such natural ease.

Jewel.

She glanced up at the Winter King. The height of the ceilings and the width of the doors—almost every one doubled—suited him. The rest of the surroundings did not. But the Chosen hadn't blinked when he'd walked through the doors; they paid him as much attention as they would have paid any member of her House that they considered trustworthy.

They should not consider any members of your House trustworthy, the Winter King said, amused. *But these are, for the most part, lesser times. Even I would have found it difficult to remain suspicious of your friends.*

"Yes, but you would have found it hard because you consider them helpless. Or harmless."

I do not consider them harmless within the context of your life. They hold too much of it. However, they are all but oathsworn; they will not raise hand against you. Those who I required in such close quarters on a continual basis were all oathsworn, when I ruled my lands.

"Taking an oath would make them more trustworthy?" Jewel, thinking of her den—of Duster, in particular— snorted.

In my time, yes. Such oaths were made in the presence of the Priests of Bredan, and to break them was death.

"I can think of a lot of people who'd swear oaths that would lead to death if it allowed them to fulfill their goals."

The Winter King nodded. *It is why the Priests were used. They would not accept an oath that had no meaning for the man—or woman—who swore it. The oath would not be consecrated. Any who came to the oathhalls with intent to betray were turned away in the final moment. They died,* he added, *but not because of the failure to keep their oath.*

Jewel was profoundly grateful not to be living at a time when the Winter King ruled.

He snorted.

Her personal rooms were not, as she suspected they would be, barren: there were two closets, both small rooms in their own right, one armoire that appeared to be there, judging by the craftsmanship, for display, a small desk—the larger one was in a different room—and two cabinets with long, beveled windows in their doors. The windows shone orange to her eyes; in fact, almost everything in the room did. The bed, the small bedstands that bracketed the bed to the left and right, the *rug.* She thought the latter was overdoing it.

She was aware, however, that she would never have had that thought if Amarais were still Terafin and closeted in these very fine rooms. *If it was good enough for her,* she told herself grimly, *it's good enough for me.* But the thought, though vehement, lacked conviction. She had the creeping sense of certainty that she, born Jewel Markess, wasn't worthy of this much effort; the magi, after all, did not work for free.

Well, not most of them at any rate, and Meralonne was contrary enough she'd be unlikely to get simple carpet enchantments out of him.

The closets, as she suspected they would be, were half full. No one had expected that she would refuse to take up residence in these rooms. She wondered if it were Gabriel or Barston who had seen to the contents of these closets; she suspected that Ellerson would have left the clothing in her own rooms until he knew for certain she was leaving.

The first closet contained dresses, in what were presumably her size, in various shades of blue. The cloths used also differed; some were silk, some raw silk (which she disliked; it was scratchy), some were a very fine wool. In the sister closet were dresses in colors other than House blues. They were also made from very fine cloth, and they differed in depth of neckline, height of collar, and length of sleeve. Not many immediately suggested the very full skirts that made running possible.

In this closet there were also shoes and boots. A lot of them. They ranged in color from black to white, with shades of almost everything in between. She closed the door and headed toward the standing dresser, where she was most likely to find something simple, like a nightshirt.

She did. She also found an army's worth of brushes and combs, more proof that the room had been repopulated with items meant to be useful to whomever was charged with maintaining her public appearance. She changed, although it took longer than it should have because the dress was a complicated affair. All dresses were, these days.

And then: bed.

Avandar came into the room with the stand into which a magestone was laid. The room didn't need it; there were magestones in the corners of the ceilings, and along the tops of the walls at regularly spaced intervals; they were similar in illumination to those that sat in blown-glass lampholders in the public galleries. Most private rooms, on the other hand, didn't have them; the West Wing didn't.

Avandar set the stone holder down on the bedstand to

the left of the bed anyway. He also dragged the chair beneath the small desk to the bedside, where he sat. The room was silent. Shadow often slept with her, and even when he wasn't speaking—which was rare—he made noise. He couldn't breathe silently, and he growled in his sleep.

But when he was present, she woke before nightmare drove her screaming from her dreams.

Tonight, she slid between the covers and stared at the canopy. She didn't particularly like canopies; she didn't like the curtains that could, at necessity, be drawn around the entire bed, either. She didn't care for this room, those carpets, the fireplace to her right, or the empty walls above it. She yanked the covers up under her chin.

She *was* tired, and knew it. Her legs and back ached, because she'd clenched every muscle in them while holding so desperately on to Snow in flight. It seemed like that had happened yesterday or the day before. It hadn't. And tomorrow would come, regardless of sleep. She took deep, even breaths and closed her eyes.

Some people reliably fell asleep this way; Jewel, one of nature's worriers, didn't. In the darkness, with no other emergencies to demand her attention, she could think. In the dark, when it felt like she hadn't slept for days, thoughts were always informed by fear. Rymark. The meeting tomorrow—tomorrow!—in the Hall of The Ten. The meeting after that—if she managed to survive it—with the Exalted, the Kings, the magi, and Duvari. So much could go wrong there. The first time she'd met the Kings, the most important thing she had to do was keep her mouth shut. Since she had also been of a social status which demanded full and absolute obeisance, it hadn't been too hard; if she'd spoken, she'd be talking to the floor. She'd practically be biting it.

Now? She was expected to speak with the full authority of House Terafin. She was expected to speak to men—and women—who believed her power could not be, as Sigurne so plainly stated, countenanced. She could only see one outcome, and she was too exhausted not to go there.

Jewel, two voices said at once.

She exhaled. *Sorry*, she said to her domicis and the resident stag. She thought about the uselessness of counting sheep—a favorite bit of advice given to those who had trouble sleeping, and one that had, as far as Jewel was concerned, never worked for anyone who wouldn't have fallen straight asleep anyway—and from there, she segued into the Terafin grounds. The gardens.

Her tree, with its exposed heart of fire.

She heard the sound of metallic leaves, like multiple wind chimes, blending and overlapping; she heard the wind through their movements and wondered if birds ever flew in that endless, ancient place. Sun shone at command or plea; night fell. Was there water? A brook, or a river, beyond the confines of trees that stretched so tall their heights could only be glimpsed at a distance? She could almost hear its gurgling rush as she closed her eyes and listened. She had not explored the forest. She had only seldom entered it, and then, at need.

What waited there, when she could explore it at leisure, if she dared? Peace? Privacy?

Yes, the Winter King said. *Both. But remember, Jewel: graveyards are also peaceful when the mourners depart. There is no silence where you dwell, because you bring noise with you.*

Where are the cats? she asked him quietly.

The Winter King said, *You will know.* It wasn't particularly comforting. *Come, Terafin. You will be a Queen of men.*

I don't want that, she told him. *The only people I want to obey me are the ones I can't stand. Haerrad. Rymark. I don't need to tell everyone else what to do. I don't want it.*

I know.

Did you?

Yes—but to me, all men and all women were like your Haerrad or your Rymark. All children would become them. If I did not rule them, if I was not willing to devour or destroy them, they would destroy me. Come, Jewel. It is time.

She opened her eyes.

In her dream—and she must be dreaming—light streamed through the tall windows. There were plants that crept over trellises of bamboo, shedding petals artfully against the bare, wooden floor. She heard birdsong, she felt breeze.

Dreams had their own logic. This was her room; she recognized it although she had conversely never seen it before. It felt like, looked like, home. The Winter King stood by the

window, tines gleaming; the windows were glassless. She slid
out of bed, and looked down at her arms; they were bare.
She wore a summer shift that would have been considered
dangerously immodest at any point in her life.

Turning her wrist over, she paused. "Avandar's not here,"
she told the Winter King.

No.

Neither was his mark. She pushed hair out of her eyes,
stood, inhaled. When she exhaled, she exhaled the whole of
the wretched day: demons and Councillors, Rymark, Haerrad, Gabriel's loss, Sigurne's oblique threat. All of it.

Jewel.

Yes. She walked toward where the Winter King knelt,
and she slid, without effort, onto his back. He rose.

They traveled through the forest. Trees opened into sunlight and small patches of wild grass, and as the Winter
King ran, Jewel saw, at last, the white foam of moving water; they had come to a river, not a brook. The water was
clean, here; the riverbed appeared to be sand and stone.
She had lived on the banks of the river in the holdings for
only a short time, but this river reminded her, perversely, of
that one. There was even a bridge.

Will you cross it, Jewel?

I'm not driving.

You are, he said, and he knelt. *You cannot cross this
bridge while you are mounted.*

You can't cross it? She slid off his back, following the
logic and the demand of dream, her feet touching rounded
rock. They were, she realized for the first time, as bare as her
arms. There was very little bank beneath the bridge; the water was high.

"I can," he said, and she turned.

Where the Winter King had stood, a man stood in his
place—a man with the same dark eyes. He was not a young
man, but not yet old; his lips were full, but his face seemed
long and fine-boned. It reminded her of Celleriant's face,
although this man was mortal. She had seen him once before, and she remembered it.

He smiled; lines deepened in the corners of both lips and
eyes. His smile was not a kind one, although it held no malice now.

"Winter King?" she asked, lifting a hand to touch the line of his jaw—something she would never have dared had she not been dreaming.

He allowed it, his smile deepening. He was a foot taller, if only that.

"I don't—I don't understand."

"These are not the lands of the Winter Queen," he told her quietly, gazing now at his hands, at the mounds of his palms, as if seeing them for the first time and finding them strange.

"But you're a stag in the normal world, as well."

"Yes." He held out an arm in a gesture that was familiar; after a moment, she took it. "Be prepared, Jewel."

"For what?"

"For anything. Do you not sense an intruder, here?"

She frowned, following as he led her toward the height of the bridge. "You don't cast a shadow," she pointed out, as if this were natural.

"No more do you, here; you have no love of shadow. Be ready," he said again.

She looked ahead to the far bank—and it was far, now; the bridge had elongated the moment they set foot on its solid planks. No dream she remembered clearly had ever been like this. She glanced up at the sky to see a lone black bird gliding in circles in the air overhead. As she watched, it plunged, its dark claws extended.

She frowned, watching it. Forbidding it to strike. Its talons skirted strands of her hair as it screeched, its voice at once discordant and oddly beautiful. It landed on the opposite end of the bridge, the end which the Winter King and Jewel were now approaching. She glanced at the Winter King's face; all warmth, all surprise, had drained from his expression; he was as cold as his title—the only name for him she knew.

"Intruder is a rather harsh word," the black bird said. Jewel had thought it a crow, but it was far too large for that, and in shape it looked more like a giant eagle; a bird of prey. "I prefer the word visitor."

"A visitor," the Winter King replied, "is invited."

"Not so, not so," the bird replied. "Oft visitors come without warning, and they are still welcomed."

"Or they are sent fleeing into the night."

"You don't have that ability, not here. No one does." His eyes were a very odd color; Jewel couldn't place it. Some part of her knew that color at this distance should have been impossible to discern, but she tried anyway, as if the information were important.

"No?" The Winter King said.

The bird failed to answer. He was watching Jewel as she walked. "You are not what I expected," he said at last. "Too scrawny, for one, and far too young. I should like someone harsher, tougher."

"Stringier?"

"Stringier."

"Then you are a very odd carnivore."

"Oh?" He began to preen his feathers, although he didn't look away.

She stopped walking. The Winter King's steps shadowed hers. "Will you allow me to deal with the intruder?" His voice was soft.

"No. Not yet." She waited until the bird had finished with his feathers. When he looked up, she said, "You're the Warden of Dreams, aren't you?"

The bird cackled. "I? Would the Warden of Dreams be trapped in such a diminished form as this? I am merely his sentinel."

"You're lying."

"Am I? Tell me, little human, how do you know that?"

"I just know."

"Interesting." The bird suddenly lifted both wings; they shot out, extended and extending as if they would encompass the entire horizon.

She stayed her ground, but gripped the Winter King's arm far more tightly. *Do not*, she told him, *take one step forward.*

He is a danger, Terafin, and he is here.

No, he's not. This is as far as we can safely travel.

I can see the path.

Yes. But the path you see doesn't belong to me.

It does not belong to him, either.

Can you claim it, Winter King?

He was silent. Angry, she thought. But she? She wasn't. Not yet.

"You are not what I expected," the Warden of Dreams

said again. Where a giant black eagle had stood, there now stood something that was almost a man—pale, slender, his wings spread wide, flight feathers trailing shadow.

"Why?"

"I recognize these lands. It has been long since I have seen them, but I recognize them. Look," he added, one arm rising.

She did. She looked up. The skies had darkened—but it was a dark that was not night, not shadow, not cloud; it held a depth of color not seen in a natural sky: amethyst. From its folds, snow fell.

Except that it wasn't snow.

The Winter King frowned.

"They're butterflies," Jewel said softly.

"No," The Winter King said. "They are the tears of mortal dreamers, given freedom."

Chapter Seven

THEY LOOKED LIKE BUTTERFLIES to Jewel; she didn't argue. She felt . . . at home, here. The strangeness of the Warden, of his skies, of the delicate white butterflies that seemed to crest air in a movement that was almost, but not quite falling, were distant. No, not distant; they simply felt natural; they had no power to surprise or shock.

But they had the power to move her; as she watched their delicate, crowded flight, she felt something tighten in her throat. Snow, she'd thought them. They drifted in the currents of wind; they struggled against them—perhaps they even reveled. They had no power to deny strong winds, no matter how hard they might struggle, but when the winds shifted or changed, they had control of their wings. She could see, at this distance, how the winds shifted by the movement of butterflies.

"Why did you call them tears?" she asked the Winter King, her gaze absorbed by the thin, living clouds.

"It is a phrase, no more. If I understand what we see, they are your dreamers. Your sleepers. In the streets of Averalaan, they do not wake."

She tore her gaze away from the butterflies, as if finding them strangely beautiful and compelling now made her some sort of carrion creature. The Warden of Dreams was watching the skies as well, his wings spread high, as if he might at any moment join them in their flight. "They are beautiful, are they not?" He held out the palms of his hands, and the butterfly cloud moved toward him.

But the winds buffeted them, pushing them back. She realized that even the edge of the cloud was confined by the shape of the bridge. "Let them go," she told the dark angelae. "Let them go now."

"They do not wish to leave me," he replied. "Will you force them? Will you break them?"

"They don't *know* what they want; they're *sleeping*."

"As are you." He leaped then, and his wings carried him immediately toward the cloud. He cast a shadow here that was much, much larger than his size. "You do not have to remain, bound to ground. But you do; you cling to what you know and you force the heart of these lands to obey you. Let them free, and you will see glory and wonder such as you have never seen in your waking life." His voice was so clear it sounded as if he were standing just a little bit too close to her—but she could see him, in the air, at a much greater distance.

"My waking life," she replied tightly, "is also a refuge from nightmare."

"Nightmare has its grandeur, but it exacts its price, it is true. Your waking life—their waking life—girdles them, binds them—it hurts them."

"It's because they're alive that they can be here *at all*."

"Ah. Yes, that is true. It was not always true, and in the future, it will not be. But you have come to me, tonight." He had reached the heart of the butterfly cloud, and in those heights, she could see that the butterflies—some of them—now flew to where he hovered; they lined his arms, his hands, his chest; they landed in the wild, black flow of his hair, tangling in the strands. Adorned by them, he was beautiful in a way that he had not been standing on the far side of this elongated bridge. She felt her mouth grow dry and her throat tighten; there were tears that wanted shedding.

But she was Jewel Markess. She didn't cry in public.

"Not even in your dreams?"

"Not," she said tightly, because it was the only way she could speak, "in *yours*."

He laughed and swept his arms out to his sides, and she knew—just before it happened—what he intended to do. Knew it, but bound to ground in his shadow, could do nothing to prevent it. He grabbed a handful—a literal handful—of those pale white dreams, and he crushed them.

She thought she heard screaming, but it was attenuated and distant.

"Jewel," the Winter King said, grabbing her arm. "It is time to retreat."

Eyes wide, she turned on the Winter King in sudden fury. His hand loosened; he paled, but he did not step back.

She raised both of her arms, as she had seen Avandar do, and she shouted her fear and her fury into the skies above her. She called the wild wind, as she had never called—and could never call it, in life—and it came, yanking at her hair and the flimsy fabric of her shift. It carried her away from the bridge, the Winter King, and the water; it took her out of reach of the earth. Even in dreams, wilderness had its own rules.

She had no wings; no feathers, no natural gift of flight; she had no weapons and no armor except her anger. The Warden of Dreams reached out again, and this time, the wind all but tore the butterflies out of his reach, scattering them to the far corners of the sky and destroying the cloud in which they'd congregated.

But his hands were white with dust, and his eyes—his eyes were like every night sky she had ever seen: clear, indigo, star-strewn and cloudy; red-mooned and white-mooned and heavy with rain.

"They desire this," he said, holding out his pale, dusted palm. "And I require it to live. Go back, little mortal. Go back to your drab and confined life, and hide there while you can."

His wings snapped out, spreading again, filling the sky with what she had seen in his eyes. "These are my dreamers," he said, and when he spoke his voice was the voice of thunder.

But hers, when she replied, was lightning. "They are in *my* lands."

"They are yours only for as long as you can hold them."

"I can—"

The wind dropped her.

"Stupid, stupid, *stuuuuuupid* girl!"

Jewel failed to hit the ground or the Winter King below

because Shadow inserted himself between her and the fast-approaching bridge. She had never been so grateful to see—or hear—the cat.

"What were you *thinking*, stupid girl!"

"He's going to kill them—"

"Yes, it's *what he does*. But you? You should *never* fight in the *air*. You have no *wings*!" All of the sibilants in the outraged sentence were very loud and very long. If he'd caught her with his jaws instead of his back, he would have been shaking her.

Snow and Night were in the air, circling the Warden of Dreams. Their coats gleamed in the amethyst sky, as if they, too, were gems.

"I'm sorry," she said, in a smaller voice. "I'm glad you're here."

"Of *course* we're here, *stupid* girl." He alighted on the bridge; the bridge shook. Jewel climbed off his back, although she didn't want to let him go.

"You must. I cannot fight him on the ground, but you? You *must* stand here. He has devoured some of his dreamers, and he will be stronger, now."

She tensed as Shadow leaped into the sky, gray against purple, his wings not nearly so fine as the wings of the Warden of Dreams.

"If he's become stronger because of—" she could barely speak the words, and let them drop, knowing he would hear what she couldn't bring herself to say, "what must I do to become strong?"

"Take the land, Jewel."

"But it's already mine."

"Ararath's sword is yours," the Winter King replied, "but you have never once attempted to wield it." His voice was oddly gentle as he watched Shadow join Snow and Night. They had not yet attacked the Warden, but circled him instead; the circles were growing tighter. "You have begun to understand some of the more subtle weapons in your arsenal, but they are not part of these lands, they are part of you."

"I don't understand."

"No. But you have chosen to let your den bear some of the burden it must if you are to survive. They cannot do what you can do here. The Warden of Dreams is the only enemy you now have that might take the lands you rule, and if he does . . ." He didn't finish.

She didn't ask him to finish; she could still see the crushed dust of butterfly wings on the Warden's hands. Those butterflies had scattered when the cats appeared; she could see them in ones and twos, lingering at the edges of the putative storm. But this time, she noticed where, in the sky, they flew. Not a single one crossed the boundaries set by the bridge, even in the air.

They were, each and every one of them, bound to the same lands on which she now stood.

"Yes," the Winter King said. "They are—they can be—yours. They are drawn to the Warden of Dreams because of his nature; he can gift them or curse them as they sleep. He is their only reality, now; they are not aware of the boundaries that contain them. They are mortal," he added, as if it were necessary, "and mortals seldom exist in isolation—but even here, where they congregate, they are not able to touch each other; he is the only reality."

"Even if he destroys them."

"Even so; they are lost in dreams that almost never end; what is one more death in the dreaming?"

She closed her eyes as the cats growled.

The Warden of Dreams began to sing. His wings folded, flexed, and snapped outward again, catching Snow and Night; Shadow avoided them because he folded his own and dropped like a stone. Against Snow's white coat she could see a sudden slash of red appear; she had never seen the cats bleed before.

But this was a *dream*. A dream. She turned from the Winter King and sprinted toward her side of the bridge; he did not attempt to stop her. When she reached rock, she planted her feet firmly against its surface, feeling the whole of its texture and warmth against her bare soles. A dream, she thought, but she was awake here, and the cats, like the butterflies, were hers.

Beneath her feet, the earth began its slow rumble; the ground shook.

"Jewel—" the Winter King joined her.

"It's not me."

"I know. Remember what you need, here. Remember what defines you."

She didn't have time to ask him what either of those were, because the ground's shift and tremble grew worse; it was bad enough that her knees buckled; she kept her feet beneath them.

What do you fear? the Warden asked, his voice, like a thought, emerging from within. *What do you desire? In these lands, either are open to you. Come. Choose.*

She bit her lip, tasted blood, wondered if she was bleeding in her sleep. She couldn't remember falling asleep at all.

If you will not choose, I will choose for you.

"No," she told the Warden, "you *won't*."

But she couldn't remain on her feet, the tremors were so bad; she couldn't hold onto the ground. She could see the Winter King's shadow, but she could no longer see the Winter King, and as she squinted into sunlight and amethyst sky, the world tore, as if it were thin cloth or paper.

She could see shreds of that cloth, that paper; torn, ragged pieces—and each small surface showed her some part of the world that had existed moments before: purple sky, rock, moving river. The river still flowed, rushing and gurgling high in its bed—but only in fragments. Those fragments overlapped sky, shadow, grass, bridge rail, as they fell.

She tried to catch them, aware as she did that the rock beneath her feet had been shredded as casually, as completely, as the rest of the known world; she stood—and braced herself to reach—on nothing. But the nothing supported her weight as her open hands caught the edges of one piece of amethyst sky and drew it in toward her chest. It was purple and dark, and within its now small and jagged canvas, three butterflies struggled. This wasn't a window; they didn't simply flutter out of view. But they tried; she could see them hit the boundary of the small scrap in her hand, and wondered if they were aware it was there at all, or if they perceived wind pushing them back in its stead.

She spun on her heels; the Winter King was nowhere.

She herself was nowhere; there was no landscape, no sky, no ground; there was no sound. The world was not dark, but it wasn't bright; it wasn't even gray, although gray was the color she would have used to describe the total absence of everything, if she'd had to pick one. She couldn't hear the cats; she couldn't hear the Warden of Dreams.

But she could see three butterflies, and these butterflies couldn't reach the Warden; they couldn't be found and crushed in the palms of his hands. Somewhere in the city of Averalaan—either in the holdings or on the Isle, three people slept; they had not yet died. She wanted to catch all of the butterflies then, and cup them somehow in the curved palms of her hand, as if her hands could be the wall that protected them from him.

No, no, that will not do. This is not a dream; this is the absence of dream. Come, if you will claim these lands. Dream them. Dream them into being. Create something vast and huge and impressive; make it, hold it. Nothing else will stand against me.

What, exactly, was vast, huge, and impressive to the scion of gods?

Certainly not the butterflies whose lives he had so deliberately cultivated and then extinguished.

Yes, he said. *Yes, and perhaps butterflies are the wrong seeming for them; they are like stalks of your wheat or corn; they grow, and they ripen, and in time, they are felled. They will fall anyway. I merely accept the gift of their harvest; it is that, or leave it to go to seed.*

Her hands stiffened; she couldn't curl them into fists without partially crushing the small, small bit of sky within which these butterflies flew. Vast? Huge? Impressive?

She thought of the palace of the Winter King—not hers, but the man who had reigned for centuries in the heart of his forest, with cats, stone cats, for companions during the long, long wait for his release. Had his storybook dwelling been impressive enough? It had impressed her—but it had impressed her the way the forests had: they were gold and silver and diamond, those trees, and the palace was all of glass. Or ice; it had been cold, she thought. She couldn't feel the cold now; it didn't touch her.

But no, no that would not impress the Warden of Dreams; such a castle had stood for centuries, and if it changed at all, it was slight. She thought of the fallen buildings of the undercity—the great, stone bridges now shattered although their pieces were larger than any single member of the den. What had those bridges occupied when they stood? How high off the ground had they reached? And what—or who—had walked across their chiseled, cut splendor?

Yet even that, she dismissed. City of gods, she thought—and knew it, the way one knows any facts in a dream, even a dream in which the only reality is six inches of amethyst sky and three white butterflies.

You have nothing, the Warden said. *And if you have nothing, nothing is all you can hold.*

"No," she told the Warden softly. The ground no longer bucked at her weight, because it didn't exist. Nothing did; there was no fall, no flight, no destination. The only voice she could hear was his, but without form, what threat could he be?

He chuckled. *You will see. These lands are mine now. You will have no dreams and no Companions, except those I allow—and I think I will allow you* nothing *for a very long time. It discomforts mortals,* he added.

Nothing, on the other hand, was better than some of the things she'd faced.

Oh, indeed. If you prefer it, I can give you something; not dreams, but nightmare. Endless fear, endless flight.

She shook her head. "No, you can't."

Silence.

In her hands, she held sky. It was a sky that no waking person would ever see. "I don't know who you are," Jewel said softly to the three butterflies, "but while you're here, I will do what I can to protect you."

You can do nothing.

She ignored the Warden of Dreams, and felt the wind blow cold from her right. It was her first sensation in the gray. She frowned. The gray was so much like the Between—a land where gods and mortals might meet, and where such meetings might have consequences.

Dreams had driven her to the South. Dreams of Diora. Dreams of a massacre. Dreams had given her her brief glimpses of the Cities of Man—those powerful, ancient homes in which even the dead could be trapped, and against which gods might break themselves, rather than walls. Dreams, she thought, had driven her to House Terafin: dreams of gods.

She heard the distant growl of a predator, although the

landscape remained gray and lifeless. She heard the buzzing of insects—which she viscerally detested—and the sounds of swords leaving scabbards. Small noises, but significant. She heard a child screaming; that was worse.

But it was the only truly human sound in this place.

Frowning, she reached into the scrap of handheld sky. The small piece of dream in her hand had dimension, if approached from the front. She inserted her hand among the butterflies, and to her surprise, they immediately alighted, attaching themselves to her palm, her inner wrist, and her fingers.

It wasn't the Warden of Dreams, she thought. That wasn't what they were seeking in their long sleep.

Build, he told her.

She nodded. "Tell me," she said to the butterflies. "Tell me where you live."

The butterflies had no mouths with which to speak, but mouths weren't necessary when reality was so profoundly subjective. This was the first lesson the dreamers taught Jewel. They answered her in a rush of tiny voices, and not a single voice was constrained by the need for words. They were so pale, she thought, so perfect in form—they were delicate but at this range she could see they were faintly luminescent.

Dreams were subjective. She'd had so many of them, she'd fled so many. Most of them weren't real unless she was in them. But when she was, they were the whole of the world. Conscious thought stopped; dream logic ensued instead, with its odd panoply of best friends she'd never seen or met in real life, relatives she'd lost, stations to which she had never aspired, familiar homes that she had never lived in. In dreams, it was not truth that mattered; truth couldn't be measured.

Yet, conversely, dreams worked because they felt true; there was no defense against them.

What she could dream into being was a product of every dream she had ever had. Every dream and every experience that also walked to one side of the solidity of the real world. That wasn't what she wanted now.

What she wanted now, oddly enough, was Shadow. Even in her dreams, he was still an annoying, whiny, insulting cat. He was utterly himself; he was proof against her imagination, large and small. No, she thought, she wanted to *be* Shadow, or like him. Herself, in a place where there was no other anchor.

She did not want the dreams of the butterflies; she wanted them to wake.

There is power in dreaming, the Warden said, his voice colorless and uninflected. *You dismiss it at your peril. You do not understand what you might build here.*

"No. I understand it. But it wouldn't be real."

It would be *real.*

She shook her head. "Why are you allied with the Shining Court?"

It suits my purpose.

"What do you want?"

I want freedom, he replied. *I want an end to cages and walls. I want your sunshine and your fields in which only plants grow. I want their dreams, at my leisure, and not in a hurried rush at the turn of seasons that* do not *turn.*

"You kill them."

I would not need to kill them, he said, *if I were free. There would be enough, could I but touch all dreamers. There will be enough*, he added, voice shifting again, *if I have yours.*

"But then I won't wake."

Silence.

"And if I don't wake, the House descends into war."

Then take them, take them and make these lands unassailable.

She shook her head.

Do the Kings not raise armies? he asked, his tone shifting. *Do they raise armies assuming each and every soldier will survive?*

"No."

Without armies to defend them from their enemies, will they not fall? This is not different. You will never rule well, if you do not understand the choices a ruler must make.

Anger was a texture. The gray of the landscape shifted by slow degree. Splotches of color without distinct shape or boundary began to grow. Was he wrong? Right? She started to tell him that people who joined the army *had* a choice. But had her den stayed in the streets of the twenty-fifth holding, it would be one of the only options left to those who were healthy and physically whole.

Choice was never black and white. It was informed by context, by fear, by hope, or by desperation.

The butterflies were motionless as they rested on her arm. Some of their light trailed in dust across her skin, as if they were shedding it simply by proximity. She slowly pulled her arm out of the small patch of sky, and the butterflies came with it. She let the sky go and closed her eyes.

Bread was baking. She could smell it; the scent was so sudden and so strong she could almost taste it. It was the bread her Oma would sometimes buy when she was being extravagant. Because that wasn't often, it had been special, and Jewel remembered it that way.

She heard splashing, felt water strike her cheeks and her eyelids. She didn't open them. She knew this sound, and knew it better, in some ways. It was fountain water. Someone was laughing—someone young—and as she laughed, other children laughed as well, the sound high and sharp. There was no malice in it, although there was plenty of mischief; Jewel knew which fountain they were playing in. The summer sun fell hot against her face and her arms; her feet were bare because shoes were expensive and water wasn't good for them, or at least that's what her mother said.

She could hear the sound of the magisterial guard that patrolled the Common; could hear the shrieks of running children who were not to play in the water—but who always did. You couldn't put water like that in easy reach of children and expect them to keep their hands dry.

Last, she could feel heat: not sun, but fire. She could hear its sharp, harsh crackle and above its constant din, louder cracking. Ah. Screams, screams of terror. Jewel knew what fire did to the old buildings in the hundred. She had seen an entire building consumed in flame. Although the fire had been magical, the effects were similar.

On a windy day, fire was more of a threat than dark gods.

It was to the fire that Jewel turned first, and when she opened her eyes, she could see it. She flinched; the smoke was black and thick, and the building's roof was ablaze. Wind? Yes, there was wind, and it tore parts of the burning roof away, carrying fire to other buildings—and spectators. There were buckets in a line, there were people with blankets and water and wet towels. There were men and women lying on the ground, chests heaving, eyes wild.

She didn't recognize the street—but she only knew three holdings like the back of her hand, and in dreams, all reality shifted and contorted to enfold the dreamer. It didn't *matter* what holding contained the dream, after all. It only mattered that someone was dreaming.

Jewel wondered, as she began to walk toward the fire, if this dreamer had been caught in the same dream since they had fallen asleep. Did dreams shift and change, the way they naturally did?

She didn't know. Adam had made clear to her that the sleepers he woke had no memory at all of their dreams; as far as they were concerned, they hadn't had any. Only during her flight up the side of the dream-twisted tree, and her defense of her new forest against a demon lord, did they remember their dreams. They also remembered the dreams, in fragmented, fractured images, of the first day of The Terafin's funeral.

Jewel looked at her arms; there were no butterflies here.

Only fire, fear, the streets of the holding looming large and impersonal in the face of impending loss. It was a fear she understood so well her mouth went dry. Love opened you up, always, to the possibility of loss.

The inevitability of loss.

She started to argue with the disembodied voice—but stopped herself because she was no longer certain that it was the Warden of Dreams who was speaking. Her mother was dead. Her Oma. Her father—and her father's future had shadowed her days with a terrible fear and certainty until the accident she'd foreseen had come to pass. Lefty was dead. Lefty, Fisher, Lander. Duster. Rath—gone. Alowan. Even Amarais, their shield and their savior.

You build, but it breaks. That is the nature of the world of your birth; it is a land of mortals, it is a land of death. Build where mortality does not reign if you wish to build eternity.

"It's not mortality," she whispered, her words cracked and broken by the roar of the fire.

It is.

She shook her head. She walked easily through the crowd, lifting her hand and exposing the signet that signified her position as *The* Terafin. The gesture was instinctive;

it was a sweep of hand that was, wordless, a command. A command and a promise. When had she learned that? Why did it work?

The crowd parted, although she took care to avoid the line of men hefting buckets against the roar of flame. It was like making an argument in whispers when your opponent was roaring like the very dragons of legend; it made *no difference* at all. Yet they tried, in this dreamscape.

They tried, she thought, when they were awake. She squared her shoulders. She couldn't douse this fire in reality. She could douse it in the dreaming.

No, you cannot. Unless you are willing to take her dream and make it your own, the flames will not respond to you—they are hers.

Would that be so much worse? Jewel, who'd known the fear that had created the whole of this landscape—who had known, worse, the end of that fear, and the truth of that death, wanted to say, No. No, it wouldn't be worse. This was a nightmare that plagued her conscious, waking moments; to live it for—for however long this dreamer had been trapped here—

But no. No. This was how it would start. This is often how things *did* start. Good dream or bad, it didn't matter. This was *all* dream, and it wasn't—couldn't be—hers. She reached the side of the dreamer, and knew—without knowing quite how or why—that this woman, small, stout, her face and hands lined with labor and lack of sleep, anchored this dream. Her face was red with exertion, wet with tears, her body bent with the burden of fear and the pain of hope when hope was so scant.

"Hold on," she told the woman, lifting hand, letting her see the Terafin crest on its heavy band of gold; the gems that studded it were altered in color by the hues of fire. She had seen those colors—those exact colors—before. They were hers. They were the heart of the first tree she had planted in a forest that existed in the shadows of the Terafin grounds.

The woman blinked, and then dashed tears away with the blackened backs of her blistered hands. "Terafin," she said, her knees buckling, her hands rising.

Jewel nodded. "The magi are on the way. They will be here soon."

Symbols had power, even here. Or perhaps especially here. Jewel couldn't see herself the way the dreamer saw her, but she felt strengthened by the woman's gaze — and burdened by the hope in it. Jewel was The Terafin. The Terafin was one of The Ten. If The Ten summoned the magi, the magi would come.

It wasn't the way it worked in waking life, not really. But this wasn't life; it was the detritus of life, stripped of reason. In this case, the lack of reason worked in both their favors; the magi did, indeed, arrive. They arrived in a cloud of robes, taller than life, broader of chest and grimmer of expression; they were, to a man, bearded, and those beards were white and long — yet no other encumbrance of age hindered them.

"Terafin," they said, as one.

She wanted to laugh. The magi could barely stand still in a room in groups of larger than one; they argued more frequently than they drew breath. If the real magi had come at her command, they'd be jostling for position in the streets, and arguing about the most effective way to put out the fire; the building would probably be ash by the time they finished. But her expression when she replied was the definition of gravitas. "Matteos. Send one of your men for the healer. Have the rest douse these flames — and quickly. There is a —" she glanced at the woman's face, "— a child, inside."

One man left at her command; the others converged.

It was interesting to see the magi as this woman saw them in her dreams: they acted in concert. They acted, Jewel thought, like *gods*. No natural force of fire could defy their will; their arms moved, and their voices rose in clear, heavy, intonation. The syllables made no sense, but the gravity and strength of each utterance lent them weight, force, will. What fire could stand against the combined force of such men?

Not this dreamer's.

It was not yet over. The woman was grateful, but gratitude was stifled by fear; the building was *so* damaged. The fire had burned for so long. Hope was harsh, and it cut — but Jewel had clung to scanter, in her time. What this woman was doing to herself, Jewel had also done. And she knew, if she woke, they would both do it, time and again; take the sharp, sharp edge of bitter hope, because none seemed the worse alternative.

You are foolish, still. Mortality is *death.*

"It's not about mortality," she whispered, as the woman turned wide eyes upon her. "Yes," Jewel told her, as the magi lowered their arms and the streets fell silent in the wake of guttered flame. "It's safe now. Shall we go?"

The woman swallowed. Jewel shook her head. "What is your name?"

"Leila."

"Come, Leila. Let's find your child."

And when she finds his corpse, what then?

What then, Jewel? The young Terafin ruler shook her head, and Leila stumbled into the house, shouting a name over and over. "Then," she said, as she followed, "she'll continue. It's all we can do. It's all we ever do. You don't understand," she added, as she stepped into the blackened remains of a sitting room and headed—as Leila had headed—toward stairs.

"It's not about mortality. You can't see that—maybe you can't die. I don't know what kills dreams. But it's not about the mortality. People die in the streets of this city all the time. They die in their bedrooms on the Isle. They die in the snows of Arrend, and they die in the sands of Annagar. Those deaths don't define me, and they don't break me.

"It's *not* about the deaths, Warden." She heard the woman scream, and she flinched, and her eyes teared instantly, the sound was so damn raw. "It's about love."

You could make it better. You have already—

"No. I didn't do any of that—she did. But even the power of symbols have limits." She bowed her head. "This is hers. This is what she sees. This is what she fears, or feared to face—I don't actually know. But good—or bad," and this was undeniably the latter, "it's *hers.* I don't have the right to decide it for her, one way or the other." She entered the building. "I don't know what led to this. I don't even know if she *has* a child."

The stairs were scorched and scored; Jewel climbed them anyway, avoiding the rail. As she did, she heard footsteps at her back; she turned.

Adam was standing at the foot of the stairs. His eyes widened as they met hers. "Matriarch!" he said.

The ground beneath her feet shifted, keeping time with Leila's low, broken cries. "Matriarch?"

He frowned. Seeing Jewel had apparently been natural and even expected; seeing the burned and blackened ruins of a small, strange house had only just begun to register. "Where are we?"

"I—" She walked back down the stairs, grabbed his hand, and pulled him up. He was solid. He looked *exactly* like Adam, and she knew—she *knew*—as she met his rounded, brown eyes, that he was. Somehow, Adam was in the dreaming with her.

She felt the world darken subtly, the way it sometimes did when dreams shifted into nightmare and every visual detail became vaguely and inexplicably threatening. *No*, she thought, clenching her jaw. *This is not my dream.* "Come with me," she said, forcing her grip on his hand to ease.

The stairs creaked in a dangerous way beneath both of their weights.

Geography was never fixed in dreams. Halls elongated or shortened, ceilings changed height, texture and color, rooms widened or narrowed. In dreams, nothing was fixed, but in her own dreams, the shifting landscape felt natural and unremarkable. Walking through Leila's dream was therefore unnerving. Had it not been for the visceral sounds of almost animal grief, it would have been easy to get lost trying to find her. Her voice, however, was so primal it was like the bottom of a cliff— when one had just jumped, or had been thrown off, its height. It drew Jewel inexorably toward where the heart of the dream waited.

The ceilings, by this point, were short enough that Jewel had to duck through what was otherwise a door's frame, dragging Adam with her. She was afraid to lose him here. Adam didn't seem to suffer from the fear of being lost; he was focused on the sound of Leila's pain. It was their guide, in the end.

They found her crouched over a small body; judging by its size—and at this age, size was often a poor indicator— Jewel thought the child no more than five, but possibly younger. His eyes—and he was a boy, that was the narrative of the dream—were closed. The fire that had damaged the room had not likewise damaged him, although his clothing was blackened by what appeared to be soot.

Adam started forward, and Jewel tightened her grip on his arm, pulling him back.

"This is a dream," she told him, when he turned to face her, his eyes narrowed in a younger man's anger. "The rules of healing don't apply here."

He swallowed, glanced around at the walls, the short, cramped ceilings, the very oddly shaped bed. Oh, Jewel thought, as his eyes widened; they had noticed the bed at the same time. It was long and narrow, and instead of a mattress, it held a wooden coffin. The coffin was the only thing in this room that had not been harmed by the fire—and why would it be, in the end? It was so much worse than the fact of the fire itself.

So, she thought. She released Adam's arm and approached Leila's curved back. Her shoulders were hunched as she gathered the body of her son into her arms and her lap, howling, words denied her.

"Leila," she said, touching the rough cloth of the woman's shirt. She wasn't surprised when Leila didn't react. Adam, free from restraint, made room for himself on the floor, opposite the grieving mother. His face was pale, but he was not afraid—not for her, and not of what she carried.

"Leila," he said. This time he placed a hand on one of her shaking arms.

Her low, animal moan stopped as she looked up. "Adam?"

He smiled. It was a slight smile, and it was—as Adam himself was—enormously gentle. He nodded. "Will you let me see your son?"

"Why are you here? It's too late—"

"The Terafin sent for me."

"You serve The Terafin?" As Jewel moved to stand behind Adam, she could see the woman's eyes. They were round with surprise.

Adam nodded.

"But—but—"

"Yes?"

"You woke me."

He nodded gently.

"How could you wake me if you serve her?"

"The Terafin cares for many people, Leila, not just her own."

"There is no other healer I could summon," Jewel said, quite truthfully. "Give him your son for a moment, Leila."

The woman's arms tightened instinctively around her burden. Jewel waited. She understood that her authority as The Terafin was grounded in the daily life of a citizen of Averalaan who lived and worked in the hundred holdings. But Adam's authority as healer was different; it wasn't symbolic; it was mystical. And neither of these was resident in Jewel or Adam; they were part of how Leila saw, and understood, her life.

You can change that.

She was getting really, really tired of the Warden of Dreams. But she'd had a decade or more as a member of the House Council in which to grit her teeth and ignore the truly tiresome; she put it into practice now almost instinctively. It was harder than it often was—but the House Council was composed of men—and women—not the scion of long-dead gods.

They are not dead.

"In your dreams," she replied, under her breath.

She heard the sound of his wild, harsh laughter as Leila let Adam lift her child into his own lap; he curled around the body in a posture very similar to the boy's mother's, bending his head over the boy's face. Jewel knew that healing required only the barest of physical contact; this is not what Adam now offered. But when Adam had woken Leila from a sleep that might otherwise be endless, she hadn't seen him at work; she had responded to his talent and the imperative of his gift.

This, then, was the physical representation of how that gift had felt to Leila. Jewel's actions and words had not been confined by Leila's belief in The Ten, its rulers, or its authority; she had moved, worked, and acted, in a fashion that felt natural to her. She wondered if Adam was doing the same, or if his actions here were pressed and burdened by the weight of Leila's expectations. If they were, he didn't seem to notice them.

He sat, while Leila held her breath, for what felt like an hour. When he lifted his face, his eyes were red. "Leila," he said, "I'm sorry. He's crossed the bridge. He can't come back." Sorrow made his face look so much younger.

"You can see him?" Leila asked, her voice raw and shaky.

Adam nodded. "I can. He's in no pain. He will never be in pain in this life again. He's playing," he added. "He's throwing stones into the river that runs beneath the bridge."

She looked scandalized for just a moment, her expression the expression of a mother who's caught her child throwing rocks into a fountain in the Common when the magisterial guards are on patrol nearby. "You tell him—" She froze.

"He knows where you are," Adam continued. "He knows why you can't come to him yet. But he's happy. He's not hungry, he's not cold, he's not in pain; nothing—not even a healer—can touch him on that side of the bridge. Only Mandaros."

Leila said, "but he'll get lonely waiting—"

"No, Leila, he won't." Adam rose, his expression changing; it grew darker, harder, although it was still young. Jewel recognized the judgment that age and experience often lessens—because it was almost a mirror. She had been young in the same way.

And then, she thought with a grimace, *Have I ever been anything else?*

"He is not your only child. But he is the only one who no longer needs you, and you have been sleeping and dreaming for far too long." He rose, still carrying the child's limp body. When he turned toward the coffin, Jewel almost stopped him. Almost.

But he was right.

Leila didn't rise. Leila didn't follow him. She buried her face in her hands and wept, instead. Adam very gently laid the boy's body into the empty coffin; there was no lid. "You will always remember him," he said, in a softer voice. "Nothing can take that away. But you are not a child, and it is time. Leave him here."

Jewel swallowed. "Leila," she said, her voice as even as Adam's, but far more autocratic.

Leila lowered her hands. She rose stiffly, glancing about the room as if—as if she were waking from a long, long dream. She saw the coffin; the coffin didn't change in shape or size. But the room did. The black scoring of fire and the soot of smoke evaporated, and the floors beneath either were solid. They were scuffed; this was a room that was well lived-in.

"It is time," Jewel said softly.

"Terafin." Leila bowed. It was a bow that was clumsy and graceless; it was, in fact, very much like Jewel's earliest bows in the Terafin manse. "Thank you."

Jewel said nothing. Adam came to stand by her side in the same silence. "Leila," he said, "go home. Your children are waiting."

Leila swallowed, wiped her eyes with the back of her hands, and straightened her shoulders.

The world began to evaporate. The floors faded. The walls. The windows. Even the coffin. All that remained was Leila herself; Leila in the gray of a colorless, featureless world. Like any dreamer, even Jewel, she wasn't shocked or bothered by the sudden absence of landscape; she looked mildly confused.

"Oh," she said, "they're beautiful."

Jewel frowned and looked down at her arm, following Leila's gaze; against her wrist and palm were two almost motionless, white butterflies.

"Go home," Jewel said gently. "You will always be welcome back—but don't stay so long next time."

"Terafin," Leila said, bowing. Yes, it was a rough bow, but she loved it because she knew it was a gift she didn't quite deserve.

They watched as Leila faded from view. Jewel had half expected Adam to go with her, but Adam remained stubbornly solid at her side. "If either of us is sleeping," she began.

"We are. But it is not yet dawn."

"How do you know that?"

He frowned. "Don't you?"

She shook her head.

Adam stared at her arm. No, not her arm, but her wrist and her palm.

"Matriarch," he said, his voice thicker.

"Adam, I'm not a Matriarch. There is no Markess line. If my Oma was Voyani, she never said so."

"It doesn't matter what you call yourself," he said, his

voice low. "It's what you *are*. I've seen the Matriarchs of Arkosa. I was the Matriarch's son, until her death, and the Matriarch's brother, after. You have the gift of the Matriarchs."

She didn't like the look on his face; it didn't suit his age.

"The Matriarchs," he continued, when she didn't speak, "protect their line. It's what they've done from the beginning of the Voyanne. But the protection is . . . difficult. It is not without cost." He cleared his throat. "If they are strong, they pay the cost in their own blood." He closed his eyes. "My mother saw her death. She knew she would die." He swallowed, opened his eyes. "My sister was never as harsh as my mother; it frightened her."

"Your sister?"

"My mother. She knew what the Voyanne demands of its Matriarchs, and she wasn't certain—" he shook his head. "I am sorry. I speak of things that are Arkosan, and I should not."

"You're speaking of your family," she countered. "And you're part of that; they were your life."

"I miss them." His voice was softer; his words carried far more weight than simple syllables should have. "But when I dream of my sister, now, I don't see our caravan; I see cities of ancient stone and empty, empty streets.

"My mother," he continued, turning, "did not consider herself strong enough."

"Why?"

"Because rulers must kill, Jewel. If it comes to that, they must make sacrifices—demand sacrifices—of *other* people."

She knew why he stared at the butterflies, then. "Adam, what do you see?"

"Pardon?"

"What do you see when you look at them?" She lifted her arm, and the butterflies came with it.

"What--what do I see?"

"I see white butterflies. They're small, they're very light, and they're glowing a little."

His eyes rounded. Clearly, that was not what Adam saw.

"There used to be three. I think—I think Leila was one of them. Adam—what do you see?"

"I see the sleepers," was his soft reply. "Sarah and Catherine. She hates that name," he added. "No one but her mother uses it."

"What's wrong with Catherine? Tell her to try Jewel."

"What's wrong with Jewel?" Adam asked.

She started to answer and stopped. Clearly, if this felt like an appropriate conversation in this circumstance, she *was* dreaming. "Never mind. I interrupted. I'm sorry."

"Sarah fell asleep two weeks ago. I've woken her once, since then. But Catherine has been sleeping for longer. She's lost weight, and when she wakes it's—she doesn't fully wake." He reached out slowly until his hand was almost touching hers. "What will you do with them?"

"Wake them, if I can."

He closed his eyes, exhaled, and relaxed. When he opened his eyes and caught sight of her expression, he winced. "I'm sorry," he said. "It's—the work of Matriarchs. We don't understand it, can't predict it—but we've always understood what it means. For the children," he added, as the Voyani so often did. "And for the future." He swallowed. "Did you come here to save them?"

"I don't know. When you wake, when Levec bellows you back to the Houses of Healing, you'll find that several of the sleepers died tonight. I didn't kill them," she added quickly. "The Warden of Dreams did."

"The Warden of Dreams?"

When Adam said it, it sounded vaguely ridiculous. "That's what he's called by Celleriant."

"Why did he kill them?"

"He derives power from their dreams."

"But they can't dream if they're dead."

Did Adam make this much sense when she was awake? "I don't know why he killed them," she said, after a long, thoughtful pause. "It made me angry."

Adam nodded, because that made sense to him.

None of this made sense to Jewel. She shook herself, straightening as she did. "I know why you're really here," she told Adam, grimly.

"I'm here to wake you." Adam replied, his hand still a hair's breadth from hers.

"Did I fail to wake?"

He nodded, hesitant now. "Everyone is upset. Angel is

angry." He looked at the butterflies. "But this is different from any other time I've attended the sleepers—even The Terafin herself." He met her eyes again and smiled, rueful. "Now, Levec will be angry."

"Because you've also fallen asleep."

"Yes, I think so."

"Well, that's the silver lining, then. If I don't wake, I don't get a face full of furious bear." She wanted to pace in the tight circles that helped her think, but she still carried the butterflies that Adam saw as women. "I'm certain the Warden killed the others," she finally said. "I don't know why he did. I don't know if he did it just to make me angry. I was," she added; she could almost hear the lecture Haval was no doubt preparing as she slept. "I was *so* angry." She glanced at her very fine, very patrician skirts, and missed the loose, summer sleeping shift. " . . . And I was afraid. This—this is my nightmare made small: people will die in front of me and there will be nothing I can do to prevent it.

"If I failed to wake, this is how he trapped me. And I," she added, stiffening, "am how he trapped you."

Adam shook his head. "I chose to stay, Matriarch."

"Can you just call me Jay while we're here?"

"Jay is a—is a bird?"

"It's better than an expensive rock."

"Women," he said, "have very strange ideas about their names. Margret hated hers. Elena hated hers. I don't understand it."

She grimaced. "What do you mean, you chose to stay? This is Levec's worst nightmare."

Adam smiled. "No. Being drawn to the dreaming by the sleepers was his worst nightmare."

"But you've—"

"I'm here with you. If you wake, Jewel, I will wake. You didn't stay because you were trapped by the sleepers; you stayed because you wanted to protect them."

"How do you know that?"

Adam raised a brow. "I'm young, I'm not stupid. Leila is awake now."

"Adam—"

"She won't come back. We can wake the two you now hold, if you're willing."

She nodded almost absently. Something was bothering her. *Winter King*.

Jewel. She wasn't surprised when he answered. She couldn't see him, couldn't touch him, was almost certain she couldn't force him to appear—not yet. But he was here. She was no longer lost in her own elusive dream.

Go back to my den. Go back and tell Celleriant that I'm here.

Silence.

I know he can understand you, even if the others can't.

I will not leave you here.

Adam is here. Nothing short of decapitation will kill me while Adam is with me. Maybe, she added, feeling distinctly uneasy, *not even that, if he acts quickly.* It was true.

"Yes," she told Adam, "we can wake them. But not just them." She lifted her arm—the arm that didn't contain butterflies. "Warden," she said. "Warden of Dreams, come."

Chapter Eight

INTO THE GRAY of nothing, Adam, and butterflies, the Warden of Dreams emerged. He was winged, his wings the color of the butterflies in this place; luminescent and pale. They were the shape of eagle's wings, but larger, higher. His face was long, fine, his eyes—the whites of his eyes—were golden. But the irises were not; she couldn't begin to pinpoint their color, they seemed to shift so much.

He bowed to her. It was shallow, but his expression robbed it of sarcasm. It was meant, felt. "Terafin," he said.

"Why did you kill the dreamers?" Her free hand slid from sky to hip. The butterflies remained on her arm. She'd been half afraid they would fly to meet the Warden of Dreams—and their own demise.

"There is power in dreams," he replied.

She watched his face, his eyes. Remembered that someone—Avandar? Celleriant?—had called him the two who are one. "Yes. But the dead don't dream."

"You believe that sacrifice leads to power. You believe that sacrifice of life's blood is potent and useful."

"I've seen both."

"Yet you fail to believe that the destruction of the dreamers leads to power?"

Jewel forced herself not to look at Adam. "They're no longer in the dreaming if they're dead. They go to Mandaros. If you need dreams for the power they provide, their death is the last thing you want."

"Perhaps, little mortal, I devour the parts of their sleeping minds that dream at all; perhaps it is the *ability* to dream that grants me the power, not the dreaming itself. You have seen only one such dream—but it is life made visceral, personal; it is strong."

"Yes. But there is *no* dream if the dreamer is dead. You killed the dreamers."

The Warden of Dreams lifted his hands; they were glimmering. "I did."

"Why?"

He smiled. It was an odd smile, and it changed the whole of his face—literally.

"The two who are one," she whispered.

He nodded. "There are many ways to travel through dreams. Not all of them grant power to the traveler; in fact, very few do. But if one is content to simply travel and observe, there is much to be learned."

She thought of the magi as they appeared in Leila's dreams. "Most of it isn't accurate."

"What is accuracy? The dreams are felt, their worlds are known, they are believed. In rare cases, when the dreamer wakes, the world changes."

"The three dreams."

"The dreaming wyrd, yes. Have you not felt its imperative?"

She nodded as the conversation began to drift out of her control. She brought it back, watching him. He seemed gaunter, more frail, than he had as he folded his wings across his back, changing his shape in the gray skyline.

"Why did you kill them?"

"You were not awake," he replied. "They were trapped here."

"We were trying to get them out!"

"No, Jewel. You were not. Your healer was." He turned and offered Adam a deep bow. Adam returned a nod; he was watchful, but he wasn't angry—not the way Jewel was. She reined in the anger.

"They dreamed pleasant dreams," the Warden of Dreams continued. "Their nightmares cause them endless pain, but nightmares can shift or change. So, too, happiness."

"You killed them because they were happy." It wasn't a question. It was a certainty.

He nodded. "They were at peace. They will be at peace in the halls of Mandaros. In no other way could I guarantee that their dreams would remain pleasant." He glanced into the featureless landscape in a way that suggested it wasn't featureless to him.

She stared. Her mouth opened, but words failed to emerge for a long moment. When they did, they were louder; had a butterfly not been sitting in her palm, her hands would have been fists. "Do you even understand what life is? What living *means*?"

Turning back to her, he raised a brow. "I understand the concept as it exists here. I understand what life meant before our parents chose to abandon us. I understand what life *is* on the hidden path. In no one of these places could your mortals exist for long; they are fragile, and their sanity breaks easily."

"I'm mortal."

"Yes. But you are gifted; you can touch the essence of the hidden path. You do not," he added, with a frown, "choose to do so; you stumble and drift by accident. But I am aware of who you are. I am aware, as well, of Adam. In you both, I see the End of Days."

This was not a comfort.

"You do not build, Jewel. But you must. These roads are known to your enemies; they have used them in the past, and they will use them again if you do not prevent it."

She thought of Lord Darranatos in the Common. "If I build, can I stop you from gathering the dreamers?"

"Yes."

"If you could kill them, why couldn't you *set them free*?"

He frowned. "I did."

"You *didn't*. They're *dead*!"

"They will never return here. They will never again be caught in the web. That is as much freedom as I am able to offer; I cannot yet leave the hidden ways."

"And you want to leave."

He smiled. "We want to leave, yes. It has been long indeed since we have walked among mortals, in mortal seeming. My brother thought if he trapped you here, it might be enough. But you are not so easily trapped; you see too clearly. He was not pleased at the deaths of the dreamers," he added softly.

"Neither was I."

"Yes. What will you do?"

"What must I do, to stop you?"

He smiled. "Stop dreaming."

She shook her head. "No. You are in *my* lands, now." She gestured and the forest grew up around them both, with trunks the size of two men abreast as bars of an ancient cage.

"I have no desire to harm you," the Warden said, as his wings once again expanded, his feathers shearing whatever they touched. Bark flew; chips of wood rained down. Only the trees of diamond were spared. Those, Jewel thought, and the lone tree of fire, around which no other trees grew. It was to the fire that she was drawn; Adam was her shadow. She couldn't see the Winter King; nor were the cats immediately obvious.

"Yes," the Warden said. Although his wings were extended, he made no attempt to fly; he waited as Jewel approached; he was standing now beneath the bowers of burning branches, his face upturned as if he desired the fire's warmth.

"This is the only thing that is truly yours in this landscape," he told her, lowering his face. The whites of his eyes were still golden, but the irises were the color of reflected flame. "Do you understand what it signifies?"

"No. It's a burning tree."

"Ah, yes—but the fire did not come from you, little mortal; it was meant to kill you. The echoes of its intent cause its leaves to tremble—but not a single one of them has dropped. It is yours, in this place; it is singly yours. Not even the Lord who sought your death by fire could touch this tree now.

"You made it, Jewel. You took his intent, and you fashioned it into something that could stand against him. It could stand against even the most powerful of the *Kialli*, unbound. Without it, you would have failed in your charge."

"What charge?"

He did not answer. Instead, he lifted one wing, as if the wings were prehensile, and touched the lowest of the branches that shadowed his face. The wing did not sever branch; the fire did not burn wing. "Once," he said, his voice even softer, "I knew a woman who could make such trees. She loved the irony of their shape: wood of fire, wood that burns and is never consumed. But she could make vines of shadow and towers of nightmare; she could make beds of water, and cradles of stone; she could make whole homes of air, although she could never fly."

"Was she mortal?"

"Of course. She was mortal, and she was Sen. She founded the first of the great Cities of Man. It is long in the past; it is forgotten by all—all save the firstborn."

"The gods—"

"The gods do not remember as we remember; they no longer live in a world in which time rules event. And they do not speak to us," he added bitterly. "Only to mortals."

"There is one god—"

"You speak of Allasakar?"

She did, but couldn't bring herself to use his name. Not here, where so much was laid bare. As she walked, the butterflies grew restless. "Adam."

Adam stepped forward, emerging from her shadow. She held out her arm, and he placed his hands directly in front of both butterflies; after a moment, they crawled into them. They did not attempt to fly. She was grateful. When both of the dreamers were safely in Adam's hands, she, too, approached the tree of fire. She reached out and laid her palm against the trunk; it felt like warm bark. It sounded like bonfire.

"Yes. It cannot burn you, cannot harm you; the whole of its power faces outward. Were I to touch the bark of this tree in the fashion you have just done, I would burn."

"There is one god in this world."

"There are two," he replied. "Allasakar is not at the height of his power; he lives where mortals might, with difficulty, live. He can touch the wild roads; he can walk them. But he is not master of what they are, not yet—nor do I think he will ever be. The unnamed god wrought well, here. But even his work must fail, in the end; anything that is part of the world is subject to the ravages of time and change, even the hidden ways.

"Do you wish to know what the world was like when the gods walked? Live here, and learn."

Jewel shook her head. "I've seen enough of it."

"Oh?"

"In dreams." She was aware of the irony of the statement, and his smile indicated acknowledgment. "The dreams were enough, for me."

"Do you know why the Cities of Man rose?"

She shook her head.

"Then you must ask the nameless god—or his daughter. You have seen her; I sense her presence in your dreaming. She is—"

"Evayne."

He nodded. "She has long dreamed on these roads, and we have traveled to her when she is absent. Your burden is not—yet—her burden. But your burden, she cannot shoulder."

"She can't claim these lands."

"No. No more could she build what you will build. The Cities of Man were safe—for man. They were not safe, on the other hand, for you and your kind. But you built them, regardless, and those who were born with talents, some fragment of power that echoed the divine, came to the cities you had built. So, too, the god-born—but not the firstborn." He lowered his wings, bowed his head. When he lifted it again, she was ready for what she saw in his face: a different man, a different Warden.

His wings fanned out with a snap toward the branches of Jewel's tree.

Jewel didn't blink. "You can't cut fire," she told him, her voice even, her hand gripping bark. "It doesn't bleed."

"And will you now destroy me?" he asked, lips curved in a smile as sharp as his wings.

"If I could."

"I did not kill your dreamers." He lifted an arm.

"No."

"Yet it is I who bear the brunt of your anger, not my brother. That is always the way; there is only one god who has ever favored *me*. Come, then. If you will fight, fight." He gestured, and from the heights of the sky—night-sky, clear and cold—came three winged cats. They were larger than

Jewel had ever seen them; their claws were exposed, their fangs glittering as if they were made of diamond.

And why not diamond, she thought? They had once been stone.

"Come, if you will. I tire of waiting. I am nightmare; I shift and change the world until it is mine. You run in terror from the things you recognize when you enter these lands; the familiar is no comfort. There is no fear I have not seen."

It was true. She felt the air darken, as if air had a color; the night became winter cold, and in the shadows between her trees, she heard the sibilants of whisper. She shook her head. "I've done this one," she told him, remembering the Green Deepings. "My dead don't scare me."

"Perhaps not. You fear death."

"Yes."

"But not your own." He gestured, and she heard Adam's breath sharpen. Turning, she saw his eyes were wide, the whites exposed around irises that were dark in the night sky.

"You cannot kill Adam," she told the Warden of Dreams. "Any other dreamer—but not Adam. Adam of Arkosa," she added, in a tone of voice her Oma would have used. Adam blinked.

"Matriarch."

Jewel sighed and accepted the title; for Adam it had more power than being The Terafin had had for Leila.

The cats circled. They growled; they didn't speak.

"Matriarch—those beasts—"

"Yes. They're the cats. Be careful what you call them," she added. "Because when we all wake up from this—"

"You will not wake."

"—They're going to remember every word you said. They're pathetically easily insulted." Jewel shook her head; she could hear the crackle of fire as if it were a voice. She called fire, and it came; the tree's branches lengthened and sharpened.

"It is not me you will fight," the Warden of Dreams told her.

"Oh?"

"It is them."

She glanced up as he spoke, because as he spoke, the cats

came. Ebon, Ivory, and night-mist, they flew above the thermals around the tree of fire.

"I understand what your brother was attempting to tell me," she said softly. These cats were nightmare cats; they were not the cats who traipsed and sprawled across any available space in the Terafin manse, demanding attention. They did not speak; they did not batter each other with gloved claws. Their teeth gleamed orange and gold in the fire's shed light; their eyes were obsidian.

"They are not yours," he told her.

"I'm sorry. They are. They are mine the way the tree is mine; it doesn't matter how you've touched or changed them. They will not serve you."

"Then they will die."

She shook her head again. "Snow," she whispered. "Night. Shadow. *Come.*"

They came at her command, utterly silent, as if aware that their silence was vastly more threatening than their litany of complaints and verbal threats.

"Matriarch—"

They alighted on the ground between Jewel and the Warden; the tree burned above them, crackling as if in greeting. They circled her, heads low to ground, jaws open, tails twitching; the pads of their paws broke twigs and branches in the undergrowth she couldn't see. They did not look at all like the cats that babysat Ariel.

But they were.

She knew it, had perhaps always known it. They spoke and fought and broke furniture, she thought, because it was something that made them vastly more frustrating and at the same time vastly less frightening. It was a gift.

Or perhaps, a curse. They were cats, after all.

The fire traveled from her right hand across her shoulders and down her left arm. Night sprang at her, fangs bared, claws extended; they closed on flame and stopped, unable to pierce its armor. He didn't complain—he snarled. She reached out with her left hand and touched his forehead, moving past claws and fangs as if they were illusion. "Night," she whispered.

His eyes rounded; as they did, she saw black recede until they were once again golden. He blinked, as if waking from a particularly deep sleep. Aside from his eyes, nothing changed; he was still half again the size he had been the last time she'd seen him in the waking world. But he turned on his brothers as they leaped.

There were two; the fire caught them, branches lashing out like limbs. Shadow skittered across the forest floor, digging his claws into earth to stop himself. Snow, she touched, just as Night landed on his back, snarling in fury. His fur was soft; softer than it was in life; his eyes were darker. Everything about his form and shape was askew—but she knew him, the way one knows anything transformed by dream.

"Snow."

The cats really were right—they were stupid names. But they were the names she'd given them, without thought and in a rush, and they were the names by which every other member of the House now knew them. They weren't demonic names; they weren't calling cards by which the cats could be magically summoned, but they didn't have to be.

He growled, his larger throat emitting a much deeper sound than it ever had before. But he turned as Shadow stalked across the grass.

Shadow, she thought, was the hardest of the three; the least frivolous, the least easily bored—although boredom was his anthem, when he chose one. Snow and Night came to stand to either side of her, but she sent Night to guard Adam; he went without complaint. Not a single word. Even in the dreaming, it felt unnatural.

Shadow was canny; he did not spring, the way Night had, and he avoided the branches of the tree of fire.

Without taking her eyes off Shadow, she said, "Snow—the Warden."

Snow leaped, silent, streamlined. Fire flowed off his back as if it were colored water; it was her fire. The Warden of Dreams raised wings; they sounded like swords leaving sheaths. More than that, she didn't see, because as Snow leaped, Shadow did likewise.

His claws were not diamond, not ebony; they weren't solid at all. They passed through the flame that enveloped her arms and her chest. Adam cried out; she bit her lip to prevent joining him as she brought her hands forward to touch the third cat.

He was clever, this cat; her hands passed through his

body, touching nothing; the same couldn't be said for his claws; she felt them shred dress and skin. Adam cried out in Torra; a warning and a curse. She stumbled; his palms caught the back of her neck—the only exposed skin a formal dress of this nature allowed.

"Adam—don't—"

It was like telling the waking cats not to complain.

"You named him," the Warden of Dreams said; his voice surrounded her.

She'd named Night as well, but Night was, and had remained, solid. Shadow bit her arm, forcing her back; she stumbled, her hand leaving the anchor of her tree. Fire guttered around her.

Adam's hands were warm. She felt pain in her arm and across her lower abdomen; she felt heat rush from the back of her upper spine toward the wounds she had taken from this nightmare version of Shadow. They met, each diminishing in the contact. Night leaped on Shadow—and fell through him. Both cats hissed; it was as close to their normal voices as they'd yet come.

"No—Night—"

Only Night bled.

Jewel threw herself to the side, breaking Adam's contact as Shadow leaped again, claws extended. She felt the warmth of tree, but it was out of her reach, and she knew that without the fire—

No. No, she *didn't*. Her eyes snapped open. It was like a second waking. The landscape hadn't changed; it was night, contained Night, Shadow, Snow, and the Warden; there were trees that the darkness made gray at a distance, and one tree whose light, red and orange, couldn't be dimmed. She wasn't touching the tree, but it burned at the heart of this forest, and if she was in these lands, the fire was hers.

She lowered her arm and turned as Shadow landed. His tail twitched, his ears were high; his fangs glittered, wet and red. He was beautiful. She heard growling in the distance; Shadow was silent; she watched him. His fur rippled as he shifted position; she knew he would leap again.

She shook her head. In the dreamscape, her hair didn't fall into her eyes. It was such an odd detail to notice while facing death. But she'd seen death so often, now; the death that Shadow offered wasn't new. It was cloaked in magic, in mystery, in things that were older in all ways than Jewel herself—but it wasn't new.

"You were right," she told the cat as his wings flexed. "I should have named you something different. But none of the names I have would suit you, and you can't name yourself."

The moment the words left her lips, Shadow left the ground; they were both significant, but only one of the two would kill her. She leaped to the left—farther away from the tree of fire. His claws clipped her arm, but the dress was already ruined; he cut skin as neatly—as cleanly—as the sharpest of knives before he landed again.

He stood between Jewel and her tree; he meant to herd her. She didn't tell him it was pointless, not in so many words. She couldn't change his name, not here; it was the name by which he was now known. She wondered if the Winter King had ever named these three. Probably not. Names, clearly, had power.

But everything here had power. She called the fire without touching the tree, and it came. It was raiment of bonfire light, not sun, and it cloaked her, covered her, fell from her shoulders and arms as if it were a dress made by Snow. It shone in the night sky. She heard Adam's choked gasp and turned to glance at him.

"Matriarch—"

"I'm not burning," she told him gently. She turned back to Shadow. Shadow was watching, eyes unblinking; she avoided meeting his gaze for any length of time. Staring contests with cats never worked out well for her; at most, she'd get teary eyes.

She knew Shadow. He had accompanied her into her dreams before; he had walked into a vision of the past, and watched by her side as Amarais Handernesse ATerafin had placed a sword and a ring—neither magical, both of incalculable value to only two living women—into the waters of the maker-born created statuary. He had seen the desert that lay at the heart of the Sea of Sorrows, unchanged by dreaming. He had protected her from the worst of her nightmares.

She couldn't touch him here. She'd tried.

But she lifted both hands as he gathered to spring again. This time he didn't reach her. He reached only the fire, although it wore her shape. Landing in the center of flames that burned nothing, his head snapped up, his wings, out. He attempted to push himself off the ground.

"Shadows are cast things," she told him softly. "They don't exist where there's no light."

He snarled; she had never seem him look so bestial. The fire that she had worn as cloth wrapped itself around the great form of the winged predator, caressing his fur and the whole of his wings—something Jewel would never dare do in life. They weren't hands, those flames; they were light.

"Shadows," she continued, as she approached him, "can't be cast by nothing. Something has to stand in the light, to catch it, to block it."

Reaching out, she touched the top of his head, the way she did when she wanted him to settle down in public. In private, it had always been a lost cause—and what was more private, in the end, than the dreams that came with sleep? Her palm flat against the space between erect ears, she swallowed warmth and nightmare. She heard his sudden hiss as if at a great remove. "Tell me what you see," she demanded.

He growled, wings straining against flame, although Jewel's hands passed through it.

She knelt on the ground before his open jaws. "Shadow," she said, voice softer. "Tell me what you see."

His eyes widened; they were so large in his face, they reminded her of the Winter King's eyes. She could feel his fur, although she touched only the top of his head; she could feel the stretched tension of wings that were flight-feather, fur, and something other. The fire rolled along their edges, and their edges were sharp, stiff. What she had done with the fire of the demon lord, she could do—in this moment— with the heart of the cat.

She could . . . plant him. It would certainly stop him—but he would never fly at the heights of this forest again. He would never fly in her dreams.

"Shadow," she said a third time. "Tell me what you see."

He rumbled and growled; his wings flattened as he stopped struggling against the pull of the fire.

"I see," he said, his voice deeper and louder, a thing felt just as much as it was heard, "a *less* stupid girl."

She closed her eyes.

"Jewel—"

Snapped them open again, to see that he had somehow managed to break free of her containing fire. He leaped. *Catch him*, she heard, although she didn't recognize the voice immediately. *Catch him, contain him, or he will destroy you.*

It was true; his claws pierced the skirts of her dress. He was wild, here; wild, dangerous—deadly. But he had always been that. Always. She didn't see it most days, because it wasn't something she wanted to see.

But it wasn't the first time she'd held something deadly in the heart of her home. Duster had stayed, after all. Duster. So much that was wild and strange and deadly brought her back to Duster. Why had Duster stayed with her? They were so damn *different*. They'd had different parents, different families, different childhoods. Duster couldn't be caged; she couldn't be chained. The rules that Duster lived by had always been her own rules.

Or had they?

No. Yes and no. Jewel couldn't remember demanding anything from Duster, except this: Kill cleanly. Kill cleanly, and come home.

And if she had refused? There would be no home for her in the den. She couldn't make Duster into Finch or Teller— but if she could have, she wouldn't; she didn't need another Finch or another Teller; she already had one of each. She needed Duster—but she needed to know that Duster could control her rage and her violence when Jewel needed both controlled. That was it.

Duster on the other hand, had never tried to kill her. Had she, even once—

Jewel grimaced. Had she, Jewel would have accepted it; what she would never accept was Duster attempting to harm anyone else in the den. But Duster was not a cat. Duster couldn't fly.

She gestured, and the only weapon the dreamscape offered came to her hands. Had she been Celleriant, it would have been a sword of blue fire; had she been Avandar, it would have been a sword of golden light. She was Jewel Markess. She got a collar; a collar of red-and-gold flame. A collar that would fit around the throat of a hunting cat—if she could force him to stand still for long enough without losing one, or both, of her hands.

She gripped it tightly; felt her fingers press into her own palms. The flame was like Shadow; it was insubstantial to touch. Yet it rested in her palms like a demand or a promise.

"Shadow," she said, just that.

He snarled; his body compressed as he gathered to leap against the fire that had managed to—barely—contain him. There was blood on his claws and his fangs; it was hers. She wondered if she were bleeding in the waking world, or if Adam had closed the wounds there as well. She could hear shouting, muffled and wordless, in the distance.

The great cat broke free; strands of fire twined around his legs and his wings, slowing him. Muscles gleaming gray and red in the reflected light, he lunged. His teeth caught her left leg; she stumbled. Adam was there almost instantly.

This time, Shadow turned on the Voyani boy. Adam was waiting for him.

Adam, no.

I am not a child.

When he broke contact, she knew why; Shadow was upon him, jaws snapping at Adam's throat. He'd tucked his chin, lifted his arms; he knew what his body could survive—and so did Jewel.

But she rolled, rose, her leg whole, her hands still grasping the collar; it fell open, as if flowering, and she could see the ebon buckle that girded the flame. She approached Shadow and his wings swept her back, striking her at her ribs. She was already in motion, her body avoiding the blow before her mind could register the movement. She moved again, dodging, until she faced his back; he was clawing at Adam's chest, exposing the ribs and the flesh that lay beneath cloth and skin.

Adam made no sound.

Someone else did; it was muffled, attenuated—like a scream that has to pass through walls. She rolled, rose, and this time, she summoned fire, not to cage, but to burn.

Shadow shrieked; it was a sound that she had never heard him make. In this fight, on his terms, he had taken the form of his name; the fire had passed around him or through him. Even Jewel's hands had found no purchase at all. But now? Fire burned. She didn't wonder why; she *knew*.

The great cat let go of Adam, turning; fire blackened the tips of his feathers. *I'm sorry*, she thought grimly. *But*

there are some things I will never allow you to do. The fire
shifted, changing; he was once again ensnared in the flame.

Jewel was robed in it as well. She approached Shadow as
he hissed. This time, he was injured; the fire both burned
and confined. He snapped at her; he lunged. She reached
out with both hands; he tucked his chin the same way—the
exact same way—that Adam had.

But his fangs were red with blood. Some of that blood
was hers.

I have you now. In the dreaming, that blood was *of* her.
It didn't matter how it had come to adorn his fangs, his
claws. Like the fire from the burning tree, she did not need
to contain it, or touch it, to use its power.

Red liquid beaded, elongated. It congealed as she concentrated, forming a fine, beaded chain—a chain of red
mist, dark against the brighter red-orange of flame. She said
nothing at all as that chain then wrapped itself tightly
around his open jaws, cutting into his fur, cutting into his
skin—which nothing else had managed to do. Here, the cats
bled, and here, his blood blended with hers and with Adam's. He could not fight himself.

"No," she told him, voice steady, although smoke made
it rough, "here, you are mine." He attempted to batter her
with his head, but the chain tightened as he struggled; in the
end, he was forced to be still to preserve the front of his
face. She said nothing, offered no apology; she had the clarity sometimes achieved in dreams—because in dreams, she
could kill, and sometimes, in triumph, she did. Had she forgotten that?

Had she remembered only terror and the flight of the
helpless, passive observer?

She did not want to kill Shadow; she did not want to
unmake him or reduce him to something irretrievably
other. She felt the fire tighten around his form. There was a
moment at which the fire bore the shape of many branches,
and she remembered how *this* tree had come into being.
But Shadow was not a tree, not a formless act of aggression;
he was a *cat.* She had no desire to plant him, and even the
desire—sudden and visceral—to kill was gone. Adam was
alive. Adam was whole.

She slid the collar around his neck; the buckle closed itself. His breath was warm against her forehead as she bent; warm as she rose.

She stepped back from him; the fire that burned guttered. The fire that limned him otherwise did not. He ceased his struggle, and as he did the chains that bound his massive jaws slid away, once again becoming a warm, red liquid—albeit with a very different shape. She wondered, idly, if his face would be scarred by this night's work, and found, with a pang, that she cared. It surprised her. Shadow's fangs receded into the line of his jaw as he stopped his attempts to bite off her hands—or worse.

"If I extinguish all light," she told him, "you cease to exist."

"But then there is *only* darkness." His voice was recognizably his own—but deeper, fuller; it rumbled.

She nodded. "If I call the Summer, Night fades; Snow melts."

"Oh, *them*. Let me out."

"You are already free. Go help your brothers."

He dared a glance at Adam; Adam, shirt shredded, was on his feet. He was pale, but unharmed. Shadow growled.

"*Shadow.*"

"I don't *like* it when he *touches* me."

"He wasn't touching you until you tried to rip my throat out. *Go help your brothers.*"

Shadow's muscles once again shifted and tensed as he gathered his body to leap. She knew a moment of awe—not fear—as he cleared ground; the fire—her fire—surrounded his body like a halo.

Adam approached her, reached out; his hand was trembling. Before he could lower it, she caught it in both of her own, drawing him closer.

His touch took pain, gathered it, drew it from her—and with it, some part of herself—as if she was defined, in the end, by pain, and its absence left her hollow. His voice was clear; it was not—yet—a man's voice, but no longer a child's. He was fourteen years old. Fourteen, a healer, Voyani—and the only other person who could, unaltered by Winter Queen or Warden, stand on this path with her now.

"You mustn't," he told her, attempting to retrieve the hand he knew he shouldn't have raised.

She shook her head. "Not here. There, yes—there it will be hard. I think Shadow almost killed me."

"He almost killed us both," Adam replied, giving up on the struggle that owned only half of his divided heart. He stepped into the fire that surrounded her, and it opened to encompass them both. "Will we need to help them?"

"We already are," was her soft reply. "But heal them? No. I don't think you'd survive the attempt—they really can hold grudges."

"Why do they hate it so much?" As a healer, hatred was not one of the reactions that Adam was accustomed to facing.

"Because healers change the shape of what *is*."

"No—we—"

"Yes. I didn't understand that until today. Tonight. Now. They change what is, they deny what is. The reality of injury—the aftermath of it—most of us learn to live with it; we've no other choice. But when you come—or even when Levec does—you give us a different choice, and we take it because it's what we want; it's what we dream of: loss of pain, a return to wholeness."

"And the cats—"

She shook her head.

The cats had taken to, and remained in, the air; the air was not a challenge for the Warden of Dreams. Where the Warden fought, the sky shifted color and texture; there were no clouds, and the sunlight was sharp and harsh—lances and spokes that hit forest floor. She had only ever seen Summer light used against demons—but what she had said was true. In the dreaming, the names she had so casually and irritably given three complaining, whining cats had a force and a power that they couldn't have in the waking world.

Snow and Night were at a disadvantage here—but Shadow was not. If he wasn't a creature of light, he existed only as an artifact of it. In the fight on the forest floor, the light had been shed by a burning tree. But in the Summer light? He was stronger, more solid.

Adam's hand in hers as if she were once again a child in the Common, she watched as the light obeyed the Warden's unspoken command, shifting in place as if it were a moving shield; darting toward Snow and Night, falling in areas where Shadow wasn't.

As they bore witness, the butterflies came. They landed on Jewel's shoulders, on her arms; they settled on Adam's head. In ones and twos, they accumulated until they were a living quilt, each element discrete. Adam's gaze was drawn to the butterflies as they landed; once or twice he whispered a name.

"Is Hannerle here?" she asked, although she couldn't remove her gaze from the sharp, staccato aerial dance of the Warden and the three cats. The cats were black, white, gray; the Warden was a moving swirl of colors, most of which she could not name. His wings caught Snow and Night; Snow bled. She thought Night might have, too, but the red was lost to the color of his coat, the sheen of it bright and reflective. The Warden's wings passed through Shadow as they stiffened, hardening; flight feathers dropped away from their stretched width.

What was left was leathery; bat wings, not eagle's; there were rents and tears beneath the pinions, but the wings were dream wings; they obeyed no physical dictates. When they started to burn, she held her breath; they were echoes of the wings of Lord Darranatos. To the Warden's hands came whip and sword. They were not red; nor were they blue or gold.

They were leather, she thought; leather and steel; plain, workaday weapons that any House Guard might wield in the line of duty. Except, perhaps, for the whip.

But dreams found reality and made it larger, smaller, or just plain stranger than life. In his hands, the weapons were enough. Snow shrieked and fell, spinning in place as he plummeted. Night roared; Shadow fell utterly silent.

Jewel extricated her hand from Adam's; she ran; at her back, his voice followed.

Above her head as she approached, Night, Shadow, and the Warden were circling; the tight, cramped space of fang and claws had been widened by the reach of whip and sword. Snow lay beneath the Warden's feet, against the undergrowth; above his open eyes, diamond leaves fell. She reached his side in a rush of outstretched hands and bent knees, skidding to a stop in the undergrowth against his supine back.

"Snow!"

He was so much larger than her Snow, and he was silent. She couldn't imagine this cat creating a dress that even the Winter Queen might be proud to wear; couldn't imagine this cat slashing the legs of a chair into hard-wood splinters because he was annoyed with Night.

But she could imagine him dying. She could imagine his absence. They opened before her like the sudden and unexpected plunge of unseen cliff. "Snow."

The great cat wheezed.

Above her head she heard the sudden sharp intake of breath and she looked up in time for blood to adorn her cheek. A drop or two, heralding, as rain did, the start of summer storm in the Common.

This was not the Common. The blood was Night's. His fall was not as uncontrolled as Snow's; he managed a glide into the lowest of a silver tree's branches. They broke; silver rained. Night did not rise again.

This was *not* what Jewel wanted. Here, in dream, she struggled against the sudden, visceral terror of the worst of her nightmares, and she lost ground almost instantly.

The cats ate too much; they broke plates; they gouged tables in the guest room out of sheer boredom. They had wings. They could fly, and speak. There *was no place* for them in the Terafin manse—but regardless, they had made one.

They were hers, these cats; they were part of her den. They fit more easily into the West Wing and its environs in two months than Avandar had in a decade. They weren't human, no; they were clearly immortal. They were beautiful in silence and in their sleek and perfect movements—when they could *be* silent, which was so infrequent.

He would kill them.

He would kill them, and she would never find them again, not even in dreams; the Warden wouldn't allow her the peculiar grace of that nocturnal haunting.

Above her head, Shadow growled—this growl contained words. "*Stupid* girl! Think! Look at his *weapons*!"

Of the three, he was the only one she had forced to find his voice. She wanted to hear it again. She didn't even *mind* that he called her stupid; it was like a sign of affection. But she looked up at the Warden, and at Shadow, limned in red-gold light; her fire was burning, there. It wasn't her fire she'd been told to examine.

She looked at the Warden's weapons. At this distance, they were even more ordinary than they had been when she had observed them by Adam's side; she could see that the sword's blade was notched—and that, the House Guard would only tolerate immediately *after* a fight. The whip flew; she couldn't examine its many tongues, but she could see that the grip was shiny and dark, the way aged leather was when it had been handled by too many hands.

She frowned. Snow lifted his head and dropped it in her lap, and she grunted; it was heavy.

But it was deliberate. She met his golden eyes, heard his wheezing breath, tried not to see the wound and the blood that fell from it. She was no healer, not even in her dreams; what Adam could do, she couldn't. And Adam couldn't touch the cats; they would die first.

They would die.

No. No, *think*, damn it. What was Shadow trying to tell her? And why, she thought, shunting fear aside for a deep, deep irritation, was he being so damn oblique? His life hung in the balance; Snow and Night were already too injured to fight—or to fly—and he was giving her disparaging *hints* as if this were still a game.

It is always a game, with cats. The mice do not understand this.

The voice was familiar, but unrecognizable, and she accepted its presence the way she accepted anything in her dreams; it was a fact of the now, very like a fact of life. She looked at the weapons again; there was nothing to mark them as extraordinary, except for the fact of their wielder.

Oh. She shifted Snow's head off her lap and rose. "Adam," she said, raising her voice without looking back. She held out a hand, and he came to her side, trailing butterflies. "I understand."

"What must I do?" he asked.

"Hold my hand. This is going to be a little rough."

He was happy to catch and hold the hand she offered him; she felt his palm. It was warm, rough, and slightly sweaty. She closed her eyes; heard the growl and hiss of one flying cat, and the labored breathing of another; Night was too far away.

Adam's breath sharpened. "You are going to wake us," he said.

"Yes," she replied, squeezing his fingers between her own where they were interlaced, "and no."

Since the fighting had started, she had heard muffled, distant voices. She hadn't listened carefully; a face full of Shadow's fangs made distant voices almost irrelevant. She listened now.

She knew whose voices they were. She knew she was abed, in the Terafin's personal chambers; she knew that the Chosen would be there. Angel. She was less certain of Teller or Finch; Finch would be at the Merchant Authority, if this were morning.

But was it? Was it only morning?

"Adam, when did they send for you?" Her breath tightened. "Were they careful? Was Levec there?"

"They sent for Levec in a panic," he replied. "Levec came with me, as he did every day we woke The Terafin while you were gone."

"Was it morning?"

"It was late morning."

"I hope we haven't been sleeping for too long."

Something about the way his eyes slid to the side caught her attention. "It was late morning when you arrived."

"Yes."

"Earlier you said it wasn't yet morning. Adam—"

"It is not yet morning," he told her. "Of the second day."

Her knuckles were white; she was afraid. Waking from a nightmare didn't frighten her, of course. But this wasn't waking. It was something other, something different, and if it didn't work, or if it worked out badly, she might never wake again. Not fully. Neither would Adam.

The Warden of Dreams laughed, and she looked up; Shadow was caught in a web—a web that looked as if it were spun by a giant spider, or several, between the overlapping branches of the great trees. She reached out with fire, and fire began to burn its edges.

"I've missed the Council of The Ten."

Adam's expression made clear that he thought she'd momentarily taken leave of her senses.

"And the meeting with the Kings."

"Jewel, now is *not* the time."

No, she thought, it wasn't. She once again focused on the voices, on the muffled words, because Shadow was utterly silent. Familiar voices. Familiar—and unfamiliar at the same time—bed and room. Night, not day; moonlight not sunlight. Adam's hand was probably half its normal width by this time, she was crushing it so hard—but it was better Adam than butterflies. Shadow couldn't—hadn't—killed him; nothing Jewel could do to him would be worse.

She closed her eyes, and the sounds—as they often did when her eyes were closed—became louder and more distinct. "Can you hear them?"

"Yes."

"It's time."

"Time?"

"To wake up." She swallowed. With a free hand, she reached for Snow and felt his unnaturally soft fur. "Snow?"

Snow didn't answer. His breath was rough and wheezy.

What did the Terafin's bedroom really look like? What did it *feel* like? Was it large? Yes. And the ceilings were high. The floors were a sharp and gleaming wood, over which rugs had been laid. There were windows limned in a subtle orange glow that did away with the need for bars.

There was a desk, a small desk. Two closets of different sizes. A ... dresser, a thing in which important and small personal items could be placed. Were there paintings? She tried—and failed—to remember; she often didn't notice art after a brief glance, and nothing in the room had demanded her attention. Magelights. There were magelights. The room never *had* to be dark; the light that it contained didn't have to be filled, fueled, watched.

She bent head, bracing herself as if to accept a heavy weight.

This was the heart of her forest. The tree of fire, surrounded by the *Ellariannatte*, silver, gold, and diamond. She had identified the forest—and its heart—as the trees. But it wasn't. It was the land on which the trees stood, sometimes bisected by footpaths, sometimes by cobbled roads.

The land was hers.

It was, in some fashion, *her*. Dreaming or waking, it didn't matter. She was asleep now, in the waking world; in the realm of the Exalted, the Kings, The Ten, she had failed to wake. But she was not a simple dreamer. She was dreaming, but it was lucid.

And the test of lucid dreaming was volition and understanding. It was time to *wake*.

Chapter Nine

SHE OPENED HER EYES to ceiling. She opened them to walls and the glimpse of a window that she knew was subtly wrong. Adam lay by her side on his back, his hand in hers. His lashes—which had always been ridiculously long—began to flutter and tremble as he, too, opened his eyes.

She turned her head to the side Adam didn't occupy and saw that Snow was aground just beside the bed; his wings were jerking. Beneath Snow, rug was being shredded because his claws were extended and they were also opening and closing almost at random. He had not diminished in size in the transition between the waking and dreaming worlds.

Beyond Snow, Angel stood; Arann, in armor; Avandar in his usual domicis robes. Everything seemed suspended, still, as if the room were a painting without any of the usual artistry of composition.

Several things happened at once; she heard Angel shout. She heard Avandar shout.

They weren't shouting about the same thing, because if the voices that had been so indistinct and muffled had suddenly become clearly audible, the sounds of the forest and the dream hadn't diminished—at all. Shadow and the Warden of Dreams now stood in the room, by the wall farthest from the bed; the cat remained mired in burning webs, he

was still large, and he was enraged. Rage did not tear the
webbing down, although the fire ate away at it steadily.

The Warden, however, was no longer concerned with
Shadow. He turned, eyes widening, as he took in the sudden
shift in surroundings; gone were the trees, the undergrowth,
the forest floor; gone were the butterflies—and that caused
Jewel's heart to sink. Where trees had stood, there were
men—the armored Chosen.

She heard—felt—the drawing of a single sword and
knew Celleriant was very close by. Shadow was no longer in
the air—but neither was the Warden of Dreams.

In his hands were an ordinary sword, an ordinary whip;
in the room, in less than a minute, other ordinary swords
were drawn. One of them was Arann's,

The Warden's wings expanded suddenly, as if he were
still in the dream world and they could encompass the
whole of a deep, clear purple sky. There were walls on all
sides and ceilings above; the wings hit wall and parts of the
wall crumbled. They hit swords, but the swords did not
break.

"Nightmare," she said, pushing herself up, "is rooted in
reality."

"It is *stronger* than reality."

"Not here," she told the Warden. "Never here, again. It's
true that I cannot destroy you."

Celleriant entered the room at a graceful, deadly run; he
saw the Warden, but he did not slow. A shield girded arm—it
was the same blue as the sword in his right hand. The Warden's wings once again shot out, unbalancing two of the
Chosen; they did not shear armor, but they dented it.

Once, Jewel would have said that the Warden was beyond the Chosen; the Chosen were men, and the Warden a
child of living gods. She would have left the Warden to
Celleriant, Avandar, and the cats, because in some fashion,
they were part of the same story; not mortal, not human—or
in Avandar's case, only barely—imbued with magics that
were wilder, greater, and ultimately incomprehensible to
those who did not possess the same.

But the Warden's sword was *not* an Arianni sword; it was
not a golden one; it did not come from the forges immortals—or gods—might use, if they needed them at all to create. That sword, and the swords that were now raised against

him—all save one—had come from the dead earth, or the sleeping earth; they had been forged in fires that obeyed the whim of *men*, in heated, enclosed rooms that smelled of sweat and coal and fire and oil. They were wielded by men and women whose oaths of service were simple words, not binding ones.

And here, it was enough. It was enough because they were as real as the people who wielded them.

Celleriant's sword swung in from the left, and the Warden's whip caught its blade as if the tongues were prehensile. It was not, therefore, Celleriant's sword that struck the first blow—it was Torvan's. The Warden's eyes widened as blade pierced flesh; his blood fell. It was not red, not crimson; it was gold, and thick, like amber honey.

The walls shifted shape where the Warden's wings touched them; plaster cracked and shattered; paper, laid across it, tore so quickly the color of the room changed every time the Warden struck. Armor took dents as the Chosen struggled to maintain their footing; Celleriant's sword finally managed to slice the bindings of leather.

Wind howled in the contained space, its voice growing as it responded to the Warden's summons.

No, Jewel told it. *Not here, and not now. Remember?*

And the Wind fell silent. As it did, the bits and pieces of detritus it had gathered fell as well; inkstand, inkwell, quill, stoneholder, and magestone itself; two trays and the contents of two large pitchers, brushes, one small mirror, quivered a moment before crashing to the ground.

Avandar lifted his hands in a wide, sweeping arc; light trailed down the length of his arms like a bright, thick liquid.

Avandar, wait.

He is—

He is the child of absent gods; I don't think we can kill him—

It is possible now.

But she hesitated, and he lowered his arms at her unspoken plea. It wasn't a command.

"You are," Jewel told the Warden, her voice clear and cold, "like the wild air, the wild earth, the wild water or the very fire. You are *not* welcome in my lands without my permission. I cannot kill you—not yet—but I can contain you;

you will take root in my garden and you will grow branches and when I sit under your bowers, the dreams I have will be yours. No more.

"Is this what you wanted? I am awake, Warden, and I am *still dreaming*. I understand the ways in which the dreaming world has its roots—and its heart—in the waking one. These men and women are mine; they will grant you no purchase here, and they will hurt you. But they will not kill you. Leave the dreamers; they *are* mine. Leave the gardens. If you need to return, you will ask my permission. Chosen," she said, in a sharper voice.

They stepped back, swords still readied; they did not look in Jewel's direction once.

The Warden of Dreams lowered his weapons in response, although he reserved most of his attention for Celleriant; the Arianni prince did not look peaceful.

"Lord Celleriant."

His gaze, when he turned to her, was cold; unlike the Chosen, he treated the Warden of Dreams as if he were almost inconsequential. "Lord."

He stepped back, crossing the subtle line the Chosen made. He was not pleased, and she knew why; like the cats, combat defined him; it was his most visceral joy.

The Warden of Dreams retreated two steps; his back touched the wall that had been shredded by the force of his wings' multiple blows; it framed him. "Jewel," he said, his voice changing, his expression altering the lines of his face.

"Does he always leave when—"

"He is like your Lord Celleriant. This is his crucible, his testing ground."

"And if he's losing?"

The Warden smiled. "He does not acknowledge loss; all loss, therefore, is mine."

To Jewel's surprise, Celleriant immediately put up his sword; the blade and the shield vanished as he tendered the Warden a deep bow. She had never seen Celleriant employ sarcasm, and assumed the gesture of respect was genuine.

"It is over, for now," the Warden told her.

"Almost," she replied. She turned to Adam, who was sitting up; he was pale, but grim. "I am grateful to you, but you are inseparable from your brother, and where he cannot go, you cannot go."

"We are not forbidden the dreams of men," was the Warden's grave reply.

"You're forbidden them in my domain."

He shook his head. "You do not have that power—even in this place. We cannot entrap the dreamers; we cannot compel them. But the visions we have carried to you, we will carry if it becomes necessary. You are not asleep now," he told her. "But you will never fully wake again. The dreams will be stronger, and they have the power to harm you, now."

She knew. They had had the power to harm her from the moment the cats had appeared; Shadow had told her that months ago. She hadn't believed him—not while she was awake. And in dreams, belief didn't matter. Everything was true.

"Can you tell me one thing before you leave?"

"If it is within my power."

"How do I get the cats to change back?"

The Warden frowned; he looked genuinely puzzled. "Change back?"

"Yes. To what they were before—before last night."

Shadow was now free of the webbing; it had vanished when the Warden of Dreams had once again turned the other face. He didn't look particularly *happy* about the shift in personality, but like Celleriant, he seemed to recognize it instantly.

"Are they different?" the Warden finally asked.

"They're half again as large as they were and they look extremely dangerous."

The Warden bent to the bristling Shadow and whispered a few words that Jewel's hearing wasn't acute enough to pick up. The cat hissed. It was a lower, louder version of his laughter.

"He says they are not changed," the Warden told her gravely.

"But they—"

"They do not appear altered, to me. Perhaps my vision and yours depend on different things." His frown deepened. "But you are Sen, and it is the way of the Sen to see things as they *are*. It is vexing."

Shadow's hiss increased in volume; the sides of his lengthy body began to heave. "She is less *stupid*," he finally managed. "But not by *much*." He rose and padded across the room to where Snow lay. Jewel gasped as he jumped *on* the injured cat, hissing in a totally different tone.

"If you break the bed," she told them both, raising her voice to be heard over the cats—Snow, not to be outdone, had begun to hiss back, "I will—"

"Yesssssss?" Both cats said, swiveling to face her, their own brief spat suspended. "What *will* you do?"

"I'll have to think about it. Turning you to stone has a certain appeal."

Snow hissed, his eyes widening. Shadow, however, snorted.

"Stop fighting in my room and go find your brother."

"Oh, *him*."

"I mean it. Find Night and bring him back." She paused and then added, "Do *not* fight with each other in the manse if you don't intend to leave by the window."

The room was silent after the cats had departed; they left through the doors. The window was apparently not to their liking.

The Warden of Dreams watched them go.

"Will they be able to find Night?" she asked.

"If that is your desire, yes. You did not, as you fear, leave him behind."

"And the dreamers?"

"More difficult, but you have begun the work you must do to find them. They will find you," he added, "if it is possible."

"In my dreams?"

"There, yes; possibly while you wake. It has been long indeed since I walked through the streets of such a city. I will not counsel caution; you do not require it." But he turned once more. "Viandaran."

Avandar stiffened, but nodded.

"You have not yet found the answers you seek."

"No."

"And have you now set the search aside? You serve the Sen. I remember when—"

"Enough." The word was a single, sharp, command. It sounded like thunder.

The Warden raised a brow. "Do you think she does not know?" he asked.

Avandar did not reply.

"The time is coming, Viandaran. We will meet again."

"No doubt."

The Warden turned last to Adam. He bowed. "And you, Adam. We will meet again, on the far road. Your sister dreams of you—you must go home, soon."

Jewel frowned.

"It is the Wyrd, Terafin. It is not just you who bear the burden of dreams of fate."

"How am I to get home?" Adam asked.

"You will know." He bowed to them all and when he rose, he vanished. It did not happen all at once; he thinned and grayed, becoming translucent, transparent. "It is good that you are here," he told Jewel. "Remember it, in the end. There are others who have seen the coming war, and they have surrendered more than their lives to prevent what is almost an inevitable outcome."

"What outcome?" She demanded.

"There is a god upon the plane. Do you think he will remain in his frozen splendor forever?"

The Chosen turned toward her in the silence. She stared at the space that had, moments before, been occupied by the Warden of Dreams. She felt curiously hollow. Isolated. Without thought, she turned toward Adam; Adam was watching her with wide eyes. Vulnerable eyes.

"Well done, Terafin," Avandar said, in a pinched tone of voice that implied the opposite.

"I think there'll be no new sleepers," she said, speaking to the halfway point between Adam and Avandar. Her eyelids felt heavy.

Angel was at her side just before her knees collapsed. She didn't faint; she didn't lose consciousness, but the world felt suddenly both fragile and untenable, somehow. Angel caught her, lifted her; the Chosen began to converge and paused as she lifted a hand, palm out. The words that should have preceded the gesture wouldn't come.

"Is Levec in the manse?"

"He's in the West Wing," Torvan replied crisply.

"Get him. Tell him—tell him Adam needs to leave the rooms."

Adam stiffened and then bit his lip; the gesture made him look so much younger. It was strange; she knew that the healer and the healed were somehow joined; that the healer had to see, to *know*, the person who skirted the outer edge of life to even call them back. She knew that Arann had been called back from the brink of death by Alowan, and when Arann had awakened, he *knew* Alowan as well as Alowan knew himself—and Alowan, in turn, had the same knowledge of Arann. It was because Alowan had healed Arann that Alowan had developed an instant affection and respect for the young Jewel Markess and her den.

Yet Jewel, at this moment, did not feel that she knew any more about Adam than she had before she had inadvertently dragged him into the dreaming with her. She wondered what Adam now knew about her, and wondered if—in part—this was why he looked so strained. The Matriarchs did not suffer their secrets to be known; she wondered if Matriarchs ever put themselves into the hands of the healer-born.

Levec came so quickly time barely seemed to pass. The two Chosen who were still on guard duty in the room barred his entrance until Jewel commanded them to let him enter.

He looked like hell.

Jewel suddenly became aware that she probably looked worse. Sure enough, her night robes were stiff with caked blood—and not a small amount of it, either. They weren't torn; they weren't the dress she'd ended up wearing after visiting the world of Leila's dreams.

Avandar bowed. "Allow me."

She nodded but approached Levec directly as the Chosen fell to either side of her. "I'm sorry," she said, without preamble. "Adam is awake now."

"I can see that."

Adam's clothing was *also* stiff with blood that had mostly dried. He glanced at Levec, no more; his face was pale, and his eyes were anchored to Jewel. Levec's single brow bunched more tightly across the bridge of his prominent nose. "You will tell me what happened."

Since Jewel had seen Levec talk to *Duvari* that way, it

was hard to find the demand insulting. The Chosen clearly didn't care for his tone. Neither did Jewel, if it came to that—but in this case, she felt it justified.

"We had a little trouble with the dreaming," she said.

"Your definition of 'little' in this case leaves much to be desired. Adam, did you heal her?"

Adam nodded.

Levec exhaled. "I will not tell you that you were foolish."

"She was fighting for the sleepers," Adam continued, when Jewel failed to insert any further words of her own. "There is at least one who has woken, and will not fall asleep again."

"Which one?"

"Leila."

"You are certain?"

Adam nodded again.

"If every time a sleeper is permanently woken it causes injuries that would absolutely be fatal without the intervention of the healer-born, I am not certain it is worth the risk."

Adam drew breath, expanding his slender chest; his arms slid down, to their full length, and his hands tightened. It was clear he found Levec intimidating, but clear, as well, that intimidation was not terror. "I am."

"No doubt. No doubt she is as well."

"The Terafin," Adam continued, emphasizing each syllable in a way Jewel herself wouldn't have dared, "is."

"Adam—"

"It's not something I know because of the healing, Levec. It's what she is. It's what she's always been. In the streets of the twenty-fifth holding—"

"And how do you know that? You are not a native, and you have lived in the Houses of Healing and the Terafin manse, nowhere else."

"Finch told me. Finch, Teller, Carver."

Levec's skepticism tightened his brow. It was amazing how much of a weather vane that brow could be.

"It's probably true," Jewel offered. "It's Finch, after all." She hesitated. She did not want Adam removed from the manse, but dim memories of Alowan's enforced separation from Arann haunted her. Adam had saved her life; she owed him. But what she owed him now was uncertain. On the other hand, that's what Levec was here to tell her.

Levec, however, shoved both of his blocky hands behind his back as he approached Adam. "I will return to the Houses of Healing," he said. "I do not doubt you; Leila will no doubt be awake. If it is safe, I will send her back to her family. I would like you to visit."

Not a demand.

"Can you now wake the others in the same fashion?"

Adam turned to Jewel. "I cannot do it myself," he told Levec. "Jewel must help."

"Jewel—The Terafin—is in much demand at the moment. There is some uproar occurring in *Avantari*, and rumors persist throughout the holdings."

"About my death?"

"I did not say they were well-founded." Glaring pointedly at the front of a dress that was more blood than cloth, he added, "but had Adam not been present, they would have been." He exhaled. That conceded, he returned his full attention to the younger man. "I know what the sleepers have come to mean to you. I will not tell you you are wrong; you are strong, Adam.

"But you must stay in the West Wing, and The Terafin must remain in her own rooms. If you cannot do even this, you will return to the Houses of Healing for at least a month."

"I can do this," Adam replied. His Weston then deserted him as he turned to Jewel. "I don't think we'll be able to wake the sleepers from the Houses of Healing."

Jewel nodded; she wasn't certain, either.

It was Avandar, carrying a dress with care over his left arm, who said, "If The Terafin decides to exercise her power, it should be possible. Those who were struck with the sleeping sickness came from across the holdings as well as the Isle; they did not come from the Terafin manse. If they could be ensnared in the holdings, they can, in theory, be wakened from the holdings as well."

Adam wilted.

Jewel, however, put an arm around his shoulder—or started to; Levec *barked*, and both she and Adam froze like children caught playing in the fountains in the Common by annoyed magisterial guards.

"I must be getting old," he muttered, as he caught Adam by the arm and dragged him toward the door. "When I was younger, I would never have allowed any of my healers to take this great a risk at his age."

Jewel said, once Levec had cleared the door, "I like him."

"Adam?" Angel asked; he'd remained silent throughout Levec's visit.

"Levec. He reminds me of my Oma—and there aren't many men who can do that." She turned to Avandar and removed the dress he was carrying from his arms. Lifting her arms, she allowed her domicis to lever the nightdress over her head. "How bad is it going to be?" she asked, some of the syllables muffled as the dress passed over her face.

"Survivable. The Kings, however, have expressed concern at your absence."

She had slept through the command appearance with the Exalted in the Hall of Wise Counsel. "Did they send it through Duvari?"

"No, Terafin." He glanced at the windows; dawn was slowly brightening the sky. "But there are several messages in the right-kin's office, none of which can safely be consigned to the nebulous future."

Jewel nodded absently and turned toward Angel. "Did the room always look like this? I mean—before the walls were shredded?"

Avandar's brows rose. Angel's didn't, but the rest of his expression froze.

". . . No," Avandar replied.

Now that she was awake and no one was trying to kill her—or anyone else—she looked with care at the windows, the flooring, the bed itself. The walls were a mess, so it was harder to assess their original length. Or height. But the ceilings, she thought, looked wrong; they made her feel much shorter.

She glanced up, and up again. Angel caught her before she toppled backward.

What had once been ceiling in the normal sense of the word was gone; instead, the bowers of trees—or vines, it was hard to tell, they were so thick—now interceded between open sky and the rest of the bedroom. The leaves were of silver, gold, and diamond, but wound around and through them, the green and golden leaves of the trees in the Common, edged in a frill of ivory.

"I'm awake, aren't I?" she asked.

Angel pushed her back to standing. "You're awake."

"When did this—"

"It wasn't like this when you were sleeping, but given the choice, I'll take this."

"The window—"

"I wasn't paying much attention to the window," Angel admitted. "And I haven't seen this room that often—"

"It is markedly different," Avandar said.

"The wall—"

"It is my suspicion that the wall will correct itself overnight."

"Have you been outside of this room? Did anything else change?"

"You are the person who can best answer that question."

Clearly, she thought with some irritation, she couldn't. She dressed quickly, allowing Avandar to fuss with her hair; he was neither as thorough nor as painful as Ellerson could be. Dressed, cleaned up to the degree that was possible when time was of the essence, Jewel approached the open doors of the room. The Chosen fell in behind her. In any other rooms in the manse, they would form up around her. Angel took up the right, leaving Avandar his customary position to the left.

Before she could leave the room—the glimpse of the hall implied that at least the hall was normal—the three cats sauntered in. They were still the wrong size, subtly the wrong shape, but were now hissing and squabbling, in admittedly lower voices.

Angel signed, moving his hands without raising his arms.

Night ignored him; Shadow gave him the evil eye, or the cat variant of same. Snow stepped on Night's tail, and since they were blocking the door, it was not the optimum place for a scuffle. Not that that seemed to deter them on most days. "Gentlemen," Jewel said, dropping hands to her hips and glaring.

Shadow tilted his head to the side. "Yessss?"

"We're leaving. You're in the way."

The three cats stopped snapping at each other. Snow examined his paws; they were also larger. Night, however, pushed his head around the corner of the doorframe, hissed, and drew back. "Why are *they* allowed to scratch the *walls*?"

"They didn't. The Warden of Dreams did. Anytime you're the Warden of Dreams, I promise not to complain if you destroy the walls."

Avandar cleared his throat.

"Cosmetically speaking."

Night appeared to think about this, inasmuch as cats ever did. "So," he said slyly, "if *we* try to—"

"No." She exhaled. "You don't seem hurt."

"Of *course* not."

Neither did Snow.

"Do you remember what happened?"

They all stared at her as if she had just said the most idiotic thing they had ever heard. Then again, on a bad day, every sentence she uttered was, by acclaim, the most idiotic thing they'd ever heard, and it seemed there was no lower limit to her idiocy.

"Did I change your shape?"

Once again a look bounced between the three of them. "What do *you* think?" Snow asked.

At this very moment, she was wondering how she had managed to miss them in their absence. Memory was obviously kind. "I think I preferred your former shapes. At this point, I think I would prefer something *much* smaller."

They hissed in unison, but they got out of the way. Unfortunately, they then joined what was rapidly becoming a procession, and she could hear the hissing of laughter at her back. Since the cats generally laughed at someone else's expense—or, to be fair, at each other's—this was not a comfort.

"Do *not* bother the Chosen," she told them. The hall was as she remembered it; the same pale color, the same baseboards and detail work in the corners of the ceiling. There were no branches here, no leaves or vines. She exhaled and glanced at Avandar.

"I would suggest we visit the library before we repair to the right-kin's office."

The last thing she wanted was to see the library altered in any way. It was one of the first rooms she had seen; it was the room in which Ellerson had taken his leave, and the room in which she had been ordered to accept Avandar as her domicis. She glanced at him, lips curving in a smile; he raised a brow in response.

"You look almost feline, Terafin; I would be cautious about the expressions you adopt from your cats, were I you."

Her smile broadened, but she ducked her head to hide the worst—or the best—of it, as Angel opened the doors—the unchanged doors—at the end of the hall.

"I don't understand," she whispered. No one else said a word, if the cats were discounted. Even Angel's hands were still. The library was *not* the library she remembered. She could understand why the bedroom had altered in dimensions, why the windows were different; she had had to *struggle* to remember them; to force her dreaming self and her waking self to merge. But she had not once thought of the library; that wasn't where her body lay.

This room—if it could even be called that, anymore—was in no way the library of The Terafin. Oh, there were books; she could see them at a distance. The long, pristine table at which The Terafin had often worked, books piled to either side, was gone. The shelves, cataloged and tended by Terafin librarians, were gone as well, although shelving of a sort remained. There were no rugs, there were no paintings, and above them, as her gaze reached for the skylight through which moons and sun could be glimpsed, she saw that there *was no roof.*

"Terafin."

"I don't understand."

Avandar said nothing. The Chosen said nothing. Jewel stood, almost frozen, until Shadow nudged her upper back with the flat of his head. "Go on, go on," he said, practically purring. "Go *look* at it."

He was as heavy as he looked; she stumbled in a way Amarais would never have stumbled during her stewardship, her rulership, of the House. The floor was of bleached wood; it was harder than its color suggested, and very, very smooth. It stretched across a span of floor so large the doors appeared to have been moved—or done away with all together. Since they were the doors that led *into* the entire suite of rooms, this was a disaster.

"It's not, you know," Shadow whispered. It sounded like a growl. "I think you could do *better*," he added, as he stepped heavily on Angel's foot and shouldered him out of the way. Angel's gestures were, while in den-sign, also universal.

There were trees in the library. They seemed to rise up from the perfect and pristine hardwood as if the whole of the floor was their roots. They grew at the ends of what had once been shelves, and indeed, shelves rested between their locked branches; they did not look particularly stable at first glance. She didn't want to see the archivist's reaction — she thought he would die of apoplexy. But these trees were not gold, not silver, and certainly not diamond; nor were they the great trees that encircled and shadowed the Common. White bark girded them as they rose, and their leaves were a pale, pale green; they seemed new, and young.

She swallowed. "Please tell me," she said, in the faintest of voices she had yet used, "that that's not water I hear."

Angel winced.

"Clearly I need a better class of liar."

Avandar did not seem as troubled as Angel, and of course if the Chosen were worried, they would keep it to themselves while on duty. They took this duty, given the appearance of the Warden, very seriously, although Jewel did not feel they were in any danger here — not until the archivist actually visited.

She glanced up at the sky and frowned.

"Tell me the sky isn't purple."

"Let me get Jester," Angel offered.

She cursed. There was *no* roof. There was a sky, but no sun, and the color was amethyst. She walked more quickly toward the sound of water, although she paused in front of the shelves that were bracketed by trees. To her surprise, the shelves grew like *branches* from the trunks.

"A maker couldn't have done this," Angel whispered.

"An Artisan could," Jewel replied.

"A very few Artisans," Avandar agreed. He was not, damn him, disturbed at all.

She couldn't help herself; she ran her fingers across the lip of the shelving, and then reached up hesitantly to pull down a leather-bound tome. She recognized the book; it was one of the many left by previous rulers as guidance, as history, and — in some cases — bitter complaint. She checked the rest of the shelf and felt the knot of tension between her shoulder blades relaxing. "The books are the same."

Avandar raised a brow, but knew her well enough to offer no other disagreement.

Shadow was almost bouncing. His claws clicked against the wood and she winced; the floors wouldn't stay pristine for very long if the cats came and went as they pleased. As if to underscore this concern, Night and Snow started to snarl—at each other—and paws were raised, claws extended.

I missed them, she told herself. *I missed having them here.* She must be insane. On the other hand, they had not yet knocked over a tree and they avoided shoving each other into the shelving, for which she tried to be grateful.

The shelves—which were now much more widely spaced than they had been, continued like a long hall across the pale floors, and if the skies were a purple not normally associated with bright light, it was day, here, and the shadows they cast were short enough it might have been close to midday, on either side. There was no undergrowth; the trees did not imply the whole of a forest.

As they reached the end of the shelving, the floor continued, like a field that hasn't yet begun to sprout the seeds that have been planted. She could see that the shelves themselves continued on the far side of the open space, but that wasn't what caught her eye.

In the center of the library—and she *knew* it was the center—were two things: the long, spare table that she associated with Amarais at work, and a fountain.

Jewel did not cry in public. It was a lesson she'd learned early in childhood from her Oma, and it clung—or she did; at a remove it was hard to separate the two. Reinforced by Amarais and her absolute control over the emotions she revealed, it was at the core of how Jewel defined strength.

She was therefore silent as she approached the long table; she did not dare, for minutes, to speak at all, because she knew that tears would follow words. Avandar was silent to her left; Angel silent in a different way to her right. The Chosen were *always* silent while on duty. The only noise in the room came from the cats.

There was rather a lot of it. Even had they chosen silence, their claws made noise; a constant patter of little clicks broken by words and the occasional petty shoving.

But their voices, lower in register, were comfortingly familiar; their arguments, their jostling for position, their insults—they were the same as they would have been in any corner of the world. Real, magical, surreal—the cats walked through worlds, their essence unchanged.

"You are not *too* stupid to *learn* this," Shadow said, leaving Night and Snow to bicker.

She knew she hadn't spoken aloud. The fact that he answered should have disturbed her—but it's not like she had much privacy as The Terafin, regardless. "I'll have to learn."

"Yessss." His head was at the height of her shoulder, now.

"I really, really want you to go back to your former size."

Night sneezed. Snow's tail narrowly avoided Night's snapping jaws a few seconds later. Jewel glared at them, and they ignored her, but her heart wasn't in it; she turned once again to the table. Shadow shouldered Avandar out of the way and slid between the domicis and Jewel; Shadow was the only one who followed closely as she walked the last few yards to the table itself. There were four chairs at this table; they were also unaltered by the transformation that had overtaken the rest of what could no longer be called a room.

"If you scratch this table," Jewel told the much larger, gray cat, "I will kill you myself."

Shadow hissed.

"The chairs?" Snow asked, sidling up on the right.

"The chairs, too."

She approached the chair at the head of the table; it was the chair in which The Terafin sat when she desired privacy in which to work. Two months, more, she'd been buried— but death didn't change the past, and the past was so strong here it was almost alive. Jewel could no more take that chair than she could have when The Terafin occupied it. She took, instead, the chair to the left—it was, on the occasions she'd been commanded to join The Terafin, hers.

There were almost no scratches on the table's surface; it was oiled to a gleaming shine, especially beneath a midday sky—even a purple one. But there were books on the table, in a haphazard pile, one left open as if the person studying it had taken a momentary break from its dry, procedural words.

And she wanted that woman to come back from stretching her legs, to resume her seat, to focus once again on those words and the work at hand. Her eyes did sting; she closed them for a long moment. When she opened them again, the chair was occupied.

But it was not occupied by The Terafin. Not even her dreams would be that kind.

No, it was occupied by a woman she had seen only a handful of times in her life — and each was burned into memory, like a brand burned skin, claiming forever some part of what it touched.

"Evayne."

"Terafin."

Her face was hooded, but she lifted her hands and drew the folds of midnight from the contours of her face. She was a woman, not a girl; she was not quite of an age with Amarais at the height of her power, but she was close. Her eyes were violet and unblinking, but Jewel thought them a lesser shade of the same color that now adorned the sky — as if the seer were a window and Jewel was looking through its haze.

The cats, bickering and whining about how *unfair* Jewel was, fell instantly silent; they turned — as one, which was always disturbing — toward Evayne. Evayne, however, did not effect to notice their presence. Had she been anyone else, this would have been a poor choice — but there was something about this woman, with her raven hair and its one shock of white, her strong chin, her piercing gaze, that kept even the cats at bay.

Evayne rose. "My apologies," she said. "It has been some time since I have seen this place."

"It's new, to me. New, now," she added.

"And The Terafin's death is also still fresh."

Jewel swallowed and nodded. The desire to cry at the sight of the unexpected familiarity of a simple table and four chairs vanished; she could at least be grateful for that.

"Why are you here?"

Evayne frowned. "What is the date?"

"It's the —" she glanced back at Avandar.

"It is the ninth day of Fabril, in the year four hundred and twenty-eight."

Two days had passed in a landscape that allowed for no

natural passage of time. Evayne nodded. "Terafin." She offered Jewel a very correct bow. It felt wrong; Evayne had
always seemed above the strictly procedural forms of etiquette, to Jewel. "Your surroundings have changed."

"You noticed. Have you seen this room before?"

"I have seen the manse, both before and after. I am here,
I believe, to ask your permission to cross your borders."

Jewel blinked, and the older seer smiled.

"Is it required?"

"It will make my passage simpler, yes. At the moment,
your borders are tenuous; they are ill-defined. It is not the
gravest threat you will face—but the threat you will face is
one I cannot clearly see." As she spoke, she drew the orb
from her robes. It rested in her hands like a luminous, crystal heart. "There are only two possible reasons that the path
is so difficult to see or trace. The first is positive, the second,
markedly less so."

"Tell me about the second."

Evayne lifted a brow. "That was—and is—your way; you
dwell on the darkness."

"I don't. But if those are the two outcomes you sense, it's
the bad one I have to worry about. Or avoid."

"Do you understand what has happened here?" She
glanced at the distant shelves, made of living trees, as she
spoke.

"Yes and no. I understand that I'm connected to these
lands; that they're mine in some visceral way." She fell silent
for a moment, gazing at the surface of a sturdy, fine table
that was nonetheless untouched in all ways by the magic of
transformation. "I had to wake up—and there was only one
way *I* could see to do that at the time."

"An interesting approach," Evayne replied. "This table—"

"Yes. It's real. It's solid. I've seen it used for over a
decade—but it's been *in* use for far longer. Whatever I build
here requires the real at its heart; it's what everything else
is rooted in."

Evayne raised a brow. "You have been speaking," she
said, after a long pause, "with the Warden of Dreams."

"Both of them."

"He has told you more than he generally volunteers."

"He didn't volunteer it in so many words; he relied on

my intuition. I'm seer-born; intuition comes almost naturally."

Shadow coughed. Loudly.

Evayne glanced at Shadow. She seemed entirely unaffected by the cats, and they seemed, in turn, entirely disinterested in her. Since they were only disinterested when they were trying to make a point, this implied that they, at least, had some inkling of who she was.

"Do you know my cats?"

Evayne did not reply, not directly. Instead, she said, "It is an unusual choice."

"Pardon?"

"To allow them this freedom of form; they are almost entirely unbound, here. Do you understand how dangerous they are?"

Jewel nodded, but felt compelled to add, "It's hard to remember, when they're talking. Shadow almost killed me—there's no way to salvage what I was wearing, there's so much damn blood—"

"You are remarkably whole for someone who came close to death in that fashion."

"I had a healer."

"Adam."

Jewel nodded, stiffening.

"He will not be with you for very long, unless there is a disaster." Evayne closed her eyes. "And I have wandered. I did not speak of your manse and your city when I asked if you understood the significance. The path is breaking; what moored it in the hidden wilderness is, as the Oracle predicted, finally crumbling.

"You have met the Warden, and you have met the cats—the cats, at least, I fear you could not avoid, given the nature of your forest—but they are the least of the difficulty that now comes."

Shadow hissed. No, they all hissed, but Shadow was faster off the mark.

"And I become more limited in my travels as we approach the end of the time I have seen." She closed her eyes for a long moment; the orb in her hand began to glow. At its center, clouds folded in on each other, looking a little like milk dropped into golden oil before it reaches the bottom of the glass. "You have gazed into this orb before—although both you and I have changed since then. Will you dare its depths again?"

Jewel shook her head. "I know what I'll see."

Evayne raised a brow. "What do you fear?"

The younger seer laughed. It was a quiet sound, broken in parts by both bitterness and genuine amusement as she met the violet eyes of the elder. "I think I fear your life."

This caused the seer's other brow to join the first one before both descended. She was not insulted, not offended. "There is perhaps much to fear in it, although by the time I had reached your age, I had fully accepted the choice I made as a youth."

"As how old a youth?"

"I was, I think, a year older than you were when you first arrived at the gates of the Terafin manse."

"I was sixteen."

"Ah. Then perhaps I was your age. Exactly sixteen. I am not that girl now, but some part of her remains in me."

Jewel nodded. She placed a palm against the surface of the table; it was cool to the touch, the way shade was cool at the height of midday. "You want me to talk to the Oracle."

"I . . . have my disagreements with the Oracle, and no path that leads to the Oracle is pleasant; no path that leads to the Oracle is painless—if it can be survived at all. But I do not see how you will build what must be built and survive what must be survived unless you make that journey."

"You can't see that future?"

"Not easily, now. It is too close."

"But you . . ."

"Yes." Evayne smiled again. It was odd; Jewel found each smile surprising, as if the face it rested on seldom wore one. "Yes, I am sent from one century to another; I walk between your past, your present and your future as if time is a path on which I am trapped and forced to wander.

"I see death—almost always—and I remember it, and I work to prevent what *can* be prevented. That's simple. It's clean. It's the deaths that can't be prevented, the deaths that *must* occur, that are harder. I confess that I do not understand why I am here today. You are not yet ready to walk the Oracle's path; if I am not mistaken, you will not even be able to find it, yet.

"You are not in danger, and were you, you have all of your escort." She glanced at the table again, and this time, she paused. "Terafin."

"Call me Jewel."

"That is not what you have said in my past and your future."

Jewel folded her hands together to prevent them from trembling. "No, probably not. You don't tend to appear when things are either peaceful or happy. The previous Terafin wasn't easily angered. I am. What I say in anger—"

"Or sorrow, or loss," the seer said softly.

Thinking of Arann and what Lefty's loss had done to him, she said, "Or sorrow, or loss." Her fingers tightened in their loose clasp, as if she were praying. She suddenly knew that she could not be—or do—what Evayne a'Nolan had been and done. No flash of visceral insight followed; she didn't know if Evayne's choices were the right ones or the wrong ones. She only knew they were acts of desperation.

Evayne once again turned her attention to the table—or rather, to the books stacked in a careful pile in front of The Terafin's chair. "Jewel," she said, although it was clear the name did not come easily, "these books—do you recognize them?"

Jewel frowned. "I haven't had a chance to inspect the library; both I and the library only just arrived here. But at least a shelf's worth of books are the same." A creeping anxiety made her turn to look over her shoulder at the shelves she had passed. ". . . I won't know until I'm brave enough to summon the archivists. Why?"

"At least three of these texts are forbidden works."

Jewel frowned. "Forbidden?" The frown opened into something rounder. "You mean, as in forbidden by the Order of Knowledge?"

"Yes. I thought them all destroyed," she added.

"You've seen these books before."

"Yes—but not in the current incarnation of this city." She reached out and touched one page of the open book. Violet light, sharp and sudden, struck both book and reader, encircling them. "I see."

"Evayne, are you—"

"I am unharmed. The book is unharmed."

Jewel quickly approached Evayne's side. This time, all

three of the cats stayed put. They didn't exactly move out of the way, but for the cats, they were positively well-behaved. Evayne withdrew her hand and the light faded—but it was slow to fade, and it left an afterimage, the way sun did if you looked at it for too long.

"What is this book?" Jewel asked, without touching it. She felt—of all things—resentful. No part of her believed that these books had been any part of the Terafin collection. The library had already been so transformed, the sight of a familiar *table* had brought her to the brink of tears.

Evayne didn't reply; Jewel wasn't certain that she had even heard the question. She was staring at a page that seemed to have been written by a man—or woman—in a hurry. The ink was faded but remained dark enough to read; the hand was a strong scrawl in places, but cramped, precise and tiny in others.

"Evayne?" Jewel reached out to touch the older woman's arm to catch her attention; her palm froze an inch from a swath of midnight blue. Evayne's eyes widened as folds of cloth began to rustle at her feet. Jewel quickly withdrew her hand.

"I'm sorry."

"It is . . . not safe . . . to touch me if I am not prepared."

"The robes?"

Evayne nodded.

"I could have used those, once."

"In the streets of a different city," was the quiet reply.

"In the streets of this one." It was a declaration they both understood. "Is it safe?"

Evayne nodded and Jewel brushed past her, but only as far as the table's edge. There, the book lay, two pages exposed, as if it were any other personal journal. There were dates, but she recognized neither the month nor the year; she knew them as dates because of the numbers and the placement—and the numbers, she *did* recognize.

"This looks like Torra."

"Not to my eyes, although perhaps it is a variant of that tongue."

Jewel reached for the book, stopped, and took the chair that she had avoided when she'd first approached the table. There, she sat, and there, she lifted her chin to gaze at the books and the length of the otherwise pristine and unoccupied stretch of gleaming, dark wood. When she reached for the tome, Shadow growled. It was a thing more felt than heard—and everyone heard it.

Remembering the flare of violet, she hesitated. Evayne, however, offered no warning.

"It won't hurt *me*," she finally told the large gray cat.

"Maybe it's not *you* he's worried about," Snow suggested.

She ignored the comment—not always wise when it came to the cats—and reached for the book again. Nothing happened. Her hands were on either side of the book, beneath its oddly textured front and back covers, and there was no resultant light, no flash of magic, nothing. "Maybe it's the chair?"

"Was the chair significant to you?"

"To me? No. But it's where The Terafin sat when she worked at this table. This is where she did most of the work that didn't require constant interruption and visitors."

"That sounds like a yes, in this place."

Jewel set the book down and stood. She then picked it up again; it was, in her hands, a book, no more. "Not the chair."

"No. Can you read the book?"

Jewel closed the book first. The odd texture of the covers against her two palms didn't change in any way, but a cursory examination of the cover made her eyes water. "Do you see it?" She asked Evayne.

"The book? Certainly."

"The light. The magic."

"Yes."

"What *is* it?" She looked to Avandar for the first time since she'd laid eyes on the table in the center of this clearing.

"I do not see as you see, Terafin. I consider it unwise in the extreme to examine that book with magic, but if you wish an attempt made—"

"No," Evayne said, before he could finish. "It is, as you say, unwise in the extreme." But she looked at the cover of the book in silence for a long moment. "If you wish, Terafin, I can hold that book for you against future need."

"You can't touch it without—"

"I would not have to touch it again," she replied. "My

robes were made in the far, far past by an Artisan who . . .
liked to travel, and was often forced to do so in less than
ideal circumstances."

"Is the book dangerous to me?"

"I cannot fully say. Will it harm you directly? No. I am
almost certain it will not. But knowledge has oft been considered dangerous when it is unbalanced, and ancient
knowledge is *never* balanced. The world that existed when
you were born, and the world that existed thousands of
years before it, are not the same."

"Birth and death are."

Evayne nodded. "And to those who lived thousands of
years ago, their world *was* normal, and a room such as this
might exist in manors and caves across the Isle." She
glanced at the amethyst sky. "Your permission, Terafin, to
travel as I must through your lands?"

Shadow hissed before Jewel could answer. "Tell her *no*."

Chapter Ten

"**H**USH, YOU."

He is not wrong, Jewel, the Winter King said. As he spoke, he appeared, walking in a measured, graceful way between two rows of distant shelving, as if emerging from a forest. *Such permission should be granted only in emergency, and only at the direst of need even then.*

Notably, none of her currently human attendants said a word. Jewel's hands fell to hips, which they did when she was getting frustrated; it was her Oma's most frequently adopted posture. "And you don't consider the Lord of the Hells to *be* a dire emergency?"

I would consider him such were he to stand outside of your lands at the head of an army of Kialli.

"We'd like to stop him from ever *reaching* that stage."

Yes, understood.

"People are walking all over my lands as we speak; they'd certainly better be working in the manse in my absence."

Those people you cannot compel. They exist outside of your realm; you may draw them in and trap them there should you desire it; you might contain them permanently. But they are mortal, and the mortals do not bend easily to the subtle magics and rules that bind these lands. The rules are written in a tongue that they cannot read, cannot hear, and could never, therefore, bring themselves to speak.

"Evayne is mortal."

The Winter King turned his gaze upon Evayne; his eyes were round, large, dark—and for a moment, entirely unblinking. To her great surprise, she realized that the Winter King was angry. She glanced at Avandar, and found that he was staring at Evayne in a similar fashion.

"Viandaran," Evayne said softly.

He said nothing.

"Tor Amanion."

It was Jewel's turn to stare, gaze riveted, at the Winter King. He raised his head, reminding everyone present of the tines that were now his only crown.

"I did not lie to you, when we met," Evayne told him softly. "But at least in your case, I do not have to wonder what atrocity I will commit in future to earn your present hatred. You will serve a Lord who will stand, in the end, against the Lord of the Hells, as promised."

"You knew him?" Jewel asked.

"No; that is far too broad a statement. But we have spoken, in the past, and we speak, briefly, now." She left the table's side and walked toward the Winter King, pausing less than two feet from his lifted face. What she said to him, Jewel couldn't hear, and if she received a reply at all, that, too, was lost. But she turned her back upon the Winter King. Given the Winter King's anger, Jewel wouldn't have.

"Your permission, Terafin."

Shadow stepped on Jewel's foot. Jewel ground her teeth.

"She is *dangerous*," the gray cat growled.

"So are *you* and you come and go as you bloody well please."

"You could force them to leave," Evayne said.

"How? They're cats."

"Yes, but they are your cats, at the moment—inasmuch as they are anyone's. If you so chose, you could limit their movement in your lands; you could deny the Winter King; you could order Lord Celleriant into the heart of the wilderness. Without your permission, none could return."

"The god-born?"

"No. And yes. You could force me from your roads if you so chose."

"Because you're a seer?"

"No. Because *my* father is on the plane, and was at my

birth. They are not wrong in their advice; I am a danger, and a threat. Our goals, in a broad sense, overlap, as do our gifts and some of our skills. But there are choices I will make—and have made in the past—that you would never countenance in pursuit of those goals. There are battles and wars that I have seen—and participated in—that you have yet to witness, and if we are very, very lucky, might never occur at all. I have your gift, and you mine, but that is not all that separates us. There is no one, nothing, that I have not considered sacrificing in order to ensure the survival of Man.

"And that will not change, Terafin. Grant your permission, or no, I will do what I must."

"You already know that I've granted you that permission."

Evayne said nothing.

"You have to know, if you've seen my lands in the future, unless you haven't been able to walk them. Why are you even here to ask at all?"

"Because permission, now, must be granted."

"And you couldn't have asked as a younger Evayne? You faced a *god* when you were ten years younger than I am now."

"I do not choose the age at which I appear, Jewel. But had I been younger, had I dared to touch that book as I did today, it would have taken months to recover—if I could recover at all. The robes are not proof against injury, and my power at that age was so new I might have lit a fire in my own defense, no more."

Is this how we change the future? Jewel thought, watching Evayne in silence. *Is this a game that I want to play, given what's at stake?*

"Terafin," Avandar said. "You must come to a decision. If time does not pass in a recognizable way in the hidden realm, it passes—quickly—in this one; the Kings will need to know that you have once again resumed your duties; The Ten will likewise need to be informed."

"Understood." She hadn't taken her eyes off Evayne's shuttered expression. "I want you to explain something to me before I grant what you ask."

"There are matters of which I am forbidden speech," Evayne replied, "although perhaps that will matter less in the scant years remaining."

"You've seen this book before."

The seer nodded.

"Where?"

Evayne turned toward the Winter King. "With your permission, Tor Amanion?"

The Winter King inclined his head as he turned to face Jewel. Jewel, who rode him, who listened to his advice even when it was frequently unwelcome.

"In the Tor Amanion," Evayne said, after a pause. "In the Sanctum of the Sen."

"Give her the book," Avandar said. No one else had yet spoken a word, not even the cats. "Give the book into her keeping, Terafin."

Jewel's grip on the heavy volume tightened.

"I will guarantee that that book was no part of the library of the former Terafin—any one of them. No more are the other books now placed with such haphazard care upon this table, and should Sigurne Mellifas happen upon them, you will place the whole of your House in grave danger."

Jewel shook her head instinctively in denial. "I think we may need them."

"And the book you now hold?"

"I don't know, Avandar."

"She'll keep it," Angel said, braving words beneath these unnatural, open skies. "I know that tone of voice. Tor Amanion is an Annagarian city?"

"I think," Jewel replied, "that Tor Amanion must have been one of the cities that once existed where the desert now stands. It doesn't exist now. I don't know what the Sanctum of the Sen is—or was." She couldn't, at this point, guess. But she could guess that the Winter King had once ruled that city. He had never offered her the name he had used when he had been a ruler of men, and even having heard it, she could not bring herself to use it—because in order to *be* the Winter King, he would have had to walk away from everything he had managed to build.

I did not build that city, he told her, his voice soft. *I did not found it. But I ruled it, in my time, and yes, Terafin, I left it for the Winter Queen. For the Wild Hunt. For the Winter.*

What she heard in his voice then, she had never heard before, and she almost took a step back at the force of it, although the words were so soft. "Do you recognize the book?"

No. Caution plays little part in my history, he added, with just a glimmer of humor. *If it is safe with anyone, it is safe with Evayne—but safety has never been her concern. She is, in her fashion, worthy of admiration.*

I know what you consider worthy of admiration.

Yes.

"Yes," she said, gazing at Evayne. "You have my permission. While you work to prevent the Lord of the Hells from transforming the world into the hells, you can come and go at need."

Shadow hissed; Jewel placed one palm between his eyes.

Before Evayne moved, Celleriant raised voice. Jewel had almost forgotten he was present, and given his stature, that was hard to do. "Seer."

Evayne nodded, as if she'd expected the interruption, or had been waiting for it.

"What of the Summer Court?"

Evayne bowed her head. "There is no Summer Court."

Celleriant drew one sharp breath; his hands were fists, his knuckles paler than his fair skin. "I am . . . aware of that. But—"

"Ariane cannot convene that Court now. There is no path that leads to it, and there will be none until—unless—she is given the last of the Summer trees."

"There is one?"

"There is," Evayne replied.

Celleriant closed his Winter eyes.

"But Lord Celleriant, there is only one. Against need, against all hope, it has been gathered; it sleeps at the behest of the bard-born until the appointed moment."

"And who appoints that moment," he said sharply, opening those eyes again, "If not the Summer Queen?"

Evayne made no reply. "My gratitude, Terafin, for permission to traverse your lands. May I give you no cause to regret it."

Jewel said nothing; she knew that there were events in life which caused sorrow and regret for all concerned—friend or foe. And she knew, watching Evayne's completely composed expression, knew it in a way that she knew breath or sleep or hunger, that had the salvation of the world rested on the shoulders of Jewel Markess ATerafin, The Terafin, it would crumble into tortured ruin.

She could not ever be or do what this woman had.

I will hate her for it, Jewel thought. But she thought it without vehemence.

"Evayne."

Evayne said, "You do not understand the significance of the ring you wear."

Jewel glanced at the Terafin signet. And then, drawn by something in Evayne's voice, she lifted the other hand; on it, she wore the signet of House Handernesse.

"Yes, that ring. It is not that it is on your hand, or even that it reached the hand of Amarais before you; it was the ring Ararath wore on the final night of his life—but even that signifies little. You found it," she continued, when Jewel failed to speak.

"He was wearing this ring when he died?" she finally managed.

"As I said, it signifies little."

She felt her hands take the shape of fists, which was inconvenient because she almost dropped the book she was holding. She set it on the table. When she looked up again, Evayne a'Nolan was gone.

Getting out of the library should have been difficult, because there was no obvious far wall in which the regular doors were embedded. There was, at the moment, a stretch of open floor, with a table, four chairs and a fountain in the distance. As it was, it took ten minutes, five of those occupied by Jewel's attempt not to say any of what she was now thinking. Her hands were shaking in exactly the wrong way; it had been half a life since she'd last seen Rath, but at this moment, he was the only thing on her mind.

And he couldn't be. He couldn't remain that way. But— Evayne knew how, and where, he had died. Jewel was as certain of it as she'd been certain of anything in her life. *Does it matter?* She told herself, jaws clenching around pointless words. *He's dead. How he died, where he died— does it really matter?*

The answer was no. Of course not.

But it was also *yes*, and the yes was more visceral. She was aware on most days that people made little sense, and today, she was going to be one of them, although she struggled to be fair. How much did she care about the death of a stranger?

"Jewel," Avandar said quietly. She raised her head; Avandar never called her by her name in front of other people—and the Chosen were here.

He attempted to gain your attention by referring to your correct title, the Winter King told her. *And Viandaran is only willing to pursue correct form so often before he chooses the practical, instead.*

"Apologies, Avandar," she said, stiffly, because that was how she could speak at the moment. "I was distracted."

"It is past time to return to the manse and the right-kin's office."

She nodded, although her hands were still clenched. She almost asked him how—how to leave the new library, how to return to the manse—but the Chosen *were* here. Instead, she began to walk, casting one glance at the table as she moved around it. She heard birdsong. In the library. She wondered if these deep, purple skies shed rain—that would be a disaster, given the lack of a roof.

But . . . she liked the light, and after the initial shock of seeing the trees growing out of wooden slat flooring, she liked the shelving. She liked the sound of the fountain; it reminded her of the healerie, in the old days, when she had had the time to visit Alowan.

She walked past them, through the wide gaps between shelves, and paused to retrieve a fallen leaf. When she rose, she continued to walk. Angel was once again on her right; Avandar on her left. The cats were snarling at each other in the rear, which meant the Chosen were, for the moment, free of harassment. When they cleared the shelving, there was no wall—but a standing arch, made of delicate filigreed black iron, waited some yards ahead. It was not a doorframe; it didn't contain doors. Vines were wrapped around its posts, and small, white blossoms adorned them.

"This is the exit," she said. She walked toward it, lifted a hand to touch the flowers, as if uncertain they were real; they were. Through the arch itself, she could see the familiar halls of the manse proper. The lighting there was dimmer; it seemed unnatural in comparison.

Letting her shoulders slide down her back as she readjusted her posture, she took a step through the arch.

"I hope Levec and Adam found their way out," Angel said, as he appeared, once again, to her right.

Jewel's eyes widened.

"I believe that the transformation had not yet occurred," Avandar replied, from her left. "Had it, I am certain Levec would have returned—in angry haste—to your room."

From this side of the hall, the doors looked like normal doors. The Chosen joined them a few seconds later, the cats almost literally on their feet. The Chosen stationed on the normal side of the doors saluted Torvan.

"As you were," Torvan replied. "They're the same winged cats—just larger."

As if to drive this point home, Night stepped heavily on Snow's tail. Jewel did not tell either of the two to shut up or play nicely, because the reaction of the Chosen had been—for the Chosen—extreme. The residents of the House had had a few months to get used to the cats in their previous incarnation—and they'd done it because the cats never shut up and always insulted each other where at all possible. These cats had lower voices, longer, more prominent fangs, and longer claws; they were taller by at least a head, and probably weighed significantly more.

But they *sounded* the same if you listened to their words, and frankly, when they were being pissy with each other, the only way to avoid hearing them was to plug your ears and run.

Lord Celleriant and the Winter King chose to remain in the library when Jewel was forced—by her awareness of the demands of a House that had probably held its collective breath for at least two days—to leave it.

The halls of the manse were exactly as she remembered them; given the mess that was the bedroom, this wasn't as comforting as it should have been. Nothing in the halls, and nothing in the public gallery seemed unnatural, though, and the window into the Courtyard showed an exterior world that felt stolid and real. The hangings and paintings had not magically been made over, and the servants all looked familiar—or better.

Word of her presence had obviously been carried from the doors that led to her personal chambers to the rest of the manse at large; she could almost *touch* the relief she saw in the various servants, it was so palpable. Even the altered size and the shape of the cats did nothing to dampen it.

The right-kin's office was not, as she'd half-hoped it would be, empty. There were guests in the various chairs in the external room, and Barston, as always, behind his desk. He rose when the doors opened and he saw who stood in their frame. He also bowed. It wasn't necessary, although given her current station, it couldn't be considered simpering or obsequious.

"Terafin."

"My apologies, Barston. I imagine the right-kin has much of import to discuss."

"Indeed. If you will follow, I am certain he will see you now." The last three words were louder; they had to be. Snow and Night had reached the point of shouting. It drew the attention of everyone else in the room; Barston had had decades with which to perfect the art of ignoring the unworthy and failed, in any other way, to notice them.

He led the way past the seated visitors, knocked on the very closed doors, and opened them without waiting for a reply. There were two House Guards bracketing the door.

Jewel entered the room, which was not unoccupied. Teller, she'd expected. She had not expected Sigurne Mellifas or Meralonne APhaniel, although the latter, at least, should have come as no surprise; she'd practically given him permission to live on the grounds without interference.

Sigurne offered Jewel a bow.

Meralonne bowed as well. The fact that no pipe graced the mage's hand was a clear indication that the guildmaster was not in the best of tempers. Jewel signed, quickly and briefly.

Teller's response was a nod. None of his frustration reached his expression. Neither did the profound relief his gesture had conveyed. Sleeping for three days—and bleeding profusely on the edge of death while doing so—might happen all the time in the Terafin manse, given the neutral cast of his face.

He did not bow. He inclined his head, and even that was

a gesture offered familiar equals. It made a point—but Jewel wasn't certain to whom. She turned to the cats and said, each syllable clearly annunciated, "Now is *not* the time."

They fell silent.

Winged cats, over the past two months, had become rather commonplace in the manse. Winged cats that were now half again as heavy, and more obviously fanged and clawed, were not. Sigurne lifted one brow.

Jewel entered the room and moved quickly toward Teller, passing between the visitors to do so. Avandar followed her; Angel took up position by the door, a position that became crowded as the Chosen entered.

Gabriel's office had always been a large one. Today, she understood why.

"Terafin," Teller said.

"I need to reschedule the meeting of The Ten," she told him, without apology or preamble.

He nodded. "The Kalakar and The Morriset have made themselves available for a Council of The Ten at your earliest convenience; they require only notification of the time."

Two of nine. Jewel kept her grimace to herself and nodded.

Exhaling, she turned to Sigurne. "Matteos is not in attendance?"

"Matteos is in attendance in my Tower." Sigurne smiled. It was a small, wintry smile of a type that didn't generally adorn her face. "Meralonne, however, is to be in attendance while I am on the Terafin grounds, unless an emergency of a magical nature demands his presence." A nod to his position as the Terafin House Mage. "Rumors of your demise were greatly exaggerated."

"Not greatly," Jewel replied. She felt Avandar's disapproval.

I was absent from a full Council of The Ten; I was absent from a command performance with the Exalted. I understand that you feel acknowledgment of any danger or threat weakens me—but not even Amarais could have missed either of those meetings without cause.

"You were asleep." It was not a question.

"I was. I am awake now. The waking was of my volition; I will not sleep again in a like fashion."

"The Houses of Healing will be interested in this."

"They will, indeed. I have already had some contact with Levec."

Sigurne winced. "You have my profound sympathies. A man less likely to be a healer could not be found if one searched for decades." She glanced at the cats, who had been almost preternaturally still *and* silent. "They are much changed."

"They are. It wasn't my choice," she added, in a softer voice.

"Do you have control of their appearance?"

She wanted to say no, but did not. Nor did Sigurne repeat the question when an answer failed to materialize. "How bad is it?" Jewel asked, instead.

Sigurne lifted a white brow, and then glanced at Meralonne. "Yes," she told him, in a more irritable—and therefore more familiar—tone of voice. "You may smoke, if that is acceptable to the right-kin and The Terafin.

"The Exalted *are* extremely concerned. Because they are concerned, the Kings are likewise concerned."

"What has happened to increase their concern?" she asked. She wasn't certain she would receive an answer now; she was certain one would be forthcoming when she traveled to *Avantari* to meet with the Exalted.

"You will no doubt be informed soon. Am I permitted to ask what occurred?"

Shadow growled. Jewel turned and said, "If you cannot be civil, you will wait outside. Outside," she added quickly, "in the hall. You are not to terrorize any guest who is not currently—and obviously—attempting to kill me. Is that clear?"

The growling abated; the lecture she'd half-expected failed to follow. Shadow was watching Sigurne as if she were a truly inimitable foe; it was unsettling. Snow and Night had remained silent, but she noted, as she glanced at them, that they were watching Sigurne as well.

"You are permitted to ask," Jewel replied, as if the correction of the cats hadn't actually happened. "But given the circumstances—and the confusion that surrounds them—I would ask for more time to prepare a comprehensive reply. It will no doubt be required by the Exalted and the Kings, and you will no doubt be in attendance at that meeting."

Sigurne inclined her head; it was the answer she expected. She turned to Teller and offered him the nod that passed between polite equals. "ATerafin. Our apologies for taking up so much of your time."

Teller returned the grave nod, but added a smile. "Given the list of visitors to the office, Guildmaster Mellifas, your presence was a blessing."

"Meralonne?"

"If it pleases you, Guildmaster, I will remain. I have a few questions to ask The Terafin."

Jewel nodded assent.

"Very well. I believe Matteos will forgive you if you fail to escort me to the Order."

One platinum brow rose in obvious dismissal of Matteos Corvel. Jewel had never entirely understood the relationship between the two guild members. Sigurne passed between the cats without apparent concern. She paused before she opened the door. "Terafin."

"Sigurne." It was painful to Jewel to keep her distance from the Guildmaster of the Order of Knowledge; she was an older woman with a spine of steel, a pragmatism born of harsh experience and an utter lack of desire to accumulate power for its own sake—and she reminded Jewel of her Oma, a woman given to much harsher phrasing.

Sigurne Mellifas said, "While it is not likely that the subject will arise when you venture into *Avantari*, I feel it is germane. There have been odd reports that have emerged from the Western Kingdoms and the trade routes into Arrend."

"Odd reports?"

"Unusual sightings."

Jewel waited.

"And at least two unexplained disappearances."

"When?"

"The exact dates are not yet known. The Order of Knowledge has sent out its investigators from the Western Kingdoms; they are less easily sent into Arrend."

"Sigurne—what was reported? Demons?"

"Ah, no. Demons, of course, would be taken seriously—but as we are aware that we face the demonic, they would cause vastly less unease in some quarters. We are not entirely certain that we do *not* face the demonic; demons are not entirely confined in the shape they take when they materialize upon the plane. It is our hope that they will prove to be demonic."

"But it's not your expectation."

"You are, as expected, perceptive. No, Terafin, it is not my expectation—nor is it the expectation of Member APhaniel. I would be obliged to you if you would cede him to this investigation for—"

"I am not interested, Sigurne." Meralonne accompanied his flat statement with smoke rings and a look of implacable boredom.

"Meralonne," Jewel began.

"I am not interested, Terafin. The source of the request matters little."

"If there are demons working on the roads to—and from—the Western Kingdoms, you have the best chance of discerning their location and nature."

He nodded. "I do not believe they are demons."

"What *exactly* was described?"

Sigurne pursed her lips. "Unicorns."

Jewel would have laughed, but the guildmaster's expression robbed the single word of the humor it should have contained: there was an unutterable weariness in the older woman's eyes, as if this—this impossibility was the final straw, a weight that she could not lift, could not carry, toward her journey's inevitable conclusion.

"Unicorns," Meralonne repeated, "and a single great, golden stag."

"You both believe that what was reported has some bearing on the truth." The last word was meant to rise in tone, to make the words a question; it didn't. The sentence came out as flat and unadorned as Sigurne's single word.

"Yes, Terafin." Meralonne examined the bowl of his pipe. "We do."

Sigurne left the office.

When she was gone, Teller rearranged the books on the shelf closest to the window. His movements were economical and deliberate; Jewel studied those volumes and their order and saw the subtle nimbus of magic: orange and violet. He caught her watching and lifted a brow.

"I don't *like* her," Shadow announced.

"Well, *I* do."

"She is dangerous."

"We're all dangerous."

Snow hissed. He was laughing. "Teller isn't dangerous," he said, strolling across the room to where Teller had just finished rearranging the shelves. He almost knocked the right-kin over in his demand for instant attention; Teller, trained by his own small—and thankfully nonverbal—cats dropped a hand to Snow's white head. His brows rose. "They're softer," he said.

She waited until Teller finished, although she cleared her throat to indicate it should happen soon.

"Meralonne, *unicorns*? Seriously?"

"I assume you are underslept and addled, so I will take no offense at your obvious attempt to belittle my opinion. Nor will I evince the annoyance your skepticism richly deserves—although I will say, Terafin, that were you my student and not my employer, more than harsh words would now be exchanged." He turned to meet Shadow's intent and unblinking gaze. "I see you have recovered some of your physical majesty. It does not help your master."

"It *will*."

Jewel grimaced and approached Teller, who had come to stand to one side of his desk, rather than taking refuge—as Gabriel so often did—behind it. "Can you reach The Ten?"

Teller smiled. He indicated a stack of meticulously penned papers to his right. "They require your signature and your seal as official correspondence between the rulers of The Ten, and not their internal offices."

"What date did I agree on?"

"You offered tomorrow at dawn—or at any time of the day. The specifics of the time would need to be negotiated, but in this circumstance, I believe The Ten will abide by any firm time you choose; one or two may quibble."

She exhaled. "Of course." They'd quibble in a burning building instead of saving the argument for the open—and safe—air. "Do you have any idea of the timing for the audience the Exalted are demanding?"

"Requesting," was his automatic correction. "Due to the nature of your illness, they have left the timing open. They have, however, been forceful in their request to see you at your earliest possible convenience."

"Where convenience is defined as breathing, awake, and mobile?"

"I believe mobility is not their concern; if you are both breathing and awake, they will no doubt offer to arrange suitable conveyance."

Jewel's brows rose, and then she laughed. "You sound just like Barston."

He smiled. "It's come in useful. I don't know what I would have done these past three days without him."

"I'm sorry," she whispered.

He turned instantly to her, but before he could speak, Avandar cleared his throat. Loudly. Teller withdrew immediately, the concern and the brief vulnerability once again buried beneath the face—the adult face—of the right-kin of House Terafin. Jewel took a few moments to do the same, but honestly, she resented the effort more; there was no one dangerous in the room.

Meralonne APhaniel is present, Avandar told her, his internal voice heated and sharp.

I've known him since I was sixteen. He hasn't changed at all.

No. He has not. But he will. *He is what he is, and unless— and until—you receive from him, in full measure, the vow you received from Lord Celleriant, you* will *practice caution.*

Meralonne cleared his throat, in much the same fashion as Avandar had done. "You were lost on the hidden path." It wasn't a question.

"I wasn't lost," she replied. "I ran into the Warden of Dreams."

His brows rose and his pipe stilled as he stared at her; she could have grown an extra head to less effect. He approached her, and to her surprise, Avandar quickly stepped between them.

Meralonne's eyes narrowed, replacing surprise with something akin to annoyance, but more dangerous. "Viandaran."

"Illaraphaniel."

Gods damn it. "*Gentlemen.*"

They both turned to look at her. Shadow snickered.

"The Warden of Dreams," she continued, her voice as even as her Oma's would have been—and about as friendly. "Is now forbidden access to these lands—but the sleepers still need to be disentangled from the dreaming and returned to themselves." She folded her arms across her chest.

"You . . . spoke with the Warden of Dreams."

"Yes. Both of him." When he failed to reply, she said, "Meralonne, you told me to find him. You told me to—"

"Terafin, do you understand what he is?"

"No." She almost added, *and I don't care*, because it was viscerally true. But it wasn't helpful. "And yes. He's the child of the gods that once walked the world. He lives only on the hidden path, or in the hidden lands. The sleeping sickness was caused by him."

"And you have driven him from the lands in your keeping."

She nodded.

"How?"

"They're *my* lands."

"The rumors were true, then."

"Which ones?"

"You were asleep for almost three days; you could not be woken."

She glanced at Teller, whose face was a marvel of inscrutability.

"They were true. They will never be relevant again, but they were true."

"How did you wake?"

She thought he knew. "Does it matter? I am awake now, and I will not sleep in a like fashion again."

"It matters, Terafin. Sigurne was not present because you slept; Levec was called—by the House—which furthered speculation about your fate."

"The magi *have* been involved in the fate of the sleepers," Jewel replied.

"They have been peripherally involved as observers. But as I said, it was not because of those rumors that Sigurne traveled to the manse today."

"Then why?"

"You are aware that I am a member of the Council of the Magi?"

She nodded.

"A mage of the First Circle?"

She nodded again, failing to see significance in either statement.

"You are also aware that I have chosen to devote myself to House Terafin as its House Mage."

"I am aware that you are the Terafin House Mage, yes."

"Some shift has occurred within the manse, Terafin."

"What do you mean, shift?"

"I feel that you are in a position to answer that question far, far more accurately than even I."

She stared at him. Turned to Avandar. "Is there some difference, besides the obvious, in the manse?"

"I have been with you, Terafin. I have had no call to examine the magics upon the rest of the manse."

"No, you have not. But *I* have—and as I have been granted blanket permission in things magical, I have done so. Some of the containing magics, and one of the most complicated contingencies, have been utterly destroyed; no hint of their prior existence can be found at all."

"Could another mage—"

"No. Not the last one. It was removed. It was . . . unraveled, Terafin."

"How would one normally remove an enchantment?"

Meralonne and Avandar exchanged a glance. "If one was the enchanter, it would be trivial," the domicis said. "If not, it is possible—but most enchantments of that nature are created to collapse in more obvious ways. We can safely assume that Member APhaniel was not the architect of the spell's dismantling."

She frowned. "Was the spell the one that exists in the chambers of the Chosen?"

"Very good," the mage replied, in exactly the tone of voice one would use on a difficult student. He had used far, far less respectful tones with Amarais herself; Jewel didn't expect better. She looked across the room to Torvan. "Captain?"

Torvan nodded. "The loss of the enchantment was of concern, given the circumstances."

"I didn't remove the enchantment."

"You did not deliberately remove it," Meralonne replied. He emptied his pipe and returned it to his pouch. "But it is no longer extant. Any attempt to recreate it—and it is an arduous casting—has met with . . . resistance."

"The enchantments in the right-kin's office are functional."

He raised a brow. "They are. Terafin, what have you done?"

She started to say *I don't know*, but what came out instead was, "I made my lands secure." And then, because she knew Meralonne APhaniel would serve her for some time yet, she added, "Let us adjourn to my personal quarters."

Avandar stiffened, but didn't demur.

Teller left strict instructions with Barston, but their tone was more plea than command. Barston looked slightly pained, but didn't correct the right-kin in public; given the slight downward turn of Teller's shoulders as he left his own office, private correction would be forthcoming.

"I'm sorry," he told her. "I won't have much time. I have an appointment in half an hour."

"With?"

"A very important representative of one of the merchant houses."

She nodded, aware that the world didn't come to a grinding halt for her own emergencies. It hadn't come to a halt during the darkest of Hendens, either.

Meralonne was silent as they traversed the grand and public halls; he was silent when they mounted the wide stairs that led to The Terafin's chambers. The silence assumed an entirely different quality when they at last entered the very ordinary doors that led to the library—and the rest of the interior rooms that she hadn't fully examined. Had he been carrying his pipe, she was suddenly certain he would have dropped it. She had never seen Meralonne adopt the expression that transformed his face.

The Winter King was there to greet them when they emerged into the forest of books beneath a sky that had not shifted significantly in color; Celleriant was not.

He is exploring the library, the Winter King told her. *He is not entirely certain it is safe.*

Nor was she.

The cats, however, fanned out when they emerged beneath the canopy of that sky; Night actually took to the air. She watched as he flexed wings and haunches, leaping upward as if intent on pouncing. Nothing met him in mid-air.

"Nothing *yet*," Snow told her. He was much more desultory in his own flight, but he joined the black cat in the air above. Shadow chose to stay by her side, a mixed blessing at best.

"Jewel," Meralonne said, his face upturned, his eyes like silver coins in the ivory of his face.

"I didn't choose the sky," she said. "I didn't choose the shelving; I certainly didn't choose the dimensions of the room." It wasn't even technically *a* room anymore, although it seemed to occupy the same space as the previous library had, at least as far as the manse itself was concerned.

"And you wonder why the gods are concerned."

"Since no one ran from here to the Exalted to *tell them* what happened to my library, yes, I do."

"No one needed to do so," he replied, slowly lowering his gaze, although it didn't return to Jewel. It went, instead, to the shelving made of living trees. "The books were not harmed?"

Since it had been her first concern, she didn't begrudge the question. "I won't know until I'm willing to let the archivists examine the collection—if any of the archivists are still willing to work here at all. I imagine they'll find it unsettling."

"I can assure you," he said, as he began to walk toward the shelves, "that if your archivists are too timid, there are at least a dozen highly qualified members of the Order of Knowledge who would willingly offer their services. You would not even be required to pay them—although it would further tarnish your reputation among the guild's membership."

She froze as she recalled the books that now lay across the table in what she assumed was the library's heart. "I don't think that would be possible."

"Oh?" He did turn to face her then.

"Some of the—not all of the books here—were here before the—before I—"

Avandar raised a hand to the bridge of his nose; Shadow snickered. Teller, however, offered her a very brief gesture of sympathy. It was all he could spare. "Does it rain here?" he asked, in a hushed voice.

"I don't know. I hope not."

"That is likely to depend on Jewel," Meralonne said, dispensing entirely with formality at her expense. "But I gather that not all of the books in your current collection existed in the collection you inherited from The Terafin."

"No. At least not that I'm aware of. I didn't spend a lot of time in the library, and very little of it involved searching the stacks."

They reached the first row of shelving. Meralonne spared these books a glance, no more; they were, his cursory gesture made clear, of little interest. These, she thought, were likely to have been owned by The Terafin or her predecessors. He continued to walk, and she let him. Snow and Night didn't land, but Shadow was clearly amused enough at her discomfort that he felt no need to join them in their careening flight. It wasn't silent, either; they were trying to occupy the same patch of sky, with predictable results.

They cleared the shelving and entered the wide, empty plane of wooden slats, table, chairs, and a fountain. It was to the fountain that Meralonne went, which surprised Jewel, because the books were still in an ungainly pile on the table, all save one, which lay open, as it was left.

When he reached the fountain, he paused. She expected him to draw pipe; he did not. Instead, he bowed head a moment; his hair suddenly broke free of its braid. She had seen this happen a number of times, but all of them had involved combat; there was no danger here.

But wind came, as if summoned. She heard no voice, felt no animosity, none of the presence she associated with the wild, the elemental, air—but absent these, it still lifted Meralonne's hair, trailing strands across his upturned cheeks.

When he finally turned, his eyes were wide, clear, bright. "You do not recognize this fountain."

"No." She had barely looked at the table the first time, caught instead by the table, by Evayne, by the amethyst skies, the strange but familiar cats, the trees—the things that had changed her life in ways she knew she hadn't yet begun to fully understand.

"Come, Jewel. Leave the books; they are yours, if I understand what I have seen correctly, and they will not vanish. You have seen the marvel that the library has become, but you have failed to understand what it presages. Come."

She joined him. Angel, silent in a way that made him almost invisible in spite of his hair, came with her, as did

Teller. Avandar stood back, and to her surprise, Shadow stayed with him. Meralonne glanced at the three of them, and something in the look — not condescension, and not the arrogance so often adopted by the mage-born — made Jewel once again feel as if she, Angel, and Teller had just arrived at the front gates of the manse in their terrified flight from the streets of the twenty-fifth holding. Young, she thought. Young, shadowed by death, but still caught by desperate, frenzied hope.

He smiled, as if he could hear what she would never again put into words. "Right-kin," he said, granting Teller the respect of title and station. "What do you see when you look at this fountain? Do you see a fountain?"

Teller frowned; his hands folded into a brief question.

Yes, she signed back. *Real.*

"A fountain."

"Describe it for me."

Teller took a breath; Angel signed, wait. To Meralonne, Angel said, "We'll answer your questions." It wasn't an offer.

Meralonne raised a brow.

"If you tell us, in turn, what you see."

At that, the mage smiled. It was a strange smile; it felt like arrogance would feel if it were charming, natural, inevitable. It felt almost like the smile of a god. "Very well. But I would hear your answer first."

"I see a fountain. It's stone, and it's larger than it looked at a distance."

"And?"

"The stone is rough. It looks old."

"In the center?"

"I see a . . . a pillar? I think its the rough shape of a man, but it's hard to tell; it looks unfinished. The water is falling from its hands; its hands are lifted."

"It?"

"I can't tell if it's a small man or a woman; there are no distinguishing characteristics; I think it's meant to be wearing robes — but honestly, it doesn't have a face."

Angel was watching Teller carefully. He said nothing, but Meralonne was magi; he noticed the way in which that nothing was significant. His brows folded in curiosity. "ATerafin."

Jewel said, "He's not ATerafin."

"Is he not?"

"No."

"Ah. My apologies."

"No apologies are necessary," she replied, because his apology had been offered to her, not to Angel. "He could have taken the House Name at any time he wanted it in the last sixteen years."

"There is clearly a tale in that," Meralonne replied, inclining his head. "And it may be, in the end, that his tale is entwined in yours."

Her brows rose. "Is there any question? *All* of our stories are entwined."

"Not all are entwined in the same way." He turned to Angel. "My apologies, Angel. I am unaware of your formal name, and will use the familiar in its place if that does not cause offense."

Angel nodded. He was staring at the fountain.

"What do you see?"

"Water."

"Water?"

"It's not a fountain, to my eyes—not the way Teller sees it."

"To your eyes?"

"It's a well."

Meralonne's brows rose. "You were not born and raised in the city." It wasn't a question.

"No." It had been a long time since mention of the Free Towns made Angel flinch, but his expression was somber; the echoes of old losses could be seen in the downturn of his lips, the brief, slight gather of his brows. "No. There's a chain," he said. "The well looks old to me—old, but solid; the stones are worn in the direction we're facing. There's a bucket," he added, "attached to the chain; it's a large bucket, and it definitely looks as if it needs replacement. Sun-bleached, the wood is warped." He shook his head. Jewel knew that he had used a well similar to this in his time, although it surprised her. She knew very, very little about life in a farming village.

"Jay." Angel turned toward her. A smile touched his face, adding to the aura of loss, instead of alleviating it. She knew the expression; it came to her when she thought of her

Oma. Or of Duster. She signed; he signed back. "What do you see?"

"I see a fountain," she replied.

"Same as Teller's?"

She shook her head. "It's made of stone, yes. But it's edged in iron, as if the outer edge is meant to be a bench. The iron isn't solid; it's worked, and there's a pattern in the flat that looks almost like a—a sculpture." She hesitated, and then said, "There are gems in the iron. They're set in either silver or—some other metal; they're large, and they're not all the same." She approached the iron edging and frowned.

"It is not iron," Meralonne said softly.

"It's black, like wrought-iron fences are black." She reached out to touch it, but stopped just shy of contact. "This is diamond," she said, pointing instead. "That's ruby. That's sapphire, I think. That one is amethyst, that's beryl. Topaz. Pink diamond, blue diamond." She wasn't certain about the colored diamonds, but the light they caught and reflected was bright enough, strong enough. "Pretty fancy bench. The Kings could sit on it and be at home."

"No," Meralonne said, "they could not. You have not finished. What do you see in the fountain's center?"

She hesitated for a long moment, as if this were a test and failure would cause a loss of face so profound it would injure all aspects of her future. She forced herself to let the fear go. She was Terafin, yes, but she was no longer walking a path prescribed by the experience of any other ruler of this House—not even the Terafin spirit himself; ignorance was, must, be assumed and accepted. There was only one way to alleviate ignorance.

Who had said that? Not her Oma, a woman who expected common sense to be a birth trait, and took its lack as a personal insult. Ah, she thought. Rath. Rath had said it.

So many ghosts, here. "I see water," she told the mage. "It's contained by the shape of the fountain—and it's falling—but it's not falling *from* anything. I can't hear its voice," she added. "If there's a statue in its center, I can't see it—but small man or woman is wrong for the length of its fall."

The words did not trouble Meralonne.

"What do you see, APhaniel?" Angel asked softly.

"Winter," he replied.

"The water's not frozen."

"No. But fountains such as this did not freeze in the Winter and did not evaporate in the Summer. Do you understand what this is?"

A glance was passed around the three den-kin as if it were too hot to retain. It was Teller who spoke first, and Jewel was aware that it shouldn't have been. "It was made by the maker-born."

"Indeed," was the soft reply. "By an Artisan, if I am not mistaken."

"I haven't seen enough of an Artisan's work to judge." Teller bent and touched the surface of rippling water with the tips of tentative fingers. Meralonne did not object. "I have seen some of the work of the maker-born; the fountain on the terrace is one such piece."

"It is not the only such piece within the manse, but it is the most public, and the most notable. This," he added softly, "was gifted to Terafin."

"How do you know?" Jewel asked, bending in turn to touch the water. It was so cold she wondered that it wasn't frozen.

"I can see the maker's mark," he replied. "It is not a wonder to me that you cannot, although given your gift, there was a chance that you might."

"Is it magical in nature?"

"It is, of course, magical in nature—the workings of the Artisans always are. But it is not a magic that is simple or mechanistic, and there are very, very few of the mage-born who might achieve its like, should they devote their time and energy to replicate it."

"Are all Artisan works so marked?"

"No, ATerafin. Only the works that are made in the wilderness, and they are marked as a courtesy and a warning. As a courtesy," he continued, before anyone could ask, "to those who might assume such artifacts the detritus of the passage of ancient gods, and as a warning, in the same measure: they are made for a purpose, and that purpose is not . . . mine, in this case.

"The Artisans," he continued, after an unbroken pause, "are as close to the gods as it is given any creature in this world to be. They are driven, and they are wild, vessels for their talent and its strange compulsion. But if they possess some small part of the power the gods once possessed, they are nonetheless mortal. It has never been clear to me whether or not they work at the insistence of the echoes of the gods' lingering voices, or from a compulsion entirely their own."

She said, "Fabril made this."

Chapter Eleven

ONE BROW ROSE. Or rather, five brows, but only one was Meralonne's. "You are certain?"

She nodded. "I can't see the mark. I trust that there is one — but it doesn't matter. Fabril made this."

"Yes. And he gifted it, if I am not mistaken, to The Terafin of the time. It has waited long to be revealed. Do you understand its purpose?"

"No."

"No more do I, before you ask. But it is a work, Jewel. On some level, he must have known what your House would face." He exhaled, a strange, small smile at play around the corners of his lips. Although nothing about his appearance had markedly changed, he looked wild, elemental; she would not have been surprised to see him draw sword, here. Sword, armor, even horn.

"You will have to arm them," he told her softly. "If they are to walk your lands, they will need arms, armor."

She shook her head, knowing that he spoke of the Chosen, her den — the people who lived in the manse and who worked to defend it in all ways, some subtle and some markedly less so. "They're armed, Meralonne."

"They are not —"

"They *are*. It was not Lord Celleriant who injured the Warden of Dreams: it was Torvan, one of the Captains of the Chosen."

"Impossible."

"No, Member APhaniel, it's not. The weapons wielded by the Warden of Dreams were not the weapons wielded by the *Arianni* or the *Kialli*. They were mortal weapons— sword and whip."

"I tell you again, Terafin, that that is not possible."

"And *I* tell you it *is*. In this manse, on these grounds, the weapons of the Chosen *are* the weapons by which the House—and its ruler—is defended."

"Terafin—"

"Maybe it wasn't true, before I woke. It is true now."

His eyes widened. "Do you understand what you are saying?"

"Yes."

Be cautious, Jewel.

I am, damn it.

You do not understand it, and it is unwise in the extreme to lie to the magi.

I can't explain it. I understand it. My home is not home to gods or immortals or firstborn or wild elements. It's home to my den, to my Chosen, my servants, my House Guards and my counselors. It has stood for centuries on the backs of people exactly like them, and it will continue to stand in the same way.

You do not understand what you face.

I don't have to understand it. The Warden of Dreams made that clear. I only have to understand my home and my people, my enemies and my kin. They don't have to be more than they are; they have to be all *that they are.* She turned and left two of her den at the side of Meralonne APhaniel, and walked over to the table where the book that had caught Evayne's attention lay open for her inspection.

She lifted it with care. "Do you understand where you stand, APhaniel?"

"It is my belief that I understand it better than you, Terafin."

She smiled. Shadow came to stand by her side, his wings a little on the high side. "This House is my House. The Library is part of the House, and it's part of what I can see and touch. I can't control it, not consciously. But I understand it in a way that you don't, or can't. I've lived here. I've worked here. I've learned here." She lifted the book. "Evayne came to me. She couldn't touch this book; I can."

He said nothing.

She drew breath and continued. "Averalaan was built at the crossroads of the wild paths. It's how the demons arrived, how they stayed. It's not the only way they can—but it's the most natural, or it was. But if I understand the Warden of Dreams, if I understand the sleepers and what they signify, I understand what Averalaan is, and will be."

"And that?" The question was soft, almost gentle.

"A city," she replied. Her hands were shaking; she forced them to still. "A City of Man."

"Do you think that the men in those ancient—and buried—cities wielded what you refer to as swords?" He did not dispute her statement; he failed to acknowledge it in any other way. "Ask Viandaran."

She had seen the weapon that Avandar wielded when he stood so close to the edge of his personal abyss. She did not wish to see it wielded again. "I have no need to ask him."

He is correct, Jewel, the Winter King told her.

No, he's not. You ruled the Tor Amanion. You bore its name. But you didn't build it. It wasn't truly yours.

Do you think you built this library?

She carried the book to the edge of the fountain and sat on the metal bench that encircled it. It was warm. *No. Not all of it. Some part of it was built by The Terafin, and The Terafin before her. Some part of it was designed by The Terafin who rode to offer his sword and his fealty to the two sons of Veralaan the Founder. Fabril labored for the Twin Kings—he gave, into their hands, the Rod and the Sword with which they rode to war.*

But Fabril was here. He wasn't immortal. He wasn't Arianni or Kialli. He wasn't a King. He wasn't even a ruler of one of The Ten. He was talent-born, and he offered his talents to the Empire. She let her fingers trail across the gentle swell of moving water. It was still damn cold, but the cold was bracing, not chilling. *Do you understand? The Cities of Man existed* because *of people like Fabril.*

They did not exist as your cities exist now; these would have barely been considered farms.

She controlled her sudden anger with difficulty. "These

are the cities of men as they live now. Yes, you find them pathetic; yes, you consider them beneath notice and devoid of wonder.

"You don't—either of you—know how to *look*."

They were both staring now, with the usual dismissive arrogance that colored all of their interactions with the merely mortal. She remembered Farmer Hanson, her hands curling into fists. Was he talent-born? No. No more were Angel, Teller, Finch—any of her den. The Terafin who had changed the course of the den's life had been without the graceful and unnatural talents that marked Jewel, the mage-born, the bard-born.

So had Torvan, Arrendas, Arann.

Jewel understood why magic was so compelling to the tens of thousands that lived within the borders of Averalaan. She even understood why so many people secretly— or openly—yearned to be touched by a talent. People wanted what they didn't have; they wanted to be elevated by the other, because magic had no easily perceived rules. It didn't cling to class, to money, to status; it was a force outside of the familiar ones that conspired to keep them in their place, whatever that place was.

But there *was* wonder in the mortal. There was a depth of humanity in Farmer Hanson and his attempts to quietly and unobtrusively help the street children who had crossed his path—often in an attempt to steal enough food to see tomorrow. It was larger than life—but it was larger than a small life, a single life. It could only touch what it could see.

"Your cities were built by men who envied the gods."

"And in the end," Meralonne said softly, "could rival them."

She uncurled her hands. "I didn't grow up in a land where the gods ran wild. I didn't see the tens of thousands of deaths they *must* have caused when they threw tantrums at each other. I understand that a god is now preparing to walk across the whole of the world—but I don't need to be a god to stand against him."

She felt a warmth touch the space between her collarbones and startled. Looking down, she saw that the pendant given her by Snow—as the only accoutrement worthy of *his* dress—had begun to glow. "Shadow, what is it doing?"

"How should *I* know? Ask Snow."

"Go and get him."

Shadow hissed, but the wings across his substantial back unfolded. He clipped Meralonne on the fly-by.

"You do not even understand how to build, Terafin," the mage continued, ignoring the cat with minimal effort.

"No. But I understand what *can* be built here."

"Do you think they will thank you?"

"Pardon?"

"Do you think the rabble of humanity to which you no doubt intend to somehow defer will be grateful for your interference? You have spent three decades within the streets of this city, in one locale or another. You have always given orders, even if they are not acknowledged as such. You *lead*, Jewel. You think of what you desire *as* a leader."

He turned to Teller. "Do you feel that the people who toil in the streets of the hundred holdings, in ignorance of what awaits, would *thank* your leader should they be given the responsibility of defending their homes, their children, and their lives from the very god?"

Teller was silent.

Angel was not. "What she'll be giving them—if I understand what's been said at all—is the *chance* to defend their homes, their children, and their lives. The god will come *anyway*."

"No matter what she does, they have no chance of standing against the god himself. Most will flee at the *sight* of armed men—men who are, in all ways, their theoretical equals. I ask again, do you think they'll be grateful?"

Jewel shook her head, exhaling heavily. "I don't think it matters." She turned to Torvan. "Captain, would you prefer to cower behind me in the hope that I might understand enough of the paradigm of this strange power to save your life? Or would you fight?" Her voice was cool, measured; it was a match for Amarais' in this place.

"We are your Chosen," he replied.

"Yes." She turned to Meralonne, and to the Winter King, who had come to join him. "These men are mine, all of them. They will keep me safe, or they will die in the attempt."

"They are not the citizens of the holdings."

"They *are*. But that isn't all that they are. Maybe we'll surprise you," she added. She could have continued, but didn't. She was aware that Meralonne was not wrong. But neither was she. There were people who would die before they took up the mantle of even limited responsibility. There had *always* been people who made that choice, knowing or unknowing. But not all people made that choice, and not all people made that choice all of the time.

"We are mortals," she said simply. "And the world, for better or worse, was left to us."

"It will not remain that way."

"I know." She closed the book carefully. "I have an appointment—or will have soon—with the Exalted and The Ten. What will you counsel?"

"I? I will counsel as I have. I feel you are foolish, impractical, and naive—but in spite of those traits, you are necessary. And, Terafin," he added, his gaze once again passing beyond and above her, "you have already surprised me; it may be that, in the end, you and your kin will continue to do so." He offered her a perfect and unexpected bow. He rose quickly, however, when Snow and Shadow landed; they weren't careful about who happened to be standing beneath them.

Or no, she thought, they were—they did not appear to care for Meralonne APhaniel. Meralonne, in his turn, singed their feathers with a casual, almost bored, gesture.

Shadow said, curtly, "He didn't *want* to come."

She could see that; the white cat was looking at anything in the huge room that wasn't Jewel.

"Snow."

He stared at her feet. It was almost impressive that he could fit that much body into such a shrinking space, but he managed. "The necklace," she said.

"What necklace?"

She lifted the chain, exposing the gem to the amethyst sky and the eyes of all observers, including one very reluctant cat.

"Oh, *that*. You shouldn't *wear* it."

"You insisted that I wear it."

"That was *then*. You won't *wear* my dress now, so you don't *need* it."

Meralonne was staring at the gem as it slowly rotated on the dangled chain. "Terafin," his voice was almost a whisper. "Where did you come by that necklace?"

"Snow," was her curt reply.

The mage turned to the cat, who cringed. "Please tell me that you did not take that necklace from—"

The cat screeched, drowning out the question. "It's not *safe* to mention him," he hissed, when Meralonne stopped speaking.

The mage was utterly silent for one long, awkward moment.

It was Teller who spoke, and he spoke to the mage. "Are you regretting your acceptance of the role of Terafin House Mage, Member APhaniel?"

Meralonne blinked, as if slowly returning to the world. He smiled. The smile was transformative. "I?" he said, his grave tone at odds with his expression. "No, right-kin. But even I had not imagined what it might entail." He turned to the fountain, and then away. "Terafin, the book?"

She shook her head. "Evayne couldn't touch it."

He did not immediately dismiss her concern, although his expression darkened and cooled. "At what age did she make the attempt?"

"I'm not sure. She was older than I, but not quite as old as The Terafin."

"The former Terafin."

She nodded, aware of the gaffe, but willing to let it stand with no sense of fault whatsoever.

"I am intrigued. Might I—"

She hesitated. She felt the Winter King's curiosity, although he fell short of urging her to allow the mage to take that risk. In the end, she chose to demur, and returned to the table which served as a shelf. "There are other books here," she said quietly, acutely aware that they were all transgressions of the Order's very strict code.

Meralonne did not appear to care, although he made a show of inspecting the volumes. "Sigurne is unlikely to be pleased by their inclusion in your library. If possible, avoid antagonizing her. She is unlikely to believe, given the nature of the drastic changes within your personal quarters—and the fountain itself—that these have always been resident in your library; she is, however, likely to demand they leave with her. I do not think that will be so easily accomplished, even if you choose to accede to her request."

It wasn't likely to be a request. "We could compromise; she could destroy them here."

"Be careful, Jewel. If you are ruler here, you are also custodian." His eyes narrowed. "You have no intention of destroying them."

"After I read them, I won't object. Or," she added, "after you do. I think there is information here that may be of use to us."

"Us?" His smile was slight and strange. "I very much doubt, Terafin, that there is anything in books—even these—that will enlighten or surprise *me*. But there is wonder here, and it is not a subtle wonder. Here," he swept out an arm, "one does not have to stand still, to close eyes, to conjure some image of the distant glories of a faded past: it is *here*, and it lives, it breathes.

"Fashion what you will out of mortal clay; build as you desire. You do not understand the whole of what you wish to invoke—because that is the nature of magics such as these. No laboratory, no paper, no dry discussion and dissection, no lesson, will ever explain it all."

"I would not have expected to hear such words from a member of the Order of Knowledge," Jewel replied quietly, "and never spoken with such exultation." She lowered the necklace into the folds of her dress. "How dangerous is it to wear this?" she asked softly.

"A wise man would not," he replied. "But a wise man would *never* accept a gift from the cats. They are vain and idle, but cunning when they so choose. If you are asking whether or not you might leave the necklace in a place of safety, the answer is no. I would counsel it anyway, but given your personal predilections, I will not; if anyone can survive the bearing of such a burden, it is one who is Sen.

"But he will search for it now."

"Who?"

Snow yowled, and Meralonne grinned. "I am afraid, at the insistence of your Snow, I cannot answer that question."

"The hells you—" Avandar cleared his throat, and Jewel reddened.

He is correct, Jewel, the Winter King said. *No good will come of the naming, if it is as I now suspect.*

Is it dangerous?

No, or not in that way; it is dangerous because another owner claims it, and he will want it back.

Can't I just make Snow return it?

*I very much doubt that Snow would survive the attempt;
I am surprised that he survived the item's retrieval. I would
not, however, be upset should you order him to attempt it.*

Snow's fur was standing on end, and Jewel placed a hand
on his head. It was, as Teller said, much softer—and given
the rest of the transformation, it shouldn't have been. Then
again, the cats often made no logical sense. "He's teasing
you," she said, as if he were a child.

"When *he* teases, it is death," Shadow replied; Snow was
hissing quietly.

Meralonne nodded. "I am here," he told the cats, "as her
House Mage."

"You are *not* hers."

"No. I will never be hers." He glanced up as the wind
changed; it carried Celleriant in its folds. The Arianni Prince
stepped out of the air and onto the ground by the fountain's
side. He bore both sword and shield.

"She would not demand it," Celleriant told Meralonne,
as if he had always been part of the conversation, even in
his absence. "Will you hide at the edge of the wilderness
like a timid stripling?"

Platinum brows rose, but no anger followed the question. "I am no longer so young that I might rush off into
every dell, every glade, on a wild hunt."

Celleriant laughed. "You are ageless, but dulled by your
long exposure to the petty squabbling and tired noise of the
mortals. Come, *come*, Illaraphaniel. Can you not hear it?
Even the trees that consent to serve as shelving are speaking."

Jewel couldn't hear the trees talk. Given the excitement
barely contained in Celleriant's words, she almost regretted
it. But Meralonne did as the Arianni Lord bid; he listened.
As he did, his expression shifted, changing by slow degree.

"I fear that my presence will be demanded soon," he said
softly.

Celleriant waited.

"Terafin—"

"Go," she told him. "Whenever Celleriant is this joyful,
it means death. I will not spend the Chosen in the wilderness if the wilderness does not attempt to spend itself on
me."

"Tell Sigurne, should you see her, that the breaking of
the enchantments was, in its entirety, your doing."

"I didn't—"

"Ignorance excuses nothing. But tell her, as well, that I am far less troubled than I was."

Celleriant laughed. "Do not trust him," he told Jewel, clearly enjoying himself. "The hidden world is waking, Lord, and you have announced your presence more clearly than even the Winter Queen might, should she ride at the head of the Wild Hunt. They will come."

Jewel froze.

"They will come," he said, "and they will test themselves against your borders. If you are strong, they will hold, and while they hold, we will fight."

"In my name." It wasn't a question.

"In your name, while you live. Your name will be *known*."

Jewel turned to the Winter King. "Yes," she said softly, although he had said, had asked, nothing. "If you desire it, join them."

And Viandaran?

"No. I need him here." All three turned to her in an instant, some of their wild exuberance dimmed.

"What concerns you?" Lord Celleriant asked.

"It is nothing to do with the wilderness," she replied. "Snow, find Night, and go with them."

"And me?" Shadow asked.

"I want you with me."

"Why?"

"Because before we meet The Ten or the Exalted, we're going to speak with Rymark ATerafin."

Celleriant called the wind, and Jewel felt it respond; nor did she stop it in its wild, affectionate rush. The Winter King stepped into the air, and it held him; Snow leaped past its sentient folds and into the purple skies. But Meralonne APhaniel lowered his hand, closed his eyes, and bowed his head.

"Lord Celleriant."

Celleriant's lips lost the curve of his smile.

"Terafin."

"I don't need—"

"No, you don't. But if you are to speak with Rymark ATerafin, I will accompany you."

"I have Avandar."

"Avandar is not a First Circle member of the Council of

the Magi; nor is Avandar the guildmaster's designated agent in this regard. She has been concerned about Rymark ATerafin for some time, and with cause. It is possible that my presence may prove critical."

"How? Even if Rymark intends to attack—or kill—me, he's going to have to do it himself; a demon can't just walk here and join him at his behest."

"I did not say that. The *Kialli* are capable of reaching both the Isle and your manse; they will not be able to do so with the speed and the secrecy to which they are accustomed. If you feel no *Kialli* watch Averalaan, you are naive. Or have you found them all, Terafin? Have you found them and ordered their destruction?"

"No."

"I will accompany you."

"You don't feel Avandar is capable of defending me."

"I do not feel that defense is necessarily the issue. It grieves me far, far more than you know."

Jewel turned to Teller. "Can you reschedule your meeting?"

He winced. "Not easily, no. Among other things, Finch will be upset."

"Finch? How important is this merchant?"

"He is Hectore of Araven."

Jewel knew the name; it was hard to be responsible for any of the merchant operations within the House and remain entirely in ignorance. Teller was right: Finch would not be pleased. She would understand, because she always did—but ruffling the feathers of Hectore of Araven was unlikely to be considered wise within the Merchant Authority. "Fine. Hectore of Araven first. Rymark second."

Hectore arrived on time. It was not against his personal beliefs to do so, but time was one of the subtle ways in which favor—or disfavor—might be shown. Too late, and someone of The Terafin's import might consider his timing a slight; too early, and he would, of course, appear far too eager. Either of these choices set a tone, and as Hectore had not had time to speak with and assess the young woman who had taken the Terafin mantle, he had not yet reached a decision about the tone he wished to set; he therefore chose to set none.

His brief meeting with Jarven had gone about as well as either of the two men expected; Hectore had spent far longer in his carriage waiting for the correct moment to disembark to achieve this perfect timeliness. Andrei was, of course, waiting beyond the open carriage door, his impeccable posture nevertheless suggesting the barest hint of impatience. Hectore occasionally enjoyed tweaking the inimitable Andrei, but knew, from long years of practice, his limits. He dismounted, accepting Andrei's offered hand. He frowned.

"Andrei."

"Patris."

The tone of the word caused Hectore to slow; he looked at the justifiably pretentious front drive of a manse that was arguably home to the most powerful woman in the Empire, excepting only the Queens and the Exalted. Andrei was . . . tense. Concerned. Given Andrei and the circumstances— The Terafin was in no way an enemy to House Araven— that concern was unexpected. House Terafin was only barely a rival, in the few concerns in which their merchant operations overlapped. They had not been involved in open trade hostilities for two decades, perhaps a touch more, and even then, the depth of the hostilities had never extended to overt physical harm.

"You put great faith in the Order of Knowledge," Hectore told his servant.

"I put an appropriate level of faith in their prognostications," was Andrei's suitably subdued response. He was too alert for verbal fencing.

"Andrei, please."

This evoked a raised brow. "Very well, Patris Araven. The *Astari* are here."

"Wonderful. If they are here to speak with The Terafin, they can wait."

"I do not see Duvari," Andrei replied. "If they are here at all, it is to observe. But they *are* here, Hectore."

"Very well. I will be on my best behavior. Will that suffice?"

"Yes. The magi have been here as well."

"Andrei, you are making me regret breakfast. Come, or we will be late."

Andrei tactfully said nothing further, but he had a way

of saying nothing that was actually quite loud. Hectore had gone to some difficulty to arrange this meeting. To his surprise, Jarven had proved as slippery and noncommittal as he would at any negotiation of grave import to the House. To his consternation, he was not at all certain that Jarven would have intervened had it not been for the young woman commonly considered his most important aide in the Merchant Authority.

She was, however, everything that Jarven was not; direct, but politic, deferential within the easy limits of polite power, and gracious enough to offer him tea. The tea had been greatly appreciated—but not, apparently, by Jarven, a man renowned for his love of teas.

"Finch ATerafin," Andrei had informed him. "She is a junior member of the House Council, which is, of course, significant. Of more interest, however, is her adoption into the House."

"She is one of Jewel ATerafin's people."

"She is. She arrived at the manse at the side of Jewel ATerafin. As, rumor suggests, did the current right-kin, Teller ATerafin."

"Teller? An unusual name."

"It is. Teller has no other family name."

"You are certain this Terafin paragon is merely mortal?" He chuckled.

Andrei, sadly, did not. He was not, by nature, a merchant; he was not, by nature, a gambler. The risks he chose to take, he took because there were no other options. Hectore understood the game of risk and chance, and if pressed, would honestly admit that it was one of the few that made him feel fully alive. There were other things that moved him in entirely different ways, of course.

And one of them had brought him here.

The right-kin's office was not empty; nor was it in appreciable disarray, although Andrei had informed Hectore that Teller was very recently installed in the position. Hectore had had very few reasons to personally visit The Terafin in the past decade; he had done so as a courtesy, of course, but he was, in any estimation, well enough established that being seen visiting The Terafin personally did nothing to further his reputation.

He therefore allowed Andrei to introduce him to the right-kin's secretary before taking a seat. Two Priests were likewise seated; they were not god-born, but they were, to his practiced eye, men accustomed to the cathedrals of the Isle. Ah. Three messengers, all wearing the livery of their Houses: Berrilya, Garisar, and Korisamis.

Hectore glanced at Andrei, who nodded; no further words were exchanged. Andrei preferred to play the dedicated and exceptional servant in the presence of any outsiders. The secretary did not move from his desk, and as Hectore was on time, this said something. What it said had yet to be determined; if Hectore was not needlessly punitive, he had a clear sense of his own worth—and the respect that worth demanded. The Ten did not specialize in obsequiousness; nor would Hectore expect it—but he expected to be treated as an important guest.

Important guests, of course, were not left waiting unless they were preceded by guests of notably greater import. Hectore would therefore judge the level of discourtesy when the right-kin's office opened and the guest who had clearly overstayed his or her welcome departed.

Except that that was not how it went. Doors did open, but they were not the doors that led to the right-kin's office; they were the doors that led to—and from—the external rooms in which the secretary held the world at bay.

Into the room walked a handful of men and women. Half of these were the justifiably respected Terafin Chosen, but for the rest? A man from Arrend, a younger man and woman, an older man cut in the style of severe servanting that was Andrei on a tear, and—a member of the Order of Knowledge. Hectore did not deal directly with the Order of Knowledge except at large gatherings; he was not therefore immediately familiar with this one.

Andrei, however, was. He gestured and Hectore's gaze sharpened as the young woman and the young man resolved themselves into the current Terafin and her right-kin. The young man now separated himself from his group and approached Hectore, tendering a perfect, and slightly deeper-than-necessary bow.

"Patris Araven," he said, rising. "Please accept my apologies for the delay."

Hectore was gracious, and dismissed the obvious, notable delay with a wave of the hand. "I do not believe we've met," he said, extending a hand. "I am Hectore of House Araven."

"Teller ATerafin," the right-kin replied. "Please, join me in my office."

Hectore, however, had turned toward the woman at the center of this hub.

The ATerafin right-kin likewise turned; it would have been awkward to do less. "My apologies again," he said, with a wry smile. "Patris Araven, The Terafin."

The Terafin took a step forward just as the doors flew open at such speed it spoke well of their hinges. Hectore's brows rose; through long practice, his mouth remained closed.

"They didn't *want* to let me *in*," the newest visitor growled. Speech, in the offices in which politics were the practiced game, was not unexpected—but a giant panther with wings, golden eyes, and fangs that seemed longer than daggers, was. This was not the white cat that eluded memory so neatly, like a dream on the edge of waking. This was nightmare. But, Hectore had to admit, it was a whiny nightmare.

The Terafin wheeled on the spot, composure forgotten, her hands falling to her hips. "Shadow, I told you to stay outside."

"You *asked*," the great beast replied. "It was *boring* in the hall."

"You were in the hall for all of a minute," she replied, in a voice tight with irritation.

"Everyone *else* is having *fun*." He turned to look around the room at large, and his eyes came to rest not upon Hectore, but Andrei. "Who is *this*?"

Andrei, ever the impeccable servant, had taken stock of the situation—which involved a giant cat with large wings and unfortunate fangs—and failed to answer. He did, however, glance at Hectore.

"He is my servant," Hectore replied, speaking directly to the cat.

The cat turned his golden eyes upon the Patris of Araven; it was disconcerting. "Who are *you*?"

The Terafin dropped hand onto the cat's head, from enough of a height that its landing was not notably gentle. "*He* is my guest."

"Oh, *guests*."

"My deepest apologies, Patris Araven," the young woman then said, regaining the composure she had set aside to admonish the creature—as if Hectore, in this room, were more of a danger than the cat.

"Accepted," Hectore replied, staring at the cat and his master for a long moment before he smiled. "I have seldom seen talking animals before, and never outside of these grounds."

The cat growled. The Terafin's knuckles whitened.

"I am therefore uncertain as to the level of manners such a creature would be expected to display." He now turned the full force of his attention upon The Terafin. Jewel Markess ATerafin. Hanging from a slender golden chain looped around her neck, was a ring Hectore recognized; it was the Signet of House Handernesse. So. Andrei was, as usual, correct.

She was shrewd, this young woman; she noted the direction of his gaze, and its length, and she lifted her hand from the cat's head. She did not, however, slide the necklace and its ring beneath the folds of her dress. He considered his options with care. Sometimes he chose to rely on his instincts, but he had amassed a wealth of experience, much of it in the company of competent young women, and on occasion he allowed that experience to be his guide.

"The ring you wear," he said quietly.

She stiffened, but nodded; there was nothing uncontrolled about the gesture. Her eyes were wide, her gaze clear. She intended to meet him, he thought.

"It is the signet usually worn by the Handernesse. As I have seen that young man at a funeral recently, I can be relatively certain that it is not, in fact, the crest of Handernesse. But at this distance, Terafin—and my eyes are not what they once were—it bears a remarkable resemblance."

"It was left to me," she told him evenly, "by Amarais Handernesse ATerafin upon her death. It, and a sword."

She did not, by tone, refer to the House Sword. "I am . . . surprised . . . that she had that ring in her keeping. Her departure from the house of her birth was not without consequence."

"I doubt very much," was the surprisingly bitter reply, "that she received this ring from Handernesse."

He inhaled, exhaled, and threw a brief warning glance at Andrei. "I should tell you, Terafin, that I was Ararath Handernesse's godfather."

Her eyes widened; she did not yet have the composure to pull back from the expression that adorned her open face. *So*, he thought.

"You knew Rath?"

"That is not what I called him, although that was his preference; he allowed much to a fond, old man. Yes, Terafin. I knew Rath. I knew him as a child in House Handernesse; it was to me he came when his sister chose to withdraw from the House of her birth to accept adoption into House Terafin. I saw him seldom in his later years, but he was kind enough to visit, and on occasion, to write."

He felt no qualms about exposing his open affection for Ararath; he seldom felt qualms about using the truth to achieve his own goals. Lies were trickier things, although he was adept at their use as well. She was young. She was, he thought, too young.

But she surprised him; she turned toward Andrei, and her eyes narrowed, her brow creasing in open concentration before her eyes widened.

Andrei bowed to her; it was, for one who knew Andrei, surprisingly genuine. "Yes, Terafin," he said, as he rose. "We have met before. You were younger, and I? I was not so finely dressed."

"Who *is* he?" The cat growled again.

"I don't know," she replied. There was no suspicion in her, not for Andrei, which was surprising. "But he came to help Rath when Rath needed help."

"As, I believe, did you. And you were not of age, Terafin, at that time. The others who were with you?"

"They're here. Not *right* here," she added, as his glance shifted. "But they live here. They work within the Terafin manse, and they are all ATerafin."

Andrei shocked Hectore—although Hectore was far, far too accomplished to allow it to show. He smiled. "Ararath wore that ring."

It was only barely a question. But The Terafin's expression changed. "That is my belief, yes. I don't know for certain."

"But you suspect it."

"I do. Another acquaintance of Rath's—of Ararath's—led me to believe that this was the case. She is seldom mistaken." The words were bitter.

"I did not travel here with the intent of speaking about my godson," Hectore said gently, "and I am aware that your time is in great demand, if rumors are to be believed."

"What rumors?"

"Jarven ATerafin did not wish to disturb you, given the nature of 'The Terafin's extremely significant schedule.'" Andrei frowned; he disliked it when Hectore publicly impersonated the dignitaries of his acquaintance.

The Terafin, however, chuckled. "Yes, that would be Jarven." She was in no obvious way similar to the woman who had previously held the House. Too warm, Hectore thought. But she had noticed Andrei, and she had been utterly certain that he was the same man she had seen in the dark of an evening half her life ago. "I am very busy," she added, her voice dropping.

Her domicis gave her a look that would have been at home on Andrei's face, and given his mimicry of the head of Terafin operations in the Merchant Authority, probably was. "You are understandably in demand, even by successful old men such as myself."

"If you didn't come here to talk about Rath—"

"No. Ararath was not kindly viewed by most of the society in which he would have otherwise made his home. There are few indeed who remember him, and of those, fewer who do so kindly. I did not speak to The Terafin about her brother."

"She loved him," Jewel replied. "Even if she didn't speak of him often. I would not be here if not for her continued affection. It wasn't The Terafin who disavowed Rath—it was Rath. Had he come here—had he *ever* come here, she would have welcomed him. She would—" she swallowed and stemmed the tide of her words.

I have you, he thought, without malice. "Ararath was proud in a way that few men are. It was his strength," he added, "but it was costly. What he loved, he loved—but he brooked no betrayal. I am grateful that matters of trade brought me to your House, Terafin, although those matters are no longer uppermost in my thoughts. I realize you are much in demand, but even the Kings require sustenance.

"If it is not too bold, might I request a dinner in the near future? I have a few mementos of my wayward godson, and I believe they should go to you."

"I think Jarven will be displeased," she replied.

"Oh, undoubtedly, but it keeps him moving, and it would be a welcome change from the doddering dotard he plays on most days."

Andrei's expression was glacial; its chill could barely be avoided. Hectore smiled, enjoying himself greatly.

"Yes, I would love that." She turned to the right-kin. "Teller, could you—"

"Of course, Terafin."

"Not tomorrow; if I get out of *Avantari* before dawn, it will be a miracle. Not a small one," she added. "But perhaps the day after? The late dinner hour?"

"I would be honored. Will you join me in Araven, or should I return to the manse?"

"The manse," she replied.

"Terafin," her domicis said stiffly, and the girl froze. But she weathered his disapproval and whatever lay beneath it.

"Very well," Hectore said, bowing. "I will be at your service the day after tomorrow, and perhaps discussions of trade may commence—in a casual way—at that time."

Andrei did not speak a word until they were well ensconced in the carriage, and a silence stone had been invoked—with a heavier hand than Hectore felt circumstance required. "That was unwise in the extreme," he said dourly.

"Which part?"

"You will, without a doubt, offend Jarven—and while our dealings with Terafin are not broad, Jarven has been known to cause trouble beyond his holdings when it suits him."

"And we have survived it passingly well until now, Andrei."

"She is not a fool. She seems young to you now, but she is a danger."

"She is sentimental," Hectore replied, gazing out the window. "But *I* am sentimental, Andrei. I think we may be of comfort to each other. It is clear to me that she and Amarais spoke of Ararath on more than one occasion—and that Amarais left the ring to her. I did not lie to her."

"Not in so many words, no. You will find maneuvering far more difficult than you expect if you do not regard her as the power she demonstrably *is*."

"I am perfectly capable of acknowledging both power and sentiment, Andrei."

Andrei said nothing for a long moment. "I mistrust your instincts in this. You have built a small empire, Hectore — but you are not interested in The Terafin for reasons of expansion or defense. Sentiment clouds judgment when it is the only motivation."

Hectore's smile dimmed. "Jarven is, as you saw, interested — personally interested — in The Terafin."

"Jarven has nothing to lose." When Hectore raised brow, Andrei continued. "There is very little within the Terafin merchant arm that he feels responsible for, now. But where Jarven plays, there is death."

"Exaggeration, surely."

"I have misgivings, Hectore. On the eve that I first made the acquaintance of Jewel Markess, as she must have been styled then, I thought her mage-born, and dangerously early into her power. Ararath made clear that it was not a subject for my concern — but that further interest on my part would be a grave difficulty. For him. I believe he thought of killing me —"

"Not this again, Andrei."

Andrei frowned. "I trust you to know your business. Trust me to know my own."

Hectore conceded, but with ruffled grace. "Ararath was many things, and I acknowledged them when forced to do so. You, however, are accusing him of gross, inconceivable stupidity."

"I merely said he considered it. However, you evade the point."

Hectore sighed and turned to his servant. "And that?"

"You trust me to know my business. I trust you to know yours. But this is not a gambit in a desperate trade war. This is outside of our experience. Leave it, Hectore. Talk to her, if you must, about Ararath — your instincts there are remarkably sound. But leave the rest."

The merchant prince smiled benignly. "I will know what caused my granddaughter's death, Andrei."

"And if it were, inadvertently, The Terafin?"

"Then she will, in all likelihood, die."

Jewel was silent for a long moment after Patris Araven's departure. She had not expected to speak about Rath—in public, no less—today, and the mention of his name—by a man who claimed to be his godfather—had unbalanced her in a way that even the library's transformation had failed to do.

She understood, from Shadow's reaction, that it was the servant, not the merchant, who was the obvious threat—but she *wanted* to talk to the merchant. She wanted to hear what he had to say. Rath had never mentioned a godfather, but that was Rath.

Do not let your affection for a dead man cause a misstep.

Hectore of Araven is significant in his own right, she argued. *And he was genuinely fond of Rath.* It was true. She knew it the way she knew anything of import to her.

She was aware of House Araven; it would be hard to be a merchant of any standing and remain in complete ignorance of Hectore. But their concerns only peripherally clashed with Terafin's. "Send word to Finch," she told her right-kin, "and ask for pertinent information on Araven and its possible new concerns."

Jewel turned to face the messengers who waited. She accepted their messages—verbal, all—in the right-kin's office, mindful of the need for rudimentary caution. Avandar let her know that her definition of rudimentary would not pass muster unless the audience was under the age of four. He was annoyed.

She grimaced; Korisamis was reluctant to commit to the meeting time, and she had little leverage. "Tell your lord," she said, in a carefully modulated tone of respect, "That my timing in this is not entirely of my own choosing." She considered dragging Duvari's name into the message, but decided against it; the Korisamis could not easily be moved by common enemy. "The matters to be discussed affect not only The Ten, but the hundred. I called Council given the severity of the difficulty, but it is not a negotiable difficulty. It is what it is.

"The meeting will therefore occur. I will, of course,

understand if his own concerns prevent participation, but feel that if this is the case, a suitable member of the Korisamis Council would not be remiss."

The messenger bowed stiffly; the stiff bow was a custom maintained within Korisamis. "And the timing?"

"I have been summoned to an audience with the Exalted," she replied. "Therefore, no earlier accommodation can be reached. The Exalted are aware of the prior Council session, and they will not interfere."

He bowed again and retreated.

She turned to Teller. "Rymark."

Teller nodded.

"Here, in my office, or in my library?"

Meralonne said, "In your library, Terafin," before Teller could respond. Jewel nodded acknowledgment, not assent, and turned to her domicis. The polite fiction of a one-sided relationship between master and servant was not, at this point, practical.

"If you are reasonably confident that there will be no trouble—or that trouble, in a public venue, would be to your advantage, I would counsel the use of the right-kin's office. Inviting—or commanding—Rymark ATerafin's presence in your inner sanctum will be noted by the whole of the House Council."

"And if I have no clear idea of how this discussion will proceed?"

He was verbally silent. *You control the conversation,* he told her. *You therefore must have some clear idea of how you would* like *it to proceed.*

They waited. *Begin,* her Oma said, *as you mean to continue.* "The library."

Jewel arrived in the library before Rymark, as intended. She did not proceed to the interior of the library, but waited at the wrought-iron gateway. The breeze was stronger than it had been, and her hair, never the most tidy, had fallen in her eyes. She considered—not for the first time—shaving her head. The Korisamis was bald, and no one blinked.

Meralonne APhaniel waited by her side. He carried no pipe; nor did he ask if a pipe was permissible. His mood was grim; he stood at his full height. Seen like this—as he so seldom was—it was impossible to be unaware of his power, although he wielded no obvious magic.

The subtle, of course, was present; he did not trust Rymark. His robes were overlaid in translucent, orange light. Jewel thought it wise. There was nothing in her memories to gentle her reaction to Rymark; they were not kind. In response, she was unkind; she waited. She did not choose to give him any privacy—at all—in which to experience the drastic transformation.

"Terafin," Meralonne said quietly.

She glanced at him, but said nothing. Avandar remained close at hand; Angel stood back. Shadow was the only bored personage in the room, although he made enough noise to compensate for everyone else's silence.

Did you kill her? Did you kill Amarais? It was the only question that mattered. She clasped her hands loosely behind her back to stop herself from pushing hair out of her eyes. It was a nervous gesture Avandar decried. What he was willing to tolerate in even a member of the Terafin Council, he was unwilling to accept in The Terafin.

Rymark ATerafin appeared beneath the center of the arch. He appeared—to her deep surprise—without his guards. She watched his expression with care, uncertain as to what she hoped to see there. His eyes widened as he gazed into the distance of shelving that was now very odd forest. Of all the things she would have predicted, triumph wasn't on the list. But there was, about the smile that transformed his face, triumph.

"Terafin." His bow was deep, graceful, and a touch too long. He noted Meralonne APhaniel—he couldn't help but notice him—with the curt nod reserved for questionable equals in social gatherings. "The library is . . . much changed."

"It is, although it is of lesser concern at the moment." That dragged his attention away from the depths of purple sky. "You requested an interview."

He glanced more tellingly at Meralonne APhaniel. "Terafin. The matter is wholly of interest to the House."

"Member APhaniel is the House Mage, and as such, indispensable at this time. He is not present as a member of the Order of Knowledge or its internal Council."

"He is nonetheless a member of both."

"I will not play these games," she replied. "I do not desire his absence, and his contract is to the House."

"My position in the Order is tenuous," Rymark replied. He spoke without apparent concern, and kept his gaze on the Lord of his House. "The Council of the Magi is politically sensitive. If Member APhaniel remains, I will seek your ear at another time."

"You will not," she replied. "I am not, now, so desperate for information that I will allow the games of the Order of Knowledge to interfere with my schedule and my priorities. You mentioned, in passing, the subject of the interview. It is a subject of grave concern and interest—which is why I have made room in my schedule to speak with you.

"But it is not, at the moment, of grave enough concern that I will dismiss my mage at your behest; if he serves as nothing else, he serves as witness."

Rymark's eyes rather predictably narrowed. "And an external witness is now considered a necessity in a matter that has direct bearing upon House affairs?"

"There are some magics, as you must well know, that are not subject to the legal exemptions that otherwise govern House Law."

His eyes narrowed further.

She lifted a hand. "I'm unwilling to play games with you. You are not here at my request, but at your own, and if you have come to posture, I will retire to better prepare for my interview with the Exalted on the morrow."

Chapter Twelve

"**Y**OU SAID YOU HAD INFORMATION about the Shining Court."

Rymark stiffened, but did not glance at Meralonne. Jewel did. The mage's silver eyes were narrowed, but betrayed no surprise. "I did."

"I am less concerned with the Shining Court than I have ever been."

"That is unwise," Rymark replied. "You do not know who presides over the Lords of that Court."

"I think I do. What I don't know is the composition of the rest of the Court, although I imagine there are *Kialli* among its numbers."

"The Court matters little. The composition of the Court—with a few key exceptions—is not specifically of note. What matters is the Lord of the Shining City."

"Allasakar."

Shadow hissed; the hiss deepened into a low rumble of sound and motion. Even Rymark looked surprised and ill-pleased to hear the god's name spoken so bluntly. He fell silent; they all did, except for Shadow.

"House Law," Meralonne said, into that silence, "does not provide exemptions for acts of treason."

Rymark said nothing, adopting—where Meralonne was concerned—his usual arrogant disdain. This required

flexibility, as he had adopted a much, much more concilia-
tory approach to The Terafin.

"Assassination of a member of House Terafin is not an
act of treason," Jewel said, in his stead.

"No, indeed," the mage agreed. "Consorting with demo-
nologists, being a demonologist, or colluding with demons,
however, is. If we agree that the method of assassination
was, in fact, demonic—and there are credible witnesses to
that effect, among them the Kings, we must also therefore
agree that the act was treasonous."

Jewel glanced at Meralonne. "Member APhaniel, I believe I said I was done—for the day—with games. They offer me little and cost me a great deal of time." She forced
her hands to remain by her sides, although they were creeping up toward their perch on her hips.

"Very well. ATerafin, you have claimed knowledge of the
Shining Court, however indirectly. The Shining Court is the
body politic of the Shining City; it serves Allasakar in all
ways."

Rymark again said nothing.

"I will not ask you how you come to have that knowledge, since we are to dispense with pretense. I will ask, instead, why you have kept it to yourself until now."

"Perhaps I did not think it relevant," Rymark replied,
turning once again to Jewel. "Might we retire to your office?".

Jewel raised a brow. "I have no idea where the office now
is, if it currently exists at all. I have felt no need for it; the
meetings that have occurred in the library so far have been
of a private nature." She considered the table and the fountain, and glanced at Avandar.

No. I consider it unwise.

Why? She had her own reasons.

*You do not, of course, trust him; that is both fair and wise.
But you have not yet decided, Jewel, whether or not he will
leave this room alive. If he does not, it doesn't matter what he
sees; if he does, it is much more of a concern.*

What do you counsel?

*I? Caution. No more, no less. I have frequently allowed
those who meant me harm to live. I have not always chosen
to do so; it depended entirely on their relative power and the
advantage to be gained by either action on my part.*

You want to know what he knows.

No, Jewel; I consider what he knows to be, as you have implied, of trivial value. You want to know what he knows.

She did. She felt a horrible traitor for choosing the politics of the moment—and of the future—over the need for the justice for which the House Sword was named. "Very well. Let us look," she told Rymark and Meralonne, "for the offices that once occupied space within my personal rooms."

Meralonne did not object, and that should have been a warning. Nor did he reach for his pipe—and Jewel was probably the only woman of any consequence with whom he dealt who didn't strongly dislike it. He nodded to Rymark; Rymark passed him by, as if his presence were, in the end, of little consequence.

Jewel frequently considered Meralonne a colossal inconvenience; she never considered him inconsequential. She didn't, now; he was gazing up at the sky, his eyes slightly narrowed, as if he expected something to emerge from its purple folds. Nothing did, not even clouds, but wind swept strands of his hair from his face. She noted only then that he hadn't bothered to rebraid it.

He had been one of the first people of any import she'd been introduced to upon her arrival in the manse, and she had been forced to work with him for weeks, crawling and digging through the dirt while he smoked his pipe and looked alternately bored, annoyed, or lazy. She had had long conversations across the breakfast nook in the West Wing about his approach to their joint investigation; she had seen him all but scream at The Terafin in frustration and fury.

And she had never seen him, she knew, the way others did. Meralonne did not age. He hadn't aged a minute in the sixteen years since their first introduction. But sometimes she could see what lay behind the patina of mercurial, slightly vindictive mage: something ancient, something wild, something ultimately unconcerned with the petty day-to-day world in which the majority of her heart lay bound.

She had seen it the first time Meralonne APhaniel had faced a demon lord; she had seen it each and every time thereafter. Something in him came alive only then, as if such life-and-death struggles were the only thing into which he could throw the whole of his heart.

She saw that in him, now. She had always considered it compelling. Finch thought it beautiful, but cold. She shook herself, turned away, thinking of her office, of the room that had been an office. It was small, tastefully furnished, and almost never used.

It was not the place for Meralonne APhaniel.

She learned at least one thing from Rymark's presence in her inner sanctum: he was not the force, either consciously or subconsciously, that Meralonne APhaniel had become. She had known *of* Rymark for almost as long, had seen him, resentful and dismissive, from her first tentative entry into the House Council meetings at the unfortunate age of sixteen, but she had never been forced to work by his side in any significant way.

She had never seen him wield the magic in which his sense of his own power was based. Oh, she'd seen him call fire—but there was something about it that had seemed, to her eyes, almost mundane in comparison with APhaniel's magic—or Sigurne's. Had he pulled sword or dagger, it would have had the same effect as his fire did: it was a threat, a danger, but it was entirely and quintessentially a human one.

He was just a man she liked to hate, not more, not less.

An arch, very similar to the one that led from the library to the manse, appeared some thirty yards ahead. The one marked difference, to Jewel's eye, was the adornment. Where the arch that led to the manse was covered in creeping vines that were nonetheless leafy and delicate to the eye, these were marked by thorns and flowers that looked almost like roses.

Meralonne approached them first, his gray eyes wide. "Have a care with the thorns," he said softly.

"Do you recognize the flower?"

"I do. I have not seen them in a long, long time." He pulled back, but not far; they had captured his attention more thoroughly than Rymark. Or at least they held it. "I find it interesting that they grace this arch."

"Given the amount of interesting we've had in the past few months, that isn't a comfort."

"In all probability, no." He bowed to her. While techni-

cally a bow upon greeting and departure was not outside of
the bounds of polite society given his relative rank in the
Order of Knowledge, and her absolute rank in House Terafin, it was also seldom offered by Meralonne, a man to
whom etiquette mattered only in the presence of the Kings.

Rymark noticed, of course; Jewel wondered if that had
been the point. She was accustomed to watching the House
Council for obvious—and subtle—social interaction. She
was not accustomed to watching Meralonne in the same
fashion.

Avandar was silent in every possible way as she approached the arch, taking a deep, grounding breath. Shadow
shouldered Angel aside, and given Angel's expression, she
thought he would fill in for Snow or Night and push back;
to avoid this, she stopped stalling and walked through the
arch.

The office was not the office she had last seen, and given
how little she expected it to be used, the last sighting had
occurred during Amarais' reign. It was also unlike the
sparsely furnished room in which Teller held most of the
official meetings the House required. The sweep of warm
wood, covered mostly by expensive rugs, had been eschewed in favor of stone; the stone was not the marble of
the foyer or any of the public areas within the manse.

It was gray and chill; footsteps across its breadth sounded
like thunder, even Jewel's.

There was, however, a long, wide runner that led from
the door to a table that was better suited to a council of war
than an office; if the room contained a desk, she couldn't see
it. There were no shelves on the walls to either side of the
door; nor was there one on the far wall. The lack on the far
wall, however, was because there was no space; it was occupied by a window that seemed to go on forever. Light entered the room from that window, but it was a sharp light
that fell in spokes and revealed every mote of dust in the air
as it did.

There were weapons on the walls in place of the shelving
that contained strategic books in the right-kin's office. She
recognized some of them, but not all, and as she couldn't
use any of them, she left them well alone. Meralonne, however, approached the walls to Jewel's right; Jewel walked

past the table to the window. When she reached it, she stopped.

Shadow nudged her back with his head; she stepped aside so that he could join her, since he clearly hadn't noticed the width of the window and the lack of anyone standing in front of any other part of it. Both she and her unobservant cat gazed out. It wasn't the horizon of sea and sky that caught Jewel's attention, because even if it was the wrong sea and the wrong coast—lacking, among other things, a harbor—it was far enough away not to be cause for concern.

No, it was the sudden drop; the window looked out and down. She could see the sides of a cliff or a gorge, and beneath it, at the full length of its drop, a green valley that ran parallel to the horizon for as far as the eye could see. The sky beyond the window wasn't amethyst, but azure; there wasn't a cloud in sight. There were birds, or what she assumed were birds until Shadow began to growl.

"APhaniel?" she said, her voice muted.

He came away from his inspection of the weapons and joined her at the window in silence. It was an electric silence.

"You recognized the weapons," she said softly.

"Not all of them, Terafin, but two, yes."

"Do I want to know?"

"Their previous wielders are unlikely to return to either haunt you or accuse you of their theft, if that is your concern."

"Were they mortal?"

"I will decline to answer that."

"Why?"

"Because it is of little consequence. At least two of the weapons in your collection would cause enterprising thieves to spend the rest of their natural lives in an attempt to remove them; they were made by Artisans."

Jewel's jaw felt unhinged. She closed it with difficulty. She didn't even ask him how he was so certain, because Rymark had wheeled to look over his shoulder at the walls and their suddenly more valuable adornments.

"What valley is that?" she asked.

"Do you not recognize it, Terafin?"

"No, not from this remove. I have spent most of my life in the city."

"But not all, and I would guess not the most significant part of it, to date." He raised a hand to the glass; his hand passed through it. Her eyes widened, but his did not. His were bright now. "Do you recognize the coastline?"

"No, not in any way."

"Then perhaps your journey did not bring you to this remote place. I did not expect it," he added, his voice soft, Rymark and the necessities of the Order of Knowledge all but forgotten. "I confess I am surprised at the shape and the composition of this room. You said you sought your office?"

She nodded.

"Clearly you have long considered your office a place of battle." A pale brow rose, along with the corners of his lips. "Shadow," he said, addressing the cat without bothering to look at him. "Can you fly and return?"

"*Maybe.*"

"I don't think that's wise," Jewel said, before she considered the audience. Shadow hissed and immediately leaped up—and through—what Jewel would have sworn looked like glass. Nothing shattered as he left. "Did you do that on purpose?"

Meralonne smiled. "I did not, in the end, do anything; he was responding—predictably—to you." He turned. "You have let them grow wild." It wasn't an accusation, but only barely missed that mark.

"I didn't choose their forms. I'm not sure they did, either. The Warden of Dreams saw no difference—at all—between this Shadow and Shadow as he first appeared." She paused as a thought struck her. "Are they going to get any bigger?"

"They are capable of far more visible ferocity," he replied, after a thoughtful pause.

"How did they become cats?"

"I believe that their essential nature does not notably change. They are alarmingly at home in the halls of your manse; I am not certain it bodes well for the future. Have they killed here?" He might have been asking if they destroyed carpets by his tone of voice.

"Only assassins."

"You are certain?"

"Yes. They've destroyed three beds, six chairs, and the baseboards in four rooms, if that counts."

"It does not, as you well know. You must now watch

yourself with care; what you deny yourself, Terafin, they will accept as a natural limitation on their own behavior. Waver, and they will waver."

"It is not my habit to go around killing people," she replied, heat entering the chill of the response.

"No. But power affects the powerful in different—and unpredictable—ways. The rules that have governed your life up to this point are much changed, and what is acceptable in times of war has oft been unacceptable in times of peace." Having made his point, he underscored it: he turned, at last, to Rymark ATerafin, who stood on the other side of Jewel, staring into the vast panorama of unnatural wilderness beneath them all.

"ATerafin."

Rymark turned slowly. He was pale, but smiling, his eyes wide with something that might have been wonder on any other face. "So," he said softly, acknowledging Meralonne. "It is true."

Meralonne said nothing.

Jewel however said, "What is true?"

"What they fear, Terafin. You will raise a city in this place that could rival the cities once built by gods."

He came to stand before her, without Shadow to intervene. Avandar remained where he was, but Angel moved. Angel, however, was not considered the threat that Avandar was; Rymark ignored him—just as he ignored the Chosen. She was prepared for his bow, but that's not what he chose to offer; he dropped to one knee and bowed his head.

She froze; she almost took a step back, she found the obeisance so unsettling. But she held her ground, forcing her hands to remain by her sides. "Explain yourself, Rymark," she said.

He lifted his head; he did not rise. He bore an uncanny resemblance to Celleriant when the Arianni prince had adopted the same posture, which reinforced her discomfort.

"I have been, as you must certainly suspect, a member of the Shining Court." He said it baldly; he made no apologies for what would undeniably be considered an act of treason.

"Have been?" She resisted the urge to tell him to stand up. "And you've had a miraculous change of heart?" She didn't bother to dull the edge in the words.

"Terafin, do you understand what a god is? Not the gods who speak to their children across the divide—but a god who lives, walks, breathes, and feeds in *this* world?"

"I believe I have some idea, yes."

"I would have told you that you could not, a scant hour ago. But now ... perhaps. You did not come into this power during your years as The Terafin's aide."

"Demonstrably not."

"It is new, to you. Before this, before you created your library and this—this war room—did you honestly suppose that we might prevail against a living god?"

"Yes."

"Perhaps your talent gives you some guidance that I myself lacked. I am not a fool; I have never been one. I understand power—and I understand the ways in which the magical, the mystical, grant a deeper, stranger power than mere money does."

"Money pays armies."

"It does. Do you honestly think the Kings' armies can stand on a field that the god has claimed as his own?"

"Not alone, no. But they do not stand alone."

"They will," he replied evenly. "Ariane cannot leave her domain; she will not ride to the aid of the mortals."

Jewel had just enough warning—instinctive, visceral warning—to grab Meralonne's arm as he lifted it, pointing. The floor shattered to the left of where Rymark now knelt. To his credit, Rymark barely flinched.

"Terafin," Meralonne said, each syllable distinct and staccato. "My arm."

"No. Execute him for treason; execute him for the practice of forbidden arts. Execute him at my command as The Terafin, if you are willing to allow the death to remain behind the shield of House Law. I will grant permission for no other death, here."

Avandar now stepped between Rymark and Meralonne.

"Viandaran, stand aside," Meralonne told him. Jewel's knuckles were white; she hadn't surrendered her grip on his arm, but at this point, it made no difference. He could have lifted her off her feet without effort, concern, or possibly even awareness.

Avandar neither complied nor replied. Jewel wondered if it bothered him to form a shield for Rymark.

No, Jewel. It bothers you. I would stand between APhaniel and any member of your House should you give a command that the magi wished to ignore. I would possibly allow the cats to be singed.

"Member APhaniel, if you will not abide by my decisions, you are free to leave. You will not, however, be free to return in the future."

He lowered his arm slowly, his eyes a flashing silver-gray, narrowed to slits. "Terafin."

Avandar did not notably relax; nor did he move.

"You believed we had no chance against Allasakar," Jewel said, turning a cool gaze upon Rymark.

"It is not a belief, Terafin; it is fact."

"And so you chose to serve?"

"Better to serve the god than to perish in the conflagration of those who defy him. You would do the same, if you better understood his power."

She almost kicked him; her hands had gathered into fists in spite of her determination to remain cool and distant. She said nothing; had she spoken, she wouldn't have stopped for an hour, and anything useful Rymark might have said would be lost.

"We defeated him once before."

"You stymied him once before; it is not the same. He has gathered power in the Northern Wastes; he has built his Court; he has built an army."

"That army was not notably successful in the South," she countered. "And in the South, the god-born are killed at birth."

He said nothing for a long moment, and he chose this moment to rise. "Were it not for the folly and treachery of Lord Isladar, the army would not have failed."

Jewel froze at the mention of that name. "Lord Isladar is *Kialli*," she said.

"He is. You have encountered him?"

"Yes. He attempted to kill me once." And he had left an injured girl in her care the second time. She failed to mention Ariel. "Where is he now?"

"His location is unknown; they search for him. It is irrelevant; were it not for his part in the battle, the Shining Court would rule the Dominion now. Depending on the treachery of the *Kialli* in order to secure what was barely a victory is foolish in the extreme."

"Depending on any victory, according to your words, is foolish in the extreme."

He smiled and turned, once again, toward the window. "No, Terafin. It was. The *Kialli* do not speak of the reasons they fear the Voyani, but the human members of the Court have whispered the words: The Cities of Man. I thought them fables," he added, "until the first city rose: the Tor Arkosa."

She had seen it. She said nothing.

"And the second, Lyserra, has also risen. The *Kialli* were displeased. When I last visited the Shining City, they had been dispersed to hunt—and kill—the Voyani Matriarchs who remained."

"They won't find that easy, if it is possible at all," Jewel replied, thinking of the terrifying and indomitable Yollana.

"No, and that is strange. But the god does not yet choose to walk in the Dominion, much to the regret of the Lord's Fist. The time is coming, but the god's eyes are turned toward the Holy Isle and the city of Averalaan. To us," he added. "And here you stand. You have already begun to build what must be built, and there is now a chance that it is the mortals who will stand against the god and his armies.

"You are the first sign of hope I have seen in my years of service to the Shining Court; the first indication—at all— that men's knees will not bend, or break, in the presence of god." His eyes were wide as he spoke the last word, and what he saw Jewel hoped she would *never* see. He closed them, composing himself. "I have always been a pragmatic man. I would not throw my life away on futile resistance."

"I don't particularly care if you throw your own life away," Jewel replied. "But with people like you, it's never just your own life."

"People like me?" He raised a brow. "Do you truly consider yourself different in any way?"

"In every conceivable way. If you need explanations of how, I'm not sure you're perceptive enough to have information of value—to anyone."

"And yet," he continued, undaunted, "you are now The Terafin; you preside over the most powerful House in the

Empire, second only to the Kings and the Exalted. Do you mean to tell me that you occupy that position by luck and merit?"

"No."

He inclined his head.

"I mean to tell you I *don't* occupy it because of treachery, deceit, and probable blackmail." He did not appear to find the response amusing. "I am disappointed in you."

"Because I have been honest?"

"If that's what you call it, and no. I am disappointed because you have successfully worked as an agent for the god most of us won't even name, for at least a decade and quite probably longer—and yet you cannot understand me well enough to at least dissemble intelligently. Instead, you offer insults in the guise of honesty, when you have yet to demonstrate that you understand the meaning of the word."

He stiffened. "I intended," he told her curtly, "to survive."

"So did—and do—I. But I intend for far more than just myself to survive."

"You have power that I did not—and do not—possess. It is ludicrously simple for you to make that claim. You intend to fight a war with the god. I have offered you my services, should you choose to accept them."

"As a spy?"

"As an ally, Terafin."

"What do you bring to the table that I don't already have?"

"Knowledge. Names. The interior workings of the Shining Court. A not inconsiderable power."

Avandar raised a brow, but held his peace. The gesture was enough.

"And in exchange for this?"

He smiled as he once again glanced toward the window. "Knowledge, Terafin. Knowledge and security. When you take and remake this city in your own image, I want lands and title commensurate with the aid I will offer you."

Avandar.

Yes?

Tell me not to kill him.

Avandar was very clearly amused. *His offer is reasonable, Jewel. If it is true that he has information regarding the composition of the Court—at least in its human variant—the information will aid us enormously. The Shining Court convenes in the Northern Wastes, but the human Lords do not live there—and here, they are vulnerable.*

He's implying that I'll have the power to grant him anything except his miserable life.

Avandar chose not to respond to this.

He's implying—no, he believes—that I'll unseat the Kings.

Again, Avandar was silent; this silence, however, he chose to break. *How do you intend,* he asked her softly, *to transform a city that must be transformed if it is to survive without overriding the Kings?*

By asking them, she replied coolly.

You will understand why Rymark considers both the asking and the permission highly unlikely.

Because he's Rymark, and no, actually, I don't *understand why. I accept it. I can work around it. But I'm not used to working with people I can't, and will never be able to, trust.*

Learn. You do not trust the House Council, now.

I trust them to have the interests of the House at heart, even if they don't give a rat's ass about mine. *I understand that they would never just expose their throats to the god. They certainly wouldn't help him.*

"I will consider your offer of aid with care," she said, each word even and enunciated. "I regret to inform you, however, that grant of land and titles that are not already held by Terafin are not within my power to promise."

"Not at the moment. But in future?"

"Titles such as you desire—and they are vanities, surely—can only be granted by the Kings, and they are unlikely to take any request I make for such a grant seriously." She glanced deliberately at the silent Meralonne APhaniel.

Rymark took her meaning, or rather, took *a* meaning, and immediately sunk into a formal bow.

"ATerafin," she said, as he rose.

"Terafin."

"I will ask one question which I hope you will offer as a sign of your future commitment to my cause."

"And that?"

"Are there any other members of my House involved with the Shining Court?"

"No, Terafin."

"Thank you." She turned to Torvan and Gordon. "Please see the Councillor safely back to the manse."

Torvan saluted, sharply, and left. His steps were far heavier than Rymark's as he crossed the stone floor, and they echoed as if the room were hollow. "Member APhaniel, I apologize for necessitating your involvement in what is *clearly* an internal House affair."

He raised one pale brow.

"It would not be the first time, through the auspices of contract, that you have neglected to inform the Kings of *all* that has happened or is suspected."

"It would not. May I point out that, in the last instance, I was correct?"

"You may. I will consider everything you say with as much care and deliberation as my predecessor showed."

"Your predecessor would have considered my intervention at this point — given the incontrovertible confession of treachery — to be a gift. It would rid her of a man she could not and did not trust, and it would leave no blood on her hands."

"It would only have that effect if Rymark made his confession in front of the House Council. In the absence of that, it would appear that I had surrendered a House difficulty to external authority. Especially given the presence of Haerrad on said Council."

Meralonne smiled; he was, if chilly, genuinely amused. "I believe, in this case, my inclination is to hear what he has to say, to test it for veracity, and to proceed from there. It is your inclination, Terafin, that will cause trouble."

"I wasn't the one who almost killed him."

"If his defenses were that insignificant, the power he offers is beneath notice," was the much chillier reply. "It was a lapse. I do not care to hear the Winter Queen dismissed by a mortal such as Rymark ATerafin. I will tell you now that the gods will have severe reservations in this."

"I know."

"And the Kings will therefore have — "

"The Kings are *not* gods, Meralonne."

"They are beholden to their parents in the same fashion so many mortals are."

"They are, but Rymark's parent is Gabriel, and two more

different men could not be found within the House. I believe the Kings will listen, in the end, to reason."

"And if they do not?"

"I'll cross that bridge when I come to it," she replied
firmly.

"Indeed you will. I suggest," he added, "that you arm
your Chosen with some of the weapons to be found in this
room."

"Noted."

Torvan and Gordon returned without Rymark. They were
grim and silent when they rejoined their Lord. Jewel understood why. She had deliberately failed to ask Rymark
about The Terafin's death, because there was no answer he
could give that would not push her into a murderous rage.
She had not taken into account the reactions of the Chosen, which was a grave oversight.

They had sworn their lives to Amarais. Jewel had loved
and served her, but it wasn't the same, and she knew it. She
had no words of comfort, and no promise, to offer them; if
she accepted Rymark's offer, she could not then plan to
have him executed.

Could you not? Avandar asked softly.

No.

*Yet if you make trade treaties with The Ten, you will honor
them only until it puts you at grave disadvantage.*

It's different.

*Yes, to you, it is. Accept Rymark's offer inasmuch as it can
be accepted, and he will serve you—but the moment a different, or better, opportunity arrives, he will take it. He will
swear no oath to you, and even if he does, it will never bind
him.*

My *oaths have to mean something*, she replied.

You will make no oaths to Rymark.

She was silent for a long moment. Folding her arms, she
turned to Avandar, and said distinctly, "I think I'm well past
the age where I offer something while crossing my fingers
behind my damn back."

"That is not what I said."

"That's *exactly* what you said."

Meralonne, for the first time since he'd entered the room,

retrieved his pipe from his satchel, and set about stuffing the bowl with dried leaf. He glanced at Angel, who had taken up position by the window; Angel shook his head. "I don't smoke."

"And you have been Jewel's companion for at least half your life? I suggest you try it. It is remarkably calming in situations of this nature."

Angel almost laughed; he didn't, but his expression made it clear his silence took some effort. The Chosen were, however, uniformly grim and composed.

"I suppose," the magi continued, having completed his task, "you approached your negotiations with regards to the merchant routes you supervised in the same manner you now intend to deal with Rymark?"

She couldn't hold on to her anger, which was probably for the best; her arms relaxed. "No. Usually with the merchants, there was more swearing and more insults. But I didn't promise them anything I couldn't deliver, either. In general," she added, slowing, "I didn't promise them anything; I implied they should feel honored to be offered a chance to work with Terafin. At all."

"Indeed."

"Rymark is, in theory, part of the House already."

"Yes. As are you. But you are in an unusual position. I suggest—if you will take my advice in these affairs at all— that you consider them in the same light: it is an honor to work with you. If you listen to *my* colleagues," he added, with a genuine grin, "it is an *expensive* honor."

She did laugh, then. He was working for free, after all. "What will you tell Sigurne?"

"That is more troublesome. I will rely on your permission—or lack thereof—to discuss anything with her at all."

Jewel snorted. "You will not."

"Perhaps not. But we will rely on it to act."

"What would she counsel?"

"I am not entirely certain." He inhaled. When he exhaled, he exhaled rings. They eddied up toward the ceiling in the still air, and she watched them as if she were simple audience in the streets of the holdings, although in those streets, she wouldn't have dared to get this close. "I would, of course, be delighted to remove him from consideration.

"He is not, however, wrong."

"In what way?"

"You will build a city here. It will encompass the whole of the Isle and the hundred before you are done; anything less, and you will surrender a part of your domain to the Lord of the Hells. That was bold, by the way."

"His name?"

Meralonne nodded. "I would suggest a more extreme form of caution in this place."

"I was angry."

"And anger will serve neither of us."

"What will the Kings do?"

"I do not know. In their position, I would now be very, very cautious."

"Cautious enough to have me executed?"

"I am not the Kings. Their Empire is not an Empire that could have existed in ancient times; it is too diverse, too easily lost. They are as concerned as you are with the welfare of their citizens. You are correct; mortals did not survive overlong in the ancient cities.

"Yet in the Cities of Man—should they reach them— they could. They did not often survive as lords, but the citizens of the hundred are no lords now, and if I am not mistaken, they are the prize that the Lord of the Hells seeks. They are also his sustenance. Do not think that even your city will survive without loss; people will die. You cannot prevent it. You will meet the Kings, if I am not mistaken, on the morrow."

"Will you be there?"

He smiled. "I will, with the guildmaster's permission. If nothing else, it promises a lack of boredom seldom found in the usual bickering for near invisible improvements in position."

"My life's ambition is not to make yours less boring."

"No; it is a happy consequence." He lifted the pipe and he gazed out of the window that had never quite lost the whole of his attention. "I believe we may have some difficulty."

Jewel's eyes narrowed as she immediately sought whatever had caught his gaze. Shadow. Or rather, what occupied the air in pursuit of the great, winged cat. At a distance, she had mistaken wings for birds. Shadow was not at a distance—and neither were his pursuers. This close to the window—and at the speed of his flight, growing closer with each passing second—such a mistake was impossible.

"Avandar!"

He was already in motion. Meralonne turned to Angel and handed him his pipe. "I am very attached to that pipe," he said, as he threw his arms wide. "Terafin, your permission?"

"You have it. Are they demons?"

Meralonne laughed. "No, Terafin, they are not; they are the natural denizens of the skies in this place."

They looked like demons to Jewel; they were, in shape—absent their wings—roughly human, in that they had faces, necks, arms and legs. But the arms and legs seemed covered in fur or feathers, and their faces would look normal only if by normal one meant enraged, insane, and dangerous. That, and they were screeching.

"Avandar?"

They are not demonic, no. They are natural.

But—they have tails.

Yes, Terafin. Come away from the window.

She couldn't. She indicated that the Chosen should stand back—but of course, if she didn't, *they* couldn't. It didn't matter. Wind swept through the window, reaching for Meralonne, who had opened his arms wide to embrace it. He rose—no, he leaped—through what still appeared as glass to Jewel's eye, and the sky became his terrain.

She knew why Finch thought he was beautiful, then. He was not a mage who had taken to the skies; he was, at that moment, *of* them. His hair swept out behind him, like a pale, perfect cape. He drew no shield, no sword, but watching him, she couldn't imagine he needed them.

"Terafin," Torvan said—because the Chosen had drawn swords. "Please. Retreat."

She shook her head. "If they can breach the windows," she replied, unable to look away from Meralonne APhaniel, "we need to know. This is where we'll be living." She heard the rough crackle of Avandar's magic, as lightning flew toward the skies beyond the magi. The bolt struck the closest of the three creatures.

"It's about *time,*" Shadow roared. He did not, however, come through the window, but veered up at the last second. At, in fact, a last second Jewel would have bet half the

House against. He rose immediately beyond her view, at such a sharp angle he seemed to be running up the outside of the building.

Meralonne, however, had control of the wind beyond that window; she could hear it, although she couldn't even feel it as breeze. One of the remaining two pursuers—one that wasn't smoldering—suddenly froze, dropping back as the air snarled its wings. It turned to face Meralonne, probably because it didn't have any choice.

Avandar's magic struck again. The creature turned and headed directly toward them. Its feathers were singed, and its fur, blackened—but the lightning that had slowed it hadn't slowed it *enough*.

"Terafin," Avandar barked.

She threw herself toward Angel as the creature breached window and landed, screeching in fury, in the middle of a room that suddenly seemed much smaller. She wheeled as the Chosen turned to face it.

Avandar caught her shoulder as she started to run toward them. *Be still*, he told her. *And watch.*

It broke through—

Yes. You allowed it.

I didn't—

Jewel, you did. *These men will be part of your first line of defense in this place. If they cannot stand against such a trivial opponent, they will not serve well. They have seen much in the past decade—but they require experience, and there is no other way they will gain it. I am here,* he added. *And Adam is within your reach. They will not die if they fall— trust them.*

She drew a deep breath, and tried not to hold it as the Captain of her Chosen closed with the creature.

The Chosen weren't stupid. They had *never* been stupid. They were cautious, they moved slowly, they kept themselves grounded firmly over their feet. The ceilings here were so high, they didn't impede the creature's wings; those wings were weapons. The creature had the long claws of an animal, and at this distance, Jewel could see its very generous fangs. If it could speak, it didn't.

Torvan barked what sounded like orders, although the words failed to register for Jewel. The Chosen, however, moved in concert, fanning out in a semicircle around the creature. It wavered almost immediately as the creature lunged; swords parried the strike that Jewel herself could barely see, the creature moved so damn fast. The act of parrying drove the sword back several steps; Torvan immediately closed the gap by attacking the outstretched arm before the creature could pull it back.

She was certain, from the sound the blade made, that the edge would be notched.

"Avandar—"

No, Jewel.

Do you even know what it is?

Yes. You have given them weapons that can harm the firstborn, but the weapons do not make the men. Watch and wait.

She inhaled. *I will never forgive you if they die.*

No, you won't. I clearly have more confidence in your Chosen than you do. It is a confidence that you must *build. They serve as your shield and your sword, but neither of these are meant to be toys or children's tools. If you* will not *trust them, you must let them go.*

I trust *them.*

You trust them not to harm you, yes. You trust them to obey you, yes. Neither will serve in this case. You trust me to deal with this creature. You did not blink when Meralonne chose to ride the wild wind into these foreign skies. You are not concerned for the fate of Shadow. But you are terrified for your Chosen.

They're just men. *They're not like you or Meralonne; they're not like Shadow—*

They are like, very like, you yourself. You trust yourself.

I— she lost the words as the creature's tail suddenly shot to the left, moving independently of the long reach of its claws. Armor buckled as it struck; she thought she heard ribs crack. She certainly saw blood as it trailed, suddenly, from Gordon's lips.

Avandar caught her arm. *Your presence will not help them. Your death is the* only *thing they truly fear.*

Gordon remained on his feet; the Chosen used the creature's overextension to land two solid blows. The first bounced, with the sword-notching resonance she'd heard when Torvan struck the creature's arm; the second, however, landed. The creature's thighs were not armored in the same way its arm appeared to be.

She held her breath, but she remained at Avandar's side, the whole of her attention on the Chosen; because it was, she was unprepared when Angel darted into the fray.

Swords didn't have the necessary reach. Angel, no master of the sword, could see this clearly; he could also see that the Chosen weren't armed with anything else. They wore the polished breastplates their duty as functional honor guards demanded, but they carried neither ranged weapons nor weapons that would give them the greater reach.

He could see the powerful muscles that underlay the creature's wings, because the creature kept them high enough they could be used as blunt weapons should the Chosen come too close. They also kept the creature airborne in staggered intervals; its leaps weren't dictated by simple gravity. Angel didn't carry a sword; given the Chosen, it wasn't normally necessary or desired.

He didn't need one. Glancing down the wall, where weapons—not paintings or tapestry—adorned solid stone, he sprinted to the right; in the center of the wall were pole arms. Angel had no training with edged pole arms, but one of these, crossed over a halberd, was a spear. Its head was long and tapered, widest at midpoint; it had two wide lugs at the base of the head, each tapering to points that bent up, in the direction of the blade.

Reaching, he pulled it down off the wall, expecting the weapon with which it was crossed to tumble after it; it didn't. The pole of the spear was thick and solid, but the spear itself wasn't as heavy as he'd expected it to be. He wondered if it were meant to be decorative; the spearhead looked solid—but at this weight?

He turned, the question unanswered because it didn't matter. This was what he had. In the time it had taken to run to the weapon, pull it down, and turn back, two of the Chosen had taken injuries grave enough they were lagging; they hadn't fallen, but their place in formation was weak. The winged creature continued its up and down flight; it moved fast, striking and leaping back, where its wings buoyed it, lending its jump both height and distance.

Angel didn't join the Chosen; no point. They had the creature's attention, and he wanted them to keep it for a few minutes longer. He came round the back, moving as silently as a man his height could. He'd learned that, in the holdings. This room and those streets had nothing in common.

Nothing but Jay, who stood and watched, Avandar's hand on her right arm holding her back. Angel was grateful for the domicis; none of the den would have dared. He watched, waiting for the creature to strike—there—and retreat, leaping, wings spread, back toward the windows. Its voice was a hiss, a garbled series of syllables that almost implied speech, but never quite attained it.

Its wing tips grazed ceiling as it lunged, bringing itself as close to ground as it ever reached. It protected its bleeding thigh, attacking the two men it had already injured. Angel saw the beginning of its ascent, its positioning, and he ran, past Jay, past Avandar, out of reach of the direct light that streamed in through the windows so harshly.

He didn't brace himself; he didn't stop. He had seconds before the creature once again leaped out of the range of the spear he carried. Wings were high; if the creature turned, Angel thought they had a good chance of snapping the spear's haft, they were that powerful. He wore no armor; he had a freedom of movement the Chosen didn't.

He was also vulnerable in ways they weren't.

There. The creature's wings snapped open as it slashed with its claws. Angel leaped seconds before the creature did. The spearhead pierced the flesh between its shoulders; whatever armored its forearms didn't protect the flesh between those wings. Angel tightened his grip on the haft of the spear as the creature screeched and attempted to wheel; the jagged edge of the weapon's bladed tip cut a rent in its back as it slid off the spear. It was the first significant wound the creature had taken, and in turning to face Angel, it exposed its back to the Chosen.

Angel raised the spear and kept it between himself and his opponent; Torvan and Marave closed immediately from behind, taking care to avoid the wide, powerful sweep of its wings. Marave was driven back; Torvan managed to duck under the range of the wings, and his sword bit far deeper than Angel's spear had, although he was struck to the side by the creature's tail.

There was no decisive blow. Angel's was not; Torvan's was not. But the cumulative effect of the concerted attacks slowed the creature enough that the fight became a combat of attrition.

Avandar released Jewel's arm. She was silent as she watched. Demons didn't *bleed* the way this creature did, and if they roared, it was in anger, not pain. They offered words—often insults—in place of syllabic animal sounds, and the grandeur of their presence was not based on sheer physical strength. They also tended to dissolve into a fine layer of ash when they at last collapsed.

This creature did not; it was reduced, slowly, to a slashed, bloodied corpse, and the reduction seemed to go on forever.

Yes, Avandar said. *This is death. It is ugly and visceral, and you will see it time and again in the coming years. But it is the death the Chosen would have faced if they had fallen. There is no pity or mercy in a predator; they are driven, always, by the need for sustenance.*

Thank you, she replied, *for the lecture.*

You do not kill your own food. You do not kill your own criminals; they are executed, as if execution were the end of a ritual. But some of your Chosen have seen war, and the rules of the battlefield are different.

The Kings' Laws—

Do not be naive, Jewel. Yes, the Kings' Laws govern some part of the armies—but not during battles. After the fact, perhaps—but even then, the rules are judiciously applied, and a blind eye equally judiciously turned. Laws exist because men accept them; where men choose not to accept them, such laws become no more than theory. Here, the only law is survival.

It is not.

When they fight, Jewel, it is.

She had seen battle, in the South. She had seen the village of Damar, under siege by elemental water and demon, both. She knew what battle looked like. She had seen the foyer of her own manse destroyed, and she had seen the bodies of the fallen House Guard and Chosen, the bodies of their nameless enemies.

It is not different?

It was. He knew it. What she couldn't say, as silence returned to the chamber, was why.

It is your home, now; it bears the whole of your name, or you bear the whole of it. When war comes to your home, it is always more personal. You travel to war, and you maintain the illusion that the life you left behind is safe.

The Terafin died.

He nodded.

"Captain," she said.

Torvan saluted.

"Take Gordon and Marave to the infirmary."

He glanced at the Chosen and nodded. They left. He remained. It was not quite insubordination, and Jewel accepted it. She turned, once again, toward the open skies; Meralonne stood in midair alone, gazing down upon the valley. If something had fallen from the skies to the distant earth beneath his feet, it was invisible. She couldn't see Shadow. But Avandar was right; she felt no visceral fear *for* the cat, although echoes of her reaction on the night the manse had altered were still present.

She turned, last, to look at Angel. He was not one of the Chosen. He followed no strict chain of command. She could give him orders—and had, in the past—but they were orders demanded by the events of the moment; they were hardly premeditated. She wanted to tell him *I never want to see you do that again.*

What came out instead was, "Nice spear."

He glanced up at its head. "It's technically yours. I pulled it down from the wall."

"You probably want to clean it before you put it back." Turning to the window, she raised her voice. "Meralonne! If you're finished there?"

He wheeled, a lazy, graceful motion, and then drifted toward the window as if the whole of his weight were insubstantial. Wind caught his hair, and light brightened it; his eyes were silver, his skin almost white. She could not imagine this man smoking a pipe which would have met with her Oma's approval. But he had.

He landed ten feet from where she stood, shadowed by Avandar.

"Shadow?"

"He will return on his own. Or not. He is not mine," Meralonne added, lifting a brow. "I would not own a creature who paid so little heed to my commands." His hair settled down his back as the breeze left the room, but his eyes remained bright and a little too sharp. He glanced at the corpse. "They will need to learn basic anatomy," he said. He turned toward Angel and stilled.

Chapter Thirteen

"**Y**OU WERE NOT ARMED when you entered this chamber," the mage said softly.

"No."

"And you simply chose a weapon with which to enter the fray?"

"I chose a weapon with greater reach than a sword, yes. No one else was using it, and it wasn't doing much good as a substitute painting."

At that, the mage smiled. "No, I imagine it wasn't. It is, if I am not mistaken, an interesting choice. Will you leave it here?"

Angel nodded. "Are we likely to see more of these creatures soon?"

"If by that, you mean, are they likely to attack you in the library? No; I think it very, very unlikely. But this room does not exist in quite the same place, and yes, it is entirely probable. They will not attack unless provoked."

Jewel grimaced. "I'll have a word with Shadow—if he gets back."

"I *heard* that." Of course he had. Shadow was perched—precariously, given his size—in the window. He leaped to the ground, and curled himself around Jewel. "Wait, *why* is he holding *that*?"

"It fell off the wall."

Shadow hissed. "Well, *tell him* to put it *back*."

Angel's eyes narrowed. He gestured in brief den-sign. Jewel laughed, and got a nose full of Shadow's tail in response.

"But—clean it first?"

Meralonne, however, said, "The blade does not need cleaning, as you can see. Where did you retrieve it from, Angel?"

Angel turned. "There," he said.

But Jewel already understood why Meralonne had asked. "Is this ever going to stop?" she asked softly. There was no empty space on the wall; the wall was still fully adorned with weapons of various descriptions.

Angel headed toward the wall, carrying the spear.

Avandar, watching, said, "I do not believe your Angel will find a mount on the wall for that spear."

"Do you recognize it?" she asked.

"The spear? No, not as such. Illaraphaniel?"

Meralonne, however, was watching Angel, a strange smile at play around his lips. "Yes," he said softly, "I believe I do. Did he truly just grab a random long weapon from the wall?"

"The wall he was standing closest to, yes."

"I suggest that, as Terafin is already accustomed to the unusual sight of Rendish hair, they might accept an equally unusual weapon."

"Terafin will. I imagine the Kings—and any of the rest of The Ten—won't, if he's out in public. It's not going to hurt him, is it?"

"It will cause him far less harm than those against whom it is wielded. Did you watch him fight?"

She nodded.

"Did anything strike you as unusual?"

"Besides the shrieking, half-armored winged creature that flew through the window?"

"Besides that, yes."

"No. I didn't expect to see him leap into the fight . . . but no. He stayed at the reach of the spear, and he never tried anything beyond pointing, stabbing, and getting out of the way."

"You noticed nothing unusual—at all—about the weapon or its blade?"

"Nothing. Nothing besides the fact that it cut through

part of the creature's spine." She turned to Shadow. "Now you can go join your brothers."

Angel found no place to put the spear. He walked up and down the length of the wall three times, stopping at the spot where he was certain he'd jumped to grab it; there was no empty space where it might have been. "This would be a damn impressive armory," he said. "It replenishes itself."

He put the spear up, letting most of its weight rest against the flat stone.

"No armor," Jay said, approaching him. Shadow came with her; he took a swipe at the spear. Angel moved it before his claws connected. Jay clamped a hand on the gray cat's head.

"Oh, *fine.*"

"You don't like the spear?" Angel asked. It was possibly the best reason offered to keep it.

"I don't *need* a spear."

"You don't need to play with a spear, either," Jay told him. "We need to head back to Teller so I can find out just how bad my day is going to be."

"And the spear?"

She hesitated; he marked it. "It's up to you."

"If it were you holding the spear?"

"Unless it belonged to an ancient ancestor—or my Oma—I'd hide it under the table and pretend I'd never touched it."

He laughed, and she signed, *I'm serious.*

She returned to the right-kin's office by way of the healerie. It was not generally considered the most direct route there, but Jewel wanted to check in on the Chosen before she spoke with Teller. Daine and his two assistants were in the infirmary, and she left Torvan outside of the healerie doors. If Alowan was gone—and he so undeniably was, it was still difficult to cross the threshold without a sense of mourning—Daine had happily adapted to the rules by which the healerie had been run under his command. Weapons were not allowed in the healerie.

The Chosen did not disarm themselves when in the presence of The Terafin.

Angel, who was perfectly happy to disarm himself gave

the wooden box on the wall a very dubious glance; it was meant for daggers and short weapons. It had no room for long swords and it certainly wasn't meant for pole arms.

Leave it? He gestured at Jewel.

No.

She left him in the hall beside Torvan and the three Chosen who had come to replace those he'd ordered to the healerie. As Avandar and Meralonne were by her side, the Chosen were willing to remain there. It was, however, grudging. Jewel well understood why, but could not bring herself to order Daine to abandon Alowan's rules.

He was waiting for her when she made her way around the fountain in the arboretum.

"Gordon?" she asked, without preamble.

"Three broken ribs, a lot of bruising."

"Did he—"

"Two ribs pierced lung, but only one lung. He accepted my aid."

She swallowed and nodded. "When will he be ready to return to active duty?"

"If you accept his own medical estimation, now."

She smiled. "I will accept the estimate given me by his healer."

"In two days."

"Is it safe for you to have him here?"

"Yes. He wasn't in any immediate danger. If you could have his captain threaten to demote him if he doesn't sit still, though, you'd have my gratitude."

She laughed. Shadow, who had been expressly forbidden to come within six inches of anything green and growing in the healerie, nudged Daine. It was, given the way Daine staggered, like being gently nudged by a battering ram. Daine, like the rest of the den, had grown accustomed to the cats' demands for due deference. He dropped a hand to the cat's gray fur.

"Torvan won't enter the healerie without his sword; he's on duty."

"A pity, then." Daine smiled. His smile surprised her; it was solid, the edges slightly hard. The healerie *was* Daine's, now. He was ten years her junior, but he had chosen his domain. Its rules and customs had been handed down by Alowan, a man beloved by almost everyone except the Chosen, and he had accepted their weight.

She saw, now, that it wasn't just acceptance. Those rules and those customs were home to Daine, just as the Terafin laws were at the core of Jewel, although she had had no hand in their creation. "Will you," she asked him softly, "accept the House Name? It is mine to offer, now." Amarais had not, in part for Daine's safety.

In part, Jewel realized, with a pang, for this moment. Amarais was not seer-born, not talent-born, but she understood the human heart, even if her entire life had necessitated that she hide her own.

"What answer do you think I should give you?"

"Yes."

"What answer do you think I will?"

"You will give me Alowan's answer."

Daine nodded. "I didn't understand it when I first met Alowan. I understand it, now. Alowan was The Terafin's, Jay. He was hers. He served her. But he served her entirely within his own paradigm as healer. He was not without temper. He was not without steel. He served Terafin because he chose to offer her the support he could, but he was not *of* Terafin."

"And you?"

"I know what some of Terafin is," he replied, his expression darkening. "But I know what *The* Terafin stands for. I'm not Alowan."

"No."

"But I hope, in time, to be like him. And no, that's not why I won't use the House Name. I know you; you won't order me to do anything that would damage the healerie, or myself. But . . . I am not Terafin. I am healer-born. I never understood why Angel refused the House Name."

"You understand now."

"Yes. I even feel guilty for thinking of him as an idiot."

"*I* don't," Shadow interjected.

They both ignored him. As long as Daine was actively scratching behind his ears, he was likely to let them continue. "Levec would be happier if you left this place."

"No, he wouldn't. He doesn't even believe he would be, anymore. I'm not trapped in Terafin; I'm not a prisoner. He believes everyone who isn't healer-born is a threat to those who are—but he understands the ways in which the healed and the healer-born are tied. What I now want to build, I can't build in the Houses of Healing. If, however, I allow myself to be assassinated, he's going to hold a grudge against you forever."

"If only that long. I'll leave you with Gordon. If you'd like, *I* can tell him he'll be demoted."

"That, in my opinion, would not help. It would be effective . . . but no."

"Marave?"

"Her injuries were superficial enough that I saw no need to detain her. Gordon was not impressed." He hesitated. "Jay."

She waited.

"The House Name isn't about the House. It's about me. I know its value. I know what it means to walk the city streets as ATerafin. I know what men—and women—believe themselves willing to do to gain it. Some of me wants it as well. And this is how I'll know where my priorities are. It's a check."

Daine was not, and would never be, Alowan. For just this moment, though, she loved him as if he were.

Angel was still waiting, spear conspicuous against the wall, when she emerged.

"Go back to the West Wing," she told him softly.

"I don't—"

"I'm going to talk to Teller. And Barston. I have no prior appointments for the rest of the day, and if I'm lucky, I won't have to look at Duvari. If I'm unlucky," she continued, as he lifted his spear, "and I expect that, given my day, I'll be mired in appointment making and veiled or not-so-veiled threats, none of which will come to fruition now.

"Go back to the Wing and tell the others what happened."

When she arrived in the right-kin's office, Barston had the expression of a man under siege, although the office was almost empty. He rose the minute she stepped across the threshold and tendered her a perfect bow. It was one of the few ways in which he expressed annoyance. Barston did not stoop to obvious incivility where relative rank demanded none; he merely sharpened every polite gesture in his arsenal.

Given he was Barston, that arsenal included obeisances that probably hadn't been used at Court for two centuries.

"Is it very bad?" she asked when he rose.

"Teller has granted the Lord of the Compact an audience. They are in the right-kin's office now."

Duvari—and a woman Jewel didn't immediately recognize—were waiting in Teller's office. Teller was seated behind his desk. He rose when Jewel entered the room, and offered her a full bow. Carrying a large, crudely painted sign about the high levels of danger would probably have been a less effective warning.

Jewel, forewarned, nodded him back into his chair before she turned to face Duvari. "Lord of the Compact," she said, inclining only her chin. She glanced at the woman.

"Terafin," Duvari replied. "May I introduce Birgide Viranyi." It was, in theory a question; it sounded like a command. The woman, however, now turned to Jewel, and offered her a full, flat-backed bow. She was about six inches taller than Jewel; her hair was cropped. She had two visible scars on her face, one along the line of her jaw and one just under her left ear. She was not particularly finely dressed, but of more relevance, she was not dressed as a member of the patriciate at all.

"You are a member of the *Astari*, Birgide?"

Birgide said nothing.

"She is," Duvari replied. "That is not to be discussed outside of this office."

"If she arrived with you, it will be."

"It is not to be discussed by you or your right-kin outside of this office. As it happens, she did not arrive with me."

Jewel turned to Teller. "Under what pretext was she granted an appointment?"

". . . As a possible new member of the gardening staff."

Jewel stared at him for a full fifteen seconds before she turned back to Duvari. "Out of the question." Duvari clearly expected this.

"She is, in fact, renowned for her skill in gardens across the Empire."

"At her age?"

"Even so. She is only two years older than you, yourself, and you are now known as the ruler of the most powerful of The Ten."

"The gardening staff is decided upon by the Master Gardener."

"I wish you to introduce Birgide to that Master Gardener—and allow him to make his own decision with regard to her employ."

"Duvari, you have at least three members of your *Astari* in various positions in my House. Why—why on earth—would you now plant a fourth here as a *gardener*?"

Avandar coughed into his hand.

Birgide lifted her chin. "It was not the request of the Lord of the Compact," she said. Her voice was low, but it was musical. "It was entirely my own; he has reservations."

"Yours?"

"Entirely. I am aware that the *Astari* form part of the Household Staff for any of The Ten—as you yourself are. I am not considered martial enough to join the Kings' Swords."

Jewel folded her arms across her chest and raised a brow.

"I don't do my best work in heavy armor. Until last week, I worked on the edge of the Empire's border, near the Free Towns."

"And you are here now?"

"I heard, of course," Birgide replied, "Of the *Ellariannatte*. I wished to study them."

"I'm surprised Duvari cared."

"Strictly speaking, he does not. I will not be forced upon your House. I have brought a resume, and a few samples of my work, and I am willing to approach the Master Gardener with only an introduction and no pressure on your part."

Jewel almost pinched herself, she felt so dumbfounded. "The grounds here are unusual," she finally said. She turned to the Lord of the Compact. "This is the sum total of the reason you are now in this office?"

"No, Terafin. It is an adjunct of little significance. I am here to deliver an invitation."

"Invitation?"

"A royal command. Tomorrow, in the morning, you are to present yourself to the Kings in the Hall of Wise Counsel in *Avantari*. The Exalted will also be present; they have chosen to allow the concerns of the Kings to outweigh their demands for your presence. If you are once again severely indisposed, the Kings have chosen to take the unusual step of visiting you, within the Terafin audience chambers."

Jewel let the words settle into a stiff silence before she held out her left hand. Duvari placed a heavy scroll case in the fold of her palm; she twisted it open and removed what lay within. It was parchment, but its texture was more cloth than leather, and it bore two seals, both of which were instantly recognizable to anyone standing in the room. She broke those seals, and to her great surprise, *heard* the command; it was spoken as she unfurled the scroll.

It was also written, but the written words were like an afterthought. The voices were undeniably those of the Twin Kings. Duvari had not exaggerated; his only tendency in that regard he saved for the Kings he served.

Duvari waited. Jewel was content, for the moment, to let him wait; it was the only way to signal theoretical defiance.

"Birgide," she said. "Why did you not simply approach the Master Gardener directly? Why did you choose to accompany Duvari at all?"

"The choice was not mine. It is my belief that the Master Gardener would be willing to accept my work. I believe that Duvari has some hopes that you will deny my petition."

"I . . . see."

"And if you do not, you will have a clearer understanding of the ways in which you might support me should support be required. I do not understand the change in your grounds, but I believe they are extensive."

"And my acceptance of your employ in this regard would be a concession to the concerns of the Lord of the Compact."

Birgide's smile was wry; it transformed her face, an acknowledgment of the fact that no concession would address the concerns of that man. It made the *Astari* difficult, for Jewel. If the *Astari* were all like Duvari, dismissing them out of hand would be a simple matter of introduction. Devon was not like Duvari. Inasmuch as a man could devote his life and his intellect to two masters, Devon had. She had no doubt at all that he would continue to do so, providing only that the interests of Terafin did not clash directly with the interests of the Kings.

Jewel admired the Kings; she honored them. She had no difficulty believing that men and women of integrity and intelligence would choose to do the same. Nor did she have any difficulty believing that those men and women might dedicate the whole of their lives to the Kings, as the Chosen did to The Terafin. She had some issues with some of what the *Astari* purportedly *did* in that service, but as that was hearsay, she attempted to suspend judgment. Birgide's wry smile made it easier than it should have been.

She exhaled. "Lord of the Compact, you may offer my acknowledgment of the Kings' command, and my acceptance of their right, as sovereigns, to command me. I will, barring a situation not of my own making, present myself before the thrones in the Hall of Wise Counsel directly after the early breakfast hour in the morning, if that is acceptable." She turned to Birgide. "The Master Gardener is extremely important to the House—and extremely particular. If you are willing to meet him on short notice, I will take you there myself."

Birgide had not lied; she had several baskets of different weight and textures which required attention; the walk to the Master Gardener's office was not particularly brisk. As Birgide insisted on carrying a clay urn of some weight in her own arms, Jewel slowed her customary pace to walk by her side. "How is it," she asked, "that Duvari, a man who defines the absence of charm, has managed to gather people who exemplify it to his service?"

Birgide chuckled. "We obey Duvari," she said, the lines around her mouth clearly marked, over time, by that smile. "But we serve the Kings. We are aware—in a way that Duvari will never openly acknowledge—that your interference in *Avantari* preserved the lives of the Princes of the Blood; you served as the only effective defense of the future Kings we will *also* serve, should we survive to do so.

"It is why," she added, the smile fading as her expression became much graver, "word of the . . . changes . . . in the physical structure of *Avantari* itself have been minimized where possible. Had those alterations occurred in *any* other circumstance . . ." she failed to finish the sentence, and because she carried something heavy in both hands, also failed to shrug.

Jewel accepted the implied shrug in its place. "I know you probably can't answer this, but I haven't been to

Avantari. I wasn't technically there the day the changes occurred, either."

"That is part of the concern," Birgide replied. "Your question?"

"How . . . notable . . . are those changes?"

Birgide raised a brow. "You really haven't traveled to the Kings' palace since then."

"No."

"And you were not informed?"

"I was informed that some structural changes had occurred at the end of the battle; I was also told that they were, architecturally, superior. They strengthened the halls, rather than weakening them."

"But you were not given a sketch of the actual differences?"

"No. This may come as a surprise to you, given the import of House Terafin, but I have not spent most of my adult life traversing those halls. I am familiar with the Trade Commission's offices, and with the galleries and the halls that lead to—and from it—but I have seldom entered the Hall of The Ten. I was not right-kin."

Birgide raised brow, no more; to reach the Master Gardener's offices, they had to pass by the large doors that led to the main terrace. Jewel paused there, and Birgide turned as well, to look out on the trees that she had correctly named: *Ellariannatte.*

"So," she said softly. "It was not mere rumor."

"No."

"I had some thought that the trees were misidentified, but one of my sources was impeccable." Her eyes were wide and unblinking as she lifted her gaze, exposing the whole of a surprisingly long throat to do so. She lowered her head slowly, and turned. "You do not know how these trees came to be here."

"I don't understand the mechanics, no."

"A subtle difference."

Jewel nodded.

"The changes within *Avantari* are not as immediately striking—or were not, to me, but architecture is not my area of specialty. To some, however, they are the same; some of the pillars are notably different, and one section of wall has been reworked in a way that has been difficult to suppress.

There are apparently two rooms that have undergone large changes, but those rooms did not see heavy use; I do not know if you will be required to view them. They are the most significant transformation, however, and I believe access has been extremely limited since then. Thank you," she added, nodding, as she pulled her gaze from the height of those trees. "Where it does not come into conflict with my duties and my oaths of allegiance, Terafin, I will repay courtesy with courtesy."

Jewel introduced Birgide to the Master Gardener with some stiffness; she found the Master Gardener about as easygoing as the Master of the Household Staff, and she was very careful about how she impinged on either's territory. Birgide, however, was Birgide Viranyi, a name which meant nothing to Jewel, and apparently a *great* deal to the Master Gardener. When Jewel informed him that Birgide wished to be considered for employ on the Household Staff, she thought his eyes would fall out of their sockets. He could not safely enthuse in front of The Terafin of course, but indicated that he wished to waste no more of her precious time, and all but ushered her out of his interior office.

Avandar was amused, but he was grave as they once again walked the halls that led back to Teller's office. "You will, of course, have a new gardener on your staff before the day is done."

"I know."

"You accepted her."

"In part, because Duvari didn't like it." Jewel glanced back over her shoulder. "And frankly, I'm relieved that I did; I cannot imagine what the Master Gardener would have said—or done—had I dismissed her and word reached his ears."

Avandar raised a brow.

"And in part, yes, because I liked her. I believed her; she wanted to work on our grounds and in our gardens, and she wanted it the way—the way makers want to make. I personally don't care for plants I can't eat; I have learned, at some expense, to appreciate some of their names and their finer qualities because it's *expected*. But something about Birgide makes me want to learn about them from *her*. They're not about status, to her, and not even just about beauty. She sees something in them that I don't."

"That can be said about many people, and many things."

"Yes. Hopefully, one of them won't be politics."

The meeting with The Ten was to occur two hours after the start of the meeting with the Kings. Jewel was certain that the Exalted, Sigurne Mellifas, and possibly the Bardmaster of Senniel College would also be in attendance. She glanced at a message delivered from House Araven and grimaced.

"How long do you feel the Council meeting will last?"

"Given The Kalakar's letter? It may well last until the following morning. It won't be the first time The Ten have met, recessed, and reconvened the following day. I'm slightly more concerned that the audience granted me by the Kings—"

Teller gestured in colorful den-sign.

Jewel laughed, although it was grim. "I know. But I don't want to clash with Duvari about the timing of the Council meeting."

"If the gods are called," Avandar interjected, "time is less of an issue for anyone who is not otherwise involved in their discussions."

"You think it likely?" As he raised a brow, she nodded. "I'm concerned about the rooms."

"That was deftly done," Avandar said, surprising her. "While I feel your role as Terafin requires a rigid formality, your instincts are good. Birgide's information was useful. Why are the rooms of concern to you?"

"I'm . . . not certain. But they are. I have no intention of contesting the Kings' sovereignty," she added, as if it were necessary. Given Avandar, it probably was.

"You will take Teller with you to the Council meeting."

"He is right-kin. Yes."

"Will you consider the inclusion of Lord Celleriant?"

"No. You'll be there, and I may second Meralonne APhaniel as House Mage, if only to keep him from Sigurne's side."

"I do not consider that wise."

"He'll worm his way in regardless. I may have some say over his behavior, this way."

"Your natural optimism is not, in this case, commendable."

"Thank you, Avandar."

They left the right-kin's office and entered the external office. Barston, seated behind his desk, rose instantly, which was never a good sign. He tendered a perfect, but brief bow. "Terafin. A possible difficulty in the Household Staff has arisen—"

Jewel turned immediately to see the white hair and grim expression of the Master of the Household Staff. She was, to Jewel's surprise, seated, although she rose the minute Jewel caught sight of her. She instantly regretted the absence of Duvari, the Exalted, or any other crisis, because nothing stood between them. The Master of the Household Staff performed as exquisite a bow as "a woman of her advanced years"—a phrase which struck terror in the heart of anyone *else* who lived in the manse when she used it—could.

"Terafin," she said, in clipped, very formal syllables.

"Master of the Household Staff." Jewel had once—only once—responded "ATerafin." "Has there been some difficulty which requires my immediate attention?"

"There has apparently been some difficulty which required mine," was the even chillier response. "The Household Staff was, of course, informed of your change of residence within the manse."

Jewel froze. Of all the difficulties she anticipated would be caused by the severe transformation of The Terafin's personal quarters, this one had entirely escaped her.

"It is customary to inform me of extensive renovations or reconstruction undertaken in the manse. Given your unexpected illness, it is possible you overlooked this responsibility."

She had. She considered it now. The servants' halls and passages, used for discreet attention to the various chambers in which the business of the manse was conducted, were present throughout the manse itself. They were—had been—present within The Terafin's chambers, although only Carver knew the exact layout; access to those halls required a seniority that most of the servants would never achieve.

"The renovations, as you have noted, were extensive. They were also almost immediate. Please extend my apologies to the Household Staff."

This was not, clearly, enough. It was, on the other hand, more than enough for Barston, who had never particularly cared for the Master of the Household Staff, although he made haste to grant her all due respect.

"The full extent of those alterations is not yet known."

This august woman raised a gray brow. Only her brows retained any color at all. "Was the House Mage involved in this endeavor?"

It was not a question she had a right to ask. "I am not at liberty to say," Jewel replied. "But I will make haste to offer instructions and a floor plan, where one exists, within the next week. Until then, it is entirely understood if the Household Staff cannot navigate my rooms at all. My domicis—"

"You are to meet with the Kings and The Ten on the morrow," was the even chillier response. "Your domicis is not, I feel, up to the task of your personal care with regards to that meeting. If you will request Ellerson's intervention at this time, I will excuse your personal attendants from their duties without prejudice for . . . the week."

"Thank you. Please make an appointment with Barston for a week hence, where we will discuss the changes in the duties of my personal attendants."

The Master of the Household Staff did not slam the doors on her way out. Jewel was surprised they didn't shatter anyway.

Teller emerged from his office almost immediately, a sure sign that some of the magic in the interior office allowed him a glimpse of the contents of the exterior one. He signed, grimacing; Jewel shrugged in response.

"On the bright side, if the Kings do demand my execution, that's one thing I'll be spared."

Barston coughed.

Ellerson was not Avandar. He didn't even blink when he entered what had once been the library. He had Carver by his side, and Carver was carrying—with exaggerated care—the official wardrobe for the following morning.

"You could just stay in our Wing," he pointed out.

"I would—but as I didn't deliberately cause *these* changes, I don't want to inadvertently change the West Wing." She hesitated, and then less flippantly added, "I can't be seen to be afraid of the changes that *have* been made."

"Why not? Everyone else is."

"How bad is it in the back halls?"

"You've managed to upend the absolute upper echelons of the Household Staff. There is no higher rank, among servants, than to be assigned to the personal detail of The Terafin herself. If you don't consider disenfranchising the oldest and most elite members of your staff—"

She raised a hand in surrender.

"I am certain," Ellerson said, "That she had larger worries to contend with."

"So was I," Jewel admitted. "I'm rethinking that, now."

"You spoke with the Master of the Household Staff."

"She spoke with me."

Carver cringed—but he cringed carefully, under Ellerson's watchful eye. Unlike Ellerson, he had no reason to treat the library as if it were still somehow just a library; he stared at everything, and whistled a couple of times.

"How bad are the back halls? Carver?"

"Sorry. Do you mean the servants or the halls themselves?"

"The physical halls."

"If you're speaking of the rest of the manse, they haven't changed at all, as far as I could tell. It wasn't as easy to cut through them though. The dragon was actually there."

"Master Carver."

"Sorry. She's reduced a third of the staff to stammering wrecks, though."

"That is not The Terafin's concern," was Ellerson's stiff reply.

"Merry?" Jewel asked, ignoring Ellerson's comment.

"Not one of them, but she's not in the senior tier, and her duties could be accomplished with very little interruption."

"Can you get into the back halls from here?"

"I don't know."

"What do you mean?"

"If you asked me that question two days ago, I would have said no." He glanced at the Chosen.

"You would have been lying."

He grinned. "Well, yes. But today? I'm not even sure there *are* back halls anymore. No one is."

"By no one—"

"No one. The Master of the Household Staff has relieved

her most senior servants from their duties for a week. No one's dared to ask her about the fate of the upper halls because anyone with a shred of luck has managed to avoid her."

"Rumors?"

"They're gone."

Jewel nodded. She walked across the much expanded library, toward the doubled set of doors on the wall at the far end. They seemed to be where she remembered leaving them in the morning, which was a relief. Ellerson followed, as did the Chosen; Carver lagged behind a bit. "I'm guessing the back halls are definitely gone," he said, as Avandar opened the doors.

"That is now my biggest nightmare," Jewel replied. "I don't think I've ever seen the Master of the Household Staff so angry, and I can't afford to have her resign in fury. I know just barely enough to know how much of a nightmare it would be to attempt to replace her with someone of half her competence."

Beyond the double doors, the rooms looked very similar to the rooms The Terafin had occupied for all of Jewel's life in the manse. "Is the library subject to constant change, or is its geography now dependable?" Ellerson asked. He removed the dresses from Carver's arms and hung them, with care, in the large closet; he set up the various brushes, combs and clips that were the bane of her morning existence, and made her hate the sight of her own hair.

While he worked Jewel pulled Carver away.

"Exercise caution," Avandar said. "I wish to ascertain that the room is materially magically unaltered, and that it is . . . predictable."

"I will exercise as much caution as the current situation allows," Jewel replied. She turned to Carver, the Chosen almost invisible to her now, although they were present. "Where?"

"There are no direct entrances into the bedchamber," Carver replied. He gestured in den-sign, and she replied: *take the lead.* As he headed into the hall, she added, "I haven't examined any of the other rooms, and the former private office was . . . greatly changed."

"Angel told us. He also showed us the spear. I'm not sure Ellerson approved."

"I'm sure he didn't." She followed as Carver opened the doors that led to the larger room at the end of the hall. It was used for informal meetings—where informal generally meant private, and of a critical nature. Jewel had seen it twice. She held her breath as Carver entered the room, and entered it hesitantly at his back. Or rather, entered hesitantly at Torvan's back; if he was willing to allow Carver free run of suspect rooms, he did *not* extend the same courtesy to his Lord.

It looked, to her eyes, like the same room. She exhaled.

"Don't be relieved yet," Carver said quietly, discerning both her anxiety and the slackening of its grip. "I don't recognize that door."

"The very ordinary door to the left?"

"The very ordinary door that wasn't here the last time I made a pass through these rooms."

"Carver . . ."

He offered no apology, his expression hardening. "You were going to be Terafin," he said, as if there had never been any question. "If you survived the South, if you came back to us—you were going to be The Terafin."

Torvan said nothing, but she expected no interruption from that quarter.

"Access to these rooms from the back halls is severely restricted, so I didn't come here often."

"And you didn't come here with permission. Does Merry know?"

"I've never asked her. But that door wasn't here the last time I was. Captain?"

Torvan said, "It's new."

It looked like a nondescript interior door, admittedly in the personal rooms of the ruler of House Terafin; it was dark, fine, the lintel of its frame engraved with the horizontal relief of the House Sword, as the interior doors in these rooms often were. There were wall sconces to either side of the frame, meant to contain magestones, although no stones occupied them at present. The handle was brass.

Jewel approached the door; Torvan stepped in her way. "Captain," she said softly, "If there is any immediate danger offered me by the door—or by what lies beyond it—*I* will know. If there is danger to you, or to my Chosen, I cannot guarantee that."

She spoke in very precise Weston; he failed to hear a word of it, although he did nod.

"Torvan—"

"Understand, Terafin," he said, relenting, "that it is not your gift that defines you. You are The Terafin. We are the Chosen. We are not, as you are, seer-born; it is not considered a grave deficit. The Chosen have existed for centuries without the talent-born among our ranks. If our survival had depended upon the gift of foresight, the House would not have survived to *become* one of The Ten."

"It seems a needless risk—"

"It is a necessary risk. It is always a necessary risk."

She swallowed, met his gaze, and nodded, remembering Avandar's words. The Chosen were not children; they were not orphans and runaways gathered in the holdings. They were shield, defense, and personal army; they were not, and could not be reduced to, retainers, attendants, and men who . . . waited.

Carver seemed to understand this already. He gestured in brief den-sign, and she nodded. *Yes, hard.*

"Was that anywhere near where the servants' entrance was?"

Carver shook his head.

"Is the servants' entrance in this room now?"

"No." He moved away from the wall as Torvan opened the door, and froze in its frame for a few seconds too long. Torvan didn't enter the room; he didn't order the Chosen forward. But he didn't immediately draw sword, and he didn't speak a word when Jewel walked toward his back. He did, however, enter then.

Jewel followed and stopped at the doorjamb, lifting one hand to the frame to steady herself.

"Jay?"

She laughed. It was an uneven laugh, an expression not of mirth, but surprise. Or shock, or outrage. "Carver, come here."

"What is it?"

"You tell me. Tell me what you see."

He came to join her, but didn't laugh; he swore, instead. Jewel lowered her arm, and Carver moved past her, just as the Chosen had done, walking single file down the hall that led from the door because it wasn't wide enough for two. It wasn't wide enough for the swords the Chosen carried, either; it was wide enough for Carver's daggers. Or Jewel's, although she was not, at this moment, wearing them.

"Terafin?" Torvan asked, the word drifting back to where she stood.

"It's the thirty-fifth holding," she said, forcing strength into the words. "It's an apartment in the thirty-fifth holding."

Torvan didn't argue. Carver, who'd ducked into the tiny kitchen to the right, reappeared and entered the room to the left. She thought she should stop him, because she knew that these rooms, this apartment, could not *possibly* be as they appeared. Instead, she drifted into the hall herself. The door did not slam shut behind them.

Carver came out after a brief moment, met her eyes, and once again moved down the hall. He went to the next door on the left. Jewel herself followed him, but diverged at the door on the right. Torvan and the Chosen had opened all of the doors, even this one, in some confusion. She could well understand why. If they had not expected the sudden, grandiose transformations of the library or the small, personal office, it was of a piece with the sudden appearance of the Common's fabled trees in their backyard; it meshed with the existence of three voluble, giant, winged cats, a silent white stag, and the demons who had assassinated The Terafin, and had failed—by a hair—to assassinate Jewel.

This?

It was of inferior workmanship. The ceilings were low, the halls narrow; the planking on the floor was old enough that it creaked no matter who walked across it. The rugs, where they existed, were threadbare and patchy, the cupboards scarred and slightly warped. There were few windows, and little light, and the windows were at the height of the short walls. They were barred, of course, and the bars were excellent—and new.

In the room at the right end of the hall was a familiar desk, a familiar table, and a familiar set of shelves on the wall. The shelves should have been empty, but they weren't. She hesitated, and then knelt by the bed-side.

"Jay?" Carver's voice was slightly muffled by the bed. "This is—"

"Yes," she said, knowing her voice would sound muffled

in the same way. "It's Rath's. It's Rath's last home." She pulled a small chest from under the bed, and dusted the skirts of her dress off as she rose. "There's a chest at the end of the bed," she said. "That probably contained most of his clothing, his makeup, and his wigs."

"You speak of Ararath Handernesse?" Torvan asked softly.

Jewel assumed that the Chosen knew almost as much as their Lord. "Yes. This is where I lived, for a few short years. This is where—" She shook her head. As it was for Torvan, the unexplained majesty of the shifting architecture of manse and gardens had almost become the norm; if she could not predict what she would see—or find—she expected things ancient, wild, and unknown.

Not this. She could look at the floor and see where the scuffs and scrapes were, because she'd traced them with her eyes so often while Rath lectured her on the names of the Houses, the names of the important merchant families, the lineage of Kings. She could see the faded patches of color on the wall, and knew which of the floor boards were so thinned with weight they were almost loose. She knew where the grate was, knew where the lamp stand was, and knew that the magestone holder would be tucked to one side of the top of the desk.

There was paper, and ink, a blotter. There was sealing wax and the seals, as well, of different families, which Rath could use when necessary. There were letters of note, some assigning him a specific role in relation to a specific merchant house. Rath had not troubled to remain within the bounds of legality.

"The room?" she asked, voice faint.

"It's the sparring room," Carver replied.

"The exact room?"

"It looks the same, to me. The wooden swords are there," he added.

She touched nothing, took nothing. The magestone holder was empty. Rising, she left the room, and walked the length of hall to the room she'd been given when Rath had first moved here. She'd been ill, then, feverish and uncertain of her surroundings. There'd been no bed for her—but a bed had arrived, and indeed, it stood by the wall farthest from the door. It was made, its sheets pulled tight. There were bedrolls against the wall. Finch's. Teller's. Duster's.

She closed her eyes. The air was thick with dust—dust, she thought, just dust. But she couldn't breathe for one long moment, and didn't even try.

Chapter Fourteen

SHE ALLOWED HERSELF only that minute, and during it, she wrestled with the severe disorientation of stepping back in time. She was still attired as The Terafin; her clothing was worthy of the High Market, although it came from the Common. She wore the House ring. She was Jewel Markess ATerafin—The Terafin of record.

But she was surprised at how much this hurt her.

She closed her eyes as Carver approached the bedroom; he didn't speak, didn't touch her. Instead, he waited until she opened her eyes; waited a little longer, until she turned. His expression was grave and silent; had he been Jester, he would have said or done something ridiculous at this point. He wasn't, and didn't.

"The last door?" she asked softly.

"I asked the captain not to open it yet."

"Did he listen?"

"It was a request, not an order. Jay—" he glanced at the floor and the very tidy bedrolls, and he knew what she remembered and fell silent again.

"I'm not that girl," Jewel told him softly. "But ... I *am*." She took a deep breath and straightened her shoulders. "Let's go."

"Where?"

"To the basement, Carver. Let's see where it leads us now."

The Chosen had, as Carver requested, waited; the door was closed. Jewel approached them.

"It's locked," one of the Captains of her Chosen told her. She almost laughed, and gestured—briefly—at Carver, who rolled his eyes.

"Yes, he used to lock the front door and this one." They were the only ways to enter the apartment.

"The key?"

She hadn't had one for a decade or more, but it didn't matter; she knew where a key could be found. She entered Rath's room, approached the desk, and opened a drawer; she pulled the fitted, false bottom up. She was not at all surprised to see two keys nestled beneath its flat surface, and didn't hesitate to take them both.

The end of the hall was very crowded as she slid between the Chosen. Carver, as usual, stood back.

She considered handing Torvan the keys, and decided against it, unlocking the door while he looked on. She did not, however, open the door. "Rath didn't need the keys," she told Torvan. After a brief pause she added, "By the end of our stay here, neither did I. We did, on the other hand, need light."

She glanced at Carver, and he smiled; it was sly and bold and brief. He drew a hand out of a jacket pocket, and she saw that he carried a magestone. Just one, but that was all he needed—it was all the den had really needed as well. He whispered it to a bright, steady glow—the halls themselves were shadowed by the lack of windows. He lifted his arm, raising the light, and Torvan opened the door.

She wasn't certain what she'd expected. Given the details of the apartment itself, the door should have opened up into a storeroom, and from there, into a basement, a sub-basement, and tunnels. Those tunnels had been unmade shortly after Jewel's arrival at the Terafin manse—but the apartment had been ransacked as well, drawers overturned, the contents of the chest spread across the room, books torn from their shelves. Her last sight of Rath's home had been entirely unlike this one: everything was in its place, even the clothing habitually strewn—with some care—over the backs of chairs and chests.

There were stairs, but they were not stairs that Jewel had ever seen in this apartment; they were of carved stone, and although they were narrow where the door met the landing, they widened considerably as they disappeared into the darkness below. "Not the back halls," she said.

The Chosen entered before her, and Carver pulled up the rear. The grandeur that had been entirely lacking in the apartment itself was in evidence in the stairs. They were rough, the way hewn stone can be, but it was a deliberate roughness, a texture. At the left and right edges of the steps, there were small engravings; they looked like letters, to Jewel's eye—although they didn't look like Weston, Torra, or even the Old Weston that she had sometimes seen in the undercity.

"How far down do they go?" Carver asked softly. He whispered the magelight to its full brightness.

"They end just ahead," Torvan replied. His voice was oddly muted; the stone deadened it. The Chosen could now fan out across the stairs; they drew swords as they continued their descent.

Jewel turned to Carver. He carried the magelight in one hand, and in the other—a dagger. She reached out and offered him her upturned palm, and he placed the light into it. She had no daggers to draw. Carver then descended, walking beneath the light. Jewel started to follow him.

Her legs locked. Her knees. The light dimmed as both hands became involuntary fists.

"Captain," she said, as Torvan cleared the last step.

He turned.

"That's enough. I know where this leads now."

Carver gestured.

"Yes," she said softly. "It leads to the undercity—but not the one we knew." She was cold, felt cold; the hair on the back of her neck must have been standing on end.

"You think—you think this is what the entrances used to look like?"

"I think they weren't always underground," she replied. "But yes. I think this is what they must have looked like. These stairs. That arch—and beyond it, cloisters. The streets might even be the same length, the same general shape—but we won't be walking over rubble."

Carver started down the stairs again and she caught his arm with her left hand. "No," she said, no hand free for signing. "We've lost enough to that city."

"Jay, the apartment's not real. The undercity here—it's probably like your library."

But she shook her head. "Not yet, Carver. If we come here—at all—we bring the cats, Celleriant, Meralonne."

"Why?"

She said nothing for a long moment.

And Carver, because he was Carver, acquiesced. The Chosen returned to her in silence. As a group, they retreated up the stairs, to the perfect replica of Rath's apartment.

Did I build this? she thought, as she glanced through the now open door of his room.

Avandar was standing in the frame of the apartment's entrance. *Jewel.* He glanced down the hall, his brows furrowing. "This is not the usual workmanship one expects of House Terafin."

She laughed. It was too wild; she brought it under control as she saw his expression shift. "No," she told him. "This is, however, the architecture commonly seen in the thirty-fifth holding."

"It was not, if I am not mistaken, part of these rooms."

She nodded.

"Why is it here, Jewel?" His voice was softer, but it was a deceptive softness; his eyes were bright.

"I . . . don't know. Does it matter?"

"Yes, Terafin, it does. You are at the heart of your domain, in this place." The ceilings were so low here he appeared to have gained a foot's worth of height. "If you are not careful, if you are not *deliberate*, no ground where you stand, sleep, or dream will be solid." He frowned. "You said the thirty-fifth holding?"

She nodded.

"Your previous domicile was in the twenty-fifth holding, if I recall your history correctly."

"It was."

"And this?"

"It was my first home without my family." She opened the door to her bedroom. "This was my room. I shared it, in the end, with Teller, Finch, and Duster. Before Duster came, Lefty would sleep here sometimes."

Avandar was silent as he entered the room. He touched nothing, and to her surprise, he stayed by her side. "The bed?"

"Rath bought it. For me," she added, as if it were necessary.

"What was at the end of the hall?"

Her throat was dry. She swallowed. "When I lived with Rath—when we lived here—it was an entrance into the subbasement. And that led to the undercity."

He turned toward the hall. "And now?"

"It leads to—" she shook her head.

"Terafin."

"It leads to the undercity—but not the one I knew."

"How, then, do you know this?"

"I just *know*," was her almost inaudible reply.

"Do you fear the *Kialli*?"

Anyone sane did. But she understood the question. She couldn't answer it for a long moment, because no answer came. On a visceral level, she *did*. She was afraid to enter that city, because the undercity had taken *so much* from her and she had sworn she would never enter it again. But that was the wrong answer. It wasn't the *Kialli* she feared. It wasn't even their Lord—although their Lord had found entrance to her world in the heart of what remained of the ancient city.

He was not there now. His demons were not there.

What do you fear, Jewel?

She had no answer to give. She lingered for a moment in the room that had once been hers, her domicis—no part of that early life—by her side.

"What will you do with this apartment?" he finally asked.

"Leave it," she replied, stepping out of the room. "I have the key."

"The only key?"

"Yes—but I have a suspicion that several of us won't need it."

Carver, waiting for her in the conference room, said, "Why Rath's place?"

"I don't know." It was not her first home. It was not the den's first home, not in any real sense. It was Rath's home. But in Rath's home, for a while, they had found safety—safety, that beguiling illusion, that fevered dream, that child's hope. After a pause, she said, "it was the only place we lived that had a basement we could access."

"You're worried."

"I am. And about the wrong thing. If the two meetings on the morrow don't go well, it won't matter. And if we don't have answers for the Master of the Household Staff . . ."

"You'll wish the meeting with the Kings had gone badly?"

"Something like that." She squared her shoulders. "There are no other doors here that I can see."

Carver nodded.

"And none in the bedroom?"

"There *weren't* any, before."

"Might as well start there, then. There's another room, and the baths. Nearer to the office, there used to be the small dining room, for The Terafin's more intimate acquaintances."

"Did she have any?"

Jewel snorted. Avandar frowned at that; she let him. She wasn't cursing, and the only witness was Carver. "Near the personal office is the small dining room. There's the rooftop." She stopped. "I don't know if the rooftop remains as it was."

"Let's check the baths and the bedchamber."

The baths were, to Jewel's profound relief, normal. The bedchamber had undergone some changes, but those were changes she had forced on it in her desperate attempt to wake up. The corners of the ceiling were, for instance, corniced, but not in a way that was consistent with the rest of the cornices within the manse, where they existed at all. The ceiling was taller. The height of the ceiling rounded in a way that matched the decorative flourishes, but not the previous shape of the roof. The bed was materially unaltered, as were the sheets; the closets were standing in pretty much the same place, as was the dresser with its ornate, oval mirror. Ellerson's working additions of brushes, combs, and clips were reflected there, as was Jewel's instinctive grimace.

Carver entered the closet closest to the doors. Jewel, not much taken by prayer, spared one anyway. It was ridiculous, and she knew it: one servant could not be weighed in balance against mages, Kings, and gods.

"We can *eat* her."

She looked up. Shadow was standing in the door, his wings folded across his back.

"Unless you can clean every room in this mansion, feed every person who lives—or works in it—and tend to every guest of *any* significance whatsoever in an entirely invisible and appropriate way, no, you can't."

"We can *eat* the *guests*."

"Only if they're entirely uninvited. Or trying to kill me. I let you eat the demon."

Shadow hissed, but entered the room, where he bumped against Jewel's arm until she scratched the top of his head. His purr was a self-satisfied rumble. When Carver emerged from the closet, the cat tilted his head, as if he needed to position his ears to listen.

"Carver?"

"No. It's a big damn closet," he added.

"Bigger than it should be?"

Carver didn't reply. Instead he headed for the second closet.

"What is he *looking* for?" Shadow asked.

"A way into these rooms. For the servants," she added.

"In the *closet*?"

Jewel did not particularly relish attempting an explanation of the back halls to Shadow. They made sense to her because they had existed for her entire life in the manse; they made sense because they existed in other grand mansions across the Isle—and in the larger homes of moneyed merchants on the mainland. She compromised. "They're usually tucked away out of obvious sight."

"Why?"

She exhaled heavily. "Ask Ellerson." To avoid more questions, Jewel headed toward the closet into which Carver had disappeared.

"Where *is* Ellerson?"

Jewel frowned and turned, slowly, to look at the whole of the room. "Avandar, where is Ellerson?"

When he failed to reply, she wheeled. She still held Carver's magestone as if it were her own; its light reddened her fingers and her knuckles, no more, her hands were so tight. "Avandar."

He didn't answer, but looked toward the closet into which Carver had just walked.

Gods, gods, gods. She ran across the room, comportment and title and Kings and Shadow forgotten. Only the last one followed her. Unclenching her right hand, she yanked the closet door open. The sight of dresses, in neat rows, did not calm her; something was wrong with the way they caught light, although she couldn't immediately say what.

What she could say, no what she *couldn't* bring herself to say, was that Carver was nowhere in sight. She had seen him open the closet, had seen him enter it. When had the door shut behind him? Why hadn't she *noticed*?

Shadow started to growl, and the sound of his voice dropped the temperature in the room so severely her fingers felt winter. Avandar said, "A moment, Jewel."

But there *were* no moments left. She heard armor, movement, understood that the Chosen were arrayed behind her, and that her presence in the small frame of the door blocked their way.

Jewel.

She didn't argue. She moved. But she moved *into* the closet, and not away. She understood what The Terafin needed—but in this moment, hand clutching magestone, she wasn't The Terafin; she was Jewel Markess, and Carver had stepped into an unknown that should have been safe. And wasn't. It *wasn't*.

Shadow shouldered her to one side. Rows of colorful cloth brushed against her face, her hands, her throat, as she stumbled. He was still growling, and what she wouldn't surrender to the Chosen, he'd taken: point.

"Stupid, *stupid*, girl," he said, over his shoulder. The arch of his wings was higher, but the wings themselves were constrained by the width of the closet. She heard two things at her back. The first, the slow creak of a door closing. The second, the sharp crack of splintering wood. The latter was followed by smoke, dust, and the flying bits of wood that generally followed that sound.

This is not a game, Jewel.

Where the door had been, Avandar stood. *Come back, now. There is something at play here that is beyond you.*

Her right arm began to throb; she felt the brand on the skin of her inner wrist, and knew, if she ignored it, it would bleed. She ignored it, willing to divert some of the wild and endless fear she felt to instant, mutinous rage. Rage, she could

handle. She inhaled and exhaled evenly as she continued to
follow Shadow. She did not descend into pointless argument;
she didn't speak to Avandar at all. But it was better. Rage was
always better than fear. Anything was.

Carver.

Anything, anything, anything. The closet gave way—as it
must—to hall, the wooden floor becoming cold stone so
suddenly, it felt as if it were the edge of a precipice. As it did,
the hall widened, lengthened; the ceilings disappeared into
darkness above her head. She felt exposed in so many ways
the darkness didn't frighten her. She forced her right fingers
to loose their grip on the magestone, and stumbled over the
syllables that would bring it, instantly, to the harshest of
light it could shed.

Shadow was silent. Light sharpened the lines of his
flight-feathers as his wings spread; light gentled the shape
of his shoulders, the musculature of his legs, his back. Ahead
of his rising wings, the hall continued into darkness; the
magestone she held couldn't penetrate it at this distance.

The floor was dusty, the air, stale. But the walls were unadorned by even the simplest of sconces or markings.

Light grew as Avandar approached. Given the width of
the halls she could no longer block his passage, and didn't
try; he came to stand to her left. His eyes, in the poor light,
were black. The Chosen were not far behind; their blades
caught and reflected light as they walked, adding motion to
the walls in the darkness.

Shadow padded forward, leaving paw prints in the dust.
"Shadow, stop—the floor—"

He glanced balefully over his shoulder. "It isn't that *simple*," he told her, adding his usual opinion of her intellect as
an afterthought. "Do you think they *ran away*?"

She wanted to say yes. She said nothing. He lifted his
head and roared; the sound reverberated off the walls, shaking the air. Jewel forced herself not to take a step back as
his upper lip slid down over prominent teeth. She inched
forward instead until she stood by his side; he hadn't moved.

"Shadow?"

He hissed. "Are *they* here *yet*?"

"I don't think—"

She heard the clatter of armor and turned. Snow and
Night had barreled their way through the Chosen.

"Everyone *important* is here," Night said.

"Many *unimportant* people are here, too," Snow added. "Why are *they* here? Take the *ugly* one and tell the others to go *away*." He paused, thought about this for a second, and then said, "No, send the *ugly* one away too."

She felt the knot between her shoulder blades loosen as Snow then stepped firmly on Shadow's tail, even when it predictably descended into a biting, scratching contest she doubted most of her friends would have survived. She let them squabble for five long minutes before dropping a hand on Snow's head.

"Why *me*?" he asked, aggrieved.

She lifted the hand that held the magelight. "One free hand, not two."

"It was *his* fault. He didn't *move* his *tail*."

Night snickered as he approached; they surrounded her. Avandar couldn't get close.

I could.

She laughed. Turning to Torvan, she said, "Captain, if it is acceptable to you, I will allow the cats to take point."

Torvan nodded.

It was interesting, to watch the cats proceed. Shadow was in the lead; Snow and Night walked a few yards behind, in lockstep to either side of Jewel. They did not step on her feet or the skirts of her dress.

"Where is this?" she asked them, when their silence grew too oppressive.

"Don't *you* know?"

"If I knew, I wouldn't ask."

"You are asking the *wrong person*," Snow replied.

"Who should I ask?"

Snow shrugged. "Ask *him*."

"Shadow?"

The great, gray cat hissed. He disliked ignorance, but never complained about his own; he merely avoided exposing it. "You shouldn't let people play here." Sidestepping the question, he began a low growl.

The air here was now so cold Jewel could see her own breath; it hung like a motionless cloud in the still air. She expected to see snow, and if snow did not magically appear, wind did, traveling down the hall in a gale. "Avandar."

"Yes," was the soft reply.

"You are *not* in your home," Shadow said, voice a growl. "The library is yours. The war room. The big house. The forest. This is not yours, not yet. If the wind comes, it will not *hear* you. If you *make yourself* heard, what will you *do with it*? Be quiet, stupid girl."

"Shadow, where are we?"

"You should know. You should *know* when you open a door. You will not survive if you do not *learn*."

"I didn't open this door."

He snorted, and his breath created a much larger cloud. "You did. If you ask me *how*, I will *bite* you."

The air grew colder still, and the wind did not relent; the snow that Jewel had almost expected now arrived in its folds. It seldom snowed in Averalaan, and when it did, people died. None of the people in this hall—with the exception of the cats—were attired for winter.

Without thought, without deliberation, she called The Winter King. She did not envisage his ride through the manse; did not imagine that he could force his way through the splintered door of her second closet. She had no idea—at all—how he traveled or where he went when he chose to vanish, and at this point, it didn't matter.

He came. She heard his hooves clattering against the stone floors of the hall through which they'd walked, and almost before she could turn to face him, he was there, scattering Snow and Night, who made their displeasure clear— but without drawing blood.

His eyes were wide and dark, his fur glittering, as if dusted with frosted crystals. He knelt—there was room for him to kneel—and she climbed, with as much grace as shivering allowed—onto his back.

Jewel.

I'm sorry. I'm sorry—I don't know where we are, but I— she swallowed. *I think Ellerson and Carver are lost here. I need you to find them. I need you to carry them—home.*

Jewel.

You carried Ramdan, she said softly. *He was a slave; he was not a warrior, not a Matriarch. But you carried him. Carry them. Carry them, and I'll walk, I'll learn to walk wherever you can run.* She hesitated, and when she spoke next, it was aloud, although that had not been her intent.

"Find them. Carry them. Bring them back to me. I will

ride you to the edge of the Summer Court, and if you desire it, I will force her to release you."

And if I do not seek that release?

"I will offer her no other Summer King."

The cats hissed in unison.

And can you promise that, Jewel? Can you promise that much?

"*Yes*. Because if she will not grant this, there will be *no* Summer." The words fell out of her open lips like a doom; she understood, as she spoke them, that they were *true*. How, why, *when*, were beyond her, but that was the way, with her gift. Her curse.

She met his eyes, and in their depths, she saw the man he had been in the dreaming; tall, proud, past the immediacy of youth, but not—never—beyond the bounds of certain power. *Do you understand,* he asked softly, *the fate of the Summer King?*

"No. But I understand that it is still the whole of your desire." She glanced down the cold, dark hall. "And at the moment, Winter King, Tor Amanion, what I ask of you is the whole of mine."

You are a fool, he replied. *If you can even manage what you offer—and you are Sen, Jewel, it is not impossible, although I do not see how it will be achieved—you will have no mount. You will walk the wildest and most ancient of ways on mortal feet, if you can traverse those lands at all. You will lose one of the very, very few who is bound to you completely; I will not be beneath you or beside you, and I will raise no weapon in your cause or for your honor.*

"My honor does not require your weapons, and given what you ruled—and how—I very much doubt that *my* sense of honor would be served by yours." She swallowed; her throat was dry. The cold did not numb her while she sat upon the Winter King's back.

No. But it will, Terafin. You understand the heart of my desire. I understand the heart of yours. But mine, Jewel, is worthy of the gods themselves at the height of their glory. Yours, only the weakest of children would privilege. I say again, you are a fool.

"Why are we even arguing?"

Because I was tasked to serve you, little one. To serve, fully and completely. It was her command, and her binding. Yes, I want what you offer. But I am compelled to offer you the counsel that my service demands *of me. Order it, and I will carry you to them—if they can be found here at all. There is no need for such negotiation.*

His voice. It was winter ice and fire's fury, night and day.

"I can't," she said softly. She did not want to leave his back, because he *was* warm, and she was cold in so many ways. But she did, slowly, treacherous hand clinging to the warmth of his fur in spite of her intention. "I understand what you're telling me. I believe it. But I cannot ride you."

Why?

"If I am on your back, you will never find them."

She felt the small huff of his breath across her forehead. *What do you see, Jewel?*

"They will stop me, if they can; they come for me now. You can pass them, unseen, but not if I am your rider."

And you will not send the cats.

"I would send the cats in an instant," was her quiet reply. "But if you cannot find them, I'm not certain anyone can." She reached up with her right hand, and caught the side of his face. "Give me what I desire, Tor Amanion, and I will give you what you desire. I swear it."

He bowed, then. She felt his sudden, visceral joy—and his derision, his contempt. She accepted both; they were, like the seasons, what they were.

You don't understand why I prize them more highly, she told him. *I don't think you* can. *It made you the ruler you were. It makes me the ruler I am. But think: In the end, if you obtain what you desire, it will not be because you were the ruler you were.*

She let him go.

Avandar's silence was a very familiar one, but he did not fill it—not with a lecture. "What is coming, Jewel?"

"Winter's heralds," she replied. "If Ariane cannot leave her sequestered Court, her lords can."

She carried no weapons on her person; she had the Chosen, and she accepted the risk they faced; it was hers. They were mortal.

But she accepted, as well, Shadow's words. These lands were not hers. Not yet. She felt it as truth, beneath her feet; the stone was simple—and cold—stone. The wind's voice was beyond her, and hers was too quiet to command it. She had the things that had defined her life: loss, and the fear of its permanence. Here, no tree of fire warmed her, and the world did not respond to her urgent imperatives.

But the cats had grown six inches, given the way their fur had risen, and they growled in low unison; it was like a visceral, ugly, *living* song. She placed a hand on Snow's white head; felt the almost dreamlike quality of his fur, it was so soft.

"Can we kill?" he asked, his voice shorn of the inflection that lent it character and made it almost comical.

She said nothing, waiting; the world seemed to hold its breath. *Ellerson*, she thought. *Carver*.

She feared to see their corpses, and lifted her chin. What came, what would come, was in theory so much worse—but she welcomed it: war, violence, death: as long as it wasn't theirs. As long as she could *see it* coming, as long as she could stand in its way, as long as she could *do something*. Anything. Even die.

Shadow said, "Walk away from death, or it will devour you."

"I am not walking to my death."

"That's not what I *meant*. Life—your life—will *always* have loss. It is not your death you fear; when your death is almost upon you, you are *too busy* to be *afraid*. It is theirs."

She said nothing.

"This is *why* rulers disavow love and friendship. It *eats* them."

"I would never have come this far without friends."

He growled again. "Perhaps. But if you continue this way, you will fall. And what remains of your city after your fall might make even the gods weep. You *must* learn." He spit as the wind changed. "You have sent *him* away. If you confront *her*, and she accepts him, you will regret his absence. He goes where even we cannot safely go."

"You go," she replied, "where he cannot safely go."

"Pffft. He is a man. *We* are cats. But there are places where he may run that we may not fly. There is no place—save one—that *she* has gone that he cannot traverse. She doesn't *like* cats."

"I can't imagine why."

He opened his mouth to continue—because Shadow,

unlike Avandar, could lecture in the face of attacking demon lords. Or so she would have said—but he turned away as the wind in the hall—in, Jewel thought, the tunnel the hall had become—died into stillness.

Jewel.

From the darkness of the distant hall came three riders.

They carried moonlight with them; it silvered their armor and the white, white fall of their unbraided hair. It wasn't magelight; it was grayer and softer. But it spread evenly across the long, long hall, at a distance that magelight failed to touch.

Three, mounted, not on stags, but horses, or creatures very like them; the mounts seemed, to Jewel, to be too fine, too slender, but they had the broader, longer heads, and the wild manes. The riders carried long spears; the man in the lead carried a silent horn. There were no banners, but the heraldry of the *Arianni* was almost unknown to a woman who had spent years memorizing human variants. The absence made no difference; she *knew* this man.

And he, she thought, knew her. He did not slow; instead, he leveled the blade of his pole arm, and spurred his mount to greater speed; hooves clattered across stone as if they could shatter it. They might, she thought. But she made no attempt to evade him; not even at Torvan's urgent command. It *was* command; she lifted a hand to stay it as the *Arianni* drew closer, closer.

"No, Captain." She did not order the Chosen to stand down, but something in her tone gave them pause—and it should. In the end, it should. Even the den had come to trust her word and mood in times of grave danger and conflict; if the Chosen were her armor and shield, they must come to do the same.

Shadow leaped before the last syllable faded. Night flanked him; Snow moved to stand in front of her. Jewel herself did not take a step, either forward or away; had it not been for the damnable cold, she would have been motionless.

Wind roared, returning to the hall in a rush.

It came, however, from behind them; she heard the clang of armor as the Chosen turned. Only the Chosen moved; Avandar, by her side, seemed made of living ice. Around her feet, however, a circle of orange and blue appeared, glowing faintly. A like circle did not appear around his; he stood outside of its boundary.

Avandar.

He didn't even raise a brow in response.

Shadow leaped as the horses approached; the leveled spear wavered briefly in the gray cat's direction. Jewel held breath, remembering: the cats were no longer creatures of stone.

"Stone forms would not prevent their injury," Avandar said. "Not against this opponent."

The horse did not slow, but the spear snapped to the side as Night now leaped, changing the mount's trajectory by landing on his side. A different rider would have been unseated by his mount's fall; this one jumped and the air caught him before he could land. It carried him, in a rush, over the two cats, but not past the third, who now sprang from his position in front of Jewel.

She watched, hands by her sides; they were looser now than they'd been since she had entered the closet that was not a closet. She raised chin, drew breath, exhaled; breath made a veil of mist through which the cat and the first assailant clashed. There was no blood; there was sound and fury; the wind drove cat and man apart, but it failed to dash the cat against the nearest wall.

Ah, no, she thought, there was blood; it was scant—a scratch across a perfect, Winter cheek. She caught a glimpse of it as he turned, dropping spear to draw sword. It was—of course it was—pale, perfect blue, a thing of light and motion. She expected shield, and it followed, instantly adorning the arm bent to bear it. That shield took the full force of Snow's extended claws, and the blow sent the *Arianni* back.

Jewel grimaced. She knew where back was in this fight: toward her. The *Arianni* Lord had positioned himself *perfectly*, and the force of Snow's almost aerial blows pushed him exactly where he wanted to go. Had his opponent been Shadow—who was now embroiled in his own fight farther down the hall—such a tactic would have been pointless. But Snow and Night were not the tacticians Shadow was; Jewel stood her ground as the *Arianni* Lord spun in air, sword raised. It came down in a flashing sweep that looked, to her eyes, like handheld lightning.

A hand's span from her neck, the blade slammed into a second, similar sword.

Celleriant had arrived.

Jewel felt no triumph at all.

"Mordanant," Celleriant said, as the echoes of steel striking steel faded. They did not put their swords up; they strained, blade against blade. All of the *Arianni* looked alike to Jewel—cold and perfect and Other. She could not see beyond that similarity to a family resemblance, although she knew they were brothers.

"Will you defend her here?" Mordanant demanded. "If she dies, you are *free*."

"If she dies while I stand," Celleriant replied, "I have failed."

Mordanant's eyes widened. "Impossible," he said, the last syllable almost inaudible. "It is *impossible*."

Celleriant remained unmoved by the disbelief, the shock, the pain, in Mordanant's voice. Jewel did not, but she had a decade of practice at hiding pain in public.

"Why do you think she waits?" Celleriant asked. "She has not moved; she has not ordered her guards forward. She knew that I would be here before your sword fell."

Mordanant was rigid. "How did she force this upon you?"

He shook his head. "She could not, as you well know. There is only one who can."

"Then *why*? Why, brother?"

Celleriant, arms locked to prevent the downward fall of his brother's sword, shook his head. "Does it matter?"

Mordanant did not reply.

"She is mortal. She has lived half her life; the handful of years left her—"

Mordanant's gaze slid from Celleriant's face to Jewel's. She stood, chin lifted, watching some point beyond his back. Snow, struggling free of the wind's grasp, padded deliberately toward Mordanant's back. "No, Snow. Not yet." The *Arianni* Lord's pale brows rose.

"Do you think I fear *cats*?"

"*Snow*. Come to me now." Growling, the cat did as she ordered—but it was a struggle. His fangs appeared to occupy most of his face. He moved to stand between her and

Avandar, bristling. She did not answer Mordanant's question.

"He came to *kill* you," Snow told her. She dropped a hand on the top of his head.

"Believe that I'm aware of that."

"Then *why* do I have to stand *here*?"

"Because he is Lord Celleriant's brother."

"*I* would have killed *mine*."

"Enough, Snow."

Mordanant was staring at her. To the cat, he said, "You serve *her*?"

Snow's wings rose in his version of an extremely antagonistic shrug.

"You serve the mortal? You do not serve Viandaran?"

Incredulous, Snow's head swiveled to the side beneath Jewel's palm. "No," he replied. "He's *too ugly*."

Only then did Mordanant lower his sword. Celleriant's fell with it, although he did not relax. To Jewel, Mordanant said, "Release him."

"I wouldn't even know how," she replied. It was truth, but it was not all of the truth.

"If you hold him in any regard, if you value any service he has rendered to you, release him."

"Mordanant," Celleriant said softly.

His brother turned to face him. "We have come this way for this purpose—and one other."

"Order your men to retreat," Jewel told him. "I will call the cats back."

Snow hissed.

Mordanant ignored her.

"Who sent you onto the Winter roads, Mordanant?"

Mordanant's sword faded from view. "The Winter Queen," he said softly.

"She did not send you to kill this mortal and relieve me of my burden."

His brother lowered chin; it was brief. "There is danger."

"And it is a danger from which you have ridden?"

"I? No. If there is difficulty, it will not fall upon me."

Silence.

Jewel.

She nodded.

Something is wrong here.

She resisted the urge to employ sarcasm. The wind was cold, here, and the chill had settled into her so thoroughly she thought she might never feel warm again.

"What endangers my Lord?" Celleriant's sword had not vanished, and he raised it as if it were punctuation.

Mordanant flinched. "Only once in our long history did the *Arianni* swear such vows to a mortal. Have you forgotten?"

"I am not as they were."

"No," Mordanant said, voice so low Jewel almost missed the word. "You are not."

"I chose, brother. They did not; they were given orders, and they swore the oaths they swore—but their service was never truly *given* to a mortal. It was *my* choice. Not hers; it was given to her to accept—or reject—what I offered."

"And what mortal would reject you?"

"What mortal indeed?" Celleriant's smile was sharp and cold. Jewel's hands curved in numb fists at the sight of it. "And yet you have asked her to release me from a vow she only barely understands."

"She understood it well enough to call you, brother."

"That is not understanding; it is instinct. I am not," he said again, "as they were."

"No. But it is coming."

Celleriant froze.

"They are waking, Celleriant. They are waking, and they will visit endless anger upon this pathetic, mortal city. Upon," he added, "the Lord you now serve. Will you stand against them? You will perish."

Celleriant threw back his head as he laughed. It was a wild, mirthless laughter, almost the antithesis of joy; his expression as it left him was fevered, too-bright. "And for this, you wish me to be *released* from my oath?"

"Where will I go, brother? Back to a Court that is hampered by lack of Summer? Back to the slumbering lands when the world—at last—begins to wake? Back to a Queen who might never again lead the host?"

Mordanant stepped forward, his anger quick and sudden; Celleriant did not move.

"Walk a moment in my Lord's gardens, and you will hear the voices of the ancients raised at last in their endless whispers."

"Celleriant—you are the youngest of our number; I am among the oldest remaining. I tell you now that you cannot stand against them. You will know the briefest of glory and your eternity will end. If you will end thus, return to us; even hampered as she is, she *is* the White Lady, and her anger is ancient and endless. We stand, and will stand, against those who have betrayed her, and if we fall, we fall in glory. We will meet them; do not do so by the orders of— the whim of—a mortal who does not, and can never, understand." He raised a hand toward his brother, but turned, once again, to Jewel. His expression was almost enough to make her take a step back. "I say again, release him."

Celleriant shook his head. "She will not give you what you desire unless it is clear that I also desire it. It is not your request she will honor, but mine."

"Then *ask her*, brother. We have been sent to hunt their heralds; to find and destroy their servants before those servants set foot upon the path that leads to where they slumber."

"The heralds are abroad?"

"They are."

"They will not find that path easily," Avandar said, speaking for the first time. "Not in this place."

"They will find it," Mordanant whispered.

"How do you know this?"

"The Winter Queen entertained a guest. Her guest has seen what must follow if they are not apprehended. They will find what they seek."

Jewel surprised herself; she spoke. "Was her guest Evayne?"

"Evayne a'Neamis," he replied.

"I don't understand. Do you speak of the Sleepers?"

The three men turned to face her; she might have uttered the most foul of curses to far less effect.

Celleriant said, "Yes, Lord. But we speak softly, if at all. Do not name them here. Do not name them at all if it is within your power."

"I don't understand."

"No," Mordanant replied. "You do not. Viandaran?"

Avandar said nothing for a long moment. Into his silence, Jewel continued. "They're meant to sleep until—until Moorelas rides again."

"Given that he was mortal, and given that he is long dead, that is unlikely." Mordanant glanced at Celleriant. "What tales do mortals now tell?"

"They tell few indeed that I have heard."

Avandar said, "the oldest of their legends—most forgotten—tell the tale of their betrayal of Moorelas in the Shining City. Four princes rode by his side, but only one fulfilled the oaths made to the wielder of the godslayer. For their betrayal, they were entombed, alive but unmoving, until the day Moorelas returns, when they will redeem themselves, at last, in the mortal's endless quest to bring death to the Lord of the Hells."

Mordanant's brows rose as his silver eyes rounded. "That is the story they tell?"

"That is the story that was once told. Fragments of it remain in the sayings and superstitions of the Empire, no more."

Jewel said, softly, "'When the Sleepers wake' heralds the end of time. The end of the world. It means 'never.'"

"Never is come upon you," Mordanant replied. "Speak, now, to Illaraphaniel. He is the only hope you have."

"He is in her service," Celleriant said.

"Not in the way you are. I would have felt it a hundred leagues away." He frowned. "Brother, among those who tracked, you were second to none. Our Lady has need of you."

"Did the Winter Queen ask this of you, Mordanant?"

Mordanant did not reply. Answer enough, Jewel knew. And she knew that if Mordanant had said yes, Celleriant would have asked for his freedom. *Knew* it. But Mordanant did not lie.

In the distance, Jewel heard the long, resonant note of a horn's call.

"Come with us," Mordanant said, speaking both softly and without hope.

Celleriant smiled; it was pained. "Survive, brother. Survive and we will meet again in the Summer Court."

"There is no—"

But Jewel said, "There will be a Summer Court if we survive what is to follow."

"How can you—"

"She is seer-born," Celleriant replied, the words strangely

hushed. "The White Lady was not the only one to entertain Evayne as guest. Mortality does not guarantee that she speaks truth; she is mortal, and as any, is full capable of choosing words without recourse to fact."

Mordanant did not reply. His expression had shifted as he regarded Jewel. She couldn't read it.

Celleriant, however, could. "Do you still counsel me to abandon her, brother?"

"You do not serve her because you view her as our hope."

"Does it matter?"

"It matters to me," was the soft reply. "Because there is now a thorn in the side of our hope, if you believe her words to be true."

"She is not full capable of a lie, although she has learned to use silence in its stead. Regardless, she cannot now lie to me." He turned to her, and fell to one knee. "Lord," he said. It was a posture she disliked; she suspected he knew it. "When you speak of the Summer Court, what do you envisage?"

"Ariane," Jewel replied. "In the heart of a forest that is also a city. It's . . . not strong. It's certain."

"Can you not look?" Mordanant almost demanded. There was a desperation in the words that underlay the sudden eagerness.

"No," she said, understanding the question. "I do not have a seer's crystal."

"You have not walked the Oracle's path. You have not survived her test." It was not a question. "Celleriant, come away. Hunt with us. There is no guarantee that she will survive the testing; most of the mortals did not."

Celleriant smiled. "She will survive. Do you forget, brother? She stood upon the hidden path and *held* it, in her ignorance, against the Queen's host. *Ellariannatte* grow in the lee of her mortal manse, and they speak."

Mordanant's eyes widened. Of all the things Celleriant had said, this was the only thing that seemed, to Jewel's eye, to be significant to him.

"My Lord," Celleriant continued, "will survive."

The distant horn sounded again. Mordanant hesitated for a long moment, and then nodded. A smile graced his face as he looked at his brother; it vanished as he looked down, at Jewel.

Before he could speak, she said, "Do not embarrass your brother. He does not require my protection."

Celleriant laughed, and this laugh was shorn of edge. It was almost—for one of the *Arianni*—rueful. He bowed to his brother. "Go," he said softly. "But if you can—if it is possible after this long night—return and I will show you the heart of my Lord's domain." He turned to Jewel. "With your permission and your leave."

"I am loath to grant that leave to a Lord who has sworn to kill me," she replied, voice cool. "But I might be moved to allow much to such a man in return for a favor."

"What favor, mortal?" Mordanant's eyes narrowed; his face was all of Winter.

"We came this way seeking *my* kin."

"Yours?"

She nodded.

"Lady, if you seek mortals on this night, you seek in vain."

"What is special about this night?"

"Those who can hunt are abroad," he replied. "The wilds are waking, and they present a challenge we have not seen in some time. How were your kin separated from your party?"

"They walked through a door in my mansion."

"A door?"

"A closet door."

He frowned. "No one lives in this place, certainly no mortals. What road did you travel to reach it?"

"The same one. A closet door."

"Little mortal," he said softly, "if you do not open the ways, you must become someone who can sense their existence. You have claimed lands, and if my brother chose to offer you his service, he believes them to *be* yours. But if the ways are opening without your permission and without your knowledge, your grasp is tenuous.

"I have not seen stray mortals; only you, yourself."

"And if you do?"

He smiled. It was exquisitely unpleasant.

Shadow, however, growled. "If *we* are not allowed to *play* with them, we will *kill you all* before you do."

"You will have to find me. Remember: I came to your Lord; she did not come to me."

Mordanant turned and leaped. He did not land. The air carried the whole of his weight, tugging at his hair. It spun him around to face Celleriant. He said nothing for a long moment, and into that silence trudged two cats—one black, one gray. It was Night who took a pointless swipe at him on the way past. He looked down at the cat in every possible way, and then he vanished into the darkness and the cold.

"Why didn't you *eat* him?" Night demanded of Snow.

"She wouldn't *let* me."

"Oh?" Shadow looked up at Jewel. "Why *not*?"

"He's Celleriant's brother. I wouldn't let you kill each other, either."

Shadow hissed. "There are others," he told her, his voice dropping.

"Yes. But I want you here. You can play with them on your own time."

"And when is *that*? Go *there*. Stand *here*. Don't *play*."

Jewel almost laughed. "Shadow, is it Winter everywhere?"

He tilted his head. "It is Winter almost *nowhere*," he replied. "They carry it *with* them. But it will not last."

Celleriant rose. To Shadow, without preamble, he said, "They are waking."

Shadow hissed. Ignoring Celleriant—which is what he generally did—he shouldered Snow aside. Avandar adroitly sidestepped most of Shadow's gray bulk. "Terafin?"

Jewel exhaled, staring down the long hall as if, by will alone, she could pierce all of the darknesses that occupied it. "No," she finally said. "We're not done yet."

Jewel, Avandar said.

She raised a hand in shaky den-sign.

Avandar, of course, hadn't lifted hand or raised voice. *Jewel*. The voice he did use was softer. *If it is not winter, it is cold, and you are—in all ways—too exposed. Return to the manse. Attire yourself for the weather and allow your Chosen to do the same.*

I can't. I can't leave without them.

Will you find them? Will you find them if we remain?

The hall stretched on forever. *Don't.* "Don't. Don't ask that here." But he had. He had, and as she formed the loose and shaking fists that the cold allowed her, she knew what the answer was. But she was Jewel; she denied it until Shadow stepped—gently, for the cat—on her foot.

"They are not here," he said, in a soft voice. "It is not through this door that you will find them."

"Will he?" she whispered. "Will the Winter King?"

Shadow growled. His eyes were gold, their light the only warm light as far as the eye could see.

"You don't *need* them," Snow said, tail flicking in the still air. "We're *better*. You have *us*."

"She wants *them*," Night said, shouldering the white cat out of the way. He looked up—or across—to meet her gaze.

"But why? She has *us*."

"She's *stupid*. But we *knew* that."

She couldn't even tell them to stop. Shadow leaned into her side; she was compressed a moment between his bulk and Snow's. The Chosen were silent. Avandar was silent. The air was dry and cold. They stood that way for five minutes, until Jewel closed her eyes.

Shadow inhaled. She felt it. He exhaled a roar that was loud enough to shake ground. "Go," he said. "Go and *find* them."

"Why *us*?"

He said, in a voice free of whine, "She is shaping her world. All things affect its shape: all. Find them."

"What if they're *dead*?"

"Alive would be *better*." Shadow bumped her again, and Jewel opened her eyes; he was staring at her face. "Alive would be better," he repeated. "But dead would be better than lost." He turned to Celleriant. "I will protect her," he said. "But these roads are not my roads, and I carry no Winter with me."

Celleriant said nothing for a long moment. "If the roads are closed, I cannot travel at need to her side."

"Summer and Winter are at the heart of your Queen," Shadow replied, voice grave and low. "The mortals are at the heart of *mine*. While you serve her, you *must* understand *this*."

Jewel watched him, afraid to speak. Afraid of what it would reveal of her heart and her fear. The cats and the *Arianni* were part of this empty, terrible wilderness. Carver and Ellerson were not.

"Would you have me leave your side in this search?" Celleriant finally asked.

"If you can find them, if you can bring them back—" she faltered. She was afraid of hope, here. Afraid of the cost of it.

He knelt. "I will go with your cats and your only true mount. But call me, Lady, and I will return. Do not touch the hidden paths if I am not by your side. I ask it; I cannot command you."

Jewel nodded. "I—I will try."

"Come," Shadow told her, in a tone of voice better suited to her domicis. "It is time to go home and be warm. You must tell the others. I will go with you," he added, as if his presence would help.

As if it would make the task of telling the den that Carver and Ellerson were missing any easier. She swallowed, dropped a hand to his head, and then nodded.

Chapter Fifteen

9th of Fabril, 428 A.A.
Order of Knowledge, Averalaan Aramarelas

SIGURNE STOOD behind her desk, facing the world that slept beyond her Tower windows. In the absence of The Terafin, the world now held its breath—although the Exalted did not do so in silence. Nor, it must be admitted, did the Kings, although they were far more gracious than the Lord of the Compact. Had she not known how grave the situation was, she would have inferred it from Duvari's carriage and attitude; he had come to *her*. He had not done so with any notable humility, but Sigurne was old enough to expect no miracles.

Tell me, Guildmaster, that you trust The Terafin.

"I trust her." She had expected argument; Duvari accepted no counsel from the Order. All of the argument he offered was silence.

"You have seen *Avantari*."

"I have seen it, as you well know."

"You have seen *Avantari*, you understand that the changes made in its structure could not have been accomplished in less than a decade at the hands of any but the maker-born."

Sigurne privately felt that he underestimated the labor involved. She nodded, but offered him this grace; she spoke.

"I am also aware that it was accomplished in less than a day."

"She did not set foot in the palace."

"No. I was at her side at the time. I heard every word she spoke, Lord of the Compact, and none of those words were an order to rearrange the structure of *Avantari*."

"At the Kings' request, you will arrive before The Terafin does." He reached into the pouch at his side and pulled out a single, long tube. Sigurne had seen its like only a handful of times. She accepted it without comment or expression.

"No writ of exemption is required when you serve at the command of the Kings."

"And I am to serve in what capacity?"

"At the Kings' Command, should the need arise, you are to render The Terafin immobile. If she cannot be rendered harmless without injury or death, you will kill her."

"At the Kings' Command, Lord of the Compact. Not at yours." But her hands gripped the tube tightly. There had been much discussion in the Hall of Wise Counsel; none, so far, had led to this. "The Kings have yet to give such a command."

"Read their message," he replied, voice cool.

She broke the tube's seal. Duvari was many things. Sigurne had no doubt at all that he was an accomplished liar, but he had never condescended to do so in her presence. He was suspicious, yes; he routinely made clear that everyone in any position of authority or power was a threat. He did not view the polity as anyone reasonable would—but that was not his duty.

She was therefore unsurprised when she read what was penned. The Kings had not yet reached a decision, but they had compromised in one thing: they required her obedient service—as First Circle mage—should Jewel ATerafin's existence finally be deemed too much of a danger.

"Very well. I will, of course, make myself available at the Kings' pleasure."

She was surprised when he acknowledged her weary tone by an abrupt shift in topic. "Where is Meralonne APhaniel?"

"Lord of the Compact, I have been as forthcoming as I can; it has been a very long day. I am aware that you are *well* aware of his current disposition; he has accepted the offer of employ as the Terafin House Mage."

"Exclusively."

"Given that, where do you think he is to be found?"

"I have been to the Terafin manse. He is not there."

"Pardon?"

"He is not present. He is not to be found upon the grounds; the Master Gardener could not locate him, although he did make the attempt at my request."

Sigurne exhaled. "He has not returned to his Tower rooms."

"He has not. It was the second place I visited." Duvari surprised her, then. He took a seat. He took a seat before the long, polished table in the rooms in which Sigurne habitually entertained visitors of import who presented a clear and obvious danger. "Are you aware of . . . structural changes within the Terafin manse upon the Isle?"

She was not, and suspected Duvari knew it. She considered a declaration of honest ignorance, and decided against it, although it was difficult. He had tied the changes to one of her own, and ignorance in that case would be politically unwise.

She had not, in truth, slept easily since the day of The Terafin's funeral. She had spent far more time than was her wont in the company of the god-born—Exalted and Kings, both. When the affairs of the Order were calm, she considered it part of her duty. Since the appearance of the *Kialli* lord during the victory parade, she considered it detrimental in the extreme. The Kings required none of her expertise and none of her advice; she had offered them three First Circle magi who might attend their various Courts in her stead, and they had all been politely declined.

But she understood two things: Duvari had all but demanded that Jewel Markess ATerafin be removed. Solran Marten, the Senniel bardmaster made clear that he had not been as subtle in the privacy of the Kings' chambers. Sigurne had not asked her how she had come by the knowledge; it was best not to know.

"Are they relevant to my current work, Duvari?" she finally asked.

"I would have you answer that question."

"Very well. I consider it inconsequential in comparison to the danger we now face."

"A demon, Sigurne."

"You do not understand what you saw," she replied softly. "The demons we have seen in the city within the last year are insignificant in comparison."

"You hope to find him."

"I hope to find his summoner, if that is possible." She lied, of course. She understood what she had seen. She knew that he had not *been* summoned by anything less than the Lord of the Hells himself; no other would have survived it. What concerned her was the exact timing of his arrival at the heart of the Common. In that fact, she could see the hand of one of her own. And if not that . . . she exhaled, and met Duvari's steady gaze. "Every moment I spend in your company, or in the company of my Kings, is a moment lost to me—and the trail, so very slender to begin with, grows cold and stale.

"I will attend the Kings in the Hall of Wise Counsel on the morrow."

One did not dismiss Duvari without a great deal of effort if he did not wish to be moved. Were he in the presence of the Kings, it would be much simpler; the Kings would not allow him to overstep his bounds because it implied a strong lack of courtesy on their part. Absent the Kings, Duvari could not as easily be contained. "I ask you again, Sigurne: Where is Meralonne APhaniel?"

"I am not his keeper, Lord of the Compact."

Duvari rose. "You do not know."

"I am not," she agreed, "aware of his exact disposition, no."

"Guildmaster." Duvari bowed; it was not the gesture she was expecting, and some hint of a cool smile adorned his lips as he rose. "Perhaps the time has come that such ignorance now presents a danger to us."

"If I am certain of nothing else, I am certain of this: Meralonne APhaniel had no part to play in the appearance of the demon in the Common. Nor had he any part to play in the architectural transformation of *Avantari*."

"And I have mentioned neither, Guildmaster."

She stiffened, drawing herself to her full height almost instinctively.

Duvari's eyes narrowed, as if her posture answered a question he'd not yet asked. "On the morrow, then."

She nodded, and escorted him out of the room. She resisted the urge to escort him off the premises, in large part because the walk to the doors and back was long and involved a not inconsiderable number of stairs. She did, however, make certain he left.

Only once she was certain did she retire to her own Tower once again. Duvari did not let information slip; it was not his way. Nor did he trade information in any obvious way; he absorbed it, filtered it through his constant and enduring suspicion, inferring—from any gesture, any word, any pause—what best suited his purposes.

He therefore offered information in a like fashion. That he was suspicious of Meralonne was not a surprise; Duvari was suspicious of any man—or woman—of power in the Empire who was not one of the Twin Kings. Even the Princes were not immune until their fathers passed on. But he had come seeking Meralonne when he was almost certain Meralonne was not present in the Tower.

It offered either criticism or warning—and given Duvari, one could hardly avoid the former. The latter, however, was telling.

Oh, it was cold in this room. She paced the floor, glancing at the grate in which the embers of a fire burned low. Decades of conservative use of magic stayed her hand; she had cast only one spell, and waited its outcome now. In the long years since she had taken the helm of the Order, she had used it only a handful of times. The time was coming, she thought, when it would cease to have any effect at all.

Perhaps tonight was that night.

Not yet, she thought. *Not now*. She had not lied to Duvari; the presence of the *Kialli* lord in the Common was her greatest concern. She had not been entirely truthful, however; if she was not aware of the minutiae of the changes that occurred in the Terafin manse, she understood that it presaged a shift of power that no one could have predicted. It compelled Meralonne, fascinated him; had she had any hope of keeping him away from Terafin, she would have forbidden his acceptance of the offered contract.

She would have failed, and knew it.

But that failure, she could accept. Walking over to the

Tower's windows, she stared into the deepening darkness of night sky, seeing the clarity of stars, of moons. It had been an hour. Two. Meralonne had failed to answer her summons—but delay was not unusual; if he condescended to obey, he did so in a way that did not, in his own eyes, either demean him or elevate her.

At the end of a third hour, she surrendered. It was now late enough that the sleep she required for the audience on the morrow would be sacrificed if she continued to pace. Exhaling, she left her office, moving with economy and a surprising speed toward her bedchamber. Of the rooms in the Tower it was the smallest; Sigurne had always been practical, and very little of her day was given to sleep. It contained one bed and one chair, a small bedside table, and a dresser upon which an oval mirror sat. The mirror had gathered dust, but the dust did not diminish its use: when pressed, she could communicate through its silvered surface.

It was not her mirror of choice, given its location.

She opened the door, a complicated affair that involved two keys and a subtle unwinding of protective spells. Although she seldom faced danger while asleep, she was at her most vulnerable in that state, and the odd ambitious mage had taken it upon himself to speed her passage into the Halls of Mandaros in a way that would not immediately cause suspicion.

The door opened, and even had the frame not suddenly shifted color in her vision, she would have understood the danger: Meralonne APhaniel had taken up residence in her room's single chair. He appeared to be stuffing the bowl of his pipe.

Relief warred with annoyance, and as neither immediately won, she was silent.

He lifted his as yet unlit pipe. "Sigurne, do come in."

"This is not the room in which I normally entertain guests."

"Ah."

"And certainly not guests who insist on smoking."

"It seemed late enough that you would be found here."

"How long have you been waiting?"

"Not more than an hour."

He looked, sounded, and moved as if he were still the very frustrating individual she had always known, and after a moment, she did enter her room; the door closed at her back, but not by her hand. "Do *not* use magic upon this door," she told him tersely.

"I am, obviously, conversant with the way the door operates, or I would not be here."

"I have some questions about that," she replied, "but they will have to wait."

"Oh?"

"If you desired my death, Meralonne, I would have been dead decades past. There is, therefore, no point in exercising that kind of caution where you are concerned. I would *ask* that you preserve the illusion that I have that choice, at least where other members of the Order are concerned."

"You don't want Matteos to worry."

"No, I don't. He is not as young as he once was, but his pride is ferocious, and he has never been much impressed with your various eccentricities." She passed him and sat on the edge of the bed, which was high enough off the ground she considered standing instead.

"I did start a fire," he pointed out. He had; with the door closed, the room was warm.

The warmth enveloped her, and she lifted a hand. "Yes, you can smoke if you must—but, Meralonne, I am not a child. I do not need to be coddled or lulled into a momentary and entirely false security."

"Ah. Were you ever that child, Sigurne?"

"No, but we were a harsher people."

"You summoned me."

"I did."

"Why?"

"Because," she said, exhaling, "I wanted to ascertain for myself whether or not I still could. I have long privileged pragmatism as a way of navigating the world, but I feel as if the pragmatic is at last unraveling, and everything I have struggled to build will crumble with it.

"Duvari came tonight."

"For?"

"You."

His gaze turned to the pipe he now lifted, and he frowned for a long, long moment. Sigurne had *never* liked the pipe,

and although Meralonne had experimented with a variety
of leaf over the decades, he had never found one that could
change her mind. Yet watching him now, she was afraid—
truly, viscerally afraid—that he would set that pipe aside
and never return to it.

As if he could read the fear, he smiled; his lips touched
the pipe's stem, and his fingers delivered fire to the leaf the
bowl contained. "Yes," he said, exhaling familiar rings. "It is
almost time, Sigurne."

Folding her hands in her lap to keep them still and
steady, she met his gaze. "I remember the first time I saw
you." It was not what she'd intended, but she had no easy
way to address the words he had just spoken. "I did not
know your name. I did not know that I would survive you;
nothing else did." She smiled as she spoke; every word was
true, and it was true in a way that time had not changed. "I
thought you so beautiful then: you were like the northern
winds. I thought you were death.

"I remember that you arrived first, and at your back in
the growing distance, the magi, straggling, hesitant, casting
their protective shields and barriers. It is what I do now—
but I thought, watching them, that they seemed so very frail,
so very timid, in comparison.

"And I remember your sword, APhaniel, and your shield.
I remember the way you leaped into the winds—and the
way they carried you. You were, then, the most beautiful
thing I had ever seen."

"In the North, beauty and deadliness are oft the same."

"Beauty does not imply safety, comfort, or peace, no. But
at that time, nothing in my life did. I thought I would die."

"You were prepared to die. Perhaps if you had cried or
pleaded, you would have." His smile was slender, and
watching it, she was aware that her youth and his were separated by so many years, and so many experiences, she
barely touched the surface of his life.

"You did not kill me."

"No, and where I would not kill, the others would not."
His smile deepened into a more familiar, vexing expression.
"But I, too, remember. They are coming, Sigurne. Darranatos was the first, but in the end, not the most significant." He
lifted his head, and wind played in his hair, and it was a cold,
cold wind.

"Duvari suspects," she said softly.

"Duvari suspects his own shadow," was the dismissive reply. "Do you know what Jewel ATerafin is creating?"

She almost corrected him, but knew it was pointless, and kept her peace. "No."

"To me, she is like, and unlike, you in your youth. Every accepted rule we have been handed demands her death—but without her, what we face will be far, far worse."

"How much worse? You know that I am fond of the girl, and in some ways protecting her is the only responsibility left me by—" she shook her head. "But she frightens Duvari, and the Exalted all but pale at the mention of her name. I would not be surprised to see another attempt on her life." She considered discussing the Kings' missive.

"It will fail."

Considered it, and rejected it. "She must travel from her stronghold to *Avantari* on the morrow—which is fast approaching."

"She will face danger and death soon enough, Sigurne. If it will comfort you, let that death be on another's head."

"What will you do if the Kings demand her execution?"

"What will you command?" he countered.

"I am a citizen of the Empire; I owe my allegiance to the Kings."

"And I am a member of the Order of Knowledge."

It was not an answer; she knew it. But Sigurne was watching the rise and fall of strands of his platinum hair. She was, she knew, afraid, and it was an odd fear. She knew that Meralonne APhaniel would never harm her unless it were necessary, and if it were necessary, he would kill her as quickly and as painlessly as she allowed. She was not afraid of death at his hands—just as she had not been afraid of death so very, very long ago on the edge of the Northern Wastes.

She was afraid, of course, of treachery. She was afraid that the coming night would transform him utterly. She turned toward the dresser, and toward the small jewelry box on its upper right corner. She touched the engraved surface of its lid in silence. "Meralonne—"

Words, written in luminescent orange light, began to trace themselves across the wall directly behind that dresser, and she watched it as if it were cloud or rain: a thing that was natural, and unwelcome, and no part of her. "APhaniel."

"Sigurne."

She could not turn to face him. Instead, she lifted the lid of the simple box. It wasn't even hinged. "You have served us for so long," she said, still unable to face him.

He said nothing.

"Was it always, and only, a cage?"

The chair protested as he abandoned it.

"I have told no one of my fears," she continued. "But the Exalted know, and the Kings; they know what the gods know. What will you do?" She reached into the sparsely occupied box and pulled out one item: a ring, and it lay a moment in her palm, catching magelight and reflecting it. It seemed, at first, a simple ring; it was not heavy, and it had no signet; it had a single gem, embedded into the curved band. In the dim light of the room, it was not clear what the gemstone was; Sigurne had never asked.

"I will do what I have done. Wait," he added, "for the coming of my enemy."

"Meralonne—"

"It was not a cage, Sigurne."

She turned to find him a foot away, his pipe in his hand. "I chose. I was offered the choice, and I might have chosen to sleep until the appointed moment. Instead, I chose to watch. To watch, to wait. It was—it has been—tedious, but there have been surprising glimpses of the ancient and the wild, even in the constraints of your world." He glanced to the right, as if he were looking out a window; he was looking, instead, at solid stone.

Sigurne did not find this disconcerting; had she, she would have had difficulty with over half of the members of the Order of Knowledge. But in Meralonne's case, she wanted to know what he saw. She had never been, even as a child, one who could ask.

Turning, she lifted the ring. He looked down at it for a long, long moment. "No," he finally said. "Not yet. Not yet, Sigurne, but soon."

"Will I know?"

"Do you not know already?" he countered softly. "Jewel has touched the slumbering wilderness, and it is waking at her call."

"Jewel did not—"

"She did. She is not aware of *all* that she has touched, and she is not in control of most of it, but the ancient world feels twinges of her presence in its sleep."

"How much will things change?" she asked, bracing herself for the answer.

"They are changing now, in subtle ways. Even the Order of Knowledge will not—cannot—remain unaffected."

She stiffened.

"I will tell you what the gods will not: it is time—past time—for your mages and your magi to take remedial classes."

"Pardon?"

"They will require them. The magic they have nurtured and honed until now was not a stream; it was a drip. That will change, Sigurne; it is changing. If they are not careful, it will devour them. They will make beginner's mistakes—but the consequences of those mistakes will be large and unmistakable.

"Word must travel to the makers, to the bards."

"And the healer-born?"

He was silent for a long moment. "Word will travel to the healers."

"Meralonne—"

He smiled. "I will attend you on the morrow in the Hall of Wise Counsel, at the side of The Terafin. I do not think you face the danger you fear to name yet; but it is coming, and when the Lord of the Hells stands outside of the city's walls—and they *will* be walls, Sigurne, not the scattered, broken demi-walls that suggest its outline to the dim and the foreign—it will be full time, and the questions of the ages will be answered."

She closed her eyes. Eyes closed, she asked the question she had avoided asking even herself. "Meralonne, what of the Sleepers?"

When she opened her eyes, he was gone. She put the ring back in the jewelry box, and prepared for a sleep that would elude her for some time yet. In the morning, she would begin the onerous and ugly fighting that remedial classes would no doubt involve. No, she thought, sliding between the sheets, in the *afternoon*, she would begin. The morning involved gods, wary Kings, the Exalted, The Terafin, and *Avantari*.

The afternoon, only fractious, bitter, aggrieved mages. The thought gave her some comfort; given the tedium of the afternoon, the morning seemed less dire in comparison.

10th of Fabril, 428 A.A.
Terafin Manse, Averalaan Aramarelas

Jewel woke to the gray of early dawn; the sun had not yet crested the horizon. If, she thought, sun did in these rooms.

The Chosen had advised—strongly—that she repair to other quarters in the manse. It was advice she herself would have given had she been in their position; it was advice she could not take. "It's not about Carver and Ellerson," she told them softly. "Word has traveled. I can't now flee in terror from the rooms I was meant to occupy."

"You chose not to occupy them for almost three months," Torvan pointed out. The words were sharp.

"Yes. And had I never entered these rooms at all, I—" Carver would not be lost. She inhaled. "I would have that option. I have, and I do not have it now. I will," she added, as he opened his mouth again, "allow the Chosen to stand guard *in* the room in which I sleep. That is the only compromise I can offer."

It was also, they both knew, necessary. Had she forbidden it, they would be in this room regardless. She knew Torvan was angry, because Arrendas joined him shortly after their return to lend his voice to their argument in progress. Arrendas, however, was silent; he observed for fifteen minutes, and then turned to Torvan and said, "Shall I work out the guard details?"

When Torvan failed to reply, he continued. "She is right, as are you. But she is The Terafin."

"She is taking an unnecessary risk."

"She is taking a risk she feels is necessary."

The other Chosen were content to let their captains speak in their stead—but their stance and expressions made clear that they were in agreement with their captains.

"We are not The Terafin; we serve her. If she is committed—

and Torvan, she is—we put our energy into minimizing the risks she feels it necessary to take."

Torvan opened his mouth, but this time he closed it without ejecting further words. He then left the room with Arrendas, and after forty-five minutes, four Chosen entered the room and took up their positions around the mouth of the splintered closet. Jewel had forbidden its removal, although she feared the way would never be open again—not through that door.

It was not as hard to sleep in a room full of armed guards as she feared it might be; they were hers, after all, and she had spent half her life sleeping in far more crowded rooms.

Shadow, however, was not amused to see them, and made it known.

Avandar was waiting, and at Avandar's side, one of the servants, an older woman whose name escaped the fragmented memory dreams left in their wake. Shadow was on the bed. He wasn't precisely sitting on her, but he was sitting on the counterpane, and she couldn't easily move. It was a blessing.

It was a blessing she couldn't afford.

"Shadow," Avandar said.

Shadow nonchalantly climbed down. He did not, however, stray far from Jewel's side as she slid out from beneath the covers and into the waking world. The closet door—the door Avandar had splintered in his haste to make room for the Chosen—and himself—to follow her into the darkness, had not yet been replaced; its splintered ruins were a reminder she didn't need.

Four of the Chosen were standing in front of it.

"It is a closet," he told her quietly. "No more."

She stiffened. She stiffened, but did not immediately run to the closet. Instead, she put herself into the hands of a woman who was not Ellerson, understanding what Avandar did not say: she was to meet with the Kings and the Exalted this morn, and if by some small miracle her death was not instantly demanded, she would spend the rest of the day fencing with The Ten.

Carver.

She inhaled. Exhaled. She moved to the dresser where

the servant was waiting in a starched silence not even Ellerson could maintain. She put her appearance into the hands of a stranger as Avandar laid out the layers of clothing she was expected, as Terafin, to wear.

The knock at the door surprised her; the Chosen answered.

Teller was let into the room after clearly stating his business.

"Is there word from *Avantari*?" she asked, facing the mirror while her hair was tortured, with steam and oil, into an entirely unnatural shape.

He shook his head, and met her gaze across the reflective surface of silvered glass. She raised her hands in careful den-sign. His remained by his sides.

She was The Terafin. He was her chosen right-kin. They were to meet with the Kings as near-equals, and it mattered. But not in the way she imagined it would. Carver was gone. Her only comfort—and it was scant—was that she did not, as she had in the case of Lefty, *know* that he was dead. Her peculiar instinct, the talent for which she was so highly prized that she had been adopted into Terafin and made a member of its House Council at the age of sixteen, told her nothing.

She was afraid that nothing was the best she could hope for.

Teller handed her a small stack of papers, which, given the ministrations of her attendant, she couldn't actually read. "Beyond the expected, is there an emergency buried in this stack?"

"No. There are some concerns with The Morriset's recent ventures and the Royal Trade Commission; Darias has filed paperwork with the Port Authority about 'irregularities' in the manifestos of two of our shipping partners."

Jewel nodded. Neither of these difficulties were substantial enough to justify a full Council meeting in the Halls in *Avantari*. Teller knew it as well.

"The last reports," he said, "do not involve trade concessions, demands, or accusations."

"So they're worse."

"They're worse."

"*Avantari*?"

"It was surprisingly difficult to acquire accurate information about the structural changes within the palace; the pillars and the foundations are, however, visible to any visitor."

"These are—"

"Descriptions of the two rooms, yes. They are verbal; no sketch was done, and no attempt to magically capture the images was made—not by Terafin agents." He hesitated, and then said, "Meralonne stopped by."

"This early in the morning?"

"He's waiting outside the door of your personal chambers; the Chosen did not feel that your grant of unquestioned access to the grounds encompassed unquestioned access to the . . . library."

"Was he smoking his pipe?"

"No. I'm not sure he cares whether or not he annoys the Chosen."

Jewel grimaced. She rose with care as the servant stepped back, indicating by clipped movement of chin that she was free to do so. She was, Jewel had to admit, less *painful* than Ellerson could be. She dressed quickly, allowing Avandar to choose appropriate jewelry. She would not, however, remove the strand of gold around which the Handernesse ring hung; nor did he insist.

Shadow then began his litany of the things that bored him. The servant did not appear to notice, but she tensed the first few times he spoke. After about the hundredth, she seemed as relaxed as anyone else in the room except the Chosen.

Meralonne met them as they entered the standing arch that led to the Terafin manse. If Jewel and Teller were dressed for an audience with Kings, Meralonne was not. His presence, in his opinion, was enough of a boon. He nodded. "Terafin."

"APhaniel," she replied.

Shadow stepped between them and flexed his wings. Or rather, flexed one—the one on the mage's side. Meralonne did not leap out of the way; he *caught* the wing and held it as Shadow hissed. Jewel dropped her hand to his head as Avandar frowned. "Shadow. Now is not the time."

"It *is*," the cat replied.

"APhaniel, please." Meralonne released Shadow's wing without meeting Jewel's gaze.

"Today," he told the cat, "is not the day to play games."

But Shadow said, again, "It *is*." His lips had drawn up, exposing his prominent fangs; his fur rose.

"*Shadow.*" At the tone of her voice, he turned away from the mage—but he stayed between them, allowing Avandar his position to her left. This left no room for Teller, but given Shadow's expression—and the grimmer cast of Meralonne's—Jewel did not push the point.

Teller, however, did. He slid between Jewel and Shadow—which took flexibility, as he didn't step on her skirts in the process—and placed a hand on the cat's head, just behind Jewel's. "In the presence of the Kings and the Exalted," he said, speaking both softly and with respect, "she faces her greatest challenge."

Shadow hissed. He rarely called Teller stupid. "*Stupid* girl," he said instead.

But Teller, divining his reasoning because he had always liked cats, said, "It is not a challenge for you; it is not a challenge for Meralonne APhaniel. It is a challenge for The Terafin. They will not attack her; they will not attempt to harm her. But if the audience goes poorly, they may decide that she is a danger to the Empire."

"What Empire?"

"The Empire," Teller replied, before Jewel could, "in which we now reside. You have seen some of it. The Common, the whole of the manse. The Empire is part of the world in which mortals live. The Terafin—and almost all who serve her—are mortal."

"But not the *important* ones."

"No," was his grave reply.

Jewel wanted to kick Shadow; she refrained. "They're important to me," she said, as a compromise.

"And we're *not*?"

"Of course you are," the right-kin replied before Jewel could. Teller lifted his free hand, signing. She signed back, but briefly; he was right. She was worried; that worry would sink roots and grow as the day progressed. She was much like her Oma: if worried, she was always on edge, and she dulled the edge by snapping or snarling, something she could not afford today. Today, she had to be perfect.

"Will you accompany us, APhaniel, or will you return to the guildmaster?"

"I will accompany The Terafin as the Terafin House Mage," he replied, eyes narrowing. "Terafin, did something remiss occur in the evening?"

Damn him, anyway. "I will answer the question, APhaniel, if you will answer the questions that arise from the events."

He raised a pale brow. "I believe you have already answered in a general sense."

"I have never met a mage who was satisfied with a general answer. On the contrary it only serves to pique their curiosity and sharpen their interest."

He chuckled. To Avandar, to her surprise, he said, "She has grown into her role."

Avandar didn't even crack a smile. *No, Jewel*, he said, although she hadn't voiced her surprise in any way. *You are correct; today you must be perfect. But I ask you to consider one possibility.*

She waited.

What if the Kings decide that your existence is a threat to their Empire? What, then, will you do? I will not stand by and allow the Kings their execution.

I know. I have no desire to walk to my own death.

Will you countenance theirs?

. . . No.

It was the answer he expected. It was not, however, the answer he wanted.

"Terafin?" Meralonne said.

"Accompany us."

The Chosen were horsed; they numbered twelve. Four rode ahead of the Terafin carriage, four behind. Two flanked the carriage on either side. Meralonne joined Jewel in the carriage, taking the seat beside Teller. Shadow flew. Both of the mages were tinted orange in Jewel's vision; Meralonne also had a subtle sheen of gray that overlapped it. Jewel's protections were scant in comparison. One, a hairpin, had come from Haval, delivered alongside dire warnings about her future should she misplace it. The other was the House Ring itself. Her peculiar talent provided the immediate protections necessary to survive for long enough that the Chosen could come into play.

Gazing out the window—and noting the emptiness of the early morning streets as they passed—she said, "Member APhaniel?"

"I will accept your formality," he replied, "if I am permitted to smoke."

"I have no objections; if you're hoping to cause minor and politically safe irritation, you'll need to find another habit."

"I find it calming," he replied, in exactly the wrong tone of voice. She gave over the window view to look at his shadowed face; his eyes were glinting. "It is a habit that is entirely of this world."

"Smoke, then. It reminds mē of my grandmother."

His brows rose, but he lined the bowl of his pipe as the carriage moved; its procession was stately, to Jewel's mind a more pretentious way of saying slow. "What occurred in the evening, if I may be so bold?"

"I'm not entirely certain," she replied, her voice soft, the words stiff. "A closet door was opened; it led into the darkness of a long, stone hall."

His hand stilled in the act of carrying leaf to pipe. "You opened this door?"

"No. Not in any sense of the word. It was a closet. Closets in the Terafin manse contain clothing, no more."

"Where was this closet situated?"

"In my personal rooms." She drew breath, held it for a moment too long. "Meralonne, who are the heralds?"

"What an odd question. Whose heralds?"

"No names were given. But if I were to convey the message that the heralds are abroad, what would that mean to you?"

"It would mean little without knowledge of the messenger," he replied. He glanced at the bowl of the pipe, but did not light it.

"His name is Mordanant. I had the impression that he knew you."

The mage set the pipe aside. "You ventured into the world into which your closet opened."

"I wouldn't," she replied, "but I had little choice. It was not I who opened the closet, and therefore not I lost to it. But, yes, we met there. It's not the first time," she added. "And it was not an accident; he knew where I was."

"And he came to you."

"Yes."

"To deliver a message to me?"

"No. He was sent to hunt the heralds, whoever they are."

"He was sent?"

She nodded. "And if he was, there's only one person who could have sent him." She hesitated. He marked it. "He came for his brother, Lord Celleriant. He was . . . concerned that his placement, here, would be his doom." Silence; it was cold in the carriage. "But he counseled Lord Celleriant to speak—with you."

"Those were his words?"

"They were not his exact words; I've stripped the patina of desperation from them."

At that, he smiled. It was not a friendly smile. He glanced at the carriage wall behind her, as if it were a window. "The heralds are not a concern," he said, "if they cannot reach their Lords. They have searched."

She didn't mention the Sleepers. Not directly. Instead, she said, "You know where they lie."

"I have always known, but I was never herald."

"Can the heralds wake them?"

"Not yet. Not yet, Terafin, but soon it will not matter." He glanced at the pipe in his hand, frowning.

Avandar, light the pipe. Light it now.

What he tolerates from you, he will not likewise tolerate from me.

Please, just do it.

Avandar glanced at the leaves in the bowl and they began to smolder. Meralonne's eyes rounded; he looked down at the now orange leaves. To Jewel's surprise, he laughed. His glance returned to her as he lifted the pipe's stem to his lips. "Lord Mordanant—and he is Lord in the Queen's Court, Winter or Summer—may overestimate my abilities. Did he speak of the Winter Queen?"

"Yes."

Rings of smoke rose in the air between them. "And?"

"Evayne visited her."

His grip on the pipe tightened; it was subtle, but he had the whole of Jewel's attention. "And?"

She exhaled. "I won't play games with you now."

Jewel. Whatever he has been to you in the past, the time is coming; he will change; he will become something that you cannot touch, reach, or trust.

Why?

If you do not already know the answer, you suspect it.

And you know.

He did not answer, not directly. *Be cautious. Believe that he will step beyond your reach or the reach of either your words or your history. Do not trust him.*

You don't think I should trust anyone.

You understand the difference.

She did. She studied the mage's shuttered face for a long moment, weighing the benefits and the cost of silence. Lifting her arm, she pulled up the edge of her sleeve; around her wrist sat a bracelet made of three strands of platinum hair.

His eyes widened. He was not Haval; he almost never forced his expression into shuttered neutrality, although he made the occasional attempt. He made no such attempt now. Pipe smoke, like a ragged veil, streamed up around his face; his eyes were silver and unblinking.

"I don't understand why you're here. I don't understand why you serve the Order of Knowledge."

"Such understanding is not a necessity."

"No." She looked away, letting her sleeve fall.

"Where did you acquire your . . . bracelet?"

"In the Tor Leonne," she replied, gazing at empty streets, at stone buildings, at trees that were in every way junior to the trees that now girded the Terafin manse.

"You were foolish enough to ask?"

"Me?" She looked down at hands that were brown with sun and pale with winter dryness. "I wouldn't have dared."

"She did not offer." It wasn't a question.

"No, Meralonne. She doesn't give gifts. Not in Winter." Speaking the words, she felt them as immutable truth.

"You did not steal them."

She shook her head. "When she turned from me — when she turned to give word to her host — three strands of her hair brushed across my open palm. I didn't mean to raise a hand — I couldn't help it. I wanted to — " she shook her head. "I don't know what I wanted. I don't trust beauty," she added. "Not the Winter Queen's; it seems too much like death to me; it's too cold and too distant. But even without trust, I wanted to hold it in place for just a moment longer. I—"

"You feared to lose it."

It was true. She knew she could never love Winter. She knew she would never love or admire its Queen. But there was a hollowness, an empty space, that existed whenever she thought of Ariane. A yearning for things wild and ancient that she would never, *ever*, want in her home.

"I closed my hand on the strands," she continued, her voice dropping. "And they remained in my palm. I braided them." She inhaled, and turned to face him again, expecting disappointment, possibly condemnation.

She found neither. Meralonne lifted the stem of the pipe to his lips, losing some of his sharp rigidity in the process. "She is death, for you."

"I know."

"But mortals have oft walked willingly to that death. Inasmuch as she gifts any mortal, she gifted you; she will not acknowledge that gift in any way, but the lack frees you from obligation." He blew rings of amorphous smoke. "Would you be parted from them?"

"No."

"Wise, indeed. It is never safe to be cavalier with such gifts." His eyes narrowed. "What do you seek to offer me, Terafin?"

"Summer," she replied.

He was rigid for a long moment after the word had died into silence. He smoked in that silence, and she took comfort from it, although he appeared not to notice the pipe itself. "You cannot offer that; it is not within your power."

"It is not yet within my power."

"And will it be, Terafin?" He leaned forward; Avandar stiffened.

"It will." As she spoke the words, she knew them for truth. They had taken root in the winter in the Tor Leonne, and they had grown.

"You will not serve as Summer King," was his gentle reply. "She would not take you."

"No."

"If you can reach her—and of the mortals here, I think you are the only one who might—you cannot force the roads to accept her; she has not offered what they require. She exists outside of their season."

Jewel nodded, as if this made sense. "If I can offer you Summer, Meralonne—if that is within my power—what will you offer me in turn?"

"What would you ask of me? I will not insult you by pretending that it is of little interest."

"You have served Sigurne Mellifas for her entire tenure as guildmaster. You have advised Kings, and trained warriors within the Order's heart."

He shrugged, as if each were inconsequential.

"Mordanant felt that our only hope of survival lay with you."

He laughed, then. It was not, in any way, a happy sound. "The Kings do not command my loyalty," he said, when he chose to speak again. "No more does Sigurne, although I am fond of the guildmaster. I will not vow to serve you in any way that matters; not even in return for Summer. Given that, what would you have of me? For what you offer, I have little of value to offer in return. You play games so poorly it is hard to discern a game at all."

"That has always been her failing," Avandar said. Teller had not spoken a word.

"It has. Terafin, I will tell you now that any hope of survival you have does not rest in my hands; Mordanant is wise, but he has never lived among mortals. Even when man was at the apex of his power, he little understood that the power they held *was* their own; he assumed—as do many of his kin—that it was granted by gods. The fate of this City is your burden, if you can see it in time to shoulder it. You are not what you were; you are not yet what you must be." He reached through the window and emptied his pipe.

"How? How can I protect the city?"

"Do not ask me the question. It is yours, and only yours, to answer." He began to fill his pipe again. "And if the condition for your offer is the safety of the City, it is not an offer I am willing to accept."

Avandar was surprised. She sensed it, although he failed to express it in any other way.

Yes, he said, his gaze on Meralonne alone. *It is a matter of little significance to promise little in return for much. I would expect—I did expect—such an offer, and I would have counseled against its acceptance. Inasmuch as he can, he understands you, or those like you; he understands your fears and your desires. But Jewel, he has not. He grants the import of what you offer, and he is unwilling to lessen it.*

"Can you walk the paths, Meralonne?"

"In safety, Terafin?"

"I don't think safety matters to you."

His smile was sharp as a blade. "Indeed. If you mean can I walk those paths to reach that court, the answer is no. Could I, I would not find the way into its heart; it is forbidden to one such as I." His glance fell again to the wrist around which Ariane's memento was twined. "But if you mean can I traverse those roads which open into your domain with so little warning, yes. The best defense you could offer those who dwell within your manse was your ignorance, but in waking from the trap laid by the Warden of Dreams, you *are* awake.

"Now, the only defense you can offer is knowledge, and it is a knowledge you fear. Shall I tell you why?"

"Do you know?"

"I cannot perceive the whole of your thought," he replied, as he lit his pipe, "but I have watched Sigurne Mellifas since she first entered the Order; she was only slightly older than you yourself were when you entered The Terafin's service. She walks—has always walked—a very delicate edge; it has scarred her, in ways you cannot see.

"Had she desired it, she might have become a mage with few peers; her power is not insignificant. She might have taken the bitter lessons of her captive youth and fashioned a place for herself that not even the Kings could rival. Do not interrupt me," he added, when Jewel opened her mouth. "When I speak of the possibility, it is just that; it is idle, it is speculation. The Northern mage did not kill her; the first— and the most significant—of her early teachers did not, although he came closer than she will admit to either of us, in my estimation.

"She has, instead, devoted her considerable knowledge to denying any other the benefit of the knowledge she gained, and she has walked the narrow road, always, as sentinel. I see some of her in you now. What she fears, you also fear—but your fear is stronger. And that is wise; the danger is greater."

"What—what fear?"

"You fear to be more than you are."

"I don't—"

"You fear, then, to lose what you are. You are wed to mortality, and you do not wish to leave it."

She glanced at Avandar. "Could I?" she asked softly.

He did not pretend to misunderstand her. "Mortals have oft chased the dream of immortality; it is a costly gift to grant—but the granting is less costly than the acceptance. I believe you are well aware of the latter cost."

She turned, once again, to the streets, glancing at the Chosen who kept pace with the carriage. "Immortality just seems like another way of being abandoned. Unless my friends are also immortal, what's the point?"

"The point for men of power—"

"They don't *have any* friends. The Winter King had rivals, enemies, and the allies he accepted for the sake of mutual convenience. Was he powerful? Yes. Far more than I'll ever be. What did it do for him? He faces eternity as a ground mount for a woman he can no longer touch."

"You attempt to shift the conversation in a direction it was not meant to go. The responsibility—if it can be met at all—will be in your hands. You have not," he added, lifting pipe to his lips, "been invited to *Avantari* since your predecessor's death. You will not have seen the changes within the palace itself."

"I'm aware that changes have been made."

"Good. The Kings are undecided because the gods are undecided. I ask you again, what would you have of me for what you offer?"

"If you will not stay within the Order's walls, take up residence within mine. I will open a room for you in the upper floor."

He lowered the pipe, although tobacco still burned in its bowl, and turned to face her. "I don't believe your House Council will approve."

"It's not up to the House Council," was her sharp reply. "It's up to me. If there were obvious expenses associated with your residence, I would have to justify them, yes—but there won't be."

"Why is this of import to you? I have already stated that I will offer you no oath and no pledge of service."

"I want you to walk those roads with me."

"I have already told you that it is not safe to even open their doors. Will you ignore advice that is meant entirely to bolster your chances for survival?"

"Yes," was her stark reply. "I sent the Winter King into the wilderness, and with him Snow and Night."

"To what end?" he asked, in a tone that made clear his astonishment at her utter lack of sense.

"I told you. I didn't open the door that led to the hidden roads."

Understanding, then. "Yes," he said softly.

"Yes you'll—"

"I will accept your offer, although it is singularly unwise. I will hunt, by your side, for those who have gone missing. They are not, of course, of value to me; no more, in the end, than all but a handful of mortals who have once called this City home. But they are, in my view, as valuable to you as what you have offered me. I will not lay down my life for theirs; I will not offer it in your stead. But what I can divert in this endeavor, I will." He looked as if he were finished, but he lifted pipe again. "Call back your cats. Have the Winter King return to your side."

But she shook her head. "I have Shadow. The cats might return, but they were bored, as you might have noticed. The Winter King *will* lay down his life in this quest."

"He will not."

"He will; what I have offered him for the chance of success is of far more import—to him. While you are in my domain, Meralonne, close the doors that you see opening if I don't perceive them. Stop my people—my mortal people—from stepping foot upon those byways."

He nodded again. "You understand," he said, as he emptied his pipe out the carriage window, "that if you fail in *Avantari*, the fate of those I save will be no kinder than the fate they will meet in the end?"

"But you'll save them *now*. What we face in the end, we face." She folded her hands in her lap. "Tell me, Meralonne."

"Yes?"

"What happens when the Sleepers wake?"

"It is said—"

"I don't care what's said. I want to know what will happen."

"They will see the ruins of a city," he replied, "infested

with carrion. Their anger at your presumption will know few bounds, and they will scour the earth of you and your kind. They will not serve our enemy," he added, "but that will be of little consolation to you."

"Can they?" she asked. "The demons themselves have chosen to approach Averalaan with caution; they do not bring armies to the city."

"Not yet. But the time for caution is passing. Come, Terafin. We have Kings to meet."

Chapter Sixteen

THE HALL OF WISE COUNSEL was, in all ways, a remarkable room. Most of the characteristics that made it unusual were not immediately obvious to a casual visitor. It was an audience chamber fit for the Crowns, a huge room the height of which instantly dwarfed any who walked through its doors. At any time of day or night, the room was brightly lit. The windows, stained glass, and almost of a piece with the intimidating architecture, shifted hue in keeping with external light, implying natural elements that did not, in any way, reach the room.

Various protective enchantments had been laid against both windows and walls; the floor was a mosaic of magical color if one knew how to look. Sigurne Mellifas did. She was intimately aware of perhaps three quarters of the enchantments; she would never be given leave to examine them all. Nor had she need.

What the hall lacked in an appreciable sense was silence. The doors and the walls did not permit sound to travel beyond their perimeters—but within the room itself, the acoustics carried spoken word, enlarging it.

When the steward opened the doors to the hall, raised voices escaped. Sigurne exhaled. She did not ask the stew-

ard how long the Kings had been resident in the hall; nor
did she ask to remain outside while the heated discussion
continued. It would not, in the past two months, be the first
time voices had been raised in this room.

Today, there were several. The Kings and the Exalted
were not seated upon their thrones; they stood in a tight
group, made wider by the obvious divergence of opinion.
The Queens were present, but they were excluded from the
debate. Sigurne had some small hope that she would be
likewise spared.

It was a vain hope. Before she had reached the halfway
point of the room, the Lord of the Compact turned. Duvari
was not a man to raise his voice in anger; he lowered it, in
times of duress. He reminded Sigurne of nothing so much
as a guard dog; the barking, one could safely ignore; the
growling, at one's peril.

"Guildmaster," the Lord of the Compact said.

"Lord of the Compact."

"— And may I remind you again, brother, that we are not
beholden to the gods' every whim; we are mortal, and mortals rule here." King Reymalyn's voice echoed in the ceilings above.

"So you have said. Nor have I disagreed; the decision is
not in the gods' hands; it is in ours. But the gods have made
clear the danger a single citizen poses to the rest of the
Empire. They have a history—"

"It is a history that has been offered us piecemeal, and it
is irrelevant. The Terafin has not contravened the laws of
this land. If we are to execute—or assassinate—every person who poses a possible threat, there would be no city
when the Lord of the Hells at last approached the gates!"

"The nonexistent gates, surely?" the Exalted of the
Mother said to King Cormalyn. He looked every bit as ill-
pleased as the god-born son of Justice. Sigurne did not envy
them this argument. On the contrary, as she had little place
in it, she would have been grateful to be excluded.

But she knew that variations of this argument had tied the
Kings' hands, extending the life of The Terafin. Rumors implied that it had not likewise bound the hands of the *Astari*.

"If she were the danger feared by the gods, she would
not have had to flee the Common when the demon attacked."

The Lord of the Compact bowed. It was a graceful, economical motion, and it brought the argument to a temporary halt. "I have received a report," he said, into the ensuing, bitter silence. Duvari was perhaps the only man who would have dared interrupt; the Queens, as Sigurne, were silent.

King Reymalyn nodded brusquely.

"There is some evidence that there are recent—and notable—structural changes within the Terafin manse." All eyes now fell on Duvari, who weathered the inspection as if it were irrelevant. "The changes involve The Terafin's personal chambers."

"Are they as impressive as the architectural changes within the Palace?" the Mother's Daughter asked.

"They are as complete."

"That is an evasion," Sigurne said.

Duvari glanced in her direction. "My sources have not yet accessed The Terafin's personal rooms. But the access points that were meant for the use of highly placed servants have vanished."

"Pardon?"

"They no longer exist. There are no back halls and no back stairs that lead into them; they vanished overnight."

"Which night?" The question was sharper, harsher; King Cormalyn was the speaker.

"The night The Terafin woke. The external building has not significantly changed; the upper floors remain intact. There is only one exception; the glass dome that once overlooked The Terafin's personal libraries."

"It is gone?"

"No. But the glass is now opaque." He hesitated, and then added, "It is not, to our knowledge, glass at all."

Silence.

The Exalted of Cormaris spoke. "If it is true the gods give us an incomplete history, it is also true that much of it has been irrelevant to our rule. That, I fear is changing. You know what we counsel. If it is to be effective, you are running out of time; it is a commodity of import to the merely mortal."

"Can we demonstrate," King Cormalyn said, "that The Terafin is now, in effect, a very real threat to the Empire?" He turned to Sigurne.

She was silent. She knew that the rooms in the upper reach were not the only difference to the manse, and knew further that the *Astari* had not infiltrated the Chosen. "If you mean to take this evidence to The Ten, no."

"Would The Ten agree to meet with the gods in the Between?"

"That will, in my opinion, depend entirely on the meeting of The Ten. But if you intend her death to have the fewest repercussions, you will have her executed before that meeting. You will not receive dispensation from The Ten; if she is dead, however, they will have little recourse."

"Very well. Her domicis is reputed to be a mage without parallel."

"I have not tested him," Sigurne replied. "But we are aware, and we are watchful. Member APhaniel does not believe he constitutes a threat unless and until any harm is offered his Lord."

"The cats?"

"Are deadly. I do not think the *Astari* would be sufficient to contain them." She hesitated. It was noted.

"Speak freely."

"The gods appeared to recognize the cats; it is of the gods, not of the Guildmaster of the Order of Knowledge, that you must ask that question. The cats do not fear the demons; they do not fear assassins. Nor, in my opinion, should they."

"Lord of the Compact, is the room ready?"

"It is."

"Guildmaster, The Terafin brings a member of the First Circle as her attendant."

"He will not interfere."

The Exalted of the Mother lifted her head. She glanced at the Queens; Siodonay was stiff and pale, her hands in fists above the fabric of her very practical skirts. "I have one request," she said, smiling the kindly smile of an aged matriarch—an expression Sigurne knew well in all its significance, she had used it so often herself.

"Ask," the Kings said, in unison.

"I would like to show The Terafin some evidence of what she unintentionally wrought."

Sigurne tensed. "I do not consider that wise," she said.

Duvari added, "I concur."

"And the request was not, with all due respect, made of either the guildmaster or the Lord of the Compact. The most difficult element of this decision has always been the character of The Terafin. The rooms are unusual. Like the work of Artisans, they do not conform in expected ways to the vision of their visitors.

"But The Terafin will not harm the Kings until it is clear they mean her death—and perhaps not then."

"What do you hope to gain?"

"Information, as always, Your Majesty. The Terafin is the only seer born in the Empire of which we are aware. What she sees might give us a glimpse of what we face in an increasingly unpredictable future—and if we mean to have her removed, it is the only such glimpse we might receive."

Jewel did not arrive in *Avantari* as a penitent; she had considered that approach, but had chosen to discard it. What had been done in *Avantari*, without her conscious consent or intent, was done. She had, through Avandar and Celleriant, two men bound in different ways to her service, preserved the lives of the Princes—men who would one day occupy the thrones of the Twin Kings. She did not intend to apologize or grovel for that.

Nor did she feel either would be advantageous; had she, she would have put aside—with difficulty—the pride required to rule. But her demeanor, from the moment she exited the enclosed confines of the Terafin carriage, was being watched, gauged, and judged. It was judged by the Kings' Swords and the *Astari*—as well as the servants of the royal palace; it was not these that concerned her as she made her way up the wide and grand stairs of the palace, and had it been only those who labored in service to the Crowns, she might have modulated her bearing, her carriage, the stiff tone of her voice when she spoke at all. No, among the servants here, and no doubt among the Swords, were those who might pass on word of what they witnessed to The Ten.

What the Kings demanded—or perhaps what Duvari demanded—was in direct opposition to what The Ten required. She could not be seen to accept censure with either grace or ease.

Shadow landed on the stairs and inserted himself behind

the Chosen to her left, forcing Avandar to fall back. He did not, however, step on Avandar's feet or on Jewel's skirts, and he did not speak at all. She in turn accepted his presence by her side as if it were natural, sharply aware of his change in visible stature. She'd grown accustomed to it in such a short period of time it should have been disturbing.

No, it *was* disturbing. But at heart he was the same creature who'd dogged her steps for months.

Perhaps because of his size and the Swords' inevitable lack of exposure to guards that moved on four paws, had wings, fangs, and looked like walking death, the Kings' Swords were present in greater number than Jewel remembered them being on any prior occasion. She accepted their presence without comment and without acknowledgment; inasmuch as armored and armed men by the dozen could be beneath notice, these were.

The steward who met her at the head of the Swords offered her a deep bow; it was not exaggerated for effect, but it was not brief.

"Terafin."

She inclined head, no more.

"Please, follow."

Jewel was not a frequent visitor to the Hall of Wise Counsel, but she had never entered that room and found the Kings waiting. The Kings remained in a separate chamber until summoned, probably by the *Astari*. The Exalted, however, were less paranoid.

Cautious, Avandar said.

I didn't say it out loud. Is it necessary to correct my thoughts?

His answer was clearly yes. She followed the steward from the large, intimidating halls into the first of the public galleries. Prepared for what she saw, she didn't miss a step—but that took work. It was hard to both gape and pretend that nothing was noteworthy; she managed something in between.

The floors in the hall were adorned with long rugs. The rugs caught the eye, but beneath them, the stone stretched out from one end to the other in a single piece, unbroken by anything as everyday as seams. These, she could have ignored with little effort.

It was the pillars that would have been hard to ignore. No,

she thought, impossible. They were, as the floors, of a single piece, and they rose from floor to the height of the beginning of arched vaulting. But they were a darker stone than the floors. They were not polished, although they appeared smoothly ground; flecks of color caught and reflected light. In and of itself, this would not have been remarkable—but the shape of the pillars had changed; they now looked like the trunks of enormous trees, over which the vaulting ceiling served as branches reaching, always, for the sky.

She wanted to ask if they were all like this, all of the pillars, but couldn't. Here, where there were no other speakers, her voice would carry her ignorance to whoever listened.

The walls, however, did not appear hugely changed. They were still adorned by tapestries and paintings. The statues, however, caught her eye. They were, in theory, carved likenesses of the gods—although having seen them in the Between, Jewel was aware that only an Artisan might truly capture some part of their essential nature—but they were not the statues with which she was familiar. No; they were so finely chiseled, and so elegantly adorned, they seemed almost alive. They were taller by a good three feet than they had been the last time she'd seen them.

Taller, prouder, and—to Jewel's eye—crueler in seeming.

She forced herself to keep her eyes on the steward; she asked no questions, and made no comments.

Duvari was, of course, waiting for Jewel in the Hall of Wise Counsel. Sigurne Mellifas was also present; she looked both weary and alert. Five minutes with Duvari could easily account for that level of weariness, but in this case, that was wishful thinking on Jewel's part. The steward announced The Terafin; the Swords spread out along the back wall, leaving Avandar, Teller, Meralonne, and Shadow standing at the foot of a long blue runner that led to the dais upon which the Exalted were seated.

Jewel, mindful of Amarais' prior behavior, tendered the Exalted a perfect obeisance. She held it until the Mother's Daughter bid her rise. The Mother's Daughter was not old, but at this moment, looked it. Her golden eyes were ringed with dark circles, and her lips, creased deeply at the corners.

"We were both alarmed and concerned when we received word of your cancellation of our last audience. What caused your absence, Terafin?" she asked, coming directly to the point. The new point. The pillars, the floors, and the unmentioned statues now seemed to be of lesser concern.

Jewel had intended to dismiss her absence as a House affair—an emergency; given that it was semi-public knowledge that she had been targeted by assassins five times in the last few months, it was almost plausible. Instead, she found herself saying, "If we might wait upon the Kings and the Queens? The Ten meet in *Avantari* today, and the explanation required might take some time."

This was not to the liking of the Exalted of Reymaris. "The Kings are also extremely busy."

"Understood, Exalted." She did not, however, answer the question; she chose to wait.

Duvari walked to Sigurne's side; they conversed briefly. In the silent room, none of their words reached Jewel. This surprised her; if silence was used as a defensive precaution— and it was—it was seldom used in such an obvious way; not in this room.

"APhaniel," the guildmaster finally said.

"I consider it safe," the mage replied. He looked bored. He was not, however, holding his pipe.

Duvari spoke to Sigurne again; Sigurne looked as pleased at the exchange as any notable man or woman of power in the Empire might. But if Duvari was not satisfied— and in this room, he seldom was—he nodded.

The carved reliefs along the back of the room began their slow fade, announcing in silence the arrival of the Kings and Queens. They entered the room flanked by two men and two women who were dressed as minor aides, wearing the gray that characterized the Swords, but absent the tabard and obvious armor. They were, in Jewel's opinion, *Astari*.

The Queens offered Jewel a shallow bow, which surprised her; the Kings confined themselves to a stiff, minimal nod, which did not. They took their thrones.

Jewel turned to the Exalted of the Mother. "My thanks, Exalted," she said, meaning it. "And my deep apologies for absenting myself from our last meeting. I was indisposed in such a way that I was not aware of the passage of time, and were I, I was nonetheless not in a position to attend." She drew breath as they waited, watching her.

She placed a hand on Shadow's head when she caught the twitch of his ears from the corner of her eye; she did not take her eyes away from the god-born and the Queens. "In the estimation of Levec, I was felled by the sleeping sickness." She couldn't tell if this was news to them or not; she assumed that word had reached Duvari through Devon.

"He woke you?"

"No. It was not necessary."

"It was not *possible*," Shadow hissed.

She felt Avandar's anger. The god-born, however, did not seem annoyed by the interruption.

"Without the intervention of healers, the sleepers do not waken."

"One has," Jewel replied calmly. "She woke shortly before I woke."

The Kings glanced at Duvari, who nodded. "Are we to understand from this that you had some hand not only in your own waking, but in theirs as well?"

"Yes."

"We await your explanation."

"The sleeping sickness has, on occasion, been called the dreaming plague. Given that the sleepers, when wakened by healers, have no memory of their dreams, I'm not certain why. But reason aside, the second name is the more appropriate. I'm not certain how the victims were chosen—I know only that they all dwell within *Averalaan*."

"It is the only distinguishing feature; there is no uniformity of location, age, or gender."

Jewel nodded again. "They were found in their sleep. They were found," she continued, "in their dreams, and while dreaming, they were caught and trapped."

"Terafin."

"Exalted."

"You speak with certainty."

"With as much certainty as I can; I am certain the information is not complete. I, too, was caught while dreaming."

"But you were aware."

"I am seer-born," she replied, without a trace of the bitterness that often accompanied the word. "And often the strongest or most complete warnings come to me in my dreams. I seldom forget dreams for that reason, and even when I am caught in them, I can ... observe."

"That is unusual, but the explanation seems reasonable," the Exalted of Cormaris said, speaking for the first time. "Continue."

"While sleeping the night before my previous audience with the Exalted, I dreamed. In that dream I met a ... man ... who called himself the Warden of Dreams. He was within the confines of my dream—but he exists beyond it."

"And not as a figment or a creation of your dreams?"

"No. He identified himself as one of the firstborn."

Silence.

After a long pause, the Exalted of the Mother said, "Please continue."

"The Warden of Dreams is not, as he appears, one person; he is not, however, two distinct entities. Both of those entities occupy the same physical form, even in the dreaming; both appear to have their own plans and their own goals—which in this case did not entirely coincide. I think of them as Dream and Nightmare, but for purposes of this discussion, I will use Warden of Dreams, if that is acceptable." When no objections were raised, she continued.

"If the dreamers are killed in the dreaming, they die. During my sleep," she added, forcing her voice to retain both volume and steadiness, "he demonstrated this."

"How many?" King Reymalyn asked. "How many did he kill?"

"I don't know, I'm sorry. At the time, the dreamers had taken the form of butterflies; they flew to him, and he crushed a handful. I wasn't close enough to interfere."

"Five died," Duvari said.

She accepted the information without acknowledging it.

"But no others have awakened without intervention."

"No. Leading them out of their dreams is not a trivial undertaking. The healer who attempted to wake me was dragged into the dreaming with me."

King Cormalyn glanced at Duvari. At a Duvari who was clearly not *pleased* to be offered information he didn't already possess. Audiences like this were a test, for the Lord of the Compact; he wished to know all pertinent facts before they occurred, so he could gauge not only the lies offered, but the shades of truth. He did not, however, accuse her of lying.

"How, then, did you wake?"

"I was within the heart of my own domain," she replied. "The Warden of Dreams might kill me in my sleep, but he could not hold me there."

"And the healer?"

"He was with me," she said. "He was, in the waking world, in constant contact with me; when I woke, he woke as well. There will be no new sleepers," she continued. "And I am in discussion with the Houses of Healing—although Healer Levec is extraordinarily busy—to arrange a schedule whereby the others might be released. It is, as I said, not a trivial undertaking, and some internal House difficulties require a vigilance that does not lend itself to ad hoc intervention."

King Cormalyn offered a slight, pained smile. "If the assassins sent against you are similar to the demon in the Common, I imagine Levec has all but forbidden you access to the Houses of Healing."

"He was not markedly enthusiastic, no."

"And we come to one of the gravest of difficulties in untangling the question of your fate."

"My fate?" Jewel asked, voice cool.

The King did not reply. Not directly. "In the opinion of the Guildmaster of the Order of Knowledge, no demonic attack has been so much of a threat to the Empire. Were the demon who appeared during the victory parade not so focused on your destruction, many of The Ten would now be without their leaders, and the most trusted members of their governing Council." Of the threat to the Kings, he did not speak.

Nor did Jewel.

"But he was focused upon your demise, and when you retreated, he chose to pursue. What you did to drive him off—unless you claim his destruction—you could not have done in the Common."

Shadow growled.

"If you cannot behave," Jewel whispered, "you will wait outside in the hall."

He compromised; he lay down, curling his body around her skirts.

Sigurne lifted hand; King Cormalyn nodded. "I believe that supposition to be in error," she said.

"Guildmaster?"

"I believe that it is possible for her to do exactly that—in the Common, certainly. There is some evidence that she could do the same within *Avantari*, and given the protections laid against the very stones of the palace, it implies that she could stand her ground anywhere upon the Isle. I am less certain that her influence would extend to the entirety of the hundred holdings."

Shadow said, "It will."

The King fixed the cat with a golden stare. "Why are you so certain?" he asked, speaking to the cat as if he was at least as worthy of respect as the Guildmaster of the entire Order of Knowledge.

"These are *her* lands," Shadow replied.

Jewel opened her mouth to disagree, vehemently, with his assertion. She closed it, in silence. She could not bring herself to speak the words of denial. They would not comfort Duvari—at this point, nothing short of her death would. Instead, after a pause in which she had not expected to speak, she said, "The lands that the demon walks are not the lands that you govern. They overlap," she added quickly, "but they are not the same.

"The lands that I walked in my dream *are* the lands that the demons have used to enter our city. To enter the palace, the manse, and even the Common. I have claimed them as mine. They are mine. It is not a claim that is understood by lawyers, merchants, or the patriciate."

"I believe almost all notable members of the patriciate were present at The Terafin's funeral," King Reymalyn pointed out. "What you said during the ... unusual ... first day rites, they heard. What you said," he continued, when she failed to reply, "was heard across the Isle. It was, our investigations imply, heard across the hundred holdings. If you feel that your claim does not coexist with the realm of the citizens of Averalaan, you took no care to diminish it."

She hadn't. She'd no idea at the time that the words would carry so damn far. Nor could she now safely own that ignorance.

"You are aware that alterations were made within *Avantari*

itself, without the permission of the Crowns." It was not a question.

She nodded.

"Are you aware of the extent of those alterations?"

"I have not had the opportunity to view them all."

"We will now provide you with that opportunity." King Cormalyn rose. King Reymalyn joined him; the Queens, utterly silent, rose as well. King Cormalyn turned to the Exalted. As one, they rose. "Lord of the Compact."

Duvari bowed stiffly.

School your expression with more care, Avandar warned her.

She didn't argue. She understood what was at stake. The doors at the end of the hall rolled open as the Kings approached; waiting in the hall were Swords in perfect formation. The Kings exited the room, followed by Duvari, the Exalted, and the Queens, in that order. Sigurne Mellifas waited as Jewel, Teller to her right and Avandar to her left, also joined the procession. They left little room for Shadow, but he corrected this oversight by inserting himself between Jewel and her domicis. As he told her often, he *liked* Teller.

Her Chosen fell in behind, and with them, Sigurne and Meralonne.

The floors and the columns Jewel had seen, she passed above and between without comment. The Kings did not speak; nor did they pause to watch her reaction. They led, and she followed, matching their stately pace. Funeral marches were more cheerful. The wide halls allowed for easy passage of both guards and guarded, but when they left the public galleries, they entered a part of the palace that was unfamiliar to Jewel.

We have not entered this wing before, Avandar confirmed.

She looked for signs, and found none; there were, above one arch, engraved letters. They were Old Weston, by look; she couldn't read them beyond that. Nor did she ask Avandar if he could.

Teller was silent; he appeared to be entirely at ease. She knew it as a front, but it wasn't one she herself could manage.

The halls here were narrower; the formation of the procession changed, the flow of progress slowing to accommo-

date the shifting of the Swords. The Chosen were likewise
forced to walk no more than two abreast; Teller fell back,
and as he did, he tapped Shadow's shoulder. Shadow sighed;
it was, with the exception of the heavy sounds of booted
feet, the only audible expression.

She did not recognize the halls; they were sparer in all
ways than the halls that had preceded them. The ceilings
were vaulted, the walls stone; no wood adorned them. They
were gray, tall, and broken only at the heights and at the
pillars—unaltered, to her relief—that served to support
those heights. Here, the decor was decidedly martial; there
were gleaming weapons across the walls where tapestries
and paintings might otherwise be displayed. The weapons,
however, were ornate; they did not seem like they were
meant for use.

Given the presence of Swords—not to mention Duvari
himself—they wouldn't be necessary.

She wasn't prepared for the stairs. That the palace had
stairs was not a surprise; the Terafin manse had many, and
many of those were hidden behind the rooms occupied by
the House members. But these stairs lay to the left of the
martial hall, as if they were an afterthought; there were no
visible doors, no possible reason for the existence of the
stairs themselves implied by the otherwise impressive, if
spare, architecture.

The Kings Swords' led the way, and the Kings followed,
as did the Exalted, the Queens, and the Lord of the Compact. Jewel, however, reached the top of the stairs and froze
there, placing her hand against the nearest wall to steady
herself.

"Terafin?" Sigurne said. She had pushed her way past
the Chosen, Teller, and Shadow; Avandar had stepped aside
to allow her passage.

The stairs were wide and flat; they did not curve—as
stairs often did within the palace. They traveled down, in a
gentle slope, the darkness alleviated by magestones. There
were no rails, stone or otherwise; they were hugged by wall
on either side. But their end, from their height, could not be
seen.

"Jewel."

She swallowed.

"What is it? What do you see?"

She shook herself. "Stairs," she said softly. "Were they—were they always like this, these stairs? Or did they—did they change when the columns changed?" She looked past the guildmaster. Avandar, Shadow, and Teller were waiting; it was Teller's gaze she sought. He lifted a hand in exquisitely graceful den-sign: *Yes, same.* He knew what she saw, here; he knew what it reminded her of: the undercity.

She could not, and did not, say as much, although Sigurne's presence by her side made clear the full failure of her composure.

"These stairs are, to my knowledge, unchanged. They are not remarkable, and they are not, beyond the magic required for illumination, enchanted in any way the Order could discern." Sigurne frowned as Jewel slowly withdrew her hand. "Why are they of concern?"

Jewel shook her head. Perhaps because she spoke with Sigurne, and not with the Kings, she said, "I've seen stairs like this before. The same stone. The same slope. They're not as wide, but—" She shook her head again. With the marching order, such as it was, changed by Jewel's hesitance and Sigurne's concern, she continued down the stairs in the wake of the Kings.

The descent was not steep, nor was it short. Jewel was aware that basements were often used for food storage, and for records storage when records considered of minor import were retired for filing considerations. The Terafin manse had several such rooms. She assumed the palace had more.

But basement rooms did not often require the height the descent implied. The Chosen could, once again, walk four abreast; Avandar continued to hold his position to Jewel's left, but Sigurne now took the right, and Jewel granted it because Sigurne was much older and could use the wall as a rail. Jewel, in theory, didn't require the support.

The air was cool. It was not damp; it was dry. A hint of a breeze blew up the stairs, chilling her. She glanced at Avandar. *Did you feel that?*

He nodded. His jaw had set in a tighter line. No one who was not familiar with the domicis would mark it. Shadow shoved Avandar out of the way. Jewel glared at the cat, but his eyes—eyes that were as golden, now, as the Kings', failed to meet hers; they were scanning the stairs ahead.

"Terafin," Sigurne said. "We tarry."

Jewel nodded and began to walk more quickly. The air grew colder; she was not attired for the outdoors.

"Be careful," Shadow told her, voice dropping into a low growl.

"Did the stairs always descend this far?" she asked Sigurne. When the guildmaster failed to answer, she turned. "Meralonne." She couldn't see him; he was behind the line of Chosen, themselves behind Teller and Avandar.

"I have never been asked to study *Avantari* in any depth," the mage replied. "I cannot therefore answer your question. Trust your instincts here."

Her instincts told her to turn around and head back up the stairs, leaving the god-born and the Kings' Swords to their exploration.

"These stairs are old," Meralonne continued, as she forced herself to ignore his advice. "I would have said, if asked, that they predate the Empire of the Twin Kings."

"And the Blood Barons?"

"Even so. I do not think they now lead to dungeons."

"Did they, once, in your opinion?"

He was silent.

She continued down the stairs. "If it were Summer," she asked, "would it be so damn cold all of the time?"

To her surprise, he laughed. His laughter bounced off bare stone to either side; Shadow's growl deepened. She understood why; there was something in Meralonne's laughter that felt diametrically opposed to mirth or amusement.

To her surprise, and to her great relief, the stairs came to an end. The flat, smooth gray of descending stone gave way to a floor that was not much different; the walls continued to either side. Magelights in ornate brass claws were spaced evenly three quarters of the way up the walls; the ceilings were high, but flat. Jewel placed a hand on Shadow's head and left it there because the cat was warm. He radiated heat.

The Kings' Swords could now be seen in the distance, and Jewel, mindful of dignity, closed the gap between them as quickly as she could. If the stairs had been long, and the descent deep, the hall was shorter. It ended in an arch that was a carved relief protruding from otherwise featureless stone. No runes, in any language, graced it.

To the right and left of this arch, two similar arches stood; they, however, opened into something other than gray stone. The Kings' Swords separated, standing with their backs to either side of the hall, facing outward. Jewel, Shadow, and Sigurne passed between them, followed by the rest of the Terafin party.

Only when she stood between the two open arches did Jewel stop. She glanced to the left and right, and saw that the Kings and the Exalted currently occupied the room on the left. She wanted to ask Sigurne how drastic the changes in these rooms were, because the answer might tell her how the rooms had once been used. Instead, she passed beneath the arch of the leftmost room, entering it.

It was illuminated from within, and the light was bright and even; there were no obvious magestones along the walls, none embedded, as was the current spare style, in the ceiling. The ceiling itself was high, but unlike the one that capped the hall, it wasn't flat. The Kings stood in what Jewel assumed, upon entry, was the center of the room; the Exalted were not far behind. They were silent as they watched her enter.

The walls were not flat, bare stone; they were, like the back wall of the Hall of Wise Counsel, intricately carved. Unlike the wall in the Hall of Wise Counsel, none of the reliefs in this room shed the ambient glow that spoke of enchantment. Like the Hall, these walls were adorned by figures who seemed to be emerging from the wall itself. Some were faint, a hint of clothing or armor, a slight protrusion of hand; their faces were delineated by nose, chin, eyelids. But others were carved so completely they almost appeared to be standing statues set as close to the wall as possible. Were it not for the continuity of the relief, they might appear to be entirely separate from it.

The Crowns watched as Jewel passed them and began to walk around the room's perimeter, the great cat by her side. Avandar followed behind, his eye on the panorama of figures that had been carved here by—it appeared—the hands of the earth itself. Teller chose to stand beside Sigurne in silence. He wasn't watching her; his gaze was absorbed, whole, by the room itself, and judging from his expression, was likely to remain that way unless the room suddenly disgorged a demon—or worse.

The floor was of stone, but it wasn't gray; it was a dull copper color. It was flat and smooth, except where runes had been engraved across its seamless surface. She glanced at the partial figures as she walked, and stopped once: she recognized the woman carved in stone. Almost without thought, she lifted her hand, her fingers stopping a hair's breadth from the hands of the figure itself.

"Ariane," she said, the word rising slightly, as if there were any question at all of her identity. Of the figures, she was the most prominent; she wore armor the color of her skin; her left arm was lifted as if in greeting or farewell. She wore sword, and a slender horn; neither of these were remarkable. But her hair seemed to move as it trailed down her back; strands of fine stone raised in a wind that touched only her.

Shadow hissed. "I don't *like* her."

"I'm certain the feeling is mutual," Jewel told him. She stepped away from the Winter Queen, wondering as she did what the Summer Queen might look like. She didn't ask. Instead, she followed the curve of the wall—and it was curved; it followed no straight edges—until she reached a second figure she recognized. This one was not yet free of the confines of stone; her back was part of the wall. But her hair, like Ariane's, flowed freely over her shoulders, curling in its fall toward her waist.

"Calliastra."

She continued to walk.

"Corallonne." Of the three she had named, Corallonne was the most remote. And of the three, she was the only one Jewel actually touched; she rested her fingertips against fingertips of stone, mirroring the tentative gesture. Where Ariane was cold and forbidding, Corallonne was not. It wasn't that she looked weak; she didn't. But there was, to her, the hard, weathered quality not of stone, but of ancient trees; she endured, and in enduring, she might offer shelter from blistering heat or driving wind.

Jewel continued to walk. At the curve of the wall farthest from where the Kings now stood she approached the figure of a man. He had no wings, but she recognized him anyway. The Warden of Dreams. She wondered, then, if he had a name at all. She felt no need to stop; she was awake. She

walked, glancing up at the ceiling; it was shadowed in a way
that suggested a dome, the only part of the room that was
not well lit.

She stopped again, not because she recognized what she
approached; she didn't. She wasn't certain anyone could. It
was roughly the height of the rest of the reliefs, and it had
limbs, one of which was a normal leg. It had feathers, which
implied wings, and a face—of a type. Scales, leather, short
fur, hair, combined in a way that defined chaos.

"Shadow, do you know what this is?"

Shadow growled. "It is *nothing*," he said, batting it with
his right forepaw before stalking ahead. "It is nothing *and*
it *smells bad*." Jewel followed in his slightly noisy wake,
glancing once over her shoulder at the creature he'd dismissed. Shadow nudged her. She almost fell over, righting
herself in silence because the words she wanted to say were
so far beneath the dignity of her position as Terafin, she
might just as well slit her own wrists as speak.

Shadow came to a stop.

Jewel looked into the hooded face of a person she had
never seen before, but knew instantly. Her features were
curiously muted, almost nondescript; she wore loose, flowing robes, folds carved in stone that completely obscured
her feet. Her hands were raised and cupped over her heart's
center, her head bent in their direction; if she had hair at all
it was completely obscured by the fall of her hood.

Her hands were empty.

Jewel took an involuntary step back; if Avandar had not
smoothly done the same, they would have collided.

Jewel.

She didn't—couldn't answer him. She was watching the
statue, in relief, a prayer to *Kalliaris* on her lips. It didn't
help. The statue raised its head, brought its hands to its
chest, and took a step forward, separating, in that motion,
from the wall that still contained everything else.

"Terafin," it said, which was worse.

"Oracle," Jewel replied, above the sharp cutting chill of
winter wind.

The semblance of stone never left the Oracle's visage; nor
did her hands, exposed and empty, suddenly become flesh
and blood. Yet robes of gray did move at the behest of the

chill wind, and where folds of stone cloth rubbed against each other, they produced the sound of chisel against hard rock. Jewel stood her ground as the Oracle approached. She was no longer certain that what she saw could be seen by any of the other observers.

The Oracle lifted her chin. "Your Majesties," she said. "Exalted."

Jewel turned then. The Kings stood behind Duvari and three of their attendants; they were rigid. Duvari was not. If the appearance of a speaking, moving stone sculpture was unexpected, his expression betrayed no surprise. What it did betray was business, calculation of risk. He spoke; his words didn't carry to Jewel's ears, although she saw the movement of his lips.

"No," King Reymalyn replied. "Your objections are noted, but we will remain."

King Cormalyn added, "Your recommendation is also noted, Lord of the Compact, but we have our reasons for limiting access to these rooms. Sigurne Mellifas is present, as is Member APhaniel; we will place our safety in their hands should protection of an arcane nature be required. As to the rest, we are not without defense here, in the lee of winter." He smiled. It was the sharpest edge of a smile Jewel had ever seen on the face of either King. As he turned the whole of his attention to this unexpected visitor, the smile dulled. "You are the first of the firstborn."

"Am I?"

"I have heard it said."

Rock folded as she inclined her head. "I beg your indulgence and your forgiveness for my intrusion; I offer no disrespect, and no threat; indeed, I offer what the future offers: scant hope, and slender. But if you are here in this room, and The Terafin is by your side, you are coming to understand just how slender that hope will be, ere the end."

"You have come to deliver a message to The Terafin?"

"Not a message, no." She offered Jewel one hand: her left. Her right fell to her side. "A path. You do not yet understand what she presages, but you will. You fear her." It was not an accusation made to Kings, and indeed, the Oracle posed her question to the Exalted instead, as if she understood that Kings must be considered above something so petty as fear.

The Son of Cormaris replied. "Should we not? The changes wrought in this room—this and one other—were made, in a moment, at her command, although they are contained within *Avantari*, the palace of Kings, and she stood in the grounds of the Terafin manse, several miles away."

The Oracle nodded. "I will not argue with the facts you have presented; they are demonstrably true. But if I understand where I now stand—and when—I will say this: you have the choice of ills, and there is true safety in neither. You may judge The Terafin by her intent, but intent is not proof against great acts of evil."

He nodded. The daughter of the Mother said, "And you foresee great acts of evil?"

"I foresee devastation and destruction," was the serene reply. "The Terafin has a bold heart, but it is not a fortress, and things might move her to action that would be better ignored. Nor will she see the cost of action—or inaction—in her ignorance."

"You do not counsel us to destroy her."

Jewel, silent, fell still at the word *destroy*. She understood that this interview would decide her future; she had understood it when she had dressed and prepared for the audience. But it had never been stated so baldly, and she was surprised at what she now felt: anger. She mastered it, aware as she did that she had not come here to lie down and die at the command of Kings, should that be their desired outcome.

She had come here to convince those Kings that she was less of a threat than a walking god; that she served the interests of the Empire, and she would defend it more capably than the Kings' armies.

And your proof?

She had no proof, of course. In this room, with its living, talking statue, there was evidence that her reach was far, far too long, and worse, far too *wild*. Nothing here was of use to the Kings in their governance of, and defense of, their Empire. The chill wind, in fact, implied the opposite: it was dangerous. It was deadly.

Carver and Ellerson had been swallowed by the wind. Their voices could not be heard above its howl. Instead of walking those hidden, wild paths to find them, she was *here*. And the only thing that kept her here, the *only* thing, was the knowledge that, were it not for Jewel Markess ATerafin, were it not for *her*, those doors would never have opened, and those paths would never have swallowed two of her own. She couldn't even be certain they were alive. It was cold—cold enough, with long exposure and no shelter, that survival wasn't guaranteed. If the cold couldn't kill, lack of food and water would.

But if she couldn't take control of a power she only barely understood, more doors would open, and more people—people with no connection to these ancient and remote magics—would open doors to closets, sheds, rooms, and disappear simply by entering them.

If she didn't understand enough to take that control, people might wake in homes that bore no resemblance to the buildings that architects had planned and carpenters and stonemasons had crafted; they might wake beneath purple skies, to the sounds of screeching predators; they might wake to an endless field of snow and the horns of the Wild Hunt.

She swallowed anger.

Because if she never had both knowledge and control, the Kings were *right*. It would be better for their city and their Empire if she simply failed to exist at all. Accepting the truth was as simple as giving the danger faces she knew and loved: Carver. Ellerson. She trusted her own intent— but trust or no, they were gone.

She became aware that the room had gone silent in that expectant way. *Avandar, what did I miss?*

A question or two. I believe they are waiting on your answer.

What question?

He was silent.

Avandar. She glanced at him; he met her gaze and held it without expression. In the end, it was Jewel who looked away. Shadow, however, had had enough. Jewel saw that he had, in silence and unnoticed by her, approached the Oracle, at whom he was now bristling. "We won't *let* her."

Jewel immediately approached the cat and laid a hand rather harder than was necessary on his head. He hissed, and his wings rose in threat.

"Are you master now?" the Oracle asked softly.

Shadow sidestepped the question. "*You* are not *her* master."

"Perhaps not." The Oracle's voice was glacial. "But she is mortal; all mortals choose a master, in one way or another. Is that not so, Viandaran?"

Jewel cleared her throat. "Avandar, don't answer that question."

"He obeys you now, Terafin?"

"It's irrelevant. If he doesn't obey me, he doesn't attend you."

Silence. The Oracle slowly lowered her arm. "You are not yet ready," she said, her voice once again smooth and implacable. "But, Terafin, if you desire it—"

"I don't."

The Oracle fell silent. After a much longer pause, she turned to the Kings. "What The Terafin has rejected, I now offer to you: a glimpse of the future I hold in my hands. It is not yet true, but neither is it lie; it is built—as all things are—on the foundations of the present."

King Cormalyn said, "I will look."

Duvari raised chin, but the Justice-born King, watching the Lord of the Compact, shook his head. "It is a risk we will take. If you do not understand the speaker—"

"I understand who the ... speaker claims to be. I am not convinced that there is truth in these claims; of a certainty there is magery."

Sigurne Mellifas said, "There is not."

His brows rose. "Do you attempt to tell me, Guildmaster, that there is no enchantment upon the stone? Stone that appears to be speaking entirely naturally?"

"I *am* telling you there is no discernible enchantment. APhaniel?"

Meralonne didn't so much as gesture. "There is none. If you wish my opinion, Guildmaster, I will offer it."

"Your Majesties?"

King Cormalyn inclined his head.

"She is as she appears; present, but of stone. I have never explored the basements and catacombs of *Avantari*, and I suggest that you have the *Astari* do so when time and their duties permit. If I am not mistaken, you will find few rooms like this one."

"We will," King Cormalyn replied, with just the hint of a smile, "find only two, unless further transformations have occurred."

"Your point, Majesty. I refer not to the architectural changes, but the stone itself."

"The stone was not deemed remarkable; it is simple stone; sandstone or a variant, according to our experts."

"Your experts, while laudable—"

"Two are members of your Order."

"Be that as it may," he replied, in a way which made Sigurne's lips tighten briefly, "they are entirely in the wrong, in this case. The quarries that would produce this stone have not been mined by men since the sundering; nor can they in safety be mined now, although the time is coming when that option may, once again, be a possibility. But I digress. As I am forbidden my pipe by both The Terafin and the guildmaster, digressions are notably less pleasant. I will therefore come to the point: She is the Oracle in any relevant fashion."

"The irrelevant?"

"If you destroy the sculpture, you will not materially harm the Oracle."

"It would not be entirely without cost," the statue said, her lips curving in a smile not dissimilar to King Cormalyn's. "And I will therefore look unkindly upon the attempt. Lord of the Compact, I am not your enemy here."

"If you can, without warning—and without necessary security precautions—emerge from a section of wall within the heart of the palace, you are not a friend."

"Will it offer you comfort if you know that I cannot appear unless The Terafin is present?"

"Scant," was his grim reply. "But not none." He met the statue's gaze, and Jewel had little doubt that he could win a staring contest with stone: he was Duvari. He was not, however, unleashed at the moment; King Cormayln stepped past him, and Duvari grudgingly allowed this.

"In times of war," the King said, with obvious respect, "harsh measures are taken, and those who might otherwise be friends are seen, always, in the least favorable of light."

"Caution is necessary," the Oracle replied, still mildly amused—but by what, Jewel couldn't discern. "And I will, therefore, take no insult from it, although clearly lack of insult is not the Lord of the Compact's first responsibility."

"He is not a court diplomat, no. If he has not given unacceptable offense, we will accept your offered gift."

"I did not say it was a gift. None can tell, before they look, whether the vision itself is bane or boon."

"None? If you say this, who saw first and will see last, we will believe it; we will, however, take that risk. It appears," he added, glancing briefly at Jewel, "that we already entertain one such."

"Indeed. I will say now that she will never be all of one thing or all of another, although her intentions are beyond reproach." She glanced at the cat, and added, "She must come to me in her time, and her time—as you are well aware—grows short."

"*She* will not die *here*," Shadow hissed. He was shaking—whether in fear or anger wasn't clear.

The Oracle shook her head; folds of her robes scraped against each other, which caused the cat's fur to rise further. "It is not for herself that she is concerned. Understand what she fears to lose before you attempt to protect her. She will not thank you."

"She *never* thanks us," Shadow hissed. To Jewel he said, "It is not *safe* to walk where *she* walks."

"It's not safe," Jewel replied, "to walk where *I* walk."

"You have no *choice*. You *are* you. But you are not *hers*."

"Shadow, I'm going to throw you out of this room if you don't stop. I am not going anywhere right now; the Kings are speaking with the Oracle and we are *interrupting them*."

The Mother's Daughter chuckled. "You are, indeed," she said to Shadow. "And if I am not mistaken, we are not the only appointment The Terafin has today; we are merely the first. Come."

To Jewel's surprise, he obeyed, his fur slowly settling. The god-born did not appear to trouble him; the firstborn, clearly, did. She glanced at Meralonne, and from there, to Sigurne; they were silent. They did not approach the Oracle; only the Kings did. Even the Exalted remained as they were, observing, their expressions remote.

The Oracle lifted both of her hands and pressed them into the folds of stone robes, compressing their fall against her chest. This was not disturbing, but what followed was: she pushed her hands slowly and evenly into that chest. Jewel was suddenly grateful that the Oracle wasn't here in the flesh. Even in stone, it looked painful; the Oracle's lips

were twisted—and etched—in pain. But they were closed;
no sound escaped her.

What she failed to acknowledge, the Kings likewise
failed to acknowledge. They waited, until the Oracle's hands
were once again visible; they emerged from stone robes
wrapped around something, and the stone itself flowed over
the gaping hole before it could be examined. She lowered
her arms, and with them, her hands; when she opened her
palms, a crystal lay cupped between them. It was not, as she
was, of stone. It was clear, and the light it cast was the color
of sky when the sun had burned away all cloud.

The clouds existed in the crystal's heart, their edges in
constant motion. What lay within them, Jewel couldn't see;
nor did she try. She had nightmares and dreams of her own,
and she knew they would come to her at need.

Terafin.

Will you look? she asked him.

*No. The Oracle offers with one hand, and only one, but
what she carries in the other, hidden, is only a danger if one
accepts her gifts.*

Jewel stiffened.

Believe that the Kings will weather it, he said sharply.
*They carry the weight of the Empire upon their brows; there
is no eventuality that they have not considered since the arrival of* Allasakar. *If she shows them their great city in ruins,
it will confirm their fear, but it will not deter them in their
rule. You have sworn to uphold their laws and their rule—
can you have done so without fully understanding their measure?*

If they see the end of their Empire because of me?

I think it likely, he replied, with just a touch of frustration, *that they may well see some element of that. Everything
that the Kings have said, every concern they have voiced—
and some concerns they have not—are concerns you accept
as valid. But the future is not fixed; it is not immutable. Even
were it, it would be valuable; it allows for contingencies.*

Jewel nodded and exhaled. It came to her as she watched
that the first time she had been in the royal audience chambers, she had come to do her utmost to convince the Kings
of the existence of a threat to the Empire; she was now here
to do the exact opposite. As diplomatic—and necessary—
missions went, this one was not going well.

King Reymalyn stiffened visibly; he did not speak. King Cormalyn said nothing. Neither King blinked; neither moved. They hovered above the crystal as if the whole of their rule was contained within its heart. After what felt like an hour, they moved. They looked first to each other, and then to the Oracle herself.

"Do you see what we see when we look into the crystal?" King Reymalyn asked.

She nodded. "It is not the first time I have seen some of these visions; they are subtly changed, no more."

"How much of what we have seen will come to pass?"

"Without intervention? All of it. It is the future that extends from this moment onward."

"And The Terafin? Will she become . . . what she was?"

"Without intervention, yes. I have offered what intervention it is permitted to offer. She will accept it, or reject it."

"And is it only your intervention," Meralonne asked, although he had not been given leave to speak, "that will prevent it, firstborn?"

There was a long, long pause. The mage turned to the Kings. "Ask her what I have asked," he told them; it could not be considered a request, although it was just shy of a command in tone.

King Reymalyn complied.

The Oracle exhaled. "No." Her tone was cold. "But I warn you: she is mortal, as are you all, and your time grows short. Illaraphaniel cannot give her the guidance she requires if you are to avoid the . . . transformation you have seen. If you cannot avoid it, hope still remains for your city; but there will be no way to defend the whole of your Empire.

"Nor will your city survive long if you choose to exile—or destroy—her. You speak with your parents across the divide. Ask them how the Cities of Man were created, and then ask them how they were ruled."

The Kings bowed in concert; they bowed to the Oracle. Jewel could not remember ever seeing them bow to *anyone.* "We are in your debt," King Cormalyn told her.

"Then I ask a boon," the Oracle replied. She stood, light from the crystal illuminating the whole of her body.

"Ask. If it is within our power, we will grant it."

"Do not destroy this room—or the other. Guard them if

you will, and as you must; observe them in like fashion. But if The Terafin petitions you, grant her the access she will request."

"Very well." He turned, then, to glance at Jewel, and she stiffened at the unexpected pity his gaze held. King Reymalyn did not meet her gaze at all. He glanced at the Wisdomborn King and they made their way to the door, Duvari preceding them. The Exalted followed, although Shadow simply waited until Jewel approached.

"I like *her*," he said, watching the back of the Mother's Daughter as it receded.

Jewel was grateful for small mercies. Sigurne waited until the god-born had cleared the door before indicating that Jewel might safely join her.

"Is the other room like this one?"

"The other room is almost entirely unlike this one," was the grave reply. "But I believe the Kings will adjourn at this point; they have much to discuss."

"Will you join them?"

"I will almost certainly be summoned, although it will not be for some hours yet, if I understood King Cormalyn's expression. Will you release Member APhaniel to my service?"

"I would prefer you did not," the mage said.

"You have a preference for a meeting of The Ten?"

His lips pursed in genuine distaste. "You make an excellent point, Terafin. I will, with your leave, accompany the guildmaster. It is my hope that the meeting of The Ten will take less time than the meeting of Kings; I may then avoid both their summons and two meetings of questionable interest."

"APhaniel," Sigurne said, in a tone of resigned disapproval.

Jewel glanced at the Chosen. "Please tell the Kings' Swords that I will accept their escort momentarily."

Jewel approached the Oracle as the Kings withdrew. So, too, did Teller. He offered the statue the very bow he would have—and had—offered the Exalted. When he rose, his hands were in motion; it was brief and pointed.

Jewel shook her head, but Teller didn't spare her a glance. "What price must I pay," he asked, "to see what the Kings have just seen?"

The Oracle considered him with care; the crystal remained in her open palms. "What price?" she asked at last, as if musing. "You are Teller ATerafin?"

"I am. And you are?"

Her stone eyes rounded at the question, and then she laughed. Her laughter was like sunlight, caught and given voice; it was bright, harsh; it made deserts. But it also, at winter's height, provided warmth. "You will not survive the long road ahead of you if you so carelessly ask such intimate questions of powerful strangers." She was clearly still amused. "Yes," she said, as if the gift of amusement were enough of a payment—and given her existence, perhaps it was. "I will take your thoughtless courtesy, Teller ATerafin. I would take more—but you will pay, and pay again, before you at last release the burdens you have shouldered.

"You do not yet know how heavy they will be. But come; I see you have borne heavy burdens in your time, and at a much younger age."

He stilled. He didn't stiffen—Jewel did that—but for a moment, the grace of motion was denied him; it returned, first, to his lips. "Can you choose what I see?"

"Yes. The wise are aware of this, when they ask for a glimpse of the future. They understand that they are never given the whole of it."

"They couldn't be," was his reasonable reply. "The future is just the present; if we were to see it all—we would have to live as long as the gods do."

"Indeed. Or as long as the Oracle." Her smile faded as the clouds at the heart of the crystal began, once again, to shift.

Shadow hissed. His fur rose, adding inches to his height, all of the calm the Mother's Daughter had briefly bestowed on him undone. "Don't *let* him."

"He serves me," Jewel replied. "But I don't—and can't—own him."

"He *obeys* you."

It was true. She wanted to order him to stop, but the words wouldn't leave her mouth. The thought of them returned echoes of her conversation with Haval: Teller was right-kin and she needed to trust him. "He is not a child," she told the cat, more of an edge in her voice than there should have been. At least the Kings were no longer here to witness it.

"Can I choose what I see?"

"Not easily, ATerafin. The wise do not make the attempt." Before he could ask why, and clearly he intended to do so, she added, "The future is one part of a story that shifts in the unfolding; it answers no direct or simple questions. It is not a small stream into which you might dip cup or bucket to quench your thirst—it is an ocean."

No one attempted to quench their thirst by drinking from the ocean.

Teller nodded, his gaze upon the crystal; its light was harsh and bright as those clouds opened. Jewel bitterly regretted her decision to abstain; she could not see what Teller saw, and the only echoes the crystal permitted her were engraved in his expression; it was rigid.

He raised hand once, and only once, reaching for the crystal; the Oracle caught his wrist before he could touch it. "Never touch a crystal such as this one," she told him, although Jewel wasn't certain that he heard her. Her gaze slid from Teller's face to the Oracle's; her hands folded into fists which she managed to keep by her sides. The winds had become stronger as Teller gazed into the crystal, and the emptier room was now winter cold.

Shadow leaned into her side; she gratefully rested one hand on his offered head. He was as stiff as Teller. Minutes passed. The Oracle did not release Teller's wrist; nor did he seek to free himself. But she watched him, her lips compressing, her eyes—all of stone—narrowing. Only when the light emitted by the crystal began to fade did she release him.

"You are bold," she whispered. "I would have once said you were foolish."

Teller did not reply.

"I will leave you now, ATerafin. Viandaran."

He bowed. "Firstborn." He was the only person in the room who remained unaffected by the events he had witnessed.

"There are three endings that I see for you. Will you hear them?"

"No. What my Lord will not countenance on her own behalf, I will likewise deny myself."

"Very well. Let me say this: roads are opening to her which you yourself could never master, when mastery was your chief concern. If you do not cleave tightly to her, you will fail utterly in your charge." She cupped both palms around the crystal, returning it to her chest in a fashion that was at least as disturbing as its withdrawal. "Yes, Terafin. There is pain. There is always pain. And there is exposure. You will come to understand this, if you survive."

"I've been told—"

"That you exist in the future? You do. But not in *all* futures; no one of us, but one, does. Return to me." Before Jewel could reply, the wall shifted in place, flowing outward to engulf her. Teller took three quick steps back as the Oracle became submerged in stone, until she, like the other statues, remained half-chiseled in place.

Even then, he didn't turn to face Jewel for a long, long moment.

Chapter Seventeen

SHADOW ACCOMPANIED JEWEL down the hall that led to the grand Council chamber. So did Teller and Avandar, but it was the cat who drew obvious attention—and given the very strict standards imposed upon visible servants in *Avantari*, obvious was perhaps the wrong word. The Kings' Swords were notably more numerous, but Jewel found this neither surprising nor distressing.

The one good thing about Duvari was it was very hard to take his suspicion and disdain personally. To do so required work. Although there were men and women of notable power across the Empire who were willing to make the effort, Jewel was not one of them. She didn't like the Lord of the Compact, but she understood his loyalty to, and his concern for, the Kings. She couldn't despise it.

She hoped, at this point, to survive it.

Duvari was not a man who liked to take risks. Men like Jarven appeared to live for them, and given the two approaches, Jewel found herself in sympathy with the Lord of the Compact's, something she would never say aloud.

Even thinking it, she felt Avandar's glacial disapproval, although she knew her domicis respected Duvari.

What I mean by the word respect is not, sadly, what you mean by it. You will be early.

Jewel nodded and glanced at Teller. *Probably better that way; it will give everyone else less chance to reach difficult agreements about the subject of the meeting behind my back.*

The door of the Council chamber was open, and Jewel, flanked by Shadow and Teller, entered; the room was not empty. She was surprised, but she suppressed all outward signs, passing beneath the door's frame with a confidence she did not feel.

The Kalakar, seated, rose to greet her, and with her, Verrus Korama. Had Ellora been Terafin, Korama would be right-kin; there was no like position within House Kalakar, and very few woman like Ellora. She lifted brow at Shadow. "Your cat appears to be larger."

"We're overfeeding him," Jewel replied.

"I imagine that must be expensive."

"Not really. He has his pick of the assassins that seem so ubiquitous within my manse."

Jewel.

But Ellora laughed. The stiff formality of proffered bow slowly deserted her, although her posture would never descend to the slouch in which Jewel most often worked. "It has been an eventful few months for House Terafin." As she spoke the last word, her expression shifted. "I am not enamored of the politics required by House governance." She once again resumed her seat.

Korama moved papers laid out against the great table, which Jewel presumed was his show of disapproval. His expression gave nothing away.

"But I regret my absence at The Terafin's funeral. Amarais was cunning, but graceful when she stooped to conquer. I think even she would find the current situation difficult. You are here rather earlier than expected."

"As are you."

"I arrived at *Avantari* in my role as one of the three Commanders of the Kings' armies; there has been much study and discussion about the final battle in the Dominion. There is some concern that we did not leave the war behind when we returned."

"The Berrilya?"

"Is an entire council of war on his own. He will be present, but I do not expect him before the session begins." She studied Shadow, who, aware of her regard, returned it, tilting his head until it practically touched shoulder. "You understand that you will be the subject of this meeting?"

Bold and blunt. Ellora was capable of finesse when it suited her; she clearly felt no need for it now. If she were The Darias or The Berrilya, her choice of words would constitute a challenge, a command, a statement of relative position within the Council hall. Amarais had, in Jewel's opinion, been the indisputable head of this table.

Jewel, Ellora implied, was not Amaris. Fair enough. Amarais might—just might—have been able to control the direction the meeting took. Jewel could not, in The Kalakar's opinion. It was a warning.

Jewel accepted it. "Yes."

"Have you seen—"

"The basement? Yes. I was there at the behest of the Twin Kings and the Exalted; it is from those rooms I have come. I assume The Berrilya has also been shown the rooms."

"You would be incorrect in your assumption; if you assume that I have seen the rooms in question, you would likewise be incorrect. The Kings have closed the entire wing; only the most senior of the palace's servants are given access to the halls. They have consulted with the Exalted, and with the Guildmaster of the Order of Knowledge; they have also—to my surprise and considerable curiosity, requested the attendance of the Guildmaster of the Order of Makers." She glanced at Korama, who immediately stopped fussing with the unread papers.

"You were absent when The Ten last attempted to convene."

Jewel nodded. She said nothing.

"Given the last assassination attempt of which we are personally aware, your absence has become the possible subject of Imperial concern."

"It was not the first time a demon has attempted to kill me since my acclamation as Terafin," Jewel replied evenly.

"No?"

When Jewel met—and held—The Kalakar's gaze, Ellora shrugged, a half smile on her lips. "No, then. My reports in this regard are of necessity less factual than ideal. Were such an assassination attempt made against me within the confines of the Kalakar manse, you would likewise be informed."

Jewel inclined her head. She liked Ellora; she always had. But she had never gone head-to-head with her over a matter of import to her House; Amarais had, but seldom. Instead, they had circled each other, making agreements outside of the Council chamber to avoid just such collisions. In public, neither woman bowed.

"A demonic assassin would be of concern to the Crowns, given the Henden of 410; it would be of concern to The Ten. But the creature that came to the Common was of grave, grave concern to the woman whose knowledge of the forbidden is without parallel."

"Sigurne Mellifas spoke to you?"

"No, Terafin. Nor had she need. I have had discussions with the guildmaster in my tenure as The Kalakar, and I understand her measure. What she saw that day was the death not of you, not even of Kings, but of Empire.

"I will not minimize the difficulties we faced in the South. Were it not for one Kalakar House Guard, I do not think we would have survived what came; it was not, in any way, human."

"Which House Guard?"

"Kiriel," The Kalakar replied. "Kiriel di'Ashaf." Her eyes narrowed as she watched Jewel's open book of an expression.

Kiriel. "Did she survive?"

"Yes. She attends the Tyr'agar as one of his personal guard."

"She is not in the North."

"No. She is no longer in my service," The Kalakar continued. "But I have not forgotten. You spoke for her." Ellora glanced down at her hands. "I was not present for The Terafin's funeral," she said again, in a voice entirely free from the regret she had first expressed. "But I am tolerably well informed of what occurred in *Avantari* on the first day rites: an assassination attempt upon the Princes.

"It is rumored that the Kings' Swords hold you personally responsible for its failure."

Jewel said nothing.

"The Kings, however, have not chosen to publicly acknowledge any part you played."

"They can't. They haven't chosen to publicly acknowledge that an attempt was made."

The Kalakar nodded. "But given your role in saving the future Kings, I would expect your reception to be less chilly." She exhaled, looking up to meet Jewel's steady gaze. "There was not a man or woman alive on the Isle who did not hear your voice at the height of what should have been funereal services.

"Reports about the events have been uneven and conflicted; I find that even the eight present are reluctant to speak of it at all—saving, of course, The Wayelyn, who appears by all accounts to have written a song."

". . . A song."

"Yes. It has received notable attention from the younger bards at Senniel College. Judging by your expression, you have yet to hear the piece in question. You may therefore assume it an irrelevant piece of entertainment by a man who is politically irreverent. Devran is unamused—and may bring the topic into today's committee meeting."

Which would serve Jewel's interests. She frowned. "You have heard the song?"

"Indeed."

"You don't consider it apolitical."

"No, Terafin, I do not. I consider it disturbing. The bardmaster has been uncooperative in attempts to restrict venues in which the song is played; it is rumored that the Kings have mentioned their concern about its appropriateness."

"One does not rebuff the Crowns."

"No, indeed. But the song has clearly escaped its cage." She lifted hand before Jewel could reply, taking unsubtle control of the conversation. Unsubtle, Jewel thought, and unconscious; she was accustomed to both rule and respect. Jewel was willing, Avandar's sharp warning notwithstanding, to cede both in the privacy of this room.

It is not private; if you do not believe that the Astari *listen—*

Of course they listen. And what they note, now, is that The Kalakar has all but declared herself my ally.

She has not. She is here to gather information.

She's here to gather information to make an informed choice; she is willing to give Terafin the benefit of the doubt.

She may not be willing to continue to do so if you do not choose your approach with caution.

"Yes, if the Bardmaster of Senniel commanded it, the song would cease its travel. But, Terafin, it has been heard across the breadth of the city—in drawing rooms, in taverns, in the Common. It has traveled to Morniel College, and from there, west."

"Will we hear it today?"

The Kalakar's brows rose at the question. Jewel, however, was clearly serious. "If The Wayelyn enters the Council chamber with a lute, we might; I do not think even he will dare such an open display of disrespect at a meeting of this gravity."

Jewel, having met the man several times, was far less certain. "You think the bardmaster chose to disseminate this bit of political irreverence as widely—and swiftly—as she possibly could."

"Yes. As I said, I find it disturbing. The Kings appear to concur with my assessment." She folded her hands behind her back. "I have, of course, seen the transformation of floors and pillars within the palace. In and of themselves, they would be unsettling; we *all* live upon the Isle, and our homes are far less protected against magical intrusion than *Avantari* itself. We are aware that while such changes can be seen as largely positive—given rumors that *Avantari* retained structural damage during the assassination attempt— changes of a largely negative nature could likewise be made.

"And if so, Terafin, we are all at the mercy of your largesse and your benevolence. You can imagine—"

"That it is not to your liking."

"An understatement."

Jewel walked toward the end of the table at which the Terafin House Seat was situated. "If the meeting is to revolve around me—me, personally, not the House over which I preside—what would the desired outcome be?"

"For Terafin?"

"No. Believe that I understand Terafin's concerns in this regard. For The Ten."

"The Ten are insular," The Kalakar replied, after a long pause.

"You do not consider yourself insular."

"I do. But I have spent months in the Dominion with the Kings' armies, and I have seen the smallest part of what we face. We did not fight a war, Terafin; we fought a battle. The thing we most fear did not take to the roads he built—at great cost; he sent his scouts. Against those scouts, without the grace of ancient weapons and the god-born, we would have fallen. Devran—The Berrilya—does not agree with my assessment of the situation.

"But it is clear to me that at least some of the bards on the field did."

"Because of the song."

"Because of the spread of a song the Kings wished to suppress, yes. What I do not understand—what I am certain I will never fully understand—is why you have chosen to involve yourself—and by extension the whole of your House—in affairs that are almost entirely beyond the ken of the merely political."

"And if I said that the choice was not entirely my own?"

"It would be the least favorable response you could tender."

Jewel lowered her chin, understanding what Ellora did not put into words: she should lie. She should lie so convincingly that The Ten and the Kings might take comfort from it. Avowal of innocence, of ignorance, of the harmlessness of intent—those were the tools of a coddled or desperate child, and they had *no place* in this room.

"You have never served in the army." It was not a question.

"No."

"When I went to the Dominion, I expected to see demons; nor was that expectation disappointed. When the men under my command went to the Dominion, they likewise expected some hint of the demonic—but most of these men had heard stories and third- or fourth-hand reports. We found demons.

"We were prepared for them. What we were not prepared for was the final battle in Averda. There, the forces we faced were comprised entirely of the kin. They did not choose to disguise their nature, and one—at least one—could wake the very earth, changing in an instant the shape of the battlefield.

"It is said no plan of battle survives first contact with the enemy. It is sometimes said in jest, but it is largely true: battle plans are plans of contingencies, of what-ifs. Could we predict that a beast whose very voice would terrify every horse on the field, and whose step would break earth, opening chasms beneath the feet of our units, would appear?" She waited.

"I will assume the answer is no."

"The answer is no. No more did I expect to have, within the ranks of my House Guard, the daughter of our greatest enemy. She was critical to our success in that war, and she was almost the singular cause of our failure. In ignorance, I made decisions. I issued orders. Those orders can be evaluated after the fact; at the time, they were almost certainly going to cost lives. I understood that. My duties on the field were not—are *not*—to preserve those lives. My duties are not to feed the men, to tend to the horses, to make or break camp. They are not, in the end, to form and stand in the lines of defense which have to hold; nor are they to kill enemy soldiers.

"My duties as leader are simple: to make decisions. To issue orders. To appear to *be* in command of a situation that is otherwise volatile and chaotic. I am mortal. I cannot stand and face a creature that is, if I understand the magi, scion of ancient, wild gods. My men know this—but regardless, it is my ability to assert control and command in the face of such a creature that holds the army together. Do I have doubts? Yes. All leaders do. But if those doubts are the only thing I convey, I have utterly failed those under my command."

"May I then point out, Kalakar, that you are not under my command?"

"You may. It is, of course, true. But The Berrilya is not under *my* command, and he understands that we share a responsibility and a duty. You are our peer; you are our equal. If you wish to maintain that footing, you, too, must shoulder a similar burden. Or you may choose to hand the burden of decision and command to a higher power. If you make that choice, you have an option: the Kings."

Jewel stiffened. When she turned to face The Kalakar, she was angry. She could not afford to vent her momentary rage upon this woman. "That is perilously close to insult," she said, keeping her voice steady and even.

The Kalakar smiled. "In this room, and among the people who will fill it, it is not close to insult; it *is* an insult."

"Understood." Jewel took the seat reserved for the House; it was—had been—Amarais'. Amarais had left the House—and everything she had built within it—in Jewel's care, and Jewel did not intend to abandon it. Nor would she fail it easily. It was true that Amarais had not accidentally restructured parts of *Avantari*; had she, what would she have done? Would she have dissembled? Would she have been forced into defensive denials of her own power?

No. Think, Jay. Think. What would she have done? Would she have failed? No. No, of course not. Lifting her chin, she said, "The floors were broken in much the same way the earth was broken in your battle."

The Kalakar nodded; Verrus Korama came to stand by her side. Neither spoke.

"The pillars were also cracked in the same way—a casualty of the shift of earth and stone beneath them. The damage was not cosmetic."

"You are certain."

"Yes. I have not been given leave to discuss the sensitive nature of other possible alterations. But when the earth broke through the marble, it did not magically assert itself; it drew itself up from beneath the architecture built upon it." As she spoke, she knew this was true, and knew, as well, that it was not only the two rooms she'd been asked to inspect that had been rebuilt. "Changes were therefore made belowground, with the same intent: to make certain the whole of the building was sound.

"I am the architect of these changes." She smiled; it was slender, and there was no amusement in it. "And, Kalakar, as Commander, I did not trifle with the details. I did not choose the stone; nor did I labor with artists and artisans over the flourishes that are carved upon the pillars. Perhaps in future circumstances, this might be wise, but I did not have the luxury of time."

"Could you, with ease, cause such changes in the future?"

"Not with ease, no. Perhaps not at all. I did not summon the wild earth."

"But you commanded it. How?" The word was sharper, harsher.

Jewel's smile was serene. "These lands, in a way the earth understands, are mine. While the earth wakes here, my commands have precedence over all others, even those who chose to summon it." She lifted a hand before The Kalakar could speak. "Before you ask, Kalakar, the earth does not understand the claims of mortal Kings; no more does it understand the claims of The Ten, even Terafin.

"But if you mean 'how did I command the earth,' it was simple: I spoke."

"Could the Kings now claim what you have claimed?"

"No."

"You are certain of this."

Jewel nodded.

"I see that you have started the heart of the proceedings without waiting upon the attendance of the Council in full."

Jewel turned as The Berrilya strode into the room. He wore the uniform of the Kings' armies, and not the more patrician clothing—in House colors—that the rest of The Ten would wear. Even The Kalakar had forgone military dress.

"We have not," she replied, before The Kalakar could. Her voice was cool. "We engage in discussions of a collegial nature between peers."

"And such discussions now include assessment of the competencies of Kings?" He entered the room before his adjutant, a younger man of military bearing. He, as Korama, was Verrus.

"Not the competencies, surely," was her equally chill reply.

The Berrilya took his chair as well. Although he wasn't above productive, informal conversation, that was clearly not his intent today. He wore his uniform as if he expected to preside over armies upon a field of battle. Given The Kalakar's expression, he probably did. Jewel had never completely understood the hostility between the two—its foundation appeared to be a solid, if grudging, mutual respect. That respect did not, however, prevent arguments.

And clearly, from The Berrilya's expression, one of those arguments had occurred prior to the meeting of The Ten. "You are aware, Terafin," he said, turning to her, "that the bardmaster has petitioned for permission to sit in observance?"

"It wouldn't be the first time," Jewel replied, although the actual answer was No. No, she had not been aware. Permission was not dependent upon any one House, although in theory The Ten could force a vote for privacy, which would require the bardmaster to remove herself. Solran Marten was not, however, a woman one wished to offend. She had the ears of the Kings and their Queens, and her reach, if subtle, extended across the breadth of the Empire and beyond the Empire's borders.

"I will tell you now," The Berrilya continued, "that I am against it. I will also vote to have The Wayelyn removed from the chamber if he so much as touches a musical instrument during the meeting."

Jewel did raise a brow then; it was seldom that The Berrilya, a man who defined rigid self-control and the capable use of protocol, made so bald a statement. She glanced at The Kalakar, who returned a shrug; The Wayelyn's lack of patrician comportment had never been of great concern to her. While she did not likewise indulge, she did not find it threatening. "Such votes should not be called in what is an essentially frivolous endeavor."

The Berrilya's frown deepened, adding brackets around the lines already etched in place. "It is not frivolous to remind any member of this Council that this chamber is neither a tavern nor a theater."

"If you feel Solran Marten should be excluded, you will be asked for justifications," Jewel said. "And I feel that those justifications, in this case, will of necessity be slender."

"And if my reasons are less than frivolous?"

Jewel inclined her head. "The Council will uphold them."

"Very well. I believe her interests and ours are not aligned."

"I would say that her interests and the Kings' are not aligned; I fail to see their significance to The Ten."

"You have heard?"

"That The Wayelyn has penned a song which has freely traveled? Yes."

"And the song itself?"

"I have not heard it."

The Berrilya straightened. "When you hear it, if you do, it will change your opinion in this matter."

"Kalakar?"

"I am uncertain. I believe you were—and are—unaware of the song itself. But if the song is considered significant to the bardmaster, it would be better, in my opinion, to demand the reasoning for her decision to ignore the Kings' request. Something," she added, "we cannot do if she is not present. As she will be present at her own request, we expend no political capital to receive an answer."

Jewel nodded; she agreed.

"Solran Marten is not a woman to answer demands," The Berrilya pointed out.

"No, indeed—but I have not heard that the Kings demanded an explanation. She will find it difficult to ignore such a question posed in *this* chamber." The Kalakar folded her arms.

After a long pause, The Berrilya said, "Very well. I will not, however, tolerate *song*."

Within the next half hour, The Ten filtered into the chamber. The Morriset arrived fifteen minutes early, with only an aide in tow; The Darias arrived at the side of The Fennesar, which surprised Jewel. The Fennesar was a woman similar in style to Amarais; she looked almost severe today. The Darias, however, seemed completely at ease in her company, and their conversation implied that they had been conversing for some small time before they arrived at the open doors of the Council chamber.

The Korisamis arrived five minutes before the hour. Jewel was surprised. Of The Ten, he had shown the most obvious displeasure at the need to reschedule the meeting. She had, of course, made no excuses and offered no explanations that would ameliorate his assumption of frivolity or incompetence on her part. She'd been too busy, and was also aware that admissions of any such kind had a political cost. He was, however, dressed in the southern style of Korisamis, which was the preferred formal dress for the House.

On his heels, and very much in House colors, came The Wayelyn; he did not arrive alone. Instead of advisers—of which he had many—he had chosen to escort the Bardmaster of Senniel College. Solran, silver-haired, wore the Senniel tabard. She offered a bow to the table at large before joining it at The Wayelyn's side. Jewel thought The Berrilya would object; he did not. The Wayelyn appeared to have divested himself of musical instruments, but the bardmaster more than made up for the lack. The Berrilya was not apparently pleased at this departure from the etiquette which otherwise governed the full Council meetings; nor was he the only one to look askance.

Jewel thought it clever. Clever, in her experience, always courted trouble, something The Wayelyn seemed to thrive on.

To no one's surprise, The Garisar arrived exactly on time, and to no one's surprise, The Tamalyn arrived five minutes late, looking as if he had only barely managed to dress on the way out of his manse. He looked slightly bewildered; the woman at his side looked slightly frustrated. Were he not so guileless, it would have been difficult not to assume this was orchestrated, an act designed to render those around him careless. Jewel had never understood—and, given her role in Terafin, was never likely to—how he managed to maintain his position as the head of his House.

They took their seats as the doors rolled to a close.

As they did, The Berrilya rose. Jewel glanced at Avandar; her domicis nodded. Although each of The Ten Houses held a relative rank in the eyes of merchants and bankers, it was not official. The members of the Council had devised a rotation by which each member of each House—should they so choose—had the opportunity to open the meeting. In an emergency, such protocols could be ignored, but not without cost. It was, in the parlance of the street, The Berrilya's turn.

Nor did he dissemble. "Terafin."

She inclined her head.

"You were much missed during our previous attempt to convene a full Council." If there was a question in the statement, it was inaudible. He left a beat, as if waiting for her to make an excuse or offer an apology, neither of which she could safely do. "Very well. I am certain that matters requiring your full attention conspired to prevent your attendance."

"I, however," The Garisar said, lifting chin but remaining in his chair, "would like an explanation, if one has been offered."

"So, too, would House Korisamis."

"House Darias concurs."

Three, Jewel thought, waiting. To her surprise, The Wayelyn added his voice to the chorus. Four. She glanced at The Morriset; he held his peace.

She exhaled and played the first of her cards. "My apologies. My absence was unplanned in its entirety. You have all, no doubt, been apprised of the difficulties caused by the sleeping sickness." She glanced at The Garisar as she spoke, as he was the first to voice what was tantamount to open criticism.

"We are, indeed."

"The sleep is not natural."

"That is conjecture," he replied.

"No, it is not."

"And you have proof of that?"

"I *am* proof of that," she replied, choosing words with as much care as she could, although she suspected it would avail her little, in the end.

"To what do you attribute the sleep?"

"The Warden of Dreams," she replied. "Both of them." She watched the length of the table as the words left her lips; she knew Teller was doing the same. Solran Marten stiffened. The Wayelyn's stillness was more subtle, but it was evident. To her surprise, The Korisamis frowned, a slow, deliberate folding of brows and lips. He didn't look surprised; he looked, for a moment, as if he were attempting to recall where he'd heard the words before.

The Garisar, on the other hand, merely looked annoyed. "Those words have no meaning to House Garisar. Explain them, if you intend to offer them as proof of your claim."

"Very well; the explanation will of necessity be less than brief. I have been the subject of various rumors over the past decade. Those rumors reached their height after the funeral of my predecessor. At least one of those rumors is pertinent, because at least one of them is true: I am seer-born."

Silence. She hoped the confession would buy her a few minutes; she was relatively certain it would not.

"Across the Empire one may find stories and legends that involve the seer-born; I believe that my predecessor had them unearthed from any number of sources shortly after my adoption into the House. They were not numerous, and they were not of particular use to my situation: what the seer-born in story claimed to have achieved, I have never mastered.

"The abilities of the seers in those stories are similar to the abilities of the most powerful of the magi. Some of my abilities were never the subject of stories. Suffice it to say," she added, as The Garisar opened his mouth, "that both The Terafin of the time and the Kings were convinced that my gift was a true talent, and not a clever fabrication.

"I can see demons as demons, even when they adopt mortal guise. It is a natural gift; it does not require effort. I have honed instincts," she continued, watching The Tamalyn, who appeared, to her surprise, to be listening intently—something that rarely happened in meetings of this nature. "And I have learned to trust them; instinct alone, however, is not proof of a talent, no matter how many times it has saved my life."

"How has it saved your life?" The Tamalyn asked. His tone was entirely unlike The Garisar's.

"I move before the dagger takes my eye out; I move before it pierces my heart. I fail to eat poisoned food, even if the poison is slow and subtle; I fail to drink poisoned liquid. Any of these skills could also be found among the *Astari*, but the *Astari* are not subject to full visions; they are not subject to true visions. I am.

"These occur, in strength, in dreams. You have heard of the dreaming wyrd?"

The Tamalyn nodded. "The three dreams."

"Yes. I have done more than simply hear of them; I have lived them."

Shadow started to growl, and Jewel grimaced. "A moment," she said, rising swiftly. The cat was bristling.

"What," she said, voice low, "is the problem?" She had almost forgotten the cat was in the room, he'd been so still and silent.

"I don't *trust* them."

She prevented herself from shoving her hair very forcefully out of her eyes. "You don't trust *anyone*, Shadow. They're not demons; they're not assassins. They're not going to kill me in this room."

He hissed.

"Where did you come by your cat?" The Tamalyn asked. Jewel jumped; he was standing not two feet away.

Shadow hissed more loudly. Jewel, embarrassed, returned to her seat; The Tamalyn did not, although his attendant—Michi?—was almost drilling holes between his shoulder blades with the intensity of her stare.

"My deepest apologies," she said to the table at large as she rejoined it. "I encountered Shadow and his two brothers during my absence from the House. They followed me home." She inhaled. "I spoke of true visions and the dreaming wyrd not to touch upon aspects of myth or legend, but to emphasize the delivery of those visions: they came to me—and come to me—in dreams. The visions that come are not clear, precise models of the future; they are not easily untangled until after the fact. It was one such vision that necessitated my absence from the House at a critical time."

"The Terafin was aware of the reasons for your departure," The Kalakar asked.

"Of course. She was my Lord. She understood—as we all did—that a war would be fought in the South; she understood that I had a part to play in its outcome, although neither of us could be completely certain what that role would be."

"You did not endear yourself to the Commanders by your absence," The Kalakar noted, although she was smiling. The Berrilya, notably, was not.

"No. But my part was not a part that could be played by armies."

"What part, then?"

Jewel stared at the tabletop. "It involved a walk on roads long closed to us, and a longer walk through the desert at the heart of the Dominion. I traveled with the Arkosan Voyani, and at their side, I saw a city—a literal city—rise from the desert sands. It was smaller than Averalaan, but larger than *Averalaan Aramarelas*, and it was whole. The walls could withstand any attack."

"Any?"

"Any. The city was built—and buried—in an age when gods walked the world."

The Tamalyn came back to the table; Shadow followed him. The great cat also wedged his head between The Tamalyn and his Council adviser while Jewel tried not to grind her teeth.

"I feel we wander far afield," The Garisar said pointedly. "And you add ludicrous claim to claims that were already suspect."

"I am interested," The Tamalyn replied, with more force than was his wont.

The Wayelyn likewise concurred, but more lazily, and with a good humor that was entirely unwarranted. It predictably annoyed The Garisar. It reminded Jewel of long House Council sessions.

"We may discuss the city at a later point," she told them both. "The Garisar is not incorrect. But if the city is not directly part of the explanation, I feel it will become relevant in the future." She looked across the table to The Kalakar. "In your sojourn in the Dominion, you saw the work of demons—and the work, if I am not mistaken, of gods."

"Of a god which we will not name here."

Jewel nodded. "Some part of that work affected the underpinnings of the dreaming."

"Pardon?"

"If dreams are not a literal place—and they are not— they are nonetheless the source of my strongest visions. Something within the dreaming itself—when I dream—has the force of reality. I will not make the same claim for any other dreamer; I would not hesitate to make it of any other seer."

"Of which you are the only known sample."

"One of two," she replied.

"The other?"

Jewel shook her head. "It is not relevant. What is relevant is that the quality of the dreaming changed markedly after the war. I believe it was changing while part of the war was being fought—the magic required to move armies to the cradle of Averda was not mortal magic. I do not have access to the reports of the magi, but I have, in my service, Meralonne APhaniel, who served as the leader of the magi under the Commanders."

"The reports of the magi are not yet fully assimilated, and no consensus has been reached about the accuracy of their ... guesswork." The Berrilya glanced at The Kalakar; she failed to return what was almost a glare.

"I trust Member APhaniel. If you consider the information suspect, you will likely consider my explanation suspect as well."

"Indeed."

There were days when she understood the animosity that existed between House Kalakar and House Berrilya. Exhaling, she glanced past him; Solran Marten was watching Jewel as if there were no others present. As bardmaster, Solran understood how to feign delight, irritation, or uncertainty; she knew when to play at politics and when to refuse the game. Jewel found her unwavering attention disturbing.

"The visions are stronger than they once were. They are more solid; they feel more real."

"This does not address the question of the sleepers."

"It does. The visions of my early years were transmitted through the dreaming. There are those who, without the talent which has been both bane and gift, were still subject to the dreaming wyrd."

"That is conjecture and story," The Berrilya said, clearly less than impressed.

"I have met at least one in my time in House Terafin; he did not lie. Those visions might be sent by the gods; it is hard to say. Think of the dreaming as if it were the edge of the Between."

Silence. It was more thoughtful, now. If The Berrilya wished to deny—loudly—the existence of the dreaming as a reality, he could not likewise deny the existence of the Between. "I would be interested to hear what the Exalted have to say about your designation."

"It is my belief they would concur." She wanted to stand; to stand and pace the length of the table, as if thoughts, like caged beasts, needed room to move, to breathe, to stretch. "The dreaming wyrd, and the unpredictable visions of seers, come when we touch the dreaming in our sleep. And it is through the dreaming that the sleepers within the city were entrapped."

"By the Warden of Dreams?" The Tamalyn asked. He was actually attempting to take notes.

"Yes. I do not understand how, or why—nor did he volunteer the information—but he derived some power from their capture and their presence. To allow them to wake was to lose that power."

"You found them while you slept."

She smiled. "Yes, Tamalyn. While I slept, I walked in the landscape of a very vivid dream, and I met both the sleepers and the Warden. I was asleep at the time, and I could not be easily woken."

"Could you be awakened at all?"

"Levec was summoned. He has had some small success within the Houses of Healing. But his intervention was not necessary, in the end. I woke from sleep at my own desire, although not at the time of my choosing; time passes differently between the waking world and the dreaming one."

"And the sleepers?"

"It is my next endeavor, although it is fraught: I will attempt to wake them."

Solran Marten stood, drawing every eye at the table. "May I ask, Terafin, how you intend to do so?"

"I intend to sleep," she replied evenly.

"And you may now do so in safety?"

"Yes."

"But if the Warden is no longer a threat, surely the sleepers would now wake on their own?"

This was not the direction she had hoped the discussion would take; it was hard to control all of its many strands when she herself had so few answers. "They are trapped in the dreaming. He does not hold them there, but they have been long enough away that they cannot easily find their way back."

"And you, Terafin, could."

"Yes. I am seer-born. I understood that the dreaming *was* a dream; I understood, as well, that it was real. Death in the dreaming is death."

"You understood this how?"

"I could see, Bardmaster."

"And you can see the dreamers."

"I believe, if I search for them, I can do exactly that." She met the bardmaster's gaze; it was steady, unblinking—almost an accusation. Yet it held no animosity.

"Forgive me," Solran said, to the Council table at large, "but I must now ask: Did you banish the Warden of Dreams from the dreaming in the same way you banished the wild water and the wild earth?"

You cannot avoid this, Avandar told her. *But I believe, were it not for the bardmaster and The Wayelyn, you might have succeeded in postponing the inevitable; you have given The Ten much to digest.*

"No."

"No?"

"The earth and the water are not the Warden of Dreams.

They are wild, yes, but they are forces that can, with effort, will, and appeasement, be used. They are *very* seldom used by mortals, if at all."

"Yet you ordered them to leave, and they obeyed."

Avandar was right. She wondered, idly, if she would have to give up the House to preserve it. It was a thought that she could not think in any other way; if she drew too close to it, it cut her with seven different kinds of guilt. The Ten would not easily surrender Terafin to the Kings if the Kings demanded it; they would, however, surrender Jewel if she were not the titular head of her House.

"Yes." She wanted to rise. She wanted to push herself up out of this confined chair, and this confining role—but she could only afford to do that if she was prepared to leave the Council chambers; she could not, by half measure, indulge in restless anger among these men and women.

"Do you understand that your commands were heard across the city?"

"Across the Isle."

"No, Terafin. Your voice reached across the bay. Bards cannot choose, at the distance your voice extended, such a wide audience. They cannot choose even a handful of strangers, in disparate locations, across the hundred holdings. A bard might speak in rapid succession to strategically placed people—but they cannot speak in such a fashion to people with whom they are unfamiliar; their audience would have to be in line of sight.

"Yet you did."

Jewel waited. She laid her hands, palm down, across the table, exposing, in that motion, the Terafin ring. Highlighting it.

"And of course, Terafin, the question becomes: How?"

Jewel drew breath. "You have clearly investigated the reach of my words far more thoroughly than I."

"And you are not curious."

"Were those who heard me speak harmed?" Jewel's voice was cool.

"They were not."

"Then, no, Bardmaster, I am not curious."

"Are you curious about the demon that disrupted the victory parade?"

Jewel glanced around the table; she was surprised—and

not pleasantly—by the fact that The Ten appeared content to let Solran speak.

Why would they not? She can speak freely without fear of political reprisal.

"Yes."

"Are you curious about the *Ellariannatte* that now grow within your grounds?"

"No. They are grand and glorious trees, but they harm no one, and they divert idle gossip."

The bardmaster's brows rose; she met and held Jewel's gaze, but Jewel wasn't of a mind to look away. "Is it then all fodder for the diversion of idle gossip, to you?"

"No. I was concerned about the Warden of Dreams. I *am* concerned about the *Kialli*. I *am* concerned about the god we do not name, because he has already amassed one army which he dropped in the middle of the Terrean of Averda in order to obliterate ours. I am *very* concerned about the fate of the city should the god at last decide to lead an army—in person—to the heart of the Empire." She exhaled. "He will destroy everything in his path between his home and mine.

"If you must ask about the trees," she continued, although she knew anger was propelling her words, "ask this: where is the only *other* place they now grow? In the Common, where the greatest and most powerful among our number barely care to set foot. They do not grow in the gardens or grounds of *Avantari*, where the heart and the head of the Empire reside."

"Oh, well answered, Terafin." Solran smiled. It was slender, but not devoid of warmth. "Very well. I have spoken in heat and without due respect, and I apologize if I have offered offense. The trees are of concern to the bardic colleges; they are of more concern, at the moment, than the rumors of the alterations within *Avantari*."

Jewel was surprised.

The Garisar said, "We would all, I am certain, appreciate the reasoning behind your concern." And not, his tone implied, be convinced by it.

"They grow nowhere else in the Empire. To our knowledge, they grow nowhere outside of it. Attempts, even those aided by rudimentary magic, to cause them to take root in any other soil has been met with utter failure. They are called the Kings' trees beyond the borders of this city."

"As The Terafin has pointed out, they do not grow in the Kings' gardens, or upon their grounds."

"Be that as it may, they are known as a symbol of Averalaan. Had they simply taken root upon the Terafin grounds, it would have been considered a botanical miracle; they did not. They grew, overnight, to a height that not even the trees in the Common have achieved; they did so without the obvious intervention of the Order of Knowledge and its many experts."

"I fail to see how that is of greater import than the shifting of stone within the palace itself."

"Yes," was her cool reply. "You do."

The Garisar raised his voice. "Bardmaster."

She inclined her head. "My apologies, Garisar. I understand the security concerns of the Kings."

"It does not appear, given your inability to halt the spread of an unfortunate song at the request of the Crowns, that you do."

"The song did not in any way address those concerns." Jewel had rarely seen The Garisar and the bardmaster interact. She now understood why.

"In your opinion," he countered. "But you are not the Kings."

"No. I am the Bardmaster of Senniel College. Nor was the song a song that originated within the halls over which I preside." She failed to glance at its author, who was nonetheless smiling broadly.

This irked The Berrilya. "It is a fact of which we are well aware, Bardmaster. If you will credit us with the bare minimum of intelligence, we are also aware that its reach, without your approval, would be insignificant. And as the matter has arisen, I would like to know why you felt it necessary to disregard the request of the Crowns."

"And of The Ten?"

"The Ten have not—yet—asked your bards to curtail the public renditions of the song. It is not, however, in our interests, given its source."

"He feels," The Wayelyn said dryly, "that the leader of a House should not curry favor with minstrels."

"I feel that the leader of a House should not *be* one," The Berrilya countered.

While the subject of the song in question generally detested the amount of time spent in arguments of exactly this nature, today she prayed to *Kalliaris* that this one would continue. Given the various duties of The Ten, such meetings could not go on indefinitely. But given the song's subject, she couldn't relax and let the argument unfold; she was aware that it could turn, in a second, into something far less favorable to her.

"What, then, do you feel the leader of a House should be, Berrilya? A commander of the Kings' armies? A scholar in good standing of the Order of Knowledge?" The Wayelyn asked the question with practiced ease, and Jewel understood, as she watched him, that this was an exact description: he *had* practiced this. Somehow, the conversation had devolved in the manner he had anticipated. Or perhaps it had not; perhaps the presence of Solran Marten ensured it.

Regardless, the question had edges.

He turned them now upon her. "Terafin? Should the leader of a House be a seer?"

"I fail to see how the question is relevant."

"I am bard-born," he replied, with exaggerated gravity. "But I am not, because of my duties to Wayelyn and The Ten, a bard."

"My gift, such as it is, is used in service to my duties to my House."

"And your Kings?"

"And, indeed, my Kings." She exhaled. "Wayelyn, what is your goal? My predecessor was, in matters of dignity, more inclined to take The Berrilya's position; in this, we are different. I do not require Wayelyn to behave within the confines of a rigid set of protocols in order to maintain the dignity of my own House."

The Kalakar coughed.

"I do, however, require basic respect, and the spread of a song in which my stature is, for dramatic or comedic reasons, exaggerated, is not to the liking of Terafin."

"You have not heard the song," was his flat reply.

"No. And for the sake of the rest of this meeting, this is not the place in which I will, if ever."

"Very well. You have offered us information, and I will offer information in return. You mentioned the possibility of a second seer."

She froze.

"I believe the name Evayne a'Nolan will be familiar to you. Shortly before—and after—The Terafin's funeral, she paid a visit. I will say that my House Guards were not impressed at the manner of her appearance." The smile he offered was grimmer. "During the first visit—which, of necessity, was brief—she exhorted me to watch, to listen, and to learn.

"I found her intriguing. It is not the first time we have crossed paths," he added softly. "But I do not see her with any frequency. She chooses both the time of her arrival and the time of her departure. Before the funeral, she was young; younger, I think, than you. She was not as careful in the guarding of her voice, and what lay beneath the surface of her words was alarming.

"And so I went, prepared, and, Terafin, you were like a waking dream. I will not lie; I saw echoes of ancient stories in you and your attendants." He glanced pointedly at Shadow, whose head had engulfed The Tamalyn's lap. "I saw them in the trees that girded your grounds.

"And I heard them, profoundly, in the words you spoke. But, Terafin, I heard the voices of the wilderness in the water, in the air, and in the earth. It was uncomfortably humbling, and as I did survive, I returned to my manse. I do not hear as you hear—any of you. That is my gift. It is also, at times, a curse; I could not divest myself of the echoes of grandeur; they were a song without words. I gave them voice. In truth, I would not have given them audience without the encouragement of the bardmaster.

"But when I had finished, Evayne returned. This second time, scarcely two days after her first visit, she was not so young. Her voice was steel and glass; I could not hear anything but the words she chose to offer—and those, she offered with both intensity and care."

"She told you to disseminate the song."

"She asked, it yes. And believe it or not, I was reluctant. It is not a political song; I have no quarrel with your House at the moment, and no intent to offer to public scrutiny the foibles of its leader. Had I, this would not be the song I would have chosen. When Evayne left me, I repaired to Senniel College, to seek the counsel of Solran Marten." He turned to the bardmaster.

She nodded, and resumed his tale. "The Wayelyn was not

the only person to whom Evayne a'Nolan spoke that day." She studied Jewel. "She spoke to me of the song that would soon arrive at my doorstep, and even of its singer. But that was not my concern; she spoke, as well, of the significance of the *Ellariannatte*. She talked of the god we do not name, and his many servants, and, Terafin—she spoke of the fall of the Empire.

"It is against that fall that she has labored for the whole of her life. And she felt—and feels, if I am any judge at all— that without you, the city will not stand. What you did to the palace, you might do to the city in its time of peril—but such actions might cause as much panic—and the resultant injuries and death—as the Lord of the Hells himself.

"We did not allow the song to spread on a whim; I sent it into the streets in the hands of my most gifted bards: Master Bards, all. Some have traveled beyond the limits of the city; the song will take root in places that even I cannot see. But it must. It must be heard, and it must be *felt*.

"I do not understand what you will become," she added, her voice dropping. "And in truth, I fear it. I have watched you for at least a decade. I have seen you at your best, and at your worst. You have many qualities I admire, and almost all of them were at your disposal on the day you gave command to the wild elements.

"But I know, Terafin, that such commands are not given to the wild by the merely mortal. They obeyed you. They accepted your claim. Where you walk, the *Ellariannatte* now grow. Have you heard the tales that have come to us from the West?"

Jewel was silent.

"Unicorns, Terafin. Winged creatures that are not birds. Great serpents and white stags. Trees that seem to leave the roads. Things are waking that existed only in story or song; they are walking. To where, we do not know. But I would not be at all surprised if you found them within the forest that now grows behind your manse."

"I would," Jewel replied. The Ten now watched her, not the bardmaster. "What counsel have you given the Kings?"

"I have not. Given the spread of the song, it is not the time to offer counsel; King Reymalyn was ill pleased by my decision."

"He heard the song."

"Yes. And he understands that it serves two purposes; the one: to plant the seeds of a story that might, if fate moves against us, become true. The other, to sever you, personally, from the realm of the merely political in the eyes of our people. Given the gravity of the situation, such severance might make any decisions about your freedom—or your survival—much more complicated."

Chapter Eighteen

JEWEL WAS SILENT. For a long, long moment, so was the rest of the Council—but that couldn't last; it never did. They looked to her to break the stillness, to inject her reaction, to lend color and flow to the conversation that would then evolve.

"When you speak of such severance," she said, lifting her chin, "you do not speak of the simple act of transforming me into a symbol that the people might recognize."

Solran glanced at The Wayelyn. "No," he replied, "She does not. She is well aware of the difference between the two acts; the Kings are symbols; they are, in song, larger than life. Their concerns are never about the next meal, the next job, or the next child; they are portrayed as legends in their own time—but they are twined and rooted in the shepherding of the welfare of the people they both serve and rule."

"I will hear this song," she said quietly.

The Berrilya immediately raised voice. "You will not. The Wayelyn has, thank the gods of oversight, failed to bear his instrument into the Council hall."

"He is bard trained. He does not require his instrument."

"Has anyone present, with the obvious exception of The Terafin, failed to hear the song?"

No one spoke.

Jewel frowned. "If the song and its significance are to be

discussed, Berrilya, I will not be the only Council member left in ignorance of its contents. If you will not hear the song within these chambers, I will retire from the meeting, and arrange to have it played within my own halls."

"It is not merely my distaste for The Wayelyn's particular predilections," The Berrilya said, speaking in a much more measured tone. "It is the Kings' own distaste. If the bard-master, for reasons of her own, chose to forgo their *request*, that is her choice; not even the bardmaster can with impunity flout their will in *Avantari*. I would be surprised if she were willing to sing for you. I would not, however, be at all surprised if The Wayelyn was."

"I am, of course, at your disposal, Terafin," The Wayelyn replied. "I am not the bardmaster; the Kings did not make that request of me."

"The bardmaster," Solran cut in, "is, however, here as your adjutant, and I am unwilling to, as The Berrilya suggests, fly in the face of the Kings' clearly stated preferences in this regard. My apologies," she added, to Jewel. "It had not occurred to me that you were in ignorance of the song's contents—although having said that, I can easily understand why; only The Wayelyn would be bold enough to sing it in your presence, and you have spent little time in the drawing rooms and ballrooms of the patriciate since claiming your seat."

Jewel turned to the Council. "Will we discuss other matters, or will we recess until I have been fully apprised of the contents of a bardic lay?"

She expected the Council to vote to continue. They did not.

"I would like to raise one objection," The Korisamis said. To Jewel's surprise, the comment was directed to Solran Marten—or perhaps to The Wayelyn; it was not entirely clear from where she sat. "You place her, in the eyes of the people, in a position above the Kings. You make a threat of her, and therefore of her House. While it is true that Terafin and Korisamis have frequently been in conflict over a broad range of issues, The Korisamis has *never* disputed the right of Terafin to exist.

"What you do—with the help of one of The Ten—is tantamount to that. You place Terafin in the path of the *Astari* and its overzealous, undersupervised leader. We are willing to consider and evaluate the danger The Terafin might present to the Kings—but we are not willing to cede the ruler of a House to the Kings' justice without solid proof that she represents an unchecked and uncheckable threat.

"Your song speaks to the heart of the difficulties we convened to discuss, and you have removed much of the weight of that considered discussion from the table. We are not pleased with your decision; if you wished to fashion a—whatever it is you mean her to be—you might have considered *asking* for her permission and her cooperation." He rose. "Terafin." He bowed.

He was as angry as Jewel had ever seen him. No, she thought, that wasn't true. But she had never seen him discard his perfect control in such a fashion. She fought the urge to ask him to resume his seat, because in the end, he spoke for her in a way that she could not, without some cost, speak for herself. And she was grateful for it.

Do not be; he speaks thus for his own benefit.

What possible benefit?

You are his peer, Jewel. You are his junior, yes, but nonetheless his peer. What can be done to you—without your permission—can be done in like fashion to any *of The Ten. They are not angry on your behalf, but on their own. Use it. It is the only chance you have to maintain your position here.*

"Korisamis." She rose and offered him, measure for measure, the respect he had offered her.

The Kalakar rose before she could resume her seat. "The Korisamis is, of course, correct. While the substance of this meeting has not been fully addressed, most of the issues that comprise it have been laid out in some detail. If it is acceptable to all present, I suggest we reconvene on the morrow."

The vote passed in less than a minute as Jewel watched her reflection in the table's surface. She lifted a hand, gesturing. Teller's reflection gestured in response, his fingers blurred and softened by the quality of the light. He had not spoken a word, and did not speak, holding both silence and position while The Ten rose and exited the chamber in ones and twos.

The Tamalyn lingered, and when the room was empty of all save the Terafin party, The Wayelyn and the Bardmaster of Senniel College, he rose. Shadow grumbled, but allowed it, following him as he approached Jewel. "Terafin," he said, the syllables hesitant.

"Tamalyn."

Michi ATamalyn smiled. It was a very brittle smile; Jewel had no doubt that the words spoken in the Tamalyn carriage on the return to the Tamalyn manse wouldn't exactly be friendly. The Tamalyn seemed to be unaware of this, or at least unconcerned by it. "If at all possible," he said, "and given your busy schedule, I would . . ."

"Like to see my trees?"

He smiled. It was the effusive, unfettered smile of a young child—but it looked entirely at home on his face. He nodded.

"You have my permission, and I offer it with genuine pleasure—something seldom afforded with ease in Council meetings. If you are willing to be shown the grounds by members of my House, and not me personally, you might visit at any time you find convenient. If, however, I am required—"

"No, no, not at all."

Michi ATamalyn flinched, but said nothing.

"I will speak to my secretary when I return. Is there anything else?"

"No."

When The Tamalyn had been all but dragged from the Council chambers by his counselor, Jewel turned to The Wayelyn and the Senniel bardmaster, neither of whom had made any attempt to leave the hall. She inclined her chin, allowing some of the stiffness which felt so unnatural to drain from her face.

"Wayelyn, must you outrage The Garisar and The Berrilya so casually?"

The Wayelyn smiled broadly. "Casually? That is unkind, Terafin. Believe that it is an art, and as all art, it must be nurtured and practiced with deliberation and passion."

Solran cast a look that was at once both mildly disapproving and affectionately resigned at the former Senniel bard. "I do not believe The Terafin considers the Council chambers a gallery or performance hall."

"And I believe she is full capable of speaking for herself," he replied.

"She is," Jewel agreed. "And I must commend the bardmaster on her perception."

The Wayelyn chuckled. "Come, the meeting was not a disaster."

"For your House, Wayelyn, or mine?"

"For neither of our Houses, surely." He offered Jewel an arm, and she accepted it. "I will, with your permission, escort you to your manse. If you feel such an escort is inappropriate, I will, with your permission, invite you to attend me within my own humble home."

"Will the bardmaster accompany you?"

Solran exhaled slowly. "With your permission, Terafin, I shall. I have some small business within *Avantari*, but I should be at your disposal within the hour."

"Very well. Wayelyn?"

"He will accompany me," Solran said, before he could reply.

"Then I will repair to my manse to make certain we have suitable rooms in which to receive you."

When Jewel left the Council chambers—and she was the last to do so—she was met in the hall by a man she had not expected to see. He tendered her a perfect bow—as suppliant to a superior. It put her off her stride, although she schooled her expression as she bid him rise.

Dantallon. Healer-born, he served in the Queens' healerie, and very little could force him from the stronghold he had made of that space. The sleeping sickness, however, had done just that—even if he had traveled only as far as the Houses of Healing.

"Dantallon."

"Terafin."

"You look well."

He raised a pale brow. "You are politic," he replied, a slight smile creasing the corners of his lips.

"Meaning I'm lying."

"A man in my position would never accuse a woman in yours of such an act." The smile deepened. It did nothing to remove the circles beneath his green eyes, and it did nothing to brighten the pallor of his skin. "Might we speak?"

She nodded. "We are to return to the Terafin manse. If the matter is not too private, we might speak on the way out of the palace." His silence was enough of an answer. "Or we might speak here, in a room of your choosing. The Council chamber?"

"The Queens' healerie."

The Queen's healerie was not the Terafin healerie, but there was a peace in the infirmary that implied they had sprung from the same spirit. There were fewer plants, and to Jewel's eye, no cat; there were wider beds, and cupboards that were flush with the walls into which they were set.

There was no discernible magic that protected the occupants of the room from eavesdroppers, but Jewel labored under no illusions; no words spoken within the walls of *Avantari* were private. She accepted Dantallon's choice, because all choices appeared equally suspect.

"I have spoken with Levec," he said, coming to the point. He did not mention Adam. "Levec feels cautiously optimistic about the possible future outcome for those who have fallen to the sleeping sickness."

I bet. She did not say this aloud, but her expression must have conveyed it; Dantallon chuckled, although it was pained.

"I am aware that a great deal of controversy shrouds House Terafin," he continued, when she failed to speak. "And I am more than aware of the ways in which controversy requires a great deal of both time and attention to manage efficiently."

"But you require some of the time I might spend putting out those fires."

"Not I, Terafin," was his grave reply. "In the past few days, we have had no new victims. But in the past few days, we have lost two."

Jewel stiffened.

"I do not pretend to understand the concerns of Kings," he continued. "Nor will I attempt to understand the concerns of Terafin; they are powers, and I am not. Nor will I ever be, if *Kalliaris* is kind. I am shepherd of the injured and the ill, as is Levec."

"He's the bulldog." She exhaled. "The Kings are aware—"

"The Kings are aware. But they must hold, in balance,

the demands and concerns for the entirety of the Empire; I am but one healer, and the lives in the balance are few in comparison."

"They didn't give you permission to speak with me."

"Nor is such permission required," he said. "But they did not consider the danger to be sufficient that it might hold a place within their audience with you."

"How long had you been standing outside that door?"

A ghost of a smile touched his lips. "Not more than an hour. The meeting ended more quickly than I expected."

"And I am promised to return to the Council chamber on the morrow."

"And after, Terafin?"

She wanted to say yes. She understood why Dantallon had waited. But she thought of Carver, of Ellerson, of The Ten and the possible censure—or worse—she faced from the Kings at the close of their private counsels. "I will do what I can. If the Kings do not decide—" She shook her head. "I forget myself."

You do.

"What I can do, I will do. I do not think I am required in the Houses of Healing in person, but I will travel there after the Council meeting, if I am, at that point, given leave."

"Levec will allow it."

It was not, of course, of Levec that she spoke, but this time, she remained silent.

The wide, well-kept streets of the Isle filled the carriage window as it at last left the long drive that led to *Avantari*. "It is a wonder to me that The Tamalyn has not been overthrown."

Jewel glanced at her domicis, amused by his obvious frustration. "Less so than The Wayelyn?"

"The Wayelyn is vastly underestimated, in my opinion. The Tamalyn is not."

"Any attempt to oust him would be met with resistance."

"Not on his part."

"No." She laughed, which deepened his frown. "Were I a member of his House Council, I would do everything in my power to keep him on his seat. He doesn't handle the Trade Commission, he doesn't deal with the Port Authority, and he doesn't personally oversee any of the Tamalyn concerns in the Merchant Authority. He does, however, clearly have capable and competent people who are willing to do all of those things while sitting to the side of the seat. I like him," she added.

"That is patently obvious. If you do not exercise some caution, you will no doubt have him visit your library, where he will become a permanent fixture." When he saw her expression, he added, "This is *not* a wise course of action."

"No," was her grave reply. "If he wanders too far and we lose him, we will have to answer to Tamalyn, and I, for one, do not intend to enrage his House Council. Leave it, Avandar. If someone can take genuine joy from the events of the past few months—and they aren't demonic in nature—I'm content to allow it." She turned to Teller. "How bad does the future look?"

He glanced out the window, as if the passing geography were riveting.

"Teller." He failed to turn away from that window. "You haven't spoken a word since the Oracle. I wasn't certain if you were—"

"I was paying attention to the discussion in the Council chambers," he replied. "And while I understand what you hoped to achieve, I'm uncertain. The Korisamis was a surprise. He has never been a dependable ally, but in this, he was definitively in our court."

Jewel nodded. "The Oracle—"

"Let me think about what I saw. I know what your visions are like, and I know they're open to interpretation." He exhaled and met her gaze. "They're mostly open to misinterpretation, if we're being honest, until after the fact. They point you in the right direction—but that's the sum total of their use. You understand them only as you're moving through them."

"You think the Oracle's gift to you is the same?"

"I think it's the same, but in some ways worse. With your visions, I had words, no more. You described what you saw. I transcribed your description. But I've never seen what you saw. Looking into her crystal—it must be like dreaming the three dreams. It's large, it's raw, everything is sharply defined—but none of it makes any sense from here. I don't think it's about the near future."

"Teller."

He nodded.

"You haven't told me what you saw."

"No."

She waited. Several minutes passed before she realized he had no intention of telling her. "Teller—"

Four claws pierced the ceiling; they looked like curved, long knives. Shadow growled, to underscore his point.

"Shadow, we can't afford the destruction of *all* of our carriages; the expense tells against *me*."

"The vision was *his*, not *yours*. What he saw—or what he didn't see—is his. I *told* you not to *trust* her."

"You did." She exhaled. "But I don't have to trust her. I only have to trust Teller." She transferred her gaze to a different window.

It was a quiet ride back to the manse; only Shadow talked, and for the most part, he mumbled about boredom. He did, on the other hand, pull his claws out of the roof.

Jewel reached her mansion ahead of The Wayelyn and the Bardmaster of Senniel College. Flanked by the Chosen, she entered her manse, to find Meralonne APhaniel leaning against the banister of the elegant stairs in the foyer. He was smoking his pipe. Sigurne was not in attendance as the mage joined her.

"The Wayelyn," she told him, continuing to walk, "will be arriving shortly."

"Council business?"

"In a manner of speaking. Have you by any chance heard the song that has purportedly spread throughout the hundred holdings in the past two months?"

A white brow rose. "A minstrel's song? I have spent little time in the Common or the taverns that surround it; between my duties to the Kings' armies and the Order of Knowledge, I have been very heavily occupied."

"Then you will attend me when The Wayelyn arrives."

"He is coming to . . . sing?" Circles of smoke rose, like a lopsided halo.

"He is. It is not an entirely frivolous visit," she added. "The song was almost the sole focus of discussion in the Council hall in *Avantari*. Enough so that a recess has been called that I might hear it; I am the only member of The Ten the song appears to have avoided." As she spoke, she cut across the public gallery. Given the recess, she had half a day ahead of her, which she fully intended to spend catching up with the small emergencies that no doubt littered her desk at Barston's discretion.

Unwise, Avandar told her. *If The Wayelyn is to perform, he should perform for the House Council.*

Jewel had a strong aversion to what might be public humiliation in front of her gathered Council. In particular, she wished to avoid Haerrad. Haerrad's sense of the respect necessary to preserve House dignity was an order of magnitude greater than her own, and she did not wish to clash over something as trivial as The Wayelyn's handling of House Terafin in a *song*.

She made her way to the right-kin's office, entering it as if it were an oasis. It was, and at the moment, it wasn't a particularly crowded one. Barston rose as she entered.

"The Wayelyn and the Bardmaster of Senniel College will be arriving shortly," she told him without delay.

"Terafin." He waited until Teller separated himself from Jewel's entourage and approached the desk. "There has been one message from House Tamalyn which is marked urgent. My apologies, but I cannot see how the contents suit the designation. If there is no good political reason to consider it so—"

Teller lifted a hand. "It is urgent to The Tamalyn," he told his secretary. "And if that is the sum of the urgent communiques received in my absence, I will make offerings at all three shrines before the day is out."

"It is, as you suspect, the only such missive that might be handled with less care." He lowered his voice. "The Master of the Household Staff would like a word with you."

Teller cringed, as she wasn't standing in the waiting room. "Is she in my office?"

"No. She has asked to be informed of your arrival." He glanced at The Terafin.

Jewel failed to hear him, but that took effort.

"Where will you entertain your guests? In your personal chambers?"

"No. For the moment, I think that unwise, and it may well lengthen the meeting beyond its time constraints." She glanced at Torvan. "The large office?"

"Might I suggest the reading room? It is well-insulated,

and if the bardmaster chooses to play, it will contain her music," Barston said.

"It is not, in this case, the bardmaster I fear, and if The Wayelyn desires to be heard, no amount of insulation will prevent him from finding an audience." She exhaled. "Very well. It might suit; it is meant to be a collegial, casual meeting."

"Very well, Terafin."

"I shall repair to my quarters to prepare for my guests. APhaniel, will you wait in the large office? You may accompany me if that is your preference."

"I will, with your permission, wait in the library."

Shadow, silent until that moment, hissed. Jewel dropped a hand on his head and he subsided, although his teeth were rather more prominent than they had been for most of the day—or at least the parts that did not include the Oracle.

When Jewel repaired to her quarters, she found one of the servants waiting ten yards from her closed doors. As she approached, she recognized her, and froze. It was Merry.

Merry folded instantly into the most obeisant of curtsies that didn't involve hugging the ground with most of her body. Jewel would have taken a knife wound with more grace; she flinched. Merry, trained by the indomitable—and hugely unforgiving—Master of the Household Staff, noticed instantly, and paled.

Jewel hated it. "Merry," she said, breaking at least two of said Master's iron rules, "please—don't. I know I'm not in the West Wing anymore, but it's been a long day, and I cannot endure—" she stopped. Composed herself. "My apologies. Did the Master of the Household Staff send you?"

Merry shook her head. As if she were mute.

As if she had come all this way, and had waited for gods knew how long, only to find speech had deserted her. She was pale, and her eyes implied that she'd chosen to forgo sleep for at least a day. Jewel nodded at the Chosen, and they opened the doors that had once led to a very conventional library. "Please," she told the servant, "join me."

Merry's silence shifted when she passed through the doors. Her posture didn't. She was not here as a visitor or a guest, and knew it. But it was hard to observe the strict etiquette demanded of servants who had been granted the House Name when faced with so much beyond the ken of the House which had offered it. She lifted her chin and her eyes touched the deep amethyst of the endless skies above; they drifted to trees that had taken the shape of bookcases, and paused at freestanding iron arches. The floors were pale plank, but they were silent beneath passing feet, no matter how heavily the steps might fall.

"Does the Master of the Household Staff know you're here?" Jewel asked, as she led the way past the forest of books. It wasn't a question she should have asked, and she regretted it the minute the words left her mouth.

But she *had* asked.

"It's my half-day off," Merry replied.

Jewel wanted to apologize for prying, but it would only make things worse. It was frustrating; Merry *knew* where the den had come from. But knowing it changed nothing. Jewel was The Terafin.

She led, and Merry followed. Jewel didn't trust the library, with its open table and its equally open sky. To underscore this point, Shadow leaped up, wings unfolding as he gained sky. He roared. There was nothing in the sound that reminded anyone listening of the smaller variety of silent feline.

Merry's attention was drawn to the sky, her gaze following Shadow; Jewel's eyes were drawn, instead, to the servant. She knew why Merry was here. Should have known the instant she saw her in the hall, waiting in the strained and terrible silence of her isolated fear. It was a fear that Jewel shared, but such fears made the poorest of bridges; Merry was not here to offer comfort, but to receive it.

And Jewel was not comforting by nature.

"APhaniel," she said, surprising the mage. "Please. Attend us."

One pale brow rose, but he offered no resistance. He looked at home in the library, now. Jewel thought she had never seen him suit an environment so perfectly; it framed him, it brought out the silver edge of gray eyes, the perfect winter of platinum hair. Even cloaked as he was in the robes of the Order of Knowledge, he seemed taller, prouder, a scion of ancient lineage.

Yes, he was at home in her library; he was at home as the

Terafin Mage. And she? She accepted his presence as if it were natural. She turned and held out a hand to Merry, who, plump and pale and red-haired, cleaved to the duty of cleaning and tidying as if it were a vocation. Merry swallowed and took the offered hand, aware that the Master of the Household Staff was not here, and would never see it.

Both hands shook.

Jewel forced her own to be steady as she led Merry across the wilderness toward the familiar doors of her rooms, as if her rooms were an oasis in this place. They might have been, once—but it was not to the wild of open, amethyst sky and unnatural trees, nor the savagery of winged predators, that she had lost Carver and Ellerson.

It was something as simple, as inconsequential, as a closet. An open door that led to *dresses*. Because it was important that she dress *appropriately*. She swallowed, realizing that her grip had tightened; she forced it to relax, but did not let go of Merry's hand. She would have to. She knew she would have to, or it would alarm Merry, and gods only knew what tales she would then take to the back halls.

And that, she thought, was unfair. "It's a bit intimidating," she said. "The open skies. I keep expecting thunderclouds to destroy the books in the library—but so far, there's been no rain."

"Not yet," Meralonne said, watching Shadow, who was now a moving fleck of darkness in the sky.

The doors rolled open before Jewel could touch them. She thought about speaking with Merry in the small conference room, but decided against it. She had come to her room to change into less uncomfortably formal attire. If The Wayelyn and the Senniel bardmaster were significant guests, they did not require the stiff, almost architectural formality that the Kings required.

"I'm sorry," she told the servant, meaning it. "The Wayelyn and the bardmaster will be arriving at the manse shortly, and I do not wish to greet them in attire fit only for the Kings'. Will you—will you help me?"

Merry hesitated as Jewel released her hand. "I'm not trained as a manservant," she finally said. "And I've no experience with your type of hair."

"My domicis can see to my hair, for the moment."

"The Master of the Household Staff—"

"I am aware of her opinions, but at the moment, I am without Ellerson, and the woman she elected to serve in his place was not expecting my early return." This didn't mean that the woman would not, like magic, appear; Jewel had no doubt whatsoever that the entire serving staff of any seniority was aware that she had returned.

"That would be Miriam," Merry said quietly. Her tone was completely neutral. "She'll be here soon. I'm surprised—" She stopped, remembering to whom she was speaking. "She'll be here."

Jewel did not want to wait. She almost said as much. But the sudden and inexplicable changes to the third-floor rooms of the manse had already thrown the upper echelons of the Household Staff into turmoil; she couldn't afford, at this juncture, to offer any further offense to the woman who ruled them all.

"How angry is the Master of the Household Staff?"

Merry hesitated. "Very."

"Will she resign?"

The shocked look the question engendered was more of a comfort than any words would have been—which was good; Merry didn't offer them.

They fell silent as Avandar approached the closet. The doors had been removed entirely—given they were mostly broken wood and jagged splinters, this was to be expected. Jewel watched his back as he began, with deliberation, the choosing of an appropriate dress.

"What happened?" Merry asked, while Jewel watched. Her voice was low; it was not hesitant.

"Ellerson was responsible for my attire; the Master of the Household Staff was willing to allow me his attendance, over a servant of her own choosing. I regret it," she added. "I regret depriving the West Wing of his guidance. He came to these rooms, through that library, without blinking; he set his irons and his damnable brushes and combs on the dresser, and he entered the closet to choose a dress.

"He did not emerge. Carver followed him."

Merry walked toward the doorless closet, where Avandar was still visible.

"It is a closet," Jewel continued, her voice almost flat with the effort to keep it steady. "It was, for a few hours, a passage. When we realized what had happened, we entered that passage in search of them; the hall that awaited us was long, tall, a thing of stone and emptiness. There was no sign of either Ellerson or Carver."

Merry stepped aside as Avandar withdrew, dress over his left arm. It was a slate blue, with highlights of a darker, richer color; Jewel noticed nothing else about it. As Merry approached the closet, she drew closer as well, and before the servant could enter it, she held out a hand.

It was not in denial. Merry hesitated, and then slid her right hand into Jewel's left.

"Terafin, I do not consider this wise," Meralonne said.

Merry froze.

"Why?" Jewel asked him, without looking back. "Will the passage that severed me from my kin once again swallow us?"

"The wisest among us could not answer that question, Terafin. In this place, at this time, it is unwise to make the wilderness aware of your desire."

"Is it remotely possible," Jewel asked softly, "that that desire might remain unknown?" She approached the doorless entrance of the closet.

"Yes. Not only is it possible, Terafin, it is imperative. What the servant wants is of no consequence."

Jewel's grip tightened briefly; Merry did not react at all. "APhaniel."

He had armed himself with his pipe. Nor did he set it aside at her command; instead, he frowned and made his way to the open closet. "You will want a door here," he told her curtly. He entered first, and Jewel allowed it. She could see the rustle of hanging cloth that spoke of his passage through her expensive garments.

"You don't know where he is," Merry said, voice low.

Jewel shook her head. "I intend to find him. To find them both. Snow and Night are searching for him; the Winter King is on the road—the white stag," she added. "So, too, is Lord Celleriant. They have been searching for Carver and Ellerson since their disappearance."

"They haven't found them."

". . . No." She turned to face Merry. "And until the matter of Kings and The Ten is settled, I cannot join them. But I give you my word, upon the House crest, that I will."

"Will you call me, when you leave?"

Jewel stiffened. She withdrew the hand she had offered in comfort, or in need of it. "I would not risk you, Merry. The Master of the Household Staff is angry enough. You are ATerafin; you have been for half your life."

"You are The Terafin."

"Yes. The responsibility for the House—and its losses—are mine." She paused. "I can't with certainty say the cats and Lord Celleriant will survive their search, but they search the lands that birthed them."

"You think I'll be a liability. You don't think I can help."

Jewel nodded. "Believe that I understand the need to act; I feel it now, and I am, instead, to attend The Wayelyn and the Bardmaster of Senniel College. I am to travel to the Houses of Healing."

Meralonne emerged from the closet. 'The way is closed," he said.

Something in his tone had her lips in a frown before she could smooth it away. "Can you open it, APhaniel?"

In reply, he lit his pipe.

"If I receive any word—for good or ill—I will summon you to the West Wing," she told Merry.

"The West Wing?"

"Yes. Because if I have any word, it is to the West Wing I will carry it. The den are my kin; they are Carver's kin. If he has any other living, he has never mentioned them."

Merry swallowed and nodded. She had an expressive face, but attempted to mute the expression that now crushed it. It was an act of kindness.

"Avandar, please escort—"

"No," Merry said quickly. "I require no escort."

"The library—"

"And if I accept one, I'll lose my job. I might keep the House Name," she added, just as quickly, "but it won't matter. I won't be able to do the only work I've been trained to do."

Miriam arrived some ten minutes after Merry left. She abjured all of the things Merry did not, chief among them openness or friendliness. Dour and stiff as the Master of the Household Staff, she offered Jewel a very formal, very precise bow. Jewel ignored it. Miriam was not Merry; nor was she one of the servants who tended and—in subtle ways—guided the den through the politics of the patriciate. She was one of the elite within the Household Staff, and she set boundaries that only the blind or willful breached. Jewel did not have the energy to be either at this moment.

"APhaniel," she said, as Miriam began to work on the unruly mass of curls which was her hair, "You did not answer my question."

"No, Terafin, I did not. I considered it unwise at the time."

"And now?"

"I consider it unwise, but I will accept the terms of my employment if you demand an answer."

"I do. Can the way that was closed be opened?"

"Yes."

"By me?"

"By you, certainly, although your lack of knowledge poses a very real threat to the security of your House."

"By you, then."

"Possibly." He paused to blow rings of smoke into the still air. "Is it your desire that I make the attempt immediately?"

"No," she replied, voice low; it felt like a yes. "What I desire, for the moment, is your expertise. I wish to know if there are other, similar, passages open to lands beyond my control within the lands that are.

"There is one other that I am aware of," she continued, when he failed to speak. "You will not touch it; you will not explore it; you will not cast magic upon it in *any* way."

She could see the lift of a brow in the mirror. It was followed by concentric circles of pale, translucent smoke. "Where is this passage of yours?"

"Beyond the small meeting room."

"I admit my curiosity is piqued."

"Do not attempt to satisfy it except in my presence." She glanced at Torvan in the mirror; he nodded. It was a slight dip of motion, and she almost regretted the command; he didn't need a fractious, temperamental mage dropped on his head. Sadly, she did.

Miriam worked quickly; Ellerson might have done the same, had she not felt the need to converse—or complain— while he worked. She was the perfect master to Miriam's stiff and proper servant; she allowed the older woman to be a competent, prominent shadow. When her hair was considered thoroughly presentable, Jewel dressed; she allowed Miriam to fuss with the dress, its laces, its buttons, and the fall of its hem. She exchanged one pair of boots for shoes that were only slightly more comfortable, and allowed a change of jewelry. Jewelry was the one thing she frequently failed to take into consideration.

It was a deliberate failure, and this, too, she set aside.

When Miriam was done—and she made this clear by a curt nod and a visible, physical retreat from The Terafin's presence—Jewel made her way back through the small hall and wide doors and into the library proper. Meralonne accompanied her, pausing beneath the open sky as Shadow made his way down, in a wide, lazy spiral, to join her.

He landed on Torvan's foot and shouldered the mage out of the way, but did so without insulting either man. For Shadow, this was an act of enormous self-restraint; Jewel therefore placed a hand *gently* on the top of his head. He hissed anyway.

Avandar walked behind her, as he usually did within the manse; Meralonne, eyes a flash of silver, chose to ignore the cat's insulting behavior and walked to Jewel's right. He gazed up at the sky, his expression carefully neutral.

"I believe I am annoyed," he told her.

"By?"

"The Wayelyn, of course. You will not put him off or have him sent to his own unremarkable manse, and you will not give me the tour I seek until his business is done."

"No. If it is any consolation, it is not The Wayelyn that I fear to offend; it is Solran Marten. She has the ears of the Kings and the Queens, and the loyalty of the only master bard who can sing to the wind and hear its answer."

"You speak of Kallandras."

"Do I?" She smiled. "Yes. I wish you had brought him with you from the South."

"Why?"

"Because he has some part to play in what is to come."

"Of that," the mage agreed, "I have no doubt whatsoever. Many, however, have some part—large or small—to play."

"He'll survive it."

Meralonne raised a brow.

"Solran has often said that nothing can kill Kallandras; she's certain she could send him alone and unarmed into the midst of a fully mobilized army, and he'd pass through the other side without injury."

"She thinks highly of him."

"She does. You do, as well."

"Do I, now? Have I become so transparent?"

"No, APhaniel. Never that. Attend me," she added, as a page approached her. "The Wayelyn and the bardmaster are now within the manse."

The Wayelyn had not retired to his own manse to change; nor, apparently, had the bardmaster. Jewel found them in the rooms she had asked be prepared for the purpose of entertaining them, and refreshments had been served. Teller sat beside Solran, and the two appeared to be engrossed in the type of conversation that bored the titular head of Wayelyn; he brightened when he saw The Terafin standing between the open doors.

"My apologies," she told them, nodding as she entered the room. "I was delayed. I hope you have not been kept waiting long."

"We have," The Wayelyn said, amusement filling the spaces in his lovely, low voice. "But the right-kin has opened the wine cellars of Terafin in recompense for our time, and, I must say, you do not husband your vintages with any great care; the wine is excellent."

Solran's glass, full, had not been touched; Teller's had, but only in sufficient quantity to assure that The Wayelyn was not left to drink on his own. The bardmaster glanced at Shadow as he padded across carpet, taking very little care not to damage it. It was one of the ways in which the cats were expensive. He sniffed the glass on the table, his nose wrinkling. He then sneezed into it. Jewel inhaled sharply, but the bardmaster merely raised a brow.

"Do you sing?" she asked the great cat.

Shadow hissed.

"Shadow."

He glanced over his shoulder at Jewel.

"It was not a challenge," she told him. "Nor was it meant as an insult."

"Then why did she *ask*?"

"She sings. She teaches the greatest minstrels of the Empire, and they answer—when they answer at all—to her."

"I don't answer to *anyone*."

"Believe that we are aware of this," she replied, with some exasperation. He had, in common with the felines kept as pets across the hundred, an ego that was at once ferocious and delicate. Crossing the room, she took a chair; Meralonne did likewise, pausing to tender both The Wayelyn and the bardmaster a bow. It was not an obeisance, but for a member of the Order, it was respectful.

She had chosen the reading room not because she might put distance between herself and her guests, but because of all of the rooms within the manse proper, it had the strongest magical defenses; no one listened here without her express permission unless they were also in the room. She had taken the liberty of invoking the extensive protections before the doors had opened. She was aware that the *Astari* had spies within her manse—Duvari's reach was such that it could safely be assumed he had spies within any House of power. Let him work for the information she did not choose to hand him.

It would, no doubt, make him far less suspicious of said information when it at last crossed his desk.

Shadow sat heavily beside Jewel's chair, staring at the bardmaster. She impressed Jewel; she met his gaze as if he were a wearisome child. "I remember a white cat," she said, the words trailing up in question.

"You remember correctly. Snow is not present at the moment. This," she added, "is Shadow. Of the three brothers—"

"We are *not* brothers," he hissed.

"—He is the most cunning." This met with Shadow's approval, although he stared at her with suspicion, as if looking for the hidden insult in the words.

"Do you guard her dreams, Shadow?" the bardmaster asked softly.

The question appeared to surprise the cat; it certainly surprised Jewel. It was, however, Jewel who answered. "He does."

The Wayelyn bent and retrieved a large, worn case from the floor to one side of his chair. It was a natural leather, but cracked in places, and darker in color around the handle and the edges that touched floor. Opening it, he retrieved his lute. It, like the case, was of obvious age, but no cracks could be seen anywhere upon its wooden body. He began to tune the strings, and as he did, Solran spoke, as if to accompaniment.

"Understand, Terafin, that I mean no disrespect either to your office or your House. I allowed the song to be widely disseminated without regard to either."

Jewel nodded, watching Solran with care.

Meralonne emptied his pipe and began to fill it.

"I ask a boon," the bardmaster continued.

Jewel stiffened. "Ask."

"I would have you hear The Wayelyn's song—but I would have you hear it in a less . . . confined . . . space."

"You do not intend to gather an audience?"

"Not as such. But I wish to return to the grounds for which House Terafin has become famed in so short a time, and I believe they would be a suitable location in which to sing. Or to listen."

Jewel considered the request with care. The song itself, Duvari had heard. Of that, she had no doubt. But any comments she might make with regard to the song would be severely limited in such unguarded environs.

You are wrong, Avandar told her. *Should you desire it, none—not even the firstborn—would be witness to what was said or spoken within your grounds. You rely on the magics of the Order, here, but even within your manse, they are the lesser power.*

The greater power, unknown and unharnessed, led to closets that devoured her kin. She did not say this aloud; instead, she rose. "Very well, Bardmaster. Wayelyn. If you will accompany me, we will take your song to the *Ellariannatte.* APhaniel?" she added, when he failed to rise.

"I speak as your House Mage," he replied, "but I will tell you now that I am not certain this is wise."

"Are you certain it is unwise?" she countered.

"No, Terafin. I feel there is some risk, but it is possible that there will be some benefit." He rose then. "And you are willing to take that risk."

"I am. I am unwilling, at this point, to take such a risk anywhere else within my domain—but within the forest, I am comfortable."

The trees for which Terafin had achieved such instant awe and fame were visible before the small party had cleared the manse; The Wayelyn and Solran Marten stood on the terrace to one side of the fount, looking up at the heights the *Ellariannatte* graced. Wind could be seen in the movement of branches and leaves; the air around the terrace itself was still.

Shadow nudged Jewel. She braced herself and maintained her footing. She expected either admonition or criticism, but the cat glanced at her visitors and remained silent. He did step on Avandar's feet, but Avandar didn't so much as blink.

There is a risk, her domicis told her.

What risk? The last thing I need is difficulty while The Wayelyn is present.

I judge the possibility of mortal danger to be low; this is the heart of your domain, and only the very, very powerful will attempt to breach it.

She was tired of riddles. As she nodded to The Wayelyn, she examined the warning, turning it over as she looked for hidden barbs. Avandar, however, had no need to rely on the hidden to make his point. She was not yet concerned with any future but tomorrow's, and even were she, tomorrow would take precedence. The rule of her House depended on it.

And not your life?

They will not kill me, she replied. As the words left her, wrapped in the intimacy of silence, she realized they were true. It should have been a comfort. But she glanced at the set of The Wayelyn's uncharacteristically still jaw, and felt uneasy instead.

"They are the marvel that I remember," Solran said, her face upturned, her voice hushed. "I envy you your grounds, Terafin. Do not tell me they are not worthy of envy; I assume they exact a price, the whole of which I might never know. But they are peaceful; they contain the quiet of a day without conflict or the burden of responsibility."

"How would you recognize such a day?" Jewel asked, with a wry smile. "Given The Wayelyn and the only other master bard with whom I'm familiar, I imagine that you don't have many of them."

Solran laughed. Her laugh was a surprise; it was low,

deep, and suggested reserves of genuine delight. "Have I done something shocking, Terafin?"

"No, Bardmaster. I apologize for staring—you are familiar with my early history. Occasionally, the strict etiquette demanded by the patriciate is beyond my grasp."

"Your grasp has grown stronger, with the passage of time—and your reach, longer. If it eases you at all, Terafin, I trust you implicitly."

"On so little acquaintance?"

"Yes. I am surrounded by the bard-born, and not a single one of them has heard more than the hint of a lie in your words when you choose to speak in their hearing."

"And I so casually came up in conversation?"

"Not casually, no," the bardmaster replied, the last of the joy once again completely submerged. She stopped walking, her mouth half-open.

Chapter Nineteen

JEWEL STOPPED AS WELL. She had—she would swear she had—followed the bardmaster into the grounds transcribed by the Master Gardener and his staff. She glanced at the path beneath her feet; it was made of interlocking stone. In shape, in width, in length, it was very like the paths that wound their way through the garden of contemplation. It was adorned by short, standing lamps, their round, glass globes surrounding small magestones, keyed to radiate light when evening fell. Flower beds were laid, in careful order, to either side of the walk, although the garden would not reach the full riot of its tended color for weeks.

She hadn't stepped off the path, but apparently it no longer mattered. Where the small, cultivated trees so dwarfed by the *Ellariannatte* had once stood, there now stood trees of living silver and gold. Standing among them was a solitary tree on which roses were in bud. It should have looked ridiculous; it didn't. Accents of red—for the buds were a deep, deep red—glinted off silver, were warmed when seen in gold; it was almost as if the trees had grown around this single bush in a ring, to give it glory.

"Your garden has grown wild since the funeral," Solran said.

"Since just before," Jewel replied. She felt Avandar's disapproval. "But they didn't take root here. Not initially." She lowered her head. "Don't touch the trees," she said softly.

"I would not dream of doing so. Neither, I am *certain*, would The Wayelyn." The Wayelyn so mentioned was approaching the trees, but stopped, armoring himself with his lute and an unrepentant smile better suited to a child than a man of wealth, experience, and power.

"You are incorrigible," Solran said, her tone equal parts affection and exasperation. "We have come this far to play to an audience of one—but for all that, an extremely significant audience. This is not perhaps the stage we would have chosen, but it seems fitting."

"I'm not certain—"

"No, Terafin, you are not—but it appears that roses can grow encircled by such wilderness, and even remain unharmed and unaltered. They are not, to my eye, remarkable, but they are—like the rarest of gems—in their perfect setting. Is it because of you?"

Jewel shook her head. "I've always thought gardens like this were a waste of time and money."

Solran appeared to be genuinely surprised; The Wayelyn laughed. "You would prefer, perhaps, a farm?"

"I would, truth be told. I am aware of all the reasons why it would be highly inappropriate; apparently to maintain wealth and power, one must exercise it in obvious and ostentatious ways. Growing food is not one of them. If you think my own attitude toward decorative flowers is at the heart of this ... encroachment, I admit that I fail to see how." She turned to The Wayelyn. "Apologies, Wayelyn, but I have one more appointment this eve, and my time grows short."

"Is it significant?"

"Although my advisers would be appalled, I will answer: I am to meet with Hectore of Araven. I am new in my tenure as head of this House, and relations between Araven and Terafin have not always been the most cordial; it is an opportunity I cannot afford to pass over."

"Indeed." He lifted his lute and once again played a series of short scales; he touched none of the knobs to either loosen or tighten strings. Instead, he frowned, and touched the strings again. He played something longer, faster, sliding up and down the scales. Jewel knew very little about music and musical instruments; she knew, in a time-honored way, what she liked—and for the most part, it was "lamentably common." But it sounded to her untrained ear as if he'd started out with a series of exercises and those exercises had gotten away from the fingers that played them.

She could hear the notes—fast, light, deliberate—as they echoed; as if they, like the glints of deep red, were being reflected by the silver and the gold. She thought, as she listened, that the notes changed, not in pitch, but in *texture*, as if the lute could somehow invoke from the heart of her forest the sounds of other instruments.

She was surprised when his voice joined the sound of a rising orchestra. She didn't understand the first words he sang; she didn't recognize the language. It wasn't Torra, and it certainly wasn't Weston. She glanced at Avandar, who seemed suddenly transfixed by the song—Avandar, whose hands had fallen, loose, to his sides. To one who wasn't familiar with him, there was no change in his outward appearance.

But Jewel knew. She knew that the words that were beyond her would not remain that way; she wasn't even certain if The Wayelyn was aware that what he sang was not what she heard.

"Bardmaster, what do you hear?"

Solran had the expression that Avandar lacked; her eyes were wide, unblinking, her pallor considerably paler. "This is not the song that has spread across Averalaan," Solran whispered.

"Do you recognize the language?"

"No, Terafin."

"Avandar?"

Her domicis did not appear to hear anything but the song itself; he didn't even spare her a glance. The Chosen listened, but Torvan was less enchanted and more alert; his gaze slid off and around The Wayelyn, who had taken up a position directly in front of the roses, not the fairy-tale trees themselves.

With sinking heart, she glanced at Meralonne. She was not surprised to see that his pale, platinum hair now flew in a strong breeze that seemed to touch nothing else in the garden, not even the leaves. His eyes were rounded, as were Solran's; unlike Solran, his lips were turned up in the faintest edge of a smile. He was the heart of winter, in this place;

she almost felt the ice forming in the air around him. Around them all.

So it was to Shadow that her gaze went, and it stayed there. The great cat's wings were high, and as she watched, he gathered himself, haunches rippling as his hind legs bent and tensed for leaping.

"*Shadow!*" Her voice was strong enough, sharp enough, to rouse Avandar from his fascination, and he turned instantly.

He didn't attack Shadow. Instead, Jewel saw a sheen of brilliant orange light spring up in a sphere around where The Wayelyn, back turned to his audience, now stood. If he was aware of it at all, he did nothing to betray it; his song did not pause. Instead, it soared.

Shadow bounced off him. Jewel grabbed his pinions— never a wise thing to do—as he tensed again. "Make him *stop*," the cat growled. "Make him stop, or I will kill Viandaran in order to stop him *myself*."

"What is he doing?" Jewel demanded, shouting to be heard. Pointing out that Avandar was deathless, while factual, was pointless. She accepted the fury of the cat's intent.

"He is *singing, stupid, stupid* girl. He is *singing*. The land *hears* him. It hears him and it will carry his song to places not even *we* can reach. They will *hear* it, and they will hear it too *soon*. You are not *ready*."

She knew, as she listened, that he told no lies. "Bardmaster—"

Solran shook herself. "Wayelyn. Cease."

Shadow sputtered in outrage. Jewel tightened her grip on his wings. "*Her* words are *nothing*! Use *yours*!"

Jewel opened her mouth, and shut it hard enough to clip the inside of her cheek. Shadow was right. He was viscerally, immediately *right*. But he was a wild, winged version of beautiful, glittering death. He didn't belong in the world of the Twin Kings, the Terafin manse, the hundred holdings. His only connection to them was Jewel.

But Jewel was *of* them. Even standing here, surrounded by silver-and-golden trees, the voice of the bard-born laden with the ancient, she was of them. Yes, this land was hers. She'd claimed it, and she'd claimed it in the only way the land itself understood. But she wasn't Shadow or Celleriant. The closest model at hand was Avandar, a man who had walked away from the defense of a city, to see it fall to the god they would face, sooner or later, in war.

She wanted to be neither.

She wanted to be Jewel Markess ATerafin for just a while longer. "Bardmaster!"

Solran didn't even look at Jewel. Her lips were compressed in a thin, white line.

"I understand what I need to understand," Jewel told the Master of Senniel College. "And if necessary, I will hear his song in a tavern, or in the market square."

The bardmaster walked to where The Wayelyn stood. What Shadow's claws and fangs couldn't penetrate, her hands could. Jewel saw the orange barrier part to let her hand through. Just one. She didn't touch The Wayelyn; instead, she laid her hands against the strings of his lute, stilling their vibration.

His fingers continued to move below her palm. "Wayelyn," she said. And then, when his voice failed to stop, she added, "Ernest."

He blinked, his voice faltering for the first time. His song banked, dwindling until Jewel could understand the words he sang: they were Weston, modern Weston.

"*And she, as fair, as fair as winter's heart, as pale as sun's light*

"*Will stand upon the walls, while winged heralds from that height*

"*Speak her name. But it is not their voices that she hears*

"*But ours, raised in our mortal song, above our fears*

"*Will lend her the strength only she requires.*"

"Walls?" Jewel asked, as The Wayelyn at last fell silent and turned toward her. His face was shining with sweat, his pupils slightly dilated, as if he'd just stepped out from a dark, dark room into full sunlight. "We don't have walls."

He blinked rapidly. "Your garden," he said, his voice cracked and dry, "is colder than I realized at this time of year. It is a wild and perilous place—but beautiful, for all that." Color returned to his cheeks, and the smile that was at once charming and self-indulgent returned to his lips. "Beauty is oft deadly, but we are moths, Terafin. You, in your white dress, with your winter cat and your glorious, ancient trees—you are the beginning of a story made flesh. It is not our story. It can't be.

"But . . ." He pivoted far too lightly on his feet for a man of his age. "APhaniel owns some part of it; look at him now. His hair is the color of your dress on that day."

"Why did you write that song?"

"Because, Terafin," he said, entirely devoid of his usual humor, "You will build those walls. No one else now can; we don't have the time. Do you understand what you heard?"

"Do you," she countered, "understand what you sang?"

"Only the last few phrases."

She was momentarily nonplussed. "Did you intend to sing whatever it was you *did* sing in this place?"

He turned to the bardmaster. Solran said—in a voice that made winter seem warm, "Ernest, you will answer her question. It is much on my mind, now."

Solran held his gaze, hers unblinking, until he looked away. "No, Terafin. No, but I suspected I might. The bard-born voice is sometimes strong in the wilderness. I cannot lie with it; the words themselves might be false, but what lies at the heart of the song *I* sing? Never. Solran is not bard-born. She understands the limitations and the capabilities of our kind more thoroughly than many born to the voice—but not all.

"Word has come to Senniel—and to Morniel and Attariel as well—that strange creatures now walk the roads. Whole caravans have been lost—much to the anger and bewilderment of the merchant houses, and lives lost as well, to things which are not easily explained away.

"We have had no word from Brekenhurst or Linden, although we expect word will come; they are furthest from Averalaan."

Solran's gaze never left his face, but her expression had shuttered; Jewel couldn't tell if she were angry. Nor did it at this point matter; The Wayelyn had not yet finished, and he could not now be stopped. "You have seen demons, Terafin. You have seen the Wild Hunt. You have taken into the heart of your domain the winged cats, and you ride a beast that the Queen of the Wild Hunt herself might ride.

"Against the creatures that now enter the Empire, you have some chance. If they were to attack you here, you would, in all likelihood survive. Am I wrong?"

"No. You are not wrong."

"What hope does a farmer have? What magic, what wild

power, comes to his defense? Does he lift his scythe? The iron in it might be some protection, but not against all creatures. And what do we know about those creatures? Stories. Legends. Bardic lays. We can learn the truth now—and we are—but what we're learning is merely how people disappear or die. There are very few credible witnesses. The bardic colleges have sent out even journeymen to the North and West; we have master bards on the roads to the South."

"We?"

"The bardic colleges. If I have not offended the bardmaster, I am still a member of the Collegiate Council."

Jewel was not completely familiar with the internal structure of the bardic colleges; she was surprised that something official existed at all. Nor was it the time to discuss it. "Very well. Bards have been sent across the Empire, and beyond its bounds. They've tendered reports."

"It is not just bards," Meralonne said. "The Members of the Order of Knowledge in the various kingdoms have begun investigations, and they have been in constant contact with the guildmaster; if the bardic colleges have a loose and collegial governing structure, the Order of Knowledge does not. What The Wayelyn says is substantiated by reports from the Order's members."

Jewel said; "The paths are opening." It was a whisper.

"Yes, Terafin. I believe we have discussed this," Meralonne added. He was watching The Wayelyn in open appraisal. "You came here deliberately."

"Yes. Here. I stood here on the day of The Terafin's funeral. I stood here while the storm came—and, Terafin, I heard you command it to leave. No one speaks openly of what happened on that day. If it is mentioned at all, it is mentioned in whispers, and it is never mentioned among the very powerful.

"I chose to speak of it in the only acceptable way I could."

"Why?"

"Because of what I witnessed. If they come here, Terafin—if the wild, lost, deadly creatures come *here*, you have some chance of stopping them."

She stared at him as if one of them were mad.

"Do not pretend," he said, as if her stare was of no consequence, "that I am wrong." Before she could answer, he turned to Meralonne APhaniel. "Do you know the lay of the Sleepers?"

"I know many, Wayelyn." The answer was cool and neutral, although given the manners of the magi in general, it wasn't rude. "And I will tell you now, if you ask, that singing any one of them in this place, at this time, would be dangerously unwise."

"Two words that have oft been used to describe me," was The Wayelyn's unrepentant reply. "But seldom by the magi. I will therefore refrain."

"Where did you come upon those lays?" The question sounded casual. The accompanying expression made it less so.

"They were taught to me long after I retired from Senniel's active lists."

"Kallandras."

"Indeed. You've met, I take it?"

Meralonne nodded. "I shall have words with him upon his return." To the bardmaster, he added, "I assume he is expected shortly."

"If you consider two weeks 'shortly,' yes. He remained in the Dominion for the coronation of the Kai Leonne, but is on the road as we speak."

"You have sent him no word, then."

"I have sent word, APhaniel, but if he is nigh invulnerable, he is mortal; he cannot travel as the most powerful of the magi do; he must therefore contend with terrain and weather."

Meralonne nodded; his gaze had not left The Wayelyn's pale face. "You have taken a risk at Terafin's expense."

The Wayelyn nodded. "Do you fear it?"

Meralonne *laughed*. It was a wild, cold sound that reminded Jewel of wind in winter. His hair flew around his shoulders. "Fear it? Wayelyn, I anticipate it. There have been battles of significance waged in this city within the past two decades—but they will be almost as nothing compared to what must come.

"You are not wrong. They will hear your song; it will travel from land to land, and it will grow in the telling. But it will grow deep. I cannot say whether or not what you hope will come to pass, but the lands are waking to the sound of your song."

Shadow hissed. Meralonne spared him an unfriendly glance. "She is Lord here," he said. "And if she is willing to take the risk, she will take it."

"She is *stupid*," the cat hissed in reply.

Solran chuckled. "I have always wondered what cats would say, could they but speak."

"You own cats?"

"Two," she replied. "And I must say my guesses were not far off." She frowned. "Terafin—there is fire in the distance."

Jewel exhaled. "Yes. But it doesn't burn. I have not explored the whole of this forest, but I know what lies at its heart. Come, if you would see it." To The Wayelyn she added, "Don't feel compelled to add another verse to your song."

He laughed. "As you say, Terafin. The song itself was exacting and it is not easily revised."

Jewel led them to the tree of fire, stepping off a path that both defined the garden and no longer served as its boundary. Shadow once again inserted himself to her right, leaving no room for her guests. She started to argue, but stopped; her dignity was no doubt at historic levels of low for House Terafin, and arguing with a cat would not materially improve it. "He is," she told the bardmaster, "an exceptional guard in all ways."

"So I have heard."

The fire that she had seen at too vast a distance grew in brilliance and heat as they at last approached the lone tree of fire within her forest; the light changed the color of Solran's skin; it lent a blush to The Wayelyn's, but didn't touch Meralonne's appearance at all.

Solran approached the tree with caution; The Wayelyn did not choose to approach it. "Will it burn?" she asked, as she slowly held out one hand, reaching for the lowest of its many-leaved branches.

"No. Unless I will it, it burns nothing."

The bardmaster touched a ruby leaf with edges—and a heart—of flame. Her eyes widened. "It does not feel like fire."

"Fire generally causes pain at that distance."

"It does—but this feels almost like . . ." Solran shook her head. "It feels too solid for flame, and although it is warm, it is not hot. What does this tree signify?"

"I don't know. It is some part of the elemental fire, and some part of an enemy's power; it is some part *Ellariannatte*, and some part dream. There is no safer place for me to stand than beneath these boughs." Shadow was hissing. "The cats are not greatly enamored of it, although they frequently play with the logs in the *actual* fireplaces in the West Wing."

The Wayelyn was staring. He turned to face her as Solran retreated from the tree of fire. "Do you not understand the choice we have made, Terafin? Is it truly incomprehensible?"

"I fear you have far too much confidence in my abilities," she replied softly.

"Yes. You do fear it. I fear it as well, for different reasons."

"And those?"

"You are capable of doing what must be done; I have been told as much, and I believe it, given the source."

"But?"

"Power is never freely given; it is taken, and it is paid for. If those below us do not or cannot see the cost, it changes little. The power you must have—the power you must summon—is beyond the reach of The Ten. It is beyond the reach of the Kings, and of the magi. Perhaps, in the long history of the Artisans, there are one or two who might have been your peers—but they are long dead."

"And while they lived were considered completely insane."

"Even so."

"What will you do, Wayelyn?" Jewel asked, as she led them toward the House shrine, and the safety of the Terafin grounds—if they could now be said to be safe.

He did not pretend to misunderstand her. "I will offer you unconditional support," he replied. "Against any decision the Kings make, in regard to House Terafin, or to your office. I am not afraid of your power, although I understand the assessment of the *Astari*."

"If the decision were now in the hands of the Lord of the Compact, I would be dead before I woke."

Shadow growled; Jewel dropped her hand to his head. "I did not say he would find it easy to kill me; I merely said that would be his decision."

"Why won't you let *us* kill *him*?"

"Because he keeps the Kings alive."

"Who *needs* Kings?"

Solran coughed politely.

"We do," Jewel replied.

"*You* don't."

"I do. I cannot rule an Empire. I can only barely rule a House. If I am—as The Wayelyn suggests—to somehow build walls and fortify a port city, I cannot attend to its thousands of citizens at the same time."

Solran glanced at The Wayelyn.

"You are not supposed to *attend* them; they are supposed to serve *you.*"

Thinking of the Master of the Household Staff, Jewel winced. "The Kings exist to serve all of their people in aggregate. I don't care if you think it's stupid. You think we're *all* stupid."

"Some of you are more stupid than others."

The Wayelyn chuckled. "The cats have the duty of keeping you humble, I see."

"Yes, and they are very, very good at it. Next time, I'll be less exacting in my demands. You will support my House?"

"Yes, Terafin. And I will urge The Ten over whom I have any influence to do likewise. Regardless of their stated fear, you have broken no laws. The possibility of danger exists— but the possibility that any given person will commit murder, theft, or treason *also* exists. We are The Ten; the Kings our ancestors risked their lives and their lineages to serve are forces of Justice and Wisdom—and choosing to act before a crime has been committed is an act of fear."

"Of caution, surely?" Jewel asked.

"Of fear. It is not the Kings of Fear we serve; not the Kings of Fear for whom we reaffirm our loyalty yearly in the Ten days that commemorate the Gathering of The Ten.

"The Exalted fear what you presage; the gods fear it as well. There are things buried beneath this city that they do not wish to see rise anew."

"That has oft been their concern," Meralonne said. "And it is both a grave concern, and a wise one."

"What will the Order of Knowledge do, APhaniel?"

"They will do what their guildmaster orders," he replied. "She is aware, as the Kings and the Exalted are aware, of the possible dangers. She understands the ways in which the current Terafin is a graver danger than any we have faced excepting only the Henden of 410. Power is always a risk when it is not your own."

"It's a risk even when it is," Jewel said. "Bardmaster?"

"I understood what I heard on the day of Amarais Handernesse ATerafin's funeral. If the city and its defense were to be given into any hands that are not the Kings, I can think of few whose hands I would fear less; perhaps Sigurne's."

"She would not accept that responsibility," Meralonne said quietly.

"No one who is counted wise would," the bardmaster replied, her smile deepening. "I certainly would not. I would abandon the city I have loved for most of my life first—and bards are famously adept at disappearing when a situation turns unexpectedly grim." She hesitated.

The Terafin marked it. "Speak plainly, Solran; I have."

"It would perhaps be best for the House you have sworn to serve—and lead—were you to retire your claim to the seat."

Jewel stiffened. But she had demanded plain speech; she could not now take umbrage at obedience. Instead, she turned to gaze at the trees—her trees. The shadows of the forest beyond the distortion of the air that flames caused were far darker than she remembered. Darker, denser; the forest, she sensed, had grown.

Was she angry? Yes. She forced the clench of fists from her hands. Anger would not help her, here—if it ever would again. "Is it true that you have never felt less than respect for a foundling from the hundred?"

"It is."

"You were not bardmaster when the honor—and responsibility—of the House Name was first conferred upon me."

Solran Marten did not reply.

"I was raised by my Oma—and a more ferocious woman, I have never met." She hesitated. "Perhaps one, but you will not know of her."

"Not The Terafin?"

"No. I speak of Yollana of the Havalla Voyani."

Silence. "I have heard of Yollana," Solran said. The

words were entirely neutral. "And if you compare your grandmother to that woman, she must have been ferocious indeed."

"She was. And she was as far from the patriciate as it is possible to be while occupying the same Empire. I struggled, upon adoption into the House, to learn to live among people she would have despised."

"Despised?"

"They disavow their blood relations; they desert their families. They take a name to which they were not born. Had any of my family lived—had she—she would have hated to see me here. But they did not. If she watches—if she waits by the bridge until I am forced to cross it—she will nonetheless understand why I cannot do what you consider wise. My predecessor knew what awaited her. She *knew*."

"Did you?"

"Yes." A hundred words rushed to leave her mouth—but they were excuses, rationalizations, a way to make her departure seem acceptable to a woman who had no right to judge her. They were not words *any* Terafin before her would ever have used; nor could Jewel. "I owed—and owe—her my life. She sheltered and protected everything that I had ever—or will ever—value. In return, before my departure, I offered her the only comfort I could: I promised to shelter, to protect and to uphold the thing she valued above all else. I promised I would *be* The Terafin.

"I *am* The Terafin. Until my death, I will remain The Terafin." She turned. "And if what you believe—if what APhaniel believes—is true, I can't turn from it. My life in the twenty-fifth holding, my life before that with my parents, and my life as ATerafin are what bind me to this city. They're what binds this city to *me*.

"I cannot turn my back on any part of it."

"Terafin—"

Meralonne lifted a hand. Wind lifted strands of his hair. "Jewel."

She faced him.

"You are wiser than you know." He bowed; it was deep. "And you are correct."

"Is she?" The Wayelyn asked. His voice was hoarse.

"You are familiar with the skills of the maker-born," Meralonne replied—if it was a reply. He had found his pipe.

Shadow watched him as if he were a particularly odious rodent. Then again, he generally did. "And you have heard—as a bard, there is little way of avoiding it—of the madness and power of the Artisans."

The Wayelyn glanced at Solran before he nodded.

"You may perhaps have heard songs or bardic lays which imply that immortal Artisans were very nearly gods."

The Wayelyn nodded again.

"They were—and will always be—wrong. There has never been an Artisan who was not mortal; nor will there be. Magic—as studied and as it is understood in your Empire—is, and was, a force that could be invoked by all: mortal, immortal, god. It can—and could—be studied; it can—and could—be mastered. But the Artisans of the Hidden Courts were, and will always be, mortal. Among the immortals were craftsmen of great renown; among the firstborn, those who could create items of beauty that outlasted their makers. Those items, were you to see them now, might seem the work of Artisans—and perhaps, to your eyes, there would be no discernible difference.

"But to the eyes of the firstborn, the differences would be immediately obvious." The mage set leaf to pipe as he spoke. "If you are fortunate, you will never have cause to evaluate the difference—but I believe the time for such fortune is passing as we speak.

"The Artisans—and even in the history of the Empire they have been few—are not considered sane by even the makers that shelter them. Yet it is in the hands of dead Artisans that so much of the future now lies. Have you visited Fabril's reach, within the Guild of Makers?"

"No. I am surprised that you have; the maker-born do not welcome outsiders into the heart of their domain."

"I have had reason to venture there." He lit his pipe. "And in future, no doubt, I will visit again. But I digress. I speak of the maker-born because you have seen their work. And I speak of the maker-born because they are, at the height of their power, the closest example to hand. Mortals exist, from birth, for one fate: death. They live to die. No achievement, no power, no worthiness—or lack thereof—can prevent it. You see the distinctions between classes when you traverse the hundred holdings—but it is an arbitrary distinction."

"It is not," Jewel said, her voice much colder than his. "Having lived both lives, APhaniel, I will tell you now you speak from the position of power and privilege."

"Indeed." His smile was sharp, but he was genuinely amused. "Your sensibilities aside, Terafin, I have stated simple fact. A life of comfort is to be preferred to a life of starvation, but neither—comfort nor starvation—changes the inevitable.

"Death is your muse."

"It is *not* mine."

"Is it not? You have so little time, yet you spend much of it attempting to protect those you love from the fate that nonetheless awaits. At best, you extend life by a few decades. At worst, there is no extension. You love ferociously, you love widely, but love—which I am certain you would claim as your motivation—changes nothing. They will die. Every person who walks the streets of the city today, will die. You cannot see it, of course. You cannot see beyond your experience.

"But blind or no, you stand in death's shadow; every minute is borrowed. In that shadow, in a desperation that you cannot even *perceive* when you feel safe or secure, mortals create. What they create might long outlive them—but it is rooted in the subtlety of an existence that is—that will always be—the art of dying.

"And you love fiercely because you can. You create with the whole of your will when will is bent to create. You sing, and we hear in your song what we see in the flowers that gird your gardens: life. It is a life that is celebrated *because* it is brief. It must be watched, because it is otherwise over so swiftly it cannot be experienced by those it cannot otherwise touch.

"The Terafin is not an exception. Should she somehow live up to the song you have issued as challenge, Wayelyn, she will remain unexceptional. She has lived among the dying in the hundred holdings; she has lived among the dying in Terafin. She has lived briefly among the dying in the Southern Dominion.

"She can make this land hers because of the lives she has lived; she is certain of each of them. It is not the experience that defines her ability, but the certainty. Break that in any way, and she will falter."

*   *   *

The Wayelyn and the bardmaster left the grounds at Jewel's side; they did not, however, remain in the manse. They were silent. The Wayelyn was so subdued Jewel almost offered him the services of the Terafin healerie. She understood that the song he'd offered—the song she barely understood—had required the use of his talent, and it had not been short. Bards, like mages—or anyone born with a talent—suffered mage fevers from overexertion.

"With your permission, Terafin, I may request that the recess of the Council meeting last three days."

"My permission is not required," she replied. "But I confess I would be grateful for the time." She hesitated for a long moment, and then exhaled. "The structural changes within *Avantari* were not the only substantive architectural changes upon the Isle."

Solran raised a brow, no more. Meralonne, however, coughed. It was a warning. To whom, Jewel was not certain.

"My own House is in some minor disarray, and as things will, minor will segue into major if I am not to attend to the difficulties—but the Kings have not been entirely patient. With cause," she added. "I am uncertain that the rest of The Ten will find the request as welcome as Terafin does."

"I believe the Kings and the Exalted will," Solran said. "But I am not one of The Ten, and perhaps I am less cautious in voicing opinion than I might otherwise be. Your grounds are magnificent, Terafin." Her glance fell to Shadow, who, aptly named, would not separate himself from Jewel's side.

The Wayelyn offered the bardmaster his arm, which drew a raised brow. She did, however, set her hand upon it.

Only when they were gone did Meralonne speak. Avandar had been speaking, in the privacy of silence, for some five minutes. "I would not have granted him the three days."

"Oh?"

"He will support you. It is my belief that The Ten will support you as well, if not unanimously. The support of The Ten will have some weight with the Kings, if they have not yet made their decision. In like fashion, the decision of the Kings will have grave weight for The Ten. You cede control of the field to the Kings by agreeing to a prolonged recess."

"I cede some control," Jewel agreed. "But if I have three

days, I can pay my respects to Levec at the Houses of Healing. I did not lie to the bardmaster; time is a commodity that I do not have in any abundance."

"Lord Celleriant has not returned."

"No." Nor had Snow, Night, or the Winter King.

"You will require his presence, Terafin. You will require his vigilance. The Wayelyn's song will travel in ways — and to places — you cannot comprehend. You are a threat that the Shining Court could not have foreseen, but you are not yet unassailable."

"Will I ever be?" she asked. The question was almost flippant.

The answer was not. "It is a possibility, Terafin."

She did not ask him what he meant; she knew. "I will visit the Houses of Healing upon the morrow. I will, with Levec's permission, spend some time there." She glanced down the public gallery; it was almost deserted. "And I will spend some time in the office of the right-kin before dinner. Thank you, APhaniel. I do not believe your services will be required."

She spent two hours in Teller's office, perched on the edge of his desk. Finch was at the Merchant Authority, or Jewel would have asked her to join them. She filled her right-kin in on the only events of the day he'd missed, took his reports, and discussed Jarven ATerafin and his demand that he be ceded the open Council chair. In Finch's absence, that discussion was of necessity brief.

"Write to Levec and ask if I may be permitted to visit the Houses of Healing within the next two days," Jewel said, rising. "I have a guest."

"Hectore of Araven."

She glanced at the signet ring that sat so heavily upon her finger and smiled. "Yes. I should cancel the dinner; there is too much that requires time and attention."

He did not speak of Carver or Ellerson; nor did Jewel.

"House Araven is one of the most important of the merchant houses," Teller replied. "But Terafin and Araven have never enjoyed a close relationship. It would be very much to your benefit were that to change in the near future."

"That's not why I want to see him."

"I know."

* * *

Jewel returned to her rooms. The library had not markedly changed; there were no storm clouds upon the horizon of the amethyst skies that opened above it. Shadow, silent, was on the prowl; he did not take to the skies as she left the unaltered portion of the manse that had been her home for over half her life.

Her maid was waiting for her when she reached her rooms. She had selected three possible gowns for the dinner hour, along with three pairs of shoes, and hair ornaments that were sturdy enough to remain in the tangle of Jewel's hair. Jewel selected one of each in near silence, and the woman nodded. She was brisk; she oozed competence.

She did not, however, do so with any warmth or affection.

Amarais had not required it. Amarais, Jewel thought, required exactly what this senior member of the Household Staff now offered. Thinking of Ellerson and his inexplicable absence, Jewel thought she finally understood why. She did not want to become attached to this stiff, cold woman. She did not want to feel the warmth of attachment if it came hand in hand with the bitter pain of its loss.

She allowed her hair to be taken down, to be ironed again, and to be bound; she allowed the woman to help her with the fiddly parts of a dress she didn't like. She allowed her to choose and place ornaments for her hair, to brush her face with faintly scented powder, to carefully clean her hands.

She did not, however, allow her to choose jewelry. Jewel already wore the only two pieces of any significance: the House signet of Terafin, and the House ring of Handernesse, the latter on a long, golden chain around her neck. She wore a bracelet of hair that might be worth more than any piece of jewelry in the Empire, but like the two rings, no money, no power, would persuade her to part from it.

But she thought she would give them up, *all* of them, if they were the price demanded for the return of Carver and Ellerson, den-kin and domicis. She rose when the maid stepped back. She did not declare herself satisfied; she simply retreated to a wall, and stood with her back against it.

Shadow, banished to the same wall, sauntered across the

carpet, no doubt adding years to the wear and tear simply by walking.

"Avandar," she said, for the benefit of the maid, "we will take dinner in my personal dining room."

He bowed. He had a few words to say, but none of the sentiment seeped into his perfectly neutral expression.

It was a bold choice of venue, and Jewel regretted it the moment she left her rooms and found herself in the library. She had not yet entered the informal room in which she and The Terafin had frequently dined, and she therefore couldn't be certain it was still there. She should have chosen a different room. The Terafin manse had a lot of them, many for public entertainment. Any of those rooms were more accessible to the servants than her personal rooms had become.

She looked up at the sky. It was a paler shade of purple. She had yet to see sunlight or moonlight, a sign of beginning or end. No clouds troubled the sky, and she wondered if they ever would. Knew, as the thought flitted past, that they would. That there would be dawn and twilight. She froze.

Shadow butted the space between her shoulders, and she stumbled in a very unpatrician way. She also spoke a few choice words in low Torra, to which Shadow hissed in reply. "Cut it out," she said, again in Torra. "I need to *find* the dining room."

The office—which was now a forbidding stone armory, with a table meant for war, not dinner—had been replaced by a single, freestanding arch made of black iron; she expected the new entrance to the dining room to be similar, if it existed at all. What had she been thinking?

But she knew, as she walked in the direction of the war room's arch. The only place in the Terafin manse where Rath's name had not been forbidden was that small dining room. The only person to whom Jewel had been willing to speak it was The Terafin herself, and The Terafin had summoned her for that purpose. Amarais was Rath's beloved sister. Amarais was Rath's betrayer. She had loved him, as sisters might, and she had left—as any who sought power within The Ten must.

Her only connection with the brother of her childhood and youth was Jewel. They had both loved him, in entirely different ways, and they both grieved at his death.

Hectore of Araven had been Rath's godfather. What Jewel wanted from Hectore was what Amarais had wanted from Jewel: Rath. Memories of Rath that were not her own, because those memories made him real. They made him relevant to someone who was not her.

And did it matter? With the whole of the House hanging upon the Kings, The Ten, with Carver and Ellerson gone, with Celleriant, Snow, Night, and the Winter King likewise silent and absent, could she indulge the melancholy she felt for one dead man? She could justify it, certainly. Hectore of Araven was a wealthy, powerful merchant. His reach was long, and the danger he could present, obvious. As an ally, he was invaluable; none could argue against closer ties with Araven.

She was grasping for justification as she came, at last, to another arch. To her surprise, it was not like the arches that led to the manse or the war room; it was far too simple for that. On first glance, it seemed a very quaint gate of the type that would grace small homes, and small plots: it was wooden, with simple hinges, and it reached Jewel's shoulders, no more. It hung on a thick beam that was unadorned in every way.

"This?" Avandar asked.

She nodded.

"If you will wait," he said, making of the request a command, "I will inform your maid of its location." Before she could reply, he added, "The Master of the Household Staff will require at least that much information; she will not receive it immediately if you insist upon entering that room—if it leads to a room—without me, because I will not convey the message."

She waited. She would rather face demonic assassins every morning over breakfast than an angry—well, angrier—Master of the Household Staff. But when Avandar returned, she swung the gate open and entered the room first. Shadow was by her side, close enough that he could easily step on her skirt. He did.

When Hectore of Araven entered the foyer of the Terafin manse, he was surprised to see The Terafin herself waiting for him. She was not, of course, alone, but in no other manse in the world would her attendant have been a sleek and very dangerous large cat. He was gray, winged, and unfortunately fanged; those fangs caught rather more of the chandelier light than ideal.

The Chosen, of course, were also present, but Hectore was more than capable of ignoring them as part of the scenery or the architecture; he was likewise fully capable of disregarding the domicis who stood farther back. Even in meetings considered completely private, she would not divest herself of the latter. Hectore was not a close personal friend; nor was he a trusted ally. He would have been surprised, and possibly unnecessarily suspicious, had she appeared without them.

Andrei immediately took a step back, to occupy the theoretically invisible space to his master's left. Although Araven did employ House Guards, they were purely for show, and if Hectore would have felt discomfited to greet The Terafin shorn of her Chosen and her servants, he had no compunctions about presenting himself in a way that implied both trust and vulnerability. He was not, cat aside, afraid of this girl.

He tendered The Terafin a bow that implied healthy respect, a sign of caution. He then offered her his arm. She placed her hand upon it; it was not entirely steady. So, he made her nervous, did he? He smiled.

"I am filled with gratitude," he told her, as she led him to the staircase that was the visual center of the foyer, "that you have taken the time to dine with me; I am aware that you are much in demand at the moment."

She lifted a brow and he chuckled. "My right-kin insists," she replied, "that I eat. And if I am to fulfill that responsibility, I see no reason to do so in isolation." She hesitated. He marked it. "You might be unaware of some of the architectural changes—within my own manse—that have occurred since I took power."

Interesting. "I am impressed that you have had the time, Terafin. You make me feel every year of my age."

She hesitated again. The hesitations were slight; in a larger group, they might have passed beneath his notice. They walked in silence up a considerable number of stairs, and from there, down a hall that was wide enough to be public. The hall itself, with the exception of the Chosen stationed at double doors, was empty, excluding present company. The walls were adorned with paintings, all of figures, all historical rulers of the House this young woman currently called her own.

The Chosen stepped aside. They saluted The Terafin, but did not otherwise speak. She did, and the doors rolled open. Hand still upon Hectore's arm, The Terafin stepped through the opened doors; Hectore came with her.

"This," she said, speaking softly, "is my library."

Hectore was, for a moment, speechless. He stood beneath a ceiling of amethyst which looked, to his eye, to be *sky*. He saw trees in the distance, and as his eyes accustomed themselves to the brilliance of the light, saw that shelves grew from them, in neat and even rows, as if they were simply branches. The floor beneath his feet was the only thing in the room that appeared normal, although it was pale in color.

"I hope," he said, as he found his voice, "that I have not been gaping."

"You have not," was her grave reply.

It was impossible, as he stood in this room, not to feel dwarfed. He could barely see wall, and at that, only in one direction. Nor was it an interior wall. He lowered his arm, and she withdrew her hand.

"Can that possibly be sky?" he asked.

In answer, the great, gray cat leaped, wings spreading in a snap of motion. He rose, becoming smaller and smaller as Hectore watched. "Architectural changes?" he asked, and then, when she failed to answer, he laughed.

He might have continued to do so, but his gaze fell upon Andrei.

Andrei was pale and still; it was exactly the wrong sort of stillness. "Are we in any danger, Terafin?" he asked, sobering.

"Not at present."

"And were we, would you have warning?"

"Yes. It would not be a subtle warning; some of my servants are incapable of subtlety." She glanced, briefly, at the sky.

"Are we then to picnic in your library?"

"No, Patris Araven; I believe the entire House Council would frown—severely—on so informal a meal with such an illustrious guest. Please, follow me."

Andrei's utter silence reminded Hectore of why he had come. Had it not, the existence of this place, this *library*, would have. The Terafin had, indirectly, been linked to the fate of those felled by the sleeping sickness. That sickness had taken from Hectore a beloved grandchild. Had he been inclined to dismiss the connection—a connection Andrei considered tenuous—this visit would have destroyed the inclination in its entirety.

Hectore had survived a tumultuous life, sometimes with difficulty. He had learned, at an early age, to trust his instincts; they were all but shouting now. But they were shouting at cross purposes. This young woman—and to Hectore, she was young—he liked. She had the polish of the patriciate, but it did not come easily to her; she labored under its dictates, the way one might labor to speak clearly in a language other than one's mother tongue.

He did not believe she would knowingly be responsible for his granddaughter's death.

But this *library*, as she had called it, was in its entirety a thing beyond Hectore's vast experience. He was, by nature, a gambler—as most merchants must be at heart. He would have bet a large amount of his vast, personal fortune that this library was also beyond her experience. He had ties, after all, to the Guild of Makers, and he had, twice, seen the interior of Fabril's reach. He had seen things made, things crafted, by people whose link to sanity was tenuous on a slow day—and nonexistent, otherwise—and he had seen the results of their glorious, disturbing madness.

He had seen nothing to compare to this. The trees here grew *shelves*. The ceiling was *sky*, and at that, a sky under which no mortals labored. Only the floors beneath his feet had the solidity of the mundane. He did not doubt that death could be found in the stacks here. Nor did he doubt that knowledge was tucked across its vast shelves. What he doubted, as he glanced at The Terafin, was that *she* could contain it.

"You were raised in the hundred?" he asked, as he walked, her hand on his arm.

She nodded. He doubted that she'd noted the effort it took to ignore the absolute grandeur of her personal "rooms." But he wondered, as he followed her lead, his arm once again anchored by her hand, why she had chosen to bring him here. She could not entertain here often; had she, the whole of *Averalaan Aramarelas* would be buzzing with hushed gossip. Hectore did not often condescend to gossip, but he was human; he listened when gossip was offered.

He glanced at Andrei, and frowned. Andrei was the perfect servant. Araven's fortune not only allowed for the hire of such perfection, it demanded it. Tonight, for the first time in living memory, Andrei did not exude the cultured aura of invisibility as he walked to Hectore's left. The whole of Andrei's attention was focused, not on Hectore, but on the room itself, as if at any time he expected attack or ambush.

Andrei was fully capable of dealing with assassins. He was capable of dealing with the unfortunate bandits that cropped up along more isolated roads in a dry season, when the threat of starvation made the lure of banditry appealing. He handled both as if he were pressing shirts. Tonight, he expected a different class of threat. It was almost embarrassing.

"Andrei," Hectore said, the tone of the single word a command.

Andrei glanced at his master.

"My apologies, Terafin," Hectore said. "We are unaccustomed to grandeur of this nature. It is breathtaking."

"And intimidating?"

"And that." He chuckled. "You do not entertain here often."

"No."

"Why did you choose to honor Araven in such a fashion?"

"Truthfully?"

"We are both merchants, Terafin."

She did laugh, then. It was a rueful laugh, but warm with genuine amusement. In answer, she reached for a slender chain she wore around her neck; she pulled it up, out of the folds of her very correct dress. In the light of bright, violet day he could see the ring that weighted the chain down. It was the signet of Handernesse.

"Did you know her, when she was not ATerafin?"

Hectore considered dissembling. He chose against it. "Yes, Terafin. I first met her as a babe in arms. She had a considerable voice, at that age, to her father's consternation."

The Terafin's smile deepened. "I do not think I ever heard her raise voice—not in that way."

"No. By the time she was four years of age, she had mastered that much control."

They came, as they spoke, to a gate so simple it would not be considered appropriate for even the Araven sheds. It was rough, and it appeared to be freestanding. Yet it did not look entirely out of place, for all that. "Was she an indulged child?" She rested her right hand upon the top of the gate.

"She was shamelessly indulged. Her grandfather adored her. It was entirely because of her grandfather that she was allowed to learn from the swordmaster hired for Ararath's education. Her mother did not approve."

She pushed the gate open, and took a step through it; Hectore lowered his arm, as the gate was not wide enough to allow two to enter with any grace. He watched as she vanished from sight in the blink of an eye. He glanced at Andrei.

Andrei offered a controlled nod in response, no more. He was extremely wary, as was Hectore, but he did not expect treachery. And would treachery be necessary, Hectore wondered, as he lifted his face to the open skies, wondering what flew at their heights.

Chapter Twenty

THE ROOM into which Hectore stepped was not large. Nor was it—as one might expect from the gate—an undistinguished mudroom. The floors were of a much darker wood, the planks narrower; they gleamed where they could be seen beneath the deep blue of the rug. There were two standing hutches against the far wall, and a long, wide sideboard; there was a small chandelier that, lit, echoed some of the glory of the chandelier that ruled the manse's foyer. It hung suspended above a rectangular table that was a shade lighter than the floor.

It was a small table; it might, in a pinch, seat eight—if they were slender. Tonight, it was meant to seat two. The Terafin's domicis was waiting by the sideboard; Andrei chose to occupy the wall nearest the exit—which was, on this side, a door, adorned at its height by a simple, double-edged sword.

"Please," The Terafin said, "Join me."

"This *is* informal," he replied. "I feel honored."

"And suspicious?"

He chuckled. "I prefer the word cautious, Terafin." He sat. The domicis offered both water and wine. Hectore chose the wine. The Terafin joined him, although she did not drink.

"Perhaps this is unwise," she said. "You said, when you appeared in the office of my right-kin, that you had matters of trade you wished to discuss. I am not adverse to being part of such a discussion, but such a discussion would be best undertaken in the Merchant Authority."

"You've been speaking with Jarven."

"I have not," she said, with a grimace, "but it isn't necessary; I know what he would say. You must, as well."

He inclined his head. "He would not, of course, approve of this meeting; he would strongly disapprove of any discussions of substance to which he was not a party." She did not bridle; she did not immediately claim that his approval or disapproval was beneath concern.

"You said that you had not come to speak of your godson."

"Not upon my arrival, no."

"You cannot have thought me so inexperienced that you could, without consequence, go above Jarven's head to discuss matters of trade."

He raised a gray brow. To be fair, the thought had not crossed his mind. He waited, interested in spite of himself.

"What, then, brought you to Terafin directly?"

Ah. "Tonight, Terafin, my godson."

"And yesterday?"

He let the smile fall away from his expression; he could not be certain what was left on his face. "The sleepers," he said abruptly.

This was not, clearly, the answer she had expected. "Your pardon, Patris Araven—"

"Hectore."

"Hectore, then. Did you say the sleepers?" Her face had lost color.

"Those who have been felled," he said, clarifying the word, "by the sleeping sickness."

She relaxed, exhaling sharply. She was not a woman to whom the careful neutrality of a born patrician came naturally, if at all. He wondered what she feared. "Someone you know sleeps?"

"Someone I knew," he replied. "My granddaughter. She did not survive."

She flinched. "My condolences," she said softly. "What brought you to Terafin?"

"I spent as much time by my granddaughter's side as I could. Given Levec, that was precious little. He is the most territorial, obdurate man it has been my displeasure to deal with."

Bread arrived, and with it, narrow slices of fish, laid against leaves and decorated by a drizzle of some sauce Hectore could not name without tasting it. He was not, at the moment, greatly interested in eating.

"I chose to entrust the care of my granddaughter to the Houses of Healing. It was only in Levec's care that any of the sleepers awakened at all."

She stiffened, but ate; Hectore joined her, aware that he did injustice to the Terafin kitchens tonight.

"I was allowed—barely—to sit; to give my granddaughter water and broth. I spent more time in the Houses of Healing than one not healer-born, and I noticed something strange, Terafin."

"Adam." She surprised him.

"Adam, indeed. He seemed an unschooled boy, to my eye; imagine my surprise when he informed me that he was resident within the Terafin manse upon the Isle. You will not dissemble."

"Say rather that I will not insult your intelligence. Adam is kin to me. I do not value him as a healer, but as a younger brother." She offered a warning.

"Your Adam could wake the sleepers. They did not wake when he was not upon the premises. I did not," he added, "question Levec about him; I do not think Levec would have allowed me anywhere near his domain had the boy's name left my lips. And I understand Levec's caution. To Levec, all healers are in dire need of protection against the demands and the predations of the powerful and the moneyed."

"He is not wrong."

"No, sadly, he is not. I mean no harm to your boy; I have discussed him with no others."

She glanced pointedly at Andrei. Hectore raised a brow in genuine surprise. "Andrei is my servant, and in all ways that matter, he is domicis, and bound to me for life."

"He is not domicis."

"No. And I will not speak of him as if he were a third party in whom I had only a passing interest."

She lifted a wineglass; Hectore did likewise, wine being more to his liking at the moment than the food. "You came to speak to me of Adam?"

"No. I came to speak to you of the sleepers, and in particular, of their deaths."

She set the glass down. Burgundy light played across the fingers of her unsteady hand. "When did she die?"

"On the sixteenth day of Henden." Hectore could be charming. He could be avuncular. But he could, on occasion, be far, far grimmer than passing acquaintance implied.

She exhaled. "I was not responsible for your granddaughter's death." She spoke with certainty. Too much certainty. Andrei stepped away from the wall, approaching the table with the quiet deference and grace of the highest class of servant.

So, too, did the domicis.

"What, then, was responsible for it?" he asked.

She was silent.

"Terafin, allow me to make myself clear—"

"You have made yourself clear, Patris Araven. Spare us both your descent into threats, veiled or otherwise. If it is vengeance—"

"It is *justice*."

"Even so. If it is justice you seek, you will not find it."

He lifted his glass. "You speak with certainty."

She nodded.

"And without surprise. Do you find it so easy to believe that I am here for my stated reasons?"

"It did not occur to me to disbelieve you."

She meant it. "Your predecessor would, of course, maintain the polite fiction of belief; she would not have believed it."

"Of you? Although she had known you since she was a child? I think you underestimate her."

He offered her a genuine smile—the first. "She was not a woman it was wise to underestimate, but in this, I believe I am correct. She would attempt, of course, to discern the truth, to see what lay beyond the simple, sentimental cloak. She would look for strategy."

"I was not raised in the same elevated circles to which she was born," Jewel replied. "I was raised, in large part, by my Oma—a woman who would have come here for just such a purpose, and would not have been easily dissuaded. If at all. Am I correct in assuming that you believed I had some hand in the death of your granddaughter?"

"I entertained it as a possibility."

"May I ask why?"

Andrei cleared his throat. Hectore grimaced. "I note that your domicis is full capable of remaining neutral in such a discussion."

The Terafin snorted.

Hectore laughed. He laughed, and he once again resumed eating. "The sleepers, to my knowledge, woke twice of their own accord. Each time they did so, they spoke of a shared dream. It was clear to me that although their accounts differed, they differed because they did not have the words to describe what they had seen. But their dreams and the events at The Terafin's funeral were, to my mind, connected. The Order of Knowledge is concerned about both your secrecy and your existence. It is rumored that the Kings themselves, and their *Astari*, are likewise concerned."

"More than a rumor, I'm afraid. They are."

"Ah. It would seem, to the untutored eye, that you are at the heart of a storm—a storm into which my innocent granddaughter was swept. She did not survive. Tell me, then, that it was not a storm of your making."

"It was not. It is my hope, within the next three days, that the sleepers will waken, and that their sleep from this point on will be natural."

"Too late for my grandchild."

She closed her eyes. "Yes. I am sorry."

"Very well, Terafin. I have seen your . . . library. I have seen the giant, winged beast you call a cat. I have heard the song the Senniel bards have been singing at every available venue. I do not consider that wise, by the way."

"I like it even less than you."

"It is clear to me that you have information that I lack. You are not a callow child; you are The Terafin. I am willing to offer certain considerations in exchange for that information."

"And those considerations?"

"They are not to be easily codified, of course. You will, by informing me, put me in your debt. I will owe you a favor." He glanced, briefly, at Andrei. He had not retreated to the wall, but he was no longer attempting to offer unsubtle criticism; he was watching The Terafin intently, his eyes slightly narrowed, his posture disturbing.

"What information?" she asked.

"Who was responsible for the death of my grandchild? The illness was not a natural one, in both my opinion and the endless, bickering opinions of the mages who happened to linger like vultures within the healerie."

"Patris Araven—"

"Hectore."

"Hectore. If I were to tell you that gods were responsible for your granddaughter's death, how then would you proceed?"

"If you were to tell me that gods were, indeed responsible, and if you were to name them?"

She nodded.

"I would do all within my power to beggar their churches within the Empire. And beyond it."

Her brows rose; he had surprised her. He had not surprised Andrei, but then again, little did.

"Perhaps that was a bad example. If I were to tell you that the water, the wind, or a similar elemental force was to blame, would you then attempt to destroy the ocean?"

"No. I do what is within my means, no more. But I will not allow you to decide that something is beyond my means. I have heard," he said, when she did not immediately reply, "that you have been targeted by an unfortunate number of assassins since you were acclaimed as Terafin."

"I would consider *one* to be an unfortunate number," she replied. "But I will not deny it."

"I have also heard that some of these assassins were not human."

"Given the debacle at the planned victory parade, I will not even question your sources. It is true."

Jewel. Be cautious.

"The collection—of both inhuman and very human assassins—implies something to a man of my means."

"And that?"

"There is a blend of mortal and immortal interests. The mortal assassins were not merely conjured and sent to die at the hands of your Chosen. They were approached and they were paid. They were not paid in empty, elemental promises, I assure you."

"Can you?"

Andrei would, Hectore had no doubt, be tight-lipped

and rigid for the next three days at the contents of this discussion. "I can. You are The Terafin. Your House and the politics of its position are something I understand almost intimately. It is clear that unnatural forces are interested in those politics, but they are playing a portion of their game in an arena of which I am master.

"Give me information, Terafin. I will put my considerable resources toward locating your hidden enemies. I will, if they can be found, beggar them in my ire."

She was silent for a long moment. When she lifted her chin, she looked troubled, to Hectore's eye. "I would appreciate your help, Hectore. I would appreciate it more than I can adequately say; I have heard rumors that you've bested Jarven in his own games at the height of his power."

Before he could answer, she lifted a hand. "Let them remain rumors. I have had some difficulty with Jarven in recent weeks, and it has not yet drawn to a satisfactory close for either of us; he will, no doubt, be annoyed with your presence in my personal chambers.

"Let me repeat myself: I would appreciate your help, and the indirect access to your considerable, and unnamed, resources. But I will not have you offer that aid under false pretenses. You grieve for your grandchild—and I admire and respect that; it is rare, among the patriciate. But I do not think you addled with grief, and I will not condescend to use that grief for my own purposes."

He smiled. He had to smile; there was something in the girl that reminded him much of her predecessor in her youth. "You must learn," he said, as if he was speaking to that girl, and not the woman who ruled House Terafin, "to align your needs with the needs of those who might be of use to you. If you choose to use my rage, it will, in the end, benefit us both."

Andrei cleared his throat.

Hectore looked pained. He was; he simply allowed his annoyance to show. "Andrei. Note the remarkable restraint shown by The Terafin's domicis." He did not look at his servant. Nor did Andrei speak, although the clearing of throat implied that he might, which would be its own class of disaster. It was not a disaster that the current Terafin would find offensive, in his estimation.

"I am not certain that the forces that robbed you of your

granddaughter are aligned with the forces that conspire against me in such obvious—and public—ways."

"Are you not?"

She inhaled. Exhaled. "Have you heard of the Warden of Dreams?"

He frowned. "Andrei, have I?"

"Perhaps in your youth."

"You are familiar with the title."

"I am, Patris." He came into view of the table. "You claim that Patris Araven lost a grandchild to the machinations of the Warden of Dreams?"

The Terafin nodded gravely, as if she were entirely accustomed to answering the questions posed her by impertinent servants. "I do not understand how, but the Warden of Dream derives power from those who dream. The sleepers across the city—and on the Isle—were caught in a web of his making."

"If that were the case, why have we not seen similar, historical outbreaks?"

"Perhaps we have; records were not always closely kept during the reign of the Blood Barons."

"And so we might have seen such an epidemic some five centuries in the past, or more?"

She pursed her lips. "I do not know. I admit that I have not done the research that you appear to have done; I was—and am—concerned with the present. I do not believe that the Warden of Dreams is entirely allied with the Lord of the Hells." She did not speak the god's name.

Andrei continued to speak, glancing once at Hectore, who nodded. "Not entirely allied, or not allied at all? They are, as you must be aware, different statements."

"The Warden of Dreams is not one entity, but two."

"Nightmare and Dream."

Her brows rose. She glanced at her own domicis, but thought better of drawing him into the conversation that Andrei should have had the bearing to likewise avoid. "Yes."

Andrei's expression was made harsher by the light from above. "The power was gathered in order to allow some attack to be made during The Terafin's funeral." It was not a question.

The Terafin nodded slowly. "That is my understanding—

but my understanding is a superficial thing. I understand the effects of a storm, without understanding the events that bring a storm into being. I use utensils such as these," she continued, lifting a fork, "every day, but I cannot tell you how the metals that comprise them are extracted from the mines in which they are found. I can you tell you they *are*; I can act on that fact.

"I do not think that death was the desired end of the entrapment. I do not think he considered it at all; it is no part of his dominion. And I do not think it possible to be avenged against him; I am not even certain how you would try."

"Do you have some guess as to how you would?"

She blinked as Hectore entered the conversation. "No." She glanced at her wrist, and then back. "I can hate the Lord of the Hells," she said. "I can devote my life—and everything that entails—to fighting him. But it isn't personal. He is a god. I'm not. I'm so far beneath his notice I might capture his attention for a few seconds, the way birdsong captures ours. I would feel relief if he was destroyed, but . . ."

"But no personal satisfaction."

She closed her eyes. "I remember the Henden of 410. But even so, no."

"And this Warden is like a god, to you?"

"Or like the Wild Hunt. He is not like my cats." She paused. "And yet, to you, he must be."

"Very well. This is excellent wine. You are not entirely open, and that is perhaps as it should be. I have promised my daughter that I will see her daughter avenged, and I have made a reputation as a man who lives up to—or perhaps down to—his vows. Your own satisfaction, your own sense of the personal, matters little to me. Andrei's words have a weight for me that yours have not yet achieved. The power that was gathered was meant to be used on the first day of The Terafin's funeral rites. It was meant to be brought to bear upon the powerful and noteworthy; it was meant to encompass even the Kings.

"That it did not, in the end, was due in large part to your interference—an interference that cannot be explained to anyone's satisfaction by the Order of Knowledge or the god-born. The sons of Teos will not answer questions about the event; I know. I have tried to ask them. Do you understand your interference in any greater detail than you understand your fork?"

Her brows rose; her lips turned up in an unexpected—and possibly unwanted—smile. Only a fool would clearly announce ignorance about such a gallingly unexpected power. She was not—quite—a fool. "Certainly more than that."

"Everyone who comes to a negotiation of any difficulty brings to the table his or her own motives, desires, and concessions. I have perhaps been more open than my *servant* would like; I have made clear what my desire and my motivations are. You are uncertain that my desires will be satisfied should I choose to ally myself with you—and I should use that uncertainty to my advantage in our negotiations. But as you have been so disarmingly *honest*, I will not.

"My enemy has an interest in your House. He has an interest in you. He has an interest in the death of the Kings—and no man of any sanity wants that. If I cannot kill this Warden, if I cannot damage him upon his own ground, I *can* damage him in other ways."

"The Warden—"

"The Warden served interests that were not his own. You may be uncertain; I am not."

The Terafin fell silent as the next course was delivered. It was a soup, in a low, flat bowl, from which steam rose.

"These dishes are enchanted?" Hectore asked.

"To preserve heat. If the soup is poisoned," she added, smiling, "the dishes will either crack or discolor."

"Which?"

"In this case, they will crack. We will apologize for the inferiority of our dishes, and we will clear them. It is not for the latter property that they're used here; my rooms are as far from the kitchens as it's possible to get while still remaining within the same building."

"And are we?"

"In the same building? Yes." Her expression hardened as she lifted a spoon. "What would you have of me, then? I can tell you of my encounters with the Warden and the dreamers. Of necessity, my explanations will be lacking; I am not a member of the Order of Knowledge, and I am not considered particularly learned."

"I would, at the minimum, require that information," Hectore replied, lifting his own spoon. The soup was hot. "I would not limit myself to that information, however. You spoke of the public assassination attempt. It was not clear that the creature that made its attack during the victory parade was there for you; it is assumed in many circles that it meant to kill the Kings."

"That may well have been some part of the demon's mission," she replied. "Demons were sent to *Avantari* during the funeral." She hesitated again. "I'm not good at negotiating without objective measures. I have no way of assessing the value of the information I provide; I have no way of assessing the value of the aid you offer. To be honest—"

"A phrase generally used when honesty is not offered."

She grimaced. "Not by me. I can't see how the information I might provide will be of any practical use to you at all."

"No. You have your own information networks. You are aware of the nature of the assassins sent against you; I am not. But as I pointed out, the assassins are paid. Even the most expensive and elusive of assassins require a fee, and the fee is not conjured by magic. Nor is the sum of money inconsiderable. Have you tracked down possible sources?"

"Only a few, and those possible sources are not, I'm afraid, on the table."

They must, in her estimation, be internal.

"I would be comfortable having this conversation in the Merchant Authority," she said.

"The Merchant Authority over which Jarven presides?"

"The same. It's not for Jarven's sake, but my own. One of the junior members of my House Council has worked under his auspices for years. If we are to reach any solid agreement, I want her there."

"You refer to Finch ATerafin?"

The Terafin nodded.

"And you would expect any dealings between our two Houses to go through Finch?"

"If that's acceptable to you, yes."

"May I ask why?"

"We came from the same place. I don't trust Jarven the way I trust Finch."

"If you've any sense, you won't trust him at all."

She smiled. "Amarais trusted him."

"Amarais was content to let him run loose, secure in the knowledge that *most* of the damage he caused was aimed outward. Very well. Finch, then."

The Terafin fell silent again. Then she looked across the table and said, "Tell me about your godson."

"Ararath?"

"I called him Rath. Some of the information I have goes all the way back to our first meeting." She lifted the chain that hung around her neck, and exposed the Handernesse signet to the light. "Amarais left this for me; I believe it was Rath's."

"It was not Ararath's."

"He was wearing it when he died."

"How did he die?"

"Demons." There was no doubt at all in her voice.

"When?"

"Just before I came to the Terafin manse. Sixteen years ago, maybe seventeen. You must have known some of what he was involved in," she added.

"I assure you he did not discuss his business with me."

"No?" She looked pointedly at Andrei. "Avandar," she said, her gaze still fixed on Hectore's servant, "Please, set a third place at the table, and inform the kitchen."

Andrei glanced at Hectore, who sighed. "Very well. But I will remind you that I am speaking with The Terafin, and preservation of my dignity is therefore a necessity. This is Andrei. He has been with me for decades; he is only slightly less necessary to my household than my cooks."

"You came to save Rath," she said to Andrei.

"That was the result of my meeting with Ararath; it was not my intent. But, yes, Terafin, the enemies that he had inadvertently gained showed considerable power. You were unexpected. I believe your interference was responsible for saving his life that night; had you not arrived, I would have arrived too late. You are seer-born?"

"I am. The powers of the seer-born in story are greatly exaggerated. You came prepared for magical difficulty."

Andrei said nothing.

The Terafin accepted this. "At that time, a merchant—Patris AMatie—was involved. He had shown a great interest in artifacts that Rath had collected. He was not without power, and not without countenance. His merchant concerns were both genuine and legitimate. We assume that funding—for assassins, for intelligence—comes from similar sources."

"But you are not aware of who those genuine and legitimate sources are." It was not a question. "Patris AMatie was a shrewd and somewhat ruthless businessman. He disappeared."

"Yes. His concerns were absorbed by his patron, Lord Cordufar."

It had been years since Hectore had heard that name. "The last time I saw my godson alive," he said quietly, "was the night of the last Cordufar ball. I received no further word from him, and I am aware of the eventual fate of the Cordufar family and its manse. Were you aware, at the time, that Ararath had dealings with the Cordufar family?"

"No. I was aware of almost nothing, at the time. Rath did his best not to involve me in his personal business; I remained ignorant until some of that business arrived in my home in the twenty-fifth holding. He'd left one letter for me, and it brought me here."

"You feel Ararath's death is connected, in the end, to your assassins."

"I feel, in the end, that everything is connected. The events in Cordufar, Rath's death, the slow rumbling of the war in the South—which was only tenuously concluded in our favor. Meralonne feels it a staying action, not a decisive victory. The Terafin's death. The events at The Terafin's funeral. Even the sleeping sickness. I've spent over half my life involved peripherally with the plans of demons and those who've summoned them.

"Even the ascension to the House Seat did not decrease that involvement; I think nothing short of death would do so. My death," she added. "The plans themselves will continue."

"Give Andrei the specifics of the attempts against you, if you are willing to trust us that far. And tell me how you came by that ring."

"Amarais left it for me. I believe she came by the ring honestly; it was still on Rath's body when what was left of that body came to the Terafin manse. He arrived the same day I did." She closed her eyes briefly. "I have the sword he was given by his grandfather. I have almost nothing else of him.

"But without Rath, I would not now be The Terafin."

"No." They ate in silence for several minutes. Andrei joined them mid-course.

"Andrei, what do you know of demons?"

"Not more than the Guildmaster of the Order of Knowledge."

"And not less?"

He didn't answer. But when dinner was brought, he said, "Hectore, you meddle in things you do not understand."

"I don't need to understand them; that's why I pay you." He concentrated on the food in front of him as he considered what he had offered The Terafin. She was quiet, stiff. He understood that the conversation had taken several turns she had not expected; the visit itself had thoroughly unsettled Hectore. He wished to spend some of his time in the library, perusing its vast shelves; he did not ask. Instead, displaying the patience which he'd learned, at some cost in his youth, to cultivate, he began to speak of his godson.

And his godson's sister.

She fell silent, listening; her face lost its brittle neutrality. He was a capable conversationalist, and in truth, speaking about Ararath was no burden: he had loved the boy almost as a son, and he understood that her interest in Ararath was all but a child's interest in the life of a parent—one lost to death, early. She laughed several times—an open laugh that robbed her of years and necessary dignity; nor did she remain silent. She offered Hectore proof that the Ararath he knew and the Rath who had rescued her were connected by recognizable character traits.

When the dinner drew to a close—and at a far later hour than was Hectore's norm—he rose. "When you have more time, Terafin, I would love to peruse your library, if it is at all possible; I would also like to visit your grounds. At the moment, an invitation to do so would elevate me above my peers and increase my consequence."

She laughed. She had an open laugh that was in no way delicate. "Would you actually care?"

"About the grounds, yes. About the consequence, as you have divined, no. I have reached a position in life in which, absent severe catastrophe, I can ignore such things in safety."

"I haven't," was her rueful reply.

"No. If I desire it, I may gain the ear of almost any of The Ten just by asking. But you have entered the loftiest of social circles, and every movement you make, every dress you wear, every word you utter, will be examined and judged. In time, Terafin, you will grow accustomed to this."

She smiled; the smile made her look altogether too fragile. The fact that the appearance of fragility was entirely unconscious on her part was unfortunate, but he understood why: Ararath had built a bridge between them. Nor was she, in truth, fragile; had she been, her reign would have been measured in days. He understood why she had succeeded Amarais. After The Terafin's funeral, the House Council had little choice. She spoke with the voice of command, and it was a command that not even the Kings could utter with an expectation of obedience.

Any patrician of any consequence whatsoever had heard her words. Against this public display of her disturbing authority, any sane ambitions must give way. Yet she did not understand this herself; that much was evident. Nor did she completely understand the awe her winged cats inspired.

"Ararath would be proud of you," he told her, as he turned toward the doors.

Her smile was almost heartbreaking. "He wouldn't."

"Believe that he would."

"He despised the patriciate. And he hated Terafin above all, for what it cost him and his family."

"Yet in his moment of desperation, he sent you to the sister who abandoned Handernesse and achieved so much outside of its bounds. He might have sent you to *me*."

Her smile deepened. "And would you have opened Araven and its resources to my den?"

"Jewel—if I may be permitted the impertinence of your name—understand that Amarais did not do so purely out of the goodness of her heart. I will allow for the possibility of sentiment, although she was not prone to act upon it in her later years. She understood what you were. Housing a handful of undemanding urchins in return for the only known seer in the Empire was a bargain. I would have done the same, but sadly, a godfather is not a beloved and resented older sister."

"She would have welcomed him," The Terafin said, in the softest of voices. "She would have opened her doors to him."

"Yes," Hectore replied. "That is the tragedy. Ararath had a ferocious and almost unequaled pride. You were the closest he could come to either apology or forgiveness. Do not, in your time, let pride become a wall without windows or doors.

"I must thank you for this dinner. I saw little of my godson in his later years—and not for lack of trying on my part. He cut all ties with Handernesse; he made no attempt to create a family of his own—until you. You were his child, Jewel. What I could not do for Ararath, in the end, I will do—in his name—for you."

"He would not—"

"No, of course not. He loved his sister to the end and could not force himself to reach out to her; he asked almost nothing of me. But it is true that we often desire to give to those who will ask for nothing, especially when they take all burdens upon their own shoulders. What I could not do for your Rath, I will do for you. He would, I think, be gratified." He lifted a hand before she could speak again. "I am an old man, now."

Andrei coughed.

"An old man with a servant who appears to have taken poorly to the chill. I enjoy a position among the Houses that few reach, and I have maintained that position for over a decade. Let me put it to use; if I can, I will have justified lean decades of effort. Let me fancy, in so doing, that you will be my godson's daughter when we are together."

She hesitated. She *bit her lip*. Hectore stole a glance at her domicis, and was highly amused at the rigidity of that man's expression. "I'd like you to meet my den," she said, as if she were still a child of the holdings. She closed her eyes, and added, "My kin."

"I will. I will make an appointment to speak with Finch ATerafin at her earliest convenience. Do you wish to be present for the first of our meetings?"

"If I can," she replied. "I will see you out," she added, as he offered her an arm.

He had not lied to her: he intended to devote his attention to the difficulties she faced, where it was possible to do so. He expected Andrei to argue against such interference. But he felt, this eve, his many failures: the failure to protect his granddaughter, and by so doing, to shield his daughter from the pain of grief and loss; his failure to succor his difficult, proud godson. In truth, given his suspicions, he had not expected to *like* The Terafin. On the day of the funeral she had been unapproachable; everything about her had been so perfect, so utterly rigid, she seemed above the foible and folly of simply being mortal.

But he knew, having met and conversed with her in such an intimate, familial way, that she would, without thought, throw herself against the Warden of Dreams to save even the lowliest of citizens. His granddaughter would have been safe in her hands.

It was a luxury to wake in the morning in her own bed without facing the prospect of a full Council of The Ten, which made rising and dressing an act of war. The Kings had not, as of late last evening, demanded her presence. She had had an almost entirely self-indulgent dinner with a man who knew most of the details of Rath's early life—a man who had come to visit because of the loss of a beloved grandchild. She *liked* Hectore.

Far, far too much for such a short acquaintance, and far too openly.

"Good morning, Avandar." She crawled out from under Shadow's wing; it lay across the whole of her upper body. "You," she said, attempting to push him out of the bed, and having the luck she usually did, "have to go visit Ariel."

Shadow rolled his great, golden eyes and leaped surprisingly lightly to the carpeted floor. He headed toward the door, which opened to allow him to leave.

"Has Barston sent up today's schedule?"

"He has. You have a meeting with Levec after the late lunch hour—at the Houses of Healing. I've taken the liberty of informing Adam." Avandar laid out the dress she was to wear for the day, and she grimaced.

"I'm not meeting Kings," she said, "only an irritable bear of a healer."

"You are The Terafin," a familiar voice interjected. "You are expected to dress as if you *are* a royal."

"Good morning, Haval." Judging from his expression, it wasn't going to remain that way. She accepted Avandar's choice, and dressed quickly.

The dressmaker inclined his head.

"Stay with Hannerle this afternoon?" she asked, as she sat before her mirror. The maidservant was waiting, brush in hand. Beside it, heating, were irons.

"Do you believe she will wake?"

"I have hopes that she'll wake and stay that way."

Haval's brow rose. Nothing else about his expression changed—but Haval could be dying of an excess of joy without giving any of it away. As if to bolster this assessment, he said, "Rumor has it that you spent last evening with Hectore of Araven in your personal quarters."

"I did."

"You are aware that Hectore is one of a scant handful of people who have bested Jarven at his own game?"

"I am. Hectore implied that it was not the only outcome when they clashed."

"Indeed, it was not. What did Patris Araven come here to discuss?"

"His granddaughter, and his godson."

"His godson would be Ararath of Handernesse."

". . . Yes."

"Was there a reason—beyond the obviously sentimental—that you chose to entertain Patris Araven in your personal chambers?"

Clearly not a good one, in Haval's opinion. "Haval, eventually people are going to have to know. I intend to use these rooms as my predecessor did, while it is safe to do so."

"And you considered it safe to do so? With Patris Araven?"

"Tell me why you feel this was the wrong decision."

"Patris Araven is known for his sentimentality. In most men of power, it would be a remarkable failing; that it is not is due in no small part to his cunning. He *is* a threat. How much of your personal quarters did he see?"

"He saw the library—there's no way to reach the dining chamber without traversing a large part of it."

"And what did you discuss?"

"Mostly? Ararath." She hesitated. "We also discussed the assassination attempts and the possibility that Hectore might use Araven's resources to curtail some of them. Rath was his godson. Rath is the reason I'm part of House Terafin."

"In how much detail did you discuss the assassination attempts?"

"Very little."

"The gods are to be thanked for small mercies. Tell me what occurred during your visit to *Avantari* yesterday."

She frowned. "Haval, it's unusual for you to come directly here."

He nodded. "It appears that the audience with the Kings was eventful. Your head is apparently still attached to your neck; it was therefore not disastrous. What happened?"

She told him. Avandar was willing to supply details she had overlooked, none of which changed Haval's severe expression. "And the song?"

"You've already heard it." It wasn't a question.

"I have. I considered it unfortunate, but given The Wayelyn, survivable. I am no longer certain that is the case. A game is being played, Terafin."

Jewel nodded. "Games are always being played."

Haval inclined his head.

She sat in a brittle silence until the maid had finished with her hair. She then dismissed the maid; her room now contained her domicis, her Chosen, and the world's most difficult dressmaker. "There is one game being played that I haven't had time to mention."

"There is surely more than one," Haval replied.

"Sit, Haval. You are making me nervous."

He did as bid, but without any marked enthusiasm for making her *less* nervous.

"Rymark."

He lifted a brow, his expression shuttered.

"Rymark came to me two days ago. He made me an offer."

"And that offer?"

"He has worked, for an indeterminate length of time, as an agent of the Shining Court."

Haval did not appear to be surprised at all. The disappointment Jewel felt was unworthy of her title. "And he has offered information about that august body to you in return for a commensurate reward." It wasn't even a question.

"What information of value do you believe he offers the House?"

"The House?" She frowned. "In a concrete sense, very little. But the information might be relayed to the Kings, and I believe it to be of value to the Empire."

"How so?"

"He knows the names of the mortal members of the Shining Court; he knows, almost certainly, the names of the *Kialli*. If we knew who willingly served the Court, we might feed information to the North, or we might cut them off entirely."

Haval nodded. "Has he also volunteered to detail his acts against the House, in service to the Court? Or his acts among his colleagues in the Order of Knowledge?"

"He has offered everything."

"And in return you are to reward him with?"

"I honestly don't know. He expects that I will be able to gift him with land and an appropriate title, although I am not the Kings."

"You are not telling me the whole of what he asked."

"I *am*, Haval."

"Very well. Let us assume that the offer made for services rendered to the Shining Court was similar. In the event that the Lord of the Shining Court is victorious, and Rymark continues in his service, there would be no Kings with which to contend. The whole of the city might be laid to waste."

"He considered that inevitable when he joined the Shining Court. He was beguiled by a living god, and felt that our survival — the survival of any of us — was an impossibility. He could serve the god or he could perish. He chose to serve." Her lips twisted. Even speaking the words recalled the rage they'd engendered.

"Very well, Terafin. What game do you believe he plays?"

She was silent. After a moment, she rose; Haval did not join her. Standing or seated, he was the more intimidating of the two.

"He did not make his offer — and its implied confession — to you without reason. You may not credit his reason, but that is not at issue, at the moment. He made the opening move in his negotiation because he believes it will be in your power to grant what he has asked."

"I believe I made clear that I do not."

"He therefore believes he knows more about your ability than you do, Terafin. It is likely he knows what the Shining Court fears."

She was silent. After a pause, she said, "Come to the library with me, Haval. I need to walk."

"If you are attempting to shock me," he said, as he walked sedately by her side, "you may stop. I was sufficiently impressed by the rearrangement of the Terafin library that I spent some moments composing myself before I entered your chambers. They, at least, seem to be spared as obvious a physical transformation."

"Rymark saw the library."

"Ah."

"He also saw the former private office; I now call it the war room."

"Is it as impressive as the library?"

"Differently impressive. It appears to be a large, stone room, set into the side of a building at the height of a cliff, given the distance to the nearest visible ground. It has one open window, the width of the wall, through which my cats can fly. And through which other things can likewise fly. I believe it was that room that fully convinced Rymark that his attempt to offer his services was worthwhile."

"How necessary do you feel the information is?"

She shrugged uneasily. "We've managed so far."

"I suppose there is no hope that you will accept the information and dispense with the informer?"

She glanced at him. "Why are you even asking the question?"

"A fair response. If I understand your hesitance correctly, you wish the information — but you also wish to execute Rymark for, among other things, treason to the House."

She exhaled. "I do."

"Understandable, Terafin. You believe him responsible for your predecessor's death?"

"Yes."

"Very well. I believe it unwise to accept his offer."

"You don't trust it?"

"It is not a matter of trust — at least on my part. He is dangerous. There have been multiple attempts on your life in the past several weeks; there is very little chance, in my opinion, that Rymark ATerafin did not play a part in most of them. I believe you will find the alliance, such as it is, costly to you."

"In my position what would you do?"

"I? I would accept what he offers."

"But you counsel against *my* acceptance."

"I am not you, Jewel. Were you a different person, we would not even be having this discussion. I understand the politics of alliance; it is, by and large, amoral. Expedience and mutual goals are all that I require. You freight your negotiations with sentiment."

"As does Hectore of Araven, but you feel he is both canny and competent."

"I feel he is *exceptionally* canny and *exceptionally* competent, yes. In your position, however, Patris Araven would accept; he is far too curious to do otherwise. Regardless, you are not Haval, Hectore, or Jarven. You are willing to play games; you are fully aware that to sidestep them courts the disaster of ignorance. But there are elements at play which are not negotiable, chief among them your sense of honor.

"Your sense of honor may well preclude justice, regardless."

"How so?"

"You cannot bring yourself to have him killed. You feel that his vulnerability was entirely his choice; he made his offer in good faith."

Every word was true.

"I believe Rymark is well aware of the effect his honesty will have upon you. But the deaths in which he has participated, if indirectly, were and are of grave personal import to you; he is taking a calculated risk. What does he expect you to do, Jewel?"

"Build a city," she replied. She had reached the long table with its multiple chairs, all empty, and its haphazard stack of books. "He expects me to build a city that can withstand the full force of a god's power."

True to form, Haval's expression remained neutral. It was an act of courtesy on his part; a sign of genuine respect for her. Given how their early morning conversation had begun, Jewel was surprised he still had any.

"I note, by your reaction, that you do not find this laughable."

"I do," she replied. Before he could lecture her on the quality of her lies—a favorite theme of Haval's—she added, "But I understand how it might, in theory, be possible."

Haval was staring at the fountain on the other side of the library's table; his eyes were slightly narrowed. She didn't ask him what he saw when he looked at it; instead she said, "Meralonne believes it was crafted by Fabril himself."

"And even a humble dressmaker is aware of some of Fabril's many legacies. Rymark feels you can do—to a city—what you did here?"

"I didn't ask him. But it's the only thing that makes sense of his behavior."

Haval turned to face her. "Can you do it?"

"Not consciously."

"That is the worst possible answer you could now offer me. You did not design this library."

"No. The only room that reflects my conscious attempt to visualize is my bedchamber."

"Why?"

"Because I was sleeping, and I knew if I didn't wake, I'd die. I could hear people shouting. I could recognize their voices. I knew where I must be, and what I must look like—in the waking world. Sadly, I was trapped in the dreaming." She gazed at her reflection across the table's surface, obscured in part by books. "I forced myself to wake."

"And you brought the dreaming with you."

She was surprised. But instead of answering, she thought about what he'd said. "I don't know. Maybe."

"I confess I am not an expert in ancient lore. Before you tell me that it is not your specialty, answer a question. If the god we do not name were to appear at the borders of Averalaan as it is now, what would happen to the city?"

"Anything he wanted to happen." She hesitated. "I think parts of the Isle could stand against him, at least for a while—the Guild of Makers, the Order of Knowledge, the inner sanctums of the Exalted."

"*Avantari*?"

"I don't know, Haval. If you're asking me whether or not I think the god could destroy this city, the short answer is yes."

"Give me the longer answer."

"Yes."

Haval exhaled and turned to Avandar. To Jewel's surprise, he tendered Avandar a bow. It was not a shallow bow; there was nothing in the graceful bend that was perfunctory.

Avandar glanced at Jewel as Haval rose.

"With your permission," the dressmaker said, "I would like to speak with your domicis."

"Why?"

Haval frowned. "The answer to the question is obvious, but I am not entirely in an instructive mood. I will not, therefore, make you answer it yourself. I wish to speak with Avandar because I believe he will not, of necessity, resort to monosyllabic answers." When she did not immediately respond, he added, "We have little time, Jewel. You have spent far too much of your life believing in relative strata of power. I will not argue the merits of this belief; in most cases, it is wise.

"I know very little of gods; I know very little of the ancient. Before today—ah, no, before The Terafin's funeral, the knowledge was esoterica; I did not require it. Now, I believe I do."

"Haval—our enemy is a *god*."

"Indeed."

"You can't treat him as if he's—"

"An opponent? Of course I can. It is what you yourself are beginning to understand. It does not matter that he is a god; it matters only that his goals and ours are mutually exclusive. Had he no need for subtlety, it is highly unlikely that a Shining Court—a Court comprised in part of mortals—would exist at all." He turned to Avandar. "If it is acceptable to leave you with your Chosen, I require a few moments of your domicis' time."

Avandar did not look to Jewel; he regarded Haval for a long, motionless moment before nodding.

"If we may use the small conference room within your suite, I would prefer it. I dislike these open skies."

Jewel rose.

"I wish to speak with your domicis alone."

"Haval—"

"Jewel—you are afraid. You are afraid of the gods, afraid of the wilderness, afraid of the shadow your own power casts. I understand—I can even commend—that emotion. I cannot, however, conduct a conversation through it. You are aware that your domicis is unusual. You are aware that he has a length and breadth of experience that is relevant to our current struggles. Any conversation I will have with him should contain a fraction of the information the two of you have shared.

"But it will not. You are afraid of—or for—him; I cannot readily discern between the two, at the moment. I cannot afford to be either if I am to serve you. If you accompany us, there will be almost no conversation. I cannot command him, nor will I try. But I will be unaffected by any answers he chooses to give—and you will not."

Go to the right-kin's office. If I am not to be with you, I do not trust the library. When we are finished conversing, I will meet you in the dining hall.

I have my Chosen.

Yes. And in the lower manse, that is all you will require.

Jewel did not head to the right-kin's office immediately. Instead, she chose to visit the West Wing. Ellerson did not magically answer the door; Jester did. She signed a brief question; his expression was answer enough. Carver and Ellerson had not returned. Shadow was in Ariel's room with Adam; Arann was sleeping.

Angel was in his room. She was surprised that he was awake, although his eyes were ringed and his face the wrong kind of pale.

"You haven't been sleeping."

"Not much. Teller told us about your visit to *Avantari.*"

"How much did he tell you?"

"Enough." It was evasive.

"I have to go back."

"To the room with the statues."

She nodded. "I have a few things to do before I return there." In den-sign, she added, *be ready*.

"For what, Jay?"

"Anything. I have to speak with the Oracle, and I'm not entirely certain what will happen when I do."

"But you have suspicions."

"Yes." She hesitated, and then said, "I promised I'd do my best not to go where you couldn't follow. If I leave, and it's possible, I'll take you with me."

He closed his eyes, displaying a fan of platinum lashes. But when he opened them, he nodded. "Can I visit your war room before we go?"

"As often as you'd like. If you can avoid mentioning it to Meralonne, I'd appreciate it."

"How big will this get?"

"I don't know. It probably won't be worse than running up the side of a tree and fighting gravity the whole way." She grimaced. "But it probably won't be a lot better, either."

"When, Jay?"

"With luck? A week."

"Without it?"

"When the Kings reach a decision and command my attendance. I have to face the Council of The Ten in two days, and I have to face Levec this afternoon." She glanced at the Chosen, and added, "And I have to speak with Rymark somewhere in between."

"How prepared do you want me to be?"

"Think of the things I won't have time to think of. Angel—" She stopped speaking; the silence was abrupt and uneasy. In the end, she chose not to break it.

Chapter Twenty-one

11th of Fabril, 428 A.A.
Houses of Healing, Averalaan

JEWEL ATTEMPTED to tell Adam, for perhaps the hundredth time, that she was *not* the Matriarch of Terafin. The hundredth attempt was as successful as the ninety-ninth—or the first. He attempted to use the correct word, but his Weston was not up to the task, and any conversation that slid into Torra included the word Matriarch.

"I don't understand," he said, the last word broken when the carriage wheels hit an unfortunate absence of cobbled stone. "You *are* Matriarch. I can use a foreign word, but the word doesn't change what you *are*."

"No, it doesn't. But I know what the word means to you—and I am not a Matriarch. I'm not Yollana."

He paled. "You are not. But my mother was not Yollana. My sister Margret is not Yollana. You remind me of my sister," he added. "You are the same age, and you have the same temper."

Remembering Margret, Jewel winced. She did not deny it.

"How is it different?" He was frustrated. He had been frustrated for most of the day—or the parts that included breakfast, a change of clothing, and any activity that didn't bring them closer to Levec and the sleepers.

"Matriarchs rely on secrecy. Among my den, I don't. I know less than many of the people who serve me, and I rely on their knowledge and understanding. Among the Voyani, no one knows more than the Matriarch."

Adam nodded. It was not, however, in agreement; he appeared to be waiting for her to make a definitive point. "Matriarchs see. You see. Matriarchs can walk the hidden roads—with cost. You can create them, Jewel. If Yollana were here, she would call you Matriarch—I think. She would see the Voyanne in your gardens. I do not think she would enter them.

"I will try to remember," Adam added, turning to stick his head out the open window. The first time he had ridden in a Weston carriage, he had been suspicious and a little appalled. It had seemed a waste—of space, of large wheels, of horses—to pull something that was basically two cushioned benches, with doors on either side. Voyani wagons were tiny homes, pieces of territory to a people that otherwise claimed none. They were not simply conveyances.

But he had grown accustomed to them, if slowly; he had acclimatized himself to the Terafin manse, the Isle, and the continuous presence of the sea. He had even grown used to the press of people, although he still found them difficult. Only during the Festival of the Moon were crowds as dense—and harmless—as the daily foot traffic in Averalaan.

Nowhere in the cities of the South was there a man to compare to Levec.

"You are worried about Levec," Adam said, glancing back into the cabin's interior.

"Am I being that obvious?"

"He is intimidating."

"He's certainly that."

"But you like him."

"Say rather that I admire him. I admire what he does for his healers. He's like a mother and a guardian and a domicis rolled into one large, angry man. Large, angry, *suspicious* man."

"He is not suspicious without cause."

She was silent for a moment, as she often was. "No, never that."

"Why are you worried today? Today, Levec will be happy."

"Levec is never happy."

"But we will wake the sleepers."

"Yes. Adam . . . do you have any idea *how* we're going to achieve that?"

His dark brows rose in surprise, before descending into a bunched furrow. "You don't know?"

"I have ideas—but that's all they are. I'm not in my manse; I'm not on *my* ground. I don't know what I'll see, if I see anything at all. I'm hoping that maybe you can wake them, and they'll just stay that way."

He shook his head.

"You don't think so, either."

"No. I think—I think if that worked, it would have worked at any other time."

"But the Warden of Dreams is gone—"

"Yes. But I think it is like a spider's web. The spider is gone; the web remains. They are trapped in a web."

"But we woke Leila."

He nodded.

"We don't have time to wake them all the way we woke Leila."

"If we have no other choice, we will make time, no?"

"No, Adam. Time is the one thing I don't have. If I spend the time here, I'm not sure what it will cost in future—but it won't be good."

"You see this?" His eyes were bright, curious.

She shook her head. "It's not vision; it's instinct." The carriage came to a halt beyond the heavy fence and manned gates behind which the Houses of Healing resided. Exhaling heavily, Jewel waited until the carriage door was opened, dismounting with a great deal more dignity than she felt as Avandar, silent and uncommunicative on all fronts, offered her a hand. Adam, on the other hand, leaped free of the cabin the second there was no danger he'd collide with her on landing.

She knew he was older than most of her den had been when she'd first found them, but he seemed so young to her now; she smiled as she made her way to the guard. Adam did not run around her; he waited, although he wasn't exactly standing still. He was genuinely fond of Levec.

The guards knew him, of course; they knew her, as well. They were therefore slightly less curt than was their wont.

Given their employer, they were perhaps the only guards in the city who could afford to offend The Terafin with impunity. She didn't begrudge them. They took their lead from Levec, and compared to Levec, they were the soul of tact and kindness.

He was waiting when the front doors opened, which was unusual. He was also scowling. "Adam," he said curtly, "you will enter the infirmary immediately. I will have words with The Terafin."

"Avandar, Torvan, please accompany him."

The domicis nodded.

"Terafin, my office." The healer turned neatly on heel and stalked down the length of wide hall. Jewel followed. Her Chosen also followed, which caused the frown on the healer's face to deepen when he looked back. The Chosen did not walk silently.

Levec's office was not a grand space; it was, however, large enough to accommodate the head of a House and the minimal number of guards required. Levec's desk was cluttered in a way that suggested correspondence was not his forte—or perhaps his problem. He sat, indicating an empty chair that had seen better days. Jewel joined him at the side of the desk.

He could clearly *find* correspondence; he pulled out one letter. Jewel could see the broken remnants of the Terafin seal along its outer edge. "I am not in the habit," Levec told her, rattling the sheet in her direction, "of opening my healerie to The Ten. I've just about had it with the damn mages, and I swear I will strangle the *Astari* if their leader pokes an inch of his nose across my threshold again."

"What was said in the request for a meeting?"

"Nothing of value."

"Given your feelings about the patriciate, Healer Levec, that covers a wide range."

He raised one half of a continuous brow before he handed the letter to her. She recognized Teller's distinct hand—and accepted Levec's dismissal. Teller had asked for an appointment for The Terafin at Levec's earliest possible convenience. He had not mentioned the reason for the visit; he merely stated that it was urgent. No wonder Levec was annoyed.

He was not, however, angry; not yet. "My apologies,

Levec. I thought Adam might have mentioned the reason for my presence."

"What does Adam have to do with it?"

"Clearly, he has not. Leila was one of your patients, I believe?"

He frowned. His frown was the whole of his answer.

"She woke. She has been discharged?"

"A few days earlier than I would have liked, but yes. Adam insisted that she was no longer in danger."

"And has she suffered a relapse?"

"No."

"I am here to attempt to wake the rest of your sleepers."

"And how exactly," Levec said, leaning across the breadth of his desk as if it no longer existed, "are you going to do that?"

It was just like Levec to cut to the heart of the matter. Jewel rose. "If you will lead me to the healerie?"

"Your guards stay outside."

Torvan stiffened.

"Agreed. My domicis, however, will be with me."

It was clear Levec wanted to argue. Jewel was almost surprised when he didn't. He rose as well; his chair creaked more.

"You'll find either three or four people awake when you arrive. They will likely be confined to bed; they've lost weight and strength because they've eaten so little. They were woken in the usual way."

"The rest?"

"Sleeping. I have some of my trainees working in the healerie. Don't touch them, don't bother them. Don't ask them questions; if you have questions, ask me." He growled. Jewel almost laughed, the sound was so unexpected; his expression forbade mirth. "And do not speak a single word to the damn mages. Not one."

"The magi are here?"

"Yes. By Royal command."

She had hoped, walking into the healerie, that an answer to Levec's earlier question would present itself. She had hoped that she might see the sleepers as Adam saw them. She didn't. She saw people in beds across the great room, almost all of them asleep. Levec had possibly a dozen assistants who sat in the very small spaces between those beds, trickling water into the mouths of those who would otherwise die of its lack.

They looked exhausted. Jewel, glancing at Levec—who was glaring back at her—instantly forgave his ill-humor. The fact that many of these people were alive at all was no doubt due to the ministrations of the healers here; had they been left at home, she wasn't certain they would have survived.

But they had. She saw Adam in the farthest corner of the room visible from the door and headed toward him. He was seated beside the bed of an elderly woman; she was awake. Her left hand was clasped in both of his, and he was bent over her, listening to her speak. Jewel guessed she was speaking in Torra, which was confirmed as she drew close.

She waited until Adam noticed her. He didn't, until the old woman did.

Jewel shook her head as he made to rise. "Introduce us?"

Remembering his manners, Adam reddened. "I'm sorry. This is Maria. Maria, this is Jewel." The old woman inclined her head. If she noticed the Terafin signet, she said nothing—and Jewel thought there was a decent chance she wouldn't recognize it if she had.

Speaking Weston, Jewel said, "Is there anything different today?"

"No." Adam hesitated. "I want to you to try something."

"What?"

"I want you to take her other hand."

Jewel really wished she'd insisted on wearing practical clothing; there wasn't much space between the beds, and even standing, her skirts were pressed over the edge of the next patient.

She asked—in Torra—permission to do as Adam had suggested; the woman did not have the energy to radiate the suspicion Jewel was certain her Oma would have. She lifted her left hand, and Jewel caught it in both of hers.

Adam closed his eyes. Jewel watched him, holding her breath. Nothing changed. The room looked the same. The old woman was staring—fondly—at Adam's face. "He is a good boy," she told Jewel, in Torra. "There are so few of those."

"There are," Jewel said, smiling. She closed her eyes.

In the red-tinged darkness of closed eyelids, sounds, as always, were sharper. She could hear Levec's impatient snap at the mages who habitually invaded his healerie. He wanted no interference with anyone in the healerie; he ordered them to leave The Terafin alone. She was unreasonably happy to note that the magi—at least at the moment—were lower on the scale of acceptable guests than The Terafin.

She heard the magi's sharp response, but didn't recognize the voices; there were at least three. Their voices tended to overlap; one woman, two men.

They faded into the background as she continued to listen. She could hear the sound of hands in water, of buckets being lifted—with a grunt—and set down. Closer and softer, she could hear the gentle murmur of Torra in a voice that seemed ancient, but the syllables refused to coalesce into words.

She could hear the sound of wind; of breeze through heavy leaves. Like the Torra, it was a soft, gentle sound, and like the Torra, it almost implied words, without the harsher edge of syllables to contain them. Unlike the Torra, however, it didn't come from the healerie.

Jewel opened her eyes. The first thing she saw was Adam; he was seated across from her, his eyes closed, his cheeks faintly flushed. His hands were still entwined with the old woman's—as were Jewel's. She shifted gaze to see Maria, head propped up against a stack of pillows, blankets of varying weight covering the rest of her frail body.

But the bed was no longer bracketed by other beds; nor was it flush against a wall. Like the shelves in The Terafin's personal library, it appeared to have grown out of the trunk of a very large tree. Above the bed, swaying in a warm breeze, were branches; the tree was *Ellariannatte*.

"Adam," Jewel said. "Open your eyes."

He did. They widened as he looked beyond her shoulder. The only person who didn't appear surprised by her surroundings was Maria, possibly because her vision wasn't that good.

"Where are we?" Adam asked—in Weston.

Maria frowned. If Weston was not her mother-tongue, or even her preferred one, she wasn't an idiot; the question was very basic. "We are in the forest," she said. "Help me stand, Adam." Her voice was stronger than it had been in the healerie, the tone of command sharper. Adam, accustomed to autocratic women, immediately slid an arm beneath her shoulders, supporting her weight as she sat. She slid her hand out of Jewel's, and swiveling, placed her feet against the forest floor; they were bare.

She was not, however; she wore clothing. Jewel was certain she'd been wearing a simple shift a moment ago, but that was gone; she wore a dress, a loose and comfortably practical one. It was a heavy cotton, a russet brown that had seen better years, and it was protected by an apron of many pockets.

"Are we ready?" she asked him. He looked confused; he was good at that.

"Where are your shoes?" Jewel asked.

Maria pursed her lips in a frown. "We don't need shoes here," she declared, with the vast authority of age.

"Where are we?" Adam asked.

"Don't you know?" One white brow rose in a distinctive arch.

"No, Ona Maria. I'm sorry."

She tsked as she set her bare feet firmly against the ground. "It can't be helped." Her arm dropped, but she still held Adam's hand; he looked like a much younger boy as she began to lead him away from the bedside. But she paused and turned a speculative eye upon Jewel. "You had better join us, I think."

Jewel, afraid to confess the same ignorance that afflicted Adam in Maria's opinion, rose instantly. She noted that her dress, her signet ring, and her short boots remained unchanged. So, for that matter, did Adam's clothing. The bed, however, dissolved, absorbed whole into the trunk of the great tree.

Maria apparently knew where she was going, which was good. Adam looked as apprehensive as Jewel felt. She wanted to speak to him, but was afraid to offend Maria.

"Where are we going?" Adam asked.

"To the Festival gates," Maria replied. "They won't be far from here. Can you hear the music?"

Until the old woman had mentioned it, there'd been no music. But Jewel could hear it now; lute, she thought, and pipe. She could hear the baritone of a man's voice, but couldn't make out the words.

"This is like Leila," Adam said.

It seemed that way to Jewel, but she said, "No," before half a thought had formed.

He didn't argue and he didn't question. Nor did Maria speak; she was now looking ahead, a smile deepening the lines around the corners of her mouth. The music grew in volume, and with it, the sounds of other voices: there was a crowd gathered here. Maria slid her hand free of Adam's, and gave him a gentle shove forward. "Go," she told him. "And have fun."

"Maria—"

"It will be over soon enough," the old woman told Jewel. She joined the gathered crowd and was soon lost to it. Adam and Jewel remained at its outer edge.

Adam, eyes narrowed, scanned the crowd. Crowds were a common element of dreaming; they had certainly existed in Leila's world. But something about this crowd felt different to Jewel. It wasn't their clothing, although they wore distinctive dresses, robes, and tunics—clearly, this was a festive gathering, and all of the participants understood as much. They all lacked shoes, which Jewel found odd. She almost considered taking hers off.

No, she thought, it was their voices. The sound of each voice, caught briefly before the sense of its individuality was lost, was sharp, clear, distinct. It didn't matter that some of those voices were childish and youthful, and some ancient and weathered; nor did it matter that some were deep and resonant, and some shrill and strident. She felt as if she knew these voices, although she knew she had never met any of these people before, with the possible exception of Maria.

"Do you recognize them?" Jewel asked.

Adam nodded slowly. He began to reel off their names, and Jewel held up a hand to stem the tide; the names meant nothing without people to attach them to, and she knew she'd forget them the moment he moved on to the next.

Except she didn't. As he spoke each name, she saw a brief light, a brief glow, touch individual members of the crowd. Or their backs; they were facing away from Jewel and Adam. What they saw, she couldn't see. Taking Adam's left hand in her right, Jewel headed around the gathering, toward the musicians that could be heard but not seen.

"I think they're all here," Adam told her. "I don't think anyone's missing."

"There were four people who were awake."

"Three," Adam replied. "But Maria is here."

"And the other two?"

He pointed. "Cedric and Hollin. Over there."

"Does that mean they've fallen asleep again in the heal-erie?"

Adam shrugged. "Probably."

"Easy for you to say—Levec isn't going to kill *you*."

He laughed. "You know Levec likes you, right?"

"No, I really don't." She started to say more, and stopped, because she had reached the music. She had correctly identified the lute and the pipes. She had failed to identify baritone and tenor. Or rather, she'd failed to identify the source of the voices. Now, she could see them clearly: they weren't human. They weren't even close.

She had met immortals in her travels: demons and *Arianni*. But the two who now sang—male and female—were neither. They were slender, slight of build, and tall, their limbs like lithe spring branches. They were a startling shade of gold, although their hair was white, shot through with green and red; it trailed from their heads to the ground in a swirl of motion that implied breeze through leaves.

Their eyes were sky blue; there were no whites.

She felt—as she often felt when confronted with immortals—old, ugly, and ungainly. She was almost afraid to approach them—but there was nothing forbidding in their countenance, nothing like the Winter chill that lived in Celleriant's gaze. As she watched, hesitating, one of the smaller members of the audience ran free of its confines, laughing with delight, her arms outstretched.

"Oh ho!" the man said, opening his arms while the pipe—no longer held in his hands—continued to play. He lifted the girl, swung her in a wide, wild arc, and let her go. Jewel inhaled sharply and started to run, but stopped as the child began to fly. Wind bore her aloft, just above the two performers, and as she sailed in sky, dodging branches, the woman turned, smiling broadly, to meet Jewel's astonished gaze.

"And here we have the master of the green," she said, her smile so warm it was almost embarrassing. She offered a low and graceful bow. "We have been waiting for you, Jewel. We gathered your lost companions, your unknown servants, and we have entertained them in your absence.

"Have you been well, my Lord?"

Adam had come to stand by Jewel's side, although he was staring at the two strangers, his mouth open.

She laughed as she rose, transferring her gaze to the boy. "And you have brought an illustrious guest with you, have you not? Brother, cease your singing and come and greet our new arrivals."

The man laughed, lifting his arms as the child's weight returned. She fell into them in a shrieking tumble that held very little fear, and he set her small, bare feet against the ground before he heeded his companion's demand. The corners of his eyes were creased—or veined—with lines of merriment. "And so I shall." The pipes, however, continued to play, absent either his fingers or his breath across them.

He bowed to them both; his bow to Jewel was the deeper of the two, and the more flamboyant. "Jewel," he said. "And Adam. We have been waiting your return."

Jewel glanced at the crowd; they had fallen more or less silent—the less being the few children who were threading their way between the press of adult legs without fear of reprisal. "I have no memory of visiting this place before," she finally said.

"Have you not? Perhaps you do not recognize it as it is." He lifted an arm.

She lifted a hand in quick response. "No," she told him. "If you mean to pull back a curtain or somehow alter this landscape—don't. This dream is a pleasant dream; I would not see it shift into something darker."

"It is not darkness that I would offer them—or you. We understood your intent. It is why we gathered those lost in the forest and brought them here. Have you come to take them from us?"

"I have come to take them home," she replied. "They can only remain here while they live, and every hour they spend increases the chance they will not."

"Will you keep nothing of them, then?" he asked, tilting his head to one side. His companion began to walk among the crowd, much as the children had done; she was not afraid of censure in any way. But she spoke to the spectators, the gathered dreamers, as she walked, and Jewel thought she saw a nod or two in her passing.

"They are not mine."

Both brows rose. "Are they not, then?"

Adam said, "She does not understand what the word means." He was flushed. "And you will not now cast them out or claim them if she does not."

"No, Adam. We will not; we do not trouble ourselves with the surface of her words. We are not bound, unwilling, to this place, to seek freedom by twisting all meaning to better suit our purposes." He threw his arms up and out, and a rain of leaves followed in their wake. In shape and form, they were *Ellariannatte*; in composition, they were not. But they were not quite silver, gold, or diamond. They were not leaves of fire.

"No," he said softly. "They are the bones of the ancient earth." As if he could hear her thoughts. The wind caught them in its folds, as easily and as gracefully as it had caught a laughing child, and the leaves tumbled end over end above the heads of the crowd. Their hands rose as they caught them.

She watched; she wasn't certain why. But it seemed, as she watched, that each man, woman, and child reached for only one of these odd leaves—and none of them reached for the same leaf. As if, somehow, they could see something in the shape and motion of their falling flight that spoke specifically to them, and only them.

"We heard your song, Jewel."

She stiffened. "You did not hear *my* song. I have no voice to sing it, and even if I did, I would not have the words."

He laughed. "You are so tame and timid," he replied. "Is she not?"

His companion had completed her circuit of the crowd to return to his side. "She is. But endearing, and beautiful in a fashion. I heard you keep the noisy ones."

She must be speaking of the cats.

"I am indeed. I have a few words to say to the darkest of the three; I bear some of the scars of his predictable ill-temper, and I would like to return them." But she spoke while laughing. "And perhaps we will see them again. Almost certainly, we will. You have woken us, Jewel, and we have come." Her smile faded from lips, although her eyes were still full of its warmth.

"But perhaps it will not happen soon. You have heard the barest whisper of our sleeping voices, and you have called it breeze. But you will hear us now, and soon. If you call our names, we will waken, and we will come to you."

"For what purpose?" Jewel asked.

The woman laughed again. "Our roots have long been buried in the soil of the lands you have claimed as your own, and we are not displeased to be so chosen. We have known the long sleep of Winter—but now we feel the sweet warmth of Spring."

Jewel stared. Without thinking she said, "But it is Winter, still."

"It is Winter in all lands but yours. And it is not yet Summer in yours—that cannot happen, not yet." Her expression became, slowly, grave. "In truth, there should be no Spring—but you have called us, and we have woken. There is a fire at the heart of this forest that is like the young sun, to us; its warmth pierces even Winter chill and banishes the long sleep. We are not all awake, not yet—but we are waking as we speak. We are not *Arianni*. We cannot rove as they rove, or hunt as they hunt; we ride wind, if we ride at all, and our flight is brief.

"But our roots are buried deep in these lands, and if we cannot ride, Lord, we cannot easily be riven from them, not even by the hunters who traverse them. We stand as we stand, and we do so in defense of your lands because they are, now, also ours.

"We will guard the ways, when you leave this place, for as long as even one tree remains standing. And you must leave, in the end. You must seek the Summer."

"What will you be in Summer?"

She laughed. "As you see us, but more so." She turned to the man she had called brother. "It is time," she said, with more warmth than dignity. Raising her voice, she then added, "She has finally come to show you the way. But there is a price and pledge for passage, as we have told you."

"There is *not*—"

Adam lifted a hand and signed. It was den-sign. *There is*.

She frowned. Adam had not deliberately or consciously touched the dreams of the sleepers—except once. He was staring at the two, slender and other, as they moved to stand between Jewel and the waiting crowd. They turned to face each other, lifting their long and slender hands and clasping them in such a way that they formed a living arch.

"Why do you know this?" she whispered.

He shook his head. "An old story," he whispered back. "A lap story."

"I want to hear it. Later." She would have said more, but the crowd began to form into a line, the head of which stood on one side of this arch. And to Jewel's eyes, it *was* an arch, now: a thing made of slender, twined branches that reached a sharp and perfect peak well above their heads. She started to walk around it; it made her uneasy. But her legs wouldn't take the steps she intended them to take.

It was not an artifact of the dreaming, though; she stopped because she *knew*, as she pivoted to move, that she must not. To pass from the lands in which they'd been trapped, these people had to travel beneath that arch—to her. To her side, and Adam's.

The first to do so was an older man. He was beardless, but still possessed hair; his eyes were a narrowed dark brown. He bowed before the arch, straightened, and passed beneath it, carrying as he did a leaf in the palm of his hand. He stopped three feet from where Jewel and Adam stood, and bowed again, his brows furrowing as if he were seeing Jewel for the first time.

"Terafin," he said. He offered the leaf to her.

She hesitated for a long, silent moment before she held out her hand to receive it. It was cool to the touch, metallic, and sharp; it sliced her palm so cleanly she felt no pain until the blood started to well.

He said nothing, but his eyes were wide and unblinking when she looked up from her bleeding hand and the leaf it now contained. He was, she realized, waiting for her to speak. She had no idea what to say; nor did the imperative of dream come to rescue her.

After a long moment, his eyes narrowed. "You are not accustomed to command," he said, as if the concept was a novelty. Given the Terafin signet upon her finger, it should have been. "But you must learn."

"I don't like to tell other people what to do."

"No. Do you understand why?"

She started to answer. Stopped. "Not really. I expect people to be responsible enough that they don't need to be told what to do."

He smiled. It was arresting. "You have given commands in your time."

She nodded slowly, aware that he, at least, was dreaming. This was a conversation that could take place nowhere else. "Usually only in emergencies. Almost always, then."

"That is better than nothing. Perhaps you should consider all of life as an emergency." He smiled. "May I leave?"

"Yes."

He took a step forward—or tried. "It will not do. Here, Terafin, there is no room for plea. Command me."

She wanted to argue. She didn't. Shifting her shoulders down her back, she straightened, stiffened. She held out her left hand, and he bowed over it, lifting the signet ring to his lips. "Leave these lands," she told him softly, meaning it. "Wake. Return to your life."

He didn't need to take a step forward; he faded from view within seconds.

Jewel exhaled and glanced at Adam, who was staring at her. "Well?" she asked, in soft Torra. He did not reply. Nor had he time; a woman bent before the arch, and then passed through it. She held, between two fingers, as if it were verminous, the stem of a leaf. As the man had, she approached Jewel, and as he, she laid the leaf across Jewel's palm. It stung.

Jewel offered her the signet ring of Terafin, and the woman bowed over it. When she rose, Jewel ordered her to leave. To leave and to wake.

"Adam," she asked, as the woman also vanished, "will all of the dreamers survive when they return?"

He was silent. After a significant pause, he said, "I think there are two who will not."

"Let me know who they are when they arrive."

He said nothing until Jewel turned to face him. He was pale. "I understand why you ask." His Weston was stilted but perfect. "But I will not."

"I don't want to send them to their deaths."

"I know. But Jewel—if they do not die, they will never live again."

"What do you mean?"

"They will never cross the bridge. They will never enter Mandaros' Hall. They will be trapped here, in the wilderness, until even the wilderness dies."

"You're Southern. You don't even *believe* in the bridge or the gods." .

"I am healer-born, Matriarch. I have seen your bridge. I know what waits." He hesitated again, and then said, "This is like the Southern Winds, this place. They will be trapped here. While you live—while you rule it—they will be safe. But no ruler lives forever."

"I could order you to tell me."

He smiled. "Yes. You could. You are Matriarch, and even if I am not Terafin, while I am beside you here, I am yours."

She turned as a young man approached her, leaf in open palm. She *could* give the order. But she was afraid he was right, and did not.

The crowd thinned. None except the children attempted to evade the arch; they were caught and corralled by the adults who remained. Nor did they avoid it because they were frightened; they were, to Jewel's eye, bored. Had she been in charge, she would have sent them through first. Or second, after ascertaining that what waited on the other side wasn't deadly.

The last of the sleepers approached. She was young and slender. Jewel wondered if she would be gaunt and skeletal upon waking. When she passed beneath the arch, the arch unraveled, peak becoming hands and forearms before those hands unclasped. A man and a woman of indeterminate race remained; they turned from each other toward Jewel, following in the sole remaining sleeper's wake.

She carried a leaf that was lighter in color and texture than any of the previous leaves; it seemed almost blue to Jewel's eye, but not a living, growing blue.

"Terafin." She bowed. "I am Rebeccah."

Rebeccah was the first sleeper to offer her name. The only sleeper to do so, Jewel realized. "Rise," she said, and the girl unbent, her hair flying in a gentle, inexorable wind.

"I was chosen. I was chosen to tell you."

Jewel waited. When the girl offered no further words, she said, "Tell me what?"

But the girl smiled, the expression exposing dimples that made her seem much younger.

Jewel exhaled. "Tell me."

"The sleepers are part of this place, but we cannot stay." She lifted her arms briefly to indicate the two immortals, who now stood to either side of her, their arms by their sides, their eyes bright, the earlier blue gone to green that seemed endless and quick with life. "They are of this place, and they cannot leave. You, Terafin, are not *of* this place—and you must never become so."

Jewel looked, carefully, at the two who had once formed the arch through which each of the sleepers had passed. They were grave, but even in gravity, they suggested vibrant joy simply by standing.

"If I am of this place, as you put it," Jewel said, when the girl fell silent, "I would be subject to its laws? Instead of making them?"

"Yes. I remember my first dream. This is my last, and I would cling to it, if I could. In it, I have been subject to your laws and your whim."

"I did not command the guardians."

"No. They are rooted here; until you command it—and only then—they cannot leave; if they leave, they cannot return. But they understand your dreams; they understand the shape of your desires and your hopes. We do not, not without the words." She set the blue leaf atop the pile in Jewel's hands. It was a precarious pile, now—or it should have been—but until this single, blue leaf with its delicate ivory veins, was set atop the rest, it hadn't been.

This leaf, however, possessed the weight of them all. It pressed them into the hands she had exposed to receive them, and she felt the sting of new cuts in a dozen places at once. But she did not drop them; instead, she watched as the blue leaf finally came to rest. It began to glow.

"The leaves you were offered came from the oldest of dreams; they are called the bones of the earth, but I'm not sure why."

Jewel nodded. "What am I to do with them?"

"What you must."

When she was gone, the two who had served as entertainers and guardians bowed.

Jewel glanced at Adam. "If I order him to wake, will he?"

The woman laughed, as if Jewel's question were vastly humorous. The man by her side chuckled. "He is your guest, Terafin; he does not sleep. The orders you give, he chooses to follow—or not, as the case may be. You might as soon order him to sprout wings or roots as order him to wake; they will meet the same end."

Remembering what had happened the last time she had wakened to escape this place, Jewel exhaled. She turned to Adam to offer him a hand; hers were still full of leaves, and her palms were no doubt bleeding. "Grab my elbow," she told him.

He did as she asked.

When they left the clearing, it vanished. Jewel knew; she looked back not ten yards distant, and all she could see was forest. It was a forest of thick, tall trees that somehow allowed steeply slanted beams of light to touch the forest floor.

"How are we going to get back?" Adam asked.

"I don't suppose you can open your real eyes?"

"No." Before she could ask, he added, "I've tried. I've closed my eyes here, but I can't feel my waking eyelids. I can't feel Maria's hand; I can feel your elbow. I can feel the breeze. I can hear the silence of forest."

Jewel frowned. "You can't feel Maria's hand at all?"

"No. Not since we arrived here."

"The night that you found me in Leila's dream—were you aware of me?"

"Yes."

"I mean, were you aware that you were—"

"Healing you? Touching you in the waking world? Yes. I was aware."

"Could you have woken, then?"

He shook his head. "No, not then."

"And now?"

"Now is different. I am no longer holding Maria's hand in the waking world." The gravity of his expression was broken by a sudden smile. "I do not think we *are* sleeping, Matriarch. I do not think—for us—this *is* a dream."

"That's what I'm afraid of," she replied, failing to see the humor in the situation.

"Can you imagine Levec's face? Or the mages?"

"That's what's making you smile?" Her brows rose into her hairline as she considered the exact same scenario. "If I had a free hand, I'd smack you."

He laughed then. "You are very like my sister."

Jewel slid into Torra as she stepped carefully over the large, exposed roots of a tree. "She doesn't have to wear stupid dresses or watch her tongue."

"No." His laughter faded. "But like you, she will kill."

"Adam—"

"Nicu envied the Matriarchs," he continued, as he walked.

"Nicu? Your cousin?"

"Yes."

"The man who betrayed your clan?" Jewel was surprised at the lack of anger with which he spoke the name. And she shouldn't have been; she knew Adam. Adam was not a boy to whom anger or contempt clung.

"Yes. He envied Margret and Elena, because in time one of them would become Matriarch. One of them would rule Arkosa. He asked me once if I did not. Envy them," he added, as if this wasn't clear.

"He didn't know you very well," she replied. Of all the questions she might have asked Adam, that wouldn't have been the first; it wouldn't have even been on the list.

"He didn't understand *them* very well," he replied. "He understood the power the Matriarchs wield. He understood the obedience they command. My mother was not so terrifying as Yollana of the Havalla Voyani; Yollana commanded even other Matriarchs. They did not like her, but they did not disobey her."

Remembering the old woman, Jewel grimaced. "I wouldn't have dared."

"No." He tightened his hold on her elbow when she stumbled, easing his grip when she was once again steady on her feet. "She is lonely."

"Pardon?"

"Yollana. She is lonely. Margret is lonely. My mother. Nicu did not see this. He didn't understand how their responsibility isolates them. He only saw the power—and it was a power forever denied him."

"Or you."

"Or me."

"Why?"

"Why what?"

"Why can't men be Matriarchs? Well, like Matriarchs, but with a different title."

"Women guarantee the bloodline," he replied. "Men do not bear children. Their wives might carry the children of other men. But a woman's child is *of* her bloodline. There is no doubt."

"And if the Matriarch bears no daughters?"

"It does not happen. But if their daughters die, there are the daughters of their sisters."

"And if not?"

He frowned. "It doesn't happen often. But even the Matriarch's daughters are not guaranteed to become Matriarch if they do not have even a hint of the gift."

Jewel said nothing. It sounded far more complicated than becoming the ruler of one of The Ten. "You never envied your sister."

"No. You must not tell her, but sometimes I pitied her."

Jewel looked sharply at him. Pity was galling; it was *not* something one offered one's sister.

"She is like you, Jewel," he said, for the second time. "She does not want to kill. She does not want to command. She wants to be part of a family."

"Mine are all dead."

"They are not. Your den is your family." His hand tightened again, but this time, Jewel stepped over the root without almost landing on her backside. "I would spare Margret, if I could. I would take her burdens."

"Adam—"

He met her gaze and smiled. It was not a happy expression. "No," he said, although she hadn't asked, "I do not want to kill, either. But I think I could do it."

"You're healer-born," was her surprisingly gentle reply. "And the healers are not known for their ability to *end* life."

"You are wrong," was his soft reply. "They can kill." He spoke with utter certainty.

Jewel felt uneasy then. "This is *not* something to discuss outside of the Houses of Healing."

"Do you know what happened to Daine?"

"And if you *do* discuss it outside of the Houses of Healing, you *don't* discuss it with the ruler of one of The Ten."

"Finch said I am one of your den," he replied. "So it is not as Terafin that I approach you."

She had nothing to say to that. "I know what happened to Daine. He was abducted by a member of the Terafin House Council, and he was forced to heal the man."

"And that Council member?"

"He died later."

"Do you think he died by accident?"

"Daine wasn't kidnapped and forced to heal him because he was accident prone," was her bitter reply.

Adam accepted the sense of that. "Levec knew. Alowan knew."

Jewel stiffened.

"His name was Corniel ATerafin. Daine healed him, bringing him back from the brink of death. His men would have killed Daine after the healing; Corniel would not allow it."

She could not think of anyone who had been called back from the shadow of the bridge that *could*.

"Levec arranged for his assassination."

"Adam."

"Levec would have killed him, but he could not reach him. Levec is a healer."

"You are *not* Levec."

"No. But, Jewel, without Alowan's aid, without the information Alowan, as a resident of the Terafin manse, could provide, the assassins would never have reached Corniel. If I am not Levec, could I not, in time, be Alowan?"

Alowan. She stopped walking, shrugged her elbow free of what was, she realized, his protective grasp, and turned to face him fully. He was young. He was so young she couldn't remember being his age in any way except numerically. He was—he had been—gentle with the Serra Diora when she had first joined the Arkosan caravan; he had been as gentle with his furiously resentful sister. He had been exuberant and silly when given the care and the feeding of the children and he had, by presence, made life less tense between his hordes of relatives.

She had watched him do it, thinking him young and inexperienced.

She watched him now. There was no laughter in his eyes, but no fear, either. He faced a woman he thought of as Matriarch armed only with facts and a desire to protect the people he loved.

But his facts were weapons. "Why did Levec tell you this?"

"I asked."

"And he *answered*?"

"Not the first time. Not the second. But, yes, in the end, he answered. You have no trouble imagining that Levec could do what he did."

"No. It's not Levec—"

"It's Alowan. But it was Alowan who brought Daine to Terafin—to heal you. Alowan understood the damage done to Daine, and in his way, he provided Daine what he felt was the only opportunity to heal it. And he provided safety from Corniel. Do you doubt it?"

Did she? The answer she wanted to offer was *yes*. Yes, she doubted it. Alowan's healerie had been an oasis of peace, a refuge, a place of life and light.

"Do you doubt that I can become what he was?"

Yes. Yes she doubted it. But the word wouldn't leave her lips because she could see—for just a moment—the steel of the older man in the youthful lines of the younger man's face. She swallowed. "I hope you can," she said softly. "And at least you wouldn't be Levec."

He laughed, the sudden shift in expression and tone shattering the brief glimpse she had had of his future. She turned to face endless forest; he once again caught her elbow. They both understood that it was important they not be separated, although neither had said it in so many words.

They walked for half an hour before Jewel once again stopped. The forest had not substantially changed, and it was hard—for someone born and bred to city trees—to easily differentiate between the trunks of large trees; they might have been walking in a circle, for all she knew. The sun did not noticeably change; the light across the forest floor still fell at a steep incline, not a gradual one.

And Jewel was done with wandering, like lost children, in a fairy-tale landscape. These trees were part of her forest, and her forest was part of Terafin. It was to Terafin that she now walked. There was no sudden clearing, no obvious path, to follow, but it wasn't necessary. She wasn't lost, here. She could not afford to be lost.

Ahead, in the same light, she could see the sudden glint of silver leaves. "You'll like this," she told Adam, "as long as the cats aren't there."

"I like your cats."

"They'd kill you if they could."

"Yes, but they can't and they accept it." He smiled. "Ariel loves Shadow. Do you think he would kill her, if he could?"

"No."

"No?"

"She's never, ever going to be dangerous to him. You might be." The silvered leaves of impossible trees were now overhead; they caught light to the right and left for as far as the eye could see. "I don't think the cats like to terrify people. The best they could hope for with Ariel is terror and death."

"Do you think that was always true?"

"Always? I don't know. I only met them once before they arrived here." Silver gave way to gold, as it had in one other forest, the cooler color surrendering the heights to the warmer one. "They were made of stone, at the time. But they seemed the same."

"The same?"

"They stepped on each other's tails and paws and tried to nudge each other into tree branches. They tried to land in the same spot. They made a lot of noise." She sighed as gold gave way to diamond; the warmer color to ice. She didn't really care for diamonds, and never had. But the trees themselves were arresting. "They were utterly silent in the presence of the Winter King."

"They served him?"

"Yes. I think he turned them into stone; he didn't say why. Or how."

"They weren't stone when they found you again."

"No." She smiled as diamond gave way to a clearing. In its center, standing alone, was a tree of burning flame; it seemed taller than Jewel remembered it. Taller, grander, red leaves crackling in a blaze that would never consume them. "I remember my first home. Not my family's home; not Rath's, but mine. It was crowded. You couldn't walk from one end to another without tripping over someone." The fire's light spanned her cheeks as she lifted her face.

"We didn't have a day of silence. We didn't have a day where one of my den wasn't stepping on someone's foot or tripping them or stealing some of the food off someone else's plate. Some days, we had Duster in a raging fury; that made almost everyone go quiet until she stormed out.

"The cats remind me of us. They're friendlier than Duster ever was, and they're much easier to control. Don't tell them I said that," she added, with a wry smile. "They'll only feel insulted."

"Or worse."

"Or worse." Tendrils of flame reached out and wrapped themselves gently around her wrists; the ache in the palms of both hands lessened. She felt no desire to plant any of these leaves in her forest. She knew it was not here they belonged, although she couldn't say why. As she watched, the leaves of iron began to melt. They didn't become molten; they pooled instead beneath the weight of the single blue leaf. It floated, sinking as the leaves upon which it sat dissolved.

In the end, only the blue leaf remained. It now looked metallic, and the white veins were a bright light that nonetheless did not hurt to look at.

"The fire doesn't burn you."

"Not this fire, no."

"Will it burn me?"

She shook her head. "Not here. Not yet. I don't understand why this tree is at the heart of my forest. The fire from which it sprouted was *Kialli* fire, not mine; it was meant to kill, to destroy. It took root here."

"You planted it," was his quiet reply.

She turned to look over her shoulder. "Adam."

His expression, lit and warmed by the colors of flame, was grave.

"We'll walk past this tree, and the footpath will join the Terafin grounds. The magi will know. Sigurne will know."

"Could you walk this path back to the Houses of Healing?"

She shook her head.

"Will you be able to, one day?"

"I think so." It was a quiet, difficult admission.

"Levec's not going to like it."

She snorted. "If Levec isn't beating my doors down by the time we've arrived in the manse, it'll be a miracle. He won't particularly care if I've disappeared—he can't stand patricians in his house. He'll be beyond livid that *you* did." Inhaling, she drew her hands closer to her chest. "Let's go home."

It was only as they approached the manse that Jewel realized that she should have recognized at least one of the dreamers, and hadn't. Hannerle had not been among them. And it was only as they left the edge of the deep forest that she realized night had fallen.

Chapter Twenty-two

THE MERCHANT AUTHORITY functioned as a bastion of patrician power and authority that was impervious to all but extreme physical damage. Its public halls and barely defensible wickets were occupied from the moment the front doors rolled open to the moment they closed; indeed, the hours of operation were often contested by merchants who had not quite finished conducting business which any idiot could see was of vast—and superior—import.

Nothing short of cracked bearing wall could bring the Authority fully to its knees.

Sadly, the men and women who toiled within its many offices were frailer; they were subject to the usual necessities of life: food, drink, and sleep. Finch had had very little of the latter the previous night. The same was true of every member of the West Wing, with the possible exception of Ariel. Jewel and Adam had traveled by fully crested carriage to the Houses of Healing.

While a carriage did arrive, ostensibly from the Houses of Healing, it bore the insignia of the Order of Knowledge, and among its occupants neither The Terafin nor Adam could be found. The Chosen who had accompanied The

Terafin—Torvan among them—had arrived almost immediately afterward.

Finch, unsuspecting, had been cleaning teacups and discussing minor matters of import with Jarven, who had become increasingly testy and bored over the passage of a week. She arrived a full hour after either the magi or the Chosen. The West Wing was not empty; but she wasn't given time to so much as set foot within the familiar confines of her home within the manse; a page waited at the doors, pale as chalk, with an urgent message: she was summoned to the right-kin's office immediately.

There, she found Torvan, Arrendas, and Teller; Barston barely glanced at her ring before he waved her past. It wasn't necessary, of course—he knew her on sight—but he was a stickler for form, and he was especially pointed in demanding correct form from those who had suffered a deficiency in their native upbringing.

"Finch," Teller said, as she entered the room and closed the door behind her. "The Terafin has not yet returned from the Houses of Healing."

She glanced at Torvan, Captain of the Chosen. There was, about his expression, some shadow she had not seen for well over a decade. He did not speak.

"Both The Terafin and Adam were seated beside one of Levec's patients who happened to be awake. They apparently disappeared as soon as the patient suffered a relapse."

"Apparently?"

"They disappeared," Torvan said.

"You saw them vanish?"

"No, ATerafin—"

"Finch. Call me Finch while the door is closed. If I hear ATerafin one more time today I'll scream."

Torvan nodded. He did not, however, use her name. "They were present by the bedside, and then they were not. There was no blood, no injury, and no obvious use of magic; believe that the magi would have noticed the latter."

"The magi waiting in the outer office," Finch said softly. "Are they the mages who were present in the healerie?"

"Two of them. The third was sent from the Order. We are, fortunately, blessed with the presence of the House Mage." Teller's grimace made clear how mixed he thought that blessing was. The presence of the House Mage—a pipe-smoking and insouciant Meralonne at his finest—had done little to calm the magi who did arrive in Teller's office. Meralonne made clear that he thought their presence in the Terafin manse superfluous and entirely unnecessary.

Since they were mages, and since they wore medallions that indicated relative seniority within the Order, voices were raised, and hundreds of words spoken. Most of these went unheard by any but the person speaking them, and they clashed the way slightly worried men with more pride than common sense frequently did.

"Barston didn't enjoy it," Teller admitted, "but Meralonne distracted the magi by offending them all the moment he opened his mouth."

"Meralonne wasn't in the outer office when I arrived."

"No. When the man with the salt-and-pepper beard started to crackle—and I mean that literally—his two companions suggested that this was a matter for the guildmaster; Meralonne agreed and left. Instantly."

". . . Which none of our other visitors have the power to do."

"Yes. They're waiting for her here."

For the next four hours, Finch and Teller had dealt with Jay's utter absence, her inexplicable disappearance, from the Houses of Healing. The fact that every person stricken by the sleeping sickness had, one by one, woken, signified little. They remembered nothing of their dreams—if indeed they dreamed at all—but that, Adam had said, was not unusual.

Word of her disappearance had, of course, traveled, although they'd done what they could to minimize its spread. At the top of hour two, Marrick joined the magi in the outer office, and within half an hour, Elonne and Rymark joined him. At the top of the third hour, Sigurne Mellifas arrived, looking grim and haggard. She was allowed into the office, Meralonne by her side. Haerrad could not be far behind.

But Jay beat him—thank all the gods—by about ten minutes. She appeared in the open door of the right-kin's office.

Finch was halfway across the room before she remembered that Jay was now The Terafin, and *no one* hugged The Terafin or cried on her shoulder with relief. Not when the door was open and the magi were stewing and the senior members of the House Council bore witness.

The Terafin, in this case, offered a curt apology for her delayed return—to her House Council. To Sigurne and Meralonne she offered a formal nod.

"Terafin," Sigurne said, tendering her a bow. She glanced at Meralonne, who failed to notice. "Apologies for our unnecessary presence; there was some concern, but it was clearly misplaced."

"House Terafin appreciates your presence, but as you note, it is unnecessary."

The mages were more easily dismissed than the House Council; Haerrad arrived a few minutes after a page had been sent to escort them to their waiting carriage. The House Council did not receive a more detailed explanation of Jay's absence, but the lack of detail and its resultant questions had taken another three quarters of an hour, after which, Finch was starving.

If Ellerson was not present, the Terafin Household Staff was, and food was arranged. Jay hadn't eaten either. She accompanied Finch and Teller to the West Wing, and joined them. Over the meal, with the Chosen who had lost her in attendance, she had explained more fully both her sudden absence and her return. The return, Finch understood. The absence made her uneasy, because Jay didn't understand it herself.

In the end, it was not far off morning when Finch had at last crawled off to bed, and it was not far off the same morning—from the other side—when she crawled, with far less enthusiasm, out of the same bed, put her entire appearance into the hands of the maid, and made her way to the Merchant Authority.

Lucille had taken one look at her face, narrowed her eyes, lowered her voice, and sent her into the relative safety of her own small office with a pile of papers, most of which were not urgent, and all of which Finch could deal with in her sleep. The woman who was this particular office's Barston had not said a word.

But she wouldn't. Three of the four new employees installed upon the death of The Terafin had yet to resign their posts. Lucille didn't trust them, and not for the usual reasons—questionable competence, which could in most cases be forgiven, although never silently. She was certain to whom two of them reported, but had not chosen to share—or burden—Finch with that information.

Finch was certain who all three reported to, but likewise felt no need to share.

She was grateful, however, for Lucille, because curiosity about The Terafin's late night excursion extended well beyond the irritable magi, and were it not for Lucille, it would have been difficult to avoid. If Lucille, however, had an iron grip over the environs of the office itself, she did not pick and choose its visitors.

Finch, behind an intimidating amount of work, albeit otherwise uncomplicated, looked up at the knock on her door. It was a heavy knock; definitely Lucille's. She rose, setting quill aside but pausing to cap the inkwell, and approached the door as it opened; Lucille's knocks were never about permission to enter; they merely served as early warnings.

"What is it?" Finch asked, seeing Lucille's expression. "What's happened?"

"Someone has requested an appointment be made to speak with you."

"Patris Larkasir?"

"No." Whoever it was, Lucille did not approve. Finch was intrigued. Lucille was not in the habit of informing Finch of nuisance requests; she denied them herself. If she disapproved, Finch rarely heard about it until after the fact—usually from a far too amused Jarven.

This meant, of course, that immediate and offhand dismissal was not considered an option. "Who?" she asked; she was not careless enough to peer around the wall of Lucille to sneak a glimpse of the offender.

"Patris Araven."

The office was not exactly in an uproar when Finch left the privacy—and safety—of her small room. It was not a room into which a man of Hectore of Araven's stature in the Merchant Authority would ever be invited; it had room for Finch and one visitor, and Hectore was never without a servant. The other occupants of the vast space in which The Terafin's concerns were administered were silent. Silent and watchful.

That type of idle voyeurism was never encouraged by Lucille, but she apparently disliked Patris Araven enough that she didn't lay into the idlers in his presence.

Finch knew of Hectore of Araven. It was impossible to work anywhere in the Merchant Authority and remain unaware of who he was. She had seen him a handful of times at a distance, and she had, on two occasions, served him tea while he and Jarven conversed—if verbal fencing with little obvious content could be considered conversation. He had been a man very much at ease in Jarven's office, and Jarven had treated him like an equal. Like a ferocious, cunning equal. She knew that Araven and Terafin were negotiating the fees for a particular passage into the mines in the Menorans, but those negotiations were firmly in Jarven's domain, not hers.

Patris Araven was seated, not standing; his servant stood unobtrusively against the wall. Seated, he did not seem terrifying or intimidating; he was a man of middling years, and his hair was that shade of gray that looked silver. He sported a beard, and he wore a cut of clothing that deemphasized his size; he was not a small man.

But he was not a man who immediately appeared to be autocratic or arrogant; nor did he gaze about the office in well-bred disdain. His dark eyes were bright and lively as they came to rest upon Finch's face. He rose at once.

It was hard to offer his hand while Lucille was standing between them; his slightly wry smile acknowledged this.

"Finch ATerafin?"

She smiled and inclined her head. "Patris Araven."

"I am indeed that if you have annoyed me. I prefer Hectore, in other circumstances." He glanced at Lucille's expression—which Finch couldn't easily see—and the lines that bracketed his eyes and the corners of his lips deepened. "I hope I'm not interrupting anything urgent."

"All of the work we do here is considered urgent," Finch replied, a hint of amusement lurking in the gravity of her tone.

He chuckled. "And so it is. Might I have a few minutes of your time? If the office is not conducive to collegial discussion," he added, daring another glance at Lucille, "might I suggest an early lunch?"

Finch could almost feel the glacial chill in the air, and

hesitated. She was saved from the necessity of making a reply by the opening of another door—the door to the only room which *was* grand enough, and large enough, to accommodate persons of note.

Jarven entered the outer office. "Hectore," he said, smiling broadly. "What an unexpected surprise. You find me in search of my tea, I'm afraid."

"And I have no intention of interrupting such important business," was the equally jovial reply. "I am not here to trouble your day with my minor complaints."

"I have been poring over the last missive you sent, and I quibble with the use of the word minor. Lucille?"

Lucille turned to Finch. "Tea," she said quietly.

Lunch, which would have been a welcome escape, was set aside in favor of tea in the confines of Jarven's very secure office. Finch was not surprised; she was longer than usual at assembling Jarven's tea because Lucille had a few pointed words to say about Hectore, none of them particularly flattering.

"Don't be taken in by his friendly face," she said, choosing between five different varieties of jam. "And don't be taken in by his demeanor, either. Given half a chance, he'll rob you blind and leave you thanking him for it when he goes."

"The same has been said—many times—of Jarven, Lucille."

Lucille glared, but didn't argue. She adored Jarven. She was not, however, blind to his faults—if the ability to rob someone blind *and* leave them grateful for the theft *was* a fault, in a man who oversaw the Terafin concerns in the Merchant Authority. "What does he want, anyway?"

"I honestly have no idea. Did he not say?"

"No." And clearly, from the thin line of her lips, she'd asked. But there was only so much she could demand from Patris Araven. "Take the ivory set," she added, as Finch began to set cups and saucers down. "Don't use those."

Given Lucille's mood, Finch didn't argue. She put away the cups normally used for tea, and selected the cups used in less friendly negotiations in which impressing the opponent in every conceivable way was considered a minor advantage. Hectore was not the type of man who would be impressed by cups, in Finch's opinion; Lucille, however, was in a bear of a mood, and in such a case, minor compromises were to be offered wherever possible.

Lucille selected the food that would arrive with the tea, her lips thinning as she did. By the end of the preparation, the entire thing had the look and feel of a last meal—a meal offered to someone who was headed directly to his or her own execution. Finch lifted the heavy tray and Lucille preceded her into the wide and silent exterior of the office she ruled. She walked directly to Jarven's closed doors, opened one, and stepped back to allow Finch to pass her.

"Finch," Jarven said, smiling broadly. "Just the young lady we were hoping to see." He was seated behind his desk—squarely behind it. When he took tea with Finch, as he often did in the afternoons, he tended to sit to one side of the bastion, nearer to where she pulled up a chair.

There were no chairs pulled up at the side of the desk; they were arrayed in front of it, in clear—if mostly empty—positions of supplication. Hectore occupied one; his servant stood at the back of the room, near the doors Lucille had opened. She remained for a long moment, her expression grim; she glared at Jarven, glared at the back of Hectore's head, and pursed her lips at Finch as if she wanted to say more.

She probably did. When she had warnings to offer, she relied on repetition. No one, she once said, hits a nail with a hammer *once*. This nail, however, carried the tea set into Jarven's office, and a modicum of dignity was required. Finch didn't greet this with the expected relief; if Lucille was overly cautious, her instincts were seldom completely wrong.

Hectore rose as Finch approached the tea table which was seldom used; in general, Jarven allowed the tray to occupy some portion of his pristine desktop. Today, however, he would not.

"Patris Araven was telling me," Jarven said, "that he hoped to make an appointment with you, Finch." His expression was bright; his fingers were steepled beneath his chin. He did not look at Finch as he spoke.

Hectore, however, did. He tendered her a respectful nod—and appeared to mean it. Jarven raised a brow.

Finch offered tea to the two men; they accepted with almost regal condescension. It had been a long time since Finch had been a silent adornment in Jarven's office. In the first few years of her tenure here, she had served almost as a maid, at Jarven's insistence, and to Lucille's annoyance. But she soon came to understand why Jarven wanted her here; it was here that she could observe the dealings of some of the most powerful merchants within Terafin—and outside of it as well. She couldn't blunder through such interviews because she wasn't meant to speak at all.

But she observed how Jarven spoke. She observed him at his sharpest; saw when he chose to accentuate his age—and implied mental frailty—and when he chose to dispense, utterly, with pretense. On occasion, that pretense could be summed up as civility.

Today he was civil. He was, she thought, enjoying himself. Hectore seemed likewise entertained; she briefly regretted her absence from this room while the men assumed their positions on either side of the desk.

She was not, however, a young girl now. Her role was not that of a servant.

To emphasize this, Hectore shook his head. "This will not do, ATerafin," he said, choosing the title and looking at neither of the people who owned it. "Andrei, please. Pour."

The servant detached himself from the wall and took control of the tea service; Finch allowed it because Hectore was once again addressing her. "I imagine you've seen many men who now occupy my position."

"Jarven is frequently engaged in House business," she replied.

"Indeed, he is."

She waited, but he seemed to be in no hurry to divulge the reason for this highly unusual visit; his presence here would cause a day's worth of heated gossip—behind Lucille's carefully turned back—at the least. That it involved Finch in some way meant she would also be the subject of said gossip. She didn't have the option of walking away from it.

Jarven lifted a set of documents.

Hectore snorted. "I am not here about trivialities."

"You consider the concessions you've demanded trivial?"

"I consider them of as much import as you do, old friend. They are a good exercise in caution for the younger, ambitious set; they offer no new challenges or obstacles to the older generation."

Hectore was, in Finch's estimation, at least a decade younger than Jarven.

Jarven raised a white brow. He glanced once more at the documents before he set them aside, relegating them to a corner of the desk that would not see much use for the rest of the meeting. "I was attempting to offer you the slender hope of plausibility," he noted.

"It is wasted on me, of course," Hectore replied. He took the cup and saucer that Andrei offered. Jarven did likewise. Neither appeared to actually see the servant—but men frequently didn't. Very few had paid much attention to Finch when she had served in Andrei's capacity.

She was a little surprised when Andrei pulled a chair back so that she might sit in it, and she was neither Jarven nor Hectore; she startled and turned to meet his gaze. His expression was shuttered; it was so smooth and so neutral he reminded her, for an instant, of Haval. That itself was an arresting thought. She accepted the chair, sat in it, and likewise accepted the cup and saucer he offered.

"Much is wasted on you, Hectore. Tea of any quality, for one. I'm almost of a mind to offer you something stronger."

Hectore laughed. "As an excuse to drink it yourself? I really must peruse those amendments, Jarven. I probably owe some poor young man in my office a bonus."

Andrei then passed out the small, cylindrical biscuits of which Jarven was so fond. Finch took one; Jarven took three. Hectore took one but set it beside his cup with a mild frown; he was clearly not a person with an enormous sweet tooth.

Finch was. She stirred sugar into her tea, added cream—which neither of the two men touched, and dipped the end of the biscuit into the resultant hot liquid.

She was very much surprised when the cup shattered.

For a long moment, it seemed that were two streams of time in Jarven's office: one, in which the cup shattered instantly, and tea that was rather too hot splashed into the saucer and over its gold-edged rim to land in Finch's lap, and the other, in which all motion was suspended and a terrible silence, an utter stillness, enfolded every other occupant of the room.

Andrei was the first to move; he lifted Finch out of her chair and pulled the folds of her skirt away from her legs without actually revealing any of them. The shards of delicate, expensive cup were brushed down her lap onto the carpet beneath her feet, and—quick thinking on his part— the pitcher of water that also accompanied the tea set was upended onto the same skirts.

Jarven, who had lifted a biscuit, set it down without comment. His expression shuttered, the jovial air of a friendly, sharp competitor instantly doused.

Hectore's personality did not likewise retreat into a careful, blank composition of features. "This, I presume, is the point at which you apologize for the inferiority of your dishes?" He raised a brow, and set the teacup upon Jarven's desk.

Finch glanced up from the ruins of her skirt. Jarven's arctic lips had curved into a smile; had she not known him for years, it would have chilled her utterly. "It is, indeed. We seldom have guests of note in this office; the dishes are antiques, and therefore seldom used. I apologize for any discomfort caused."

Finch rose. "Let me take this away," she began.

"Do not touch it," Jarven said, without a glance in her direction.

"Do as he says," Hectore added. "But tell me, Finch, in all your years as Jarven's glorified serving girl, have you ever had occasion to apologize for the quality of Terafin's tea service?"

She felt it safe to ignore the question.

"Andrei." Hectore lifted his cup.

Andrei glanced at Jarven, but nodded.

"It is unfortunate," Jarven said. "I would suggest we repair to the Placid Sea, but Finch is no longer appropriately attired." He rose, abandoning the safety of his desk; his very posture implied it was no longer necessary. "If you will excuse me for a moment, Patris Araven?"

A glance passed between Hectore and his servant; his servant stiffened. He set the cup he had taken from his master's hand upon the empty space on one of the shelves built into the wall.

"Of course," Hectore replied, waving a careless hand. Finch noted the silence that had preceded his response; Jarven could not, therefore, have failed to do likewise. What he made of it, however, she couldn't say. He left his office, closing the door at his back.

"Will we be able to leave this room before he returns?" Hectore asked.

She glanced at the closed door. Silence was her best option. It was not, however, the one she chose. "I'm not certain." Her tone was apologetic. Her expression was not. "But I believe our suspicions are aligned."

"Andrei?"

"Yes, we can leave. It will be marked, and there may be some difficulty. Do you wish to take that risk?"

Hectore chuckled. "Why should I? I had hoped to speak to Finch, and she is here; Jarven is not. Jarven is an old opponent; he is naturally cautious and unnaturally canny. If he suspects that I had a hand in today's minor disturbance, he is clearly well into the dotage he oft feigns."

"You don't believe that."

"No. He is far too intelligent."

Finch glanced at Andrei; his back had become a wall as he turned to face the cup he'd set down. "Patris Araven, why *did* you come to the Terafin offices?"

"You have obviously spent far too much time in Jarven's company. I came, as I said, to arrange an appointment to speak with you. Did The Terafin not give you any advance warning?"

Finch stiffened. "I'm afraid it must have slipped her mind."

His eyes narrowed. "I am going to assume, for the sake of my dignity, that the wild rumors that have escaped the Houses of Healing yesterday contained some element of truth."

"I'm afraid I can't say. I haven't been privy to any of those rumors."

Hectore smiled. "You do that well."

"Pardon?"

"Lie. It is a useful trait—one that The Terafin does not

seem to possess. I was informed by the leader of your House that there have been numerous difficulties since she became The Terafin. Andrei?"

"A moment, Hectore."

Finch considered the man seated before her with care. She considered what she knew of him—which involved a large amount of draconian paperwork—and what she had heard. At the moment, with his careful and jovial smile, he didn't seem to be a man to whom Jewel would confide.

Yet she had. "Why did you wish to speak with The Terafin?"

"The Terafin and I have an old friend in common. I am not sure if you will be familiar with his name, but I will offer it anyway: Ararath of Handernesse."

Finch's eyes rounded slightly. She sat, her wet skirts falling over her lap. She didn't keep clothing of any sort in the Merchant Authority, and could not therefore change.

"I see you knew him."

She nodded slowly. "He was related to you?"

"He was my godson."

"And you've become aware of the debt we owe him."

"We?"

"House Terafin." The answer was smooth and unmarred by hesitation.

"Ah, no. I did not seek The Terafin in order to speak about debt. I asked for her aid in a particular matter, and offered my aid in return. I would, as a gesture of good faith, rework the contract that is sitting so forlornly on Jarven's desk, but I have found, with Jarven, that it is unwise to let him grow idle."

"What aid did you feel compelled to offer?"

"What aid did she feel compelled to accept? Andrei."

Andrei turned. "Two parts," he said quietly. "But it *is* a subtle combination. I do not believe it would have killed instantly, unless the imbiber were already of weak constitution."

"That's all you can tell us?"

"For the moment."

Hectore had not once so much as glanced at his servant; he watched Finch. "I did not, of course, expect any of my expertise to be of immediate relevance to you. But you are a House Council member, if a very junior one. You have been given an office of your own within the Terafin quarters in the Authority; it would not be considered a small accomplishment if one had ambitions."

Finch's brows rose. "You cannot possibly believe that today's unpleasantness was aimed at *me*?"

"I would not," he replied, his lips retaining the framework of a smile, "were it not for the fact that Jarven does."

"He can't possibly believe that. I am a minor official in the Merchant Authority."

"A minor official who serves as a full member of the House Council, and a minor official who has a permanent residence within the Terafin manse upon the Isle. Foolish of me to consider either important." His smile did not touch his eyes. "Andrei?"

"I am not entirely certain that my interference will be either welcome or acceptable, Hectore," his servant replied, the mild reproach an obvious indicator of the esteem in which Patris Araven held him.

Hectore's smile froze, and after a long, immobile moment, Andrei approached the doors Jarven had closed.

Finch held her breath as he reached for the handle and opened the door. She exhaled when the only result of the attempt *was* the open door. It closed again as he left.

"I confess a galling ignorance when it comes to ancient trees that grow—overnight—in the grounds of a manse upon the Isle. My ignorance when it comes to giant, winged cats is less galling. I am not talent-born. I felt no pressing need to learn the mysteries of the gods—any god—and I very much doubt any temple would have me, although they're all prepared to take my money.

"But I have had some experience with people, ATerafin. Not all of those experiences were pleasant, nor would I expect my life in future to be devoid of unpleasantness. It is, in part, the cost of power—but only in part. I understand that you knew The Terafin when she living in the old holdings."

Finch inclined her head.

"Then you, of course, understand that unpleasantness also proceeds from lack of power. There is no man, woman, or child—except perhaps for babes in arms—who has not experienced pain. The world scars us. Life scars us. But our ability to take scars is the cost, or perhaps the proof, that we do live.

"I claim no greater understanding of The Terafin than Jarven might; I claim a vastly smaller understanding than yours. She is new to her rank, new to the seat. She is, at this moment, at her most vulnerable. This is simple truth. It would be—and will be—true of any ruler of The Ten, in both past and future. Gaining power and retaining it are two very different struggles—and she does not, perhaps, have a background in which old alliances and former family ties will be of use.

"What she has, ATerafin, is you. She has the current right-kin, a man who has otherwise failed to distinguish himself outside of the bounds of the House. Her oathguard—her Chosen, in Terafin nomenclature—are few, in comparison to their strength while Amarais lived.

"She has managed a few clever coups; she is being watched with not a little interest in several quarters. The bards appear content to spread her fame throughout the streets of the city, where they can find any audience willing to listen; no less a mage than Meralonne APhaniel serves House Terafin exclusively. It is rumored that he has chosen to do so for free.

"While the Kings are rumored to have strong reason to fear her—and I have seen some proof of that in my recent visits to the Royal Trade Commission—they will not interfere in Terafin business. There is every reason to believe, given no less than five assassination attempts in a paltry two months that they will not have reason for long.

"But she *remains* alive. Given the nature of the fifth assassin, her survival is an act of sorcery or luck—it is entirely beyond my ken. The nature of some of the other assassins, however, is not." He glanced pointedly at the shards of cup beneath their chairs. "I assumed—and it appears it was a rash assumption—that the more visceral elements of a succession war had already been dispensed with. I assumed—and I feel this is *less* rash—that The Terafin's enemies were, in large part, outside of Terafin—and outside of the patriciate that otherwise rules this city.

"But you are not your Lord. You have not—that I am aware of—evinced any surprising or bewildering talents; you are merely a normal mortal—as am I." He frowned. "I admit that my first instinct would be to assume Jarven is the target. Jarven, however, has been famously apolitical for most of his tenure here. Even aligned, he has never been easily controlled."

"Patris Araven—"

"The Terafin asked me to speak with you; she wished you to impart details about the four attacks I did not personally witness—and perhaps about the conclusion of the one I did. Was she aware of the danger to you?"

"No. And Patris Araven—"

"Hectore."

"*Patris* Araven. If you wish my aid in any way, you will not inform her."

One brow rose as he considered her. "She will discover the facts—"

"I am not at all certain she will," Finch replied. "If I were to guess, Jarven is beyond these doors complaining bitterly to Lucille about your arrogance—with a certain arrogance of his own, of course. It is unfortunate that you sent your servant to join him; otherwise, he might be seen to capitulate to your demands for the appointment you desired—with me." She rose, her legs uncomfortably damp, and reached for the document Jarven had all but discarded. "I will return this to you, Patris Araven."

"And I will leave with it, in an obvious fashion."

"And return on the morrow with a different document, yes."

His gaze assessed her. Her skirts were an unfortunate shade of brown. But she had stood in far grimmer circumstances in far poorer garb; she met his gaze and held it.

"And Jarven?"

"Leave Jarven to me."

Both brows rose. After a gap of silent seconds, Hectore laughed out loud. "My dear," he said, rising once again, "you look like a slip of a girl; you look almost meek. Even now, were you standing in a crowded room, I might not notice you. If nothing else can be said of The Terafin, she commands attention."

"Attention, where we grew up, wasn't always desirable." She smiled. "But where it could not be avoided, we were forced to make other plans." She continued to hold out the document; Hectore took it.

"Do you know who might want you dead?"

"Not yet." Finch exhaled. "I could name perhaps half a dozen."

"And this does not disturb you?"

"No. It is not, after all, personal."

His smile deepened. "Not personal?"

"As you've said, there are always unpleasant acts of factionalism when the succession for a House is contested. But I, as you, had been under the impression that such factionalism was a thing of the past. Foolish, really. I think it best you retire for the day." She glanced at her skirts. "I will not see you out. If Jarven means to affect ignorance of this day's events, it's likely he's already sent someone to the manse with the urgent and extremely tactful request for a change of clothing—or three."

He bowed. "You are an interesting woman, Finch. I almost understand why The Terafin sent me to you."

"Don't misconstrue her motives," Finch replied, walking toward the doors.

"I have not made clear what I believe those motives to be."

"Which will save us both embarrassment. I look forward to our future dealings."

Jarven entered the room over an hour later; he found Finch in an unusual position: behind his desk. Her hands were clasped loosely in her lap, and she appeared to be examining her slightly blurred reflection on the surface of his pristine desk.

He cleared his throat, and she looked up. She did not, however, stand.

"So I am now displaced, am I?" he asked, smiling. "It *has* been a rather vexing afternoon, Finch, and I am in want of the comfort of my desk."

"And your tea?"

"And my tea, but at the moment, I believe I can do without. I trust you had a friendly chat with the Patris?"

"I did."

"And?" He looked, pointedly, at the chairs on the visitor side of the desk, and after a moment, moved one so it sat to the desk's right side.

"Why were you so certain that the intended victim of the probable poisoning was me?"

"Was I? How very odd. Come, Finch. My chair."

She rose. "I wouldn't have noticed," she replied evenly. "But it appears Patris Araven did."

At that, Jarven grimaced. He sat—heavily—in his accustomed chair while Finch occupied, with more grace, the chair he had moved for her benefit. "We will not be able to keep knowledge of this within the office for long."

She nodded, glancing at her skirts. "I thought you might have sent for clothing."

"I considered it, and did one better. You will borrow a cloak when you leave, and you will find, upon your arrival at the manse, that I have sent three or four very practical bolts of cloth to your rooms. I suggest you speak with your tailor and have him make a few dresses, at least one of which will remain on the premises against future need. I am afraid I was rather cross when speaking with Lucille, and she will, no doubt, knock on these doors within the half hour to ascertain that you are still alive."

"She thinks you're angry at *me*?"

"Given the preposterous show Hectore made of his departure? Yes. I imagine the entire office now entertains that opinion." There was an unpleasant edge to his familiar smile; it looked almost predatory.

Or perhaps it was just the contrast of lips to eyes; like Hectore, Jarven was capable of smiling in a way that suggested the opposite of warmth or amusement. "I wish you to tell me, in detail, about The Terafin's past week."

Finch said nothing.

"Finch, I am to be without tea, and without sustenance, for at least this afternoon; I am not in the mood to deal with any obstruction."

"Would it be considered obstruction if I accepted your offer of a cloak and took you to lunch at the Placid Sea?"

"It would rather spoil the appearance of displeasure I have been at pains to convey."

"No," she said softly, "it wouldn't. Lucille knows how angry you are. I know it."

"I wish the others to believe I am angry with you."

"Yes. But I wish them to believe it while I'm not hungry." She was, in fact, lying; she was not hungry at all. The thought of food—and in particular, tea—was nauseating. But Jarven *was* hungry, he needed to eat, and he had that peculiar brightness in his gaze that meant he would forget something as simple as food, if allowed.

He glared at her. "You are taking this disappointingly well."

"I can, if you prefer, cry or shiver."

"It would appeal to my ego," Jarven said, deserting his chair. "Is it necessary for me to lecture you on the subject of Patris Araven?"

"No. I know he is dangerously perceptive; I know he is canny."

"You say neither as if you mean them."

"Nonsense," she replied, retrieving his walking stick from its position in the corner of the room. "I know you are at least as dangerously perceptive, and I believe you to be more canny; you are certainly more pragmatic."

"Pragmatic?"

"Patris Araven is, in my opinion, genuinely sentimental."

"And I am not? You wound me, Finch."

She collected his coat and found the cloak of which he spoke. It was, in her estimation, too short for Jarven; she wondered whose it had once been and what it was doing in this office. It was a very, very finely textured wool, and the embroidery along every visible edge was neither simple nor inexpensive. The dye was a deep, blue-purple.

"If I am dangerous," he told her, as he allowed her to help him into his coat, "why am I being badgered into leaving my inner sanctum?"

"At the moment? You are hungry, and you are not actually angry at me." A fact for which she was, at this moment, grateful. Although Jarven's voice and mannerisms had not significantly altered, there was an edge to his expression and his posture that reminded Finch—ridiculously, and for no reason she could easily pinpoint—of Duvari. "Come, Jarven. Lunch. I would like to speak to you about the House Council seat, among other things."

"I will thank you not to bat your eyelashes at me as if I were an ignorant, gangly youth." He offered her his arm, and she laughed. They almost made it to the door before Lucille knocked—and entered.

She was angry. Her anger was a shout to Jarven's neutral whisper; her lips were set, her face pale. Before she could speak, Jarven lifted a hand. "If you are about to tell me something I already know, I would ask that you come to my office after we've closed up for the day."

"I'm not here to see you," was her curt reply. Oh, she was angry. Finch detached herself from Jarven's arm to close the distance between her and Lucille as quickly as possible. She hugged the older woman tightly.

Lucille's hug was larger in every possible way.

"I'm unharmed, Lucille," Finch said softly, as she pulled back.

Lucille said a very cold nothing. She looked down at Finch, and then looked past her shoulder. Finch had seen her this angry only a handful of times.

"Lucille, Jarven had nothing to do with what happened this afternoon."

Lucille did not reply. Jarven remained uncharacteristically silent. After a long moment, Lucille said, "Jarven may well have had something to do with it." She still wasn't looking at Finch. "And I am here to tell him that I will resign in some fury if I ever have to cart corpses out of this office in any number again." She paused and added, "Terafin corpses."

"Lucille—"

"Finch," Jarven said.

She turned toward him. He looked younger, sharper, and infinitely less pleasant than the man she habitually served tea. "Jarven, tell her—"

"I cannot tell her the only thing which would bring her any peace. You can."

Lucille snorted.

But Finch knew, then. She knew what Lucille needed to hear. And she understood, with sudden clarity, that she could not do it. Could she lie? Yes. As Hectore had surmised, Finch was far better at the art of dissembling than her den leader. But she respected Lucille too much for that. "Lucille."

Something in Finch's tone served as warning; the older woman stiffened and dragged her gaze away from Jarven. Her face was pale.

"I'm sorry. I don't know if you've understood from Jarven's demeanor that the intended victim of the poisoning was me. Jarven believes it; I'm not entirely certain I do. But if it was me, I don't think it will be the last attempt."

"Finch, *why*? We *have* a Terafin. The succession was decided the day of The Terafin's funeral. You aren't—you can't intend to take Jarven's place here."

"No. I don't."

"I fail to see why not," Jarven replied.

"You'll leave the Authority office when you die, and I'm not in a hurry to bury you," Finch replied. "I don't have your connections, and had I, I don't have the confidence to deal with them as you do. If I had been a House Council member for as long as The Terafin, I might be considered an appropriate choice—but I haven't. No, Lucille, I don't intend to take Jarven's place."

"Then why, Finch?" She was shaking; it pained Finch to see.

"Because I think this *is* about the succession. I can't explain much more than that, not yet. Maybe not ever. Jewel *is* The Terafin, but—" here she stopped.

Jarven came to her rescue, in a manner of speaking. "But The Terafin is at odds with the Kings, and at odds with the Order of Knowledge. I believe Duvari would have her disposed of if the Kings allowed it. Even if he does not, it is clear to many that she is now in command of a power that she neither controls nor fully understands. If The Terafin exceeds her authority—and let me say I do not believe she will do so consciously—someone will step in to take her place.

"I do not believe that anyone on the House Council has any intention of hurrying her demise. If the demons cannot do it, they will have little luck. But if she somehow manages to do so herself—ah, then, the field is open. The landscape has shifted, Lucille—but in reality, not by so much." Jarven frowned. "We are to lunch at the Placid Sea. If you wish to join us, Lucille, please ready yourself."

Lucille did not choose to join them. She said nothing until Finch took her hands; they were cold. "It's not the fight I would choose," Finch said, voice low. Her own hands were shaking very slightly. "But I'm not sure I can face it without you. I won't be hounded from this office—"

"You most certainly will not be," was the stern reply. Lucille's hands tightened, crushing Finch's. "You don't know how deadly things can become—"

"I worked here every day of the Henden of 410," Finch

replied. "During which I would have gladly taken poison on several occasions. I don't intend to allow myself to be the first victim in an undeclared war. It would kill Jay to lose me, too."

"I'll stay," Lucille said.

"Will you forgive Jarven? He didn't attempt to kill me. He may well be responsible, in the end, for keeping me alive."

Lucille snorted. She released Finch's hands, glared at Jarven, and made her retreat.

When the door closed on her back, Jarven heaved a theatrical sigh. "She will never forgive me if any harm comes to you," he said, offering her his arm.

Finch took it once again. "No," she said. "And it won't even be your fault."

Jarven chuckled. "You fail to understand the esteem in which Lucille holds me, Finch. In her mind, even the attempt can be attributed to my carelessness." Before Finch could reply, he added, "And she is not wrong."

The Placid Sea was quiet, as it often was at this time of year. Jarven ATerafin was a man of enough import that even had it been packed, a table would have been found; nor would it be a simple table wedged between the others in unseemly haste.

They were given a quiet booth, tucked away in the back, near where the fire burned. Given the temperature, this was a blessing. Jarven sat, and when the two were alone, he reached into a pocket and set a stone upon the table. It had a polished, black-marbled surface, which seemed to absorb more light than it reflected.

"What are your intentions, Finch?" he asked. His voice, absent the usual humor and gentle wheedling, reminded her of the stone's surface. It wasn't pleasant.

"I intend to keep coming in to work."

"You don't intend to inform The Terafin of today's events."

"No."

"May I ask why?"

"If you want to waste the time, yes." This pulled an almost unwilling smile from the corners of his lips. "You already know why, Jarven."

"Yes, I do. I believe I have said before that I consider your protective instincts in this case to be wasted."

"I don't believe that's how you put it at the time, but, yes, you've made yourself clear." Finch's smile was entirely unfettered. "I was prepared," she told him, as the smile faded, "for a House War. I've known the Captains of the Chosen since the first day I arrived at the Terafin manse; I've spoken with them.

"But even if I hadn't, I was ATerafin when Alea died. I was ATerafin when Courtne died. I was ATerafin when Captain Alayra was murdered. Those were overtures in a more unpleasant war; we all understood it." She exhaled. "We understood what we were facing. We were relieved when Jay—Jewel—was acclaimed The Terafin. We'd lived in the shadow of war, and we'd emerged."

"War casts a long shadow, and it is seldom singular."

"I know. I was there—I was present—when The Terafin died. I saw what killed her. If you ask what I intend, it hasn't changed. I intend to do everything in my power to support and strengthen the rule of Jewel Markess ATerafin."

"And you, of course, risk death to do so."

"Of course."

"You mentioned the House Council seat," he said, after a long pause.

Finch nodded. "I thought it unwise to give you the seat while you retained power in the Merchant Authority."

"And now?" Had her companion been any other man, Finch might have resented the discussion; it seemed unnecessary. But Jarven often surprised her, and regardless, could not be moved to change his pace once he had set it.

"I will recommend that it be given you."

His smile was sharp. "I will still retain far more power than The Terafin should be comfortable placing in my hands."

"Yes. I'm not entirely comfortable with it now."

"But today's little fiasco has changed your opinion?"

"It's shifted it, yes. Jarven—you'll do what you want, in the end; I think you always have. But you're angry. Lucille is angry."

"And you are not." It wasn't a question.

"No. I should be. Perhaps, when I am in the safety of my own rooms, I will be."

"You don't believe that."

She didn't. "I don't think you will work against The Terafin. I don't think you would work against me."

"You are not The Terafin."

"No."

"Has it not occurred to you, Finch, that the one certain way I have to preserve your life is to make a deal?"

She stiffened and paled. Finch was seldom angry with Jarven; she was angry now. "Do not make me the excuse for the games you might choose to play. Never, ever do that to me. I am not Lucille."

"Lucille would accept such a deal."

"No, Jarven, she wouldn't."

"And if I made such a deal to preserve Lucille's life? Or The Terafin's?"

"Nothing can kill The Terafin," she replied, with utter conviction. She did not answer the first question, and he allowed this.

"There are, however, things that can hurt her."

Finch nodded.

"Very well. I want the House Council seat, as you are well aware. I feel, given the shift in your attitude, that I have lost valuable time while I have played this excessive waiting game. I do not intend to abuse the joint power the seat will give me. What word can I give you, Finch, that you will trust?"

She shook her head. "That's not how this game will be played, Jarven. We've known each other for over half my life. Tell me what *you* want."

"At this very moment, my precocious little assistant, I want two things. I have agreed that I will accept a junior aide who will report to Lucille and The Terafin."

Finch nodded.

"I will withdraw that. I will accept, instead, a promotion— for you. You will be my adjutant, and your function in my office will not markedly change—but you will have title and responsibility within these offices that are second to none."

Her brows rose.

"Yes," he said, as wine and bread were brought to rescue them from their lack of any refreshments. "We will share a title, within the Authority."

"That is hardly likely to make me *less* of a target."

"Nothing will make you less of a target, my dear. But The Terafin trusts you; she has no doubt of your loyalty at all. I will offer her that. In fact," he added, his smile becoming the smile with which she was so familiar. "I believe I will insist on it."

Chapter Twenty-three

FINCH RETURNED two hours later than usual from the Merchant Authority, in time—barely—to catch the tail end of the late dinner hour. She entered the West Wing holding her breath, and exhaled when Ellerson failed to materialize. A brief check of Carver's room confirmed what she already knew: it was empty.

Angel was pacing; Jester was in the great room with Arann, who was off-duty. Teller had not yet returned from the right-kin's office. He was the only member of the den whose day started earlier, and often ended later, than Finch's.

"Where's Daine?"

"In the healerie. No, there was no emergency," Jester added quickly. "But he's been interviewing people for positions as assistants. He's enjoying it about as much as you'd expect."

Given Daine's age, her expectations in that regard were quite low. She spent some time chatting with Angel, who was clearly restless; Arann was his usual silent self. Jester, since Carver's inexplicable disappearance, had become almost as silent; everyone marked it more.

But it was Teller to whom Finch wanted to speak. She considered the events at the Merchant Authority dispassionately, and decided to set them aside for now. They were the subject for a kitchen council. Finch had called council before, but never when Jay was in the manse—and she was, if the environs that now constituted The Terafin's personal chambers could be considered part of the manse.

Besides, she was worried about Teller. The only person who worried in public was Jay. Everyone else's worries were more focused, more personal. She retired for the evening, but as she made her way to her own bed, she heard the doors open, and saw Teller walk into the hall. He glanced at the doors to the great room; his shoulders stiffened. Instead of entering those doors, he retreated into Finch.

That had been a tactical mistake on his part. Finch saw it in his expression, but she was willing to take advantage of it. She lifted her hands in quick den-sign, and he answered, after a significant pause, the same way. They retreated to his rooms.

"You've eaten?" she asked softly, when the door was closed.

He nodded. "Barston brought food. He doesn't approve of eating in the office," he added, with a grimace, "but forces himself to make exceptions." He sat heavily in the chair in front of his writing desk—a desk that had once been tidy, but was now cluttered with papers and ledgers.

He was pale, the lower half of his eyes accented by dark semicircles. Finch did not attempt to fill the silence that followed his last words; it descended around them both. When it had become thick enough to be uncomfortable—a rare occurrence between two of the quieter members of the den, she chose her words with care.

"You've barely spoken a word," she said softly, "since you returned from *Avantari*."

"I've spoken several thousand," he replied, with a rueful grin.

"Not to us. Not to any of us."

She waited, watching his carefully guarded expression. She had known Teller for over half her life; she could catalog the fleeting glimpses of the emotions her question invoked: fear, anger, weariness. Resignation. It was the last that held his face, and the last that held her attention.

"Teller."

He said nothing.

"I heard you, last night."

The nothing was sharper; he turned away, glancing at the papers beneath his right elbow.

"Have you slept at all?"

"Some." It was a grudging answer to an invasive question. Finch knew she should leave it alone, but knew, as well, that she couldn't.

"Teller, you haven't had nightmares like these for longer than I can remember."

He stood. She thought, for a moment, that he would ask her to leave; she wasn't sure if she would respect the request. He saved her from making that decision. "No." His voice was hollow. "I've never had nightmares like these. Not after my mother died. Not in the Henden of 410. Not even after The Terafin's death." He ran both hands through limp hair as he bowed his head.

He glanced, once again, at the papers on his desk, and Finch frowned.

"When we went to *Avantari,* we were taken to a room in the basement of the palace."

"Dungeons?" she asked, half grinning.

"Not when we arrived. I think—I think in the end dungeons would be preferable." He glanced up again. "The rooms in question either did not exist before the first day of The Terafin's funeral, or existed in an entirely different form. Jay hasn't talked much about this."

"And you didn't feel you could."

"I can talk about the rooms," he replied. "Although I shouldn't talk about them here."

"The room isn't secure enough."

He raised a brow, an expression he'd borrowed, over the past decade, from Barston. "This room is secure enough, now. Barston's been pushing me—gently—toward the suite normally occupied by the right-kin."

"You don't want to move."

"No. I'm not The Terafin; I have the luxury of refusal." Jay had refused for two months. "You've been in the library."

It sounded like a change of subject. "Yes."

It wasn't. "The room in the basement reminded me of the library. It wasn't open; there was no sky. But in every other way it felt ancient, wild. It felt like the work of Artisans; nothing about it was sane." He smiled; it aged him. "I felt like I'd stepped out of my world." He shook his head. "That's not what I mean. When we first arrived at the doorstep of the manse, I *had* stepped outside of our world. It was intimidating. But—it was only a part of our world I hadn't learned yet.

"The room, the library, the grounds—they're not part of my world. The only part of them I understand is Jay."

Finch exhaled and closed her eyes, listening to the cadence of Teller's voice.

"And they're part of her now. I'm *trying* to understand them because they're part of her."

She opened her eyes when he fell silent.

"Do you see it differently?" *Tell me I'm wrong.*

She couldn't. She didn't even try. "We've managed to accept anything we've had to accept," she said. "We can manage this."

He shook his head. "The Oracle paid us a visit while we were there."

"The Oracle?"

"The Oracle. Firstborn. Ancient. She was part of the carvings along the wall—until she wasn't. She stepped out of it, made of stone. And she held a seer's crystal in her hands." He swallowed. Finch waited. "She offered a glimpse of the future to Jay—and Jay refused it. I don't think she trusts the Oracle."

"Did you?"

"I don't think my trust matters one way or the other. What Jay wouldn't accept, she offered the Kings. The Kings agreed to look."

"They didn't speak of what they saw." It wasn't a question.

"No." He raised his chin, his lips almost white. "But I asked. I asked her to show me what the Kings had seen."

Finch whispered his name, her hands signing in silence.

"I saw a god," he whispered. "I saw the *Kialli.* I saw creatures I've never seen. I was standing in the streets of a city—but it wasn't this one. Not as it is now. I could see walls in the distance." He closed his eyes. "I could see the dead in the streets; the dead and the dying. I could see Jay," he whispered. "She was bleeding, injured; her eyes were wild." He fell silent again.

"She was alone?"

He laughed. "No. No, she wasn't alone."

She'd asked the wrong question. In silence she rose and

came to stand before Teller; after a brief hesitation, she put her arms around his neck and shoulders. "Were we with her?"

She felt him shake his head. "No. We were at a distance, and we were holding—between us—the banner of House Terafin. The Chosen were set to guard it, not her."

"Were *any* of us with her?"

"Only one. Only one of us. But—"

"But?"

"His hair. His hair was down." He tightened his grip briefly. "If these are Jay's dreams, I don't want them. I'll be grateful for their lack for the rest of my life."

"They seem clearer than Jay's dreams, to me."

"There was more."

"It doesn't matter. You understand what at least part of the vision must mean." She pulled away. "I need to talk to you about Jarven ATerafin."

"Finch—"

"And I need to tell you about my day in the Merchant Authority. It's not the stuff of dream or nightmare—not the ones you've been having. But it's not going to make you happy."

13th of Fabril, 428 A.A.
Terafin Manse, Averalaan Aramarelas

Finch woke and dressed early, with the help of a maid. She missed Ellerson. They all missed Ellerson. But the domicis had not returned. Nor had the two cats and the Winter King. While they were absent, there was hope—but hope was a special kind of pain.

She left her rooms and entered the breakfast nook; to her surprise it was empty of all save one man: Haval. He was seated along the bench against the wall. He had not, from the look of the table, come to eat.

"ATerafin," he said, rising as she entered the room. He bowed.

"Haval?" She glanced around for a glimpse of Jay; the room was otherwise empty.

"I have come to speak with you, if you have a few moments."

She frowned as breakfast arrived. "Do you mind if I eat while we speak?"

"I do not wish to deprive you of your meal," he replied, "but the conversation is of a more personal nature."

This deepened Finch's frown. Haval was Jay's adviser, but in all other ways he chose to be near invisible while within the West Wing.

"How is Hannerle?" she asked.

"She is sleeping." He said it in exactly the wrong tone of voice.

Finch, never particularly hungry in the mornings, felt the desire for food desert her completely. "It was my understanding," she said, choosing her words with care, "that the sleepers had all awakened."

"That was my understanding as well. It is true of the sleepers who convalesced within the Houses of Healing."

"Is Adam present?"

"He is, to the best of my knowledge, asleep." Haval lifted a hand. "And it is not my intent to wake him to demand answers. The questions to which I now require answers, I will ask of The Terafin directly."

"Is there anything I can do?"

"Eat. Eat, and then come to the fitting rooms, where we are less likely to suffer interruption."

Breakfast was a quick affair, and Finch left the table feeling every bite as a weight in her stomach. It had not occurred to her that Hannerle might not waken; the others had. Haval did not seem unduly angry, but that told Finch nothing. She liked the tailor, but on occasion he made her uneasy.

This morning was to be no exception. She knocked at the door, and was given leave to enter; the room was, as were most spaces in which Haval worked, a mess in progress. She could see both floor and carpet, but it was broken in many places by the various tools and materials of his trade.

"Late yesterday afternoon, bolts of fabric were delivered to the West Wing; the men who delivered them claimed that I had ordered them. I admit that I am not a man in the prime of youth, but I cannot for the life of me remember placing such an order. They are against the wall," he added.

It was necessary; they were not the only bolts of cloth present.

She considered her next words with care. "Jarven ATerafin sent them."

One gray brow rose. "Indeed. I am to assume that he meant them for your clothing?"

"Yes, I'm sorry. We had a bit of an accident in the office yesterday, and as I don't generally sleep in the Merchant Authority, I was forced to wear a tea-stained dress for the duration of the day."

Haval nodded, as if tea stains were a daily—and trivial—event. "Jarven, one assumes, chose the cloth."

She eyed the cloth with a great deal more suspicion. "Yes. My apologies, Haval. I am not a clothier of any great note, and while textiles are of course part of Terafin's trade, they are not under my direct supervision. What is significant about these bolts of cloth? They do not seem exceptional in color; the dyes seem bright, but otherwise ordinary, at least in this light."

"Jarven did not inform you."

"No."

"Then I should not. But I will say this: there is no other cloth that would have a fraction of the worth of the cloth he did choose. I quibble only at his source—a source of which you remain in ignorance."

She approached the bolts, her brow furrowed. They were not, at first glance, a rough cloth, or even a practical one; they were not, for instance, the fine linen out of which so much of her clothing had been made. "They are silk," she said.

"They are silk. They are of a composition found only within the Royal Courts, and even then, only on strict social occasions."

"I don't understand."

"No, ATerafin. What did Jarven tell you?"

"He said simply that he was sending bolts of cloth to me. I was to inform my tailor of a need for new dresses, at least one of which would remain within the Merchant Authority offices against future accidents."

Haval's expression shifted, closing like a snapped fan. What was left was a certain brightness of the eye. "Please,

ATerafin, take a seat. That one; you can remove the cloth across the chair without causing any significant damage."

"I am not certain I would not prefer to remain standing."

"Very well. Unless your measurements have changed significantly in the last two months, I do not require your cooperation in the mechanics of making such dresses. I require, perhaps, some input into the design."

"You've never required such input before."

"Have I not?"

"No. You've always chosen the designs, with Hannerle's guidance. You are aware that we are not fully cognizant of the hidden barbs presented by fashion."

"Cloth such as this is not subject to the simple dictates of fashion," he replied. "And indeed, there are very, very few tailors who are capable of working with it at all."

Finch stared at the cloth as Haval's words sunk in. "And if I ask how Jarven knew you would be one of those few?"

"I have not yet admitted that I am."

She met, and held, his gaze. "If you do not admit that you are, there is very little point in continuing this conversation. I am expected in the Authority offices this morning, and I cannot afford to be too late."

"I believe Jarven will expect some delay."

"It is not Jarven who concerns me. I do not understand your previous relationship, Haval, nor is it required."

"I wish you to tell me what occurred in the Authority offices yesterday afternoon."

"You could ask Jarven."

"I could, but I wish a reasonable answer in a reasonable length of time."

"I believe he would give you both, given your suspicions about his choice of fabric. He could hardly do otherwise."

"And you claim to have known Jarven for half your life? He has clearly mellowed."

She smiled; the expression was a merchant expression that did not reach her eyes. "Tell me about this fabric. You said it was silk?" As she spoke, she reached out to touch a fold of creased cloth. It was not, to touch, remarkable.

"Yes."

It was a heavier silk, washed and smoothed into a reflective, burgundy sheen. The color was appropriate for her Authority work. She looked up to meet his gaze. Jay trusted this man. Finch had always liked him, but she had been aware that his past was not entirely what one would expect of a tailor. She liked Hannerle without reservation—but Hannerle was not Haval.

And yet, Haval was here, and Jay listened to him. She turned once again to the bolts of cloth. Inspecting them, she said, "As you surmise, the cloth was meant for my use. Jarven must have known the conclusions you would draw upon its receipt; he did not, however, think to give me fair warning."

"A failing of his, I assure you." There was a dry humor at the bottom of those words. "He could not have come by this cloth on short notice."

"It was very short notice," she replied. The brown silk was dark enough it was striking, not drab. "I assumed it the work of an afternoon—less, in fact. I think he was out of the office for under an hour."

"And the accident in the Merchant Authority?"

"I did, indeed, spill tea all over my lap, during a significant appointment with a merchant of some import. It was embarrassing."

"Was it deliberate?"

She exhaled. "No. Had I realized that some part of our regular tea was poisoned, I would have taken care to ensure that the cup in my hand did not shatter." Sliding her hands behind her back she turned to face him. "Is the cloth proof against stains?"

"It is. It is proof against water, alcohol, and simple dirt. It is *not* for that reason that it is prized, of course; that is merely a beneficial side effect. The cloth cannot be worked with normal thread, normal needles; it cannot be cut with normal shears or scissors."

"Can it be cut at all?"

"Yes."

Finch bent, picked up a small pair of scissors, and drew the lower blade swiftly across the brown fabric. It failed to mark the cloth at all. Frowning, she removed the small knife she habitually wore secreted in her skirts; she knew the knife was sharp. Haval said nothing as she attempted to slice through the cloth. She failed.

"Does it prevent stabbing?"

"No. The cloth will not tear, but the blunt damage will occur regardless."

"Does it provide protection against magic?"

"It does. It does not provide any protection against poison. But it is armor, of a kind, against specific types of attacks. It will not preserve your life for long if you are isolated and you face an expert foe—but many assassinations are achieved in seconds. Jewel is The Terafin, and she does not own one such dress."

"She's—"

"Nor did the previous Terafin."

"Can you be certain of that?"

"Yes."

"Just how expensive *is* this cloth?"

"It is all but priceless," Haval replied. "But, as I have said, having the cloth will not guarantee its use. It would not surprise me if these bolts are quite old."

They did not look particularly old to Finch; if they were, they'd been stored in reasonable environs, not damp ones. She shook her head. Given the properties Haval attributed to this silk, it probably wouldn't matter.

"You needn't waste them on me," she told him politely. "I have survived my years in Terafin—and a few tense years before them—in cloth meant for the merely mortal. Yesterday, I managed to stain my skirts; I took no other lasting or significant damage."

He did not relax. He watched.

"Haval, if you are concerned about my welfare—"

"I was not, before these arrived. I am now concerned in a multitude of ways. Had Jarven chosen to back Jewel ATerafin's bid in its entirety—and from the start—I would not have been as surprised to see them. He is prone to extravagant gesture when the mood strikes him. But he did not. Jewel was acclaimed Terafin. You have served her for your entire tenure as ATerafin, and I did not imagine that you would make any move—political or otherwise—against her."

Finch's brows rose as the words—and the implication—became clear. Her left hand curled in a fist; the right still held the knife that she had drawn to attempt to cut cloth. She left it by her side, although it was shaking. "If you imagine that I am doing so now," she finally said, "you do not understand what I want for either The Terafin or her House." She spoke with a quiet, searing dignity.

He watched for a full minute, during which she met and held his gaze. "I believe," he said, voice soft, "that I will have to speak with Jarven after all. If you do not mind arriving at the Merchant Authority on the late side, I will join you there. I have some tools to retrieve from my sadly neglected storefront." He tendered her a brief bow.

Finch, still angry, did not offer a similar courtesy in response.

"I meant no disrespect," he said, as he rose.

"I fail to see how you could mean anything else."

"Then you are still far too naive to be put into play in this unexpected fashion."

Finch arrived at the Merchant Authority on time and unescorted. Lucille was behind her desk as Finch opened the door; her eyes instantly narrowed. Finch glanced over her shoulder to see who might be following her into the office; the hall was, aside from the two House Guards who stood to either side of the doors, empty.

She approached the desk, and Lucille handed her a small stack of papers, on top of which was a sealed letter. The seal was of House Araven. It was also unbroken.

"Is Jarven in?"

"He is. He was here before I arrived."

That was unusual. Jarven often worked late, but did not particularly care for mornings, especially the ones that started early.

"He was expecting you half an hour ago," Lucille added.

"I suppose you pointed out that this *is* the time I'm normally expected?"

"I did."

Finch sighed. "I'm sorry—that was a rather dense question. Does he have an appointment now?"

"No."

She made her way to Jarven's closed doors immediately, and knocked before she entered. Lucille was not the only person in the office who knocked to give warning, rather than to ask permission. Jarven was seated behind his desk.

She immediately joined him, taking the chair to the right of the desk. "I didn't realize you would be here this early."

"Clearly. You were otherwise occupied?"

"With breakfast and an extremely suspicious tailor."

At that, he smiled. "Ah. I see you spoke with Haval."

"It may have escaped your attention, but he maintains an unofficial residence in the West Wing. And he feels that the bolts of cloth you so cavalierly sent were a sign of . . ."

"Yes?"

"I will let him explain it himself."

"Finch, please."

"He had business to attend to at his store, but said he would come here after. If you wish to avoid him, you will probably have to either tell Lucille to send him on his way, or leave for an urgent appointment."

"I would," Jarven said, "but the cloth is rather pointless without his aid. Was he difficult?"

"He felt that gifting the cloth to me implied a desire on my part to replace The Terafin."

Jarven laughed. He was genuinely amused—and genuinely delighted. Finch felt the urge to strangle him, and allowed it to pass. This was not the first time Jarven would frustrate her; nor was it likely to be the last. "You do not seem pleased by the ridiculousness of it all."

"I was—and am—not. I found it insulting."

"It is so very seldom that Haval missteps, my dear; you must learn to appreciate it when it happens. He does not take kindly to reminders of his fallibility, and you will be able to rub his nose in it at your pleasure."

Her lips thinned as he laughed again. "Honestly, Jarven."

"He is fond of the girl."

"He is fond of *The Terafin*."

"Yes, yes. It amuses me, Finch. Surely you don't begrudge that? I have had a miserable week."

"Prior to yesterday."

"Indeed, indeed."

"You could try to be a little more circumspect, Jarven. Lucille is not pleased."

"Ah. She is no doubt ill-pleased because you arrived at the office without House Guards in tow."

"Pardon?"

"It will come as no surprise to you that Lucille takes the events of yesterday very poorly. There is some threat to your life; anyone rational who had access to House Guards—and you do, as a House Council member—would *of course* avail herself of their protection."

Finch folded arms across her chest. "That didn't save The Terafin."

"No, my dear, it did not; I was at pains to point this out to my worthy secretary; she was not amused." Jarven clearly was.

"You are capable of acting somber and serious when it suits you, Jarven. Could you not try, for Lucille's sake?"

"No." His smile faded. "It gives her a safe outlet for the fury she is otherwise feeling. Our Lucille does not like to feel helpless. In that, I believe she is very much like your Jewel."

"The Terafin." She exhaled. "Tell me where you acquired the cloth you sent to Haval."

Jarven opened a ledger and began to flip through its pages, pausing once or twice to make notations.

Finch cleared her throat, and he looked up. "Yes?"

"You wanted to speak with me."

"I did. But as you have set Haval on me, I will wait until he arrives; anything of relevance to you will no doubt be subject to his scrutiny, and I do not wish to expire of the boredom of repetition. You can make that face if you like, Finch; it is clearly much easier for you to alleviate your own boredom. I, however, am considered old and of little interest; I wield some power, but in the eyes of the patriciate, it is a *fading* power, soon to be removed by the expedience of my death—from a boring, fretful old age, no less.

"I am in want of tea," he added.

Finch nodded stiffly and went to fetch it. She had no doubt, at this point, that tea was safe. Doubt or no, when she made up the tray, she used the finer dishes. Without Lucille's aid, she returned to the office quickly.

She found Haval in the outer office. He rose as she emerged from the long back room, tray in hand, and he tendered her a perfect bow. He was dressed, head to toe, as a merchant of some standing, his jacket a blue of fine velvet, his shirt cuffs edged in tasteful frills. It was a far cry from the practical apron and somewhat dingier clothing in which he normally worked.

Lucille did not seem overjoyed to see him, but she clearly didn't consider him a threat; she took no pains to contain her pinched expression. Haval crossed the room as Finch approached Jarven's closed doors.

"If I may?" he asked.

Finch nodded. Haval opened the doors. They stood framed by them as Jarven looked up from his desk. His version of work, at the moment, was a careful study of his hands; there were no longer any open books or ledgers anywhere.

Finch preceded Haval into the room, and set the tea tray on Jarven's desk. He glanced at the side table; she ignored it.

"Please," Jarven said, his voice smooth as fine glass. "Be seated." He spoke, of course, to Haval. Haval inclined his head, his face shuttered and expressionless. He did, however, take one of the chairs Jarven indicated. Finch poured three cups of tea. Haval had not arrived with a servant, as Hectore had on the previous day. He did not refuse the tea she offered; he did refuse cream, sugar, or honey. Jarven did not.

Finch had brought biscuits. She'd chosen the same biscuits as she'd chosen on the day Hectore had come to visit. She felt no hunger at all, but as she carried the decorative plate to Haval, and then to Jarven, she smiled. She took one biscuit, as she had done the day before. Jarven took two. Haval glanced at the tray and politely declined.

And there they sat, two silent old men. Jarven did not effect his usual avuncular dotage; Haval did not affect his usual servant's invisibility. Although neither man spoke, they met and held the other's gaze; they were fencing in silence.

Finch considered dropping a cup to see if it caught either man's attention. She understood that they shared a past, and from this posturing, inferred that they had been equals. But Haval made clothing for a living; Jarven ruled the Terafin concerns in the Merchant Authority.

"Haval," she said pleasantly, when it became clear he would not be the first to speak, "Are you acquainted with Patris Araven?"

The clothier raised a brow. "I am."

"Have your dealings in the past been pleasant?"

"They have been few. Is this question relevant?"

"Only if you wish to avoid him. While you and Jarven attempt to outstare each other, he is no doubt making his way to the Terafin Authority offices. The room is clearly large enough to accommodate him; I am not certain the discussion the two of you wish to have will be."

Jarven chuckled.

Haval, notably, did not.

"If you would prefer it, I will withdraw."

Haval was silent. Jarven, however, frowned. "You are at the heart of this discussion, Finch."

"There has been no discussion," Finch replied sweetly. "And on occasion the person who is at the heart of the discussion inhibits discussion by her presence."

"You are in the lair of two decided dragons, Finch," he replied, his smile broadening. "Where we choose to speak, believe that we will not be inhibited."

"That, of course," Haval said, almost grudgingly, "is her fear. No, Finch. Jarven is correct. You are not your leader. You will inhibit us only if you choose to do so, and I believe you will do so tactically, if at all. You understand why we are here."

Finch took a chair. Jarven and Haval had confidence in her—and it was, of course, a confidence she did not share. She wanted to have this discussion in her own Wing, with Teller at the table. But she could not, without also having Jay. Teller would not speak if Jay was present—and it was likely that Finch, to spare them both, would also be reticent.

"Yes," she said quietly, lifting the cup to her lips. "I do."

"Very well." Haval exhaled and looked directly at Jarven. "Why have you chosen Finch?"

"Why not?" Jarven was enjoying himself, and took no pains to hide it. "Answer carefully, Haval. She has been under my wing for the whole of her tenure as ATerafin. She understands the Merchant Authority—and the merchants who plague it—better than anyone here, save perhaps myself."

"Lucille knows—"

"No, Finch, she does not. She knows this office. No one—not even I—understand its workings so completely. But she looks no farther than this office, and she never has. She has depended upon me to see the enemies at the gate; she has assumed that I will head them off before they trouble her domain."

"She is not a fool," Haval said.

"No. But she has come to depend on me."

"And Finch has not?"

Jarven glanced at her. "Your manners, Haval, are lacking. Finch is here; you may ask her the question yourself."

Haval nodded, but did not repeat the question.

"I depend, to a certain extent, on Jarven," Finch replied, as if he had. "But what Jarven sees is not always what I see. In the early years, the differences denoted a lack of experience on my part. I have had sixteen years in this office since then."

"And the differences now?"

"Are more subtle. There are merchants who are willing to negotiate with me, where they would not negotiate with Jarven." She lifted a hand. "I do not mean they will not speak with him; they will, of course. But they will not move, at all."

"And you have coaxed them into a flexibility Jarven cannot?"

"I rarely threaten them," she replied. "Jarven, for his own reasons, does. Perhaps he plays the foil, and they come to me because I offer respect instead. But he will not always be here, and I will. What Jarven does, I cannot do. I have never considered it wise to make the attempt. I depend on Jarven," she continued, "but I do not fully trust him."

Haval was still for a long beat. He offered her his first smile since entering this office. "Jewel does not."

"No. But if she worked at his side as I have done, she would." Finch paused, considering her words with care. "She trusts you."

Jarven laughed.

"She has reason to trust me." Haval said.

"I have reason to trust Jarven," Finch replied pleasantly, her tone implying agreement without actually ceding any. "And, Haval, I have reason to trust you. If you feel that I am suspicious, accept it as your due: with the single exception of my den, I trust no one of any power completely."

"Not even the former Terafin?" He did not, as he so often did, decry any possibility of power by pointing out that he was a simple maker of dresses.

"The dead have no need of trust."

"The living require some, Finch. It must be clear to you now—"

"That you don't trust me? Yes. It is. I'm uncertain as to

whether the greater part of your suspicion is due to Jarven's interest."

He nodded, but felt no need to enlighten her. He was, however, watching her with care; Jarven, still chuckling, failed to hold his attention. She had seen Haval concentrate upon beadwork with exactly the same expression. It told her nothing. But she understood that this interview, such as it was, was to be a test; it was a test that Jarven welcomed.

Finch almost resented it. Almost. But she understood that only by passing it would she be able to help Jay, if help was required. And by passing it, she would then open herself up to all manner of testing. Assassination was, after all, a test of intent.

Haval did not speak. Jarven fell silent; she expected the latter.

"You don't understand what I want," Finch said, the statement flat and uninflected. She didn't speak defensively. Haval was Jay's. He was here to protect *her* interests, or so Finch guessed. She could not hate him for that. She couldn't even cling to the insult of his suspicion for much longer. "But you suspect, Haval. I didn't think, this morning. I reacted, and I reacted poorly; I was angered by your implication."

"By your inference," he replied. It was a start.

"Perhaps. But if, as Jarven suspects, someone intends my death, I do myself no favor by allowing anger to govern my reactions."

He inclined his head.

"There are things of which I cannot speak."

Jarven cleared his throat.

"You have not yet been confirmed as a Councillor," Finch said serenely.

Haval raised a brow. "I do not consider that wise."

"I know. Neither, if truth be told, do I — but the risks are greater if we refuse, and I will require Jarven's support in future."

"Why?"

Finch swallowed. "She will leave us again."

"Pardon?"

"She will leave us. With luck it won't involve the destruction of parts of the Common, this time." She lifted a hand as Jarven cleared his throat. "She will not desert us. If she survives—as she did in the South—she will return."

Haval said, "Is she aware of this, Finch?"

Finch said nothing.

"She has not discussed this with you, then."

"She has discussed it with no one."

"And yet you seem to know her plans."

"I've known her for most of my life," Finch replied. "Understand, Haval, that we are all apprehensive. The changes in the gardens were intimidating. The changes in—" she glanced at Jarven. "The other changes, more so. We have lost one domicis and one den member, and no one understands how.

"We know of all of the structural changes in *Avantari*; the most impressive and disturbing of which are not on public display. We're not seer-born. We don't possess an ounce of talent between us. But we understand that something bigger than we are is happening. Beneath our feet. Outside of our walls. Within them."

She exhaled. "Teller believes we will lose the city—and with it, the Empire—if Jay doesn't leave."

"The right-kin has said this?"

"Not to her." She hesitated. "She walked from the Houses of Healing to the Terafin manse without once touching the streets of the city—and the bridges—on her way."

"I am aware of that."

"She gave The Terafin her word that she would take, and hold, the House."

"Will she appoint a regent?"

Finch shook her head. "No. She has no intention of leaving."

"You feel, intention or no, she will."

"It is not my belief, in the end, that is significant. My belief—or its lack—did not inspire an assassination attempt."

"True. You mean to hold the House in her absence."

"As de facto regent, yes."

"It would be a position that would normally fall to the right-kin."

Jarven cleared his throat again, and this time both Finch and Haval turned toward him. "The boy is worthy of respect," he told them both. "But I do not believe he can manage the current Council as constituted."

"He is hardly a boy, Jarven."

"He is deliberate, straightforward, and either honest or silent. He can handle Haerrad, Rymark, and Elonne with grace because he defers, in all ways, to The Terafin and they are aware of this. Absent The Terafin, I do not believe he will have the advantage."

"Finch will, in your opinion."

"Yes. I will be there to offer support. She understands the Merchant Authority, and she understands the various financial concerns that intersect it. She knows where the other House Council members stand in terms of their finances, and she knows which are the least defensible. It is true she is the most junior member of the Council—but so is the right-kin."

"You feel that someone else shares your opinion of her."

Finch spoke. "I don't. I think I am merely meant to carve support away from The Terafin while she learns to master the changes in her environment. I don't think they've given much thought to me as a difficulty in my own right."

"And the rest of your den?"

"We've already lost Carver. And Ellerson. The Terafin has not notably collapsed in the wake of their absence."

Haval met, and held, her gaze.

"They cannot safely assassinate anyone but me. If I succumbed to poison, it would be assumed that the intended victim was Jarven. I would have assumed it; Jay will. She'll be angry, yes. But if they assassinate the den, she'll understand that it's *personal*. I don't think they wish to engage a woman who can—who can make the changes she's made in her sleep, in an out-and-out fight."

"Not yet."

"Not ever. I don't think, unless she's demonstrably dead, that there will be a war for the seat. It's hers. It's been hers since The Terafin's funeral, and nothing that's happened since has changed that. But if she—if she becomes more embroiled in the—" Finch exhaled. "Not all of her concerns are now political. If the concerns that are greater than the House absorb her time and attention, someone else will rule in all but name."

"And if she appoints a regent and the regent dies?"

"If there is no obvious assassin, she will be forced to appoint another. We've assumed, for some time, that Haerrad and Rymark are the two Councillors most likely to kill. I would count Elonne among them; Elonne, however, will not destroy the House."

"They are not the only Councillors."

"No. They are the interior Council."

Haval rose. "I have heard enough." He bowed to Jarven. "I will make your dresses, Finch. In spite of Jarven's rather cavalier handling of the cloth required, the crafting of such dresses is not a trivial task. I will require the cooperation of the House Mage."

She said nothing for a long moment. "Haval, before you leave, I must ask one question."

"And that?"

"Will you serve The Terafin if Hannerle is the only sleeper who fails to wake?"

"Jarven," he replied, "I believe I have underestimated your protégée."

Jarven, however, rose. "It is a question best answered, Haval."

"You will have an answer within the day," the clothier replied. "For the moment, I am content to plan; if I have underestimated your student, believe that I am incapable of underestimating mine."

A knock interrupted the tense silence that followed his words.

Finch rose to answer the door; Lucille failed to open them when Jarven was in an actual meeting, unless there was an emergency. Given Lucille's expression when Finch did open said doors, she was surprised that she'd waited.

"Patris Araven, by appointment," she said stiffly, vacating the doorway.

Hectore walked into the room, Andrei three steps behind him. The servant turned and closed the doors.

"Haval Arwood," Hectore said. He smiled; it was not a particularly friendly expression.

"Patris Araven." Haval bowed. In execution it was flawless and it implied that Hectore's position was far loftier than Haval's. "My apologies for any delay in your schedule. I am about to take my leave."

Hectore lifted a hand; Andrei, who stood in front of the doors, did not move. "I did not expect to find you here, but on reflection, I am unsurprised."

"And disappointed, Hectore?" Jarven asked, chuckling. On occasion his ability to enjoy the discomforts of others was almost obscene.

"No. I am perhaps lulled by your frivolity, Jarven; you are quite the expert at making the deadly serious seem amusing and quotidian. Haval is, of course, your equal in that regard, but he at least is possessed of some personal dignity. I have come with a report, and I have come to speak with Finch ATerafin on matters of some concern."

Haval glanced at Finch.

"I did tell you," she reminded him.

"Honesty in the heart of a merchant's domain is enough of a rarity I failed to credit your warning." He turned to Hectore. "Why are you here, Patris Araven?"

"I offered The Terafin my aid," he replied. He did not smile. "She accepted. I am of the opinion that she accepted on her own behalf—but I am not entirely convinced; she sent me to Finch. Let me return the compliment, Haval. Why are *you* here?"

Haval's face was at its least expressive. "I am here on a matter of business."

"As a tailor?"

"Yes. Jarven ATerafin is, as you must be aware, frequently a difficult man, but I believe our business has been concluded for the moment." He bowed stiffly, rose, and turned toward the door.

"Haval," Hectore said, glancing at Finch. "I thought you well quit of games with a distinctly political edge."

"I have been informed, Patris Araven, that all of life is political. I can hardly have dealings with Jarven ATerafin that do not, at his whim, affect more exalted spheres than my own."

"He is, of course, correct," Jarven said. "Come, Hectore, let him leave; he has business to conduct, and I wish to see it concluded quickly."

"Andrei?"

The servant nodded. He stepped out of the way of the doors, and opened them to allow Haval to pass. When he closed the doors, however, he closed them from the outside;

this left Finch, Hectore, and Jarven in Jarven's office. Jarven was frowning. "Was that necessary?" he asked.

"In all probability, no," was Hectore's genial reply. "At the moment, however, some caution on all fronts is required."

Finch offered—and poured—tea. Hectore accepted it with casual grace. "I have, as requested, the revised trade concessions Araven is seeking." He set a stack of papers upon Jarven's desk.

"Do I need to review these?"

"It is entirely up to you," the merchant replied. "If you have fallen into the habit of trust, no."

White brows rose in a dismissive arch. "Very well. You will, of course, give me time."

"Yes. You may take the time now, if you will allow me to speak with Finch."

"Hectore, please. If you are a busy man, I am not less so. Do not waste my time."

Hectore chuckled. "Very well. Finch, I will have you speak, now, in detail."

"The assassination attempts?"

"Yes. You may offer details about other events you consider pertinent as well."

"I have only one question."

"And that?"

"Does Araven deal, in even a minor way, with members of the House Council?"

"It does, as you are well aware. I would be surprised if you could not—at this moment—tell me who they are. And I will note that Jarven does not tell *you* not to waste his time."

"That is because it is not a waste of time," Jarven said. "If you do not choose to answer, that tells us something. If you choose to answer selectively, that also gives us information. If our knowledge matches yours exactly—and disappointingly—it will nonetheless be valuable."

Hectore actually laughed. He had a deep, resonant voice. "And I am now to be schooled like the most naive of young men, am I?"

Finch said, "That was entirely for my benefit."

"Yes," the merchant replied. "But if he is willing to have you here at all, ATerafin, it is because he believes you already know it."

"Perhaps he hopes to make you think I am vastly less experienced than I am?"

"It would be exactly like Jarven to do so, yes. But I believe it will not be the strategy you choose."

"No," was her soft reply. "I am willing to trust you with the information you've requested, although it is unusual to speak of such things to those who are not highly placed within my House. I will ask for the same level of trust about matters that do concern my House."

"That was not part of my bargain with The Terafin."

"No," was her serene reply. "It was not." She folded her hands in her lap and listened as Hectore began to speak.

The office doors opened, and Andrei slid into the room. He had once again assumed the role of consummate servant, and had chosen to take up a standing position against the wall farthest from Jarven's desk. Hectore glanced at him, and then returned his gaze to Jarven and Finch.

"Two of the attempts you are not aware of—if we assume the events in the Common during the victory parade were a fifth attempt—are irrelevant."

"You are certain?"

"No," she said, smiling. "But The Terafin is. She believes that the demons who attempted to kill her weren't summoned to the manse, but outside of it. As far as we can tell, they walked through the doors. Both appeared to be human; both appeared to be tradesmen. They wouldn't have raised eyebrows, given their demeanor and the way they were dressed. Demons do not require financial compensation. No one believes they were for hire."

"No. But their presence strongly implies that the man—or woman—responsible for the merely mortal assassins that *do* require monetary compensation is in league with those who are capable of commanding demons."

Finch nodded. "We have more information on the second attempt. Four men, in the attire of House Guards—"

"Genuine?"

Finch nodded. "The uniforms appear to have been taken from the Terafin armories. The weapons were likewise taken from the armories. None of the items were in any way enchanted."

"The men were not House Guards?"

"One of the four was. He was a guard on the active duty rolls. He had been in service to the House for over a decade."

"The money went to him, I take it."

"Yes. It was found at his home when his home was searched. He was not ATerafin. There was nothing deemed remarkable about the men who made the attempt with him."

"He could not have expected he would survive."

"That's not clear. None of the four did."

"Clumsy," Hectore said, clucking his tongue.

Finch smiled. "The Terafin was not particularly impressed with the cats after that affair, no. The Chosen understood, although they didn't start out holding back. The cats, however, pounced on the would-be assassins with ferocity, and in the spirit of unfortunate competition—with each other. The amount of money was not staggeringly high, and as the man was a House Guard, it may well have accrued; we could not definitively trace its source."

"They were not in communication with anyone?"

Finch shook her head. "I do not think this was an attempt in which your aid would be required."

"No. The second attempt?"

"That, we have more information about." She glanced at Jarven, who inclined his head. "The woman met with a member of the House Council at the Placid Sea. It's a relatively secure establishment, and it presents a risk for both parties; if the House Council member chose to act against the assassin in that venue, heads would roll."

Hectore glanced, again, at Andrei—who apparently failed to notice.

"The assassin was recognized after the fact as the woman who was seen with the Council member in the Placid Sea."

"Convenient."

"Of course. Her hire was therefore less casual than that of the four men posing as House Guards. It was more costly on a number of fronts."

"Her name?"

Finch shook her head. "There are two possible names. The first is Hanna Gower. The second is Maria Giennau." Without pause she added, "You are familiar with both names."

"Andrei?"

"Yes." The servant turned to face Finch. "It is neither my place nor my desire to be part of this discussion."

"Hectore clearly feels the expertise in this case is yours."

"Clearly. The woman died?"

"By the cats, yes."

"What was her attempted method?"

"Daggers. They were contained in long pockets in the skirts of her outfit—pockets that are not generally present. The uniform was, in fabric and detail, a House uniform; it was not, however, taken from the House."

"No, it wouldn't be. When did this occur?"

"On the eighteenth of Veral, in the early morning when The Terafin was on her way to the breakfast hall."

"Poison?"

"The daggers? Yes. It was not a destructive poison or a corrosive one. We believe the poison was applied before she entered the manse; she carried no poison on her person."

"Does The Terafin never leave the manse?"

"She leaves it infrequently, and during the early days of her tenure, unpredictably, at the request of her Chosen."

"Now?"

"She has removed herself from the manse to attend the Kings; she has paid a visit, on very short notice, to the Houses of Healing. You know what occurred during the aborted victory parade. She leaves the manse seldom."

"She is wise."

"She is less vulnerable than others in a similar position. The women?"

"They are, as you surmise, the same. There are four other aliases the woman in question has assumed. Averalaan is not her home."

"If it's not her home, there must be some method of reaching her."

Andrei inclined his head. "Sending the message itself is not inexpensive, and it is not without risk."

"Would there be some record of the request?"

The servant failed to answer.

"Andrei."

"I am willing to aid you in this endeavor," Andrei replied stiffly—to his master. "But I am unwilling to continue this discussion. The woman in question is dead; the surrounding details are largely irrelevant."

Finch folded her hands in her lap. "If you wished to arrange a similar meeting," she said, tucking her chin slightly, but nonetheless meeting Andrei's steady gaze, "could you?"

He was silent for a long moment.

"I'm sorry, that was perhaps the wrong question. Let me ask a different one. If you wished to learn whether or not other such assignations had been made—in reference to this office and to Terafin—could you?"

"It is possible. I could not guarantee that I could do so before the fact." Before she could speak again, he added, "It is one of the responsibilities Hectore has asked me to undertake."

"Will you discuss the others?"

"As they become relevant, yes. At the moment, they are not."

Finch nodded. "Yesterday's poison?"

"It was clever and subtle," he replied. "It was also expensive."

"More or less expensive than the lone assassin?"

"At a guess? Slightly less."

Her eyes rounded. She knew, from Teller, what the purported sum paid to the woman—who had failed—was.

Jarven was smiling genially. "A good question, Finch. If the sum is significant, it can be traced. I do not believe the attempt will be made again, more's the pity."

"I don't consider it a pity." Her voice was soft and pleasant; her expression matched it. She did, however, tighten her hands slightly as they rested in her lap.

"If they were willing to try again, we might begin to pull a pattern out of the mathematical chaos; it is exactly the type of detective work we are, by experience, meant for." He glanced at Hectore. "I believe you wish to speak with the right-kin at your earliest convenience."

Hectore nodded. "I have made an appointment to do just that." He rose. "I will want lunch, of course, before that meeting. Are you mobile, Jarven, or will you now sit like a King in your empty office?"

Jarven smiled broadly. "If you will give me a week to look over this pernicious agreement—and honestly, Hectore, could you not find a scribe who could work at a decent letter size?—I will join you. The Placid Sea?"

"That is agreeable to me." Hectore rose as well. He

bowed to Finch. "I have a few small questions to ask about your route through the Menorans, ATerafin. Perhaps I will be forced to return in the next few days."

Finch rose as well. "I look forward to it." She watched Andrei. He had once again donned the expression and demeanor of the flawless servant. She had not asked Andrei the one question that was now uppermost in her mind. Had Hectore any need to hire an assassin, or did the servant perform that duty should Patris Araven deem it necessary? She thought she knew the answer, and did not care for it.

Chapter Twenty-four

13th of Fabril, 428 A.A.
Terafin Manse, Averalaan Aramarelas

JEWEL DISLIKED THE WAY dresses served as armor among the loftiest of the patriciate. It was, of course, a subtle armor, and it had taken her two years to accept it for what it was: a necessary act of camouflage. Every item she wore formed part of that pretense, even her hair, and the nets that bound it—decoratively, as her hair was so stiff—into place. The maid assigned to her by the Master of the Household Staff was waiting in the morning.

Shadow did not, apparently, care for her. She ignored his presence.

She ignored everyone's presence. She was stiff in all possible ways; her extreme sense of propriety and service was a wall that was either too thick to breach or too high to climb over. Jewel accepted it; Shadow grumbled. He had come to her bed when she had at last left the West Wing, and he had accompanied her into sleep and dream.

She could not remember her dreams. This morning, that was one of the few blessings she was to be allowed. When she was appropriately attired, she glanced at Avandar and he inclined his head. "The carriage will be waiting."

It was. So were Teller and the two Captains of the Chosen. Shadow lived up to his name; he would not leave her side until she reached the carriage itself. He disliked carriages—or so he declared—and chose to circle it as it made its way down the path.

"Do *not* land on the roof again," she told him, just before she climbed in.

He hissed.

Teller chuckled, because the hiss was loud enough to be heard while the doors were closed. Shadow didn't confine himself to hissing; he made clear what he thought of his *stupid* master until they'd cleared the drive. He did not, however, continue beyond that point, for which small mercy Jewel was grateful.

It was not, otherwise, a day in which gratitude was to be her chief emotion.

The Council of The Ten had, at The Wayelyn's request, agreed to convene on the thirteenth of Fabril. Jewel had lost an entire day to the Houses of Healing—which, given the results, was more than acceptable. But her realization, as she stood on the edge of Terafin's more mundane grounds—that Hannerle had not been among the sleepers—had become an almost nameless dread. Hannerle had *not* been awakened. She slept in the West Wing, tended by Haval.

Haval had not said a word. It made Jewel far more uneasy than any words he could have spoken. He had not asked *why*. Had he, what could she have said?

I don't know why Hannerle didn't wake. She wasn't with the rest of the sleepers.

It was the truth, of course. She didn't. But a suspicion had formed in the long hours of a restless night, and she would not be able to hide it from Haval; she could only barely hide it from herself.

"Jay?"

She offered Teller a wan smile. It would be safe to do so only until the carriage reached *Avantari*. The Kings had not commanded her presence in the Hall of Wise Counsel. Nor had she requested an audience—which was well within her rights. She needed the backing of the Council of The Ten before she felt it safe to do so.

Teller carried the various documents of possible relevance to a regular Council meeting in an innocuous folio;

he did not mention them because he knew—perhaps better than she—that "possible" and "probable" were worlds apart this morning. Jewel did not believe that she could grasp—and control—the shape of the meeting. She could weather it. She fully intended to tie her fate, and by extension, the fate of Terafin, to the future fates of the other nine; she was no longer certain that The Ten would believe it to be true. There were *no* prior instances of such obvious—and far-reaching—magic within either Terafin or the other Houses. Not in the hands of their rulers.

Not even during the wars of the Blood Barons had Jewel been able to find a similar magic. Demons, yes. There had been a lot of demons during the reign of the Barons. But nothing like the forest. Nothing like the library. She was tempted to say that the histories were silent on any number of concrete facts, but *knew* that had every account about every activity been preserved, she would find no similar events.

The Seneschal, along with a half dozen of the Kings' Swords, was waiting to escort the Terafin party to the chamber in *Avantari* reserved for The Ten. He tendered her a deep bow; she returned a slight nod. She dropped a hand to the back of Shadow's neck, and kept a grip on his fur. He hissed with amusement; the Kings' Swords tensed slightly. It was the only way in which they acknowledged the presence of a petty, giant cat.

Teller walked to Jewel's right; Shadow occupied the left. There had, as usual, been a jostle for position initiated entirely by the cat; it had been, on the other hand, subtle in the context of that cat. They made their way, without mishap or interruption, to the closed Council doors.

Before those doors rolled open, Jewel stiffened. Without looking at Teller, she raised her hands in brief den-sign: *Ambush.*

He understood her meaning seconds before the familiar Council table came into view: Terafin was the last of The Ten to arrive, and from the sound of the room—which stilled as she stepped into the chamber—the other nine had been in session for some time.

Jewel was not happy. She had been surprised, and she shouldn't have been. She caught the tone of voices as they faded into a silence that acknowledged the open door and the arrival of the Terafin party. It had not been an entirely cordial or civil discussion, then. She had allies on this Council, but not one of them had chosen to give her any advance warning.

Given the subject, it should not have come as a surprise; they could not discuss her without ramifications in her presence. Which is, of course, why she disliked being absent, especially today. Shadow glanced around the table but did not wander off to dump his head in the nearest friendly lap; he stood by her side, as if waiting—respectfully—for her command.

"Terafin," The Korisamis said, rising—which surprised Jewel—to offer her the shallow bow that indicated genuine respect between equals.

"My apologies for the hour of my arrival," she replied. "I was clearly misinformed of the time the meeting was to commence." She kept her expression stiff; the words had edge, but at least they were polite. She walked to her seat; Teller took his.

The Berrilya raised an iron brow. "Apologies, Terafin. It was felt that some portion of the discussion might lack the gravitas one would otherwise expect from one's peers." He glanced, pointedly, at The Wayelyn—who had not chosen to second Solran Marten as his adjutant for this meeting. The Ten had, in fact, chosen to pare down their entourages to the bare minimum of guards and a single counselor; it was what she herself had chosen to do.

"The Guildmaster of the Order of Knowledge has petitioned the Council," he continued, when The Wayelyn failed to interrupt. "She asks your permission, Terafin, to sit as observer for this discussion."

"Is she within *Avantari*?"

"She is. She can be found in Queen Marieyan's Court, and if her presence is acceptable, she will attend us without delay."

"The rest of The Ten will accept this?" Jewel asked softly.

The Garisar said, "I fail to see why we should, and I have made my objections known prior to your arrival. I would like to repeat them now."

Jewel inclined her head. "Your objection is noted. The reason?"

"The business of The Ten is not the business of the Order of Knowledge."

"Indeed, it is not," she replied. She had not herself decided how to handle Sigurne's unusual request, and wondered if that request had been prompted by another House. If it had, no one was willing to own it. She glanced over her shoulder to her domicis, who waited by the wall as if he were, in truth, just another servant.

You take a risk, if you accede.

I take a risk if I don't, she replied. *We are to discuss The Wayelyn's song, and its growing effect. We deal now in magics that no one of us understands.*

You cannot afford to own that ignorance. He was, of course, correct.

Tell the page to summon Sigurne.

He nodded stiffly.

She turned back toward the large table. "When we agreed to a recess, the topic of discussion was a song, written without my knowledge and without my consent by The Wayelyn. I could not speak of it then, as I had not heard it. I have, now. Does it remain—personal dignity aside—a matter of import to this Council?"

"It does."

"Very well. Let us speak of this when the guildmaster arrives."

Sigurne arrived at the side of Member A Phaniel. Jewel was surprised; Matteos Corvel did not seem to be in attendance. She entered the Council chambers on Meralonne's arm. As she headed toward the stairs that led to the gallery, Jewel rose.

"Guildmaster," she said. "If you would remain on the floor?" Avandar, at her silent command, had retrieved a chair from its standing place against the far wall.

"It is not my intent to guide or participate in the meeting, Terafin," she replied.

"Of course not," Jewel said, noting that Sigurne had ceased to move. "But if you are called upon to speak, it will be more dignified for all concerned if you choose to speak from the floor."

"Does the Council concur?" the older woman asked.

If they did not, no one spoke against the courtesy Jewel

had offered, not even The Garisar. Sigurne seated herself. Once she was settled, Meralonne chose to withdraw, retreating to the wall against which Avandar was standing, as if he were in truth a simple escort or attendant.

Before The Berrilya could once again speak, Jewel lifted a staying hand, her attention still given to the Guildmaster of the Order. "We will be discussing a song that is of some concern," she said. "Have you heard it?"

Sigurne inclined her head. "I have. In some circles, it is much discussed."

The Korisamis now rose. "It is not the contents of the song that we will now discuss," he said, "with apologies to The Terafin and the guildmaster. Terafin, you have now heard The Wayelyn's questionable composition."

Jewel nodded.

"At our previous meeting, the Bardmaster of Senniel College made clear that she thought the dissemination of this song was a crucial endeavor—when the Kings themselves did not concur."

She nodded again.

"We are all interested in your opinions on the matter at this point. Do you believe that the bardmaster made the correct choice?"

It was not the question Jewel had been expecting. "Given that The Wayelyn's fulsome praise is better suited to a god, it is hard to see either myself or my House in its lyrics. I consider it an impolite fiction, and feel no need to acknowledge it publicly one way or the other."

"You do not feel the contents are in any way accurate," The Korisamis said. It felt as if he was pressing a point that had already been made before her arrival.

She raised her brows slightly. "Korisamis, forgive any lack of due respect, but he describes me '*as fair, as fair as winter's heart, as pale as sun's light.*' If we ignore the details of the walls upon which I inevitably stand, and assume that by heralds he refers to the cats—"

"He does not," Shadow interjected.

Jewel turned, slowly, to stare at the gray, winged difficulty. After a few seconds, the cat dropped his gaze and gave a soft hiss. She returned her gaze to her peers. "The contents of the song itself are ridiculous. I understand that the bardmaster saw fit to speed its progress through the holdings; I understand that she—and The Wayelyn—are concerned about nebulous, future events."

"But those events are, if I understand the genesis of the song correctly, based entirely upon the visions of one who is seer-born."

The Wayelyn cleared his throat. Jewel considered speaking over him, but held her peace. "They are predicated on the visions of one who can, for all intents and purposes, travel through time. She has seen both your gardens and your personal chambers, Terafin, and she has seen what the Empire must face. It is not vision alone that guides her, but also experience."

Jewel wanted to argue further; to diminish the weight Evayne's words carried. But she accepted The Wayelyn's correction because it was true. She understood that truth and political expedience were often diametrically opposed; it was a fact she used to navigate other people's lies. Navigating her own, she had not yet mastered.

She exhaled. "Let me posit that The Wayelyn's song contained some kernel of truth, then. It is not, in any way, factual; nor, I think, was it meant to be. It does not speak to truth as I perceive it—and I live behind my grounds and the great trees that now grow there. I am guarded by large winged cats. I number, among my servants, one immortal.

"This does not make me any less Terafin; were it not for these facts, Terafin might still be ruled by a regent. It is not. I will not banish the cats; nor will I uproot the trees—if that is even possible."

"And the immortal?"

"He is, at the moment, occupied elsewhere—but he serves *me*, and I intend to retain those services. Each of our Houses contains hidden bits of history, and each of our Houses numbers, among its members, dangerous men and women. I have broken no Imperial law in my quest to gain the House Seat; I have broken no laws since I became The Terafin. I have made my pledge of allegiance to the Kings, and vowed to follow their laws in all ways that do not impact the laws of exception by which we *all* govern."

"We are aware that the alterations made to *Avantari* were not made with the express permission of the Crowns," The Garisar pointed out.

"It was my thought that they would prefer to have a

structurally sound palace from which to govern the Empire. Perhaps that was foolish. I did not feel that I had the time to consult with their wishes."

The Kalakar offered a smile that was both reluctant and genuine. "The sweeping—and obvious—changes are, of course, the reason we convene, Terafin. It has been noted that the intervention of your immortal servant was almost certainly responsible for the continued existence of the Twin Princes. The Crowns are willing to overlook much for precisely that reason—but power is a sword with two edges, at least in the Empire. And the power to restructure supporting beams, walls, and floors instantly—when you are not resident within the palace itself—is a power with which no one is comfortable."

Her words dropped like a stone into a still pond. Jewel watched their ripples. Even The Wayelyn's expression was disappointingly cautious. But he was not the author of her misfortunes; he was the author of a simple song.

"You are all in agreement, then?"

"Surely," The Morriset said, and this was a blow, "you yourself cannot advance an argument against this position? Were it to be my House, and not your own, that was author of these dubious changes and holder of this unknown power, you would yourself bring measures to counter or contain it."

Teller lifted a hand in brief, quick sign. She caught it out of the corner of her eye. "Were it not for the power you fear—"

"Fear is a harsh word," The Darias said.

"Yes. But this is, apparently, to be a harsh Council, and I will not mince words where others will not. Were it not for that power, there would in all likelihood be no Council of The Ten; there would be eight Houses ruled by unprepared regents; the demon would have destroyed all during the victory parade."

"You are so certain?" The Berrilya asked, with a softness that was sharp and cutting.

Jewel forced her hands to remain on the table's surface. It was a struggle. "I am." She exhaled sharply and stood. "So, too, the Kings, or I would not be in this Council meeting."

"Guildmaster," The Wayelyn said, turning to Sigurne,

who had become so silent it was almost possible to forget that she served as witness. "We would, if you are so inclined, have your assessment of The Terafin's claim."

"If there is no objection," Sigurne said, in the tone of voice she oft used when attempting to imply fragility and age. She looked to The Terafin.

"I object," The Terafin said. Sigurne nodded.

Meralonne, looking bored, pulled a pipe from the folds of his satchel. He watched Jewel, his silver eyes unblinking as he proved his familiarity with the shape of both the pipe's bowl and the leaves with which he lined it. He did not once glance at his hands.

"If you wish to play the game of ignorance," The Terafin continued, her voice sharpening, "play it when it does not waste my time. If you have failed to speak with the Order of Knowledge in the two months preceding this meeting, you will live for a few hours more with your ignorance. I know you all, some better than others; I can't believe that you haven't. If you wish to ask the guildmaster's advice purely for show, find a different spectator."

The Fennesar, who seldom spoke in full Council meetings, cleared her throat. "My apologies, Terafin," she said, in a voice as soft and yielding as Sigurne's had been. "I have been occupied with the concerns of my House, and I have not had the time or the inclination to speak with a member of the Order of Knowledge."

Had it been any other member who chose to speak the words, Jewel would have been blistered by her own fury. But The Fennesar had always been a modest, quiet woman. A steward, not a captain. "My apologies, Fennesar."

"Accepted. I feel that eight men and women here owe you far more courtesy than they have yet shown, and perhaps I am vain enough not to want to be included in their number; your accusation is otherwise well-founded." She rose, turned to Sigurne, and bowed. "Guildmaster?"

Sigurne once again glanced at Jewel, but this time she did not hold her gaze in any way. She nodded to The Fennesar as if certain of Jewel's response. And, Jewel thought grudgingly, she was. "What The Terafin claims is, in the opinion of the Guildmaster of the Order of Knowledge, fact. It is the truth. What she stopped—with a few very well-placed words—could not have been stopped by any member of the

Order, save perhaps one. Even in the case of the exception, it would have been the work of at least an hour, during which time, lives would inevitably have been lost."

"Thank you, Guildmaster," The Fennesar said. She resumed her seat.

Jewel did not wonder, as she often did in such a gathering of the elite and the powerful, what Amarais would do. Amarais would never have been in this position. What Jewel had promised the woman she almost revered was that she would *become* Terafin, and she would hold the House. Not more, not less. She did not, therefore, resume her seat as The Fennesar had done; she had not finished speaking. She had barely started.

Be cautious, Jewel.

Jewel did not reply.

Anger is not your friend here.

"It has been suggested, at least once, that I abdicate. It will *not* be suggested again, and if the idea is entertained by any of my peers, it will be entertained entirely in my absence. If it is a motion that is being considered, I will absent myself from the rest of this meeting because the meeting will be irrelevant to Terafin. I *am* The Terafin. I will remain The Terafin until my death."

It was The Berrilya who nodded, an odd gleam in his eyes. No one else spoke, although The Tamalyn was listening carefully to the woman who was whispering in his ear.

"I am willing to listen to your advice and your counsel; I am aware that I face the Twin Kings in a position that not one of our ancestors have ever occupied. I understand the reluctance of the Kings to merely overlook what is an obvious danger in different hands. I understand that I will be the personal magnet for the *Astari* and the Lord of the Compact while I still draw breath anywhere in this Empire. In your position I would consider that advantageous."

The Kalakar chuckled. "That is the silver lining to the storm clouds?"

"In your position, I would accept it," Jewel replied, with a slight smile. "But, in your position, I would not be concerned about Terafin."

"If you wish us to speak bluntly," The Berrilya said, "I feel that you are being disingenuous."

"I understand that the god we do not name is waiting

outside the borders of the Empire. I infer, from the brief
exchanges between the Exalted and the Order, that a god's
power is a matter of legend—and in this case, of nightmare.
None of us understands what a god can—or cannot—do.
Most of us believe there is very little of the latter. Our enemy is a *god*.

"I am a mortal. I'm human. I've lived in the humblest
streets of this city and in its most exalted. Everything I currently have, and every commitment I have undertaken, involves people. Mortals. It does not, oddly enough, involve
magic or sorcery. I cannot explain the whole of what I can
do."

Jewel.

She ignored Avandar. "But I would not give it up now,
even if that were a possibility. Not to cozen the fears of the
god-born nor the fears of The Ten. We face an enemy that
is almost beyond our comprehension. We cannot afford to
casually discard any weapons we might have, even if we do
not understand the whole of their import. I am not being
disingenuous, Berrilya. I have the seer's vision, and in my
early life—before I joined House Terafin—I saw the god we
do not name. I have lived in his shadow for all of my adult
life.

"And I would never willingly throw away a weapon unless I thought he could turn it against me. He can't."

"You are so certain of this?" The Garisar said sharply.

"I am."

"Guildmaster?"

Sigurne did not speak. Meralonne, pipe emitting tendrils
of smoke, did. "She is certain," he said, sounding bored. "If
your concern is that she is capable of turning that power
against you, it is not unfounded; she will be. If you kill her,
she will be no threat to you."

"No one," The Berrilya said, "is considering such a
death."

"Yet you play petty games, Berrilya. All of you. You play
games, and you waste time that should not be wasted."

"The governance of—"

"The governance of ten Houses—even *The Ten*—is of
little consequence if the city falls. The city is the heart of the
Empire; without the city, the Empire is lost."

"The city will not be—"

Meralonne lifted one hand—the hand that did not hold the pipe. His fingers danced in the air with practiced grace, and an image began to coalesce above the center of the table.

"APhaniel," Sigurne said, rising. "That is enough. Our opinion has been offered; more is not desirable at this time."

"Guildmaster," The Kalakar said, also rising. "In your considered opinion, is The Terafin critical to the city's survival?"

"It is the opinion of the Order of Knowledge," the guild-master replied, "that The Terafin poses a graver threat to the city than any we have encountered—as an Empire—in the past."

Silence.

"But it is also the opinion of the Order that because of that threat, she is critical to our survival. She poses a risk. Some of the members of the greater Council dislike the nebulous and unknown nature of that threat; some consider the god we do not name enough of a danger that the risk is necessary."

"But not all," The Garisar said.

"No. Not all."

"And the guildmaster?"

"I speak as the representative of the Order," she replied, as if her personal opinion counted for little. "The Terafin has made clear that she has no intention of abdicating—and in this, I must agree. The heart of her power *is* the Terafin manse. To separate her from her seat at this time would be impossible."

"If she chose—"

"She *will not* choose. The matter is not under consideration."

The Berrilya cleared his throat. "You consider such a choice unwise."

"Yes, Berrilya; you are perceptive. But it is entirely outside of my hands, for which I am grateful. She will face the Twin Kings as The Terafin. It is possible that the Twin Kings will demand her abdication."

"That is not their right," The Kalakar said stiffly.

Sigurne fell silent.

Jewel assessed the uneasy silence. Teller gestured again; this time, she nodded and drew breath. "That is the question that we face. I am Terafin. I will be summoned by the Kings. I do not know what they intend—but if they intend to demand my abdication, I will refuse. I owe loyalty to the Twin Kings and the Empire—but I owe a more binding loyalty to my House, and I will not betray it.

"If the Kings feel they have the power to force an abdication, will they not then have the power to choose who rules?"

"We are aware of the difficulty such a demand presents," The Garisar said curtly.

"And aware, as well," The Darias added, "of the exceptional circumstances in which such a demand might be made." He watched Sigurne.

The Wayelyn rose. "We have been in discussion since the crack of dawn, and we have not notably moved in anything but circles. The nature of The Ten cannot be changed; The Ten cannot vote to have one House stricken from the Council. Nine of The Ten can, should they so choose, approach the Kings to offer support should the Kings choose that option—but it would have to *be* nine.

"Wayelyn will not be among that nine." He smiled broadly as he met Jewel's stony gaze and winked.

What she signed, in a brief flick of fingers, could not be said in this Council hall, not even by a servant.

His smile faded. "You understand the import of the song. Will you find it in yourself to forgive me?"

"For singing it in my garden, yes."

"For writing it, Terafin?"

". . . I am talent-born, as you know; I understand the ways in which our talent inexplicably drives us. If I find no favor with your song, I find no deliberate malice in the writing of it. Its spread, however, is more problematic."

"You do not believe, as the bardmaster does, that it is necessary."

"No, Wayelyn, I don't. I am not, however, certain; certainty will only be reached in the future, one way or the other. If, in the end, the spread of the song works as the bardmaster intended, I will bless you for it.

"In the present, however, the song has increased the censure with which I am personally viewed by the Crowns. I am aware that there is no assurance, no treaty, no contract I can offer the Lord of the Compact that would ease his suspicion. In like fashion, I can offer little to assuage the concerns of the Council. Nor will I try."

"An attempt, at least, would be a sign of good faith," The Morriset countered.

"On my part, yes. On yours? Highly doubtful. Terafin has worked hard to amass its fortunes, and it has been intelligent in both the husbanding of its resources and the acceptance of its various treaties. I will not throw away decades of work as a sop to fear, be that fear my own or others."

He smiled. "And if we spoke, not of the usual concessions, but of some pact—in writing—that assures The Ten you will not use your inexplicable magic against us in future?"

"I would be willing to enter into a binding treaty that prevented the use of all magic by The Ten. All magic."

His smile cooled. "That is not a possibility. Terafin has chosen to retain a First Circle mage exclusively, and if other Houses do not have the incentive to offer similar contracts to the Order, they nonetheless retain the services of the magi. If The Ten chose to strip themselves of such minor—and regular—advantages, the merchant houses would not."

"No? A pity. I do not intend to surrender very real political advantage in return for theoretical support. Nor do I intend to hobble the activities of my House. There is no way to enforce conformance to such an agreement, and I am not of a mind to offer the trappings of an agreement without substance.

"I will remain Terafin. If unanimity is required to give the Kings consent to remove Terafin from the Council of The Ten and its role, in future, as one of the only Houses granted laws of exception, they will not have it."

"It would make a mess of the Gathering," The Tamalyn pointed out. Jewel nodded; she could practically hear The Berrilya grinding his teeth. "There are Ten days, one for each of The Ten. If The Terafin could be removed from the Council of The Ten, the House would still have its historical significance, and the Gathering is intended to be a reminder of the historic choices of the leaders of each of our Houses—from the first to join the banner of the first Kings, to the last."

"Yes, thank you, Tamalyn," The Berrilya said stiffly.

Shadow sidled over to The Tamalyn's chair. He glanced

once over his shoulder at Jewel, who exhaled sharply and
pursed her lips. Since she didn't actually reprimand him, he
dropped his head into The Tamalyn's lap.

It was a sign. The Korisamis rose; more than half of the
Council members were now on their feet in the sparsely
populated chamber. "It is not our habit, Terafin, to offer
trust. We are, and will remain, rivals. But we are also peers
in a very exceptional way. If you are willing to overlook The
Wayelyn's deployment, we will set the question of the song
itself aside.

"I will, as Korisamis, set aside the more pressing concerns. I understand that your cat is a ferocious guard—but
at the moment, he is only that."

Although Shadow didn't lift his head, the entire table
could hear his hiss.

"You are correct; we employ men and women who could
be—and are—considered dangerous. We consider ourselves
the masters of our own domains; we have the protection of
the laws of exemption for matters that concern only members of our own Houses. And we are, as you are aware, concerned about the structural changes within *Avantari*. Not
one of us has seen the entirety of those changes—which
deepens, rather than lessens, that concern. The Kings have
been extremely reticent, and the information that has come
from the Order of Knowledge and the few garrulous servants within the palace has been disappointingly brief and
vague.

"I will say for the record that should my House and my
heir come under the same attack that *Avantari* and the Twin
Princes faced on the first day of The Terafin's funeral, I
grant all necessary permission in advance for your intervention." His smile was dry. "I cannot say, with any certainty,
that Korisamis trusts Terafin in matters that arise between
our two Houses. I can say that I trust you to act within the
confines of the law; between two Houses, of course, laws of
exemption do not apply.

"But I will take the risk and say I trust your interests to
lie, squarely, with the Empire. I do not believe that you have
summoned demons; they seem so intent on your death I
cannot conceive of a cessation of hostilities. Intent or no,
they have failed."

"Their failure was not without cost," The Darias said.

"Were The Terafin to locate herself outside of Averalaan, the attack during the victory parade might never have taken place."

"And she would be without the ability to defend herself. Come, Darias; we do not counsel murder and we do not counsel suicide."

"It would not be the first time in our history that a Council member has ruled from beyond the hundred holdings."

"It would be, technically, the second; it would, however, be a first for House Terafin. The suggestion has already been dismissed." Throughout this discussion, The Korisamis watched The Terafin. She weathered his regard in silence.

"Given the testimony, however reluctantly offered, of the Order of Knowledge, our position must be clear. Korisamis will not countenance the removal of a legal head of House Terafin. If she will not abdicate, she will remain Terafin."

"Very well," The Berrilya said. Before he could continue, Jewel spoke.

"If you intend to call a vote, I will speak against it."

"A vote?"

"This is not a matter for Council vote. I am not present as a penitent; I am not present as a supplicant. I own my position on this Council. Working in concert, there might be some small chance of allaying the fears of the Kings should they move against my House in an unprecedented fashion; there is clearly no concerted effort here. A vote is therefore a measure that is both superfluous and insulting."

Both brows rose, but in a measured, steady way. Jewel didn't even blink. Shadow, however purred. Next time, she was going to leave the cat at home.

She reached out with her right hand, and Teller, without a pause, placed a sheaf of documents across her palm. "If we are done, we might move on to other matters of business. I have a question for The Morriset about his Western route and some difficulties that have occurred."

Less than a half hour later, the Council session was brought to a close. The Kalakar offered her congratulations with an appraising smile and a slight nod. The Tamalyn lingered to ask a few questions about the *Ellariannatte*.

She spoke briefly with The Morriset, and to her surprise,

found herself the recipient of The Berrilya's soft-spoken, "Well done, Terafin." It should not have mattered; if anything it should have annoyed her. It didn't.

Avandar was not angry; he seemed—for Avandar—pleased with Jewel's performance. He did not, of course, say so. Nor did he leave when the room emptied, because the Guildmaster of the Order and the Terafin House Mage made no move to retreat.

Sigurne offered Jewel a brief bow. "This is not over," she said softly.

It surprised Jewel. "The politics of the Council? No, of course not. It is never over."

Sigurne shook her head. "The Kings."

"You've spoken with them."

"Members of my Order have been in session with the Kings at their convenience since your last audience. Not all of the members summoned consider this a blessing, and they are at pains to point it out—to me, of course. In front of the Kings they are commendably well-behaved."

Jewel glanced at Meralonne.

"APhaniel's service has been, given his contract with Terafin, somewhat more difficult to secure. He is, however, expected to speak with the Crowns shortly." Her glance at the mage was pointed.

Meralonne, predictably, blew rings of smoke into the air in nested circles. He did not, however, contradict Sigurne's statement. Instead, after a long pause spent studying his own brief creations, he turned to Jewel. "You have not yet made your decision."

Jewel frowned. "Is there a decision, APhaniel, that I am required to make?"

His frown was sharper and more irritable. "If you play at ignorance, Terafin, I am your servant. I will allow it."

"I am not playing at ignorance," she replied. "I am not playing, at the moment, at all."

"Where is Celleriant?"

Her frown deepened.

"Where are your cats?"

Shadow, standing by the doors and complaining—in as quiet a voice as he possessed—about *boredom*, twitched.

"Where, Terafin, is your mount? You cannot leave them behind."

"They are all absent in the wilderness," she replied. "At my command."

"And you have not chosen to summon them."

"I have Shadow and I have Avandar; I have my Chosen. More is hardly required."

He let the embers of his pipe burn down as he met and held her gaze, his silver eyes unblinking. Wind moved through the nets that bound her hair; her hair was so stiff, it didn't cause any strands to land, as they often did, in her eyes.

"I will travel with you," he finally said.

"No," she replied, without pause for thought. "You will not. You are required here."

"It will not be safe," was his answer.

"If it is not safe for you, APhaniel—"

"I did not say the danger was to me." He turned and offered Sigurne his arm.

Sigurne took it. To Jewel's surprise, her hand, as it rested in the crook of the magi's elbow, was visibly trembling. Although the Council session's early start and the discussions that she had missed were upsetting, they were not nearly as unsettling as that visible sign of unease.

It is not lack of ease, Avandar said, watching as Sigurne and Meralonne at last left the chamber. *It is fear*.

The carriage was silent as it returned The Terafin and her right-kin to the Terafin manse. Shadow was not, but he was on the outside of the carriage, where he couldn't be easily corrected. Jewel wondered if passing strangers considered his inappropriate whining—for he *was* whining, and loudly—amusing, frustrating or frightening. Fear was almost beyond her.

He almost killed you.

It was true. He had. In the wilderness of her contested lands, in the lee of the Warden of Dreams, he was the only one of the three to present a very real threat. Had Adam not been by her side, he would have succeeded. Where he might then have gone—if he had retained any freedom at all—she couldn't say.

He was gentle with Ariel. He was affectionate with Teller and Finch; he treated Haval with something approaching respect. He was at his most difficult with Avandar, Celleriant, and his brothers, although he often stepped on Angel or Carver if they happened to be nearby.

Carver.

She swallowed. She had not lied to Meralonne; there was no decision demanded of her. Not by the Kings, nor by the Council of The Ten; not by her den or the House Council. But she had not been entirely truthful, either. She was waiting. She was waiting in the role of Terafin for some sign, some word, of her missing den.

She was waiting, with far more power and far more responsibility, as she had waited for some sign of Lefty in far poorer streets than the one along which the carriage ran.

It wasn't the same, of course. She had *known* that Lefty was gone. She'd known it. But knowing in that bone-deep way hadn't made the hope any easier to bear, because she did hope, and yet had none. She did not have the certain, talent-born sense that Carver would never return.

But Snow and Night had not returned. The Winter King had not. Nor had Celleriant. The odds that the two cats were actually *looking* were low. She imagined they would remember Carver between distractions, if then. But while there was any hope that Carver still lived, the Winter King would not return. He had not.

It was seldom that Jewel prayed; the silence of the carriage created a space for it. She closed her eyes and bent head. She wanted nothing so much as a glimpse of the Winter King, because—unless she commanded it—he would not return without Carver.

Teller returned to the right-kin's office, and Jewel joined him; much of her daily schedule had been put on hold because of the indeterminate length of the Council meeting. Teller, in theory, had done the same with his own, but a message indicating his absence had clearly failed to propagate; there were people waiting in the office. Jewel froze in the door, until she ascertained that none of these people were the Master of the Household Staff.

Barston was already rising to tender her a perfect bow. "Terafin."

"Barston. For the moment, the Council matters have been resolved to the satisfaction of The Ten."

His smile was slight, but genuine. "Right-kin," he said, to

catch Teller's attention. When there was anyone else in the office, he did not use Teller's name.

Teller, about to retreat into his office, pivoted and turned back to his secretary's desk.

"Patris Araven sent a message requesting an appointment."

"I see. When did he request such a meeting?"

Barston cleared his throat. "This afternoon. An hour after lunch."

Since lunch in the busy office was a moving target, Teller frowned and glanced at Jewel. Jewel flicked fingers in rapid den-sign. "You accepted?"

"I accepted contingent upon the right-kin's timely return from *Avantari*," Barston replied. "If the right-kin wishes, I will reschedule the appointment."

Teller, glancing briefly at the waiting room, shook his head.

"If you could inform the Household Staff that I'll take lunch in my quarters," Jewel told the secretary, "I would be grateful."

Barston's lips tightened. "I will inform the Household Staff," he said stiffly. He glanced pointedly over her shoulder at her domicis, and sank back into his chair. Avandar was amused, although his expression could have frozen water.

She retreated, so comfortable in the presence of her Chosen they might have been noisy shadows. They were, on the other hand, a good deal quieter than Shadow who was loudly *bored*. He gave Avandar's feet the evil eye while he complained volubly about the unending dreariness of his life.

Jewel stopped him when he started to give the same eye to the pages and servants in the galleries. She told herself firmly that there were many, many things worse than a bored cat. There weren't, however, many things as *irritating*. Irritation caused her to walk as quickly as possible up the stairs and toward the library. When she entered the doors, Shadow at her side, she froze.

Haval was waiting.

He was not wearing the apron in which he so frequently did his work; he was dressed, instead, in a velvet jacket, its deep blue collars fringed in lace that on Haval looked disturbing. His cuffs were accoutered the same way, and he wore boots that were a far cry from the practical, everyday boots he generally chose. She recognized him because she was familiar with him, but she felt a sinking suspicion that had he wished to remain unnoticed, she would have failed to notice him.

She lifted a hand as Gordon approached the clothier, and Gordon halted, hand on the hilt of a sword he had not yet drawn. Shadow interrupted his litany of the things that were boring to stare at Haval.

"Terafin," he said. He offered her a perfect, brittle bow. "I trust the Council meeting went well?"

"It went as well as could be expected given Terafin's arrival time was two hours after any other House's." She had not moved to close the distance between them. There was something about Haval, in clothing better suited to the ambitious patriciate, that was disturbing.

Shadow approached the clothier. He did not, however, do so with his usual sense of nonchalant condescension. Haval glanced at the cat, no more; he was watching Jewel. The bow was as much as he was, at the moment, willing to give her.

She found her voice. "Will you join me for lunch?" Turning to Avandar, she said, "Inform the Household Staff that I will dine with a guest."

Her domicis did not move for one long moment. The bow he tendered her before he left was exacting and perfect. *Be wary*, he told her, as he left to follow her orders.

I know, she replied. *He's angry.*

Yes. He is angry, and Jewel—he has always been a dangerous man.

There was nothing stiff about Haval; he did not carry himself in any way that suggested rage. He was more graceful, his movements more fluid, than they often were. He had not been to the small dining room within Jewel's personal quarters, but offered her his arm as she approached.

She accepted the offer in silence, placing her hand in the crook of his elbow. Shadow chose to walk by her side, rather than between them. He walked in silence, and the litany of boredom that she had found so irritating she now profoundly missed.

The room had not appreciably changed since her meal with Hectore, but it seemed smaller and more confined. Haval held out her chair, and tucked it beneath her as she sat; his manners were flawless. In no other way did he accuse her.

But she knew why he had come.

"Hannerle is not awake," she said, as he took his chair.

"No. Adam will wake her when I return."

Shadow, tail flicking, sat between them in silence, a sentinel. Two of the Chosen remained by the doors; in general, more were not required in her personal rooms. She thought, as she watched Haval, that more would make no difference.

"Let me tell you what occurred when Adam and I visited the Houses of Healing."

He inclined his head. He offered no questions, and made no accusations. He was almost entirely unlike the Haval with whom she regularly interacted. It made her uncomfortable, and she guessed that was his intent. But she had spent time with moneyed merchants—which was certainly the guise he had adopted—and she knew how to carry herself.

"Killing me," she told Haval quietly, "will not bring Hannerle back."

"That was my suspicion," he replied. The doors opened; wine arrived. Jewel glanced at it. She had never developed a taste for wine; she found it acrid and bitter to the tongue. She had, however, learned to drink it. It was the duty of the host. "Adam did not wake the sleepers."

"No. Adam could see them and he could bring them out of the dreaming, but he couldn't sever the connection between the waking and dreaming worlds."

"You did."

"Yes. Let me tell you what happened, and then you can decide—with as much information as I have—how you want to proceed."

She chose her words with care, but held nothing back; nothing except Adam's revelations about Corniel ATerafin's death. Those, she did not choose to share with anyone. She hesitated briefly before describing the leaves of iron and the bleeding cuts they had made in her palms, because no evidence of those cuts remained by the time she had stepped onto the lamp-lined footpaths of the gardens.

Haval did not interrupt her. He did not ask for clarifications, he did not pinch the bridge of his nose. He merely waited. He accepted wine when Avandar poured.

Avandar, however, did not speak, not even to Jewel. Like Haval, he was capable of containing the whole of his thought behind a perfect facade. The only person present who struggled with that was The Terafin herself.

"It was only as we approached the manse that I realized the one person I hadn't seen at the gathering was Hannerle."

"She was not present."

"No."

"These . . . individuals said they had gathered the sleepers."

She nodded.

"They had gathered them because they understood your intent and your desire, although you were, up to that point, unaware of their existence."

Jewel nodded again. Her throat was dry. Avandar poured water for her, which she accepted in almost nerveless hands. "I don't know why Hannerle wasn't there. I don't know why I didn't notice it until I was almost quit of the forest. I'm sorry."

"And you can wake her now?"

"I should be able to wake her."

"You are not certain."

"No, but, Haval, I had no idea what I would do to wake the others, either. I know what happened with Leila, the first time. I thought it would be something similar: I would have to walk into the heart of *their* dreams and force them out."

Haval lifted his wineglass by its very fine stem; he regarded the magelight through its burgundy depths. After a long pause, he lifted the glass to his lips. Jewel did the same. The silence stretched and thinned as she watched him. She had known him for over half her life, but she had never known him.

"Haval."

"Terafin."

"I will, after lunch, accompany you. I will return to the West Wing and we can try to wake her. I did not intend . . ." The words trailed into silence; they could find no purchase in his expression. She could not afford to make an enemy of this man. She did not want to make an enemy of him, and certainly not this way. She liked Hannerle, and always had.

But she wondered what Haval would become if Hannerle did not survive. She wondered what Haval had been *before* Hannerle, and what he would have become had he never met her.

"No," Haval said. "You did not intend that she continue to sleep. Were I to ask you now, Jewel, you would swear that you intended its opposite." He set the glass down.

She felt relieved, because his voice sounded almost normal, but his expression was so pleasantly neutral she could not relax.

He smiled, as if he knew. She had the absurd desire to beg him not to be angry with her, and because it was absurd, she stiffened as if to hold it in. "Tell me," he said, "about the Council of The Ten. Tell me, Jewel, about *Avantari*."

She blinked. "Haval, it's not necessary. We can eat lunch, and I can—"

"You do not understand what has happened. I do. I can put some of the blame at my own feet, although it pains me to do so." He lifted the glass again, as the doors opened. Lunch had arrived. "I will not kill you. I will not so much as make the attempt."

"It's not—"

"And it would please me to hear you tell me why."

She grimaced. "Haval—"

"The reasons should be obvious."

"Will you at least tell me what you understand that I don't?"

"We would be here all week," he replied, and he smiled again.

Jewel glanced at Shadow; Shadow had not moved. Not even his whiskers twitched. She exhaled and set her glass firmly down. "You won't kill me because if I die there's no chance—at all—that Hannerle will wake. Even if I were responsible for her continued sleep, it wouldn't matter; her life is in the balance and it's tied to mine."

"Very good. If she dies of this illness?"

"All bets are off."

"Indeed."

"Haval—what about Hannerle don't I understand?"

"I believe you understand my wife quite well; she certainly feels she understands you." As Jewel opened her mouth again, he lifted a hand. "When you first approached me and offered me the position of adviser, you attempted to threaten me."

Jewel nodded.

"I considered the attempt insulting."

She nodded again.

"My opinion in that regard has not changed, Terafin. You could not, at that time, deliberately hurt my wife; nor could you deliberately threaten her. You might—in my estimation—rise to a level of uncertainty wherein a threat against *me* is not impossible. But Hannerle has ever been determinedly apolitical, and you do not draw innocents into your battles where it can be avoided at all. Indeed, I feel your consideration in that regard is a weakness.

"But dreams, Terafin, are not deliberate. Desires are not deliberate. Our base natures are often things we struggle, for the sake of society, to repress. You walked the dreaming lands, and you found the sleepers—they had been gathered in response to a desire you had never consciously expressed. You did not know the sleepers; I am certain Adam recognized most, if not all, of them. He did not notice Hannerle's absence.

"Nor, at the time, did you. Do you think it an accident that she alone of all the sleepers was not present?" He paused, waiting for her reply.

She had no reply to offer. She had not considered the question at all—and she should have. She had had little time, of course. She had had the Council meeting to prepare for, and she had the Kings and their decision—whatever that decision might be—looming above her House. But she had had time to think about Carver and Ellerson.

Was it an accident? She had not told the strange immortals who lived in her forests to gather the sleepers; how could she when she hadn't known, until the moment she laid eyes on them, that they existed at all? They had, they said, acted on her desire. They had gathered everyone *else*, and they had kept them both amused and safe. Nightmares had not troubled them in their captivity.

But Hannerle was not there. If Hannerle was not there, did that mean they believed she didn't want Hannerle to wake? And if they believed that, *why*?

As she circled the question Haval had asked, wary of its hidden edges, she knew the answer. "No," she said, almost inaudibly.

"I have considered myself almost superfluous to you, Terafin. You are served by Devon and Gregori, and they bear the House Name; in all matters except one, they are beholden to you. Your right-kin is served by Barston, a formidably well-organized and perceptive man; your Finch is guided by Jarven." When she stiffened, he added, "I am not enamored of that connection myself, but Jarven is canny in a way you will never be.

"You have the Chosen, and if they are smaller in number than they were at the height of your predecessor's power, they are devoted to you; there are no cracks in that armor. You have your cats, and a control over the lands you have claimed that no Terafin before you has even dreamed of having. You have failed to die each of the five times assassins have been sent to end your life; I do not believe you will acquiesce when a sixth, a seventh, or even a hundredth is sent.

"You have enlisted the aid of Hectore of Araven. You think him sentimental, and you are not mistaken; you feel that sentiment, however, is proof of other sterling qualities, and in that, you are incorrect. Elonne, if I am not mistaken, serves you, and will do so unless you falter. Marrick is yours, and he will be yours until your death. Haerrad is not, but he is not a fool. That leaves only Rymark, and I believe you think to play a game with him.

"Regardless, Terafin, your House is at peace, and your rule is uncontested. My services are almost inconsequential, given the realities of your current situation."

Avandar moved to the sideboard and began to serve lunch. He was silent; even his internal nagging had been put on hold—which did not mean he thought she was on safe ground.

"I am a comfort to you because I am familiar, and because you are foolish enough to trust me."

There was no point in arguing with the last statement. Haval felt that trust in general was foolish as a matter of principle.

"But it is not for comfort, Jewel, that you would threaten Hannerle."

"I *would not* threaten Hannerle."

"I do not speak to your conscious intent. You would not; we are not in disagreement. What I did not take into account—and while I am chagrined, I do not see how I could have, given the information with which I was working—was your subconscious intent. You believe that I am necessary. It is seldom that your assessment disagrees with mine so profoundly.

"I am not a modest man. If I feel that I am superfluous, there is a reason." He laid napkin across the folds of his lap with fastidious care. "But while your impulses veer to the sentimental and the foolish, you are not a fool. Were you, it would be simpler. What am I to make of this?"

Haval could talk circles around her. He could reason her into the ground. She knew it, and knew that she could stop him if she could take control of the conversation. But she was hesitant. This Haval, she recognized; she was afraid to lose him completely.

"I will have you speak to me of *Avantari* now. The Council of The Ten I consider the lesser threat; if you cannot force them to support you as the legitimate ruler of Terafin, against any possible decision of the Kings, you will not survive the rule of your own House."

Jewel fiddled with her napkin. "Why is *Avantari* relevant?"

He smiled. "You have more information at your disposal than I, Terafin. If you will not speak of the palace, I will force you to answer that question. Changes were made in the structure of the palace. It is not spoken of in *Avantari* itself—and I admit that the Kings have a heavier hand than I suspected would be possible; it is spoken of in careful, hushed whispers outside of the palace.

"It is my suspicion that you know the full extent of the architectural changes that occurred on the day of The Terafin's funeral. When the Terafin terrace was destroyed by water, it was rebuilt in almost an instant. It is the same in shape and form; it is entirely different in construction. The Terafin gardeners are not royal gardeners; they *do* speak.

"What do you fear in *Avantari*?"

"Besides the Kings?"

"You do not fear the Kings," he replied. "You are cautious, and that is wise, but the Crowns engender no fear.

Nor do you fear Duvari, or his *Astari*. Given your particular talents, I do not feel this unwise. But you fear the palace. Why?"

"I don't fear the palace," she said, her voice sharper.

"It is my supposition that had you never ventured to *Avantari* at the Kings' behest, Hannerle would now be awake. She would be awake, in our home; she would probably be in the kitchen making lunch. Or cleaning; she will be appalled at the state of her home when—and if—she does wake." He watched her. He ate. The conversation might, given his comportment, have been about the price of cloth.

She was silent for another long beat. "When I went to the South," she finally said, "I didn't leave Averalaan the way I'd intended to leave it. I was in the Common and the Common was attacked."

"By demons, yes. They did very real damage in your absence. Were you the target?"

She did not reply.

Haval, being Haval, noticed. She thought, as she ate, that there was nothing he did not notice, but very little that he chose to bring to bear in any discussion. Hannerle stood between them like an uncomfortable ghost.

"I ended up in a mountain fortress, and the only way to leave it was to walk. The walk was entirely underground."

He waited.

"It was through stone, Haval. The Stone Deepings. I don't know if those words have any meaning for you."

"They do not. Do they now have meaning for you?"

She nodded. "They're like my gardens, in a way. Meralonne thinks that at one time, stone from the wild ways was quarried. It was used to build. Some of that stone lay in the foundations of *Avantari*."

"What properties do you ascribe to this stone?"

"Ask Meralonne. I don't know what properties the stone has; I don't know all that it can—or can't—do." She swallowed "But I do know that when I went to *Avantari* at the behest of the Kings, it was because two storage rooms had been entirely refashioned. They were much larger than they had been. I saw only one room; I was informed that both rooms had been significantly altered."

"In what way?"

"The room I saw was circular in shape; it was large. The ceiling was domed in a way that implied the basement is tall, even cavernous."

"In much the same way the doors to the library imply a library?"

"Yes. In just that way." She closed her eyes. "The walls of the room were carved. The carvings were of figures."

"Not mortal."

"No, I don't think so. Some of the carvings were reliefs, but some were almost standing statues. One of them was the Queen of the Wild Hunt." She opened her eyes again, because, eyes closed, she could see Ariane, and in this room, Haval was preferable.

"And you recognized the others?"

"Not all of them, no. But some, yes; they came to me while I walked the Stone Deepings, looking for a way out." She swallowed. "The Kings were there, in silence; the Exalted. Duvari. I don't know what I looked like to them. I don't know how composed I was. I don't know what they hoped to see me do.

"But while I was there, one of the statues stepped away from the wall and began to speak."

Chapter Twenty-five

"**I** SEE." HE TURNED, then, to Avandar, who now stood against the wall. "You recognized all of the figures." It was not a question. Had it been, Avandar would have met it the same way: in stiff silence.

"Haval—he is my domicis."

"He is far more than that. Do not look surprised; I will find it insulting. I assume that the demons that attacked the Common meant to kill him, not you. Your silences, Terafin, say as much as your words; possibly more."

"But it is my words, not his, you will have. He is part of this, but he is part of this now because I am."

"Very well. This statue?"

"The Oracle."

Haval frowned, as if in thought. "I believe I have heard that name before."

"Seers of old, if they wished control over their visions, walked the Oracle's path. Before you ask, no, I don't know what that means; I don't know if it's a physical path or a metaphorical one. I know only that she tests; the tests are harsh, and they are costly."

"Costly in what fashion?"

"They are meant, I think, to test breaking points. If you break, you fail."

"This is supposition."

"It is. But I've seen a seer's crystal before. If a seer has one, she can control her vision to some extent. I don't know how large an extent, before you ask. The crystal looks as if it is a prop. It's not. It's not separate from the seer; it's an extension of everything they are."

"You do not have one."

"No." She swallowed. "The Oracle offered the Kings a glimpse of their future. I don't know if she did it for my sake or for theirs. They accepted."

"As did Teller."

"She didn't offer the same to Teller; he asked." Jewel wanted to ask him how he knew this; she wasn't certain he would answer. And if he did, she wasn't certain she would like the answer offered; she said nothing. The table felt confining; she longed to rise and pace. After a moment, she did.

"What I did to the library, I did by accident." Her voice was low. "The whole of this place. The trees that are shelves. This room. The former office. You haven't seen it yet—it's a war room, Haval. There are weapons Meralonne feels are significant on its walls, and a long, flat table. There are windows—without glass—that open into skies that are not Averalaan's skies.

"An accident." Her lips twisted. "Carver and Ellerson disappeared when they entered a *closet*. An open door. The door led to gods only know where. Snow and Night are hunting for them now, and I *do not know* if they'll be found. I didn't intend for those doors to open. Not on *any* level. They weren't mine.

"They were part of the wilderness. Part of the ancient byways that the children of the gods and the firstborn walk. They weren't meant for an elderly domicis and a man who spends most of his free time in the servants' quarters. I think—I think, if I were Evayne, I could find them. I think I could look into my own heart and see some hint of where they might be.

"But I can't, as I am."

The rigidity of his perfect posture left him, then. "Jewel—"

"Teller thinks I don't know." Her voice had dropped almost to a whisper. "Teller thinks I can't tell what he saw. He thinks I don't know how badly it's affected him. It's true: I don't know what he saw. But I don't *need* to know; I know how it affected him. How it *still* affects him. The only thing he'll say is that he saw no sign of Carver or Ellerson."

"He is your right-kin," Haval said, as if that made sense in this conversation. When he realized that it didn't—to her—he added, "He understands your strengths and your weaknesses, Terafin. He understands them in a way that even Gabriel did not for The Terafin he served. The Oracle asked you to take this test."

"More or less."

"And you have not yet decided what you will do."

She swallowed. Paced the length of the room twice before she stopped and turned to face him. "I'm The Terafin," she whispered. "And not all those who take that test pass it. Those that don't—I don't know if they die, or if they're driven insane, but for the purposes of the House, it's one and the same.

"The Oracle believes that I am—I am—"

Haval waited. Jewel knew he exposed what he wished her to see; she knew he could feign delight or anger at the slightest of whims. She knew she couldn't trust any expression that crossed his face. But the expression he offered her now was one of compassion, and she *wanted* to believe in it.

It was Haval who had warned her to distrust her own desires. *Do not put faith in the things you want to see. Desire is the simplest way to manipulate another; it clouds vision, it impedes perception.*

"What do you believe the Oracle showed the Kings?"

She closed her eyes. "The fall of the city," she whispered. She knew what he would ask next, but waited anyway.

"Did the Oracle imply that the only hope of preventing that fall lay in you?"

Jewel lifted her chin. "Yes."

"And so you risk everything. If the city falls, Terafin falls with it, and all your oaths to the dead will amount to nothing." He frowned. It was his usual frown, and so familiar she almost smiled to see it. "You have not been entirely forthright."

"You're always annoyed when I am."

One brow rose. "What have you seen, Jewel?"

She swallowed. She had not spoken to anyone of her dreams. She had not called her den. She had not led them to the kitchen.

"You intend to take this test. You intend to walk this path."

"I am trying to think of *any* alternative, Haval. Any. But I *know* that if I stay in this manse until the end, it will *be* the end."

"And so my wife lies sleeping," he said. But he said it in the familiar cadences of the tailor.

She could not deny that fact. Hannerle was asleep. She would not wake without intervention. "Haval, I would never harm Hannerle."

"No. Not consciously. And perhaps not subconsciously. You know that she was very, very unhappy at my presence here."

Jewel had not resumed her seat; nor did she intend to do so. "I'll try to wake her now."

He smiled. It was a tired smile. "I understand, now, why she sleeps. I am not, as you have wisely observed, happy. I believe you will attempt to wake her. Tell me, Jewel, why you think I am necessary."

She pursed her lips and said, in a thicker voice, "Tell me— tell me truthfully—that you are *not*. Tell me, Haval, and make me believe it. You can; you know I want to."

He grimaced.

"If I leave Terafin—if that's what the Oracle demands of me—I leave a House that I have ruled for a bare two months. In that time, five attempts have been made on my life, and I would not have survived even the first were it not for my talent and my companions.

"The last time I took such a risk we *had* The Terafin. She knew how to prepare; she knew what to watch for. If they had not sent a demon against her, I do not think she would have died. This time? We have Haerrad and Rymark. If I can hobble Rymark, it will always—and only—be by presence. If I appoint an heir—" she swallowed. "Alea and Courtne died. I won't do that to any of mine. I can leave the seat vacant for some small period of time—perhaps weeks.

"But the Chosen are *so few*. I cannot call Snow and Night back."

"Cannot?"

"They're searching for Carver and Ellerson. To call them back—"

"Is to abandon all hope."

She swallowed again. Her throat felt thick, and she felt

so tired. It was midday. She had not yet seen to her correspondence. She had not reviewed the documents from the Merchant Authority that required her personal attention. But she wanted to sleep. She wanted to pull the covers over her face and curl up in her bed and sleep.

"Tell me that you believe you are not necessary, Haval."

"You understand," he said, rising, his plate a good deal cleaner than her own, "that I could do as you ask. You have always believed that I am an excellent prevaricator, with reason. But, Jewel, I lie seldom to you. I have no objections to lying to those who employ me, although most of my lies in these latter years have been in the form of flattery.

"But in your case, Terafin, it is my considered opinion that your talent would prevent your belief, and I am loath to make the effort where I am not relatively certain of success. You will leave your den in charge."

"Teller is right-kin."

He stared at her. After a long, silent moment, he lifted his fingers and pinched the bridge of his nose.

". . . You don't think Teller can hold the seat."

"Do you?"

She said nothing. Teller was known to the House Council; they were in frequent contact with his office. He was capable of handling their daily demands and the myriad nuisances that entailed.

"When do you plan to leave, Jewel?"

"Not before I wake Hannerle."

"You are aware that I will not remain resident in your manse when she wakes." It was not a question.

She nodded.

He smiled and offered her his arm. "What would you have me do, Terafin? You will not be present. Any aid I might have offered is entirely irrelevant on the road you feel you must travel."

"I would have you keep my home safe," she whispered.

"Your home? Not your House?"

"They are now one and the same." Her hand tightened. "I don't want to come back to a funeral. I don't want to leave at all."

"And what would you have me do? I am not in the councils of your enemies; nor is any member of your House, save perhaps one."

"It's not the demons I fear."

"Ah." He glanced down at her hand, frowned, and readjusted it. "I will speak with Hannerle."

Hectore arrived at the Terafin manse moments after the traditional lunch hour. This of course required that he sit in his carriage for an inconvenient length of time before at last ordering his driver to proceed. As was his habit, he traveled with Andrei, but no guards. While he did not disapprove of guards in theory, in practice he found them difficult. If they took the initiative, he was frequently required to smooth over the resultant difficulties; if they took *no* initiative, he found them annoying. Regardless, guards and servants often served two masters, neither particularly well.

Nor did the lack of formal guards cause difficulties; Andrei could, in an emergency, deal with anyone who meant Hectore immediate harm. Andrei, however, had never approved of the lack of guards. He felt that guards distinguished a man of means.

"They are men, not jewelry," Hectore replied—as he so often did. "I am not of The Ten; my dignity will survive a lack of guards." It always had. But it was only on visits of import that Andrei felt it necessary to return to a subject Hectore considered long closed.

The Terafin right-kin was, of course, of import.

"What pretense did we give for this visit, do you remember?" Hectore asked Andrei. He chuckled. "I can't help but notice that you don't care for the Terafin manse."

Andrei glanced briefly at his master. "I do not care for the *Astari*," he finally replied.

"They are everywhere, Andrei; you cannot expect to come to a House of any note and remain untroubled by their presence."

"They are not to be found in the Araven manse."

"Yes. I found that decision unwise, but in matters of security I am generally willing to bow to you."

"Bow in matters of dignity and I might be willing to compromise."

Patris Araven laughed. It was a bold, sharp sound, and the acoustically unforgiving ceiling carried its echoes; to the credit of the page who now led them to the right-kin's office, he didn't so much as turn or pause. "My dear Andrei, we both know you do not fully grasp the meaning of the word. Come. The servants are staring."

Teller ATerafin reminded Hectore, superficially, of Finch. If The Terafin was not nondescript—and she was not; her attendants guaranteed that—both Finch and Teller were self-contained. Their gestures were fluid but minimal, their voices smooth and inflected in a way that spoke of education, not birth. Jewel Markess ATerafin was wild-haired, dark-eyed, her skin more likely to take sun than either her right-kin's or Finch's. She stood and sat as if her energy was only barely leashed, and her frequent gestures were sharper, broader. She conveyed her meaning and her intent just by moving.

Hectore liked her. He had not expected to like her, but was not surprised; she was the only child his godson had ever taken under wing, and when he could no longer protect or contain her, he had sent her here. From her flat in the twenty-fifth holding to her seat in the Council Hall in *Avantari*, she had followed a path Ararath had set.

But Ararath disdained the patriciate, and he loathed The Ten. What would he make of the girl who had shouldered the burden of Terafin, who had become his estranged sister's heir?

"Patris Araven."

"Forgive my manners, ATerafin. I am admiring the paintings on the far wall. They are new acquisitions?"

"They are," the right-kin replied. "Barston is the expert here; I served as consultant, but the final choice was left in his hands." His own hands he clasped loosely behind his back while he waited.

Hectore then turned, nodded, and allowed the right-kin to lead him into his office. It was not an office that Hectore had had much occasion to visit, although he had, of course, seen its interior before. He was not surprised to see it remain almost unchanged.

Teller ATerafin did not immediately retreat to his desk; he paused before the shelves to the right of it. He inspected the spined books with some care, and eventually chose one. It was not a ledger, by look. He carried the book to the desk, where he placed it upon the surface on which he had clearly been working.

Hectore glanced at his servant as the right-kin opened the book. Andrei offered a controlled, minimal nod. "I see you have taken some precautions, ATerafin."

"I have. They are more complicated than the precautions taken as matter of course in this office." He sat, lifted his chin, and said, "I've spoken with Finch."

Hectore inclined his head; he was not surprised. "Have you spoken with The Terafin?"

"No. We spent much of our day in *Avantari*, and she is now in a meeting of some import."

Hectore chuckled. "You will have to tell her, you know."

The right-kin's brows rose slightly.

"I am about to offer House Terafin a joint venture of some value," the merchant said. "It is a gesture of good faith, on my part; a gesture as well of my support for the current Terafin. I would therefore like to ensure, by all means necessary, that the current Terafin retains her seat."

"In that, if nothing else, Patris Araven, we are agreed. Finch is expecting you. While I am fully capable of looking over minor trade agreements of a limited nature, almost all of the agreements of any note are undertaken by our office in the Merchant Authority."

"Of course."

"May I ask why you are here?"

"If you have spoken with Finch, you are aware that the aid I have offered is not entirely confined to the Merchant Authority. The Terafin has accepted my aid, in principle."

Teller nodded. He was more obviously reserved than Finch.

"With your permission, ATerafin, I would like to have the grounds—and the manse—searched."

"We are responsible for our own security," Teller replied. "The Terafin trusts that it is thorough."

"Indeed. I do not ask to offer insult to the men and women who serve your House. I ask for reasons of my own."

"And those?"

Hectore sighed. "Andrei."

"At least one new employee within the manse is a member of the *Astari*."

The right-kin inclined his head. After a pause, he said, "I believe there are three. We do not, at this point, distrust the *Astari*."

"Of course you do. Trust in the *Astari* is almost poor sportsmanship," Hectore said. "If it will comfort you, I am happy to attend my requested inspection; I am also happy to have it conducted in the company of any man or woman you choose."

"I admit I am confused, Patris Araven. I was uncertain what to expect when you asked for an appointment; I admit that I thought your visit would involve information."

Hectore frowned. "Of course it does." He exhaled. "Very well. I wish my servant—my personal servant—to have a more intimate knowledge of the layout of the Terafin manse. Not more and not less."

"Why?"

Andrei offered Teller a bow. It was deep. It was also unusual; servants generally remained invisible, standing against the far wall until their masters chose to leave. A bow was acknowledgment that servants did not offer. "I am tasked," he told Teller, "with protection and preservation. I informed Patris Araven that the security measures undertaken by The Terafin would be up to the task; he is, of course, less willing to trust matters that are not in his own hands."

"That is *not* what I said, Andrei. I am certain that your security is functional. It did not, at its height, prevent the previous Terafin's death."

The right-kin stiffened.

"The current Terafin has, however, survived similar threat. It is my belief that her survival is tied in some way to the . . . unusual nature of both the grounds and the manse itself. I have seen her personal quarters. Were I tasked with protection of The Terafin, I would be unconcerned.

"It is not, however, The Terafin. It is Finch."

Teller was silent.

"I believe that The Terafin intended exactly that. If Finch is capable of manipulating the same magical power that Jewel Markess ATerafin does, tell me, and I will apologize for the unpardonable waste of your time. If, however, she is not, she does not have any of the advantages The Terafin currently enjoys.

"Her enemies may, with impunity, attempt to poison her where she works; they may, with impunity, attempt to poison her here. She has no Chosen, and if I am not mistaken, she has not availed herself of the privilege of House Guards. She has no domicis, and were one to be found, he or she would never be the equal of The Terafin's.

"She has not played games in which death is practically the price of admission. But she has been drawn into them now—and so, ATerafin, have you."

"No attempts have been made on my life."

"None yet. How long do you think that will last?"

The right-kin stood. "Patris Araven, I am grateful for your concern."

"Andrei?"

The servant turned. He walked over to the bookcase and stood before it for a long moment. "Two," he said.

Teller frowned. "Two?"

"I believe one belongs to Member APhaniel. I see his signature in some of the more complicated enchantments." Hectore could hear the frown in his servant's voice, and smiled in spite of himself. Andrei would be vexed when they left.

"To be expected. The second?" Hectore grinned.

"It is subtle," the servant said, after a long pause. "Subtle enough that it appears to be one of the several protective spells that gird the room. The trace of the magic does not appear to leave the room."

"I did not realize you employed a member of the Order as a servant," the right-kin said, after a brittle pause.

"I do not. No more does The Terafin. Is it under the purview of the Lord of the Compact? It is just the type of enchantment the House Mage would ignore."

"It is exactly the type of magic he would not," Andrei replied. "Meralonne APhaniel is not known for his subtlety; nor is he known to be politic or pragmatic if he feels someone is trespassing in his domain. Not all of the enchantments that gird this room are his; I believe some laid here are older."

"They are," the right-kin said. He had not resumed his seat. Instead, he moved to stand beside Andrei. "You think there is a protective enchantment in this room that is not meant for my use."

Andrei nodded. "I believe it *is* protective in nature. But, yes, I think it is not meant to give the right-kin the advantage here."

"Can you ascertain what it is meant to do?"

"I am attempting to do just that, ATerafin. As I said, it is subtle."

"And now we come to the crux of the matter," Hectore said as he, too, rose. "Do you trust me? Do you trust my servant?"

Teller watched Hectore of Araven for a long moment; his question faded into silence, and the silence grew more pronounced as the minutes passed. It was not a question he had expected to be asked; trust was little more than a polite fiction when one dealt with people outside of the den.

It was a necessary fiction, of course; it was civil. It was politic. But he understood the risk Hectore had taken; he had chosen to deliberately reveal at least some of his servant's ability. "Can you ascertain what some of the other spells are?" The question was subdued, but measured.

Andrei replied, although his gaze never left the bookcase. "The book on your desk is a defensive spell. It does not convey silence; it conveys conversation. But it is a particular type of conversation. I believe the page to which the book is opened is relevant in this regard. You might close the book, and the conversation would be subdued and awkward; you might open it to the end of the first chapter—or perhaps section—and the conversation would be genial. Farther in, and angry words will be exchanged. They will sound natural; they will mimic the voices of the people in the room."

Teller exhaled.

"If the eavesdropper is aware of the properties of this particular spell, he may attempt to breach it. If he is not *exceptionally* skilled, he will, after some strenuous effort, be successful. But success in this case leads to a secondary line of discussion."

Teller did not stare at the servant, but it took effort. "If he is exceptionally skilled?"

"The spell has a feedback contingency. If he is competent, he will be deafened for a few hours."

"If he is not?"

"It will be far longer than a few hours."

It was all true. Every word of it. Teller's security had either been heavily compromised or Andrei was a mage of far more subtlety and expertise than most mages seconded to the Houses.

Andrei continued. "It is not, of course, the only spell woven around this room. There are basic silence spells across both doors, and spells which prevent simple projectiles from breaking the windows. There are spells of seeming upon the curtains, and if the curtain holders are twisted in a certain way, when closed, they will show a shadow of your back, as you sit at your desk and labor over your paperwork.

"The carpet and one wall have also been enchanted to respond to magic in proximity; the proximity detection has made exceptions for the convenient minor stones that men of Hectore's import frequently carry upon their person. It would be very, very difficult to enter this room unseen."

"But not impossible."

"No, A Terafin. Not impossible." He turned from the bookcase and glanced at Patris Araven. "Is that satisfactory?"

"It is not up to me, Andrei; I am not the person you need to impress at the moment."

Teller, watching them, smiled. "I think, Patris Araven, that you are. Your servant believes he is to be judged by *your* standards of what is considered impressive; he is unaware of what mine are." The smile faded. "I am aware that The Terafin has chosen to trust you."

"And that is not enough for you?"

"It is not my job to question her judgment. We do, on the other hand, have men who are paid to do just that. They are not, in my estimation, nearly as impressive as your servant. Do you seriously feel that the office of the right-kin is in danger?"

"Did you," Hectore countered, "believe that Finch was? Or has she lulled you into the belief that someone is attempting to give Jarven the death he richly deserves?"

Jay trusted this man. Without that certain knowledge, Teller was not certain he would; Hectore was far too moneyed, far too powerful; his servant was frighteningly competent. Rumor had it that Hectore did not particularly care for guards; it was attributed to his desire to be seen, somehow, as a "regular" man. The attribution was wrong. In Teller's estimation, Andrei was the equivalent of a dozen armored men. Perhaps more; he would not, in most cases, be noticed.

"No," Teller said. "Nor did she try. She was uncertain, but Jarven was not. She has worked with him for her entire tenure in the Merchant Authority, and in this, she trusts him."

"In this?"

"She understands Jarven ATerafin's peculiar foibles."

Hectore had a laugh reminiscent of Marrick's. It was full, loud, resonant; it filled the room, demanding at least the shadow of a smile in return, which was what Teller gave him.

"I would, if given the choice, prefer to have Andrei examine the Merchant Authority in a similar fashion, if you can spare him. The Merchant Authority is not entirely under the auspices of House Terafin—"

Hectore coughed, loudly. "I should hope not."

"—And therefore does not fall under our oversight. If Finch is at risk, the risk would be greatest in the Authority."

Andrei pursed his lips, but said nothing.

"You don't agree."

"No, ATerafin. Precautions have been set in place, but at this time, I feel it unlikely. If Finch—along with Jarven— were to die within the Authority offices, their deaths would fall under the laws of exemption if The Terafin did not see fit to demand a public inquiry. She will not, of course."

"If they occur within the Merchant Authority proper, the same will be true."

"You fail to understand the scrutiny under which the House has been placed. If the Crowns wish to press the issue at this time, they have a case."

"They have not pressed it in similar circumstances in the past."

"No. But in the past, they have had access to The Terafin. I do not think any of the spies who serve the Crown will gain entrance to the upper remove of this manse without express permission. Without, in fact, The Terafin's presence. They are hampered, and they are already concerned. They might use public deaths to push for very private concessions."

"Which would imply a benefit to the Crowns for such public deaths."

"Indeed."

"May I give you a tour of the manse, Patris Araven?"

"I would appreciate it. Terafin has, I am told, very fine

public galleries, but I have been so pressed for time on my previous visits that I have failed to see them."

"And would you care to dine in the dining hall?"

Patris Araven grimaced.

Andrei, however, said, "He would."

"Then let me notify Barston that we will have such an illustrious guest."

Teller's tour of the manse was thorough. Hectore lingered at some sign from his servant—but it was not a sign Teller could easily intercept. Outside of the confines of the right-kin's office, Andrei once again adopted the mute and perfect silence expected of a man of his station. Teller had some difficulty with this sudden shift. Hectore, however, did not; when Teller's gaze rested for too long upon Andrei, Hectore would ask a question.

"Do you have any desire to view the grounds?" Teller asked.

"Not today; I believe the grounds are impressive enough we would miss dinner entirely were we to venture there."

Teller nodded. He suspected that the grounds—like the library—were beyond Andrei's ken. Andrei offered no observations. If he found anything unusual, he gave no sign at all.

But they followed a course set by Teller, and it led, eventually, to the West Wing. As the doors were opened, he said, "Our rooms are currently here. There are twelve occupants, although the West Wing is capable of housing more."

"The twelve?" Andrei asked—after the doors were shut at their backs.

"The original occupants of the West Wing, one domicis, and one child."

"The child is whose?"

"An orphan," he replied. "She arrived on the day The Terafin returned from the South, and has been with us ever since."

"Are visitors entertained in this Wing?"

"Yes. Generally in the great room."

"Servants?"

"None currently resident within the Wing; the servants who care for the Wing have been working here for years."

"None are new?"

Teller shook his head.

"We will want their names," Hectore said, unexpectedly.

"They are all ATerafin," Teller replied, the tone of his voice his only offered warning. He turned toward the great room, entering it as the doors were opened. "If you wish to have a seat, we may take drinks before dinner here."

"Andrei."

Andrei turned and bowed, briefly, to Teller. "With your permission, right-kin, I would like entry to your personal rooms here."

"And Finch's?"

He nodded. "Patris Araven?"

"I have had enough exercise, I think. If you feel it necessary to accompany Andrei, please do; I will avail myself of your fireplace and your very comfortable chairs."

Jewel might have remained uncertain about Haval's mood, but Shadow was not. The large, gray cat never bothered Haval the way he did Angel, Arann, or select members of her Chosen; he was not hugely disrespectful the way he was with Celleriant, Avandar, or Meralonne. Nor did he start this afternoon—but he did attempt to step on the feet of the Chosen and he did mutter "ugly" and "stupid" under his breath while glaring at Avandar from the corner of his eyes.

He was no longer on full alert.

Haval, for his part, now looked like he was overdressed and slightly uncomfortable to be so. For Jewel, there was no slightly; she longed to return to her rooms and change into something that did not feel so confining. She didn't even ask. She understood that the lunch with Haval had been a test. She was accustomed to Haval's tests, and frequently failed them. She knew that this was not a test she could afford to fail.

It was not Haval's way to offer comfort. He offered opinion—some of it caustic, much of it frustrating—and fact. Comfort was not something that the reigning Terafin should require. Ever. He therefore said nothing as he walked by her side toward the West Wing. He frowned once at her grip on his arm, and she forced her hands to relax. More than that, he did not say; they were in public.

He trusts your intent, Avandar told her, his voice tinged

with mild frustration. *But feels you are wise enough and mature enough to understand that intent counts for little. He is also aware that his wife would be beyond upset if he were to kill you; if he chooses to act against you, he will not do it while there is any chance she will survive.*

Avandar had a sense of comfort very similar to Haval's.

She approached the West Wing, wondering if anyone, besides Adam and Ariel, would be present.

The answer was not quite what she expected; as she opened the doors and entered the hall, she saw a familiar man slide between the doors of the great room. She felt Haval stiffen and glanced at his profile.

"Andrei?" she asked, as she released the clothier's arm. His brows rose slightly. "Terafin." He bowed.

Teller entered the hall a moment later. His brows rose as he met Jewel's gaze; his hands moved briefly in den-sign.

No, she replied, in the same language. *No danger.*

He glanced to her right, where Haval stood. She grimaced. *No immediate danger.*

You're all right?

She didn't answer. She wanted an hour and real words for that. Haval did not immediately move. Neither did Andrei. Jewel cleared her throat. "Is Patris Araven here?"

Teller nodded. "He is. He's in the great room, at the moment. I took the liberty of offering him a tour of the manse."

"We don't mean to interrupt, of course. Haval is currently measuring me for two dresses—hopefully less confining than the monstrosity I'm currently wearing."

Teller almost laughed; the sound lurked in the corner of his eyes and lips.

"Haval?" Jewel said, when the tailor failed to move. He was watching Andrei. Andrei returned his regard; they might have been the only two men in the room. ". . . Or I could entertain Patris Araven if you have other pressing concerns at the moment."

"A man of Patris Araven's import," Haval surprised her by saying, "should not be left unattended. Please, Terafin, do not let the minor matter of fittings cause neglect. I will wait."

She did not stare at the side of his face, but it took effort. She knew that the resolution to this difficulty would occur only after she made an attempt to wake his wife, to return her to the waking world. She was not certain what Haval would do if she failed. "Are you certain?"

He raised one brow in a stiff arch.

"Very well. I would be delighted to entertain Patris Araven. Avandar?"

He bowed. If Andrei was a concern, he was content to leave him in Haval's hands.

"Shadow, go to Ariel."

The cat sniffed loudly. And complained. But his complaints were second class, for a cat. He considered Ariel boring. But he didn't consider her annoying; he certainly didn't consider her dangerous. That was no surprise. What was a constant surprise was that Ariel did not consider Shadow threatening. She frequently fell asleep draped across his side. She occasionally tried to stretch his wings—a crime for which other men would lose their hands. Or arms.

"Will you join us?" Jewel asked Teller.

Teller hesitated. Before he could reply, Haval said, "As right-kin, Terafin, and as host, he will of course join you."

Teller evinced no surprise. He offered The Terafin his arm; Jewel took it. Her hand was shaking. Together, they entered the great room. Hectore was seated; he glanced at the door and rose instantly.

"Terafin! I am surprised." He offered her a very correct, very formal bow.

"As am I," she replied. "I am here for a fitting. I hope you will not consider the manners of my House to be insufficient; I did not know you were here."

The smile froze, for an instant, on his face. "A fitting?"

"Indeed. At the moment, given the victory celebrations and the various functions within *Avantari*, I have a clothier in residence to see to the needs of my wardrobe."

"In . . . residence." Hectore glanced at the closed door. It opened, but Andrei did not appear in the frame; Avandar did. He carried two bottles to the sideboard as the door closed at his back.

"Please, Patris Araven, be seated."

Hectore continued to stare at the closed door. "May I ask, Terafin, if your clothier is a man named Haval Arwood?"

"He is. Is this a concern?"

". . . No. No," he added, with a smile that was not entirely forced. "It is not, of course. You ventured into the den of The Ten this morning?"

"I did." Jewel took a chair near Hectore; she clasped her hands in her lap as if she were once again at her lessons.

"I did not expect to see you here," Haval told Andrei.

"Nor I you," the Araven servant replied. They were alone in the hall, save for the presence of two of the Chosen, who now stood guard at the doors of the great room.

"Why are you here?"

"I might ask the same question."

"Yes. And if there are no answers forthcoming, we will stand in the hall like two overly cautious men. I am here as a clothier. I have the distinction of being one of the few The Terafin hires."

"I see. I am here because Patris Araven made an appointment with the right-kin."

"I was not aware that the Araven fortunes were so congenially tied to House Terafin's."

"No, indeed. You were not. It is not information that is considered vital to most clothiers."

They remained at an impasse. Haval had no intention of allowing Hannerle's condition to be spoken of in Hectore's hearing; if Hectore was unaware of Adam, he did not intend to bring Adam to the merchant's attention. It was a simple precaution; Hectore of Araven was not a particularly mendacious or cruel man. But he was a man, and like all men, had his weaknesses.

"You are inspecting the manse?" he finally said, dispensing with the pretense of affability and ignorance.

Andrei inclined his head. "Terafin security, I am told, is adequate."

"Your informant must be ATerafin. It is not, to my mind, adequate at all."

"Indeed. Might we hold this conversation in a different room?"

"As you wish. I have a workroom in the Wing; it is inconvenient to task The Terafin with travel to—and from—my shop. It is not perhaps the tidiest of spaces, and I will ask you to touch nothing."

Andrei nodded.

* * *

They entered Haval's workroom in silence, aware of the Chosen at the doors of the great room.

Andrei's frown was no doubt genuine as his gaze swept the floor of Haval's workroom. "I had not realized," he said, "that the attempt to touch nothing was to be so onerous. Will I be forgiven if I accidentally step on anything?"

"No."

The Araven servant chuckled. "You have not changed at all, Haval. You have aged, but you have not markedly changed. I did not think that decades of life as a tailor would have so little impact."

"They have not had none," he replied. "Does the manse meet your approval?"

"It does not. There are areas I feel are of significant concern."

"How thorough was your inspection?"

"It was not, given we had a spare few hours, as thorough as I would like."

"And you are done?"

"No. Hectore will dine in the dining hall with The Terafin this eve. He is not amused," Andrei added.

Haval chuckled. "No, he wouldn't be. I am surprised he agreed."

"He has taken a liking to your Terafin; he considers her, in many ways, the child of his godson."

"Which godson? He has a dozen."

"He has seven," Andrei replied firmly. "But I am not in the mood to answer questions which are superfluous. You are aware of whom I speak."

Haval nodded. If he did not trust Hectore—and he did not, but in the general misanthropic way he regarded most of humanity—it was Andrei who was his chief concern. "The Terafin has a domicis of whom even you would approve."

"My approval is also superfluous."

"Ah, I have grown clumsy. She has no need of any service you offer."

"That was my conclusion, yes. Hectore feels that The Terafin is as sentimental as he was in his youth. He has taken her acceptance of his offer to heart, and he looks, now, to the two members of the House Council who are her closest friends."

"Finch."

"And the right-kin, yes. He is willing to work with Jarven."

"I'm surprised you are."

"I am servant; Hectore is master. My preferences in this regard are inconsequential."

"Do you feel that Finch is in danger?"

Andrei did not answer.

"And the right-kin?"

"I am here, am I not?"

"If Hectore decided to arrive to celebrate the birthday of a servant's child, you would be here regardless." Haval frowned. "You have concerns about the right-kin's safety?"

Andrei bent and lifted a pair of shears. "Haval, the mess here is almost overwhelming."

"It is an ordered mess," Haval replied. "I remember where everything has been laid. I expect no hands but mine to touch anything in this room; it is arranged in a way that is convenient to me."

Andrei set the shears down. "I am here to examine the right-kin's personal quarters. He was to accompany me. Will you do the honors?"

"I will—but I expect to be informed of any difficulties you perceive."

Andrei exhaled, but nodded. "I do this not for access; I have already been granted access."

"Of course. You will tell me because you are certain that I am one of the very few people in this manse that will understand—and remember—the whole of what you say."

"Hectore will not be pleased to see you so intimately involved," Andrei said, as he stepped aside to allow Haval to leave the room.

Haval said nothing. He led Andrei to Teller's chambers; the door was not locked. Had it been, he would have opened it. They entered the room together. Haval closed the door at his back, and stood against it, observing the Araven servant as he made his way, with care, toward the office, with its shelves, its more modest desk. He touched very little.

In truth, Haval was not ill-pleased to have Andrei in the Wing. Jewel's particular abilities compensated for somewhat lax security, as did the plethora of guards with which she was often reluctantly surrounded. The cats were so swift in their response to danger, they reacted almost before she could.

He did not discount the importance of the Chosen, but he did not privilege it, either. He trusted her domicis with the protection the cats might fail to provide; they were not naturally strategic thinkers, in Haval's opinion.

Had he been certain that the cats would remain as guards for Finch and the right-kin, he might have been less concerned. The cats did not trouble either of the two with their pranks; they did, of course, share their voluble complaints, but not even Jewel escaped those.

Haval was uncertain that the leash that restrained the cats would remain in place if Jewel herself were not present; if they slipped that leash, it would be disastrous. He was not certain that The Terafin was aware of the control she exerted. The cats whined, complained, destroyed carpets and occasional pieces of furniture when they sulked—but they obeyed her. They obeyed her express commands while attempting to maintain the polite fiction that they did so voluntarily.

But they appeared, to Haval's eye, to understand the commands it did not occur to her to put into words. Shadow had never harmed Ariel. He had never attempted to frighten her. He was content—barely—to allow the girl to pull his whiskers and treat him as a large pillow. She adored the cats.

Jewel didn't question this. She saw—as she often did—what she expected to see. What she desired to see. Jewel herself was not comfortable with silent and utter obedience. She assumed that the cats were not comfortable with offering it. But in Haval's opinion, they were. They were perfectly capable of killing for sport or for distraction; they were capable of true menace.

They responded to her. They responded to the unspoken desire for familiarity. Were they more fractious than her den? Yes. And in words, far less mature. But they were not more fractious than the den, in the years of its formation, had been. More deadly, yes, but that, Haval thought, was immutable.

She controlled them the way she had controlled the spirits in her garden: without thought, without conscious word, without the need to express her desire clearly. She did not realize how much of herself she had laid open to the dreaming, to the cats, to the wilderness that she did not understand.

All of the sleepers had been gathered in Jewel's forest. They were entertained and feted while they waited for her arrival.

All but Hannerle.

How much control was it necessary for Jewel to learn? She was not, now, in full and conscious control of her manse; were she, Carver and Ellerson would not be missing. Haval presumed them dead; Jewel did not. Their disappearance was the only element that now troubled Haval. Hannerle, he understood. He dispensed with anger, compartmentalized it. He knew what had happened.

Andrei had paused for too long at the side of Teller's desk.

"I have tested the ink," Haval said.

"I don't know why you waste your time on these gambits, Haval; Hectore is not present. My concern is not, as you suspect, with the ink; I have not bothered to check it. Had I known you to be in residence here, I would have dispensed with this visit entirely."

"And that would have been a misfortune," was Haval's smooth reply. He approached the desk. "You have seen the library." It was not a question.

Andrei nodded.

"Understand that it became as it is in minutes."

The servant did not reply.

"Did you inspect the library at all?"

"In a desultory fashion."

"Did you detect magic there?"

Andrei was silent for a long moment. "No."

Haval was surprised. He allowed some of this to show. "Nothing?"

"I was not given leave to peruse the environs at my own whim—but no. There was no magic upon the gate that led to the dining room, and no discernible enchantment laid against the wrought-iron arch through which the rest of the manse is accessed. We were not invited into The Terafin's personal chambers; if there is enchantment there, I am unaware of it."

"There is almost certainly some."

"The House Mage?"

"Or the domicis."

"Does the domicis otherwise interfere with magical protections?"

Haval considered this for a moment. "No. He is not a man who lacks confidence in his own abilities. Nor does he doubt hers."

"You have personally cleared the servants."

"I have not thoroughly done so, no. I am here as a *tailor*, Andrei. That is not completely a front."

"I wish to have the desk replaced."

Haval nodded. Andrei left the desk and approached the bookcases. Teller kept many volumes in his personal rooms. He was the only one of the den to do so; he had an affinity for books that his den-kin did not share. Andrei stiffened.

"You would like to replace the bookcase?" Haval asked.

"Haval, I find this entire visit something of a trial. Please do not add to it."

"He is very attached to his books."

"I imagine this is a well-known weakness. There are three volumes here that must be removed immediately."

Haval froze. "Can you remove them safely?"

"Two, yes."

"The third?"

"I am not certain." Andrei did not touch any of them. "Leave them for the moment; let me check his room."

Haval remained in Teller's office, considering this new, and unwelcome, information. He did not doubt Andrei. But it added a layer of complication which would have to be dealt with. He considered Hannerle. He considered her anger. He considered the ways in which he might approach her, if he wished to remain involved.

He loved his wife, and understood her well; he knew her weaknesses and her strengths. He could, with little effort, step back to examine them all as if they were a topographical map and he was considering the movement of armies across its surface.

"Haval, remember to move on occasion."

"The room?"

"There is very little in the room; it is, in my estimation, clean. There are two capes which appear to be enchanted;

the enchantments, on second glance, are minor protections—against rain, perhaps. Finch's rooms?"

"The books, Andrei."

"I believe I will require the aid of the domicis or the House Mage for the third volume. I could remove it; I could not remove it with any finesse or subtlety."

Haval nodded.

Finch's rooms, in the end, were relatively clean. There were two items that Andrei considered suspect, one a necklace and one a bracelet. Finch had very little in the way of jewelry, given her status as a House Council member.

"At least one of those is a gift from a merchant," Haval said. "He currently presides over one of the mining concerns."

"Is the merchant ATerafin?"

"Yes."

Andrei closed his eyes. "Ludgar?"

Haval nodded.

"Haval, that is *not* what I wished to hear." Andrei grimaced and pocketed the necklace. "The bracelet was a gift from a similar source?"

"Almost certainly. The Terafin's closest advisers have not yet mastered the art of ostentation. They did not come to the offices they hold with any measure of wealth. They tend to hoard, rather than spend, where it is at all practical. Take the bracelet. Evaluate it at leisure. If I am not mistaken, Finch wears one necklace and no bracelet. The necklace was a joint gift from Lucille ATerafin and Jarven for one promotion or another."

"That does not make me less suspicious."

"No, of course not. But if Finch is in danger from Jarven, there is very little you will be able to do, in the end, to preserve her."

Chapter Twenty-six

AT HAVAL'S INSISTENCE, Andrei did not stop with the two suites. He was not asked to thoroughly inspect Haval's workroom, but did not seem concerned. Nor did Haval lead him to the room in which Hannerle now slept, although he considered it with care while Andrei inspected the rooms of the other den members. There were very few men who were as thorough as Andrei; there were very few who were as suspicious.

Andrei did not suffer from the natural arrogance of the mage-born. He did not consider his own skills to be up to any conceivable task. He often made the mistake of assuming too much competence on the part of erstwhile enemies, but one rarely suffered from errors of that nature.

Haval was not pleased to discover that all of the rooms—with the notable exception of Jester's—contained items of concern. None were as egregious as Teller's books, but the fact that they existed at all was troubling. Only Ellerson's much sparer quarters were pronounced completely clean.

Hannerle.

Haval was not a notably sentimental man; he had seen too many to their deaths, and if his had not always been the hand that killed them, it signified little. He had known, the day Ararath had left his store that he would never return. But he had known, on that day, that very little could dissuade his friend. Haval did not expend effort where it was fruitless.

Hannerle frequently did, but that was her nature; she was, in spite of her temper and the frequency of professed disappointment, a *hopeful* woman. Haval exhaled.

Angel's rooms were, like Jester's, sparse. Like Jester's, the closet held very little in the way of formal clothing—but not none. Angel was frequently Jewel's companion of choice. He did not seem to appreciate the clothing he was forced to wear when his den leader had inherited the title, but he kept his complaints largely on the correct side of his mouth.

One of the few differences between the rooms of these two men was the weaponry. Jester had daggers. Angel had those, but also owned a short sword, a long sword, and an ax that had seen better decades, in Haval's opinion. Given the expression on Andrei's face, he concurred.

It was not, therefore, any of these weapons that drew his attention; it was the pole arm that rested against the wall beyond the clean—and clearly unused—writing desk. Haval noted it immediately; he generally noted everything in a room immediately. Andrei came to it a few minutes later.

But Andrei's eyes widened; his lips parted. No words escaped and as Haval moved to better see his expression, he realized no words would. He had never seen Andrei so discomfited; the Araven servant could not take his eyes off the weapon.

"Haval—where did this come from? It was not in the Terafin armories."

Haval did not reply.

Andrei hesitated before he inhaled and found his customary poise. He approached the weapon, reached for its haft, and stopped. "Haval."

"You recognize this weapon?"

"Why is it here?" He spoke almost to himself.

"Andrei. The weapon?"

The servant turned. "Do you know where this weapon was obtained?"

"Yes."

Andrei's brows rose. "You had something to do with its acquisition?"

"I had nothing whatsoever to do with it. I know where it came from because I heard its owner—its current owner—discussing the fight in which it was blooded. Is it dangerous?"

"It is *lost*, Haval. You are not concerned because you do not understand what this weapon *is*."

"I am now concerned," was the mild reply, "because you apparently do."

"It cannot be what it appears to be. It cannot."

"It appears to be a bladed spear to my eyes."

Andrei reached out and gripped the haft. He released it almost instantly. The smell of burning flesh slowly permeated the otherwise still environs of Angel's room. The servant did not speak for a long moment.

"It is protected."

"Yes." Andrei glanced at his hand. "The burn is not serious; it is merely a reminder. Did The Terafin give him this weapon?"

"He chose it; he needed a weapon with reach."

"I will speak with The Terafin."

Haval stepped between Andrei and the door. "Do not assume she is an enemy, old friend."

Andrei lifted one brow. "I make no assumptions. But this is the most unwelcome news I have received in over a decade. I would ask Hectore to withdraw if I thought he would listen."

At that, Haval chuckled. He was alarmed by the servant's reaction, but felt no need to share. "There is very little chance of that. If you wish to force him to abandon The Terafin and her stray ducks, you would best be served by hiding the entirety of your concern."

Andrei shook his head. "You do not understand Hectore."

It was slightly insulting, but Haval accepted it. He did not entirely understand Andrei; Andrei's master was not difficult.

"We are not yet done, Andrei. There are two other suites I would like you to examine."

All of the obvious frustration had drained from the Araven servant, leaving a remote and silent man in its place. Haval preferred the irritation; he knew, in Andrei's case, it was genuine.

"You may, of course, bill The Terafin for your time."

Andrei's eyes narrowed. "The suites, Haval. Hectore is no doubt giving away half of his fortune and all of his secrets in my absence."

Haval chuckled. He led him to the room Adam and Ariel shared, and knocked on the door. "This room is currently occupied."

The door opened and Adam peered into the hallway. He recognized Haval, which Haval expected; he recognized Andrei, which he had not.

"My pardon, Adam," Haval said, dispensing with the need for secrecy. "We wish to search your rooms. We will touch and take nothing without your knowledge."

"Who *is* it?"

"Haval," Adam replied, opening the door to allow the two men entry into his rooms. "And Andrei."

Ariel was seated beside the great gray cat on the floor; she was leaning into his side. Shadow did not therefore move. "Why are *you* here?"

"We are looking for traces of magic," Haval replied.

"Why?"

"There are, of course, enchantments throughout the manse—and throughout the Wing; these are expected. There exists the possibility of less acceptable enchantments, and we wish to ascertain that there are none."

The cat glanced at Andrei. A low growl started in the back of his throat; Andrei did not appear to hear it.

"He is here with The Terafin's permission. If you have concerns, Shadow, you must speak with The Terafin. She will not be pleased if you injure Patris Araven's servant."

The cat hissed. To Adam, he said, "Go and tell her we don't *want* him *here*."

It was the second surprise of a long day. Haval weighed both with care. "What is the nature of your concern?" he asked the cat. Adam had made no move to leave the room. "You were not notably fond of Adam when you first arrived, but The Terafin accepts both his presence and his aid."

Shadow's hiss extended for several beats. He said, to Adam, "Touch *him*."

Adam's brows rose and fell. In Torra, he said, "I can't just touch him. He's a guest. If he were dangerous, the Matriarch would *know*."

"She is *stupid*," the cat said—in perfectly audible Weston. He growled and added, "So are *you*."

Throughout this exchange, Andrei attended to the room. Like Jester's and Angel's, it was sparsely furnished; unlike Jester's and Angel's, its closets were neatly divided and contained no clothing of exceptional worth or note.

"Shadow," Haval said, "this is not the first time you have seen Andrei."

The cat hissed. "We don't want him *here*. If she *needs* him, she can talk to him *upstairs*."

"I will impart your message," Haval replied gravely. A glance at Andrei made clear that he did not care for the cat—which, given the cat's manners was expected—and that the room passed muster.

The last room they entered was Hannerle's.

"If you speak of this to any save your master," Haval began.

"There is no need to threaten me. I understand the danger." Andrei glanced at Haval, and added, "unless, of course, the threat comforts you."

Haval took the chair beside his wife's bed. He had been from her side for several hours. There was water here, and a stack of towels that were clean; he began to tend to his wife while Andrei examined the rooms. There were two; Hannerle's merited a brief inspection, no more. It was the expected result. Haval therefore showed none of the relief he felt; in truth, the relief was embarrassing.

It faded when Andrei failed to emerge from the sitting room. Haval spoke softly to his wife as he continued to drip water between her closed lips; he watched as she swallowed. Then he set the towel aside. He should have asked Adam to sit with her, but he was still concerned about Shadow's reaction.

Andrei stood in front of a paneled wall. The seam of the hidden door was clearly visible to anyone who looked with care.

"The servant's entrance is of concern to you?"

"This one is. The others were not." He frowned. "I have always disliked the idea that servants are to be invisible in precisely this fashion. The entire manse is no doubt riddled with narrow back halls—all of which cannot be guarded."

Haval inclined his head. "It is a problem faced in *Avantari*, as well. Thus far, the Kings have failed to be assassinated by their servants—or those who attempt to infiltrate their ranks. They have also notably failed to die when assassins have attempted to utilize those corridors."

"Thank you," was the unappreciative response. "I assume your career as a tailor means you no longer play in those corridors."

"I never *played* in those corridors, Andrei. You are concerned, one assumes, for reasons that are *not* obvious to anyone who pauses to think for half a second?"

"I am. The woman in this room is your wife, is she not?"

"She is."

"Were she mine, I would have her moved."

Haval offered no argument. "Do you consider the danger theoretical?"

"All danger before the fact is theoretical. If you intend to involve yourself in Terafin affairs, be concerned, Haval."

"I am now concerned. What do you fear?"

"Let us return to Hectore. I wish to ask The Terafin for permission to open this door."

Haval did not point out that permission had not been necessary on any other occasion. "The right-kin's books."

"Those as well."

Hectore, Jewel decided, would be amused and jovial on a *battlefield*. His momentary discomfiture upon hearing that Haval was in residence in the Wing might have been a trick of a tired imagination; he greeted Haval as if he were an acquaintance of long-standing. His was one of the richest merchant houses on the Isle, and he was a powerful member of the Merchants' Guild. Yet he did not cleave to the social distinctions that both Avandar and Ellerson so prized; not for Hectore the invisible, nameless servant.

"Andrei?"

Andrei, thus named, seemed to favor Ellerson's school of thought: he winced when Hectore addressed him. Having been thus addressed, however, he could not slide into the comfortable anonymity of a servant. Jewel felt a twinge of sympathy for him; she knew the feeling well. Of course, in her case, she had desired the Terafin title—a position that all but guaranteed lack of anonymity.

He turned to Jewel and offered her a deep, graceful bow.
Nor did he rise until she had bidden him do so. "Terafin."

"Within these rooms, we seldom stand on ceremony,"
she began.

Avandar cleared his throat. Loudly.

Andrei bowed in turn to Teller. "ATerafin."

"Andrei," Hectore said, with more than a touch of impatience. "What, exactly, have you found?"

"I require your permission—and the aid of either your
House Mage or your domicis—to remove three books from
the right-kin's personal collection. I have—without permission, removed two items from the rooms of Finch ATerafin;
I do not intend to keep them or destroy them, but if I have
overstepped the bounds of the examination, I will return
them immediately to your keeping."

Jewel felt a twinge of unease. She had been off-balance
for all of the day, with the possible exception of the last half
hour in the meeting of The Ten. She had no vision to guide
her—not in this. Never in this. She resented her talent
deeply on those occasions when ignorance was a danger.

It was a danger now.

"I also feel that the entirety of the desk in the right-kin's
personal rooms requires replacement. I will—with your
permission—arrange for the replacement. In size and shape,
the desk will be roughly similar. In function, there will be no
notable difference."

Teller opened his mouth and shut it again, because Haval lifted his hand and signed. It was den-sign. It was *wrong*.
It was a language that did not belong in the hands of men
who had not lived—and lost—in the streets of holdings so
poor life was often a matter of staving off death for as long
as one possibly could.

Ellerson, Jewel knew, could read den-sign. But his great
dignity and his pride in his role as servant had prevented
him from speaking in the silent tongue.

Haval seldom angered Jewel. He made her uneasy, he
made her feel stupid, he made her feel insignificant and
sometimes incompetent. But anger? No. She was surprised,
then, to feel angry now.

But she said—and did—nothing, although the desire to
lift her own hands and pointedly offer her opinion in den-
sign was searing, it was so strong.

"That will, of course, be acceptable," Teller was saying. "I am less sanguine about the fate of my books, and I require some explanation before I will part with them."

"You are aware—perhaps more so than any other member of your House—of the enchantments that can be placed on books."

Teller nodded.

"Three of the volumes upon your somewhat cluttered and untidy shelves—"

"You will forgive him," Haval interjected. "He has always been an overly fastidious man."

"—are enchanted. They are not enchanted in a similar fashion to the books in the right-kin's office." Before Teller could speak, he added, "You have three volumes of your own that *are* similar. You have two bookends at the height of your writing desk that could have come from the right-kin's office; I assume, in fact, that they did.

"The three that I speak of are not those."

"Can you—can you neutralize the enchantments without destroying or removing the books?" Teller asked.

"Not with any certainty of safety, no."

Jewel glanced at Teller. He loved his books. It was his one expensive indulgence. Many of the volumes in his possession had been gifts from Gabriel; two had come from Barston. Some, he had chosen for himself. "May we accompany you?" she asked Andrei.

"Of course. It would be instructive to know how these volumes were acquired. There is one other difficulty," he added.

Jewel tensed.

"The servants' halls are, of course, threaded throughout the manse. It is not optimal, in my opinion, but it is certainly expected. One entry—or exit—requires somewhat more extensive attention."

"Is the room occupied?"

"Yes. I have not taken the liberty of examining the unoccupied rooms yet."

Teller's rooms were large compared to the rooms in which the den had lived for the first few years of its existence. They were large compared to some of the smaller quarters in the manse, although they were quite modest in comparison with the rooms that were his by right of his position on the House Council. They felt crowded, now. Hectore did not insist on remaining in the great room, and Haval did not insist upon retreating; both men, along with Jewel, Teller, and two of the Chosen, now entered his rooms behind Avandar and Andrei.

Andrei indicated three books. Two of them had titles that all but guaranteed sleep, in Jewel's silent opinion: one was a treatise about textiles and their history, the other about ... plants. The third, however, was not written in modern Weston. She frowned as she looked at the faded, creased spine.

"Teller—where did you get this book?" She lifted a hand to reach for it; Avandar caught her wrist. His movement was so swift, so sudden, and so unexpected that she hadn't seen its start. Its finish, however, would leave bruises.

"You see it," Andrei said softly.

"ATerafin," Avandar said, ignoring the Araven servant, "it would be best if you could answer that question."

Teller frowned. "It came into my hands through a contact in the Common. Several of the older volumes came into my hands through the same contact; I believe he deals in antiquities."

"His name?"

"Avram. Of *Avram's Society of Averalaan Historians*."

Andrei pinched the bridge of his nose. It was a gesture of frustration so similar to the one Haval usually used, Jewel wanted to laugh. "His name is not Avram. He offered this to you?"

"Yes. He said he had offered it to the magi in the Order of Knowledge, but they were unwilling to meet his price. I assumed that the magi considered it pointless or inaccurate."

"That is not," Avandar said, "a safe assumption." To Andrei, he added, "I am not familiar with the name."

"Of the man or the establishment?"

"Either."

"The establishment is a storefront in the Common. It houses antiques for those with more pretension than knowledge. On very rare occasions, its proprietor has something of worth cross his counter—but it is, I assure you, accidental on his part."

"And this volume?"

"I will pay a visit to him on the morrow."

"Is it Old Weston?" Jewel asked. *Avandar, let go of my wrist. You are embarrassing me in public.*

As you say.

Teller's handled this book, and he is obviously alive and unharmed.

From which we may assume that he is singularly fortunate.

Avandar, what do you sense? What do you think this book is meant to do?

He didn't answer. "Andrei, how old do you think this book is? I have never been much of a scholar, and books—even those considered forbidden—were not a threat in my youth."

"Not even in your youth?" the Araven servant asked.

Jewel felt Avandar stiffen. "No."

"It is my suspicion that you will recognize some part of this enchantment. The Order of Knowledge could not, combined, create such a book as this."

Hectore was watching his servant with narrowed eyes. The look was frank and assessing; it was not accompanied by words.

"Is it sentient?" Avandar asked.

"Were it, I think its effects would now be known—but I cannot be certain. ATerafin, when did this particular volume come into your possession?"

"Six weeks ago. I have handled it," he continued. "I have even taken some notes about the use of language. I am, at best, an indifferent scholar; I have the curiosity, but not the leisure to devote to ancient tongues."

"And yet this book was offered to you."

"It was offered, yes. The proprietor of Avram's is aware only of my interest in books; many of his clients who profess such an interest don't quibble about simple things like language."

Six weeks. Six weeks, Jewel thought. "After I took the House."

"After your acclamation as Terafin, yes. You understand the significance."

She nodded. "Avandar, why do you feel the book is of significance? Andrei wished to have Teller's desk removed, and you didn't blink an eye."

"The nature of the magic makes it suspect. The possible age of the volume. Books such as these were created for the use of the powerful; they were seldom created to be repositories of knowledge for future generations. What words you might find therein were not meant merely to enlighten, although any number of harmless words might be added after the fact.

"There were two known incidents of diaries being thus enchanted. They were meant to exert influence, and, Terafin, they did. If the reader was not careful, the life lived in those pages, the handwriting read, might grow to become as visceral as the reader's own memories; the reader might forget the events of his own life, and become embroiled, instead, in the life of the scribe—as if the reader were actually living it.

"It was seldom that such volumes were given to mortals."

"Mortals being easily rendered powerless in other ways?"

"Indeed." Avandar fell silent.

"They were not easily created. Among other things," Andrei continued, not taking his eyes off the book's unremarkable spine, "they required the hides of a variety of creatures to be effective. The hides were cured, dried, flattened, and bound into the book as pages—while their donors still lived. It was a requirement of the magics involved. Enchantments can, as you are aware, be laid upon the inanimate. They can less trivially be laid upon the living. But when they are laid upon the living, they are at their most potent when there is cooperation between the being and the enchanter.

"Where there is no cooperation, the enchantments are of a different nature. But even then, they are more potent where there is life. Thus, books such as this."

"Avandar—can you see what, about this book, made Andrei so certain it's—whatever he thinks it is?"

"I would not, to my chagrin, have noticed were it not for his attention; I would not have thought *to* notice. Guildmaster Mellifas might notice, if she brought the whole of her attention to bear."

"Meralonne?"

"Yes. I think he would. Shall I fetch him?"

Jewel closed her eyes. "I don't think that will be necessary," she said softly. "He is in the heart of my forest, near the tree of fire."

"You can see him?"

She couldn't. But she didn't doubt the peculiar sense of certainty. Nor did she doubt, as she concentrated on the mercurial House Mage, that he would answer a summons that no one else—not even she—could hear.

Teller signed. Jewel hesitated, and then signed in response. She turned to the Chosen to ask them to leave with the right-kin. They agreed, but made clear that they would be back—with reinforcements. "We do not need reinforcements," she told them. "Patris Araven?"

"I will accompany the right-kin; if he does not wish to be in his own rooms for the duration of this procedure, I do not feel it is my place to insist upon remaining. Terafin?"

"I'm staying. Allow me to see you back to the great room."

Torvan and Arrendas arrived with Gordon and Marave. She considered demoting them both. "Avandar and Andrei will be in the room; Avandar will not allow Hectore's *servant* to do anything that will be dangerous in any way to either me or my House. Teller and Hectore will be in the great room; I would like you to remain *with them*."

"Are you going to be in the great room, Terafin?" Torvan said, stepping forward as if to draw the brunt of her growing ire down upon only his own head.

"I will not."

"Then we will not remain in the great room. If you wish to demote us, we will, of course, obey as House Guards—but we are *your* Chosen. What you risk, we will risk."

"I am *not* at risk, Torvan!"

"Then we will likewise not be at risk. We are going to be there, or you are not."

Jewel could not remember Amarais ever dealing with this level of insubordination in her reign—from anyone.

"Avandar will be there."

"Avandar is not Chosen."

She turned to Arrendas. Arrendas was, unfortunately, standing at attention. It was deliberate, of course. On most days, Jewel hated the cats. She now reconsidered this. The cats, she could leave behind. As she opened her mouth to attempt to give orders that could not be ignored, the doors opened.

Meralonne APhaniel stood in their frame. His hair was unfettered; it fell across his shoulders and down his back, but strands were caught in a cross-breeze that no one else in this hall felt.

"Terafin," he said. He dropped to one knee, and that drove the ability *to* argue out of her grasp. When she failed to reply, he lifted his head. "You summoned me."

He did not offer her sword or fealty; she *knew* he would offer neither while he lived. But the depth of the respect he now publicly showed was very, very discomforting. "I did. A book has been discovered in Teller's room, and the man who discovered it—in a routine security sweep—did not, and does not, feel it could be safely moved."

"And Viandaran?"

"He is in the right-kin's personal rooms. He feels that you will have more knowledge of the esoteric enchantments than he does. If you feel that removal of the enchantment—or the book itself—will cause material damage to the rest of the room, give us warning and I will have the rest of the right-kin's possessions relocated."

The mage rose, frowning. "Very well. I admit a certain curiosity." He reached into his robes, and Jewel lifted a hand.

"I do not think," she told him, "that you will require your pipe."

When Meralonne entered Teller's rooms, he preceded the Chosen. Jewel, however, was sandwiched between them. She had surrendered to Torvan and Arrendas because she did not wish to continue the argument in the presence of the House Mage. She did not therefore see Meralonne's reaction to Andrei—if he even had one.

"Viandaran?" he asked.

"I am uncertain."

"Very well. I will have you stand back."

When Andrei failed to move, Meralonne coughed once. Loudly. The Araven servant swiveled to meet the mage's gaze. He held it for a long moment before inclining his head. He did not, however, retreat to the far wall; he stepped back until he was perhaps a yard away from the space now occupied by the mage.

Meralonne, without ceremony, reached out and plucked the book from the shelf. Andrei's eyes rounded; the momentary outrage in his expression was almost comical.

Jewel felt the hair on her neck begin to stand on end as Meralonne turned to face them, the book in his hands. He did not open it; instead, he closed his eyes. Before he could ask, Jewel told him when the book had entered Teller's collection, and who its source was. He did not appear to be listening.

Nor did he appear to be moving or casting, but the air grew thick and charged; it implied thunder and storm, contained on all sides by walls, floors, and ceilings. His eyes snapped open; they were bright, silver lightning.

"Where did this book come from?" he demanded. Since Jewel had already answered this question, she grimaced. He glanced at her from what appeared to be a great remove. "I heard you mention that preposterous oaf. He did not find this book on his own."

"I am to pay a visit to him on the morrow," Andrei said. "Which The Terafin *also* mentioned."

Jewel, Avandar said, *leave. Take your Chosen, and retire to the great room.*

Jewel shook her head.

"How much has this volume been handled?"

"Very little. It's written in a language Teller can't easily read." Jewel, glancing at the cover of the book, felt compelled to add, "Neither can I. It looks like Old Weston, to me—but some of the letter forms seem wrong."

"It is not Old Weston. It is the language from which Old Weston evolved. But it is not, if I am correct, only or even entirely in that tongue. The spine and the front cover, however, are. This book was meant for mortals."

"Avandar said—"

"Viandaran is one of the few who is up to the task of handling it," Meralonne replied.

"You've seen this book before."

He smiled. It was not pleasant.

"Can you neutralize it?"

"That, of course, is the question. I would suggest we retire to your library. If for no other reason than that the book will be—in my considered opinion—safe there."

Teller was not going to like it. "What about the other two?"

Meralonne frowned. "The others? Oh. Those. One is meant as an anchor; it serves as a beacon to those who might attempt to enter this room through entirely magical means. It is a relatively powerful and innocuous spell. Those of the magi who are not capable of traversing great distances in an instant can use some of the power in the beacon to bring them here."

Jewel did *not* consider this to be inconsequential.

"The other is a listening device. What is spoken here, if the book is not properly contained, will be heard by those who choose to listen. I do not believe it captures all words; it is not powerful enough for that. Neither of these are materially deadly; they can both be used to cause mischief. In your manse as it is currently constituted, I consider them both to be lesser nuisances. They may have uses, now that you are aware of their existence, and for that reason, I counsel against their destruction." He smiled. "You were correct, Terafin. I do not find myself missing my pipe at all."

Jewel chose to leave Hectore and Teller in the great room. She gave Andrei the choice of either following or remaining behind, and he chose—to her surprise—to remain behind. "Hectore is feeling maudlin," he said, by way of explanation. "And he will give away half his House on impulse in this mood."

"I am not certain it is in the interests of my House to have you there to prevent it." She smiled. Andrei did not. He had retreated into a familiar expression: that of long-suffering servant. "Thank you for the services you have rendered Terafin this afternoon. If you are willing to do so, I would have you search the other rooms." She paused. "Did you say there was an entrance into the servants' halls that you found suspicious?"

"I did. If Member APhaniel is willing to inspect it—"

"Member APhaniel is not," the mage replied, sounding both irritable and bored.

"Member APhaniel will inspect it before we retire to my library," Jewel said smoothly. She turned to Haval.

He nodded before she could ask. "I will, of course, be present for that inspection."

"And the book?"

"If you permit it, Terafin, I am curious."

When Meralonne entered the chamber in which the servants' entrance lay hidden, he stiffened. "Viandaran." He held out the book. Avandar frowned at its worn, faded cover before he accepted it. "Where is the Araven servant?"

"He is with his master," Jewel said.

"How did he ascertain that there was difficulty with this particular door?"

"I am uncertain, Meralonne. I can't tell you how he knew the book in Avandar's hands would be a problem either — I'm not a mage."

"Viandaran, do you detect any magical difficulty with this door?"

Avandar was silent for long enough Jewel thought he wouldn't answer. But he did. "No. You see what Andrei saw."

"I see, indeed, what he saw. It is possible Sigurne Mellifas would see it as well, were she alerted to the danger and told exactly where to look."

"Then it is not unlikely that Andrei might be likewise competent."

"It is, in my opinion, entirely unlikely. I know who Sigurne's master was." Meralonne turned to Jewel, who waited. "You asked me, Terafin, to watch the hidden ways. I understand, now, how you lost two to the opening of the ways."

She froze. She forgot to breathe. A hundred words slammed against her teeth as she struggled to master them.

"The servants who enter your Wing through this door will emerge into the familiar rooms they tend. If they attempt to leave the same way, however, they will not reach the back halls."

She asked the only question that mattered. "If I walk through that door now, will it open to the same lands that swallowed two members of my House?"

"Hope makes mortals foolish," was his soft reply. "You already know that it will not."

Hope made mortals bleed. Jewel said, after a pause, "Can you dispel whatever magic lays across this door?"

"Yes. You would not, however, care for the results, and I am beholden to you for some little while yet. I will therefore not make the attempt. The way is not fixed. If you board this door from the outside—with apologies to your Household Staff—the danger will pass."

But Jewel was staring at the mage. She had known him for half her life, but only seldom found him beautiful. Meralonne had taught her much about beauty, all of the lessons unintentional on his part. He was beautiful when he fought. He was beautiful when he drew sword and danced upon currents of air that he could summon with a whisper and release with a benediction. Beauty was death.

He was death, now. He was tall, proud, and very, very cold. He held no sword. He faced no foe. There were no demons to draw his attention away from the occupants of this tiny, mundane room.

"Yes," he said softly, as he met and held her gaze. "You understand."

"I—I don't."

"I cannot close the ways, Terafin; they are the dreams of sleepers far older and far more powerful than the mortal handful you hold."

"I don't hold them now."

He smiled. "Is that what you believe? I do not always understand your kind, Terafin. I am conversant with the art of prevarication; I have no qualms whatsoever about a well-placed lie. Indeed, it can alleviate drudgery and boredom. But I do not lie to myself. It is pointless."

"I don't," she repeated, with more force, "hold them now." She started to speak, but Haval gestured in broad, quick den-sign; the movements were fluid and emphatic. Although she hated to see him speak in the private language of the den, she respected his right to do so in this one case. She did not speak of Hannerle.

"I will not argue; it is pointless. Mortal belief flies in the face of fact and logic, as it so often has. You do not hold these dreamers; nor can you. But if you are foolish, if you are very, very unwise, you will wake them in your ignorance. They are close to waking now." He smiled. "I have never been particularly concerned with the Warden of Dreams before this day, and perhaps I have done them an injustice. This was clever, Terafin. It was cleverly wrought, and I did not imagine any one of the firstborn would show such effrontery.

"If the Warden of Dreams worked at the behest of the god you will not name, this one act would not be to his liking. Very much the opposite."

"Meralonne," she whispered, "where does this door lead?"

"I cannot say without opening it."

Do not allow it, Jewel. If he makes the attempt, I will be forced to counter it, and we will destroy much of your manse in the process. I cannot guarantee that any of you will survive it.

He would not destroy the manse.

No, Jewel, not yet. But he is burning, now. Call him back, Terafin. Let him play with the book he has found. Let him smoke his pipe and let him once again assume the comfortable seeming of mortality. It will not be long before it is beyond him.

"What is your command, Lady?"

"Tell me where these doors open."

"They open into the ancient wilderness," was his soft reply. "You stand, now, on part of it; you have made it substantially your own and you do not fear it. You should, but mortals seldom have the time to grow wise."

"Do you know where my den-kin are?"

"No, Terafin. I do not. They might be found in the vast winter plains, or at the heights of serpent's reach; they might find themselves in the depths of the vast, sleeping oceans. There is no place but one that cannot be accessed by doors such as these—but such openings are not deliberate; they are the random thoughts of those who sleep. They make no conscious decisions."

"Where is that one place?" she asked, although she thought she knew.

"The Winter Court, Terafin. Or the Summer. They cannot go to where she waits."

"How can they dream?"

"In truth, I do not know; I suspect it is mischief on the part of the Warden; he is firstborn. My kin do not sleep and do not dream."

"These—"

"This is not a sleep they chose, and they are not mortals, to be conveniently fettered; even in sleep, they have long been considered a threat. But not this way. I do not know if these doors exist because they are searching for a way out of their captivity—but if they are, and they find it here, you will not survive."

"How do I prevent it?"

"I do not believe you can. You might petition the Warden of Dreams—if you know how to summon him. But I am not certain he could undo the damage he has done here. If a man stabs another, he might extract his knife; he might pay wergeld for the damage done. Unless he is healer-born, he cannot in any way reverse that damage. I believe that the Warden might find such reversal problematic; they were not aware of him, before. They will be aware of him—even in their sleep—now.

"He will not face them unless the whole of his kingdom hangs in the balance. The whole of your kingdom will signify little to the firstborn."

"Then I will repeat my earliest request, APhaniel. I will ask that you find these entrances into the hidden ways; if you cannot safely seal them, I ask that you mark them as the danger they are. I wish to lose no one else until the appointed hour."

"And at that hour, Terafin, you will cede them all?"

She met his gaze without flinching. Without blinking. "Not without a fight." Without thought, she raised her wrist and pulled the cuffs of stiff sleeves up to expose what lay around it: three strands of pale, unbroken hair. "I will find her," she said. "I will find their Winter Queen, and I will ask one boon of her when I do."

"She is not under obligation to grant it," he replied; he did not laugh. He did not scoff.

"Not yet. But she will be."

"You will not reach her now. I understand the whole of your intent—but you will not reach her."

"I will," she said. "If that is the only thing that stands between this city and destruction, I will. I will pay the Oracle's price. I will walk the long roads. I will find my kin."

He bowed.

She exhaled. "Will you examine the book in my library, or are you content to leave it there?"

He glanced at the volume that remained in Avandar's hands. "I will examine the book, of course. It might provide a moment's amusement."

They returned to the library. To Jewel's surprise, Angel was waiting. He seemed as surprised to see Haval and Meralonne as she was to see him. When he lifted his hands in den-sign, she shook her head; he let his hands fall to his sides.

"What's happened?" she asked.

He shook his head. "I want to enter your armory. With your permission, I need to borrow a few of the weapons on the walls there."

"I think the one you have is significant enough," Haval surprised her by saying.

Angel met the erstwhile clothier's gaze. He then turned, without comment, to Jewel.

"Yes, of course you have it," she said. She spoke quietly, as if there were some hope that Haval would fail to hear her. It made her feel young in all the wrong ways. "We've taken a book from Teller's collection and we're about to examine it where it won't cause structural damage if it's dangerous."

"I did not say that," Meralonne told her.

"Teller's collection?"

"That was my reaction as well." She exhaled. "Hectore of Araven is in the West Wing at the moment; Teller is entertaining him. His servant, Andrei, is in attendance; they will remain for dinner."

Why are you telling me this?

She grimaced. *Early warning. Go.*

Haval waited until Angel was out of sight. "That was unwise," he said, with the type of severe frown he reserved for her most egregious acts of self-indulgence. She did not feel this was deserved.

"Why? I'm aware—Meralonne has made it clear—that the weapons in that room were and are significant. Unless they present a danger to their wielders, I can't think of a person I'd rather have wield them. I can think of a few more I would arm without reservation." She turned, then. "Torvan. Arrendas. I believe that in this space, we are not in as grave a danger as we might otherwise be. I have four Cho-

sen, and two outside my doors; I do not require more than
two. Accompany Angel, inspect the weapons on the wall. If
you find weapons that suit you, take them."

Haval's lips compressed. "Member APhaniel," he said,
turning to the mage, who was busy fetching his pipe from
the folds of his robes. "Do you have anything of material
import to add to this command?"

"The only risk these weapons pose to their wielders is
inherent in their condition."

"Pardon?"

"Fools will be fools. The Captains of the Terafin Chosen
are not—and have never been—fools. Optimists, perhaps,
but never fools. The Terafin is correct; the weapons arrayed
on the walls of that room were not crafted to be display
pieces; they were meant for use.

"They were meant for use in a time far more dangerous
and far less mundane than the lives you have collectively
led. The hidden ways are bleeding, at last, into the mortal
lands. Weapons such as these will be useful; in my opinion,
they will be necessary. And they appear to be yours to grant,
Terafin. Arm your Chosen. Arm your den. Arm yourself, if
you find a weapon that is willing to accept you." He turned
to the captains. "It is not simply a matter of choosing a
weapon. If you are not acceptable to the weapon, it will not
serve you well.

"You will know," he added. "And perhaps you will suffer
the ignominy of finding that you are considered unworthy.
It is, in my opinion, worth the risk. The weapons you carry
now will be of little use against even the foes The Terafin
has already encountered.

"The weapons you might carry would be of considerable
use. The decision is not entirely in your hands, but without
the determination and the will to wield arms in her defense,
those weapons will remain as simple, private decorations."
He had, during this speech, lined the bowl of his pipe, and
with a flick of his fingers, set the dried leaves to burning; it
was a slow, steady burn.

The Captains of the Chosen did not reply. But Torvan
turned to Jewel. "Will you arm all of the Chosen in this
fashion?"

"As many as I can, yes." She hesitated. She wanted to tell
him to take Arann. To take him first. But Arann was *part of*

the Chosen; they were his captains. She had chosen him in the streets of the twenty-fifth; she trusted him as much as she trusted Torvan and Arrendas. More. But . . . they were his captains. The decision, in the end, was not one she could make without cost.

Torvan heard what she did not say. He waited. She shook her head. "You are the Captains of my Chosen; I will trust your choice of bearers."

They both saluted.

Without another word she turned to Meralonne. "My apologies. There is a table farther in upon which books of a questionable nature appear to be safe. If you feel that opening the book will harm the table, inform me."

"The table is of import to you?"

"Yes. It has sentimental value, and is therefore irreplaceable. Inasmuch as simple objects are priceless, the table is priceless to me."

"If you speak of the table situated near the fountain, it is a flat, inanimate object made by simple carpenters."

"I believe it was."

Smoke trailed from the bowl of his pipe. He glanced at the book in Avandar's hands, and his eyes crinkled at the corner; it was Meralonne's version of a smile. It robbed his face of years, and the lack chilled her; on his face, it implied that the whole of a lifetime's experience was ephemeral, transient; he might remove it the way Jewel removed dirt in a bath. In exactly the same way.

His smile deepened as he met her gaze. "Come, come, Jewel. You stand on the precipice, now. You will see days of grandeur. You will never the see the world at the height of its youth and its beauty—but you will finally understand what true beauty *is*."

"A book made of living skin is never going to be beautiful, to me."

"You quibble."

"No, APhaniel, I don't. I speak the truth, and nothing will ever change it. I might find beauty in things that are deadly." Her throat grew dry. "I saw the Winter Queen. I touched her hair. I knew that could she, she would have run me down on the hidden path. She couldn't. Not without losing her mount. If she meets me again on the hidden road, and I attempt to stand in her way, worse—far worse—than death awaits me.

"But she *was* beautiful. If I close my eyes now, I can see her. She is always in my mind; she is like the dream I can't escape by waking. And you," she continued, her voice dropping. "I see that in you as well—but only when you fight. When you call your sword and the wind comes to take your hair and your robes shift and change and you stand like a god among men. You are beautiful."

He surprised her; he reached out and caught her chin in his slender fingers. "Yes," he said, the smile somehow gentling. "You have seen her. What you see in me is only an echo, and it is yearning, Terafin. Yearning, loss, desire. But you do not conflate beauty with desire—or love. You are unusual."

She said, without thought, "Neither does Sigurne."

He withdrew his hand, and his expression lost all warmth. "Understand that I am fond of her. She was a child of the Winter in all ways. She will die; she is aged greatly. But I do not want her to pass beyond without experiencing the grandeur and the majesty of the world. She has spent so much of her life denying its existence."

"She will not thank you."

"Oh, but she will, Terafin. You admire her. You respect her. You are even wise enough, on rare occasions, to fear her. You have both dedicated your lives to protection and guardianship. But for Sigurne, the guardianship is almost at an end; as all mortal guardians, she has outlived her usefulness. She is not you, Terafin. She dreads the laying down of her burden, but she also welcomes it. When you have done everything in your power to delay the inevitable, when you have done *more*, there is no shame, no guilt, in surrender."

"She will never surrender."

"You quibble again, but I understand why, and I will allow it; where you walk, you will not have the comfort of ignorance. She will not walk your road, but she has walked dark roads before. You feel that she is like you. She is. But your first teacher was Ararath of Handernesse. Sigurne's first teacher was not mortal. What you felt for Ararath, when you were a girl, Sigurne also felt, and it was not—it was never—safe.

"Come," he said again. He lowered his hand. "Take me to this object of sentiment." Shifting position, he offered her an arm. She stared at him for a long moment before she accepted, resting her hand lightly on the crook of his elbow.

The table was as she'd last seen it. So were the chairs. The books were in an unkempt stack. Meralonne was a member of the Order of Knowledge; he reported to Sigurne. But he was not Sigurne. The volumes of questionable origin did not trouble him in the slightest.

"Viandaran."

Avandar set the closed book on the table.

"If this book is meant to have power of any significance, it can mean only one thing."

"And that?" Jewel asked as she withdrew her hand. The Chosen took up positions at their customary distance; Avandar, however, chose to stand closer.

"The pages were crafted from the flesh of living beings. It is a potent way of creating a book, if one intends the book to be an object of magic in its own right. It is not the only book present in this library that was crafted in such a fashion. But those books are dormant now; they might cause mischief, but they do not have the power to be truly dangerous."

"You think this book is dangerous."

"I do."

"And that implies that at least one of the contributors to its many pages is somehow still alive."

"Yes, Terafin, it does. It cannot be *Kialli* flesh. In any way that matters, the *Kialli* chose death when they chose to follow their Lord."

"Demons have been used to craft weapons. Summoned demons."

"Yes, but weapons of that ilk are not meant for mortals. Too often, the mortals become the weapons; the demons, the wielders. None crafted in such a fashion reside within your armory."

"Meralonne—it can't be the skin of mortals. Not if the book is ancient, as you say."

His smile was strange. "There is no immortality waiting for your kind, although men have yearned and bartered for it since the advent *of* mortality. But there are individuals who have been granted their heart's desire. You know of one. It is possible, Terafin, that he was not the only one."

"His immortality was granted by a malevolent god."

"Malevolence was not required," Meralonne replied. Avandar did not speak. "There are ways to contain the lives of mortals; there are ways to put them beyond the simple reach of time. It is not an act that could be performed by the *Kialli*. Nor by me or my kin. But the Winter Queen could, should she desire to do so. There are bindings that are older and deeper than the simple march of years."

"The Winter King, Jewel, is ancient."

"He is no longer a man."

"No. But the Winter King that was at last hunted was ancient, endless; he had power and his dreams were cold and dark. There are ways. But your kind does not take well to immortality; one cannot be both mortal and immortal. The very essence of what you are denies eternity.

"It matters little. It is possible that mortal skin was used to craft these pages."

"To render the book harmless, we would have to find and release those mortals."

"Yes. It is possible, however, that the source of these pages was never mortal, and if that is the case, Terafin, it becomes more complicated. They are bound, in part, to the physical book. It has long remained dormant—but if the book is opened, they will know."

"Will you know?"

"It is possible. I was a warrior, in my youth. Games of this nature were not for one such as I. I did not deal in subterfuge; I did not require it."

"How much of this book requires a living donor?"

"In this age? A page, Terafin. When the book was created, I am certain that all of the pages contained that power."

"Will it affect you, Meralonne?"

"No."

That is his arrogance speaking, Avandar said. *He cannot be certain.*

You're not.

No, Terafin. I am almost certain. But I would have said that Celleriant was in no danger from a tree, no matter how rooted in dream it was, or how transformed. From what you have said, he almost perished there.

Meralonne left the book upon the table, but traced the runes across its cover.

"What is the title of the book?" Jewel asked.

His silver eyes widened. "Terafin, you missed your calling. You might have found a home in the Order itself with a question as irrelevant as that one."

Her hands found their perch on her hips again, and she forced them to slide off the fabric to rest at her sides. "If you can't read it, just say so."

His platinum brows rose at the effrontery of her suggestion, but Jewel held her ground. To her great surprise, he laughed. The rich, full sound of genuine amusement filled the air as if it were sunlight on a particularly cold winter day. Much of his laughter was barbed or edged—but not this. "You underestimate yourself in all ways, Jewel. It is a failing with mortals who shoulder responsibility. They fear that they will fail; they see the things that may cause that failure. They do not see the things that will, in the end, all but guarantee success.

"You are correct, Terafin. I did not study all of the ancient tongues, and I confess that I do not recognize this one, although I would be considered a linguistic expert in the Order itself. I will trouble you not to repeat that confession."

"Avandar," she said, voice soft, "what is the title of the book?"

Her domicis stiffened. So, too, did Meralonne.

"*The lost son of Silastrassi*," he replied.

"It is not Old Weston."

"No, Terafin. It is a variant of Ancient Torra; I do not think even the Sword of Knowledge would recognize the whole of its grammatical structure; there are very, very few extant texts over which they might work, and even had they several, the written language was fractured and individual."

"Variant?"

"The Cities of Man had, of course, written language, but their use of language diverged greatly upon the written page. Although the basic language spoken between the ambassadors of those city-states was one, the written language was not. A merchant tongue, as it was called, existed for commerce—and war—between the cities. But it was used only as discourse for quotidian business.

"For any other matter in which a man of significance and power might lift quill, the syntax of the language was unique in each city. It was not completely foreign; the Tor of one city, if presented with a poem or a literary endeavor of another, would be able to parse its content."

"You're saying this book was written in—or written by—men in the time of gods?"

"Or very shortly thereafter, yes."

"But—would that not mean that this book *was* meant for mortals?"

"Yes and no," Meralonne cut in. "Are you mortal, Terafin?"

She frowned. "Of course. You've remarked on it at least a dozen times in the past few months—let alone the decade that preceded them—and usually as an insult."

"Viandaran?"

"Bind the book," Avandar said. "Contain it. Do not open it here." His tone of voice drew the instant attention of the Chosen who nonetheless appeared to hear and see nothing.

Jewel, however, said, "You think this was meant for the Sen?"

"It was meant for the Sen of a city," Meralonne replied. "I was not certain until Viandaran spoke, but *he* is certain. He may even be able to tell you which one."

"I have not said that," Avandar replied, in a tone so chilly it would freeze whole lakes if he dropped a word in their water. "It is possible it was written by the Sen."

"But why would the Sen *need* to create a book like this?"

They both looked at her as if she were six years of age and had asked a question that proved she had never been educated. She was highly tired of this, but also accustomed to it; it was the danger of surrounding oneself with counselors of experience and power. "Look at this library," she said, her hands in loose fists. "Look at the war room. Look at my forest. And then, after you have paid attention to their existence—to their *creation*—pretend that I asked that question a second time."

Meralonne lifted a brow. "I will grant you, Terafin, that it seems a strange artifact for the founder of a great city. But Sen served as a title for the women who came after. They were not all what you are; they did not all have that power. Some of the Sen were mage-born, some seer-born. In the age of man, it was rare, but not unheard of, for a woman to be both. The Sen could speak with gods with impunity. They could hear the language of the gods and retain what little sanity they possessed. They understood how to manipulate their people, and how to best use them, to defend and enlarge their domains.

"They did not rule. But they did not serve except at their own pleasure. No Tor sought to destroy the Sen of his city, although in theory the Tors *did* rule. You imagine that the Sen were not human. You are wrong. They played their games of dangerous power. Sometimes it destroyed them; far more often it destroyed their enemies. Not even the Queen of the Wild Hunt chose to cross blades with the Sen Adepts except at great need."

She exhaled. "Why was that book given to Teller?"

"That is what we will now ascertain."

Avandar reached out and placed one hand on her left shoulder.

Meralonne gestured. A patina of orange light flared around him, overlapped in an instant by bands of green and subtle gray. After a pause, he spoke a single word, two; she heard it as language but also as thunder; the air crackled. In her gaze, his hands began to glow. The left was gloved in a golden light that superseded all others, but did not obliterate them; the right, in a black that devoured everything.

Avandar's grip tightened, and she realized that she had started to move toward the mage. *Do not touch him. Do not touch the book. If you struggle, I will be forced to act, and I will not gain the information we require.*

What information?

Who the creator of the book was.

The book was old. It looked old. Everything about it spoke of the ancient. But it was Meralonne's approach that inspired awe, for Jewel recognized the twin aspects of a magic that mortals in the Empire did not use: Summer and Winter. She had seen Meralonne use Summer magic before; she had never seen him use Winter's. Yet she was not surprised.

Terrified yes, but not surprised. She almost ordered him

to stop. A small part of her mind told her that she *could*, and he would obey. She was The Terafin; she was no longer a desperate, hungry girl from the poor holdings. But instinct kept her silent. She realized that he *must* do this. She didn't know why, and didn't argue.

Meralonne didn't touch the book's cover again; he gestured instead. It flew open, pages fanning as if caught in the gust of a strong wind. None of the other books upon the table was caught in the same wind, not even the book that had so discomfited Evayne, but she spared them a glance, no more; Avandar's hand had tightened in a death grip.

The pages did not, as Jewel expected they would, come to rest. They continued to fan up and over, until they were a blur of ivory motion, a semicircle of faintly glowing light. It wasn't white, but wasn't gold; it wasn't the black of winter. It was a color that Jewel had not yet seen magic take.

She glanced up from the book and her attention was caught and held by Meralonne's expression. His eyes, reflecting the book's light, were shining silver; his hair was caught in the wind that touched nothing else. He took a step back from the book, his expression shuttered. Gone was the delight of anticipation, although no boredom remained to take its place.

Avandar, let go.

To her surprise, he did. She walked the short distance to the table, and stood to one side—and in front—of the silent mage. When she looked at the book itself, the pages suddenly fell to one side or the other, exposing a spread of two pages. Upon the left were words. They were, to Jewel's eye, Weston. Not Old Weston, but Weston. The upper corner of the page was a detailed illumination, the paint and the ink so bright and new the book looked like it had never seen sun. Or time.

But she didn't need to read the words—although she could. The right facing page was not covered in text; it was an illustration. The paint here was as bright, as new, as that used for the illuminated letter, but it wasn't the color or the artistry that caught her attention: the illustration depicted a young man.

A familiar young man. Adam.

Chapter Twenty-seven

WHEN THE CAPTAINS of the Chosen were separated from their duty, even briefly, they were different men. They relaxed into simple things like, say, discussion. They spoke. They made the occasional joke. Angel understood this transformation better than any of the den except Arann. The others accepted it, although it was Jay who found it the most difficult, which was ironic, given she was their reason for existence.

Angel understood service. He understood it in a bone-deep way. He didn't feel the need to put that understanding into words; they'd just make Jay uncomfortable. But he had already laid down his life for her once. Only the intervention of Alowan had saved him.

He entered the war room first; Torvan and Arrendas were enumerating the Chosen by name and seniority. They had listened to Meralonne's arrogant commentary, and had accepted it as truth: not everyone who wanted to own a weapon considered significant by the mage would be able to do so.

But Angel had not been tested by the pole arm he'd grabbed from the wall. There had been no moment of judgment, no measure of his worth. He had seen the pole arm and he had realized it was the right weapon for the job at hand. The Chosen carried long swords, but the reach of the creature's wings had rendered them ineffective for anything but defense.

And offense had been required. The creature had taken out two of the Chosen—not fatally, thank *Kalliaris*—almost before the battle started. Angel glanced at Torvan; Torvan returned his regard.

"When you took the spear from the wall, did anything unusual happen?"

Angel chuckled. The Chosen were bound by rules, regulations, and customs in ways that Angel would never be—but at heart, they understood each other. "I was just wondering that myself. I didn't notice anything at the time."

"Have you attempted to wield the spear since?"

"No. We don't generally carry weapons when we're at home. We don't carry them when we leave the manse."

"You're thinking of changing that habit."

"Yes." He hesitated. Torvan marked it. Torvan, unlike Jay or Finch, didn't press the point. Angel addressed it anyway, coming at it from the side. "Has she talked with the Chosen about her future plans?"

Arrendas glanced at Torvan. Torvan was silent, but it was a measuring silence, not a refusal. "Not explicitly, no. We are aware that she may be absent from the manse for more than a few days. You intend to go with her."

Angel nodded. "The Terafin hopes this has something to do with Carver, and he owes me money."

Arrendas actually laughed. "Who doesn't Carver owe money?"

"Probably Merry. I wouldn't bet on it, though." Angel's gaze traveled across the wall. "I have an old friend in the city, and I think he's been waiting for this."

"An old friend?"

"Yes. A family friend. He's kin, by my reckoning. He's not a mage; he's not a member of the Order. He works in the Port Authority. He keeps an ancient ax under his bed; it took him a few years to get used to the lack of weaponry on the city streets." Angel smiled as he spoke. "I swear the weapons look different than they did on the first day."

"You noticed that as well."

"There are more swords. Do you think the weapons change shape somehow?"

Silence.

Angel said, uneasily, "I hope not. Can you imagine your

sword turning into an entirely unfamiliar weapon in the middle of a fight?"

"Yes," was Torvan's flat reply. He clearly took as much comfort from the thought as Angel did.

There were no chairs in this room; there were no ladders. The weapons were not at chest level; they were not even at eye level. They were—barely—within arm's reach. They were also in scabbards, for the most part. The axes—there were three—were not.

Angel's experience with an ax consisted of Terrick and brief glimpses of his father; his father had not chosen to teach Angel the art of wielding an ax. He taught sword, instead, the instruction harsh and bitter. As a farmer, he was an exacting—and frequently disappointed—weaponsmaster. Angel was one of his best students, but only because after the rest of the boys had gone back to their farms, his father continued to drill.

Angel had spent the past few years honing that rusty skill; turning the basic thrusts and parries of a youth into something more powerful and certain. He knew how to sharpen a blade, knew how to oil it, knew how to handle it. But he was almost never called upon to carry it in service to a Lord. His weapon—and the long sword he carried when a sword was allowed came from the Terafin armories— was not his measure in the eyes of that Lord. It was, like forks and quills, a tool to be picked up at need and set aside after the task was done.

Or so he had believed.

Yet he knew that were it entirely true, he would not have drilled with the Chosen and the House Guard. He would not have pushed himself. There was a reason that Terafin— and The Ten in general—*had* guards: the guards were their shields and weapons. Had he had a sword when he attempted to engage the demon that had almost killed Jay, it wouldn't have made a difference.

But he was here. He was here, at last, for a sword of *his own*. He looked at hilts. Some of the hilts looked like jewelry; they made ornaments of the sword; the scabbards were likewise overdone. If Meralonne was right, these were magic; they had survived for centuries and did not look any worse for the passage of time.

But if he was wrong in any way, scabbards like that one were a disaster waiting to happen. They'd attract the eye of every thief in range, and quite a few who would pick up the rumor. Angel wasn't certain that thieves would be an issue where Jay was going—but he'd spent enough time in the streets of the city it didn't matter.

In the bad years, one of those thieves might have been Carver or Duster. No, he thought, shaking his head and walking, slowly, past the wall. They wouldn't have been that stupid. They had known—or at least Carver had—what was out of reach.

Wind gusted through the open window. The skies were not quite as purple as the open air above the library, but they were cloudless. At a distance birds could be seen—and flying among them, winged but all the wrong shape for birds, other creatures. None of them came to the war room, but then again, there were no cats and no Meralonne APhaniel to challenge them.

Torvan said, "Is that where you think she'll be?"

"I don't know where she'll go. I don't know if I'll see what she sees. When we rode up the side of the tree, she saw a plain of untouched snow. I saw the tree." He shrugged. "We've never seen everything she can. We've bet our lives on what she does see—but we do it because we trust her.

"On the day Celleriant was caught in the tree—and if I understand what happened, the dreaming—I couldn't follow her. I would have fallen if I'd been on the back of any other mount. But she needed me to see what *we* see. Maybe that's why she wants me."

"It's not just that," Arrendas said. "You're better than Arann with a sword; he's close, but you've got grace and skill. He has everything else."

Angel paused beneath two crossed weapons. One, sheathed, was a long sword with a narrower blade than the swords found in the Terafin armory. The other, however, was an ax. The blade curved; it was heavy and entirely without blemish. The haft of the ax was simple; there were no jewels, no gold, nothing but black leather on the grip. The pommel was rounded, but seemed to be simple steel.

The scabbard of the sword was likewise simple. It looked new, but it had none of the obvious ostentation of some of the more complicated—and therefore expensive—scabbards his father would have despised. He could almost hear his father's voice as he stood beneath the intersection of these two weapons.

He could hear the question that his father had never asked. The question that Terrick had avoided. He could hear the question that Caras the god-born son of Cartanis had asked: *Tell me, Angel, Garroc's son, do you serve The Terafin?*

No.

Jay had not been Terafin, then. She had become Terafin months ago. She had offered him the House Name, and he had hesitated. Stubbornly. *Does it matter what I'm called?*

In this room, for the first time, he faced the truth. Yes, it mattered. Jewel was The Terafin. He had come to House Terafin in her service. He had served no other Lord, and no other master. He had made clear to Caras that he never would: he followed Jay.

Weyrdon didn't tell me to find a Lord that he *would be willing to follow; he told me to find one that* I *would.*

She has not taken your oath.

No. No, Angel thought, she had not—because he had never formally offered it. He knew it would embarrass her.

She knew, though. He had told her in every other way. He had explained why he would not take the House Name the first time it had been offered to the den. But as he looked at the crossed weapons, they were like a window into the future: they illuminated a truth that he had decried as unnecessary. On the paths she would walk—no, the paths *they* would walk together, he was hers. She was his Lord. And he needed to offer the formal vow to seal a future that not even Jay could see.

He reached up. His fingers could easily touch the weapons, but they were high enough that he could not grasp them firmly. The worst outcome, of course, would be that he jog them loose and have the ax come crashing down, blade first; he took that risk. He knew that these—sword and ax— were the only things in the room he wanted.

Why these two? He wondered as he stretched. In a room with walls full of weapons, why these two? He should at least look at the others. Not the extremely ostentatious ones, never that—but the other weapons. Yet it was

these two that drew the whole of his attention. The sword.
The very Northern ax.

Ah.

Why had he not offered her his binding oath?

A flash of light across the ax blade caught his eyes. The
ax was above his head, it was flat against the wall. It
shouldn't have shown him a reflection of himself—but it
did. He saw his own face, his cheekbones, his chin, and the
rising spire of his hair. He froze, arms lifted, hands touching
the hilt of the ax itself.

And he understood.

"You wield an ax?" Torvan asked, the voice coming from
somewhere over his left shoulder.

"No," he replied. "Not me."

"The friend you spoke of."

"Yes. My father's man, in every way." Still. After decades,
still the man who served Garroc. Angel's father was dead.
Angel had loved him, but he had never understood Terrick's insistence on serving a *memory*. Even Angel had not
chosen to do that.

But no, he thought, his reflection gazing back at him like
a subtle accusation. That was a lie. He could make truth of
it in only one way. He had thought he could never be Terrick. He had thought himself beyond that kind of bone-
deep theoretical service. What service, after all, did Garroc
require? He was *dead*.

But his quest? Ah. His quest was not. Whatever it was
he had dedicated his life to achieving, he had failed—but
failure was not infinite. It was not a stable state. His son,
Angel, had come to Averalaan, seeking. His son, in ignorance, had chosen to undertake the quest that had sent his
Rendish father into exile.

Terrick knew. Terrick waited. He had waited for decades.
And Angel had not yet completed the task set his father by
Weyrdon before Angel's birth. Angel had found the only
master he ever wished to serve, but it was not yet done.

He gripped the haft of the ax, standing almost on his toes
to do so; the ax came easily off the wall and did not demand
his toes in payment, although the whole of its weight suddenly dragged Angel's arm toward the floor. He knew what
this ax meant now. He knew what he had to do.

The sword came more easily to his hand, but again, there was no test, no measure taken. Only when he attempted to draw it from its sheath did the blade resist. He heard no voice, no commandment; it was a weapon.

But it was a weapon he could not draw.

"So there is something to it, after all," Arrendas observed. "Too bad you can't use axes."

Angel grimaced as he put the whole of his weight into his hands; the right on the sheath, the left on the sword's hilt. Try as he might, he could not separate the two.

"Try a different sword?" Torvan suggested.

"No. It's this sword, or no sword." Angel was not seerborn. He couldn't speak with the certainty that lifted Jay's pronouncements from the realm of the merely stubborn. But he felt that this was not mere ego on his part. This sword was meant to be his.

But not yet.

He knew what he had to do. He took the ax—which had no sheath—and tucked the sword into his belt. "I'll leave you both here," he told the Captains of the Chosen. "I have to head into the city." He began to walk toward the door, but Torvan called his name, and he halted and turned.

"You are not one of us," Torvan told him. It was not said with any disdain. "You would never surrender yourself to the Chosen. Arann did. The Chosen serve The Terafin; we exist for no other purpose. But in serving The Terafin, there are rules, regulations, there are hierarchies. The Chosen are a *unit*. But we are aware of you, Angel. We know what you mean to her. We know what you offer her—even when she doesn't see it herself.

"The Terafin is not a woman who likes to be beholden to others; nor is she a woman to whom rule comes easily. The Chosen are part of *Terafin* to your master. They are inextricably linked. Where she goes—and I see, by your decision here, that she *will* go—the Chosen cannot follow.

"I will argue for it," he added. "I will demand that she take at least a handful of the Chosen with her. I do not think in the end I will be successful."

Angel said nothing. He waited, knowing that Torvan had not yet reached the end of a speech that was difficult for him to make.

"You are, therefore, the only one of us who will accompany her."

"I am not—as you said—of the Chosen."

"Not hierarchically, no. But in spirit, you are equal to the very best of us. Perhaps you are better. We are proud of the Chosen, Angel. We are proud of what we *are* in *her* service. You exist as hers without rank. She will tolerate you. Where she walks, she will take no one *but* you, if I understand her intent at all.

"We will guard her seat in her absence. We will protect Finch and Teller as if they were The Terafin herself. We will do everything in our power to prevent a House War in her absence; we will hold the home she has vowed to both rule and protect. There is nothing more that we can offer her, and indeed, nothing she would value as much.

"We will do this because it is all she will allow us *to* do. You will, therefore, stand in our stead.

"Bring her back to us," the Captain of the Chosen commanded.

13th of Fabril, 428 A.A.
Port Authority, Averalaan

Terrick Dumarr was a man of middling years, with more gray than color in hair that had been pale to start with. He had taken on the ruddy complexion of a man who lives by wind and sun, and if his position behind the open window of a wicket in the Port Authority was not unassailable, it was not because of his demeanor; he was still a man whom the Port Authority guards found intimidating if he did not approach them with care.

It was not that he was large or threatening, although with ease he could project size and danger; it was his origins. He was, in their eyes, a friendly barbarian: a man from Arrend, the country of Northern barbarians. Time had softened the edges of the accent with which he spoke Weston; time had given him the experience—and knowledge—with which he might better blend with Averalaan society. But in truth, he had no desire to blend in. He spent some time each weekend in the Temple of Cartanis, and he spent six days a week in this wicket; he spent six days a week eating lunch in the much roomier and much quieter environs that customers of the Port Authority could not access.

He was therefore surprised when someone not wearing the teal of the Port Authority entered the lunch room and came directly over to where Terrick now sat, bread and its crumbs scattered over the table's surface. He had water in a tin mug, and half of a round cheese, although the cheese was well-aged. The meat, cured and smoked, was spare, as it often was during the colder months. The rich could afford the various spells of preservation and enchantment that meant their food was less seasonal—but if the Port Authority kept a roof over his head, it did not propel him into their ranks.

He did not recognize his visitor for a minute, although he rose instantly; the visitor was carrying a bundle—a blanket wrapped around something that was clearly not conventionally wrapped in such a fashion. The Port Authority guards might not have recognized this disguised burden; Terrick did. Instantly. But the young man carrying it did not unwrap it, did not draw it, and made no threatening moves. He simply gazed at Terrick, and then, past him, to the remainder of his lunch.

Terrick laughed.

He seldom laughed, but it was that single glance that made clear who his visitor was. "Angel."

Angel nodded. He had filled out over the past decade and a half; he no longer looked the boy. The awkward slenderness of youth was gone.

So, too, the Weyrdon crown. Terrick had seen Angel with his hair down before, but only after cleaning; he did not leave the apartment—any apartment—with his hair down. But there was no identifying spire, now. Nothing at all to mark the boy as Rendish; even the Southerners wore their hair in the nondescript braid that Angel had chosen. At least he had not sheared his hair, the way many of the Essalieyanese did. Terrick dragged a chair over to the table; he sat, and indicated Angel should join him.

He did not ask about the hair. It was far too personal a question.

Angel said, "I can't stay. I wasn't sure whether or not I should bother you at work—but I wanted to give you warning."

"Warning, is it?" Terrick asked, as he ate. He offered Angel food—bread and cheese—as he had unexpectedly lost his appetite. He had been alarmed, the first time he had seen the Weyrdon styling on Garroc's son—but he felt its loss as an unexpected blow. The chick had, at long last, left the nest.

He saw no shadow of Garroc in his son's face.

If Angel was aware of how Terrick felt, he showed no sign; instead, he ate. He could reliably eat, Terrick was certain, in any circumstance. The well-stocked larder and kitchens of the very patrician Terafin manse had not cured him of this habit.

"Warning," Angel said. "I don't know how much notice you have to give the Port Authority to leave without censure."

Terrick raised a brow. He glanced at the bundle Angel had set on the ground beside the chair. "What word have you brought, boy?"

Angel was old enough now that he did not stiffen with resentment at the word. "It's for you," he said, chewing with haste and swallowing just as quickly, as if suddenly remembering his manners. "I think you'll need it, where we're going."

"We?"

"Jewel needs to leave the city," he replied, his voice heavy with gravity. "I'm going with her when she leaves. And, Terrick, I want you with me."

"Why? Is she daft enough to travel to Arrend?"

"Not on purpose, no. But if I understand things—and I don't—she won't know where she's going until she gets there."

"You'll tell me more."

"I can't. I'd tell you everything but you'd miss the end of lunch call. And dinner. And possibly breakfast."

"So you say you want me to go with you—but you can't tell me where."

"Or when," Angel replied, grinning slightly. "I know in the old days you had to be ready to move with almost no notice. This is like those days. The only normal guards she'll have are us."

"Us, is it?"

Angel nodded. "She means to hold this city against the—"

Terrick held up one hand. "Let me see what you've brought me."

Angel laughed. His laughter was nothing like Garroc's. But there was a look in his eye, an excitement, a focus that had meant, on his father's face, that the waiting was *done*. It was time, at last, for action. Angel bent, the braid batting his cheek as he retrieved the bundle. He pushed what remained of Terrick's lunch to one side—it was mostly crumbs, and the mice would clean them up—and set the blanketed object between them.

"It's not a gift," he said, voice grave, laughter gone. "It's a burden, Terrick. It's a responsibility. I've told you what I want. Give me your answer."

"When?"

Angel fell silent.

Terrick's hands did not tremble. They ached when the sea air was cold—a sign of encroaching age—but they never trembled. They were, therefore, steady as he carefully drew back folds of heavy cloth. The dyes were shades of blue that were rare enough only the patrician Houses of note used them for something as simple as blankets.

But it was not the dye, not the blanket, that was significant. Angel's hair was styled in a *braid*. He had undertaken the last of Garroc's final mission, but he had sworn no oath to Weyrdon. Weyrdon had *asked* the boy to do what Garroc could not. He had permitted Angel to style himself a man of Weyrdon without demanding the substance.

Now, Angel had released all hold on the claim.

He served The Terafin. He served Jewel Markess.

Angel watched as the cloth fell away from the ax. He saw Terrick's reflection—and only Terrick's—across the blade's unscarred flat, but the room in reflection seemed brighter, harsher; the light was like Winter light, in the first fall of snow.

The older man stared at the ax for a long, transfixed moment. His hands were still; they touched nothing. But the edges of the blanket fell from them and over the edge of the table, like cloth meant for that purpose. Angel, watching his face, noted his loss of color.

It had not been Angel's reaction to the ax—but the ax was not meant for him. It was Terrick's. It was Terrick's, while he lived. He knew it with a certainty born of both desire and instinct. He wasn't Jay—but he didn't need to be, not here.

Terrick clasped hands behind his back as he straightened. "Where did you get this ax?"

"I took it from a wall in the Terafin manse."

"You are certain?"

"Yes."

Terrick shook his head. "You are lying."

Angel was surprised. Had he truly been Rendish, he would have been both insulted and angry to be so. "I am not. If you will see the room, I will take you there. I have permission to house you in the manse until we are due to depart; it will save us all from having to travel by Terafin carriage to the blacksmith to terrify him into opening your door." He hesitated. "It looks, to my eye, like a very, very fine ax. It doesn't look like more. You think you recognize it?"

"The blade, yes."

"How?"

Terrick was silent for long enough Angel wasn't certain he would answer. "Did Garroc teach you nothing of Arrend?"

"The language, and some few of its customs," Angel replied.

"But none of its stories."

"Some of the stories—but my mother preferred less martial tales."

"In the North, it is the women who tell tales of war to our sons," Terrick replied, sliding into Rendish as he spoke. "Women do not weep in Arrend."

"You think this ax is from those stories? Terrick, an ax is an ax."

"I am grateful on some days that your father met his end in battle," Terrick replied, through slightly gritted teeth. "Else I might be tempted to strangle him myself. There were three weapons that were granted the three sons of Arrend. Weyrdon bears one; he does not carry it if he does not ride to battle."

"You said men are always prepared for battle."

"All men are prepared to *fight*." He ran his hands through his hair, which Angel found shocking. He had never seen Terrick so discomfited. "Why did you bring this to *me*?"

"I needed a sword," Angel replied.

Terrick couldn't connect the reply to the question that had spawned it. He waited for the rest of the information that would make sense of the words.

"I needed a sword," Angel said again. "I can't wield an ax, not without cutting off my feet. I could use it to split wood—no, I'm joking, I'm joking." He exhaled. "The House Mage believes all of the weapons in the room that contained the ax are significant in some way. I asked The Terafin if I could borrow a weapon or two, and she gave permission."

"I will accept your Terafin's offer," Terrick said abruptly.

Angel forgot what he was about to say. "You will? You'll leave the smithy?"

"Yes. If you return to the Port Authority at the close of the day, you may vouch for me when I arrive at the manse; I assume you did not otherwise prepare a letter of introduction for my use."

". . . No."

"Meet me here, then. We'll go back to the smithy and I will inform the smith that I will be absent to conduct family affairs in Arrend. I will also inform the Port Authority officials."

"Terrick—"

"No, boy. I wish to see the room in which you found this ax. It is, as you imply, impossible that this ax be the ax I know it to be. When I see where you found it, I will have the answer to the only question now on my mind."

13th of Fabril, 428 A.A.
Terafin Manse, Averalaan Aramarelas

"He's older," Jewel said. She was the only person in the room who seemed inclined to speak at all; the Chosen, of course, would remain silent. She glanced up from the page and saw that Avandar was staring at her, his expression carefully neutral. His inner voice was silent.

She looked at Meralonne; what Avandar hid, the mage did not. His expression was one of active loathing. She had seen him argue, shout, wheedle, and laugh. She had never seen raw hatred on his face before. "APhaniel," she said, gentling her voice almost automatically.

"Yes."

"Yes?"

"Yes, that is a representation of Adam, and yes, he is older. He is not, by mortal reckoning, much older."

"You think this book was meant for Adam?"

"I think you do him no kindness if you make that assumption."

"Is it active, Meralonne? Is it, as you suspect, scribed in part on a page whose donor still lives?"

"It is."

"You know who the donor is."

"I do."

"And you will not tell me."

He turned, full, to face her, the book apparently forgotten. She had the instinctive urge to take a step back; it was overmastered by a second, stronger instinct: here, now, in front of this angry man, she must stand her ground as if he were the Winter Queen herself, at the head of her gathered host.

Here, now, she could. She did not even blink as his sword came into his hand; instead she moved to stand between the mage and the table; the blue glow of the blade's edge glimmered across the surface of her skirts. The Chosen drew swords; she lifted one hand in their direction although she didn't take her eyes off Meralonne.

"A long time ago," she said, when he did not immediately attempt to run her through, "the gods walked this world. They lived among us."

He said nothing.

"Above us," she amended. "They did not live as Lords over your kin."

"No. Not even the gods would have dared."

"But the gods left, Meralonne. The gods *left*. They aren't here, but they fear the Sleepers—who are. The Sleepers cannot harm the gods."

He said nothing, but his sword fell. It did not vanish.

"I understand what we have to fear. I understand that. But I don't understand *why* they sleep. I understand that the gods *left* us, but I've never understood why. We couldn't force them to leave. Even when the Cities of Man were at the height of their power, we could not kill the gods."

Jewel, be cautious.

He can't kill me here, she replied—and the minute the words were thoughts, she *knew* they were true. She wondered if he would try.

"They wished to preserve *you*," he replied. Winter voice, anger. "They warred for the entirety of their existence, shattering and remaking the landscape. There were very few enclaves in which your kind could grow; you were pets. You were favored, intelligent pets.

"But you were made in a way that the wise did not understand, and some part of your frail, animal forms contain eternity."

The air was cold. The wind curled through the fall of his hair. He was beautiful. "If mankind had a god that they could call a parent—and the gods were *not* their parents in any mortal sense of the word—he was nameless. Faceless. He was called Mystery by many; his counsels were opaque, his advice, barbed. Yet he was respected by the gods; he did not seek to encroach upon what was theirs.

"In the world before yours, that was rare. He owned no land; if his touch was felt at all beneath the ceaseless skies, it was subtle. He was like your gardeners; he created beauty but owned none of it. Or so we thought. I would have killed him," he added, voice low. "If I had known, I would have killed him."

"Meralonne—"

"But I did not know."

"And now?"

"If I could travel as my former apprentice does, if I could bespeak time and move at whim through its currents, I *would* kill him. I would salt the earth upon which he once stood. I would offer my life as curse and seal for his doom."

She said, without thinking, "He is not gone."

"No. Of the gods, he is one of two who did not willingly sign the binding Covenant. They are both present, Terafin. The author of our misfortune and the god we were sent to kill."

"The book—it's the god's flesh."

His eyes narrowed. "Can you see that?"

"No," she whispered. "It was a guess. Destroying the book won't destroy him."

"No. But I am now certain it is part of his plan. He meant the book to travel to you. He meant Adam to be here."

"If the book is meant for Adam—"

"I did not say that, Terafin. You can read it; I cannot. I do not believe the writing is legible to Viandaran, either. But I offer the god no aid, and where I can, I will thwart him. Had I realized the source of this book, I would never have brought it here."

"To where I can protect and safeguard it."

"Yes."

She had danced around the question and the suspicion so many times, once more seemed prudent. But the wind reached from his hair to hers, teasing out strands from the nets and pins that bound it. She could have sent it away; she didn't.

She glanced at Gordon and Marave; they were tense, but they waited. They knew he could strike her down before they could interfere—but in this case, their knowledge was wrong.

"Why," she asked, her hands by her sides, her chin lifted so that she might meet—and hold—his gaze, "are you not sleeping with them, Meralonne? Why do you labor here as a member of the Order of Knowledge?"

Jewel.

She didn't answer. Neither did Meralonne.

The Chosen were rigid, but they were surprised. Avandar was not, but he wouldn't be. Nor, she thought, would Celleriant, were he present. The cats knew. She was certain, at this point, that the *gods* knew; they had recognized Meralonne; they had called him by the name that only the immortals used. "Does Sigurne know?"

He inhaled once, deeply; when he exhaled, the sword was gone. The wind, however, was not; it flapped the pages at her back. "Yes, Terafin."

"Has she always known?"

"No. Not when she first came to the Order as a reluctant apprentice, and not for years after. But she is Sigurne Mellifas, and her first master—the master of her choice, if such choices exist in captivity—was not mortal. He, like she, was a captive of the Ice Mage: a *Kialli* lord. He told her much about the world in the days of his youth; about the gods in their glory, and the firstborn. About the *Kialli*, and the nature of their choice.

"He spoke about the war between the gods. He told her the names of gods who perished in those ancient conflicts; she remembers all of them. He did not speak to her of her own kind, except where it was necessary to tell the larger tale. But to speak of the fall of *Allasakar* is to speak of things mortal: He therefore spoke of the man you call Moorelas. He spoke of the blade fashioned by gods and mortal Artisans, and of its purpose.

"He told her much, much more than the gods themselves might, if they deigned to be questioned."

"But he served *Allasakar*," Jewel replied. She used the god's name, as Meralonne had done.

"Yes. You do not understand the complicated measure of their service; you do not understand the narrow, narrow line between love and hate, adoration and obsession. You do not understand the *Kialli*. Let me say only this: if a mortal child of sixteen could harm *Allasakar* because of the knowledge of one bound demon, the god no longer deserved dominion over the Hells; he deserved destruction."

"Did he speak of the Sleepers?"

"Yes. But not as you know them. He spoke of the firstborn. He spoke of Ariane, the White Lady, one of the only children born to the gods who could hold the roads against *Allasakar*. But he did not speak of the cause of their enmity; it was great, Terafin, and no concession on the part of the Lord of the Hells will ever quench it while he lives.

"To destroy him, to banish him, to sever his ties with the world into which she was born—and in which, ultimately, she was doomed to exist should the gods leave and the Covenant come into effect—she served the *gods*." The bitter, bitter cold in his voice reminded Jewel of her youth in the streets of the twenty-fifth holding.

"And we served *her*. We served the White Lady. She commanded, Terafin, and we obeyed. It was our privilege. It was our reason for existence."

His eyes were silver, and bright. His voice lost the edge of killing cold. His hair swept past his shoulders to fall in a moving drape down his back. She thought he would draw sword again, but no sword came to his hand. "She was as a god, to us, and she was deep in the councils of the nameless god.

"She was there when Moorelas' sword was forged, and she paid the price it demanded; so, too, the gods. She gave it her blood and her name and her oath. Understand that all of the gods did; all but one.

"Imagine our dismay when it became clear that such a sword, such a weapon, was meant to be wielded by a *mortal*." His tone of voice conveyed some of that dismay; he used the word mortal the way the Chosen might use the word *rabbit*, it seemed to contain so little sense. "A mortal.

"Nor was one found that could wield that sword. Many came, to be tested; the test was not a simple act. It was not a test of blood; it was not a test of lineage. A test of courage? A test of skill? No, not even that. It was not a test that the wise could comprehend. We were not privy to the methods of the test; the sword itself decided.

"And so we waited. We warred. We died and we conquered. The lands broke and changed beneath the feet of our armies, and we rode the crest of their shifting waves. But in time, a man arrived who could wield the sword, and he meant to wield it against *Allasakar*.

"He was mortal. The White Lady understood that the sword could not be wielded by any other hand, and she had waited long, in her own reckoning, for the sword to make its choice. But she did not trust mortals. She trusted the sword-bearer's intent, yes—but his competence? How could she?

"And so she came to the Princes of her court, and she chose from among them four who would journey at the side of Moorelas. Four. But we understood the whole of her intent by the time we reached the shadows cast by *Allasakar's* vast and changing fortress. We understood that *Allasakar* was the only god who stood between the cleaving of two worlds; if he could be killed, Terafin, then the Covenant *could be* signed, and the gods could depart.

"And with the gods, the wilderness of the world would be sealed, and the firstborn—those born to and of the plane—would be banished into the hidden corners; even the White Lady herself.

"And mortals would be left to crawl across the husk of the world, digging in their dirt in *peace*. No more could the

White Lady ride forth; no more could she take—and hold—the lands she desired. She would be a shadow of herself, and her lands, a tiny fraction of what they might otherwise have been.

"And she was *willing* to do this, to see her enemy destroyed. She herself would survive."

Jewel said, "They were not."

"No, Terafin. She commanded, and in this case, they *could not* obey. Obedience meant her destruction."

"She is *not* dead."

"No. But she is not what she was. They were willing to lose her in order to preserve her. They were willing to sacrifice the thing they held dear above all things. They knew her wrath would be great and endless."

"And you were not."

"I served the White Lady," he replied. After a long pause, he added, "And I would serve. If she had commanded our destruction, none of us would have resisted. But she did not ask that. She asked us to lessen *her*. She asked us to destroy almost all of her power and her endless beauty." He turned to the Chosen, which Jewel had not expected. "You serve your Lord. You have sworn your lives to the protection of all that she holds dear.

"Would you cripple her, if she commanded it? Would you break her legs and her arms?"

They were silent in the face of his words; they were only barely a question. They looked to Jewel. Jewel hesitated for a long moment, and then nodded.

Gordon did not choose to answer. But Marave stepped forward. "Yes. If she commanded it, I would obey." She said it with a trace of defiance—but that trace ran through her entire personality like tempered steel.

"Why?"

"I trust The Terafin. I entrust her with my life. She is the whole of my duty. But I am *not* The Terafin, thank the gods. Her decisions, and their consequences, are *not* mine to bear. If I did not trust her—if I did not trust her absolutely—I would never have taken the oath. And if she commanded me to injure her—or cripple her—I would hate it, but I would trust that there was a reason for the command. Even if I couldn't see a reason for it, even if none came to me—I would trust that there was one."

Her answer, rather than annoying the mage, robbed him of words for a long, long moment. What was left in their wake was a slowly kindling smile. "Even so," he said, his voice once again the voice of the mage who lived in—and served—the Order of Knowledge. He glanced, again, at Jewel.

"You have your answer," he told her softly.

"Marave," Jewel said. The Chosen nodded, waiting. "If I ordered the Chosen to do this thing, and Gordon refused, would he then be forsworn?"

Marave hesitated. It was not an obvious hesitation, but Jewel marked it. "The Chosen serve as a body. If the Chosen refused, if the Captains of the Chosen refused, we would all be forsworn. But if any one of us could achieve the task you set us, no, Terafin. We are the men and women you Chose. We are not all one thing or another. We were asked to serve with both thought and conscience; we are not simple House Guards.

"You are our Lord. But our oath to Terafin does not require that we give up our core beliefs in service to yours. We are free to speak, and we are free to disagree—at your behest. It is the foundation of the choice we are asked to make."

"Thank you, Marave." Jewel turned once again to Meralonne. "The Winter Queen is not The Terafin."

"No," was his grave reply. "She seldom forgives. Her orders are not to be questioned; her commands are absolute. I understood the choice they made, and I have never been certain that my own choice was not an act of cowardice, in the end."

Jewel was silent at the magnitude of his confession. It made him seem human, a fact she was certain he would never appreciate. "But you have not returned to the host."

"No, Terafin. There is no return for me, save by her leave; she has never given it. *Allasakar* did not perish at the end of the long war. He was gravely injured, and he was contained—as the Sleepers were contained—by the combined efforts of the gods. A seal was set upon them, and the Hells were given to *Allasakar*.

"He was therefore beyond the White Lady's reach."

"Until now."

"Until now." His smile was bitter. "And so the lost

Princes will be given a chance to redeem themselves in her eyes. She has fallen, as we feared, but she is still the White Lady, and as the bindings that hold the hidden ways separate from the mortal realms fray, you will see some echo of her ancient glory.

"I have waited against hope for that day. I have waited for my brothers to finally wake." He bowed. It was a low, graceful gesture of respect, none of it feigned. "It is not yet their time."

"Will you know?" she asked softly. "Will you know when it is? Or will the time be decided in its entirety by *Allasakar*?"

"The roads of the future were never mine to traverse," he replied. "But, yes, I believe I will know. There is one event that must occur before we have any hope of returning to the side of our Lady."

"And that?"

His smile was cool. "We must at the side of a mortal ride against the god, as we once did, under Moorelas' shadow."

The silence seemed to stretch and lengthen. Meralonne's lips framed a sharp, cutting smile; he knew what those words meant to the people in this city. To fall under Moorelas' shadow was death; even the adults who minded their children in the lee of the great statue avoided the shadows the stone figure cast.

Duster had emerged from the undercity into that shadow. Duster was dead.

She shook her head to clear it, but the image clung anyway. Duster. Duster as she was, as Jewel had last seen her. She had not aged with time, but memory did not make, of Duster, a young girl. A child.

"The sword," she whispered.

"It is said that the sword could not be destroyed except by the combined will of the gods. That act will never occur upon this plane."

"It is said?"

"The sword could not be destroyed," he replied. "Attempts were made. They failed. The best the gods could do was to bind it, bury it, and keep it hidden from all mortal knowledge. That was done, in a fashion, but without their knowledge. No god can tell you what became of the blade.

But if the gods choose to answer directly, they will admit that they do not know its fate."

"And you?"

"Not I," he replied softly. "Were I to find it, I could not wield it. It was meant for mortal hands. Nor could I find and enslave a mortal to wield the sword at my bidding. I told you: the sword tests. The sword judges. The *Kialli* have been searching since their Lord took his place upon the throne in the frozen wastes—but they have not found it.

"There is some hope that the blade itself might fail if it achieves its goal: it was meant to end *Allasakar's* life. But, Jewel," he added, forgetting himself, and forgetting a title he must viscerally consider irrelevant, "it was a blade meant to kill a god.

"It is our belief that it could be wielded against any god."

"It can't be wielded against any god that is not on the plane."

"No. But there are two who are." And one of the two, she thought, he hated. The Winter Queen had given no command in regard to that god.

What must it be like to demand the utter and absolute obedience of men like Meralonne?

You do, Avandar replied. *Or you would if you desired it. Lord Celleriant has bound himself* to you.

She knew. She *knew*. When Mordanant had come to take her life, she had not even flinched. Celleriant was not by her side when the cats had attacked his brother, but she had felt no fear. She had known on some instinctive level that Celleriant would arrive at need.

He was a match for his brother. He was possibly more than a match. Jewel frowned. "Meralonne, how are the *Arianni* born?"

Platinum brows rose in shock; she might have asked him the intimate details of his sex life to far lesser effect.

"I've never seen an *Arianni* woman before."

"You have."

"I haven't. I've seen the Winter Queen . . ."

"Yes."

"Mordanant came for his brother. He called Celleriant his kin."

"So do you call Teller and Finch yours."

"It's not the same."

"Is it not? There is only Ariane. There is no other. We are not mortal, Jewel. We are not born as you are born; we do not age as you age. Nor do we die. We do not perform acts of glory for the faint hope of a random woman's love; we do not—as your kind does—marry and bear young. We are the *Arianni*. We serve no other."

"Celleriant serves me."

Meralonne did not reply. After a pause in which he obviously discarded her comment as unworthy of note, he asked, "What will you do with the book?"

Jewel exhaled. "I'll read it, of course."

His eyes rounded. She almost laughed; she hadn't seen that particular expression since the early months of her life in the manse. "Viandaran."

"I counsel, of course, that the book be disarmed or destroyed, but she is The Terafin. She is the master I have chosen to serve."

"She is little more than a mortal child. Had Sigurne been a tenth as foolish in her youth, she would not now be the guildmaster; she would be a footnote, if that, in the annals of the Order's history."

"I don't require your permission or approval," Jewel told him firmly. "Either of you. If you're materially afraid of the outcome of such a reading, I suggest you return to the manse; you will be unlikely to feel any ill effects at that distance. If what I understand about my personal library is true, I'm the one person in the manse the book *can't* affect without permission. To me, the script is Weston. It's a familiar Weston, at that; it's not stiff and it's not formal."

"The risk is yours to take," Meralonne replied.

She nodded. She considered sending the Chosen away, but grimaced and accepted the risk to their safety; they wouldn't leave her. Not when Meralonne had already drawn a sword; not when he had implied that this book and its inexplicable contents were a threat.

Reaching out, she touched the page. It felt like dry paper; dry and slightly brittle. It looked new. Her hand shook as she turned the page. It froze in the act of turning, the page on which Adam was painted curled but not yet flattened. Beneath the leaf which contained his image was another painted figure.

Carver.

Just Carver.

Avandar was by her side before she could move. She heard two words leave his lips; she understood neither. They were a curse in a dialect that she had never heard him speak. Nor did she ask.

Carver crouched, back against a wall, his face slightly lifted. He was gaunt, and she could see a small trail of blood from the corner of lips that looked cracked. His eyes were ringed with darkness, although she could only see one; his hair covered the other. His hands were streaked red, and in one, he held a dagger.

It was not a familiar dagger. It was not a Terafin dagger.

Beyond the edge of the wall she could see white, some hint of snow—but the wall implied city; it looked like an exterior wall.

"Carver." The word was barely a whisper. She had drawn no breath to utter it, and she choked as she tried to say more—or tried to stop herself from saying more. She was The Terafin; she could not lose control here.

But she didn't know how to *keep it*. She wanted to scream at the book. To scream at the person who had delivered it. She wanted to scream at Teller for hiding it in his study for six weeks, because she had no idea *when* this had happened.

Breathe. Breathe. She had no idea *if* this had happened. It was a painting of Carver. Carver, with his patrician nose, its line less perfect than it had been the first night she'd laid eyes on it. His hair was still a drape across one eye. He didn't look any older to Jewel than he had the last time she'd seen him; he looked exhausted.

But he would be. He was nowhere near any of the homes he had known. Were there streets, where he crouched, hidden? Was there food? She whispered his name again, and this time, as the page trembled in her nerveless fingers, the image shifted. Carver *looked up*. He looked up, out of the page, and his eyes rounded as they met hers.

She was transfixed. She saw nothing, heard nothing, beneath the amethyst skies; not Avandar, not Meralonne, not the Chosen. She reached out to touch him and felt paper. Paper. Her hand could not dip below the surface to reach Carver.

But Carver could see her gesture. He didn't speak. He

didn't try. Instead, he lifted a hand in den-sign, his lips curved in a tired, steady smile. He forced exhaustion from his face as he met and held her gaze.

Can't speak, he signed. *Need silence.*

She lifted her hands. She didn't know if he could hear a word she spoke, but he could see her. *Where are you? How long?*

He shrugged. *Two hours. Maybe.* Two hours. It had been four days, here. She needed no further proof that Carver was lost on the wild roads.

They had no gesture in den-sign that meant Ellerson. They had small signs for each other, but none for the domicis. She wanted to ask. She mouthed the old man's name.

Carver shook his head. She couldn't read his expression — but she tried. She tried harder than she'd ever tried to read written language. *Where are you?*

Don't know.

You're lying.

He grimaced. *Jay, don't come. Don't follow.*

She bent the whole of her will, the whole of her desire, toward her den-kin. It had been more than a decade since she had tried to deliberately invoke her stubborn, intermittent gift. She tried now. She tried, straining against every failure she'd ever had before. It didn't help. She did not *know* where Carver was, and she could not *see* it.

But she knew it was Carver. She *knew*. He was still alive. He was somewhere cold, somewhere dangerous; he was in the shadows and on the run — but he was *alive*. She wanted to know where he was. She wanted to find him. He was, in that moment, the only thing she cared about.

She reached. She reached with both of her hands, letting the picture of Adam fall flat, face down, to one side. Carver's eyes widened in utter silence. He gestured in frantic den-sign, but she couldn't read it, couldn't take it in. He was *right there*, and that was where she wanted to be.

And then the book fell away, as did the table; the ground moved — or her feet did. She heard a snarling hiss of outraged fury as Shadow literally knocked her off her feet by landing on her.

"What are you *doing*? Stupid, *stupid* girl!"

She had landed on her side; Shadow's paws were flat against her skirt. She turned to rise, but found it difficult to move. "Get off me," she told him, voice low. It was almost as feral as the cat's.

Shadow hissed. "You are *foolish*. Why are you *reading* that book? What are you *doing*? You will wake *them* if you make that much *noise*." Without waiting for a response, he turned his massive head and said, "What were *you* doing?"

Avandar did not deign to reply.

"And *you*, what were you *thinking*?"

Meralonne raised a brow. Instead of answering the cat, he walked to the table and bent over the open book. Shadow moved, allowing Jewel to scrabble gracelessly to her feet. There was gray fur down the length of her skirt; she left it. She'd never particularly cared for this dress anyway. She approached the mage. Avandar was on his other side.

"Yes," Meralonne said, before she could speak. "I believe I know where he is. I am not entirely certain; the image contains very little in the way of either geography or architecture."

"You—you know where he is."

"I am not *certain*, Jewel. It is entirely possible that I am mistaken. If he—"

Shadow roared. It was both deafening and bracing. He inserted himself between Jewel and Meralonne, and then lifted his wings and nudged them farther apart.

"Shadow," she said, exasperated, "he is unlikely to harm me."

Shadow hissed.

"He knows where Carver is. I need to know."

Shadow flexed his wings, forcing Meralonne to step back or fall into Avandar. To Jewel's surprise, he chose to step back. Shadow was not shy about shouldering the domicis out of the way, either. He was tall enough to look down at the book. "I should *eat* this," he told her, growling.

"Do not even *think* it, Shadow."

"Why is *he* so important?"

"He's Carver," she replied, throat tight. When the cat asked again, she said, "Because he's one of *mine*."

"But—but you don't *need* him. You have *us*."

"He is not as dangerous as you are," Jewel replied, gritting her teeth but forcing her voice into something resembling reasonable calm. "But he was there for me when I needed him. He needs me now. I have to find him and bring him back."

"Why did you *let him* leave, if he was so important?"

"I didn't know that he *was* leaving. He went to the closet to find Ellerson, and he didn't come back. I sent your brothers to find him. They haven't come back either."

"Oh, *them*." Shadow snorted. "They can't find their *tails*. You can't expect them to find *anything* lost."

"You could have said this earlier, Shadow."

Shadow, however, did not reply. He was sniffing the page and snorting. It was the cat version of subverbal muttering. He hissed. He glared at Meralonne—which required some work, before he turned back to the book. "Is he *very* important?"

"Very." She hesitated. "The Winter King is looking for him."

"He *won't* find him."

"Will Snow or Night?"

"No."

"Could you?"

Shadow hissed.

"No," Meralonne said. "What he means to tell you is no."

"Meralonne, could you reach him?"

Chapter Twenty-eight

MERALONNE WAS SILENT. Silent, tall, distant: a living sculpture. "There is a danger," he finally said. It was not an answer—but it was. "If I understand the events in *Avantari* correctly, there is a path you must walk, and your time grows short. To go to where your compatriot must be is not a small undertaking; it is not even an undertaking you are guaranteed to survive.

"The Oracle lives at the heart of the wilderness, although you will not perhaps perceive it that way."

"How will I perceive it?"

"I cannot say. No invitation to one such as I has ever been extended."

"You haven't seen it."

"I did not say that. I said merely that I was not present as a guest. The Oracle's path is not the road that will lead to your lost kin—but any hope you have of walking that road requires vision, sight: it requires your ability to control and focus the wild talent to which you were born.

"Yet if you focus thus, you may be gone for months—or years—while your House waits and the city grows less and less stable; time does not pass reliably or predictably in any lands save the lands mortals call their own. If you abandon your home in the hour of its greatest need, I am not certain the city will remain; you have not yet built all that must be built because you do not understand *how*. And before you ask, Jewel, I do not understand it, either. Nor will I. Perhaps the Summer Queen might—but she is gone from the land.

"I fear she will never return."

In silence, Jewel considered the mage—and only the mage. "You did not answer my question. Could you lead me to Carver?"

"Yes."

Avandar stiffened, which caused the mage to smile. It was a bitter expression.

"But they will be aware of me the moment I set foot upon that ground; they will be aware, Terafin. If you wish them to sleep—and you do—you will not ask me to lead you to your Carver. Nor will you ask me to accompany you."

"If I asked you to go on your own?"

A pale brow rose. "The risk is the same," he finally said. "I am not in danger should I choose to do what you've asked; it is not my life that will be forfeit." He gestured at the open book. "It is his. He will pay dearly for his trespass should they become aware of it."

"Will the cats pose the same risk?"

"No."

Shadow hissed.

"May I ask why?"

"They are what they are. There is no place they cannot enter, unseen, should they so choose. You would not, of course, believe it, given the manner of their appearance and their speech in your House—but you should. You wear a pendant that was procured from a treasury that not even my brethren could reach. Their difficulty will not lie in entry, but in finding that entrance."

If not for the sight of Carver, Jewel would have been chilled by the words. She heard them. They registered. But while the book was open, she could see Carver—and only Carver. She inhaled. Exhaled. "What of Avandar?"

Meralonne considered the question for a few seconds; she might have been asking about the weather. "I am not certain. His power was considered significant among my kin; even the White Lady respected it. He is not now what he was—but it remains within him. Were I you, I would not risk it. But were I you, I would have no choice.

"What lives upon the hidden paths is not what lurks in the

darker corners of this city. I have no doubt that you have seen shadows here. But they are the streets you know; Viandaran has some experience with things vastly less mundane." He glanced once more at the book, and then turned to fully face her.

"Call back your hunter, Terafin. Summon your cats. Summon the Winter King. They search to no purpose; they will not find what you have commanded them to seek."

"Can you—can you preserve his life? Can you do *something* to help him until I can reach him?"

"I have told you," he said, in a more severe voice, "that seeking him is folly. He is one life, Terafin. One of tens of thousands. Of more. Tarry, and you risk everything."

"Can you," she repeated, adding a staccato beat between each word to prevent her voice from rising in fury, "offer. Him. Aid."

Avandar said, "No." The tone of his voice made clear to Jewel that the answer was probably yes, and that it would be costly.

"Jewel," Haval said, and she startled. She had forgotten that Haval had followed her; forgotten, until the moment he spoke, that he occupied the same space as the rest of this conversation. She hid her guilty start and turned to face him. He stood to one side of the Chosen, his hands behind his back, his expression at its most inscrutable.

"Come away. You have much to think about and much to discuss. Member APhaniel will offer nothing that he has not already offered."

"But Carver—"

"Now. You must see to my wife, and I am no longer content to wait. If you will play games of risk, play them—but play them *after* my wife is safe." When she failed to move, he held out an imperious arm.

"A moment," Meralonne said. Haval did not appear to have heard him. Jewel, twisting on hooks of bitter hope, turned immediately. She met silver eyes, and held them. "You spoke, when last we spoke of such affairs, of Summer."

She nodded, wary now.

"I cannot walk the roads you will now walk, although I offered to do that; I did not see, clearly, what those roads were and where they would lead. I can offer warnings—and

I will, should you instruct your household to heed them. I am not, as you have always understood, mortal.

"But if I feel no particular attachment to mortals as a concept, or mortality as a condition, it is my desire to hold this city while Sigurne lives. I can, as you suspect, offer aid to your kin; there is, as Viandaran suspects, a danger. But I am more subtle than the Sleepers, and I am awake.

"The action is not without cost to me. Were I to accompany you on your journey, I might see and know the truth of your offer; I will not. Bring me some proof that your intent is not the daydream of a foolish girl, and I will do everything within my power to preserve this one, mortal life."

"I need you to do it *now*," she said, voice low. "I can't wait—"

"You can. You have little choice in the matter. You do not trust me, and in this, you are to be commended. I, likewise, do not trust you. I trust your intent. I believe you to be Sen in the most ancient of ways known to man. But these lands are not likewise ancient, and you are not what man was when the Cities of Man ruled the vast majority of your kind.

"I will remain in residence in your library in your absence. I may spend some time patrolling your forests, if that is also acceptable. I believe there have been some mundane difficulties within the House and its environs, and I will make myself available should the right-kin require advice or the services it is legal for members of the Order to render.

"Matters of the Houses—and even the Kings—have no bearing, for the moment on this book, the statuary in *Avantari*, or the whole of your library. I am therefore at liberty to pursue the continued survival of your House in a manner that will offer no cause for complaint."

She stared at him. *Carver.* " . . . Is there anything you require? If you wish to move your belongings from the Order—"

He waved a hand. "I will, of course, move belongings of significance to me. I do not require Terafin baggage handling—or babysitting."

"Jewel," Haval said, lifting his arm.

This time, she bit back anger and pain and hope, and she accepted the wordless command.

Haval did not speak a word as they walked through the public galleries. He did pause once or twice to glance at a painting, as he walked in the slow, stately way an elderly man of patrician bearing would. Jewel was forced to match his pace; to stop when he stopped and to walk when he continued to move.

She found it frustrating, and was certain he knew it. Shadow found it *boring*. Haval acknowledged his boredom with a smile and a grave nod, neither of which ruffled the cat's feathers. She had originally asked Shadow to remain with Meralonne; Shadow practiced selective deafness. He failed to hear the request.

She failed to make it a command. There was very little Meralonne could do in the library that would threaten her House. Or rather, very little that he would. The time might come—would come, she feared—when that would no longer be the case.

Haval led her to the West Wing, and she was almost ashamed to find his presence a necessary comfort. She could not stop her hand from shaking.

She was a coward. She did not want to go to her den, to call kitchen, and to tell them what she had seen. She did not want them to face the days—the weeks—of waiting. They had done this before, in the darkest of the shadows of her past: they had lost Lefty, lost Fisher. In House Terafin, they had been safe from those disappearances, those shadowy losses.

She had brought them back.

"Jewel," Haval said softly.

She nodded; she didn't meet his gaze. She took deep, even breaths, forced her shoulders to fall, and lifted her chin. She was The Terafin, until she reached the West Wing. She was Jay when the doors closed at her back—but not until then. Nor did Haval otherwise admonish her. He served as an anchor as she returned to the West Wing.

When the doors opened, Jewel froze beneath their frame. Shadow, bored, nearly knocked her over as he pushed her to the side. "Why are you *standing* there?" he asked, as he sauntered over to the only other person in the hall: Angel.

For a moment, she hadn't recognized him. She had seen his face daily for over half her life, and he now looked like a stranger. His hair—his platinum hair, so similar to Meralonne's in color, so different in texture—was plaited in a single long braid.

She started to say *kitchen*, stopped as she remembered why Haval had brought her here. She stared. Just stared.

"Terrick is here," he said, into the silence of this unfathomable change. "He's in one of the guest rooms."

"Terrick?"

"My father's friend."

She nodded, gathering herself. But she flashed quick den-sign, a question.

Need to speak, Angel replied, in the same language.

Kitchen?

No.

"I have business with Haval. Since you're here, can you knock on Adam's door and ask him to join me in Hannerle's room?"

Shadow hissed. "I'll get him," he said. "Or we'll be *standing here* all day."

"Angel—when Finch comes home, tell her we're to meet after dinner in the kitchen."

"Teller?"

"Teller knows. He has a guest who will take dinner in the dining room this eve."

Adam came instantly, but as he wasn't running, Shadow pushed him from behind. Literally. Ariel had not joined them, but she seldom left her room. Jewel often wondered if she would have been happier remaining with the Voyani. But the Voyani in reach was Yollana, and the lands in which Yollana was situated were about to become a battlefield. Jewel had felt she had no choice but to bring the child home.

Yet home was not home for Ariel.

"I'm sorry to drag you away," Jewel said, in Torra. "But . . . Hannerle didn't wake with the rest of the sleepers and we need to wake her now."

Adam nodded. He didn't ask her how she intended to do this, which was a pity. She'd had no idea how she intended to wake the others, either, and that had caused a ripple-down panic, because both she and Adam had vanished from the healerie during the process.

She was certain Levec would eventually forgive her, but equally certain it wouldn't be soon.

Avandar drew two chairs to the bedside, one on the right and one on the left. Jewel took the chair farthest from the door; Adam took the empty one. Haval stood at the foot of the bed; he was offered a chair, but declined. He stood like a man of some power, hands loosely clasped behind his back; he stared down at the sleeping face of his wife with no discernible expression.

Jewel took Hannerle's slack hand in her own. She was dismayed at how much weight Hannerle had lost; Hannerle had never been a small woman. In repose, she looked fragile. It was wrong; Hannerle had never been wilting or frail. In the shop that had been her home, she had been the center of all the bustle. She nagged, it was true, but she nagged far less than Jewel's Oma, in the crowded environs of her first home.

Adam, opposite Jewel, immediately took Hannerle's other hand. Stretched between them, she formed a human line. *I'm sorry, Hannerle,* Jewel thought, as she closed her eyes.

"Sorry for what?"

Jewel opened her eyes immediately. She was no longer in the bedroom that had been Hannerle's home for many weeks. Nor was Hannerle; they were in the kitchen, in the back of the shop in which Haval had done most of his notable work until The Terafin's funeral.

Adam was seated at the table, as was Jewel; Hannerle was busy at the counter. She wore a familiar, faded apron, and the weight she had lost in the waking world girded her firmly in the dreaming one.

"Have you been letting my pest of a husband bully you again?" She turned and Jewel's eyes widened. She was ten, maybe twenty, years younger. "You need to assert yourself. He'll walk all over you if you don't." As she spoke, she set her hands on her hips. It was like and unlike the gesture that had defined Jewel's Oma at her most irritable.

"I—"

"Don't make excuses. I love him, but he'll take a mile if you give him an inch." She frowned. "What, exactly, were you apologizing for?"

"Haval hasn't been bullying me."

"Hah. He does it all the time. You don't notice because he doesn't shout. And don't think I notice you didn't answer my question."

Jewel glanced at Adam, but no help came from that quarter. Adam was, in some ways, in his element here: he was accompanied by two opinionated women, both of whose age and position gave them easy authority over him. He was expected to make no decisions or choices. Here, the floor was either Jewel's or Hannerle's; it would never become his.

Hannerle frowned. "Adam?"

He smiled. "You look well, Hannerle."

"I do." She smiled back. It was the smile one gave to a precocious child. "I'm happy to see you. Have you been given a tour of the front?"

"No."

"I should do that, then. Unless you're still hungry?" She looked pointedly at the empty plates in front of her two guests. They had not been there when Jewel had first opened her eyes, but dreams were like that, and both of the guests accepted their appearance as if this were expected and natural.

Hannerle headed to the kitchen door and called for her husband.

Jewel tensed, but no dreaming image of Haval answered her call. Hannerle was silent in the door for a long moment. When she turned to face them again, she had aged into the appearance Jewel was now familiar with. "That's right," she said, her voice shorn suddenly of all certainty. "He's not home."

Jewel rose. She rose instantly and closed the distance between that door and the woman who stood framed by it, reaching out with both of her hands to take Hannerle's into her own. She wanted to apologize again. She wanted to tell Hannerle that her husband would be home—and *stay* there—the minute she woke.

But what she said instead was, "I'm sorry. I'm sorry, Hannerle."

Hannerle's hands tightened. "Why are you apologizing? You're just a child. Haval is a man; he makes his own decisions. He always has."

Jewel shook her head. "Do you know what Haval did before he became a dressmaker?"

"Yes."

"I don't. I don't exactly know. I've asked," she added, "but he's never answered."

"I should hope not." This was said with more asperity. "He had no business doing what he did; he has no business teaching you any of it." She withdrew her hands. "Adam?"

Adam rose more slowly than Jewel had, and he glanced at Jewel, his fingers slipping into surprisingly confident densign. Jewel hadn't taught him that; she wondered who had.

Jester, he signed.

Jewel was surprised. He signed something Jewel didn't recognize. Two things. "My name," he told her. "And Ariel's."

She blinked. But Adam was older than any of the den had been when they had first come together. He was, in many ways, more competent than any of them had been, as well. He was as calm as Finch or Teller at their best, but clear-eyed and compassionate in a way that almost no one in the den had been when it came to outsiders. He was watching Hannerle now.

She reached out for one of his hands, as if he were in fact a child. He accepted the gesture without a trace of self-consciousness. "I promised I'd show him the store," she said to Jewel, by way of explanation. "Do you want to join us?"

Jewel nodded. She almost took Hannerle's free hand, but she would have felt extremely self-conscious. *You are not a child*, she told herself. It had been so long since she'd missed her mother.

Adam followed Hannerle, as he was attached; Jewel trailed behind them, gathering her words, preparing them. She realized that she wasn't comfortable in the store, although it looked—to her eye—very like the store that she had visited infrequently in her youth. Dreams had a way of shifting geography, but if this was the geography dictated by Hannerle, it was solid. It did not, had not, changed.

Hannerle, who often left Haval to his work, showed Adam the pride of her collection: the silks colored in the most expensive of dyes. One or two were a shade of blue that Jewel had never seen; she didn't think this was because Hannerle was dreaming, but couldn't be certain. Hannerle spoke of only one or two customers by House—but, of course, the most significant of these was Terafin.

Adam said, "Jewel is The Terafin," and Hannerle stopped, arrested. She turned to Jewel, and Jewel felt her clothing shift as Hannerle examined it. It was not comfortable to be a passenger in another person's dreams.

"Why, so she is. Haval has been making dresses for her, hasn't he?" She frowned. Hannerle, always pragmatic, shook her head as if to clear it. "He's been working for you." The shift in tone was wrong.

Jewel swallowed. "Hannerle."

"What have you asked him to make for you?" Her knuckles were white around Adam's hands.

"Dresses," Jewel replied. "As always. But it isn't just me he designs for; it's Finch and Teller."

Hannerle closed her eyes. Jewel was afraid the store would vanish around them; it faded, becoming momentarily transparent. But before Hannerle opened her eyes, it reasserted itself. This was Hannerle's home. This was what she had built. She was not about to let it go.

And Jewel had taken Haval from its heart, and she did not intend to relinquish him. For herself, yes. She could forgo his often caustic advice and guidance. She trusted the gift with which she'd been born to preserve her own life; it was the lives of everyone else it might fail.

She understood, as she waited for Hannerle, what Haval had understood in the intimate environs of her private dining room: She held Hannerle *here* because she did not wish to let Haval go. Haval did not lie to Hannerle. Haval had promised her that when she woke on her own, he would leave Terafin and return to their life at the shop.

"Hannerle," she said.

Hannerle opened her eyes and met Jewel's gaze. "Terafin."

Jewel didn't flinch. It took effort. "Haval will come home if you ask him."

Hannerle's lips turned up in a strange, bitter smile. "Will he?"

The question robbed Jewel of an easy answer. She thought, in that moment, Hannerle knew everything. Jewel was accustomed to this from her husband, but not from Hannerle herself. "Yes. You must know that."

"I know that I keep him here, yes. But some days I feel as if I built this. Me. I'm like a cage, Jewel. Beyond my bars, he is what he always was."

Everything. "He loves you."

"Yes."

"He always has. The only part of his past he'll speak about is you."

"I'm the only part of his past that's unlikely to kill him," was the gruff reply.

Jewel laughed; she couldn't help it. "You're the only part of his past he wouldn't stop, if you demanded his death."

"You think he's been staying with you because of me," Hannerle said, releasing Adam's hand and getting, at last, down to business. "He tells you that. You tell yourself that. Do you actually believe it?"

Jewel's automatic response was yes. She bit it back. Hannerle was not asking a rhetorical question. "I did."

"I don't."

"But—but why, Hannerle? He's run this shop since before I met him. He's good at what he does, and he's never seemed unhappy."

Hannerle snorted. "He seems to be whatever's convenient for him at the time. He could, if he wanted, treat the shop with active loathing and you'd believe it just as readily."

"I wouldn't. If he loathed this store, he wouldn't be in it. Nothing holds Haval down unless he wants to be pinned."

Hannerle folded her arms across her chest. "So. You understand."

And she did.

"What do you want from my husband? I've known you for over half your life. You haven't asked him to kill for you."

How much did Hannerle know?

"No."

"I could kill Rath myself," Hannerle continued. "But not you. I never approved of Rath; I never approved of your association with him. But you're The Terafin now; maybe I misjudged him."

Jewel shook her head. "You didn't. But if it weren't for Rath, I wouldn't be Terafin now." She exhaled. "I don't need your husband for my sake. I have my Chosen, and others besides. Inasmuch as every demon discovered in the city in the past few months has been discovered while trying to kill me, I'm safer than I've ever been."

"But?"

"It's not his advice, Hannerle. If he left the manse and returned here, I'd still commission dresses from him, and I'd still talk to him about my daily life. He takes Terafin money for his work, but it's not the money that he wants; he wants the gossip. He wants to know what happens in Houses of power.

"He'd probably be happier if he didn't have to live sequestered in the West Wing. It's much harder for him to gather information when he's not in this store, being visited by patrons of power and note from time to time."

Hannerle snorted again. "If you think he hasn't been gathering information while tucked away in the Terafin manse, you do not know my husband."

"No," Jewel agreed. "I don't. I know as much about him as he wants me to know." She hesitated. "That's unfair. I know that he's observant."

Hannerle snorted.

"I need him to be where he is."

"Why?" The single word was the sharpest word Hannerle had yet spoken.

But Jewel understood women like Hannerle. They were part of her history, her childhood, her sense of what people *were*. She was The Terafin, yes; The Terafin was meant to define autocratic. It was not, however, as Terafin that she confronted Haval's wife now. She wished, briefly, that her clothing would shift into something more appropriate, but realized as she thought this that there was nothing else she could wear.

"Because I won't be where he is for much longer."

Hannerle waited, lips compressed in a tighter line.

"I need to leave Terafin, and I don't know how long I'll be gone. I'm Terafin, yes—but I'm also the only person who can undertake this journey. I can't order someone else to take it—unless you happen to know another seer." Jewel turned to examine the bolts of cloth that Hannerle had shown Adam with such pride. "I wouldn't leave, Hannerle. Terafin is my home. The only family I have left is in Terafin.

They can't come with me, and I wouldn't take them even if it was possible.

"You've seen my cats," she said, lifting the edge of a bolt of blue silk and letting light play across its fabric. "I don't know if you've seen my forest."

"Of course I have," she replied, in an entirely different tone of voice.

Jewel turned. The store had not melted away, but Hannerle drew her—and Adam, who remained silent and watchful throughout their discussion—toward the store windows. Outside of those windows the familiar streets of the Common no longer existed; instead, there were trees of silver, of gold, and of diamond.

"I find it beautiful," Hannerle said, her voice softer. "I find your cats beautiful—but I'm glad they're yours, not mine; I think their constant whining would make me box their ears. I couldn't own a forest like this one," she added softly. "I'd forget how to live and work, I think. I'd wander through those trees looking for—for gods only know what. I'd be searching for the heart of those lands. I'd feel my own life too small and too dismal, too gray.

"Too mortal," she added. "You will not take Haval to your forest."

"No. Haval doesn't belong in it. I don't know what he'd do if he had to learn all the rules that govern and guide the wilderness; I don't think rules really exist. But I can't take my kin, either. I don't want to put them at risk there. So I leave them at risk *here*."

Hannerle turned away from the window. "Here?"

"In this city, where demons still hide and idiots still try to assassinate me. *I'll* survive," she added bitterly. "I always have. But they won't. I've lost my kin before. I've lost—" she stopped as Hannerle put an arm around her shoulder. "I'm sorry," she whispered. "But I need Haval in my House while I'm gone. Finch will need him. And Teller.

"But if I don't go—if I don't go—"

Hannerle's arm tightened, although she didn't speak.

"I know—I know you don't want to lose him."

"No," Hannerle said, "I don't. I've never liked the games he played. I didn't like what it did to him, what it made of him. I saw what he could become if he walked away—but I wanted to see that, and we both know Haval's good at controlling what people see. I don't want him to be devoured by what he was. And Jewel? He played games that only men of power play. He had no obvious power. He survived."

"Sometimes he barely survived. Tell me where you must go."

"I—" She almost told Hannerle that she couldn't speak about it, that the Kings were already so close to demanding the separation of her head from her shoulders. She didn't. "How much has Haval told you about me?"

Hannerle said, tersely, "Enough."

"I don't know enough, yet, to use my talent properly. If I can't use it, if I can't control what I see and when I see it, the city will eventually be destroyed."

Hannerle exhaled. "I've been dreaming," she said.

Jewel glanced out the window, and Hannerle grimaced. "Yes, well, Haval is a normal man," his wife continued, turning once again to gaze out at the trees.

"Yes. But if Haval is here, he can provide by dint of will and observation what I provide by random vision and gut instinct. He can probably do *better*. If he decides to keep them alive, they'll remain alive. I don't know what he'll do. I don't know *how* he'll do it. I don't know where the information will come from—and Hannerle, I *don't care*. I'm trying to care because I know what the cost might be to you. And if he loses you, I know what the cost will be to me."

"He *has* been bullying you."

Jewel smiled wanly. "With cause. If you were Finch, if you were Teller, if you were trapped sleeping while every *other* sleeper had finally awakened—I'd do the same. I'd be angry. I'd be—"

"Oh, hush. Tell him he's to stop. I don't want him to become what he was—but I like your Finch and your Teller. I like you—and he knows it. He's probably gambling that my affection for you is greater, in the end, than my fears and my needs."

"It shouldn't have to be."

"No. Not in a world that had no forests such as this one. I can't offer you any help. You're The Terafin; you're so far above me we shouldn't be having this conversation. The only help I can offer, in the end, is Haval."

But will you? Jewel almost said. She didn't. She had laid

her own need bare, and now she waited. She had left the decision in Hannerle's hands—and Hannerle knew it.

"I can't live in your manse," Hannerle continued. "I understand why you had me moved, but I can't live there. The West Wing will never be my home. Even if I could chase every servant out of the kitchen, I could never be comfortable. It's too large, and there are too many people in it.

"I want to go home."

Jewel nodded.

"I don't know whether residence in the manse will suit Haval in my absence. I don't know if it will suit his intent. He worked for a select few men in his time, and he did not dwell in their homes. But those men were not Finch or Teller. They were not you. If you weren't The Terafin, I would tell him to keep an eye out for your interests—but he'd do that anyway.

"I won't force him to abandon your den-kin. But I'm not of a mind to make it particularly *easy* for him, either. He knew I'd be angry when he had me moved. He knew I'd hate to be surrounded by people in positions of power. He expects me to be angry now, and I find with Haval it's often best to give what he expects."

Jewel frowned. "But he knows people so well, he observes so much. If he's certain—"

"I've been dreaming," Hannerle replied, voice low. "And I have seen things in my dreams that you might see only in nightmare. I've been safe. I've been here, in the heart of my home; the scenery on the outside changes. But my windows don't break, and none of the violence or death crosses my threshold; I witness it, but I'm not threatened by it.

"And I've seen enough, Jewel." She closed her eyes. "I will not speak of it, not even here. I hope, when I wake, it becomes as distant and vague as nightmare. I know—I know what you fear. I know why you must leave. It's been explained to me in a hundred different ways.

"I don't feel it's fair that you're the only hope the city has. I think it's appalling. What do we have *Kings* for, if not tasks like this? You don't deserve to bear the burden of the entire city. But we mostly don't get what we deserve in this life."

"That's what my Oma always told me."

"Smart woman."

"And scary."

"Come, Jewel. Take me to my husband."

Jewel closed her eyes.

When she opened them again, she was in the West Wing. Hannerle's hand was clasped tightly in both of her own; Adam held the other, his eyes still closed.

"Adam," Jewel said.

He opened them and met her gaze. Hannerle's eyes opened as he withdrew his hand and set it in his lap. Haval had not moved an inch. His expression shifted only as his wife's eyes narrowed in recognition.

She said, in a much creakier voice than the voice she'd used in the dreaming, "I've a few words to say to you, Haval."

His brows rose. As a greeting, it wasn't promising. "Of course. If I may ask for a moment of privacy," he added, glancing pointedly at Adam and Jewel.

Hannerle's hand tightened briefly around Jewel's. "Help me up," she said, as if The Terafin were the least significant person in the room. Jewel nodded to Adam, and Adam pulled the pillows that lay decoratively at the foot of the bed; together, they propped Hannerle up. She hardly seemed to notice; her lips had set in a thin line, and she was glaring at her husband.

Her husband, in response, seemed to wilt. The patina of self-confident patrician deserted him. Jewel *knew* this was deliberate affectation, but felt a pang of sympathy anyway.

"Don't you dare," Hannerle said, proving that if she was not as observant as Haval—and Jewel doubted anyone could be—she was still fully capable of noticing what went on beneath her nose, even if that nose happened to be pointing up beneath narrowed eyes. "I have a few words to say to you," she said.

"Hannerle—can it wait until the children are gone?"

Hannerle snorted. It was a far weaker sound than it should have been, but it didn't matter. "What have you been doing while I've been ill?"

"Making dresses, love. And two suits."

"And that's all?"

"I've had a few conversations, most with young Jewel."

"Conversations, you said?" She turned to look at Jewel. "I

think you'd better leave. I know how you feel about lying in general, and I have *some* regard for my husband's dignity."

Jewel retrieved her hand and stood far too quickly. She nodded at the Chosen, and they headed toward the door. Adam left first. Through the closed door, Jewel could hear Hannerle's voice rise in pitch and volume; she couldn't make out the words, which was probably a mercy.

Jewel did not join her den for dinner. She chose to remain in the West Wing instead, in the comfort of the great room. The great room was occupied by the Chosen who served as her shadows, her domicis, and one very bored, very whiny cat. Finch came just before the start of the middle dinner hour. They didn't have the chance to converse; Hectore was waiting, and Finch immediately joined him.

"Jarven will most likely be in the dining hall," she warned the Araven merchant.

He laughed. "That will most certainly make my evening. I suspect it will somewhat sour his." He glanced at his servant; Andrei's expression made clear that the warning meant for Hectore found favor in his eyes; he clearly disliked Jarven. But Finch found neither man off-putting. She was diffident, polite, and appeared to be entirely at ease in their company—something Teller could not feign.

"You will not be joining us, Terafin?" Hectore asked.

"No. I'm afraid the events of the afternoon have thoroughly destroyed my schedule, and there are some matters to which I must attend while I am still on my feet."

Hectore offered her a perfect bow. Andrei did not; he had retreated into the role of servant, and he looked as if he intended to stay there. The great room was therefore silent—except for whining cat. "Do *not* scratch the furniture, Shadow. The Master of the Household Staff is already angry with me." Angry was too paltry a word. Enraged? Yes, that was more suitable.

Meralonne's strict instructions on the doors that could—and could not—be used would fan the flames. Avandar brought wine; Jewel stared at it. She did not generally drink, except where social circumstance mandated it.

And the knock on the door indicated that this might be one of those occasions. "It's Haval," she told her domicis. "Please, see him in."

Haval chose to present himself as a deflated, older man. Jewel watched him. She felt sympathy for an expression that was, in all likelihood genuine; Haval's lies almost always were. She indicated that he should sit, and Avandar placed a glass of wine in his hand; he accepted it absently.

"Hannerle was angry," Jewel said.

"She was." He glanced at her and frowned.

He knows, she thought, unsurprised. Haval was one of nature's liars; Hannerle was not. People believed that any man who was thoroughly encumbered by honesty could not be lied to effectively; Jewel believed the opposite. Lies were a particular type of work, and it was work an honest man might never fully appreciate.

"What did you say to my wife?"

"I believe she will have to answer that," Jewel replied. She lifted her own glass and held it between them, looking at Haval as if through a facet-less prism. "You'll stay."

"Yes." The look of exhaustion fell away instantly, as if brushed aside. He observed her, his eyes sharp, his gaze steady. "It was cleverly done, Jewel. I will give you that. I do not think I could have achieved the same result, and I am a man of both experience and guile. What did you do?"

Jewel exhaled. She could refuse to answer the question a second time, but knew, from long experience, that he would get the information he desired in one way or another. Acceding with grace was something she could afford at the end of this bitterly long day. "I threw myself entirely upon her mercy," she replied. "It's not something you could do."

One brow rose.

"She knows you too well, Haval. If you dissembled in any fashion, she would be insulted."

He smiled. "Indeed. And she knows that you are not me. You cannot lie to save your life, Jewel. You hide none of your weaknesses; indeed, where my wife is concerned, you expose them all. You cannot be The Terafin in her presence; you have a weakness where autocratic older women are concerned.

"You will leave?"

She nodded.

"When?"

"I'm not certain, Haval. Soon. It has to be soon."

"You are waiting for something?"

She nodded.

"But you do not know what."

"No. I *know* that I'll know when the moment arrives. Until then I will try to put my House in order and prepare the people I trust for my departure."

"What will you do about Rymark?"

She shied away from the question.

"Very well. Tell me what you want, Jewel. Be explicit. Offer guidelines, and if it pleases you, strict codes of behavior. I will speak with Devon, if you will allow it."

She nodded. "Haval—"

"I will require a budget. While you are within your manse, I will report to you. I will answer any question you are adept enough to ask; I will hide nothing."

"It's not me who'll be asking the questions," she replied, deciding. "It's Finch."

"You are aware that she has already been the target of one assassination attempt?"

She froze.

"Ah. I see she failed to report it."

"How—how do you know?"

"Jarven. Finch believes Jarven found it both entertaining and even amusing."

"You don't."

"I believe Jarven is angry."

Jewel frowned. "He's not the type of man to get angry over something like that," she finally said. "I don't have the same affection for Jarven that Finch does, but I have a good sense of who he is; Finch has taken no pains to hide it." She grimaced. "He reminds me of my cats."

Shadow hissed in astonished outrage.

Haval chuckled. "An apt description. I have a great deal of respect for your cats."

"I haven't noticed, Haval, that you offered a great deal of respect to Jarven on the few occasions I've seen you together."

"Ah. Jarven is to me what your cats are to you."

Jewel laughed. Shadow looked confused. He couldn't quite tease out the insult he was certain was in the statement.

"Finch is an easy person to underestimate. It will be her chief strength in the coming months. Jarven is angry, Jewel.

Understand what his anger means. Jarven could make a game of assassination attempts—but they would be just that. If he is aware of them beforehand, they become a test. He did not see this one coming; he takes it as a personal insult.

"I do not know what he expects of Finch."

"He expects her to hold the House," Jewel replied. "In my name. For as long as it must be held."

"He expects that the first attempt will not be the last," Haval replied.

The hand in her lap tightened. She drank slowly and deliberately. "I expect her," she said, forcing her jaw to relax, "to do exactly that. She'll have Teller." Her hand tightened again.

"You are afraid."

"Haval, I'm *always* afraid." She laid the stark words between them, meeting and holding his gaze.

His smile lost its edge. "Yes," he said, "you are."

"Will you go back to the store, or will you be resident in the manor?"

"I will retain rooms in the manse for my use; I will, however, require some time to tend to my business. I have taken a select handful of commissions during my stay in House Terafin, and I must tend to them. It will also ease Hannerle's mind." He lifted his own glass and studied its contents.

"Keep them safe," she told him abruptly. "Don't treat this as another lesson, Haval. You know me. You've known me for my entire adult life. You know what's important to me. You know why it's important. I won't *be* here. You *will*. Be what I can't be. See what I can't see. *Keep them safe.* Do whatever you have to do."

"You are aware that what I might consider necessary and what you yourself would deem acceptable are not always consistent." He set his glass down. "I am not you. You have, by dint of birth and talent, survived in an environment that most men of power would consider lax. You are likely to continue to do that. Finch, however, is without many of your advantages.

"What limits will you place upon me?"

"You want me to say 'none.'"

He failed to acknowledge the statement.

"But I won't. It's true, you're not me. It's true I won't be here. But, Haval—*they* will. You told me I needed to trust them. You were right. I do. I trust them to make those decisions in my absence. Do what Finch will accept. Don't do more."

"Very well." He rose. "Terafin. Hannerle will be fit to travel in two days' time, in Adam's estimation. If you are to be present for those two days, I will content myself with waiting on my wife."

He paused at the door. "I will make one further request."

Jewel tensed but nodded. "And that?"

"One member of your den is not, in any obvious way, meaningfully employed. I wish to change that."

She frowned. "Jester?"

"Indeed. He is an interesting young man; he has mastered the art of invisibility in one of the more difficult ways."

"Jester's hardly invisible."

"Exactly."

"Jester doesn't care for the patriciate. He's fine with Terafin, because it's ours."

"It is *yours*," Haval replied.

"If he's willing," Jewel finally said. "Then, yes. I won't order him to obey you."

"No, of course not."

Chapter Twenty-nine

"ANDREI, YOU'VE BEEN positively morose all evening," Hectore said to his servant when the Araven carriage at last rolled away from the Terafin manse. "Was the Terafin dining hall so difficult?"

"I'm sure your food was excellent," was Andrei's sour reply. He did not, of course, join Hectore for the meal, although food was offered in the servants' mess. Andrei seldom joined a gathering of such servants; he had surprised Hectore by accepting the obligatory invitation.

"The company was fascinating," was Hectore's genial reply.

"I'm sure it was. The company in the back kitchen was likewise fascinating. I now live in fear that I will come to the attention of the infamous Master of the Household Staff."

"I should hope not!" Hectore was willing to cede some of Andrei's time and service to Terafin, but he had standards; Andrei was not under the auspices of any *other* Household Staff.

"You are determined, given the active presence of not only Jarven ATerafin but Haval Arwood, to continue in your present course?"

"Does that question even require an answer, Andrei? Finch is a civil and pleasant young woman; if I am not involved, Jarven will likely corrupt the poor girl."

"Hectore, please," Andrei replied, pinching the bridge of

his nose. "The girl, as you call her, is well aware of Jarven's various foibles; I cannot understand how she holds him in such great affection."

"But she clearly does. Perhaps he has mellowed."

"You don't believe that."

"Why not? I certainly have."

"You were never the man Jarven was."

"I'll take that as a compliment. Come, Andrei. What exactly did you see in your inspection that caused such a souring?"

Andrei exhaled. "The Terafin kitchens are appallingly lax in their security. The House Guard and its hiring practices are suspect. It is my belief that it wouldn't be much harder to infiltrate the House through the time-honored practice of servants than it would be to walk in through the front foyer.

"Some precautions will be required where food is involved."

"Surely we've seen that already."

"The Merchant Authority is not the manse," was his stiff reply. "The Terafin Chosen are good. I'll give them that. If the guards in your employ could be expected to serve at that standard, you would complain less about them. It is Teller who concerns me. Finch will be less at risk for a variety of reasons; the right-kin will not. Security around the right-kin is, and has been, tighter, but I am not certain he is yet at Gabriel's level of competence." He glanced, almost rigidly, out the window.

"Things will change," he said. "And we'll have little control in the end over their eventual shape."

"We'll have the control we always did," Hectore replied. "As long as we continue to be moving targets. Who hired the assassin? Was it Rymark?"

"No. If eyewitness reports—suspiciously *convenient* reports—are to be believed, Rymark did indeed meet the woman before the attempt; he was not, however, responsible for her presence."

"Who, Andrei?"

"I am not yet certain. The necessity for certainty, given your continued commitment, is now high. I will also have words with Avram on the morrow. Hectore, expect things to become unpleasant."

"How unpleasant?"

"If we are lucky, we will avoid the darkness of the Henden of 410."

Hectore fell silent and remained that way for the duration of the carriage ride home.

The kitchen that night was crowded. Jewel had slipped into clothing suitable for her early years in the West Wing, to Avandar's disapproval, and she had commandeered a chair at the head of the table. Angel sat to her left; Teller, to her right. Beside Teller, in clothing far more casual than Jewel's, sat Finch. Arann had taken the chair beside Angel; Jester sat beside Arann. Daine and Adam filled in the empty seats. Shadow wedged himself between Angel and Jewel's chair, and dropped his chin onto the table's surface.

"If you bite the table," she told him, "I'm going to be angry. Scratching counts."

He sniffed. "Tables don't *bleed*." He eyed Avandar rather malevolently.

There was an empty chair that Carver would have occupied, to one side of Jester. Jewel looked at it once, but couldn't bring herself to tell people to shuffle over. She understood why it had been left empty. It spoke of the hope—the increasingly painful hope—that he would walk through the kitchen door and take his place in their councils.

"So, what happened to your hair?" Jester asked, before Jewel could bring the meeting to a start. Since he'd asked what was probably the most pressing question in everyone's mind, she didn't speak; she looked, instead, to Angel.

Angel, predictably, shrugged. "It was time," he said, as if his hair had not been his defining characteristic for as long as they'd known him. "It was a gesture of respect for my father." He started to say more, stopped, and signed, *I'm done*.

It was understood, among the den. You shared what you wanted to share. You shared what you *could*. When you couldn't, people mostly left you alone. And some days, that was hard.

"I'm sorry I haven't called kitchen in the last few weeks," Jewel said. "Because if I'd been living here, I would have. None of you would have gotten any sleep."

Teller hesitated.

"You don't need to write it down," she told him. "I close my eyes and I can see it. I'm not going to forget—and if I did, I wouldn't want reminders.

"You all know—you've always known—that I'm talent-born. I'm seer-born. It's been useful, sometimes. I don't know if you remember Evayne, but she's seer-born as well. And she can look and see what she needs to see. I think. I've never asked her directly.

"What I did in the grounds—with the trees, what I did in *Avantari* and here, for the terrace, it's *part* of that somehow. I don't understand how, or why. Changing the shape of a garden or a palace doesn't seem to have much to do with random glimpses of the future.

"So is the library—or what the library became. The sleeping sickness wasn't my fault, but I woke the afflicted." She hesitated again, and then said, "Those sleepers aren't the only ones we have to worry about. In any real sense, we didn't have to worry about them at all."

"They would have died," Adam said quietly.

"Yes. And we saved them. But asleep they wouldn't kill. And awakened, they couldn't destroy a city. You all know the phrase 'When the Sleepers wake,' right?"

Nods, one or two murmurs. Silence that held under-standing.

"Yes. Those Sleepers. They're here. They're here, beneath Moorelas' Sanctum. The gods worked to put them to sleep—to force them to sleep—until some unspecified appointed hour. No, I don't know what that hour is. I just know that they sleep.

"We've all assumed that the demons—that the god—avoids the Empire because of the Twin Kings and the magi and the makers. We've assumed that we're somehow a threat to the god and his demons. He'll send them in ones and twos, but he's never come down here with an army—and we *know* he can field one.

"The Kings' armies faced such an army in the South. So, that part's not guesswork. But we felt confident that he wouldn't bring them here. And we were right—but not for the right reasons. He doesn't want the Sleepers to wake.

"And bringing a large army of demons to the city might be the thing that wakes them. I think the god doesn't care about *us*. He cares about them."

"What are they?" Finch asked quietly.

"The most powerful servants of the Winter Queen. The most powerful hunters of the Wild Hunt. They don't care about us, and we're living on top of them. Meralonne thinks it likely that they'll take our existence as an affront, and they'll destroy us for the presumption of playing in their bedchamber, so to speak, while they slept.

"And *they will*."

They all watched Jewel now, arrested. She swallowed and nodded. "Three dreams," she said quietly. "Three long, horrible dreams." She looked at their familiar, *living* faces as if they were anchors that could hold her in place while the storm raged around her. And they were. They always had been.

"They're beautiful," she whispered, staring into the lamp's fire. "Beautiful, flawless, and entirely without mercy. We're like rats. No, we're like cockroaches. It's *that* bad. Nothing the god-born can say will *matter*. Nothing anyone can say will matter."

"How do we stop them from waking?"

She hesitated again. "Right now? Kill me." She exhaled. "But that only works for now. It doesn't work soon. I don't know why. They take orders from one person, and one alone. Ariane. The Winter Queen. But had they obeyed her orders, they would never have been imprisoned in their long sleep. They're wild. They can't be fully tamed.

"And these are *not* their lands."

Teller said, "You can do something."

She closed her eyes. "Yes."

"Jay?"

She rose. She rose and walked away from the table, to pace at its head, her hands behind her back, her head bent. She hated fear, but she had not lied to Haval: she was always afraid. As long as fear didn't stop her from moving forward, she accepted it. "What I did to the manse, I might be able to do to the city. But if I don't learn *how*, I'll destroy it. I won't *mean* to destroy it," she whispered. "But—I'll be like a god. I'll be able to do anything I want. Do you know how I changed the palace?" She stopped and turned to face them. "I told the earth to clean up after itself before it left.

"Just that. I didn't tell the earth what to build, or how. I didn't tell the earth to wake the wild stone that was part of *Avantari's* foundation. I told it to *clean up*. No one was killed by the earth; the demons killed dozens." She spread her hands out. "I don't want to go that route. I don't want it. I don't know what I'll be. I don't even know who."

"Jay," Teller said, rising. "Tell us. Tell us what you saw."

"Three men," she whispered. "Three. They might have been gods. They had swords of blue fire. They spoke a language I don't understand, but I didn't *need* to understand it. I was home. We were *all* home. They called air, they called earth, they called water—and gods, gods, *the water*—" She shook her head. "They couldn't destroy Terafin, but the rest of the city? It was a slaughter. It was like stepping on an anthill—but worse.

"And then they came here." She closed her eyes. "They came here. There were things in my forest that I've never seen; there were people I've met only once, in a dream. Here, they were my army. They were my defenders. And they were forced to fight.

"But we weren't a match for them, not that way. If these lands weren't mine—"

"Jay—"

"And I knew. In the dream, I knew. I have to speak to the Oracle. I have to walk the Oracle's path—whatever or wherever it is—and survive it. I don't know when it was. In my dream, I mean. I don't know when—but it's soon. It's summer air. I don't know if it's months from now, or the summer after—but it's soon. It's too soon." She lifted her chin. "Adam," she said.

He met her gaze, held it. He was quiet, and reminded her absurdly of young Teller. "I am to go with you," he said.

She blinked. Nodded slowly.

"Why *him*?" Shadow cut in. "He's *scrawny* and *stupid*. He's a *kitten*."

She didn't answer.

"When?" Finch finally asked. She asked without surprise. As if she knew. Jewel glanced at Teller; he looked exhausted.

"I don't know. I don't know the exact date. I'll know when it's time to leave. I don't know how much warning I'll have, other than that. Enough time, I hope, to pack rations for overland travel. And no, I have no idea how long we'll be forced to travel. But being Terafin where I'm going isn't going get me free food." She tried for a smile.

"Angel's going with you," Teller said.

She glanced at Angel. "Yes."

"Good. What do you need us to do?"

"Survive." She grimaced. "No, I need you to do better than that. I need you to hold the House. I need Finch to become regent, if a regent is demanded."

Teller and Finch exchanged a glance.

"Will it matter?" Jester asked.

Finch frowned. "What?"

"Will it matter? If we're looking at the destruction of an entire city, will all the politicking among the powerful amount to anything?"

"It will matter." To the den's surprise—Jewel's included—it was Avandar who answered. Avandar was not a man the den interrupted under normal circumstances; they were silent, waiting for the rest of his reply.

Shadow, however, snorted. "Of *course* it matters," he said; he could not let Avandar have the final word while he was in the room. Not on matters about which he had any stray knowledge.

"She lives *here*. It is *easy* for her to get lost. She can get lost in her *dreams*. She can get lost in her forest. She can get lost in the high wilderness. Mortals are *stupid*. They get lost *anywhere*.

"But she is not *as* stupid. She is tangled up in you. In all of *you*. She is tied down by this *house*. She *needs* you to be here. She *needs* the House. Without it all, she will not be right. In the head," he added. "And if she is not right in the head, she will make monsters and *nightmares*. She will make a city that is broken like *she is*." He snorted again, and stamped his front paws.

"Tell *them*," he said, nudging Jewel hard enough that she almost lost her footing. "*Tell them*."

Jewel, having found her footing, let her hands slide to her hips. She glared at the cat. The cat, undaunted, glared back, hissing.

"She is *afraid* to be broken," he said, still returning her glare. "She is afraid to be *alone*. She is afraid she won't *know* what is real, and then *she* will break everything. So, *yes*, stupid *boy*, it *matters*."

"Thank you, Shadow," Teller said, as the cat drew another breath. "I think we understand what's at stake, now."

Jewel met Finch's gaze. "I'd transfer the House to you. I'd declare you my heir. But we both know how well that worked last time it was tried in this House." She couldn't keep the bitterness out of her voice; she didn't even try. "In theory, I'll be traveling to the Menorans. There will be some significant difficulty with the trade route and the Royal Commission, and it will require my presence.

"But I don't expect that to stand for long, because the Chosen won't be coming with me."

Teller inhaled, and Jewel held up a hand, forestalling him. "I want them here for you. They know the House. They know the guards. They know that in serving you, they best serve my interests. I expect Torvan and I will have the crowning glory of a fight about this, but it doesn't matter. I want them *here*, and in the end, they take their orders from me. While I'm gone, they'll take their orders from Finch. And you, Teller, if you've a mind to give orders.

"I might come back quickly. I don't know how time passes, where we'll be going. I might come back months from now. There's nothing I can plan for. All I can give you is the time before my departure. Haval will stay in the West Wing," she added. "At least part time.

"In my absence, my rooms will be closed. No one except Meralonne is to be granted access to them under any circumstance; Meralonne will reside within the suite."

"He's going to be living here?" Finch asked, brows rising.

"Yes. He'll perform the necessary duties of a House Mage in a crisis. If he gives you strange instructions about the doors in the manse, *listen* to him. Obey him where it won't cause bloodshed."

She resumed her seat. For a brief moment, she lowered her face into her hands, and sat in silence. Then she lifted her head and said, "Carver is still alive."

The silence broke with questions, with exclamations, with the beginning of a frenzied kind of hope that could be mistaken, at a distance, for joy. But Jewel's silence quenched it.

"He's alive. Shadow says no one will find him; not Snow or Night, not the Winter King. I believe I have some chance of finding him—but I won't, if I don't undergo the Oracle's test. The Kings won't care about Carver. I'm not sure The Ten will either—not in comparison to the fate of the rest of the city.

"But Carver is somewhere the Sleepers know. Meralonne thinks the doors that opened into unexpected places opened because the Sleepers are restless; they're almost awake. Carver is somewhere *they* know.

"Meralonne can't go. Celleriant can't. But Meralonne thinks I'm insignificant enough that I *might* be able to do it safely."

"What's unsafe entail?" Jester asked.

"The Sleepers will become aware enough of me that they'll wake."

He whistled. "That's unsafe. You're not going to mention Carver to the Kings."

"Not unless they physically torture me, no." She was silent for a full beat.

Jester's smile was a very strange one; it rested on his face like a wound. "If you're looking for arguments from me, don't. I could care less if most of the city burned in hell. Get Carver back."

"You'll be *in* the city if it burns in hell," she pointed out dryly.

He didn't even blink. "Bring him back."

"We're all in agreement?" she asked softly.

Silence. She held up her right hand and placed it on the table, palm down. Jester's followed almost instantly. Angel's was third. Shadow, who did not notably use den-sign, having among other things no hands, hit the table with both paws. And claws. Jewel ground her teeth.

Adam looked at the table, and the hands. He looked at Daine. Daine looked troubled, but took the time to explain that this was, in essence, a vote.

"Jay's not bound by the vote, but if she's asking for one, it'll have real weight."

"And we are voting on the risk? On taking the risk?" Daine nodded.

Adam looked mildly confused. Troubled. He looked up and met Jewel's clear gaze. In Torra he said, "This is a decision made by Matriarchs. Such decisions are made all the time. It is a burden placed on the leader of our people: to make the hard decisions so the rest of us aren't torn apart by guilt and the blood-demands of kin."

In the same language, Jewel asked, "What would your mother have done?"

"She would grieve," he replied, without hesitance. "But she would never risk the whole of her clan for the sake of one of its members—unless that member were her heir, and only daughter. If she asked for a vote to be taken, there could only be one outcome: we would vote to save our kin.

"We would vote, because the loss of kin is a known evil, a painful one, and the loss of everything is inconceivable. There is only one way this vote can go." He did not lay a hand on the table.

Jewel felt a brief stab of anger.

Adam said, "This is not the only time you will be faced with decisions like this one. I'm sorry. I will never be Matriarch. It's never something I've had to face."

"And Margret?"

"Margret avoided making this decision. From what you've said, it cost Arkosa Elena. I do not think she will make the same mistake again."

You don't understand, she wanted to tell him. *You didn't live with Carver. He's* not *kin to you.* But the words wouldn't leave her mouth, because she remembered Margret. She remembered Yollana. What Yollana had done in preparation for a future that only Yollana could clearly see, Jewel *could not* have done: She had sacrificed—murdered—three of her clansmen in order to keep the tiniest part of the hidden pathway open against future need. And yet, it was that, and only that, that had allowed them to elude capture by the *Kialli* and the human forces who served their purposes.

She swallowed. She noted that there were only three hands on the table. Arann, Finch, and Teller had not responded. And she struggled with the sense of bitter betrayal that gripped her as she looked at the lack of their hands.

Teller's hand came, palm down, as she thought this. "I'll trust you," he said evenly. "I'll trust you to know what risks are worth taking; we won't be there. We won't see."

As his words filled the silence, Arann's hand joined theirs, and Finch's.

Before Daine could vote, Jewel lifted her hand. "I'm sorry," she said softly. "Adam is right."

"He's not," Finch said. "He asks you to take the entire burden onto your own shoulders, one way or the other. You're not Voyani. You're not—as you always tell him—Matriarch. You're Jay. Jewel Markess ATerafin. Teller's right, of course. We trust you. But we're aware of what the risk means. If we vote against, if we *all* vote against, or if enough of us do—it spares you the pain of making that decision on your own."

Jewel shook her head. Her eyes stung. "No, it really doesn't." She rose. "I'm exhausted. If we're done, I'm going to try to sleep."

They weren't done. Or at least Jewel wasn't. When she left the kitchen, Angel followed, signing briefly. She signed in return and turned to the Chosen.

"We're going to visit the House shrine."

If they were surprised, they kept it to themselves; they had kept the entirety of the kitchen conversation to themselves as well. The den had come to accept the Chosen as almost literal shadows; they spoke freely in their presence. They were still wary of the House Guard, but that made sense.

Angel returned from his room with two things he'd failed to bring to the kitchen: the first, a sword. The second, a companion. The companion looked only vaguely familiar to Jewel. He was tall, wide, bearded; his hair was pulled back from his face in what she presumed was a Northern braid; he had the look of Arrend about his jaw and eyes. He carried an ax, on the other hand; it was a sizable and impressive weapon, and it did nothing to make him seem harmless.

"With your permission," Angel said, in Weston that sounded far too formal, "Terrick will accompany us to the shrine, and then, to the library." His smile folded into an awkward expression. "That ax came from the armory that used to be an office. He won't use it until he sees where it came from."

Jewel nodded, made awkward and stilted by the presence of a stranger. Angel wasn't likewise encumbered. But Terrick walked behind, with the Chosen; Angel walked by her side. Shadow, she sent off to Ariel's room, because she knew the girl would desperately miss the cat when they left.

She just didn't consider it wise to leave the cats behind if she wasn't present.

The walk to the House shrine involved walking past the three shrines erected to the Triumvirate: the shrine to Cormaris, lord of Wisdom, Reymaris, lord of Justice, and the Mother. Tonight, Jewel stopped to say a brief prayer at each, although she knew that the words she spoke wouldn't reach the gods. Angel waited, but did not offer like prayers. He looked slightly nervous but also determined.

She wondered what it was about.

But when she climbed the stairs to the altar at the heart of the small House shrine, she knew. He removed his scabbarded sword from his belt beneath the well-tended lamps that provided light, and he laid it upon the altar.

"My hair," he said, "marked me as a retainer of Weyrdon. My father was Weyrdon's man. He was sent into the Empire to fulfill a quest that Weyrdon himself didn't fully understand, and I—I was meant to take it up when he died before he had completed it.

"And I did. And I have."

"What—what quest?"

"To find, in the Empire, a worthy Lord. A Lord for whom I would lay down my life gladly and without hesitation. When The Terafin offered us all the House Name, I wouldn't take it. I told you then—"

"That you wouldn't become ATerafin until and unless I was The Terafin. I remember."

"Yes. Because I'd found the only person I was willing to follow."

"Angel—"

"I know. You know. You've always known. But even if I knew, I couldn't let go of the Weyrdon crown. It defined me. It was part of who I was."

"And now?"

"Nothing of me belongs to Weyrdon. I know I'm not always impressive," he added, but without self-consciousness, "but I understand you. I know who you are and what you want. I won't always agree, but blind obedience isn't part of service." He dropped to one knee, which Jewel found painfully awkward.

"Angel, don't."

"I have to," he said gravely. "Terafin, I, Angel, son of Garroc, offer you my oathsworn service." He said it without a trace of embarrassment, the gravity of his perfect tone eradicating his unnatural position. Closing his eyes, he took the scabbard and hilt in separate hands and drew the blade.

It was black.

Beneath the lamps in the shrine, it reflected no light at all.

Avandar was not at Jewel's side, but she felt him stiffen at a distance. "That sword came from the war room."

Angel nodded. It didn't, to his eyes, look like much of a sword at all; it looked like tarnished, neglected silver—but worse. "Until tonight, I've been unable to draw it from its scabbard." He hesitated, and then, without expression, drew the edge of the blade across his palm.

No matter what the sword looked like, its edge was sharp enough, clean enough, to cut. "I don't know what the House Name requires," he said. "But in the North, such an oath is made—and affirmed—in blood."

Jewel wasn't *from* the North. Neither, in any real sense, was Angel. But Terrick waited at the foot of the shrine, watching, his gaze hooded and nearly unblinking. There was a story in his presence here; Jewel felt that he had come to bear witness.

And it was not, after all, the first time she had accepted an oath such as this with blood of her own. "You will be ATerafin?"

"While you live. Only while you live."

She held out her hand. In the light of the shrine, against her palm, she could see the single line that was Celleriant's oath; white, healed, but part of the geography of her palm. Angel offered her the sword's hilt; she took it. The hilt was wrapped in leather; it was warm, but simple. She hoped that the sword did not feel the need to cut off her hand; she was far more aware of Meralonne's opinion of the blade than she had been when she had given Angel almost nonchalant permission to go into the room and find a weapon that suited him.

She made the cut, and he brought his left hand down upon hers. As their hands joined, the sword began to glow. The black surface of its flat vanished, like shadow destroyed by strong light. It was not Meralonne's sword; not Celleriant's. It didn't *look* like an impressive, magical blade. But in the instant that Jewel pronounced Angel ATerafin, in some odd blend of Northern custom and House custom, it looked whole, new, perfect.

"Does it speak to you?" she asked, as she lifted her hand.

"Not yet," he replied, as he took the hilt from her. He drew a cloth to wipe the blade's edge clean, and frowned. There was no blood on the blade.

There was, Jewel saw, no blood on his hands—and none at all on hers.

"I am so grateful," she said, quietly enough that it barely carried to Angel, "that I won't have to choose one of those damn weapons."

Terrick said nothing.

He said nothing when Angel drew the blade he had been, until that moment, unable to draw. He said nothing when Angel cut his palm and extended his bleeding hand. Nor did he speak when The Terafin took his weapon and made a like cut in her own. He might have pointed out to Angel that the customs of the South did not include—and did not privilege—blood; that instead binding oaths were legal documents.

He didn't. He listened. He bore witness. He remembered his youth. He remembered standing, as Angel now stood, before Garroc—a man he had detested on first sight; a man he had been so loath to trust. Yet in the end, Garroc had become the center of his life: the man he was willing to follow and to serve.

Garroc had not, at that time, found a Lord *he* was willing to offer such a binding oath. And when he had, Terrick had been angry. Angry and, yes, a little afraid. He was sworn to Garroc; what would become of Terrick when Garroc was absorbed into Weyrdon's service?

He remembered Garroc's oath of allegiance; he remembered Garroc's hour of cursing the first time he had attempted to tend his own hair, to style it in the Weyrdon crown. Garroc had been fastidious about braiding—

unbound hair was a hazard in combat—but the Weyrdon hair? He vented his considerable spleen at the *pretension* of it. At the stupidity of it. But he accepted it as a necessity if he wished to make his allegiance known. And he did, in the end.

But he had taken his hair down to leave Weyrdon and begin a fruitless quest in the Southern Empire of which Arrend was only theoretically a part. He had walked away from public honor and public oaths. He had walked away from everyone.

Only Terrick had followed, but he could not follow Garroc into Kalakar; he could not follow Garroc into the Southern skirmishes, although he tried. Nor could he, in the end, follow Garroc into exile in the Free Towns.

And it was exile. Garroc found a woman, married her, and began to *farm*. The great quest that had caused his public disgrace—and the private disgrace of failure—was abandoned. He could not return to Weyrdon as a failure.

Garroc died a failure in the Free Towns at the Empire's borders. And his only child, Angel, arrived in Averalaan, wearing the Weyrdon crown on his head, and on his sleeve, an anger and resentment against Weyrdon that was second only to Terrick's. Terrick had feared the consequences of the presumption of styling himself *of* Weyrdon. But Weyrdon had—against all hope—accepted Angel's hair as a profound gesture of respect for Garroc. For Garroc and his quest.

Years, Terrick had waited. Years, he'd worked behind the wicket of the Port Authority, growing older and more gray as the time passed. Garroc's death had not released him; it had not ended his service.

As The Terafin frowned and lifted the hand Terrick had just seen her cut, his eyes rounded, his breath—momentarily—stopped, as if the motion of breath was too profane for what he now witnessed. He had seen her draw the edge of the sword across her palm; he had noted the tightening of her jaw, the compression of her lips. She did not appear to be a woman accustomed to shedding blood, either her own or others.

But the hand she lifted now had not been cut. Nor had blood pooled in its multiple lines. Angel lifted his, his eyes narrowing as he confronted an equally unblemished palm.

Terrick exhaled. His hand dropped to the haft of an ax that had been given into his keeping. He could not think of it as his. Not yet. But it felt solid as he gripped it; solid, heavy, natural.

The Terafin's domicis approached on a path that Terrick had clearly heard he did not walk. His presence caught The Terafin's attention.

"Terafin."

"We're fine, Avandar."

"The sword?"

"Yes, well."

"Was there difficulty?"

"I don't think so."

The domicis was clearly not enamored of the answer. But he did not stride up the steps of the shrine, and he did not demand a full explanation. Then, again, he glanced at Terrick before he fell silent; clearly, he was not accustomed to strangers so close to this shrine.

The Terafin descended the stairs as Angel joined Terrick; she glanced once over her shoulder at the altar, as if searching for someone. Then she shook her head, straightened her shoulders, and faced Terrick gravely. "Angel says you've come to see the heart of my personal quarters."

"I wasn't aware that your personal quarters were an armory."

"It's probably not common knowledge," she replied, a slight smile changing the shape of her lips. "Although given the speed at which news travels, it wouldn't surprise me much if it were. I should warn you that my personal quarters are not architecturally consistent with the rest of the Terafin manse."

Terrick frowned and raised a brow in Angel's direction. Angel's answering smile contained a slight edge buried beneath genuine amusement. It offered warning, of a type. Angel did not feel that Terrick was in danger of losing anything but dignity.

It was Garroc's smile.

The Chosen were, in Terrick's opinion, excellent guards. They were more formal and more hierarchical than Weyrdon's closest retainers, but that was to be expected of Southern guards. He therefore expected—and received—no acknowledgment. But each of the Chosen present had noted Terrick's ax, and the subtle shift in their expression and their position told him much. They did not openly offer insult; they did not demand that he set the weapon down.

The Terafin did not; what she did not do, they would not. She was not their equal in height, and she did not yet have the presence of her predecessor, but she walked with purpose, and spoke with certainty as she led the way to her personal quarters. Terrick was uncertain what to expect when the doors opened and she entered them; what he did not expect was the way she suddenly vanished.

"It's safe," Angel said, in Rendish. "While she's here, it's safe." Without another word, Angel followed his Lord. Terrick grimaced. He had grown accustomed to the way the Southerners flaunted their magic on street corners and in expensive buildings, but he had the native Rendish distrust of enchantment. It did not stop him from following.

No, what stopped Terrick was the color of the open sky above their heads. He heard wind, felt breeze. There were no clouds; there were trees—and the trees seemed rooted in floor that was pale golden planking that extended in all directions as far as the eye could see, as if it were the plains of the Free Towns.

The trees, he saw, served as posts and shelving.

He was utterly still, his hand loose upon the haft of the ax, his jaw tight.

"This—this is where she lives?" he asked, in Rendish.

"No. This is the Terafin library. She has a suite of rooms that's almost normal in comparison."

"And the armory?"

"This way." Angel turned to The Terafin. "Will you accompany us?"

The Terafin glanced at Terrick. After a pause, she nodded, her expression thoughtful. She joined Angel; two of the Chosen led the way.

There were no obvious outbuildings in this vast, vast room; there were gates. Gates and arches that stood without benefit of adjoining fences. They seemed decorative until the moment that the Chosen entered one and vanished. Terrick grimaced, and he was surprised to hear The Terafin's chuckle.

"I couldn't stand it either, when things first changed."

"It was not always like this?"

"No, sadly. But you get used to it."

Terrick highly doubted that this was true, but kept this to himself. When Angel walked beneath the wrought-iron arch, The Terafin surprised Terrick; she offered the Rendish man an arm. Such a gesture could be construed as a severe social criticism, but her expression—and the fact she'd waited until Angel couldn't see or comment—made clear it was not. He mirrored the gesture, and she placed her hand on the crook of his arm.

And so he entered the room Angel referred to as the armory.

Unlike the library, there was ceiling in this room. There were solid walls to either side of the doors. The doors themselves appeared to be made of thick wood; the arch into which they were set was stone. The floors were stone. The massive table that commandeered the room's center was also stone. There were no chairs.

There was one window in the far wall, tall as a man, and wide enough to step through. There appeared to be no glass and no shutters to prevent this. Beyond those windows the skies were a paler shade of the amethyst that opened above the library. But the library's skies were empty and still; the skies beyond these windows were not.

Terrick could see what he assumed were birds gliding on thermals in the distance.

He could also see what no amount of poor vision could make birds. He lowered his arm and made his way to the window, where he placed both hands on its bottom edge. There, he looked down, and down again. He had entered the Terafin manse. He had walked in its galleries. He had stored his possessions in one of its rooms.

This was no part of that manse. No part of the world that contained the Port Authority, the Merchant Authority, or the Common. He released the windowsill, turning to gaze at the walls upon which a variety of weapons were mounted.

"Angel—" He froze, the rest of the words lost to a great and terrible roar. It was like thunder, given voice and a giant's throat, and as he wheeled once again for the window, he saw the flying creatures in the air suddenly dive, as if for cover.

Angel sprinted to the window; the Chosen closed ranks around The Terafin, who had the sense she was born with, and remained where she was. But her domicis came, wearily, to see what Terrick now watched, transfixed: A frostwyrm.

A giant of the wastes. Its wings were the size of ancient trees in length, its neck their equal; its body was the size of the greatest of the seafaring merchant ships, but flesh, organic, and glittering in the pale sky.

Even at this distance, the creature was majestic. Terrifying. It raised its head, opened its jaws, and roared again, and the very ground trembled beneath Terrick's feet.

And he knew, then. He *knew*. The ax Angel had, in ignorance, given into his keeping was one of the lost blades. It had to be. It was here, and so, too, one of the creatures it had been meant to slay.

His hand shook as it gripped the ax's haft; his knuckles were white.

It had been created to fight *that* creature and its kind— but what fool would attempt such a kill? Yes, the edge of the ax might wound it, might pierce its hide—but a tailor's pins and needles might pierce mortal flesh to far greater effect.

He turned to Angel, whose hand had not touched his sword; the boy was staring, as if at a painting. The roar that so alarmed Terrick might have been silent.

"Jay," he said, forgetting for a moment that Terrick was an outsider, a foreigner, and that the woman was *The Terafin*. He would have words with Angel later.

"Please tell me that's not a dragon," she said.

"It's a white dragon."

"Avandar—"

"Yes," her domicis said. He, like Angel, watched the dragon. Unlike Angel, his expression contained no awe, no wonder. It was set, grim, weary. "It is, as you suspect, a dragon. Can you see it from there?"

"I'm not sure I want to see it."

"It will not, in my opinion, be your only opportunity; it may well be your only safe one."

The Terafin came toward the window; her Chosen came with her. But she stopped before she reached them and shook her head, lifting her hand to her throat. "No," she said quietly. "I think it best to remain out of sight."

Her domicis frowned. "I will, with your permission, kill one of your cats upon his return."

"I doubt you can," she replied. "And if you insist on trying, wait until we're *out* of the manse." She turned to Terrick. "My apologies," she said. "But I do not feel it wise to remain in this room at this time."

"Are we at risk?"

"No. But I don't think he's noticed us yet, and I'd like it to remain that way." To Avandar she added, "tell me what you know about dragons."

"Very little."

"Are they immortal?"

"Yes. But they are not—entirely—invulnerable."

"Are they more dangerous or less dangerous than the wakened Sleepers?"

"The one in the air? Much less, in my opinion. Not all *Arianni* are created equal; no more are dragonkind. There is one who is equal to the Sleepers in the destruction he can unleash, should he so choose, but he is not asleep beneath the streets of your city, and he has not—yet—emerged from the hidden lands."

The Chosen retreated.

Angel joined his Lord; he lifted his hand and his fingers danced a moment. Her reply was shorter and swifter, but she spoke no words.

For the first time, Terrick thought he understood why Angel had chosen this particular Lord. She had heard—and felt—the dragon's roar, and she had not even blinked. She called it by its Southern name, and not its Rendish variant; she understood what it was. She understood what it meant.

But it was not, he saw, her concern. She was not in awe of it; she was not afraid.

"Terrick?" Angel said, and Terrick, chagrined, shook himself. "The ax?"

The older man smiled. It was a winter smile. "I understand, at last, what Garroc sacrificed his life to achieve: You, Angel." His smile was the wolf's smile; there was no kindness in it. "And I understand and forgive Weyrdon for the choice he made.

"But this ax was not, I think, meant for me. It was meant for you."

Angel shook his head. "The sword is mine. I can wield it

without cutting off my leg. I *could* use the ax to split firewood—and where we're going, that would probably be useful." He laughed at the expression on Terrick's face, but sobered quickly. "My father left Weyrdon. He left you. He offered no explanation—to you—for either act.

"You waited. You've waited for all of my life—for longer, if I think about it. You've kept yourself in fighting shape. You've endured the demanding idiots who plague the Port Authority. When I saw the ax, I thought of you. Only of you.

"I won't remain in the Terafin manse for much longer. When Jay leaves, I'm going with her. But I'll take my sword. The ax is yours. If you feel its too much for you, go home. Take it to Arrend. Deliver it to the man you feel would be worthy of its edge.

"I did. I didn't know what the blade signified when I pulled it off the wall, but I think it was crossed with this sword for a reason."

Terrick turned to The Terafin. "When you leave," he said, "do you have room in your party for one more? I am accustomed to winter camping and life on the road. Or I was before I was swallowed by the Port Authority."

"Do you understand where I must go?" she asked softly.

He glanced out the open air windows.

"Yes. There, or places much like it. I don't know what we'll encounter, if we encounter anything at all. I don't know what we'll face. We may be forced to forage for food, something I've done only in the streets of a very mortal city."

"I've done it in the North, and in the Northern snows. I doubt that a valley, even one that contains such a creature as that, will be more of a challenge."

She lifted her hands and her fingers danced again.

Angel said, clearly, "With my life."

"Then, yes, Terrick. Yes, if you are willing to take the risk and wield ax in my defense, I have room in my party, as you call it, for one more. I hope you're not allergic to cats."

Epilogue

THE MAN CAME DOWN the well-tended road on which carriages usually traveled. He walked. On his shoulder he carried a bag that had seen better years, and over it, a cloak that the road had paled with dust. His hair was likewise lank with dust, his boots caked. What he needed, at this moment, was a bath. A bath, a meal, a good night's sleep.

He highly doubted that his needs were of import.

He had received harried instructions: he was to come immediately to the Terafin manse upon his arrival in *Averalaan*. He had not; he had made one short stop at Senniel College to introduce his companion upon the road to the bardmaster. Disentangling himself from the bardmaster's questions had taken more time than ideal. Nor was Solran likely to be best pleased when he immediately took to the road again, and for that reason, he had neglected to inform her.

The sea air was cool at this time of night; the salt it carried reminded him of the small scrapes and cuts that the road almost inevitably produced. He could, if he listened with care, hear voices upon the sea breeze; he did not. Instead, he spent some time listening to the distinctive rustle of leaves.

He was bard-born; he knew that that rustle contained voices. Not so many voices as the city itself, when day was in full swing—but voices as deliberate, and far older. He found it disturbing.

She will be waiting for you. She will be waiting, and wasting time she does not have. Deliver this one item into her keeping.

He had not asked what it was. Evayne was, by nature, mysterious. She walked roads that cut across the ages, age receding and returning to her visage like an unpredictable tide. When she had met him on the road from Annagar, he had been surprised.

She was not young. In her prime—for he had never seen her close to dotage—she was a force that made the voice of the wild wind seem tame in comparison; she had come at the height of her power. She seldom arrived at such an age, and when she did there was almost always death or violence.

But not this time. This time, there was a simple box. Kallandras recognized it instantly: it had traveled, hidden and guarded, from the ancient stores of the Tor Arkosa, risen from its bed of earth, in the keeping of the Serra Diora en'Leonne. "You wish me to take this to The Terafin?"

"Yes. The current Terafin is a woman with whom you are familiar; you traveled by her side for some leagues in the Dominion."

Jewel Markess ATerafin.

"I would not task you with this; nor would I have any other bear this burden—but the ways are closed to me now. I did not realize—" she shook her head. "There are some things that cannot transcend time. While I carry this, I can only move forward. It is an anchor that I cannot afford; in the Northern Wastes, the enemy gathers. And at this time, I cannot enter lands which are all but lost; I thought to move forward, or back—but it is forbidden."

He did not ask by who; long experience had taught him there were no answers to such questions.

"While she bears this burden, Kallandras, guard her with your life. Preserve it, no matter the cost of the preservation."

"Will she understand its significance?"

"Yes. Inasmuch as she currently can, yes."

"How significant is this charge, Evayne? How much danger will she face?"

"If the Lord of the Hells knew the contents of the box existed, he would take to the wild roads himself to hunt her down. He does not know, while such knowledge can still be denied him." Her voice dropped.

He was surprised to hear the fear and the weariness in her words. At this age, she could make her voice so smooth and impenetrable that even Kallandras could take nothing from it that she did not wish to offer. There were very, very few who could deny his bard-born gift.

He did not touch Evayne; no one did. Her robes rustled at wind that touched nothing else, and her breath came out in a mist that spoke of Winter cold. "Evayne," he asked, pitching his voice so that it traveled to her ears alone, "Is it soon?"

Her smile was bitter. "Yes, Kallandras. It is soon."

"And after?"

"I do not know. I surrendered the whole of my life to stop this one event—but I was sixteen and young and isolated. I am older, and not less isolated, but the one event now seems so minor to my mind it is hard to remember *why* I chose to walk as I walk."

"You will remember," he said, gilding his voice with his gift.

But she frowned. "You cannot command it," was her soft, soft reply. "I am aware of what it might cost to save one small town on the edge of our borders. What I've seen, what I've done—it makes the fate of a handful of people almost irrelevant: so many will die." As she spoke, she reached up and grasped something that hung around her neck. It was a lily, a silver lily. Kallandras had seen it a handful of times; he had never seen Evayne without it. Nor did he ask.

Had he his lute, he might have played it; he had left it in Senniel College. He felt, for a moment, the urge to sing; he had sung for the Serra Teresa on the long walk home. But if Teresa and Evayne were almost of an age, if they were two women with spines of pure steel, there were differences. He could not reach Evayne that way, and did not try.

Once, he would have been too angry to care. But time and war had blunted some of the dangerous edges of grief-maddened youth. If the coming war had brought no peace to Evayne, it offered peace—of a kind—to Kallandras. He had abandoned the brothers of his youth in order to preserve them; he had become Evayne's reluctant, resentful agent.

But now, he understood that if he played his part—whatever that part might be—he would achieve his goal: the brothers who were lost to him would survive.

He wondered, briefly, how lost he might feel if that goal no longer held significance for him, but shunted the thought aside. He had come to the manse—to the front doors of the manse, not the tradesman's entrance.

If Kallandras did not cut a fine, patrician figure—and in his current, dust-ridden clothing that was an impossibility—his name carried weight; he used it, with little concern. "My apologies," he said, to the guards, "but I have come on a matter of some import to The Terafin. I am Kallandras of Senniel College."

His name, recognized even when he himself was not, allayed some of the obvious suspicion the guards felt. They knew that the bards traveled, often extensively, at the behest of their bardmaster, in support of the Kings. "I have only tonight reached Averalaan from the Dominion, with word that must reach her. I did not even return home before I made my way to Terafin."

"A moment," the guard said. He vanished, and was not tardy in his return; clearly the Seneschal had given instructions that the master bard was to be seen inside.

The waiting room to one side of the foyer was not large; it was, however, very finely appointed. Kallandras felt far more road-worn and weary here than he had when offering the guards his polite deference. He was aware that his errand would take some time—if The Terafin permitted him entrance at all.

He was not, however, prepared when the door opened and Meralonne APhaniel entered the small room. Given the condition of his clothing, he had chosen to remain standing.

Meralonne offered him a polite nod; Kallandras returned a smile. "I did not expect to see you here."

"No? I forget; the events of the past two months occurred when you were wasting your time in the Dominion."

"I would not call it wasting time," Kallandras replied. "You are the Terafin mage?"

"I am. I am under exclusive contract to The Terafin."

Pale brows rose. "I'm surprised. The guildmaster allowed it?"

"Kallandras, please. Unless my presence were construed as a threat to the Empire, Sigurne is not foolish enough to deny me a simple choice." He chuckled as he drew pipe from the folds of his robe. "The Council of the Magi is incensed."

Kallandras watched as the mage set about lining the bowl of his pipe. "How so?"

"I felt events within the Terafin manse were interesting enough that I considered the privilege to be in the thick of things compensation enough for my services."

Kallandras felt that the words were Weston; he was weary enough that it took a moment for them to assemble sense. "You are working for . . . free?"

"I am." Meralonne lit his pipe, chuckling. "You would think I'm personally responsible for beggaring the Order. Will you join me?"

"My pipe, along with my lute, are ensconced within Senniel, I'm afraid. I wait upon the pleasure of The Terafin."

"Yes. I have been sent to retrieve you."

The duties of House Mage did not generally overlap the duties of a senior page, but Kallandras felt no need to make this observation aloud. Meralonne, as they strolled up the vast and impressive stairs of the foyer, chose to speak of the minor problems the city had faced in the bard's absence. He spoke of the events of The Terafin's funeral, his voice soft and steady; he spoke of the shift in the structure of *Avantari*. Kallandras stared as the mage chuckled.

"There was also the matter of the *Kialli* who chose to attack the The Terafin during the victory parade. But these are minor compared to what you are about to see."

"I'm not entirely certain I anticipate major with any joy. Where exactly do you lead me?"

"The library, as it happens. You will not, however, be in danger here, and the Chosen frown upon the drawing of weapons that are not their own." He paused in front of two of the Chosen. "Master Bard Kallandras of Senniel College, to see The Terafin."

The Chosen nodded and allowed the mage to pass through the doors. Kallandras, frowning, followed.

He was silent when he entered the world. Meralonne had called it a library, and a quick glance at the standing trees in the near distance made truth of the statement; they appeared to be growing shelves, and on those shelves, books had been placed, spines of different heights, textures and colors clearly visible beneath the midday light. The sky was amethyst, not blue, but it was cloudless, and the light it shed, bright and clear.

Avandar met them at the standing arch. "The Terafin is waiting," he said, bowing. "Please follow me."

Kallandras had seen this man summon and control the wild earth; he had seen him wield a sword of gold that had a voice, however muted. He had built a bridge all of stone in a matter of minutes, and he had turned the tide of an ugly—and almost hopeless—battle singlehandedly, in the village of Damar.

Very little of that man remained in this one.

Kallandras felt wind. He could hear the whisper of its voice, distant but unmistakable. He had not summoned it; it had not come at his call. He nonetheless offered it a benediction, and felt it creep up to curl his hair. But he glanced at Meralonne as he followed the domicis, and saw that the wind also traveled through the mage's hair. In this room, beneath this sky, Meralonne APhaniel looked like a young man—dangerous with youth and passion and intent.

"Have I amused you, Master Bard?"

"I so seldom feel kinship, APhaniel; you remind me of myself as a youth."

"Perhaps you could keep this between us," the mage replied, with a smile that was all edge. "My youth—and yours—are not generally appropriate conversational fare for appointments such as this one."

Kallandras laughed. As Avandar crested the end of the rows upon rows of shelves, a plain wooden table came into view. Seated at it, her hair half in her eyes, her expression entirely despondent, was Jewel. Ah, no. The Terafin.

Avandar cleared his throat, and she looked up, bleary-eyed. Exhaustion was replaced by a surprisingly warm smile of recognition as she rose.

"Kallandras, it *is* you."

"I should hope that men don't generally apply to speak to you using my name," he replied with mock gravity. He bowed. It was a graceful, swift motion that achieved the correct depth without descent into the obsequious. He was surprised by the delight he heard in her voice; it matched her tone. She knew that he was bard-born; she held nothing back. But she had never been good at disguising her feelings beneath an unbreakable patina of words.

"You look like you've barely left the desert."

"That is unkind, Terafin. I have, however, barely left the road." He glanced past her shoulder and frowned. "You have a fountain in your library."

"It's not much of a library," she replied. "And yes. The fountain came with the trees and the open air." She held out her hands and he took them, as if both gestures were entirely natural. Then again, for the bards who occupied the courts, they often were.

"It is, as you are aware, an impressive library. It is not, however, architecturally, as ... closed ... as many. You are well?"

"I am. If you have time—and you look as if time is an issue, I'm sorry—you should come to the West Wing. Adam is there. He'd be grateful for any sight of you, I think."

"Adam is here?"

She nodded. "It's complicated. How was Diora when you left?"

"She was well. No, she was better than well; she was very cautiously happy, I think. She has grown bold, for a Serra, and Valedan delights in it. Her first public act was to acknowledge her brother and her disgraced father's wives."

"And the Serra Teresa?"

"She is also in the city."

Jewel's eyes widened. "In Averalaan?"

"Yes. I have introduced her to Solran Marten; she is to become a Senniel student."

Jewel's smile was unfettered. "I'd love to see her. She's well?"

"She is still recovering, but she is physically whole." He let the smile fade. "I wish I could have come just to bear happy tidings."

The Terafin exhaled. "So do I. What unhappy tidings do you bring?"

"On the road to Averalaan, we were met by Evayne. She was not best-pleased that I was not to be found in the city; she felt that my arrival was tardy, and time was short."

Jewel stiffened. For a moment, the weight of her title informed the whole of her bearing. "I've been waiting for you."

"So she said. She asked me to convey an item of import to you." He removed the pack from his shoulder and untied its strings. He was aware of the intensity of her stare. Jewel had never been still or quiet; she moved, often restlessly; she pushed hair out of her eyes whenever a conversation troubled her—often when the hair was not in those eyes. But when she held herself in like this, she silently demanded motion and movement from those around her.

The only motion he could offer, he did: he drew the box from the faded, travel-worn bag. It was as it had been: small enough to be a modest jewelry box for a person of middling means. It was not terribly fine; wood had been engraved with runes and symbols, but none of these were obviously portentous.

She stared at it as he held it out to her. "What—what's in it?"

"I did not ask. You may have noticed that Evayne does not often answer questions. Certainly not questions which are easily answered."

She looked at him in mild confusion.

"You could open it," he replied, his voice and smile teasing.

It drew a smile from her. He guessed that she had done very little smiling since she had taken the Terafin Seat.

"Have you eaten?"

"No. I was told that it was a matter of utmost urgency that I deliver this into your hands; I felt it necessary to settle the Serra Teresa before I came. I do not think she would thank me for bringing her to the head of one of the most powerful Houses in the Empire with no pause for a bath and fresh clothing."

"I don't think she would have cared."

"Not when she realized The Terafin and Jewel Markess were one and the same, no. But Averalaan will be strange enough, difficult enough, in the months to come." He glanced again at the fountain. Jewel had not removed the box from his hands.

She closed her eyes. To her domicis, she said, "Avandar, go to the kitchens, and to the West Wing. Tell Adam, Angel, and Terrick that they are to make preparations to travel." To Kallandras she whispered, "Hold the box for a moment."

Kallandras heard raw fear in her voice. Not in her words; she had enough mastery to mask it there. She made her way back to the table, to a book that lay open upon it. Lifting her hands above the page, she signed; it was not in a language Kallandras recognized.

"APhaniel."

Meralonne's pipe had gone out. He did not light it. "I will keep watch, Terafin."

She took the box from Kallandras' hands and drew it toward her chest; she did not attempt to remove the lid. "They're coming," she whispered.

The wind's voice rose in a howl, but it held no anger and no fear. Kallandras felt it; it was strong enough he could have danced—or fought—in its folds. The ring on his finger was cool. He glanced at Meralonne, saw the slender edge of a smile on the mage's face.

Into the library, from between the trees that served as shelves—flew two large creatures: predatory cats, in size and color. One was white, one black; were it not for their wings, they might have looked natural and dangerous.

Their wings, Kallandras thought, and their voices. They attempted to land on the same spot ten feet from where The Terafin stood, collided, rolled; their voices devolved into a series of hisses and growls that often contained no words.

The Terafin looked . . . resigned. The presence of flying, talking predators did not seem to invoke any of the wonder the bard himself felt. "Snow. Night. *We have guests*."

They paused in their not-so-playful attempt to shred each other's fur. The white cat's ears twitched. "Oh? Who?"

"This is Kallandras. He is a master bard of Senniel College. Meralonne, you know."

The white cat hissed. "Can we eat *them*?"

"I would very much like to see you try," Meralonne replied. The pipe vanished from his hand in an instant.

Jewel looked at Kallandras. "They're always like this. I'd be grateful if you found it unoffensive."

"There are no known rules of etiquette for dealing with

talking, winged cats. Were I not trained in Senniel, I might find myself at a loss for words."

Night hissed, stopped, hissed and then tilted his head. He padded across the floor toward Kallandras. Kallandras inclined his head. Night butted his side with the top of his head, and Kallandras obligingly reached down to scratch behind the great cat's ears. He had not lied; he considered them a wonder.

"Do not indulge them, brother," a new voice said, and Kallandras lifted his chin—but only his chin; he continued to scratch the cat's head. The cat, however, growled.

"Lord Celleriant."

"Kallandras of Senniel. Well met." His smile was sharp and bright and painfully familiar. But he turned and bowed to Jewel as the white stag Kallandras had last seen in the Dominion of Annagar walked into view. He looked a changed creature; his fur was matted in places, and blood crested the hair on his front hooves. Blood adorned the tines of his antlers.

He approached Jewel, head lowered.

"I'm sorry," she said, her voice so low only Kallandras could catch it. It, and all the regret it now held. "Meralonne believes that Carver is trapped in lands that only the Sleepers know."

The white stag lifted its head, eyes rounding. It was clear he could speak to Jewel, but his voice, no bard could catch. "You remember Kallandras."

Kallandras met the white stag's steady gaze; he bowed. The stag nodded.

"Tomorrow morning we will travel to *Avantari*. Most of us will go by carriage. We will not return the same way. I need to speak with the Oracle." She exhaled. "I will ask to take her test."

The stag was very still.

"I don't *like* her," Snow said. "Why do *we* have to go?"

"Because it will be very, very boring in the Terafin manse if I'm not here, and I have some sympathy for the Household Staff: they don't deserve to listen to you all complain about boredom while they're working their—while they're working so hard."

Celleriant's smile had frozen on his face at the mention of the Sleepers. "Lord," he said, "if what Illaraphaniel fears is true, you cannot go to your Carver."

"No," she replied. "I can. You can't. But I am to travel to the heart of the Oracle's domain, and for that journey, I want you with me. If—" She shook her head. "Kallandras will be joining us."

He had not said as much, although Evayne's orders were quite clear.

"What do you hold?" Celleriant asked.

Jewel gazed at the box. In answer, she lifted the lid in one shaking hand.

Light flooded the room, paling the contours of her jaw, her lips, her cheekbones. Meralonne and Celleriant froze in that instant; they were rigid, breathless, silent. They could not see the contents of the box; only Jewel could.

But vision in this case was clearly superfluous.

Meralonne whispered a word. Two. He did not speak Weston, nor Torra, nor Rendish, but Kallandras was bardborn. He understood. "This is what we searched for along the borders of Averda," Kallandras said softly.

Meralonne did not—could not—speak. Kallandras understood why; at the moment a word left his lips, he would be laid bare to the bard's talent, and he would not risk it.

"Why?" Jewel asked, staring. "Why me?"

"The trees exist in their season," Kallandras replied. "They are wed to it, bound to it. Evayne can carry coin and weapon across the divide of years—but she cannot carry this tree outside of its season. She has tried. She meant to keep and protect it, but she cannot tread time's path while she holds it safe.

"She attempted to carry it to the Hidden Court—but the way was barred; she could find no entrance, and no purchase upon the path that must lead to its heart. You have, at your side, a Lord of that court. Celleriant?"

Celleriant slowly came back to life. "No," he said. "I cannot return. Nor can Illaraphaniel."

"Evayne felt that The Terafin could," Kallandras said. "And you are tasked with the safety of what that box contains. If its existence is known—"

Jewel lifted a hand. She placed the lid firmly over the box. "I could keep it safe in the manse against all intruders," she said. "But only while I remained here. And I *can't*."

Celleriant, however, said: "You can carry it to the Hidden Court."

"If you can't go—if Meralonne can't—"

"I serve you, and Illaraphaniel—"

"Cannot return unless he is summoned, and he will never be summoned," the mage said, finally finding his voice.

"Your brother, Celleriant. Your hunters. Call them—"

"You do not understand, Lord. They ride, now. They search. They cannot return to her side unless—and until—there is Summer. The doors to the Hidden Court open but once until the turn of the seasons; they have chosen to ride. But you bear part of the White Lady upon your person. You at least might force entry—but only because of her gift."

Jewel frowned. "If it was as simple as three bloody strands of hair, why wouldn't she just make sure they *all* had them?"

Lord Celleriant stiffened. He served Jewel—which Kallandras found almost shocking. Such service had clearly not lessened the regard in which he held the Winter Queen. "It is not, as you imply, so simple."

Kallandras said, quietly, "Of what does Lord Celleriant speak?"

Jewel lifted her wrist. To Kallandras' eye, the wrist was bare, covered in part by the fabric of sleeve, no more. "Three strands of the Winter Queen's hair."

Meralonne was silent for a long moment. "Evayne and the White Lady share a parent: the father. She knew, Terafin. You hold some small part of her power around your wrist; until you die, it will not be parted from you. It cannot be transferred; it is hers. But it is also yours. Lord Celleriant is correct; while you carry what you carry, there is some small chance you will find a way into the courts that are lost to those who do not remain in their smallness by her side."

"I would travel with you, now."

Jewel shook her head. "You know why I need you here."

"The needs of your House are irrelevant."

"No, Meralonne, they're not. I need you here. If you're afraid of what happens to the box—you can keep it with you." She held it out.

"Do not play games—"

"I'm not. I'll take it with me if you remain; I'll leave it here if you follow. Those are the only choices you have."

"Illaraphaniel," Celleriant said.

Meralonne drew his sword. Jewel stared at him as if he were a particularly stupid merchant. "If you mean to threaten me — don't. Just don't. If you mean to threaten anyone else in this room because you know you can't kill me, *really, really* reconsider. I understand what's at stake for both of us."

"You will go to the Hidden Court first."

"I will not — I have no idea *where* the Hidden Court is. It's called hidden for a reason. I will go to the Oracle."

"Illaraphaniel," Celleriant said again.

Meralonne ignored him. "Do you understand what happens if that box is lost or its contents destroyed?"

"Yes. There will be no Summer Court and no Summer Queen — and if there is no Summer Queen there is almost nothing that can take and hold the field against *Allasakar*. I *understand* what's at stake. But it is not the only thing at stake for *me*. I want you here."

"Illaraphaniel."

Meralonne turned his head as Celleriant at last drew his sword. "Ask the master bard what he hears in her voice. Ask. She will not be moved. If you threaten her, she will accept it; if you seek to threaten those in her care, she will not. She will not kill you, if that is even within her power, but the battle will reverberate throughout the hidden world; it will pierce the dreams of the Sleepers.

"I will accompany her. She will ride the Winter King. If she needs to eat and sleep, the cats do not. Your presence in the world that waits will not go unnoticed; you risk everything if you are forced to reveal yourself before it is time."

"And your presence?"

"I am the youngest Prince of the Court, and I was never your equal. But I will fight you here, if that is what you demand. She is seer-born. She is *certain*. Consider what that means. You have seen the Winter Queen's gift. You understand its significance. Respect the Winter Queen's choice."

Meralonne was still; not even the wind touched him.

"Illaraphaniel," Celleriant continued, voice low, "I would have felt as you felt. Before I encountered the mortal I now willingly choose to serve, I would stand as you stand. But I have traveled with mortals, now. I have seen the glimmering of the ancient and wild in those travels. They have not turned from it; they have not fled.

"I have fought at the side of Kallandras of Senniel. I have fought at the side of The Terafin, as she styles herself among her kind. Are mortals frail? Yes. But against a Duke of the Hells, *this* mortal stood; she did not fall."

"Nor did he," was the grudging reply. "And you know why she did not; she was here, in the heart of the domain she had made her own."

"I would not serve her now if she had not been able to hold the road in the Stone Deepings against the Wild Hunt." Celleriant's voice was low, intent. His sword, as Meralonne's, had not wavered. "But she held the road. And she would have continued to hold it until Scarran had passed.

"She could not hold it indefinitely against the Winter Queen—but Illaraphaniel, neither you nor I could have held it at all. Yes, she is mortal. Yes, as mortals are, she is beset by frailty and a brief, brief span of years: but she burns, as mortals do, within that short span.

"You know that the bindings of the Covenant have been fractured. You know that the ancient is leaking, slowly, into mortal realms. You *know* what that must mean; you have lived among mortals far, far longer than I. If my Lord says she will hold this gift safe, if she says she will deliver it to where it must, after so long, be planted, I believe it." He closed his eyes, then, and the sword vanished.

"And if the Winter Queen had chosen to trust Moorelas and his sword, your brothers would not now sleep the long sleep. You understand the folly of their choice; you did not make it, although you might have chosen as they chose.

"Was the cost and the consequence of that ancient choice greater, in the end, than the possible consequence of this one? You were the pride of the *Arianni*. Even in exile, your name is carried by the wind; the earth remembers your passage above it, and the water, your calm. Of the four, you were the *only one* to hold true to the White Lady.

"I ask you: hold true now."

Meralonne closed his eyes. "You are so young," he said, as he opened them and his sword vanished. His smile was one that Jewel had never seen adorn his lips before. "You have been in the company of mortals for so short a time, Celleriant. You do not understand their history."

"Nor have I need. *Viandaran* was young when I was young, and he walks among us." He turned to look at

Kallandras, who had not moved once during this exchange. He started to speak, but stopped; no words left his mouth.

Meralonne's smile faded. He lifted chin and looked at a point beyond Celleriant's shoulder. "You did not see—or war against—the Cities of Man in that youth; you did not walk their streets or fly above their peaked heights."

"No."

The mage closed his silver, bright eyes. "I will abide, in exile, as I have chosen. When you reach the doors of the Hidden Court, give the Lady my greetings." He turned stiffly and walked away—into the depths of the library not even The Terafin had yet explored.

In the morning, in a silence that was heavy with words that her den had no way to speak, Jewel Markess ATerafin, The Terafin, left the home which was, in all ways, her foundation, and headed toward *Avantari* to meet the Oracle.

I am worried, Evayne had said. She let the fear seep into her words; in no other way did she emphasize them. *Jewel is not what I was. Watch her, Kallandras. Guide her where she will accept guidance. There are too many bad choices she can make, and very, very few good.*

She is seer-born, Evayne.

Yes. But love is no part of that, and love clouds vision. Sometimes we turn away from the truths we don't want to face when the alternative is too harsh.

He said nothing, then—or now. He understood the burdens love placed upon those who loved. He understood, as well, that absent an army and the generals familiar with the demands of battle, Jewel now rode to war.

It was not her own war that concerned her; he saw this clearly. She left her den to do battle in her absence. He hoped, for her sake, they were capable enough to wage, and win, that war.